THE ARBOR HOUSE
TREASURY OF

GREAT WESTERN STORIES

BOOKS BY JOHN JAKES

NORTH AND SOUTH
THE KENT FAMILY CHRONICLES: *The Americans* and *The Seekers*
THE BASTARD
THE REBELS
AMERICAN BICENTENNIAL SERIES: *The Titans*, *The Furies*, *The Warriors* and
The Lawless

BOOKS BY BILL PRONZINI

NOVELS
SCATTERSHOT
MASQUES
HOODWINK
LABYRINTH
BLOWBACK
GAMES
SNOWBOUND
UNDERCURRENT
THE VANISHED
PANIC!
THE SNATCH
THE STALKER

NONFICTION
GUN IN CHEEK

ANTHOLOGIES
SPECTER!
THE ARBOR HOUSE TREASURY OF MYSTERY AND SUSPENSE
  (WITH BARRY N. MALZBERG AND MARTIN H. GREENBERG)
THE ARBOR HOUSE TREASURY OF HORROR AND THE SUPERNATURAL
  (WITH BARRY N. MALZBERG AND MARTIN H. GREENBERG)
CREATURE!
THE ARBOR HOUSE NECROPOLIS
MUMMY!
VOODOO!
WEREWOLF!

OTHER BOOKS EDITED BY MARTIN H. GREENBERG

THE ARBOR HOUSE CELEBRITY BOOK OF HORROR STORIES
  (WITH CHARLES G. WAUGH)
THE ARBOR HOUSE TREASURY OF MODERN SCIENCE FICTION
  (WITH ROBERT SILVERBERG)
THE ARBOR HOUSE TREASURY OF GREAT SCIENCE FICTION SHORT NOVELS
  (WITH ROBERT SILVERBERG)
TOMORROW, INC.
RUN TO STARLIGHT: SPORTS THROUGH SCIENCE FICTION

THE ARBOR HOUSE TREASURY OF

GREAT WESTERN STORIES

EDITED BY Bill Pronzini
and Martin H. Greenberg

ARBOR HOUSE New York

Reader's Digest Fund for the Blind is publisher of the Large-Type Edition of *Reader's Digest*. For subscription information about this magazine, please contact Reader's Digest Fund for the Blind, Inc., Dept. 250, Pleasantville, N.Y. 10570.

PERMISSIONS

CONTENTS

INTRODUCTION

BY JOHN JAKES

But westward, look, the land is bright.
Arthur Hugh Clough

The word *west* is central to American reality and myth. But *west* is a chameleon. Sometimes it means a geographic region, sometimes a direction, or then again, a period of time in our national experience.

But however it's used, it brings with it a whole trove of secondary meanings. They speak an alluring language of hope; adventure; riches; escape; beginning again.

The sense of renewal and rebirth contained in *west* goes far back, to Europe and beyond. Thoreau speculated that "the island of Atlantis, and the islands and gardens of the Hesperides, a sort of terrestrial paradise, appear to have been the Great West of the ancients, enveloped in mystery and poetry." Even when the wealth of the Orient, imaginary and real, drew European explorers in that direction, the better, faster route was imagined to lie the other way, and for years, mariners tried to find this fabled western passage.

But it was a series of events on the North American continent in the nineteenth century that gave the word its final form and densely interlocked meanings:

- West—the way you go to reach the unpopulated country. The gold. Free land. Breathing room.
- West—where the buffalo roam. A vast space beyond the Mississippi.
- And West—a period of time, of roughly thirty-five to forty years duration—say, from the strike at Sutter's Mill to the massacre at Wounded Knee. Often, this time frame is called the "Old West,"

Introduction © 1982 by John Jakes

a common shorthand for the years encompassing the final explosive
thrust of the United States population, native and foreign born alike,
into and through all the empty lands from Old Northwest to the
Pacific.

Some would argue that the "Old West" is better defined by fixing its
limits at either end of the heyday of the cowboy—a span much shorter
than the first one; only a decade or so. There is something to that
argument since, in large parts of the world, the American West is definitely not the sodbuster or the railroader, the owner of the Blue Hotel or
the young reporter on the *Territorial Enterprise*. The West is the cowboy,
and vice versa, period.

No matter what time period you choose for your definition, one thing's
clear. America took *west* and put its own brand on it. Frederick Jackson
Turner saw that. In Europe, he observed, the "frontier" was traditionally
the boundary, clearly defined and often fortified, between countries; there
could be hundreds of thousands of people living settled lives along this
kind of frontier.

Eighteenth- and nineteenth-century Americans, on the other hand,
transformed the meaning of frontier to the edge of settlement, which was
sparsely populated and slowly but steadily moving as more people approached.

And if you wanted to know where to find this moving border of
civilization, you generally looked west.

The popularity of literature about the West isn't hard to explain. From
the earliest European voyages of exploration, accounts of the beauties and
perils of remote, exotic lands have exerted a strong appeal on readers.
Although some men and women always go out to the unexplored places,
wherever those happen to be, a lot more stay safely at home, preferring
to do their travelling vicariously.

There you have the reason for the success of *The principall Navigations,
Voiages and Discoveries of the English Nation,* as chronicled in three
volumes by Richard Hakluyt, the geographer. You understand why people
savored the journals and diaries of the epochal Lewis and Clark expedition. Or rushed to buy all the guidebooks to the California gold fields
(frequently written by men who had never seen them).

But we're dealing here not with advice to the gold-seeker, or descriptions of the flora of what would turn into the states of the Pacific North-

west. We're talking fiction. "The Western," to use a familiar name. Europeans and others have written them, but as a genre, Americans invented them.

The Western was, in its first life, an Eastern. Although part of our frontier almost always lay to the west—the far reaches of Virginia; the more remote and legendary Kentucky—for a while other parts lay down in the Carolinas, or up in the forests of New York. The authors in this book owe an immense debt to the authors of "Easterns"—Fenimore Cooper and all his literary kin, including his now largely forgotten colleague from the South, William Gilmore Simms. During the antebellum period, Simms's historical and frontier novels were nearly as popular as Cooper's had been. But he was a South Carolinian, and bullheaded in his defense of slavery. That and the Civil War eroded his popularity with New York editors, and with a huge segment of his public.

Neither Cooper nor Simms wrote the kind of fiction this book contains. They are its grandfathers, certainly. But who are the parents? And how did the offspring get to be so universally beloved?

Some of the reasons have already been suggested. The materials and background of the Western have an instantaneous appeal. They are colorful; exciting. And, as noted, nineteenth-century stay-at-homes were wildly curious about the country's far reaches, to which increasing numbers of their fellow citizens were rushing in search of precious metal, farmland or freedom from pursuit by law officers, wives or cuckolded husbands. People who didn't go wanted to know what it was really like out there where the sirens sang the song of manifest destiny.

So the moment was ripe for the appearance of a new kind of fiction. I would argue that three forces in nineteenth-century popular culture propelled the Western to national, then global acclaim:

The debut of the dime novel.

The fiction of Ned Buntline.

And the life of Buffalo Bill Cody.

The earliest dime novels were created in the tradition of Cooper, Simms and Sir Walter Scott. Their authors wrote of the frontier, all right, but in a manner that made at least some pretense of literary quality.

The very first of them was one of those "Easterns." *Malaeska: The Indian Wife of the White Hunter* was published in June, 1860, by the firm of Beadle and Company of William Street, New York. The work carried impeccable credentials. It had already appeared as a prize story in a magazine called *The Ladies' Companion.*

Edmund Pearson's entertaining study of dime novels gives us this description of the first offering from Beadle: ". . . a thin little book, of one hundred and twenty-eight pages . . . about six-inches-high and four-inches-broad . . . the covers were of saffron paper—the book was a 'yellow-backed Beadle.' "

The term quickly became pejorative, which Mr. Beadle resented; he also insisted his covers were orange. Whatever the hue, Beadle books went to war in many a military haversack. The soldiers couldn't get enough of them. So it wasn't long before a picture of a ten-cent piece was printed on every cover to foil Army sutlers, notorious price-gougers.

The all but unpronounceable *Malaeska* is a Cooperish frontier romance set in the Hudson River Valley in the 1700s. It opens gently—a stylistic refinement which other Beadle authors would soon demolish:

> *The traveller who has stopped at Catskill, on his way up the Hudson, will remember that a creek of no insignificant breadth washes one side of the village . . .*

The reader must wait until the second chapter to encounter the woodsman-hero, Danforth, and a fight featuring feverish dangers as well as feverish prose:

> *Sternly arose the white man's shout amid the blazing of guns and the whizzing of tomahawks, as they flashed through the air on their message of blood . . . Oh, it was fearful, that scene of slaughter. Heart to heart, and muzzle to muzzle, the white man and the red man battled in horrid strife.*

The author of this stirring stuff was no obscure hack, but an accomplished and well-regarded magazine editor (*Graham's, The Ladies' World,* etc.) and the creator of some eminently respectable novels (". . . published at the conventional price of one dollar and fifty cents, and bound, decorously, in boards"). She ran a fashionable New York salon, and received "marked attentions" from the likes of Thackeray and Dickens during an 1850 world tour. Her name was Mrs. Ann Sophia Winterbotham Stephens. She was deemed, correctly, a pillar of propriety.

Yet she did create the first work presented in a new and lusty fiction format; one which would serve as the earliest popular vehicle for Western stories.

Relatively soon, the dime novel would become—to busybody clerics, narrow-minded parents and other spoilsports—what Pearson delightfully terms "a literary pestilence." The objection was usually moralistic. Lack of quality would have been a better target. As the dime novel grew, expanding its scope to deal with all sorts of subjects and introducing series characters who solved mysteries, invented fabulous electric boats or lettered in every sport ever conceived by God or man at Yale, the writing became a lot more punchy. A typical opening instantly removed any doubt as to whether this was, or was not, a tale of derring-do:

> *Bang!*
> *Bang!*
> *Bang!*
> *Three shots rang out on the midnight air!*

I guess we can agree that it isn't your average literary prize-winning diction. But it surely gets the blood going(!!!).

The dignity and talent which a few writers such as Mrs. Stephens brought to the form were cake-icing that rapidly disappeared. But the stage was set; a means was at hand to make exciting fiction, including tales of the West, affordable and widely available.

Enter the bizarre Edward Zane Carroll Judson, alias Ned Buntline.

No author would dare invent Ned Buntline; his manuscript would be rejected as too outrageous.

"Colonel" E. Z. C. Judson was a short, stocky, slightly lame man of quick wit and tongue. He was a propagandist without peer, in print or in front of a mob. He instigated the bloody Astor Place Riot in 1849 to protest the presence on a New York stage of a famous Shakespearean actor from Britain (it robbed America's premier thespian, Forrest, of the chance to work, Judson claimed).

In the same generous vein, Judson helped organize the American Political Party, or "Know-Nothings," who stood foursquare against anything and anyone not white, Protestant and native born.

Judson served two-and-a-half years with the First New York Mounted Rifles during the Civil War. He saw no battle action, but he did see the interior of a cell in which he was placed for deserting. Over the years he had up to half a dozen wives (the records of his marriages and divorce settlements are confused), and was a bigamist at least once.

Using the Buntline pseudonym, he became an author of sensational fiction: sea stories, and adventures set in the Seminole and Mexican Wars. The firms of Beadle and Street and Smith published his material. One biographer unequivocally calls him "America's best-paid writer" during his prime years (the annual income cited in support of this claim is twenty thousand dollars).

In the summer of 1869, Buntline/Judson heard or read of a hot skirmish between Indians and cavalry at Summit Springs, Nebraska. Sioux and Cheyenne under Chief Tall Bull had been pursued by General Eugene Carr's 5th Cavalary, aided by the irregulars in Major Frank North's Pawnee scout battalion. Buntline boarded the westbound cars to see whether there might be fresh story material in it.

He hoped to interview North, the man who had reportedly killed Tall Bull. He tracked the scout to a military post, but North apparently had no wish to become grist for the fiction mill: "If you want a man to fill that bill, he's over there under the wagon."

The man snoozing in the shade was a frontier-wise young fellow, born in Iowa and revealed as tall when he stood up. One source characterizes him as "handsome as Apollo." William Frederick Cody was a veteran of the Union army, a hunter and a supplier of buffalo meat to railroad construction crews.

Although not actually present at the battle of Summit Springs—he had been on a scouting assignment for General Carr—he arrived at the Indian village soon after the engagement. He was sufficiently charmed by Mr. Buntline so that he was willing to discuss the experience.

Cody, already nicknamed Buffalo Bill by his friends, suggested they go out looking for Indians. Buntline abandoned his previously announced plan to give a temperance address (it was another way he made money; he also had a stock lecture on the subject of "Woman As Angel And Fiend," a topic he seems to have researched in some depth). Off they rode, the scout and the fiction writer, talking a blue streak. Buntline described his heroic exploits in the Seminole, Mexican and Civil Wars. Presumably the young and likable Cody was more truthful.

At the end of the research trip, Buntline went back to New York City and to work. He had seen no Indians except maybe a few hanging around the post. But he'd heard enough stories from Cody and other scouts and soldiers to send the kettle of his imagination to full boil. In December of that year, Street and Smith proudly announced a new Buntline story: *Buffalo Bill—The King of Border Men.*

The archetype of the Western hero was about to burst on the world. A young plainsman with a sense of humor, a liking for spirits (he often said that when he volunteered for the war, he was so drunk he didn't know what he was doing) and a God-given gift for showmanship, he was about to begin his journey to fame. As he went, he would carry and spread the legend of the West far beyond the shores of his own country.

The Buntline story portrayed Bill Cody not only as the greatest scout in the West, but as a staunch cold water army man; a teetotaler. Well, no law requires that the truth be told by, or about, living people, as numerous memoirs of movie stars and ex-presidents demonstrate.

Don Russell's life of Cody disputes many claims of Buntline's chief biographer, as well as subsequent exaggerations of Buffalo Bill's early career. (One has the scout simultaneously shooting Tall Bull, tipping his sombrero respectfully to the chief's white female captive, and holding the reins—"presumably with his third hand.") Russell also questions the extent and value of Cody's contribution to the Street and Smith story; he claims most of it was actually based on the adventures of another frontiersman, James Butler Hickok, and that all Buntline really got out of his meeting with the young Iowan was "the alliterative magic of the name Buffalo Bill."

Whatever the truth, the magic was more potent. The serial was a hit. Buntline churned out a few more while shuttling between a wife in Manhattan and another up in Westchester. The stories featured not only Bill and his horse Powder Face, but Bill's real-life wife Louisa, her invented sisters Lillie and Lottie and various frontier pals including "Wild Bill Hitchock" *(sic)*. Later dime novels about the famous Westerner were authored by Prentiss Ingraham.

While Buntline was still the one writing about him, Cody continued to work as a scout and guide, although the quality of his clientele improved rapidly as his fame spread. He was chosen to take General Phil Sheridan and powerful newspaper publisher James Gordon Bennett on a hunting expedition. Then came an even bigger plum. Sheridan recommended that Cody be the guide for the Grand Duke Alexis of Russia, age 19, who was making a triumphant tour of America and hankered to go on a buffalo hunt—the 1871 equivalent of a visit to Disneyland.

Cody soon succumbed to the lure of the big cities, where his name was being heard with greater and greater frequency. He went to New York, where Gordon Bennett's editors and writers treated him as a media star. He was sighed over, fussed over, fought over as a guest. He was asked to dine with the Belmonts. And from Ned Buntline's personal box at the Bowery Theatre, he watched the dramatization of his own adventures, which playwright Fred Meader had created from the half-truths and plain lies of the first Buntline story.

Something in Cody must have stirred then. He must have glimpsed El Dorado—a way to earn far more than he ever could as a cavalry scout or supplier of buffalo meat. Somewhere in the two or three years that culiminated in the Bowery Theatre premiere, Buffalo Bill the showman came to life.

He was off the army payroll by late 1872 and on his way to Chicago to star personally in a new Buntline venture—a stage extravaganza in which Ned filled the multiple roles of producer, director and actor. He also wrote the show, *The Scouts of the Plains,* which was nothing more than Meader's play slightly refurbished.

On stage, Cody didn't fool around with memorized dialogue. He just extemporized a narrative of some of his experiences. He was no actor, but he received an ovation anyway. (Buntline portrayed a white renegade; he managed to slip a temperance lecture into one of the character's long monologues.) From time to time, thrilling action broke up the talk. The scouts bravely slew a lot of Indians portrayed by "supers in cambric pants."

The reviews weren't good. The Chicago *Times* called the production "a combination of incongruous drama, execrable acting, renowned performers, intolerable stench, scalping, blood and thunder." When the show eventually arrived at Niblo's in New York, the local critics were even more unfriendly (some things never change). Said one: "As a drama it is very poor slop."

It made no difference. Buffalo Bill was an American original, and the public fell in love with him. The love affair would last a long time.

Cody was a genuinely brave man. He fought in at least sixteen battles with Indians during his lifetime, the most famous being that with the Cheyenne, Yellow Hair (not Yellow Hand), in 1876. Contemporary accounts indicate that he realized he was spoofing himself and the West, just a little, when he organized his first arena show in 1883.

It became known as Buffalo Bill's Wild West and Congress of Rough Riders of the World—and eventually brought to amphitheatres all over America, and then Europe, such sights as simulated stage robberies and personalities such as Annie Oakley and Chief Sitting Bull.

And if the show was still not exactly the truth any more than the dime novels had been, it was *enough* of the truth so that it can honestly be said that no other entertainment, and no other man, did more to implant the myth and magic of the American west in the minds of his countrymen and millions of others besides. The working cowboy did part of the job of course. But he was anonymous. (And until recent years, we've seldom seen him written about or depicted as he really was—often still in his teens, or barely out of them; frequently black.) Cody remains *the* Westerner.

Bad management cost him the fortune he made in show business. His death in 1917 was messy and unheroic; the cause was uremic poisoning. But he was a showman to the end, making his last appearance two months before he was buried.

Personal problems linked to flaws in his character vexed most of his later life. But he has a just claim to immortality, because he bequeathed the West to the whole world. The rest—from Zane Grey and Max Brand to John Ford and Sergio Leone—is history.

Exactly as great men often rise from humble circumstances, a splendid body of literature has come from the beginnings just sketched. Writers of vastly greater talent and far more serious purpose than Buntline were understandably drawn to the dramatic potential of Western characters and settings. From what resulted, the editors have cooked up a real feast.

The menu is splendid. I might have liked a complete dime novel (really little more than novelettes) as an appetizer. Or maybe, as a gourmet course, one of the many stories in *Centennial,* which I consider a great Pike's Peak of a Western novel whose unique protagonists are the land itself and the town created by all the many characters drawn to the land.

Still, the editors have done a first-rate job of capturing the scope of Western fiction by condensing it into two great periods. I expect you'll find more than one favorite author represented. The popular Louis L'Amour. The vastly underrated Steve Frazee. Jack Schaefer, whose *Shane* is one of the few fictional Westerners who approaches the status of a Buffalo Bill; Clarence Mulford's Hopalong Cassidy might be another.

I discovered a favorite of mine—William R. Cox, a fine craftsman whose yarns I devoured in the pulps as a teenager.

The backgrounds of these stories are varied, and so are the styles, ranging from the comic verbal gingerbread of O. Henry to the spare prose of Wayne Overholser, which to me rings of the Bible. You'll find the crude ore of a familiar plot refined by talent of a high order, as in A. B. Guthrie's "First Principal," a beautifully understated tale of the classic confrontation between the peaceful newcomer—a *male* schoolteacher; a marvelous fresh touch—and the town bad man, a no-good with "yellow eyes."

An authentic genius and the first American practitioner of naturalism, Stephen Crane, writes of travellers snowbound in a Nebraska hotel, and he gives the narrative knife a savage twist at the end in a novelette I have always found unforgettable.

There are plenty of cowboy stories, naturally; no such collection would be respectable without them. Emerson Hough's is a wildly funny one about a cross-eyed racing pinto. It captures the flavor of Western yarn-spinning; the tall tale. But there are veins of melancholy in it too: the old ways pass and always will and never was this truth more evident and hurtful than in the short time of the American cowboy. Movingly, Hough writes:

> *The whole country's changed, and it ain't changed for the better, either. Grass is longer, and horns is shorter, and men is triflin'er . . . a ranch foreman ain't allowed to run his own brandin' iron any more, and that takes more'n half the poetry out of the cow business.*

You'll encounter hard-edged revisionist Western writing from the fine Elmore Leonard. Even a Christmas tale, courtesy of Bret Harte.

You may single out one story that you find yourself liking best of all. I did: "High Wind," by one of the giants, Ernest Haycox. I like "High Wind" because I think it successfully encompasses the lure and the legend, the dream and the reality, in one short, powerful piece of work.

Buck LaGrange, the transplanted Connecticut grocery clerk, understands that to build a future for himself and his new bride, he will be forced to overcome difficulties of immense magnitude—which Haycox puts in the form of the killing wind that dominates the action.

And yet, although Buck must finally resort to a gun to defend his property against another enemy—men—he (and, I suspect, Haycox too) believes that the only weapons which will ultimately beat new, rough country—or *any* challenge to those who want something better—are courage and hope:

> *It's the thing we look up to. It's the thing we've all got to have. Just courage.*

> *When the herds quit coming from Texas we'll have something else better—farms.*

And the wind? *"It will pass. It always has."*

Why does a fictional clerk cling so stubbornly, maybe even crazily, to that kind of vision? For the same reason so many real ones went West:

> *There's a chance for everybody out here. I mean to take my chance— and make a go of it.*

I was pleased to be invited to write an introduction for this anthology, and contribute a story, because—in case it isn't evident by now—I've always loved the Western in all of its permutations.

Well, not *every* one. As a kid, I went faithfully, not to say eagerly, to the Saturday matinees. I couldn't see too many of those one-hour programmers from Republic and Columbia, Monogram and PRC—with one exception: the pictures featuring singing cowboys in embroidered shirts who hopped on their too-pretty horses to chase crooks driving vintage convertibles back and forth across strange hermaphroditic landscapes, half old, half new. There is a lot of never-was in Western fiction and film, but that sort of thing was too ridiculous even for a true believer.

Still, a believer I remained, thanks to pulp novels about Texas Ranger Jim Hatfield, richly detailed *Saturday Evening Post* serials by Luke Short, and Errol Flynn pictures scored in epic style by Max Steiner, a Viennese who seemed to understand the West better than most Americans.

When I broke into writing, I divided my time between science fiction and Western stories, and wrote a couple of dozen of the latter, novelettes mostly, published by the great old Popular pulps. I can still remember haunting Indiana drugstores whenever a new shipment of magazines arrived; I knew the delivery schedules by heart.

There is one thrilling moment in my memory in which, for the first time, I discovered my story, and my byline, among those featured on the cover (bright yellow, incidentally) of a magazine which proclaimed above its name:

Frontier Fiction by Tophand Authors.

I didn't really believe I was a "tophand author"—I was twenty-one or twenty-two at the time. But it was heady to find someone else saying it, even as hyperbole; and saying it about one of my Westerns to boot.

So I'm proud to have a small place in this company of men and women who, no matter how diverse their literary approaches, share belief in the verity set down by a Victorian poet and printed as the epigraph to this piece:

Westward, the land is indeed a little brighter.

Hilton Head Island
July 1, 1982

THE FIRST
FIFTY YEARS

Buck Fanshaw's Funeral

Most people don't think of Mark Twain (Samuel Langhorne Clemens; 1835–1910) as a Western writer, but he certainly qualifies as one since he wrote extensively about the influence of the frontier on the American spirit in addition to having lived for a number of years in the towns and cities of the West. His influence on American literature is immense, and his stories and novels have well stood the test of time. Although Twain's Roughing It *is an autobiographical account of his experiences on the frontier and his love for it, it's unknown whether or not the characters and action in "Buck Fanshaw's Funeral" are based on fact.*

SOMEBODY HAS SAID that in order to know a community, one must observe the style of its funerals and know what manner of men they bury with most ceremony. I cannot say which class we buried with most éclat in our "flush times," the distinguished public benefactor or the distinguished rough—possibly the two chief grades or grand divisions of society honored their illustrious dead about equally; and hence, no doubt, the philosopher I have quoted from would have needed to see two representative funerals in Virginia before forming his estimate of the people.

There was a grand time over Buck Fanshaw when he died. He was a representative citizen. He had "killed his man"—not in his own quarrel, it is true, but in defense of a stranger unfairly beset by numbers. He had kept a sumptuous saloon. He had been the proprietor of a dashing help-meet whom he could have discarded without the formality of a divorce. He had held a high position in the fire department and been a very Warwick in politics. When he died there was great lamentation throughout the town, but especially in the vast bottom-stratum of society.

On the inquest it was shown that Buck Fanshaw, in the delirium of a wasting typhoid fever, had taken arsenic, shot himself through the body, cut his throat, and jumped out of a four-story window and broken his neck—and after due deliberation, the jury, sad and tearful, but with intelligence unblinded by its sorrow, brought in a verdict of death "by the visitation of God." What could the world do without juries?

25

Prodigious preparations were made for the funeral. All the vehicles in town were hired, all the saloons put in mourning, all the municipal and fire company flags hung at half-mast, and all the firemen ordered to muster in uniform and bring their machines duly draped in black. Now—let us remark in parenthesis—as all the peoples of the earth had representative adventurers in the Silverland, and as each adventurer had brought the slang of his nation or his locality with him, the combination made the slang of Nevada the richest and the most infinitely varied and copious that had ever existed anywhere in the world, perhaps, except in the mines of California in the "early days." Slang was the language of Nevada. It was hard to preach a sermon without it, and be understood. Such phrases as "You bet!" "Oh, no, I reckon not!" "No Irish need apply," and a hundred others, became so common as to fall from the lips of a speaker unconsciously—and very often when they did not touch the subject under discussion and consequently failed to mean anything.

After Buck Fanshaw's inquest, a meeting of the short-haired brotherhood was held, for nothing can be done on the Pacific coast without a public meeting and an expression of sentiment. Regretful resolutions were passed and various committees appointed; among others, a committee of one was deputed to call on the minister, a fragile, gentle, spiritual new fledgling from an Eastern theological seminary, and as yet unacquainted with the ways of the mines. The committeeman, "Scotty" Briggs, made his visit; and in after days it was worth something to hear the minister tell about it. Scotty was a stalwart rough, whose customary suit, when on weighty official business, like committee work, was a fire helmet, flaming red flannel shirt, patent leather belt with spanner and revolver attached, coat hung over arm and pants stuffed into boot tops. He formed something of a contrast to the pale theological student. It is fair to say of Scotty, however, in passing, that he had a warm heart, and a strong love for his friends and never entered into a quarrel when he could reasonably keep out of it. Indeed, it was commonly said that whenever one of Scotty's fights was investigated, it always turned out that it had originally been no affair of his, but that out of native goodheartedness he had dropped in of his own accord to help the man who was getting the worst of it. He and Buck Fanshaw were bosom friends, for years, and had often taken adventurous "pot-luck" together. On one occasion, they had thrown off their coats and taken the weaker side in a fight among strangers, and after gaining a hard-earned victory, turned and found that the men they were helping had deserted early, and not only that, but had stolen their coats

and made off with them! But to return to Scotty's visit to the minister.
He was on a sorrowful mission, now, and his face was the picture of woe.
Being admitted to the presence he sat down before the clergyman, placed
his fire hat on an unfinished manuscript sermon under the minister's nose,
took from it a red silk handkerchief, wiped his brow and heaved a sigh
of dismal impressiveness, explanatory of his business. He choked, and even
shed tears; but with an effort he mastered his voice and said in lugubrious
tones:

"Are you the duck that runs the gospelmill next door?"

"Am I the—pardon me, I believe I do not understand."

With another sigh and a half-sob, Scotty rejoined:

"Why you see we are in a bit of trouble, and the boys thought maybe
you would give us a lift, if we'd tackle you—that is, if I've got the rights
of it and you are the head clerk of the doxologyworks next door."

"I am the shepherd in charge of the flock whose fold is next door."

"The which?"

"The spiritual adviser of the little company of believers whose sanctuary
adjoins these premises."

Scotty scratched his head, reflected a moment and then said:

"You ruther hold over me, pard. I reckon I can't call that hand. Ante
and pass the buck."

"How? I beg pardon. What did I understand you to say?"

"Well, you've ruther got the bulge on me. Or maybe we've both got
the bulge, somehow. You don't smoke me and I don't smoke you. You
see, one of the boys has passed in his checks, and we want to give him
a good send off, and so the thing I'm on now is to roust out somebody
to jerk a little chin music for us and waltz him through handsome."

"My friend, I seem to grow more and more bewildered. Your observa-
tions are wholly incomprehensible to me. Cannot you simplify them in
some way? At first I thought perhaps I understood you, but I grope now.
Would it not expedite matters if you restricted yourself to categorical
statements of fact unencumbered with obstructing accumulations of met-
aphor and allegory?"

Another pause, and more reflection. Then, said Scotty:

"I'll have to pass, I judge."

"How?"

"You've raised me out, pard."

"I still fail to catch your meaning."

"Why, that last lead of yourn is too many for me—that's the idea.

I can't neither trump nor follow suit."

The clergyman sank back in his chair perplexed. Scotty leaned his head on his hand and gave himself up to thought. Presently his face came up, sorrowful but confident.

"I've got it now, so's you can savvy," he said. "What we want is a gospel sharp. See?"

"A what?"

"Gospel sharp. Parson."

"Oh! Why did you not say so before? I am a clergyman—a parson."

"Now you talk! You see my blind and straddle it like a man. Put it there!"—extending a brawny paw, which closed over the minister's small hand and gave it a shake indicative of fraternal sympathy and fervent gratification.

"Now we're all right, pard. Let's start fresh. Don't you mind my snuffling a little—becuz we're in a power of trouble. You see, one of the boys has gone up the flume—"

"Gone where?"

"Up the flume—throwed up the sponge, you understand."

"Thrown up the sponge?"

"Yes—kicked the bucket—"

"Ah—has departed to that mysterious country from whose bourn no traveler returns."

"Return! I reckon not. Why, pard, he's *dead!*"

"Yes, I understand."

"Oh, you do? Well I thought maybe you might be getting tangled some more. Yes, you see he's dead again—"

"*Again!* Why, has he ever been dead before?"

"Dead before? No! Do you reckon a man has got as many lives as a cat? But you bet you he's awful dead now, poor old boy, and I wish I'd never seen this day. I don't want no better friend than Buck Fanshaw. I knowed him by the back; and when I know a man and like him, I freeze to him —you hear *me*. Take him all round, pard, there never was a bullier man in the mines. No man ever knowed Buck Fanshaw to go back on a friend. But it's all up, you know, it's all up. It ain't no use. They've scooped him."

"Scooped him?"

"Yes—death has. Well, well, well, we've got to give him up. Yes, indeed. It's a kind of a hard world, after all, *ain't* it? But pard, he was a rustler! You ought to seen him get started once. He was a bully boy with a glass eye! Just spit in his face and give him room according to his strength, and it was just beautiful to see him peel and go in. He was the worst son-of-a-thief that ever drawed breath. Pard, he was *on* it! He was on it bigger than an injun!"

"On it? On what?"

"On the shoot. On the shoulder. On the fight, you understand. *He* didn't give a continental for *any* body. *Beg* your pardon, friend, for coming so near saying a cussword—but you see I'm on an awful strain, in this palaver, on account of having to cramp down and draw everything so mild. But we've got to give him up. There ain't any getting around that, I don't reckon. Now if we can get you to help plant him—"

"Preach the funeral discourse? Assist at the obsequies?"

"Obs'quies is good. Yes. That's it—that's our little game. We are going to get the thing up regardless, you know. He was always nifty himself, and so you bet you his funeral ain't going to be no slouch—solid silver door-plate on his coffin, six plumes on the hearse and a nigger on the box in a biled shirt and a plug hat—how's that for high? And we'll take care of *you*, pard. We'll fix you all right. There'll be a kerridge for you; and whatever you want, you just 'scape out and we'll 'tend to it. We've got a shebang fixed up for you to stand behind, in No. 1's house, and don't you be afraid. Just go in and toot your horn, if you don't sell a clam. Put Buck through as bully as you can, pard, for anybody that knows him will tell you that he was one of the whitest men that was ever in the mines. You can't draw it too strong. He never could stand it to see things going wrong. He's done more to make this town quiet and peaceable than any man in it. I've seen him lick four greasers in eleven minutes, myself. If a thing wanted regulating, *he* warn't a man to go browsing around after somebody to do it, but he would prance in and regulate it himself. He warn't a Catholic. Scasely. He was down on 'em. His word was, 'No Irish need apply!' But it didn't make no difference about that when it came down to what a man's rights was—and so, when some roughs jumped the Catholic boneyard and started in to stake out town-lots in it he *went* for 'em! And he *cleaned* 'em, too! I was there, pard, and I seen it myself."

"That was very well indeed—at least the impulse was—whether the act was strictly defensible or not. Had deceased any religious convictions? That is to say, did he feel a dependence upon, or acknowledge allegiance to a higher power?"

More reflection.

"I reckon you've stumped me again, pard. Could you say it over once more, and say it slow?"

"Well, to simplify it somewhat, was he, or rather had he ever been connected with any organization sequestered from secular concerns and devoted to self-sacrifice in the interests of morality?"

"All down but nine—set 'em up on the other alley, pard."

"What did I understand you to say?"

"Why, you're most too many for me, you know. When you get in with your left I hunt grass every time. Every time you draw, you fill; but I don't seem to have any luck. Let's have a new deal."

"How? Begin again?"

"That's it."

"Very well. Was he a good man, and—"

"There—I see that; don't put up another chip till I look at my hand. A good man, says you? Pard, it ain't no name for it. He was the best man that ever—pard, you would have doted on that man. He could lam any galoot of his inches in America. It was him that put down the riot last election before it got a start; and everybody said he was the only man that could have done it. He waltzed in with a spanner in one hand and a trumpet in the other, and sent fourteen men home on a shutter in less than three minutes. He had that riot all broke up and prevented nice before anybody ever got a chance to strike a blow. He was always for peace, and he would *have* peace—he could not stand disturbances. Pard, he was a great loss to this town. It would please the boys if you could chip in something like that and do him justice. Here once when the Micks got to throwing stones through the Methodis' Sunday-school windows, Buck Fanshaw, all of his own notion, shut up his saloon and took a couple of six shooters and mounted guard over the Sunday school. Says he, 'No Irish need apply!' And they didn't. He was the bulliest man in the mountains, pard! He could run faster, jump higher, hit harder, and hold more tanglefoot whisky without spilling it than any man in seventeen counties. Put that in, pard—it'll please the boys more than anything you could say. And you can say, pard, that he never shook his mother."

"Never shook his mother?"

"That's it—any of the boys will tell you so."

"Well, but why *should* he shake her?"

"That's what *I* say—but some people does."

"Not people of any repute?"

"Well, some that averages pretty so-so."

"In my opinion the man that would offer personal violence to his own mother, ought to—"

"Cheese it, pard; you've banked your ball clean outside the string. What I was a drivin' at, was, that he never *throwed off* on his mother— don't you see? No indeedy. He give her a house to live in, and town lots, and plenty of money; and he looked after her and took care of her all the time; and when she was down with the smallpox I'm d—d if he didn't set up nights and nuss her himself! *Beg* your pardon for saying it, but it hopped out too quick for yours truly. You've treated me like a gentleman, pard, and I ain't the man to hurt your feelings intentional. I think you're white. I think you're a square man, pard. I like you, and I'll lick any man that don't. I'll lick him till he can't tell himself from a last year's corpse! Put it *there!*" (Another fraternal handshake—and exit.)

The obsequies were all that "the boys" could desire. Such a marvel of funeral pomp had never been seen in Virginia. The plumed hearse, the dirge-breathing brass bands, the closed marts of business, the flags droop- ing at half-mast, the long, plodding procession of uniformed secret soci- eties, military battalions and fire companies, draped engines, carriages of officials and citizens in vehicles and on foot, attracted multitudes of spectators to the sidewalks, roofs, and windows; and for years afterward, the degree of grandeur attained by any civic display in Virginia was determined by comparison with Buck Fanshaw's funeral.

Scotty Briggs, as a pall bearer and a mourner, occupied a prominent place at the funeral, and when the sermon was finished and the last sentence of the prayer for the dead man's soul ascended, he responded, in a low voice, but with feeling:

"AMEN. No Irish need apply."

As the bulk of the response was without apparent relevancy, it was probably nothing more than a humble tribute to the memory of the friend that was gone; for, as Scotty had once said, it was "his word."

Scotty Briggs, in after days, achieved the distinction of becoming the only convert to religion that was ever gathered from the Virginia roughs; and it transpired that the man who had it in him to espouse the quarrel of the weak out of inborn nobility of spirit was no mean timber whereof to construct a Christian. The making him one did not warp his generosity or diminish his courage; on the contrary it gave intelligent direction to the one and a broader field to the other. If his Sunday-school class pro- gressed faster than the other classes, was it matter for wonder? I think not. He talked to his pioneer small fry in a language they understood! It was my large privilege, a month before he died, to hear him tell the beautiful story of Joseph and his brethren to his class "without looking at the book."

I leave it to the reader to fancy what it was like, as it fell, riddled with slang, from the lips of that grave, earnest teacher, and was listened to by his little learners with a consuming interest that showed that they were as unconscious as he was that any violence was being done to the sacred proprieties!

BRET HARTE

How Santa Claus Came to Simpson's Bar

Few people realize that Bret Harte (1836–1902) was once the highest-paid short story writer in America. He achieved tremendous popularity because of his talent for capturing the sounds, sights and feel of the Old West, which provided the settings for such famous stories as "The Luck of Roaring Camp" and "The Outcasts of Poker Flat." He remains one of the great writers on the subject of pioneer California, the state that stole his heart. "How Santa Claus Came to Simpson's Bar" may not be as well-known as the two stories mentioned above, but it is every bit as good.

IT HAD BEEN RAINING in the valley of the Sacramento. The North Fork had overflowed its banks, and Rattlesnake Creek was impassable. The few boulders that had marked the summer ford at Simpson's Crossing were obliterated by a vast sheet of water stretching to the foothills. The upstage was stopped at Granger's; the last mail had been abandoned in the tules, the rider swimming for his life. "An area," remarked the *Sierra Avalanche*, with pensive local pride, "as large as the state of Massachusetts is now under water."

Nor was the weather any better in the foothills. The mud lay deep on the mountain road; wagons that neither physical force nor moral objurgation could move from the evil ways into which they had fallen encumbered the track, and the way to Simpson's Bar was indicated by broken-down teams and hard swearing. And further on, cut off and inaccessible, rained upon and bedraggled, smitten by high winds and threatened by high water, Simpson's Bar, on the eve of Christmas Day, 1862, clung like a swallow's nest to the rocky entablature and splintered capitals of Table Mountain, and shook in the blast.

As night shut down on the settlement, a few lights gleamed through the mist from the windows of cabins on either side of the highway, now crossed and gullied by lawless streams and swept by marauding winds. Happily most of the population were gathered at Thompson's store, clustered around a red-hot stove, at which they silently spat in some accepted sense of social communion that perhaps rendered conversation unnecessary. Indeed, most methods of diversion had long since been exhausted on Simpson's Bar; high water had suspended the regular occupations on gulch and on river, and a consequent lack of money and whiskey had taken the zest from most illegitimate recreation. Even Mr. Hamlin was fain to leave the bar with fifty dollars in his pocket—the only amount actually realized of the large sums won by him in the successful exercise of his arduous profession. "Ef I was asked,"—he remarked somewhat later—"ef I was asked to pint out a purty little village where a retired sport as didn't care for money could exercise hisself, frequent and lively, I'd say Simpson's Bar; but for a young man with a large family depending on his exertions, it don't pay." As Mr. Hamlin's family consisted mainly of female adults, this remark is quoted rather to show the breadth of his humor than the exact extent of his responsibilities.

Howbeit, the unconscious objects of this satire sat that evening in the listless apathy begotten of idleness and lack of excitement. Even the sudden splashing of hoofs before the door did not arouse them. Dick Bullen alone paused in the act of scraping out his pipe, and lifted his head, but no other one of the group indicated any interest in, or recognition of, the man who entered.

It was a figure familiar enough to the company, and known in Simpson's Bar as the Old Man. A man of perhaps fifty years; grizzled and scant of hair, but still fresh and youthful of complexion. A face full of ready but not very powerful sympathy, with a chameleonlike aptitude for taking on the shade and color of contiguous moods and feelings. He had evidently just left some hilarious companions, and did not at first notice the gravity of the group, but clapped the shoulder of the nearest man jocularly, and threw himself into a vacant chair.

"Jest heard the best thing out, boys! Ye know Smiley, over yar—Jim Smiley—funniest man in the bar? Well, Jim was jest telling the richest yarn about"—

"Smiley's a————fool," interrupted a gloomy voice.

"A particular————skunk," added another in sepulchral accents.

A silence followed these positive statements. The Old Man glanced quickly around the group. Then his face slowly changed. "That's so," he said reflectively, after a pause, "certainly a sort of a skunk and suthin' of a fool. In course." He was silent for a moment, as in painful contemplation of the unsavoriness and folly of the unpopular Smiley. "Dismal weather, ain't it?" he added, now fully embarked on the current of prevailing sentiment. "Mighty rough papers on the boys, and no show for money this season. And tomorrow's Christmas."

There was a movement among the men at this announcement, but whether of satisfaction or disgust was not plain. "Yes," continued the Old Man in the lugubrious tone he had within the last few moments unconsciously adopted—"yes, Christmas, and tonight's Christmas Eve. Ye see, boys, I kinder thought—that is, I sorter had an idee, jest passin' like, you know—that maybe ye'd all like to come over to my house tonight and have a sort of tear round. But I suppose, now, you wouldn't? Don't feel like it, maybe?" he added with anxious sympathy, peering into the faces of his companions.

"Well, I don't know," responded Tom Flynn with some cheerfulness. "P'r'aps we may. But how about your wife, Old Man? What does *she* say to it?"

The Old Man hesitated. His conjugal experience had not been a happy one, and the fact was known to Simpson's Bar. His first wife, a delicate, pretty little woman, had suffered keenly and secretly from the jealous suspicions of her husband, until one day he invited the whole Bar to his house to expose her infidelity. On arriving, the party found the shy, petite creature quietly engaged in her household duties, and retired abashed and discomfited. But the sensitive woman did not easily recover from the shock of this extraordinary outrage. It was with difficulty she regained her equanimity sufficiently to release her lover from the closet in which he was concealed, and escape with him. She left a boy of three years to comfort her bereaved husband. The Old Man's present wife had been his cook. She was large, loyal and aggressive.

Before he could reply, Joe Dimmick suggested with great directness that it was the "Old Man's house," and that, invoking the Divine Power, if the case were his own, he would invite whom he pleased, even if in so doing he imperiled his salvation. The Powers of Evil, he further remarked, should contend against him vainly. All this delivered with a terseness and vigor lost in this necessary translation.

"In course. Certainly. Thet's it," said the Old Man with a sympathetic frown. "Thar's no trouble about thet. It's my own house, built every stick on it myself. Don't you be afeard o' her, boys. She *may* cut up a trifle rough—ez wimmin do—but she'll come round." Secretly the Old Man trusted to the exaltation of liquor and the power of courageous example to sustain him in such an emergency.

As yet, Dick Bullen, the oracle and leader of Simpson's Bar, had not spoken. He now took his pipe from his lips. "Old Man, how's that yer Johnny gettin' on? Seems to me he didn't look so pert last time I seed him on the bluff heavin' rocks at Chinamen. Didn't seem to take much interest in it. Thar was a gang of 'em by yar yesterday—drownded out up the river—and I kinder thought o' Johnny, and how he'd miss 'em! Maybe now, we'd be in the way ef he wus sick?"

The father, evidently touched not only by this pathetic picture of Johnny's deprivation, but by the considerate delicacy of the speaker, hastened to assure him that Johnny was better, and that a "little fun might liven him up." Whereupon Dick arose, shook himself, and saying, "I'm ready. Lead the way, Old Man: here goes," himself led the way with a leap, a characteristic howl, and darted out into the night. As he passed through the outer room, he caught up a blazing brand from the hearth. The action was repeated by the rest of the partly, closely following and elbowing each other, and before the astonished proprietor of Thompson's grocery was aware of the intention of his guests, the room was deserted.

The night was pitchy dark. In the first gust of wind their temporary torches were extinguished, and only the red brands dancing and flitting in the gloom like drunken will-o'-the-wisps indicated their whereabouts. Their way led up Pine Tree Canyon, at the head of which a broad, low, bark-thatched cabin burrowed in the mountainside. It was the home of the Old Man, and the entrance to the tunnel in which he worked when he worked at all. Here the crowd paused for a moment out of delicate deference to their host, who came up panting in the rear.

"P'r'aps ye'd better hold on a second out yer, whilst I go in and see that things is all right," said the Old Man, with an indifference he was far from feeling. The suggestion was graciously accepted, the door opened and closed on the host, and the crowd, leaning their backs against the wall and cowering under the eaves, waited and listened.

For a few moments there was no sound but the dripping of water from the eaves and the stir and rustle of wrestling boughs above them. Then the men became uneasy, and whispered suggestion and suspicion passed from the one to the other. "Reckon she's caved in his head the first lick!" "Decoyed him inter the tunnel and barred him up, likely." "Got him down and sittin' on him." "Prob'ly biling suthin' to heave on us: stand clear the door, boys!" For just then the latch clicked, the door slowly opened and a voice said, "Come in out o' the wet."

The voice was neither that of the Old Man nor of his wife. It was the voice of a small boy, its weak tremble broken by that preternatural hoarseness which only vagabondage and the habit of premature self-assertion can give. It was the face of a small boy that looked up at theirs —a face that might have been pretty, and even refined, but that it was darkened by evil knowledge from within, and dirt and hard experience from without. He had a blanket around his shoulders, and had evidently just risen from his bed. "Come in," he repeated, "and don't make no noise. The Old Man's in there talking to mar," he continued, pointing to an adjacent room, which seemed to be a kitchen, from which the Old Man's voice came in deprecating accents. "Let me be," he added querulously to Dick Bullen, who had caught him up, blanket and all, and was affecting to toss him into the fire, "let go o' me, you d——d old fool, d'ye hear?"

Thus adjured, Dick Bullen lowered Johnny to the ground with a smothered laugh, while the men, entering quietly, ranged themselves around a long table of rough boards which occupied the center of the room. Johnny then gravely proceeded to a cupboard and brought out several articles, which he deposited on the table. "Thar's whiskey. And crackers. And red herons. And cheese." He took a bite of the latter on his way to the table. "And sugar." He scooped up a mouthful en route with a small and very dirty hand. "And terbacker. Thar's dried appils too on the shelf, but I don't admire 'em. Applis is swellin'. Thar," he concluded, "now wade in, and don't be afeard. *I* don't mind the old woman. She don't b'long to *me*. S'long."

He had stepped to the threshold of a small room, scarcely larger than a closet, partitioned off from the main apartment, and holding in its dim recess a small bed. He stood there a moment looking at the company, his bare feet peeping from the blanket, and nodded.

"Hello, Johnny! You ain't goin' to turn in agin, are ye?" said Dick.

"Yes, I are," responded Johnny decidedly.

"Why, wot's up, old fellow?"

"I'm sick."

"How sick?"

"I've got a fevier. And childblains. And rheumatiz," returned Johnny, and vanished within. After a moment's pause, he added in the dark, apparently from under the bedclothes—"And biles!"

There was an embarrassing silence. The men looked at each other and at the fire. Even with the appetizing banquet before them, it seemed as if they might again fall into the despondency of Thompson's grocery, when the voice of the Old Man, incautiously lifted, came deprecatingly from the kitchen.

"Certainly! Thet's so. In course they is. A gang o' lazy, drunken loafers, and that are Dick Bullen's the orneriest of all. Didn't hev no more *sabe* than to come round yar with sickness in the house and no provision. Thet's what I said: 'Bullen,' sez I, 'it's crazy drunk you are, or a fool,' sez I, 'to think o' such a thing.' 'Staples,' I sez, 'be you a man, Staples, and 'spect to raise h——ll under my roof and invalids lyin' round?' But they would come—they would. Thet's wot you must 'spect o' such trash as lays round the bar."

A burst of laughter from the men followed this unfortunate exposure. Whether it was overheard in the kitchen, or whether the Old Man's irate companion had just then exhausted all other modes of expressing her contemptuous indignation, I cannot say, but a back door was suddenly slammed with great violence. A moment later and the Old Man reappeared, haply unconscious of the cause of the late hilarious outburst, and smiled blandly.

"The old woman thought she'd jest run over to Mrs. MacFadden's for a sociable call," he explained with jaunty indifference, as he took a seat at the board.

Oddly enough it needed this untoward incident to relieve the embarrassment that was beginning to be felt by the party, and their natural audacity returned with their host. I do not propose to record the convivialities of that evening. The inquisitive reader will accept the statement that the conversation was characterized by the same intellectual exaltation, the same cautious reverence, the same fastidious delicacy, the same rhetorical precision, and the same logical and coherent discourse somewhat later in the evening which distinguish similar gatherings of the masculine sex in more civilized localities and under more favorable auspices. No glasses were broken in the absence of any; no liquor was uselessly spilled on the floor or table in the scarcity of that article.

It was nearly midnight when the festivities were interupted. "Hush," said Dick Bullen, holding up his hand. It was the querulous voice of Johnny from his adjacent closet, "Oh, dad!"

The Old Man arose hurriedly and disappeared in the closet. Presently he reappeared. "His rheumatiz is coming on agin bad," he explained, "and he wants rubbin'." He lifted the demijohn of whiskey from the table and shook it. It was empty. Dick Bullen put down his tin cup with an embarrassed laugh. So did the others. The Old Man examined their contents and said hopefully, "I reckon that's enough; he don't need much. You hold on all o' you for a spell, and I'll be back," and vanished in the closet with an old flannel shirt and the whiskey. The door closed but imperfectly, and the following dialogue was distinctly audible:

"Now, sonny, whar does she ache worst?"

"Sometimes over yar and sometimes under yer; but it's most powerful from yer to yer. Rub yer, dad."

A silence seemed to indicate a brisk rubbing. Then Johnny:

"Hevin' a good time out yer, dad?"

"Yes, sonny."

"Tomorrer's Chrismiss—ain't it?"

"Yes, sonny. How does she feel now?"

"Better. Rub a little furder down. Wot's Chrismiss, anyway? Wot's it all about?"

"Oh, it's a day."

This exhaustive definition was apparently satisfactory, for there was a silent interval of rubbing. Presently Johnny again:

"Mar sez that everywhere else but yer everybody gives things to every-body Chrismiss, and then she jist waded inter you. She sez thar's a man they call Sandy Claws, not a white man, you know, but a kind o' Chine-min, comes down the chimbley night afore Chrismiss and gives things to chillern—boys like me. Puts 'em in their butes! Thet's what she tried to play upon me. Easy now, pop, whar are you rubbin' to—thet's a mile from the place. She jest made that up, didn't she, jest to aggrewate me and you? Don't rub thar. . . . Why, dad!"

In the great quiet that seemed to have fallen upon the house, the sigh of the near pines and the drip of leaves without was very distinct. Johnny's voice, too, was lowered as he went on. "Don't you take on now, for I'm gettin' all right fast. Wot's the boys doin' out thar?"

The Old Man partly opened the door and peered through. His guests were sitting there sociably enough, and there were a few silver coins and a lean buckskin purse on the table. "Bettin' on suthin'—some little game or 'nother. They're all right," he replied to Johnny, and recommenced his rubbing.

"I'd like to take a hand and win some money," said Johnny reflectively after a pause.

The Old Man glibly repeated what was evidently a familiar formula, that if Johnny would wait until he struck it rich in the tunnel he'd have lots of money, etc., etc.

"Yes," said Johnny, "but you don't. And whether you strike it or I win it, it's about the same. It's all luck. But it's mighty cur'o's about Chrismiss —ain't it? Why do they call it Chrismiss?"

Perhaps from some instinctive deference to the overhearing of his guests, or from some vague sense of incongruity, the Old Man's reply was so low as to be inaudible beyond the room.

"Yes," said Johnny, with some slight abatement of interest, "I've heard o' *him* before. Thar, that'll do, dad. I don't ache near so bad as I did. Now wrap me tight in this yer blanket. So. Now," he added in a muffled whisper, "sit down yer by me till I go asleep." To assure himself of obedience, he disengaged one hand from the blanket, and grasping his father's sleeve, again composed himself to rest.

For some moments the Old Man waited patiently. Then the unwonted stillness of the house excited his curiosity, and without moving from the bed he cautiously opened the door with his disengaged hand, and looked into the main room. To his infinite surprise it was dark and deserted. But even then a smoldering log on the hearth broke, and by the upspringing blaze he saw the figure of Dick Bullen sitting by the dying embers.

"Hello!"

Dick started, rose and came somewhat unsteadily toward him.

"Whar's the boys?" said the Old Man.

"Gone up the canyon on a little *pasear*. They're coming back for me in a minit. I'm waitin' round for 'em. What are you starin' at, Old Man?" he added, with a forced laugh. "Do you think I'm drunk?"

The Old Man might have been pardoned the supposition, for Dick's eyes were humid and his face flushed. He loitered and lounged back to the chimney, yawned, shook himself, buttoned up his coat and laughed. "Liquor ain't so plenty as that, Old Man. Now don't you git up," he continued as the Old Man made a movement to release his sleeve from Johnny's hand. "Don't you mind manners. Sit jest whar you be; I'm goin' in a jiffy. Thar, that's them now."

There was a low tap at the door. Dick Bullen opened it quickly, nod-ded "good night" to his host, and disappeared. The Old Man would have followed him but for the hand that still unconsciously grasped his sleeve. He could have easily disengaged it: it was small, weak and emaciated. But perhaps because it *was* small, weak and emaciated he changed his mind, and drawing his chair closer to the bed, rested his head upon it. In this defenseless attitude the potency of his earlier potations surprised him. The room flickered and faded before his eyes, reappeared, faded again, went out, and left him—asleep.

Meantime Dick Bullen, closing the door, confronted his companions. "Are you ready?" said Staples. "Ready," said Dick; "what's the time?" "Past twelve," was the reply; "can you make it?—it's nigh on fifty miles, the round trip hither and yon." "I reckon," returned Dick shortly. "Whar's the mare?" "Bill and Jack's holdin' her at the crossin'." "Let 'em hold on a minit longer," said Dick.

He turned and reentered the house softly. By the light of the guttering candle and dying fire he saw that the door of the little room was open. He stepped toward it on tiptoe and looked in. The Old Man had fallen back in his chair, snoring, his helpless feet thrust out in a line with his collapsed shoulders, and his hat pulled over his eyes. Beside him, on a narrow wooden bedstead, lay Johnny, muffled tightly in a blanket that hid all save a strip of forehead and a few curls damp with perspiration. Dick Bullen made a step forward, hesitated and glanced over his shoulder into the deserted room. Everything was quiet. With a sudden resolution he parted his huge mustaches with both hands and stooped over the sleeping boy. But even as he did so, a mischievous blast, lying in wait, swooped down the chimney, rekindled the hearth and lit up the room with a shameless glow from which Dick fled in bashful terror.

His companions were already waiting for him at the crossing. Two of them were struggling in the darkness with some strange misshapen bulk, which as Dick came nearer took the semblance of a great yellow horse.

It was the mare. She was not a pretty picture. From her roman nose to her rising haunches, from her arched spine hidden by the stiff *machillas* of a Mexican saddle, to her thick, straight bony legs, there was not a line of equine grace. In her half-blind but wholly vicious white eyes, in her protruding underlip, in her monstrous color, there was nothing but ugliness and vice.

"Now then," said Staples, "stand cl'ar of her heels, boys, and up with you. Don't miss your first holt of her mane, and mind ye get your off stirrup *quick*. Ready!"

There was a leap, a scrambling struggle, a bound, a wild retreat of the crowd, a circle of flying hooves, two springless leaps that jarred the earth, a rapid play and jingle of spurs, a plunge and then the voice of Dick somewhere in the darkness. "All right!"

"Don't take the lower road back onless you're hard pushed for time! Don't hold her in downhill! We'll be at the ford at five. G'lang! Hoopa! Mula! GO!"

A splash, a spark struck from the ledge in the road, a clatter in the rocky cut beyond and Dick was gone.

Sing, O Muse, the ride of Richard Bullen! Sing, O Muse, of chivalrous men! The sacred quest, the doughty deeds, the battery of low churls, the fearsome ride and gruesome perils of the Flower of Simpson's Bar! Alack! She is dainty, this Muse! She will have none of this bucking brute and swaggering, ragged rider, and I must fain follow him in prose, afoot!

It was one o'clock, and yet he had only gained Rattlesnake Hill. For in that time Jovita had rehearsed to him all her imperfections and practiced all her vices. Thrice had she stumbled. Twice had she thrown up her roman nose in a straight line with the reins, and resisting bit and spur, struck out madly across country. Twice had she reared, and rearing, fallen backward; and twice had the agile Dick, unharmed, regained his seat before she found her vicious legs again. And a mile beyond them, at the foot of a long hill, was Rattlesnake Creek. Dick knew that here was the crucial test of his ability to perform his enterprise, set his teeth grimly, put his knees well into her flanks, and changed his defensive tactics to brisk aggression. Bullied and maddened, Jovita began the descent of the hill. Here the artful Richard pretended to hold her in with ostentatious objurgation and well-feigned cries of alarm. It is unnecessary to add that Jovita instantly ran away. Nor need I state the time made in the descent; it is written in the chronicles of Simpson's Bar. Enough that in another moment, as it seemed to Dick, she was splashing on the overflowed banks of Rattlesnake Creek. As Dick expected, the momentum she had acquired carried her beyond the point of balking, and holding her well together for a mighty leap, they dashed into the middle of the swiftly flowing current. A few moments of kicking, wading and swimming, and Dick drew a long breath on the opposite bank.

The road from Rattlesnake Creek to Red Mountain was tolerably level. Either the plunge in Rattlesnake Creek had dampened her baleful fire, or the art which led to it had shown her the superior wickedness of her rider, for Jovita no longer wasted her surplus energy in wanton conceits. Once she bucked, but it was from force of habit; once she shied, but it was from a new, freshly painted meetinghouse at the crossing of the county road. Hollows, ditches, gravelly deposits, patches of freshly springing grasses, flew from beneath her rattling hoofs. She began to smell unpleasantly, once or twice she coughed slightly, but there was no abatement of her strength or speed. By two o'clock he had passed Red Moun-

tain and begun the descent to the plain. Ten minutes later the driver of
the fast Pioneer coach was overtaken and passed by a "man on a pinto
hoss"—an event sufficiently notable for remark. At half-past two Dick
rose in his stirrups with a great shout. Stars were glittering through the
rifted clouds, and beyond him, out of the plain, rose two spires, a flagstaff
and a straggling line of black objects. Dick jingled his spurs and swung
his riata, Jovita bounded forward, and in another moment they swept into
Tuttleville and drew up before the wooden piazza of the Hotel of All
Nations.

What transpired that night at Tuttleville is not strictly a part of this
record. Briefly I may state, however, that after Jovita had been handed
over to a sleepy ostler, whom she at once kicked into unpleasant consciousness, Dick sallied out with the barkeeper for a tour of the sleeping town.
Lights still gleamed from a few saloons and gambling houses; but avoiding
these, they stopped before several closed shops and, by persistent tapping
and judicious outcry, roused the proprietors from their beds and made
them unbar the doors of their magazines and expose their wares. Sometimes they were met by curses, but oftener by interest and some concern
in their needs, and the interview was invariably concluded by a drink. It
was three o'clock before this pleasantry was given over, and with a small
waterproof bag of india rubber strapped on his shoulders, Dick returned
to the hotel. But here he was waylaid by Beauty—Beauty opulent in
charms, affluent in dress, persuasive in speech, and Spanish in accent! In
vain she repeated the invitation in Excelsior, happily scorned by all Al-
pine-climbing youth, and rejected by this child of the Sierras—a rejection
softened in this instance by a laugh and his last gold coin. And then he
sprang to the saddle and dashed down the lonely street and out into the
lonelier plain where presently the lights, the black line of houses, the spires
and the flagstaff sank into the earth behind him again and were lost in
the distance.

The storm had cleared away, the air was brisk and cold, the outlines
of adjacent landmarks were distinct, but it was half-past four before Dick
reached the meetinghouse and the crossing of the country road. To avoid
the rising grade he had taken a longer and more circuitous road, in whose
viscid mud Jovita sank fetlock-deep at every bound. It was a poor preparation for a steady ascent of five miles more; but Jovita, gathering her legs
under her, took it with her usual blind, unreasoning fury, and a half hour
later reached the long level that led to Rattlesnake Creek. Another half
hour would bring him to the creek. He threw the reins lightly upon the

neck of the mare, chirruped to her and began to sing.

Suddenly Jovita shied with a bound that would have unseated a less practiced rider. Hanging to her rein was a figure that had leaped from the bank, and, at the same time, from the road before her arose a shadowy horse and rider.

"Throw up your hands," commanded the second apparition, with an oath.

Dick felt the mare tremble, quiver and apparently sink under him. He knew what it meant and was prepared.

"Stand aside, Jack Simpson. I know you, you d——d thief! Let me pass, or—"

He did not finish the sentence. Jovita rose straight in the air with a terrific bound, throwing the figure from her bit with a single shake of her vicious head, and charged with deadly malevolence down on the impediment before her. An oath, a pistol shot, horse and highwayman rolled over in the road, and the next moment Jovita was a hundred yards away. But the good right arm of her rider, shattered by a bullet, dropped helplessly at his side.

Without slacking his speed, he shifted the reins to his left hand. But a few moments later he was obliged to halt and tighten the saddle girths that had slipped in the onset. This, in his crippled condition, took some time. He had no fear of pursuit, but looking up he saw that the eastern stars were already paling, and that the distant peaks had lost their ghostly whiteness and now stood out blackly against a lighter sky. Day was upon him. Then completely absorbed in a single idea, he forgot the pain of his wound and, mounting again, dashed on toward Rattlesnake Creek. But now Jovita's breath came broken by gasps, Dick reeled in his saddle, and brighter and brighter grew the sky.

Ride, Richard; run, Jovita; linger, O day!

For the last few rods there was a roaring in his ears. Was it exhaustion from loss of blood, or what? He was dazed and giddy as he swept down the hill, and did not recognize his surroundings. Had he taken the wrong road, or was this Rattlesnake Creek?

It was. But the brawling creek he had swum a few hours before had risen, more than doubled its volume, and now rolled a swift and resistless river between him and Rattlesnake Hill. For the first time that night Richard's heart sank within him. The river, the mountain, the quickening east, swam before his eyes. He shut them to recover his self-control. In that brief interval, by some fantastic mental process, the little room at

Simpson's Bar and the figures of the sleeping father and son rose upon him. He opened his eyes wildly, cast off his coat, pistol, boots and saddle, bound his precious pack tightly to his shoulders, grasped the bare flanks of Jovita with his bared knees, and with a shout dashed into the yellow water. A cry rose from the opposite bank as the head of a man and horse struggled for a few moments against the battling current, and then were swept away amidst uprooted trees and whirling driftwood.

The Old Man started and woke. The fire on the hearth was dead, the candle in the outer room flickering in its socket, and somebody was rapping at the door. He opened it, but fell back with a cry before the dripping, half-naked figure that reeled against the doorpost.

"Dick?"

"Hush! Is he awake yet?"

"No; but, Dick—"

"Dry up, you old fool! Get me some whiskey, *quick!*" The Old Man flew and returned with—an empty bottle! Dick would have sworn, but his strength was not equal to the occasion. He staggered, caught at the handle of the door and motioned to the Old Man.

"Thar's suthin' in my pack yer for Johnny. Take it off. I can't."

The Old Man unstrapped the pack, and laid it before the exhausted man.

"Open it, quick."

He did so with trembling fingers. It contained only a few poor toys—cheap and barbaric enough, goodness knows, but bright with paint and tinsel. One of them was broken; another, I fear, was irretrievably ruined by water, and on the third—ah me! there was a cruel spot.

"It don't look like much, that's a fact," said Dick ruefully—"but it's the best we could do—Take 'em, Old Man, and put 'em in his stocking, and tell him—tell him, you know—hold me, Old Man—" The Old Man caught at his sinking figure. "Tell him," said Dick, with a weak little laugh—"tell him Sandy Claus has come."

And even so, bedraggled, ragged, unshaven and unshorn, with one arm hanging helplessly at his side, Santa Claus came to Simpson's Bar and fell fainting on the first threshold. The Christmas dawn came slowly after, touching the remoter peaks with the rosy warmth of ineffable love. And it looked so tenderly on Simpson's Bar that the whole mountain, as if caught in a generous action, blushed to the skies.

The Blue Hotel

Stephen Crane (1871–1900) was the first American writer to use the realistic approach in fiction, paving the way for the work of such subsequent giants as Sherwood Anderson, Ernest Hemingway and Dashiell Hammett. Crane's best known literary achievement is of course The Red Badge of Courage—*the single finest novel ever written about the Civil War. Of his many stories about the Old West "The Blue Hotel" (which appeared in his collection* The Monster, *in 1899) is the longest and ranks with his oft-anthologized "The Bride Comes to Yellow Sky" as the best.*

I

THE PALACE HOTEL at Fort Romper was painted a light blue, a shade that is on the legs of a kind of heron, causing the bird to declare its position against any background. The Palace Hotel, then, was always screaming and howling in a way that made the dazzling winter landscape cf Nebraska seem only a gray swampish hush. It stood alone on the prairie, and when the snow was falling, the town two hundred yards away was not visible. But when the traveler alighted at the railway station, he was obliged to pass the Palace Hotel before he could come upon the company of low clapboard houses which composed Fort Romper, and it was not to be thought that any traveler could pass the Palace Hotel without looking at it. Pat Scully, the proprietor, had proved himself a master of strategy when he chose his paints. It is true that on clear days, when the great transcontinental expresses, long lines of swaying Pullmans, swept through Fort Romper, passengers were overcome at the sight, and the cult that knows the brown reds and the subdivisions of the dark greens of the East expressed shame, pity, horror, in a laugh. But to the citizens of this prairie town and to the people who would naturally stop there, Pat Scully had performed a feat. With this opulence and splendor, these creeds, classes, egotisms, that streamed through Romper on the rails day after day, they had no color in common.

As if the displayed delights of such a blue hotel were not sufficiently enticing, it was Scully's habit to go every morning and evening to meet the leisurely trains that stopped at Romper and work his seductions upon any man that he might see wavering, gripsack in hand.

One morning, when a snow-crusted engine dragged its long string of freight cars and its one passenger coach to the station, Scully performed the marvel of catching three men. One was a shaky and quick-eyed Swede, with a great shining cheap valise; one was a tall bronzed cowboy, who was on his way to a ranch near the Dakota line; one was a little silent man from the East, who didn't look it and didn't announce it. Scully practically made them prisoners. He was so nimble and merry and kindly that each probably felt it would be the height of brutality to try to escape. They trudged off over the creaking board sidewalks in the wake of the eager little Irishman. He wore a heavy fur cap squeezed tightly down on his head. It caused his two red ears to stick out stiffly, as if they were made of tin.

At last, Scully, elaborately, with boisterous hospitality, conducted them through the portals of the blue hotel. The room which they entered was small. It seemed to be merely a proper temple for an enormous stove, which, in the center, was humming with godlike violence. At various points on its surface, the iron had become luminous and glowed yellow from the heat. Beside the stove Scully's son Johnnie was playing high-five with an old farmer who had whiskers both gray and sandy. They were quarreling. Frequently the old farmer turned his face toward a box of sawdust—colored brown from tobacco juice—that was behind the stove, and spat with an air of great impatience and irritation. With a loud flourish of words, Scully destroyed the game of cards and bustled his son upstairs with part of the baggage of the new guests. He himself conducted them to three basins of the coldest water in the world. The cowboy and the Easterner burnished themselves fiery red with this water, until it seemed to be some kind of metal polish. The Swede, however, merely dipped his fingers gingerly and with trepidation. It was notable that throughout this series of small ceremonies, the three travelers were made to feel that Scully was very benevolent. He was conferring great favors upon them. He handed the towel from one to another with an air of philanthropic impulse.

Afterward they went to the first room, and, sitting about the stove, listened to Scully's officious clamor at his daughters, who were preparing the midday meal. They reflected in the silence of experienced men who tread carefully amid new people. Nevertheless, the old farmer, stationary, invincible in his chair near the warmest part of the stove, turned his face from the sawdust box frequently and addressed a glowing commonplace to the strangers. Usually he was answered in short but adequate sentences by either the cowboy or the Easterner. The Swede said nothing. He seemed to be occupied in making furtive estimates of each man in the room. One might have thought that he had the sense of silly suspicion which comes to guilt. He resembled a badly frightened man.

Later, at dinner, he spoke a little, addressing his conversation entirely to Scully. He volunteered that he had come from New York where for ten years he had worked as a tailor. These facts seemed to strike Scully as fascinating, and afterward he volunteered that he had lived at Romper for fourteen years. The Swede asked about the crops and the price of labor. He seemed barely to listen to Scully's extended replies. His eyes continued to rove from man to man.

Finally, with a laugh and a wink, he said that some of these Western communities were very dangerous; and after his statement he straightened his legs under the table, tilted his head and laughed again, loudly. It was plain that the demonstration had no meaning to the others. They looked at him wondering and in silence.

II

As the men trooped heavily back into the front room, the two little windows presented views of a turmoiling sea of snow. The huge arms of the wind were making attempts—mighty, circular, futile—to embrace the flakes as they sped. A gatepost like a still man with a blanched face stood aghast amid this profligate fury. In a hearty voice Scully announced the presence of a blizzard. The guests of the blue hotel, lighting their pipes, assented with grunts of lazy masculine contentment. No island of the sea could be exempt in the degree of this little room with its humming stove. Johnnie, son of Scully, in a tone which defined his opinion of his ability as a cardplayer, challenged the old farmer of both gray and sandy whiskers to a game of high-five. The farmer agreed with a contemptuous and bitter scoff. They sat close to the stove, and squared their knees under a wide board. The cowboy and the Easterner watched the game with interest. The Swede remained near the window, aloof, but with a countenance that showed signs of an inexplicable excitement.

The play of Johnnie and the graybeard was suddenly ended by another quarrel. The old man arose while casting a look of heated scorn at his adversary. He slowly buttoned his coat, and then stalked with fabulous dignity from the room. In the discreet silence of all the other men, the Swede laughed. His laughter rang somehow childish. Men by this time had begun to look at him askance, as if they wished to inquire what ailed him.

A new game was formed jocosely. The cowboy volunteered to become the partner of Johnnie, and they all then turned to ask the Swede to throw in his lot with the little Easterner. He asked some questions about the game, and, learning that it wore many names, and that he had played it when it was under an alias, he accepted the invitation. He strode toward the men nervously, as if he expected to be assaulted. Finally, seated, he gazed from face to face and laughed shrilly. This laugh was so strange that the Easterner looked up quickly, the cowboy sat intent and with his mouth open, and Johnnie paused, holding the cards with still fingers.

Afterward there was a short silence. Then Johnnie said, "Well, let's get at it. Come on, now!" They pulled their chairs forward until their knees were bunched under the board. They began to play, and their interest in the game caused the others to forget the manner of the Swede.

The cowboy was a board-whacker. Each time that he held superior cards he whanged them, one by one, with exceeding force, down upon the improvised table, and took the tricks with a glowing air of prowess and ride that sent thrills of indignation into the hearts of his opponents. A game with a board-whacker in it is sure to become intense. The countenances of the Easterner and the Swede were miserable whenever the cowboy thundered down his aces and kings, while Johnnie, his eyes gleaming with joy, chuckled and chuckled.

Because of the absorbing play none considered the strange ways of the Swede. They paid strict heed to the game. Finally, during a lull caused by a new deal, the Swede suddenly addressed Johnnie. "I suppose there have been a good many men killed in this room." The jaws of the others dropped and they looked at him.

"What in hell are you talking about?" said Johnnie.

The Swede laughed again his blatant laugh, full of a kind of false courage and defiance. "Oh, you know what I mean all right," he answered.

"I'm a liar if I do!" Johnnie protested. The card was halted, and the men stared at the Swede. Johnnie evidently felt that as the son of the proprietor he should make a direct inquiry. "Now, what might you be drivin' at, mister?" he asked. The Swede winked at him. It was a wink full of cunning. His fingers shook on the edge of the board. "Oh, maybe you think I have been to nowheres. Maybe you think I'm a tenderfoot?"

"I don't know nothin' about you," answered Johnnie, "and I don't give a damn where you've been. All I got to say is that I don't know what you're driving at. There hain't never been nobody killed in this room."

The cowboy, who had been steadily gazing at the Swede, then spoke. "What's wrong with you, mister?"

Apparently it seemed to the Swede that he was formidably menaced. He shivered and turned white near the corners of his mouth. He sent an appealing glance in the direction of the little Easterner. During these moments he did not forget to wear his air of advanced pot-valor. "They say they don't know what I mean," he remarked mockingly to the Easterner.

The latter answered after prolonged and cautious reflection. "I don't understand you," he said impassively.

The Swede made a movement then which announced that he thought he had encountered treachery from the only quarter where he had expected sympathy, if not help. "Oh, I see you are all against me. I see—"

The cowboy was in a state of deep stupefaction. "Say," he cried, as he tumbled the deck violently down upon the board, "say, what are you gittin' at, hey?"

The Swede sprang up with the celerity of a man escaping from a snake on the floor. "I don't want to fight!" he shouted. "I don't want to fight!"

The cowboy stretched his long legs indolently and deliberately. His hands were in his pockets. He spat into the sawdust box. "Well, who the hell thought you did?" he inquired.

The Swede backed rapidly toward a corner of the room. His hands were out protectingly in front of his chest, but he was making an obvious struggle to control his fright. "Gentlemen," he quavered, "I suppose I am going to be killed before I can leave this house! I suppose I am going to be killed before I can leave this house!" In his eyes was the dying-swan look. Through the windows could be seen the snow turning blue in the shadow of dusk. The wind tore at the house, and some loose thing beat regularly against the clapboards like a spirit tapping.

A door opened, and Scully himself entered. He paused in surprise as he noted the tragic attitude of the Swede. Then he said, "What's the matter here?"

The Swede answered him swiftly and eagerly, "These men are going to kill me."

"Kill you!" ejaculated Scully. "Kill you! What are you talkin'?"

The Swede made the gesture of a martyr.

Scully wheeled sternly upon his son. "What is this, Johnnie?"

The lad had grown sullen. "Damned if I know," he answered. "I can't make no sense to it." He began to shuffle the cards, fluttering them together with an angry snap. "He says a good many men have been killed in this room, or something like that. And he says he's goin' to be killed here too. I don't know what ails him. He's crazy, I shouldn't wonder."

Scully then looked for explanation to the cowboy, but the cowboy simply shrugged his shoulders.

"Kill you?" said Scully again to the Swede. "Kill you? Man, you're off your nut."

"Oh, I know," burst out the Swede. "I know what will happen. Yes, I'm crazy—yes. Yes, of course, I'm crazy—yes. But I know one thing—" There was a sort of sweat of misery and terror upon his face. "I know I won't get out of here alive."

The cowboy drew a deep breath, as if his mind was passing into the last stages of dissolution. "Well, I'm doggoned," he whispered to himself.

Scully wheeled suddenly and faced his son. "You've been troublin' this man!"

Johnnie's voice was loud with its burden of grievance. "Why, good Gawd, I ain't done nothin' to 'im."

The Swede broke in. "Gentlemen, do not disturb yourselves. I will leave this house. I will go away, because"—he accused them dramatically with his glance—"because I do not want to be killed."

Scully was furious with his son. "Will you tell me what is the matter, you young devil? What's the matter, anyhow? Speak out!"

"Blame it!" cried Johnnie in despair, "don't I tell you I don't know? He—he says we want to kill him, and that's all I know. I can't tell what ails him."

The Swede continued to repeat, "Never mind, Mr. Scully; never mind. I will leave this house. I will go away, because I do not wish to be killed. Yes, of course, I am crazy—yes. But I know one thing! I will go away. I will leave this house. Never mind, Mr. Scully; never mind. I will go away."

"You will not go 'way," said Scully. "You will not go 'way until I hear the reason of this business. If anybody has troubled you, I will take care of him. This is my house. You are under my roof, and I will not allow any peaceable man to be troubled here." He cast a terrible eye upon Johnnie, the cowboy and the Easterner.

"Never mind, Mr. Scully; never mind. I will go away. I do not wish to be killed." The Swede moved toward the door which opened upon the stairs. It was evidently his intention to go at once for his baggage.

"No, no," shouted Scully peremptorily; but the white-faced man slid by him and disappeared. "Now," said Scully severely, "what does this mean?"

Johnnie and the cowboy cried together, "Why, we didn't do nothin' to 'im!"

Scully's eyes were cold. "No," he said, "you didn't?"

Johnnie swore a deep oath. "Why, this is the wildest loon I ever see. We didn't do nothin' at all. We were just sittin' here playin' cards, and he—"

The father suddenly spoke to the Easterner. "Mr. Blanc," he asked, "what has these boys been doin'?"

The Easterner reflected again. "I didn't see anything wrong at all," he said at last slowly.

Scully began to howl. "But what does it mane?" He stared ferociously at his son. "I have a mind to lather you for this, me boy."

Johnnie was frantic. "Well, what have I done?" he bawled at his father.

III

"I think you are tongue-tied," said Scully finally to his son, the cowboy and the Easterner; and at the end of this scornful sentence, he left the room.

Upstairs the Swede was swiftly fastening the straps of his great valise. Once his back happened to be half turned toward the door, and, hearing a noise there, he wheeled and sprang up, uttering a loud cry. Scully's wrinkled visage showed grimly in the light of the small lamp he carried. This yellow effulgence, streaming upward, colored only his prominent features, and left his eyes, for instance, in mysterious shadow. He resembled a murderer.

"Man! man!" he exclaimed, "have you gone daffy?"

"Oh, no! Oh, no!" rejoined the other. "There are people in this world who know pretty nearly as much as you do—understand?"

For a moment they stood gazing at each other. Upon the Swede's deathly pale cheeks were two spots brightly crimson and sharply edged, as if they had been carefully painted. Scully placed the light on the table and sat himself on the edge of the bed. He spoke ruminatively. "By cracky, I never heard of such a thing in my life. It's a complete muddle. I can't, for the soul of me, think how you ever got this idea into your head." Presently he lifted his eyes and asked, "And did you sure think they were going to kill you?"

The Swede scanned the old man as if he wished to see into his mind. "I did," he said at last. He obviously suspected that this answer might precipitate an outbreak. As he pulled on a strap his whole arm shook, the elbow wavering like a bit of paper.

Scully banged his hand impressively on the footboard of the bed. "Why, man, we're goin' to have a line of ilictric streetcars in this town next spring."

" 'A line of electric streetcars,' " repeated the Swede stupidly.

"And," said Scully, "there's a new railroad goin' to be built down from Broken Arm to here. Not to mention the four churches and the smashin' big brick schoolhouse. Then there's the big factory, too. Why, in two years Romper'll be a met-tro-*pol*-is."

Having finished the preparation of his baggage, the Swede straightened himself. "Mr. Scully," he said, with sudden hardihood, "how much do I owe you?"

"You don't owe me anythin'," said the old man, angrily.

"Yes, I do," retorted the Swede. He took seventy-five cents from his pocket and tendered it to Scully; but the latter snapped his fingers in disdainful refusal. However, it happened that they both stood gazing in a strange fashion at three silver pieces on the Swede's open palm.

"I'll not take your money," said Scully at last. "Not after what's been goin' on here." Then a plan seemed to strike him. "Here," he cried, picking up his lamp and moving toward the door. "Here! Come with me a minute."

"No," said the Swede, in overwhelming alarm.

"Yes," urged the old man. "Come on! I want you to come and see a picter—just across the hall—in my room."

The Swede must have concluded that his hour was come. His jaw dropped and his teeth showed like a dead man's. He ultimately followed Scully across the corridor, but he had the step of one hung in chains.

Scully flashed the light high on the wall of his own chamber. There was revealed a ridiculous photograph of a little girl. She was leaning against a balustrade of gorgeous decoration, and the formidable bang to her hair was prominent. The figure was as graceful as an upright sled-stake, and, withal, it was of the hue of lead. "There," said Scully, tenderly, "that's the picter of my little girl that died. Her name was Carrie. She had the purtiest hair you ever saw. I was that fond of her, she—"

Turning then, he saw that the Swede was not contemplating the picture at all, but, instead, was keeping keen watch on the gloom in the rear.

"Look, man!" cried Scully, heartily. "That's the picter of my little gal that died. Her name was Carrie. And then here's the picter of my oldest boy, Michael. He's a lawyer in Lincoln, an' doin' well. I gave that boy a grand eddication, and I'm glad for it now. He's a fine boy. Look at 'im now. Ain't he bold as blazes, him there in Lincoln, an honored an' respicted gintelman! An honored and respected gintleman," concluded Scully with a flourish. And, so saying, he smote the Swede jovially on the back.

The Swede faintly smiled.

"Now," said the old man, "there's only one more thing." He dropped suddenly to the floor and thrust his hand beneath the bed. The Swede could hear his muffled voice. "I'd keep it under me piller if it wasn't for that boy Johnnie. Then there's the old woman—Where is it now? I never put it twice in the same place. Ah, now come out with you!"

Presently he backed clumsily from under the bed, dragging with him an old coat rolled into a bundle. "I've fetched him," he muttered. Kneeling on the floor, he unrolled the coat and extracted from its heart a large yellow brown whisky bottle.

His first maneuver was to hold the bottle up to the light. Reassured, apparently, that nobody had been tampering with it, he thrust it with a generous movement toward the Swede.

The weak-kneed Swede was about to eagerly clutch this element of strength, but he suddenly jerked his hand away and cast a look of horror upon Scully.

"Drink," said the old man affectionately. He had risen to his feet, and now stood facing the Swede.

There was a silence. Then again Scully said, "Drink!"

The Swede laughed wildly. He grabbed the bottle, put it to his mouth; and as his lips curled absurdly around the opening and his throat worked, he kept his glance, burning with hatred, upon the old man's face.

IV

After the departure of Scully the three men, with the cardboard still upon their knees, preserved for a long time an astounded silence. Then Johnnie said, "That's the daddangedest Swede I ever see."

"He ain't no Swede," said the cowboy scornfully.

"Well, what is he then?" cried Johnnie. "What is he then?"

"It's my opinion," replied the cowboy deliberately, "he's some kind of a Dutchman." It was a venerable custom of the country to entitle as Swedes all light-haired men who spoke with a heavy tongue. In consequence the idea of the cowboy was not without its daring. "Yes, sir," he repeated. "It's my opinion this feller is some kind of a Dutchman."

"Well, he says he's a Swede, anyhow," muttered Johhnie, sulkily. He turned to the Easterner. "What do you think, Mr. Blanc?"

"Oh, I don't know," replied the Easterner.

"Well, what do you think makes him act that way?" asked the cowboy.

"Why, he's frightened." The Easterner knocked his pipe against a rim of the stove. "He's clear frightened out of his boots."

"What at?" cried Johnnie and the cowboy together.

The Easterner reflected over his answer.

"What at?" cried the others again.

"Oh, I don't know, but it seems to me this man has been reading dime novels, and he thinks he's right out in the middle of it—the shootin' and stabbin' and all."

"But," said the cowboy, deeply scandalized, "this ain't Wyoming, ner none of them places. This is Nebrasker."

"Yes," added Johnnie, "an' why don't he wait till he gits *out West?*"

The traveled Easterner laughed. "It isn't different there even—not in these days. But he thinks he's right in the middle of hell."

Johnnie and the cowboy mused long.

"It's awful funny," remarked Johnnie at last.

"Yes," said the cowboy. "This is a queer game. I hope we don't git snowed in, because then we'd have to stand this here man bein' around with us all the time. That wouldn't be no good."

"I wish pop would throw him out," said Johnnie.

Presently they heard a loud stamping on the stairs, accompanied by ringing jokes in the voice of old Scully, and laughter, evidently from the Swede. The men around the stove stared vacantly at each other. "Gosh!" said the cowboy. The door flew open, and old Scully, flushed and anecdotal, came into the room. He was jabbering at the Swede, who followed him, laughing bravely. It was the entry of two roisterers from a banquet hall.

"Come now," said Scully sharply to the three seated men, "move up and give us a chance at the stove." The cowboy and the Easterner obediently sidled their chairs to make room for the newcomers. Johnnie, however, simply arranged himself in a more indolent attitude, and then remained motionless.

"Come! Git over there," said Scully.

"Plenty of room on the other side of the stove," said Johnnie.

"Do you think we want to sit in the draught?" roared the father.

But the Swede here interposed with a grandeur of confidence. "No, no. Let the boy sit where he likes," he cried in a bullying voice to the father.

"All right! All right!" said Scully, deferentially. The cowboy and the Easterner exchanged glances of wonder.

The five chairs were formed in a crescent about one side of the stove. The Swede began to talk; he talked arrogantly, profanely, angrily. Johnnie, the cowboy and the Easterner maintained a morose silence, while old Scully appeared to be receptive and eager, breaking in constantly with sympathetic ejaculations.

Finally the Swede announced that he was thirsty. He moved in his chair, and said that he would go for a drink of water.

"I'll git it for you," cried Scully at once.

"No," said the Swede, contemptuously. "I'll get it for myself." He arose and stalked with the air of an owner off into the executive parts of the hotel.

As soon as the Swede was out of hearing, Scully sprang to his feet and whispered intensely to the others, "Upstairs he thought I was tryin' to poison 'im."

"Say," said Johnnie, "this makes me sick. Why don't you throw 'im out in the snow?"

"Why, he's all right now," declared Scully. "It was only that he was from the East, and he thought this was a tough place. That's all. He's all right now."

The cowboy looked with admiration upon the Easterner. "You were straight," he said. "You were on to that there Dutchman."

"Well," said Johnnie to his father, "he may be all right now, but I don't see it. Other time he was scared, but now he's too fresh."

Scully's speech was always a combination of Irish brogue and idiom, Western twang and idiom, and scraps of curiously formal diction taken from the storybooks and newspapers. He now hurled a strange mass of language at the head of his son. "What do I keep? What do I keep? What do I keep?" he demanded, in a voice of thunder. He slapped his knee impressively, to indicate that he himself was going to make reply, and that all should heed. "I keep a hotel," he shouted. "A hotel, do you mind? A guest under my roof has sacred privileges. He is to be intimidated by none. Not one word shall he hear that would prijudice him in favor of goin' away. I'll not have it. There's no place in this here town where they can say they iver took in a guest of mine because he was afraid to stay here." He wheeled suddenly upon the cowboy and the Easterner. "Am I right?"

"Yes, Mr. Scully," said the cowboy, "I think you're right."

"Yes, Mr. Scully," said the Easterner, "I think you're right."

V

At six o'clock supper, the Swede fizzed like a fire wheel. He sometimes seemed on the point of bursting into riotous song, and in all his madness he was encouraged by old Scully. The Easterner was encased in reserve; the cowboy sat in wide-mouthed amazement, forgetting to eat, while Johnnie wrathily demolished great plates of food. The daughters of the house, when they were obliged to replenish the biscuits, approached as warily as Indians, and, having succeeded in their purpose, fled with ill-concealed trepidation. The Swede domineered the whole feast, and he gave it the appearance of a cruel bacchanal. He seemed to have grown suddenly taller; he gazed, brutally disdainful, into every face. His voice rang through the room. Once when he jabbed out harpoon-fashion with his fork to pinion a biscuit, the weapon nearly impaled the hand of the Easterner, which had been stretched quietly out for the same biscuit.

After supper, as the men filed toward the other room, the Swede smote Scully ruthlessly on the shoulder. "Well, old boy, that was a good, square meal." Johnnie looked hopefully at his father; he knew that shoulder was tender from an old fall; and, indeed, it appeared for a moment as if Scully was going to flame out over the matter, but in the end he smiled a sickly smile and remained silent. The others understood from his manner that he was admitting his responsibility for the Swede's new viewpoint.

Johnnie, however, addressed his parent in an aside. "Why don't you license somebody to kick you downstairs?" Scully scowled darkly by way of reply.

When they were gathered about the stove, the Swede insisted on another game of high-five. Scully gently deprecated the plan at first, but the Swede turned a wolfish glare upon him. The old man subsided, and the Swede canvased the others. In his tone there was always a great threat. The cowboy and the Easterner both remarked indifferently that they would play. Scully said that he would presently have to go to meet the 6:58 train, and so the Swede turned menacingly upon Johnnie. For a moment their glances crossed like blades, and then Johnnie smiled and said, "Yes, I'll play."

They formed a square, with the little board on their knees. The East-erner and the Swede were again partners. As the play went on, it was noticeable that the cowboy was not board-whacking as usual. Meanwhile, Scully, near the lamp, had put on his spectacles and, with an appearance curiously like an old priest, was reading a newspaper. In time he went out to meet the 6:58 train, and, despite his precautions, a gust of polar wind whirled into the room as he opened the door. Besides scattering the cards, it chilled the players to the marrow. The Swede cursed frightfully. When Scully returned, his entrance disturbed a cozy and friendly scene. The Swede again cursed. But presently they were once more intent, their heads bent forward and their hands moving swiftly. The Swede had adopted the fashion of board-whacking.

Scully took up his paper and for a long time remained immersed in matters which were extraordinarily remote from him. The lamp burned badly, and once he stopped to adjust the wick. The newspaper, as he turned from page to page, rustled with a slow and comfortable sound. Then suddenly he heard three terrible words. "You are cheatin'!"

Such scenes often prove that there can be little of dramatic import in environment. Any room can present a tragic front; any room can be comic. This little den was now hideous as a torture chamber. The new faces of the men themselves had changed it upon the instant the Swede held a huge fist in front of Johnnie's face, while the latter looked steadily over it into the blazing orbs of his accuser. The Easterner had grown pallid; the cowboy's jaw had dropped in that expression of bovine amazement which was one of his important mannerisms. After the three words, the first sound in the room was made by Scully's paper as it floated forgotten to his feet. His spectacles had also fallen from his nose, but by a clutch he had saved them in air. His hand, grasping the spectacles, now remained poised awkwardly and near his shoulder. He stared at the cardplayers.

Probably the silence was while a second elapsed. Then, if the floor had been suddenly twitched out from under the men, they could not have moved quicker. The five had projected themselves headlong toward a common point. It happened that Johnnie, in rising to hurl himself upon the Swede, had stumbled slightly because of his curiously instinctive care for the cards and the board. The loss of the moment allowed time for the arrival of Scully, and also allowed the cowboy time to give the Swede a great push which sent him staggering back. The men found tongue together, and hoarse shouts of rage, appeal or fear burst from every throat. The cowboy pushed and jostled feverishly at the Swede, and the Easterner and Scully clung wildly to Johnnie; but through the smoky air, above the swaying bodies of the peace-compellers, the eyes of the two warriors ever sought each other in glances of challenge that were at once hot and steely.

Of course the board had been overturned, and now the whole company of cards was scattered over the floor, where the boots of the men trampled the fat and painted kings and queens as they gazed with their silly eyes at the war that was waging above them.

Scully's voice was dominating the yells. "Stop now! Stop, I say! Stop, now—"

Johnnie, as he struggled to burst through the rank formed by Scully and the Easterner, was crying, "Well, he says I cheated! He says I cheated! I won't allow no man to say I cheated! If he says I cheated, he's a——————!"

The cowboy was telling the Swede, "Quit, now! Quit, d'ye hear—"

The screams of the Swede never ceased. "He did cheat! I saw him! I saw him—"

As for the Easterner, he was importuning in a voice that was not heeded, "Wait a moment, can't you? Oh, wait a moment. What's the good of a fight over a game of cards? Wait a moment—"

In this tumult no complete sentences were clear. "Cheat"—"quit"—"he says"—these fragments pierced the uproar and rang out sharply. It was remarkable that, whereas Scully undoubtedly made the most noise, he was the least heard of any of the riotous band.

Then suddenly there was a great cessation. It was as if each man had paused for breath; and although the room was still lighted with the anger of men, it could be seen that there was no danger of immediate conflict, and at once Johnnie, shouldering his way forward, almost succeeded in confronting the Swede. "What did you say I cheated for? What did you say I cheated for? I don't cheat, and I won't let no man say I do!"

The Swede said, "I saw you! I saw you!"

"Well," cried Johnnie, "I'll fight any man what says I cheat!"

"No, you won't," said the cowboy. "Not here."

"Ah, be still, can't you?" said Scully, coming between them.

The quiet was sufficient to allow the Easterner's voice to be heard. He was repeating, "Oh, wait a moment, can't you? What's the good of a fight over a game of cards? Wait a moment!"

Johnnie, his red face appearing above his father's shoulder, hailed the Swede again. "Did you say I cheated?"

The Swede showed his teeth. "Yes."

"Then," said Johnnie, "we must fight."

"Yes, fight," roared the Swede. He was like a demoniac. "Yes, fight! I'll show you what kind of a man I am! I'll show you who you want to fight! Maybe you think I can't fight! Maybe you think I can't! I'll show you, you skin, you cardsharp. Yes, you cheated! You cheated! You cheated!"

"Well, let's go at it, then, mister," said Johnnie coolly.

The cowboy's brow was beaded with sweat from his efforts in intercepting all sorts of raids. He turned in despair to Scully. "What are you goin' to do now?"

A change had come over the Celtic visage of the old man. He now seemed all eagerness; his eyes glowed.

"We'll let them fight," he answered, stalwartly. "I can't put up with it any longer. I've stood this damned Swede till I'm sick. We'll let them fight."

VI

The men prepared to go out of doors. The Easterner was so nervous that he had great difficulty in getting his arms into the sleeves of his new leather coat. As the cowboy drew his fur cap down over his ears, his hands trembled. In fact, Johnnie and old Scully were the only ones who displayed no agitation. These preliminaries were conducted without words.

Scully threw open the door. "Well, come on," he said. Instantly a terrific wind caused the flame of the lamp to struggle at its wick, while a puff of black smoke sprang from the chimney top. The stove was in mid-current of the blast, and its voice swelled to equal the roar of the storm. Some of the scarred and bedabbled cards were caught up from the floor and dashed helplessly against the farther wall. The men lowered their heads and plunged into the tempest as into a sea.

No snow was falling, but great whirls and clouds of flakes, swept up from the ground by the frantic winds, were streaming southward with the speed of bullets. The covered land was blue with the sheen of an unearthly satin, and there was no other hue save where, at the low black railway station—which seemed incredibly distant—one light gleamed like a tiny jewel. As the men floundered into a thigh-deep drift, it was known that the Swede was bawling out something. Scully went to him, put a hand on his shoulder and projected an ear. "What's that you say?" he shouted.

"I say," bawled the Swede again, "I won't stand much show against this gang. I know you'll all pitch on me."

Scully smote him reproachfully on the arm. "Tut, man!" he yelled. The wind tore the words from Scully's lips and scattered them far alee.

"You are all a gang of—" boomed the Swede, but the storm also seized the remainder of this sentence.

Immediately turning their backs upon the wind, the men had swung around a corner to the sheltered side of the hotel. It was the function of the little house to preserve here, amid this great devastation of snow, an irregular V-shape of heavily encrusted grass, which crackled beneath the feet. One could imagine the great drifts piled against the windward side. When the party reached the comparative peace of this spot, it was found that the Swede was still bellowing.

"Oh, I know what kind of a thing this is! I know you'll all pitch on me. I can't lick you all!"

Scully turned upon him panther-fashion. "You'll not have to whip all of us. You'll have to whip my son Johnnie. An' the man what troubles you durin' that time will have me to deal with."

The arrangements were swiftly made. The two men faced each other, obedient to the harsh commands of Scully, whose face, in the subtly luminous gloom, could be seen set in the austere impersonal lines that are pictured on the countenances of the Roman veterans. The Easterner's teeth were chattering, and he was hopping up and down like a mechanical toy. The cowboy stood rocklike.

The contestants had not stripped off any clothing. Each was in his ordinary attire. Their fists were up, and they eyed each other in a calm that had the elements of leonine cruelty in it.

During this pause, the Easterner's mind, like a film, took lasting impressions of three men—the iron-nerved master of the ceremony; the Swede, pale, motionless, terrible; and Johnnie, serene yet ferocious, brutish yet heroic. The entire prelude had in it a tragedy greater than the tragedy of action, and this aspect was accentuated by the long, mellow cry of the blizzard as it sped the tumbling and wailing flakes into the black abyss of the south.

"Now!" said Scully.

The two combatants leaped forward and crashed together like bullocks. There was heard the cushioned sound of blows, and of a curse squeezing out from between the tight teeth of one.

As for the spectators, the Easterner's pent-up breath exploded from him with a pop of relief, absolute relief from the tension of the preliminaries. The cowboy bounded into the air with a yowl. Scully was immovable as from supreme amazement and fear at the fury of the fight which he himself had permitted and arranged.

For a time the encounter in the darkness was such a perplexity of flying arms that it presented no more detail than would a swiftly revolving wheel. Occasionally, a face, as if illumined by a flash of light, would shine out, ghastly and marked with pink spots. A moment later, the men might have been known as shadows if it were not for the involuntary utterance of oaths that came from them in whispers.

Suddenly a holocaust of warlike desire caught the cowboy, and he bolted forward with the speed of a bronco. "Go it, Johnnie! Go it! Kill him! Kill him!"

Scully confronted him. "Kape back," he said; and by his glance the cowboy could tell that this man was Johnnie's father.

To the Easterner there was a monotony of unchangeable fighting that was an abomination. This confused mingling was eternal to his sense, which was concentrated in a longing for the end, the priceless end. Once the fighters lurched near him, and as he scrambled hastily backward he heard them breathe like men on the rack.

"Kill him, Johnnie! Kill him! Kill him! Kill him!" The cowboy's face was contorted like one of those agony masks in museums.

"Keep still," said Scully icily.

Then there was a sudden loud grunt, incomplete, cut short, and Johnnie's body swung away from the Swede and fell with sickening heaviness to the grass. The cowboy was barely in time to prevent the mad Swede from flinging himself upon his prone adversary. "No, you don't," said the cowboy, interposing an arm. "Wait a second."

Scully was at his son's side. "Johnnie! Johnnie, me boy!" His voice had a quality of melancholy tenderness. "Johnnie! Can you go on with it?" He looked anxiously down into the bloody, pulpy face of his son.

There was a moment of silence, and then Johnnie answered in his ordinary voice. "Yes, I—it—yes."

Assisted by his father he struggled to his feet. "Wait a bit now till you git your wind," said the old man.

A few paces away the cowboy was lecturing the Swede. "No, you don't! Wait a second!"

The Easterner was plucking at Scully's sleeve. "Oh, this is enough," he pleaded. "This is enough! Let it go as it stands. This is enough!"

"Bill," said Scully, "git out of the road." The cowboy stepped aside. "Now." The combatants were actuated by a new caution as they advanced toward collision. They glared at each other, and then the Swede aimed a lightning blow that carried with it his entire weight. Johnnie was evidently half stupid from weakness, but he miraculously dodged, and his fist sent the overbalanced Swede sprawling.

The cowboy, Scully and the Easterner burst into a cheer that was like a chorus of triumphant soldiery, but before its conclusion the Swede had scuffed agilely to his feet and come in berserk abandon at his foe. There was another perplexity of flying arms, and Johnnie's body again swung away and fell, even as a bundle might fall from a roof. The Swede instantly staggered to a little wind-waved tree and leaned upon it, breathing like an engine, while his savage and flame-lit eyes roamed from face to face as the men bent over Johnnie. There was a splendor of isolation in his situation at this time which the Easterner felt once when, lifting his eyes from the man on the ground, he beheld that mysterious and lonely figure, waiting.

"Are you any good yet, Johnnie?" asked Scully in a broken voice.

The son gasped and opened his eyes languidly. After a moment he answered, "No—I ain't—any good—any—more." Then from shame and bodily ill, he began to weep, the tears furrowing down through the bloodstains on his face. "He was too—too—heavy for me."

Scully straightened and addressed the waiting figure. "Stranger," he said, evenly, "it's all up with our side." Then his voice changed into that vibrant huskiness which is commonly the tone of the most simple and deadly announcements. "Johnnie is whipped."

Without replying, the victor moved off on the route to the front door of the hotel.

The cowboy was formulating new and unspellable blasphemies. The Easterner was startled to find that they were out in a wind that seemed to come direct from the shadowed arctic floes. He heard again the wail of the snow as it was flung to its grave in the south. He knew now that all this time the cold had been sinking into him deeper and deeper, and he wondered that he had not perished. He felt indifferent to the condition of the vanquished man.

"Johnnie, can you walk?" asked Scully.

"Did I hurt—hurt him any?" asked the son.

"Can you walk, boy? Can you walk?"

Johnnie's voice was suddenly strong. There was a robust impatience in it. "I asked you whether I hurt him any!"

"Yes, yes, Johnnie," answered the cowboy, consolingly, "he's hurt a good deal."

They raised him from the ground, and as soon as he was on his feet, he went tottering off, rebuffing all attempts at assistance. When the party rounded the corner, they were fairly blinded by the pelting of the snow. It burned their faces like fire. The cowboy carried Johnnie through the drift to the door. As they entered, some cards rose from the floor and beat against the wall.

The Easterner rushed to the stove. He was so profoundly chilled that he almost dared to embrace the glowing iron. The Swede was not in the room. Johnnie sank into a chair and, folding his arms on his knees, buried his face in them. Scully, warming one foot and then the other at the rim of the stove, muttered to himself with Celtic mournfulness. The cowboy had removed his fur cap, and with a dazed and rueful air he was running one hand through his tousled locks. From overhead they could hear the creaking of boards as the Swede tramped here and there in his room.

The sad quiet was broken by the sudden flinging open of a door that led toward the kitchen. It was instantly followed by an onrush of women. They precipitated themselves upon Johnnie amid a chorus of lamentation. Before they carried their prey off to the kitchen, there to be bathed and harangued with that mixture of sympathy and abuse which is a feat of their sex, the mother straightened herself and fixed old Scully with an eye of stern reproach. "Shame be upon you, Patrick Scully!" she cried. "Your own son, too. Shame be upon you!"

"There, now! Be quiet, now!" said the old man weakly to this slogan, sniffed disdainfully in the direction of those trembling accomplices, the cowboy and the Easterner. Presently they bore Johnnie away, and left the three men to dismal reflection.

VII

"I'd like to fight this here Dutchman myself," said the cowboy, breaking a long silence.

Scully wagged his head sadly. "No, that wouldn't do. It wouldn't be right. It wouldn't be right."

"Well, why wouldn't it?" argued the cowboy. "I don't see no harm in it."

"No," answered Scully, with mournful heroism. "It wouldn't be right. It was Johnnie's fight, and now we mustn't whip the man just because he whipped Johnnie."

"Yes, that's true enough," said the cowboy, "but—he better not get fresh with me, because I couldn't stand no more of it."

"You'll not say a word to him," commanded Scully, and even then they heard the tread of the Swede on the stairs. His entrance was made theatric. He swept the door back with a bang and swaggered to the middle of the room. No one looked at him. "Well," he cried, insolently, at Scully, "I s'pose you'll tell me now how much I owe you?"

The old man remained stolid. "You don't owe me nothin'."

"Huh!" said the Swede, "huh! Don't owe 'im nothin'."

The cowboy addressed the Swede. "Stranger, I don't see how you come to be so gay around here."

Old Scully was instantly alert. "Stop!" he shouted, holding his hand forth, fingers upward. "Bill, you shut up!"

The cowboy spat carelessly into the sawdust box. "I didn't say a word, did I?" he asked.

"Mr. Scully," called the Swede, "how much do I owe you?" It was seen that he was attired for departure, and that he had his valise in his hand.

"You don't owe me nothin'," repeated Scully in the same imperturbable way.

"Huh!" said the Swede. "I guess you're right. I guess if it was any way at all, you'd owe me somethin'. That's what I guess." He turned to the cowboy. " 'Kill him! Kill him! Kill him!' " he mimicked, and then guffawed victoriously. " 'Kill him!' " He was convulsed with ironical humor.

But he might have been jeering the dead. The three men were immovable and silent, staring with glassy eyes at the stove.

The Swede opened the door and passed into the storm, giving one derisive glance backward at the still group.

As soon as the door was closed, Scully and the cowboy leaped to their feet and began to curse. They trampled to and fro, waving their arms and smashing into the air with their fists. "Oh, but that was a hard minute!" wailed Scully. "That was a hard minute! Him there leerin' and scoffin'! One bang at his nose was worth forty dollars to me that minute! How did you stand it, Bill?"

"How did I stand it?" cried the cowboy in a quivering voice. "How did I stand it? Oh!"

The old man burst into sudden brogue. "I'd loike to take that Swade," he wailed, "and hould 'im down on a shtone flure and bate 'im to a jelly wid a shtick!"

The cowboy groaned in sympathy. "I'd like to git him by the neck and ha-ammer him"—he brought his hand down on a chair with a noise like a pistol shot—"hammer that there Dutchman until he couldn't tell himself from a dead coyote!"

"I'd bate 'im until he—"

"I'd show *him* some things—"

And then together they raised a yearning, fantastic cry—"Oh-o-oh! if we only could—"

"Yes!"

"Yes!"

"And then I'd—"

"O-o-oh!"

VIII

The Swede, tightly gripping his valise, tacked across the face of the storm as if he carried sails. He was following a line of little naked, grasping trees which, he knew, must mark the way of the road. His face, fresh from the pounding of Johnnie's fists, felt more pleasure than pain in the wind and the driving snow. A number of square shapes loomed upon him finally, and he knew them as the houses of the main body of the town. He found a street and made travel along it, leaning heavily upon the wind whenever, at a corner, a terrific blast caught him.

He might have been in a deserted village. We picture the world as thick with conquering and elate humanity, but here, with the bugles of the tempest pealing, it was hard to imagine a peopled earth. One viewed the existence of man then as a marvel, and conceded a glamour of wonder to these lice which were caused to cling to a whirling, fire-smitten, ice-locked, disease-stricken, space-lost bulb. The conceit of man was explained by this storm to be the very engine of life. One was a coxcomb not to die in it. However, the Swede found a saloon.

In front of it an indomitable red light was burning, and the snowflakes were made blood color as they flew through the circumscribed territory of the lamp's shining. The Swede pushed open the door of the saloon and entered. A sanded expanse was before him, and at the end of it four men sat about a table drinking. Down one side of the room extended a radiant bar, and its guardian was leaning upon his elbows listening to the talk of the men at the table. The Swede dropped his valise upon the floor and, smiling fraternally upon the barkeeper, said, "Gimme some whisky, will you?" The man placed a bottle, a whisky glass, and a glass of ice-thick water upon the bar. The Swede poured himself an abnormal portion of whisky and drank it in three gulps. "Pretty bad night," remarked the bartender indifferently. He was making the pretension of blindness which is usually a distinction of his class; but it could have been seen that he was furtively studying the half-erased bloodstains on the face of the Swede. "Bad night," he said again.

"Oh, it's good enough for me," replied the Swede hardily as he poured himself some more whisky. The barkeeper took his coin and maneuvered it through its reception by a highly nickeled cash-machine. A bell rang; a card labeled "20 cts." had appeared.

"No," continued the Swede, "this isn't too bad weather. It's good enough for me."

"So?" murmured the barkeeper languidly.

The copious drams made the Swede's eyes swim, and he breathed a trifle heavier. "Yes, I like this weather. I like it. It suits me." It was apparently his design to impart a deep significance to these words.

"So?" murmured the bartender again. He turned to gaze dreamily at the scroll-like birds and birdlike scrolls which had been drawn with soap upon the mirrors in back of the bar.

"Well, I guess I'll take another drink," said the Swede presently. "Have something?"

"No, thanks; I'm not drinkin'," answered the bartender. Afterward he asked, "How did you hurt your face?"

The Swede immediately began to boast loudly. "Why, in a fight. I thumped the soul out of a man down here at Scully's hotel."

The interest of the four men at the table was at last aroused.

"Who was it?" said one.

"Johnnie Scully," blustered the Swede. "Son of the man what runs it. He will be pretty near dead for some weeks, I can tell you. I made a nice thing of him, I did. He couldn't get up. They carried him in the house. Have a drink?"

Instantly the men in some subtle way encased themselves in reserve. "No, thanks," said one. The group was of curious formation. Two were prominent local business men; one was the district attorney; and one was a professional gambler of the kind known as "square." But a scrutiny of the group would not have enabled an observer to pick the gambler from the men of more reputable pursuits. He was, in fact, a man so delicate in manner when among people of fair class, and so judicious in his choice of victims, that in the strictly masculine part of the town's life he had come to be explicitly trusted and admired. People called him a thoroughbred. The fear and contempt with which his craft was regarded were undoubtedly the reason why his quiet dignity shone conspicuous above the quiet dignity of men who might be merely hatters, billiard markers or grocery clerks. Beyond an occasionally unwary traveler who came by rail, this gambler was supposed to prey solely upon reckless and senile farmers, who, when flush with good crops, drove into town in all the pride and confidence of an absolutely invulnerable stupidity. Hearing at times in circuitous fashion of the despoilment of such a farmer, the important men of Romper invariably laughed in contempt of the victim, and if they thought of the wolf at all, it was with a kind of pride at the knowledge that he would never dare think of attacking their wisdom and courage. Besides, it was popular that this gambler had a real wife and two real children in a neat cottage in a suburb, where he led an exemplary home life; and when any one even suggested a discrepancy in his character, the crowd immediately vociferated descriptions of this virtuous family circle. Then men who led exemplary home lives, and men who did not lead exemplary home lives, all subsided in a bunch, remarking that there was nothing more to be said.

However, when a restriction was placed upon him—as, for instance, when a strong clique of members of the new Polywog Club refused to permit him, even as a spectator, to appear in the rooms of the organization —the candor and gentleness with which he accepted the judgment disarmed many of his foes and made his friends more desperately partisan. He invariably distinguished between himself and a respectable Romper man so quickly and frankly that his manner actually appeared to be a continual broadcast compliment.

And one must not forget to declare the fundamental fact of his entire position in Romper. It is irrefutable that in all affairs outside his business, in all matters that occur eternally and commonly between man and man, this thieving cardplayer was so generous, so just, so moral, that in a contest he could have put to flight the consciences of nine-tenths of the citizens of Romper.

And so it happened that he was seated in this saloon with the two prominent local merchants and the district attorney.

The Swede continued to drink raw whisky, meanwhile babbling at the barkeeper and trying to induce him to indulge in potations. "Come on. Have a drink. Come on. What—no? Well, have a little one, then. By gawd, I've whipped a man tonight, and I want to celebrate. I whipped him good, too. Gentlemen," the Swede cried to the men at the table. "Have a drink?"

"Ssh!" said the barkeeper.

The group at the table, although furtively attentive, had been pretending to be deep in talk, but now a man lifted his eyes toward the Swede and said shortly, "Thanks. We don't want any more."

At this reply the Swede ruffled out his chest like a rooster. "Well," he exploded, "it seems I can't get anybody to drink with me in this town. Seems so, don't it? Well!"

"Ssh!" said the barkeeper.

"Say," snarled the Swede, "don't you try to shut me up. I won't have it. I'm a gentleman, and I want people to drink with me. And I want 'em to drink with me now. *Now*—do you understand?" He rapped the bar with his knuckles.

Years of experience had calloused the bartender. He merely grew sulky. "I hear you," he answered.

"Well," cried the Swede, "listen hard then. See those men over there? Well, they're going to drink with me, and don't you forget it. Now you watch."

"Hi!" yelled the barkeeper, "this won't do!"

"Why won't it?" demanded the Swede. He stalked over to the table, and by chance laid his hand upon the shoulder of the gambler. "How about this?" he asked wrathfully. "I asked you to drink with me."

The gambler simply twisted his head and spoke over his shoulder. "My friend, I don't know you."

"Oh, hell!" answered the Swede, "come and have a drink."

"Now, my boy," advised the gambler kindly, "take your hand off my shoulder and go 'way and mind your own business." He was a little, slim man, and it seemed strange to hear him use this tone of heroic patronage to the burly Swede. The other men at the table said nothing.

"What! You won't drink with me, you little dude? I'll make you, then! I'll make you!" The Swede had grasped the gambler frenziedly at the throat, and was dragging him from his chair. The other men sprang up. The barkeeper dashed around the corner of his bar. There was a great tumult, and then was seen a long blade in the hand of the gambler. It shot forward, and a human body, this citadel of virtue, wisdom, power, was pierced as easily as if it had been a melon. The Swede fell with a cry of supreme astonishment.

The prominent merchants and the district attorney must have at once tumbled out of the place backward. The bartender found himself hanging limply to the arm of a chair and gazing into the eyes of a murderer.

"Henry," said the latter as he wiped his knife on one of the towels that hung beneath the bar rail, "you tell 'em where to find me. I'll be home, waiting for 'em." Then he vanished. A moment afterward the barkeeper was in the street, dinning through the storm for help and, moreover, companionship.

The corpse of the Swede, alone in the saloon, had its eyes fixed upon a dreadful legend that dwelt atop of the cash-machine: "This registers the amount of your purchase."

IX

Months later the cowboy was frying pork over the stove of a little ranch near the Dakota line when there was a quick thud of hoofs outside, and presently the Easterner entered with the letters and the papers.

"Well," said the Easterner at once, "the chap that killed the Swede has got three years. Wasn't much, was it?"

"He has? Three years?" The cowboy poised his pan of pork while he ruminated upon the news. "Three years. That ain't much."

"No. It was a light sentence," replied the Easterner as he unbuckled his spurs. "Seems there was a good deal of sympathy for him in Romper."

"If the bartender had been any good," observed the cowboy thoughtfully, "he would have gone in and cracked that there Dutchman on the head with a bottle in the beginnin' of it and stopped all this here murderin'."

"Yes, a thousand things might have happened," said the Easterner tartly.

The cowboy returned his pan of pork to the fire, but his philosophy continued. "It's funny, ain't it? If he hadn't said Johnnie was cheatin', he'd be alive this minute. He was an awful fool. Game played for fun, too. Not for money. I believe he was crazy."

"I feel sorry for that gambler," said the Easterner.

"Oh, so do I," said the cowboy. "He don't deserve none of it for killin' who he did."

"The Swede might not have been killed if everything had been square."

"Might not have been killed?" exclaimed the cowboy. "Everythin' square? Why, when he said that Johnnie was cheatin' and acted like such a jackass? And then in the saloon he fairly walked up to git hurt?" With these arguments the cowboy browbeat the Easterner and reduced him to rage.

"You're a fool!" cried the Easterner, viciously. "You're a bigger jackass than the Swede by a million majority. Now let me tell you one thing. Let me tell you something. Listen! Johnnie *was* cheating!"

" 'Johnnie,' " said the cowboy, blankly. There was a minute of silence, and then he said, robustly, "Why, no. The game was only for fun."

"Fun or not," said the Easterner, "Johnnie was cheating. I saw him. I know it. I saw him. And I refused to stand up and be a man. I let the Swede fight it out alone. And you—you were simply puffing around the place and wanting to fight. And then old Scully himself! We are all in it! This poor gambler isn't even a noun. He is kind of an adverb. Every sin is the result of a collaboration. We, five of us, have collaborated in the murder of this Swede. Usually there are from a dozen to forty women really involved in every murder, but in this case it seems to be only men —you, I, Johnnie, old Scully and that fool of an unfortunate gambler came merely as a culmination, the apex of a human movement, and gets all the punishment."

The cowboy, injured and rebellious, cried out blindly into this fog of mysterious theory, "Well, I didn't do anythin', did I?"

GERTRUDE ATHERTON

The Vengeance of Padre Arroyo

San Francisco-born Gertrude Atherton (1857–1948) wrote books of fiction and nonfiction during her long life, among them the novel The Californians *(1898) and a collection of stories,* The Splendid Idle Forties *(1902), both of which expertly chronicle life in Old California. "The Vengeance of Padre Arroyo" is the cream of the stories in the latter title —a perfect short short with an O. Henry twist at the end.*

PILAR, from her little window just above the high wall surrounding the big adobe house set apart for the women neophytes of the Mission of Santa Ines, watched, morning and evening, for Andreo, as he came and went from the rancheria. The old women kept the girls busy, spinning, weaving, sewing; but age nods and youth is crafty. The tall young Indian who was renowned as the best huntsman of all the neophytes, and who supplied Padre Arroyo's table with deer and quail, never failed to keep his ardent eyes fixed upon the grating so long as it lay within the line of his vision. One day he went to Padre Arroyo and told him that Pilar was the prettiest girl behind the wall—the prettiest girl in all the Californias— and that she should be his wife. But the kind stern old padre shook his head.

"You are both too young. Wait another year, my son, and if thou art still in the same mind, thou shalt have her."

Andreo dared to make no protest, but he asked permission to prepare a home for his bride. The padre gave it willingly, and the young Indian began to make the big adobes, the bright red tiles. At the end of a month he had built him a cabin among the willows of the rancheria, a little apart from the others; he was in love, and association with his fellows was distasteful. When the cabin was builded his impatience slipped from its curb, and once more he besought the priest to allow him to marry.

Padre Arroyo was sunning himself on the corridor of the mission, shivering in his heavy brown robes, for the day was cold.

72

"Orion," he said sternly—he called all his neophytes after the celebrities of earlier days, regardless of the names given them at the font—"have I not told thee thou must wait a year? Do not be impatient, my son. She will keep. Women are like apples: when they are too young, they set the teeth on edge; when ripe and mellow, they please every sense; when they wither and turn brown, it is time to fall from the tree into a hole. Now go and shoot a deer for Sunday: the good padres from San Luis Obispo and Santa Barbara are coming to dine with me."

Andreo, dejected, left the padre. As he passed Pilar's window and saw a pair of wistful black eyes behind the grating, his heart took fire. No one was within sight. By a series of signs he made his lady understand that he would place a note beneath a certain adobe in the wall.

Pilar, as she went to and fro under the fruit trees in the garden, or sat on the long corridor weaving baskets, watched that adobe with fascinated eyes. She knew that Andreo was tunnelling it, and one day a tiny hole proclaimed that his work was accomplished. But how to get the note? The old women's eyes were very sharp when the girls were in front of the gratings. Then the civilizing development of Christianity upon the heathen intellect triumphantly asserted itself. Pilar, too, conceived a brilliant scheme. That night the padre, who encouraged any evidence of industry, no matter how eccentric, gave her a little garden of her own—a patch where she could raise sweet peas and Castilian roses.

"That is well, that is well, my Nausicaa," he said, stroking her smoky braids. "Go cut the slips and plant them where thou wilt. I will send thee a package of sweet pea seeds."

Pilar spent every spare hour bending over her "patch"; and the hole, at first no bigger than a pin's point, was larger at each setting of the sun behind the mountain. The old women, scolding on the corridor, called to her not to forget vespers.

On the third evening, kneeling on the damp ground, she drew from the little tunnel in the adobe a thin slip of wood covered with the labour of sleepless nights. She hid it in her smock—that first of California's love-letters—then ran with shaking knees and prostrated herself before the altar. That night the moon streamed through her grating, and she deciphered the fact that Andreo had loosened eight adobes above her garden, and would await her every midnight.

Pilar sat up in bed and glanced about the room with terrified delight. It took her but a moment to decide the question; love had kept her awake too many nights. The neophytes were asleep; as they turned now and again, their narrow beds of hide, suspended from the ceiling, swung too gently to awaken them. The old women snored loudly. Pilar slipped from her bed and looked through the grating. Andreo was there, the dignity and repose of primeval man in his bearing. She waved her hand and pointed downward to the wall; then, throwing on the long coarse gray smock that was her only garment, crept from the room and down the stair. The door was protected against hostile tribes by a heavy iron bar, but Pilar's small hands were hard and strong, and in a moment she stood over the adobes which had crushed her roses and sweet peas.

As she crawled through the opening, Andreo took her hand bashfully, for they had never spoken. "Come," he said; "we must be far away before dawn."

They stole past the long mission, crossing themselves as they glanced askance at the ghostly row of pillars; past the guard-house, where the sentries slept at their post; past the rancheria; then, springing upon a waiting mustang, dashed down the valley. Pilar had never been on a horse before, and she clung in terror to Andreo, who bestrode the unsaddled beast as easily as a cloud rides the wind. His arm held her closely, fear vanished, and she enjoyed the novel sensation. Glancing over Andreo's shoulder she watched the mass of brown and white buildings, the winding river, fade into the mountain. Then they began to ascend an almost perpendicular steep. The horse followed a narrow trail; the crowding trees and shrubs clutched the blankets and smocks of the riders; after a time trail and scene grew white; the snow lay on the heights.

"Where do we go?" she asked.

"To Zaca Lake, on the very top of the mountain, miles above us. No one has ever been there but myself. Often I have shot deer and birds beside it. They never will find us there."

The red sun rose over the mountains of the east. The crystal moon sank in the west. Andreo sprang from the weary mustang and carried Pilar to the lake.

A sheet of water, round as a whirlpool but calm and silver, lay amidst the sweeping willows and pine-forested peaks. The snow glittered beneath the trees, but a canoe was on the lake, a hut on the marge.

Padre Arroyo tramped up and down the corridor, smiting his hands together. The Indians bowed lower than usual, as they passed, and hastened their steps. The soldiers scoured the country for the bold violators of mission law. No one asked Padre Arroyo what he would do with the sinners, but all knew that punishment would be sharp and summary: the men hoped that Andreo's mustang had carried him beyond its reach; the girls, horrified as they were, wept and prayed in secret for Pilar.

A week later, in the early morning, Padre Arroyo sat on the corridor. The mission stood on a plateau overlooking a long valley forked and sparkled by the broad river. The valley was planted thick with olive trees, and their silver leaves glittered in the rising sun. The mountain peaks about and beyond were white with snow, but the great red poppies blossomed at their feet. The padre, exiled from the luxury and society of his dear Spain, never tired of the prospect: he loved his mission children, but he loved Nature more.

Suddenly he leaned forward on his staff and lifted the heavy brown hood of his habit from his ear. Down the road winding from the eastern mountains came the echo of galloping footfalls. He rose expectantly and waddled out upon the plaza, shading his eyes with his hand. A half-dozen soldiers, riding closely about a horse bestridden by a stalwart young Indian supporting a woman, were rapidly approaching the mission. The padre returned to his seat and awaited their coming.

The soldiers escorted the culprits to the corridor; two held the horse while they descended, then led it away, and Andreo and Pilar were alone with the priest. The bridegroom placed his arm about the bride and looked defiantly at Padre Arroyo, but Pilar drew her long hair about her face and locked her hands together.

Padre Arroyo folded his arms and regarded them with lowered brows, a sneer on his mouth.

"I have new names for you both," he said, in his thickest voice. "Antony, I hope thou hast enjoyed the honeymoon. Cleopatra, I hope thy little toes did not get frost-bitten. You both look as if food had been scarce. And your garments have gone in good part to clothe the brambles, I infer. It is too bad you could not wait a year and love in your cabin at the rancheria, by a good fire, and with plenty of frijoles and tortillas in your stomachs." He dropped his sarcastic tone, and, rising to his feet, extended his right arm with a gesture of malediction. "Do you comprehend the enormity of your sin?" he shouted. "Have you not learned on your knees that the fires of hell are the rewards of unlawful love? Do you not know that even the year of sackcloth and ashes I shall impose here on earth will not save you from those flames a million times hotter than the mountain fire, than the roaring pits in which evil Indians torture one another? A hundred years of their scorching breath, of roasting flesh, for a week of love! Oh, God of my soul!"

Andreo looked somewhat staggered, but unrepentant. Pilar burst into loud sobs of terror.

The padre stared long and gloomily at the flags of the corridor. Then he raised his head and looked sadly at his lost sheep.

"My children," he said solemnly, "my heart is wrung for you. You have broken the laws of God and of the Holy Catholic Church, and the punishments thereof are awful. Can I do anything for you, excepting to pray? You shall have my prayers, my children. But that is not enough; I cannot—ay! I cannot endure the thought that you shall be damned. Perhaps"—again he stared meditatively at the stones, then, after an impressive silence, raised his eyes. "Heaven vouchsafes me an idea, my children. I will make your punishment here so bitter that Almighty God in His mercy will give you but a few years of purgatory after death. Come with me."

He turned and led the way slowly to the rear of the mission buildings. Andreo shuddered for the first time, and tightened his arm about Pilar's shaking body. He knew that they were to be locked in the dungeons. Pilar, almost fainting, shrank back as they reached the narrow spiral stair which led downward to the cells. "Ay! I shall die, my Andreo!" she cried. "Ay! my father, have mercy!"

"I cannot, my children," said the padre, sadly. "It is for the salvation of your souls."

"Mother of God! When shall I see thee again, my Pilar?" whispered Andreo. "But, ay! the memory of that week on the mountain will keep us both alive."

Padre Arroyo descended the stair and awaited them at its foot. Separating them, and taking each by the hand, he pushed Andreo ahead and dragged Pilar down the narrow passage. At its end he took a great bunch of keys from his pocket, and raising both hands commanded them to kneel. He said a long prayer in a loud monotonous voice which echoed and re-echoed down the dark hall and made Pilar shriek with terror. Then he fairly hurled the marriage ceremony at them, and made the couple repeat after him the responses. When it was over, "Arise," he said.

The poor things stumbled to their feet, and Andre caught Pilar in a last embrace.

"Now bear your incarceration with fortitude, my children; and if you do not beat the air with your groans, I will let you out in a week. Do not hate your old father, for love alone makes him severe, but pray, pray, pray."

And then he locked them both in the same cell.

O. HENRY

The Reformation of Calliope

Many of O. Henry's (William Sydney Porter) delightful "surprises" have Western settings. His collection Heart of the West *(1904) contains nineteen of the finest of these stories, many dealing with a variety of unusual characters that are mischievous to one degree of another. Calliope Catesby, the hero of "The Reformation of Calliope," is of this ilk—a man who, when "in his humors," had been known to wreak havoc in the town of Quicksand. What happens to the "Terror of Quicksand" is O. Henry at his ironic best.*

CALLIOPE CATESBY was in his humors again. Ennui was upon him. This goodly promontory, the earth—particularly that portion of it known as Quicksand—was to him no more than a pestilent congregation of vapors. Overtaken by the megrims, the philosopher may seek relief in soliloquy; my lady find solace in tears; the flaccid Easterner scold at the millinery bills of his women folk. Such recourse was insufficient to the denizens of Quicksand. Calliope, especially, was wont to express his ennui according to his lights.

Over night Calliope had hung out signals of approaching low spirits. He had kicked his own dog on the porch of the Occidental Hotel, and refused to apologize. He had become capricious and fault-finding in conversation. While strolling about he reached often for twigs of mesquite and chewed the leaves fiercely. That was always an ominous act. Another symptom alarming to those who were familiar with the different stages of his doldrums was his increasing politeness and a tendency to use formal phrases. A husky softness succeeded the usual penetrating drawl in his tones. A dangerous courtesy marked his manners. Later his smile became crooked, the left side of his mouth slanting upward, and Quicksand got ready to stand from under.

At this stage Calliope generally began to drink. Finally, about midnight, he was seen going homeward, saluting those whom he met with exaggerated but inoffensive courtesy. Not yet was Calliope's melancholy at the danger point. He would seat himself at the window of the room he occupied over Silvester's tonsorial parlors and there chant lugubrious and tuneless ballads until morning, accompanying the noises by appropriate maltreatment of a jingling guitar. More magnanimous than Nero, he would thus give musical warning of the forthcoming municipal upheaval that Quicksand was scheduled to endure.

A quiet, amiable man was Calliope Catesby at other times—quiet to indolence, and amiable to worthlessness. At best he was a loafer and a nuisance; at worst he was the terror of Quicksand. His ostensible occupation was something subordinate in the real-estate line; he drove the beguiled Easterner in buckboards out to look over lots and ranch property. Originally he came from one of the Gulf states, his lank six feet, slurring rhythm of speech, and sectional idioms giving evidence of his birthplace.

And yet, after taking on Western adjustments, this languid pine-box whittler, cracker-barrel hugger, shady-corner lounger of the cotton fields and sumac hills of the South, became famed as a bad man among men who had made a lifelong study of the art of truculence.

At nine the next morning Calliope was fit. Inspired by his own barbarous melodies and the contents of his jug, he was ready-primed to gather fresh laurels from the diffident brow of Quicksand. Encircled and crisscrossed with cartridge belts, abundantly garnished with revolvers and copiously drunk, he poured forth into Quicksand's main street. Too chivalrous to surprise and capture a town by silent sortie, he paused at the nearest corner and emitted his slogan—that fearful, brassy yell, so reminiscent of the steam piano, that had gained for him the classic appellation that had superseded his own baptismal name. Following close upon his vociferation came three shots from his .45 by way of limbering up the guns and testing his aim. A yellow dog, the personal property of Colonel Swazey, the proprietor of the Occidental, fell feet upward in the dust with one farewell yelp. A Mexican, who was crossing the street from the Blue Front grocery carrying in his hand a bottle of kerosene, was stimulated to a sudden and admirable burst of speed, still grasping the neck of the shattered bottle. The new gilt weathercock on Judge Riley's lemon and ultramarine two-story residence shivered, flapped, and hung by a splinter, the sport of the wanton breezes.

The artillery was in trim. Calliope's hand was steady. The high, calm ecstasy of habitual battle was upon him, though slightly embittered by the sadness of Alexander in that his conquests were limited to the small world of Quicksand.

Down the street went Calliope, shooting right and left. Glass fell like hail; dogs vamoosed; chickens flew, squawking; feminine voices shrieked concernedly to youngsters at large. The din was perforated at intervals by the staccato of the Terror's guns, and was drowned periodically by the brazen screech that Quicksand knew so well. The occasions of Calliope's low spirits were legal holidays in Quicksand. All along the main street, in advance of his coming, clerks were putting up shutters and closing doors. Business would languish for a space. The right of way was Calliope's, and as he advanced, observing the dearth of opposition and the few opportunities for distraction, his ennui perceptibly increased.

But some four squares farther down, lively preparations were being made to minister to Mr. Catesby's love for interchange of compliments and repartee. On the previous night numerous messengers had hastened to advise Buck Patterson, the city marshal, of Calliope's impending eruption. The patience of that official, often strained in extending leniency toward the disturber's misdeeds, had been overtaxed. In Quicksand some indulgence was accorded the natural ebullition of human nature. Providing that the lives of the more useful citizens were not recklessly squandered or too much property needlessly laid waste, the community sentiment was against a too strict enforcement of the law. But Calliope had raised the limit. His outbursts had been two frequent and too violent to come within the classification of a normal and sanitary relaxation of spirit.

Buck Patterson had been expecting and awaiting in his little ten-by-twelve frame office that preliminary yell announcing that Calliope was feeling blue. When the signal came the city marshal rose to his feet and buckled on his guns. Two deputy sheriffs and three citizens who had proven the edible qualities of fire also stood up, ready to bandy with Calliope's leaden jocularities.

"Gather that fellow in," said Buck Patterson, setting for the lines of the campaign. "Don't have no talk, but shoot as soon as you can get a show. Keep behind cover and bring him down. He's a no-good 'un. It's up to Calliope to turn up his toes this time, I reckon. Go to him all spraddled out, boys. And don't git too reckless, for what Calliope shoots at he hits."

Buck Patterson, tall, muscular and solemn-faced, with his bright City Marshal badge shining on the breast of his blue flannel shirt, gave his posse directions for the onslaught upon Calliope. The plan was to accomplish the downfall of the Quicksand Terror without loss to the attacking party, if possible.

The splenetic Calliope, unconscious of retributive plots, was steaming down the channel, cannonading on either side, when he suddenly became aware of breakers ahead. The city marshal and one of the deputies rose up behind some dry-goods boxes half a square to the front and opened fire. At the same time the rest of the posse, divided, shelled him from two side streets up which they were cautiously maneuvering from a well-executed detour.

The first volley broke the lock of one of Calliope's guns, cut a neat underbite in his right ear and exploded a cartridge in his crossbelt, scorching his ribs as it burst. Feeling braced up by this unexpected tonic to his spiritual depression, Calliope executed a fortissimo note from his upper register, and returned the fire like an echo. The upholders of the law dodged at his flash, but a trifle too late to save one of the deputies a bullet just above the elbow, and the marshal a bleeding cheek from a splinter that a ball tore from the box he had ducked behind.

And now Calliope met the enemy's tactics in kind. Choosing with a rapid eye the street from which the weakest and least accurate fire had come, he invaded it at a double-quick, abandoning the unprotected middle of the street. With rare cunning the opposing force in that direction—one of the deputies and two of the valorous volunteers—waited, concealed by beer barrels, until Calliope had passed their retreat, and then peppered him from the rear. In another moment they were reinforced by the marshal and his other men, and then Calliope felt that in order to successfully prolong the delights of the controversy, he must find some means of reducing the great odds against him. His eye fell upon a structure that seemed to hold out this promise, providing he could reach it.

Not far away was the little railroad station, its building a strong box house, ten by twenty feet, resting upon a platform four feet above ground. Windows were in each of its walls. Something like a fort it might become to a man thus sorely pressed by superior numbers.

Calliope made a bold and rapid spurt for it, the marshal's crowd "smoking" him as he ran. He reached the haven in safety, the station agent leaving the building by a window, like a flying squirrel, as the garrison entered the door.

Patterson and his supporters halted under protection of a pile of lumber and held consultations. In the station was an unterrified desperado who was an excellent shot and carried an abundance of ammunition. For thirty yards on each side of the besieged was a stretch of bare, open ground. It was a sure thing that the man who attempted to enter that unprotected area would be stopped by one of Calliope's bullets.

The city marshal was resolved. He had decided that Calliope Catesby should no more wake the echoes of Quicksand with his strident whoop. He had so announced. Officially and personally he felt imperatively bound to put the soft pedal on that instrument of discord. It played bad tunes.

Standing near was a hand truck used in the manipulation of small freight. It stood by a shed full of sacked wool, a consignment from one of the sheep ranches. On this truck the marshal and his men piled three heavy sacks of wool. Stooping low, Buck Patterson started for Calliope's fort, slowly pushing this loaded truck before him for protection. The posse, scattering broadly, stood ready to nip the besieged in case he should show himself in an effort to repel the juggernaut of justice that was creeping upon him. Only once did Calliope make demonstration. He fired from a window, and some tufts of wool spurted from the marshal's trustworthy bulwark. The return shots from the posse pattered against the window frame of the fort. No loss resulted on either side.

The marshal was too deeply engrossed in steering his protected battleship to be aware of the approach of the morning train until he was within a few feet of the platform. The train was coming up on the other side of it. It stopped only one minute at Quicksand. What an opportunity it would offer to Calliope! He had only to step out the other door, mount the train, and away.

Abandoning his breastworks, Buck, with his gun ready, dashed up the steps and into the room, driving open the closed door with one heave of his weighty shoulder. The members of the posse heard one shot fired inside, and then there was silence.

At length the wounded man opened his eyes. After a blank space he again could see and hear and feel and think. Turning his eyes about, he found himself lying on a wooden bench. A tall man with a perplexed countenance, wearing a big badge with City Marshal engraved upon it, stood over him. A little old woman in black, with a wrinkled face and sparkling black eyes, was holding a wet handkerchief against one of his temples. He was trying to get these facts fixed in his mind and connected with past events, when the old woman began to talk.

"There now, great, big, strong man! That bullet never tetched ye! Jest skeeted along the side of your head and sort of paralyzed ye for a spell. I've heard of sech things afore; cun-cussion is what they names it. Abel Wadkins used to kill squirrels that way—barkin' em, Abe called it. You jest been barked, sir, and you'll be all right in a little bit. Feel lots better already, don't ye! You just lay still a while longer and let me bathe your head. You don't know me, I reckon, and 'tain't surprisin' that you shouldn't. I come in on that train from Alabama to see my son. Big son, ain't he? Lands! you wouldn't hardly think he'd ever been a baby, would ye? This is my son, sir."

Half turning, the old woman looked up at the standing man, her worn face lighting with a proud and wonderful smile. She reached out one veined and callused hand and took one of her son's. Then smiling cheerily down at the prostrate man, she continued to dip the handkerchief in the waiting-room in washbasin and gently apply it to his temple. She had the benevolent garrulity of old age.

"I ain't seen my son before," she continued, "in eight years. One of my nephews, Elkanah Price, he's a conductor on one of them railroads and he got me a pass to come out here. I can stay a whole week on it, and then it'll take me back again. Jest think, now, that little boy of mine has got to be a officer—a city marshal of a whole town! That's somethin' like a constable, ain't it? I never knowed he was a officer; he didn't say nothin' about it in his letters. I reckon he thought his old mother'd be skeered about the danger he was in. But, laws! I never was much of a hand to git skeered. 'Tain't no use. I heard them guns a-shootin' while I was gittin' off them cars, and I see smoke acomin' out of the depot, but I jest walked right along. Then I see son's face lookin' out through the window. I knowed him at oncet. He met me at the door and squeezed me 'most to death. And there you was, sir, a-lyin' there jest like you was dead, and I 'lowed we'd see what might be done to help sot you up."

"I think I'll sit up now," said the concussion patient. "I'm feeling pretty fair by this time."

He sat, somewhat weakly yet, leaning against the wall. He was a rugged man, big-boned and straight. His eyes, steady and keen, seemed to linger upon the face of the man standing so still above him. His look wandered often from the face he studied to the marshal's badge upon the other's breast.

"Yes, yes, you'll be all right," said the old woman, patting his arm, "if you don't get to cuttin' up agin, and havin' folks shootin' at you. Son told me about you, sir, while you was layin' senseless on the floor. Don't you take it as meddlesome fer an old woman with a son as big as you to talk about it. And you mustn't hold no grudge agin' my son for havin' to shoot at ye. A officer has got to take up for the law—it's his duty—and them that acts bad and lives wrong has to suffer. Don't blame my son any, sir —'tain't his fault. He's always been a good boy—good when he was growin' up, and kind and 'bedient and well behaved. Won't you let me advise you, sir, not to do so no more? Be a good man and leave liquor alone and live peaceably and godly. Keep away from bad company and work honest and sleep sweet."

The black-mittened hand of the old pleader gently touched the breast of the man she addressed. Very earnest and candid her old, worn face looked. In her rusty black dress and antique bonnet she sat, near the close of a long life, and epitomized the experience of the world. Still the man to whom she spoke gazed above her head, contemplating the silent son of the old mother.

"What does the marshal say?" he asked. "Does he believe the advice is good? Suppose the marshal speaks up and says if the talk's all right?"

The tall man moved uneasily. He fingered the badge on his breast for a moment, and then he put an arm around the old woman and drew her close to him. She smiled the unchanging mother smile of three-score years, and patted his big brown hand with her crooked, mittened fingers while her son spoke.

"I says this," he said, looking squarely into the eyes of the other man, "that if I was in your place I'd follow it. If I was a drunken, desp'rate character, without shame or hope, I'd follow it. If I was in your place and you was in mine, I'd say, 'Marshal, I'm willin' to swear if you'll give me the chance, I'll quit the racket. I'll drop the tanglefoot and the gun play, and won't play hoss no more. I'll be a good citizen and go to work and quit my foolishness. So help me, God!' That's what I'd say to you if you was marshal and I was in your place."

"Hear my son talkin'," said the old woman softly. "Hear him, sir. You promise to be good and he won't do you no harm. Forty-one year ago his heart first beat agin' mine, and it's beat true ever since."

The other man rose to his feet, trying his limbs and stretching his muscles.

"Then," said he, "if you was in my place and said that, and I was marshal, I'd say, 'Go free, and do your best to keep your promise.'"

"Lawsy!" exclaimed the old woman, in a sudden flutter, "ef I didn't clear forget that trunk of mine! I see a man settin' it on the platform jest as I seen son's face in the window, and it went plum out of my head. There's eight jars of homemade quince jam in that trunk that I made myself. I wouldn't have nothin' happen to them jars for a red apple."

Away to the door she trotted, spry and anxious, and then Calliope Catesby spoke out to Buck Patterson:

"I just couldn't help it, Buck. I seen her through the window a-comin' in. She never had heard a word 'bout my tough ways. I didn't have the nerve to let her know I was a worthless cuss bein' hunted down by the community. There you was lyin' where my shot laid you, like you was dead. The idea struck me sudden, and I just took your badge off and fastened it onto myself, and I fastened my reputation onto you. I told her I was the marshal and you was a holy terror. You can take your badge back now, Buck."

With shaking fingers Calliope began to unfasten the disk of metal from his shirt.

"Easy there!" said Buck Patterson. "You keep that badge right where it is, Calliope Catesby. Don't you dare to take it off till the day your mother leaves this town. You'll be city marshal of Quicksand as long as she's here to know it. After I stir around town a bit and put 'em on, I'll guarantee that nobody won't give the thing away to her. And say, you leather-headed, rip-roarin', low-down son of a locoed cyclone, you follow that advice she give me! I'm goin' to take some of it myself, too."

"Buck," said Calliope feelingly, "ef I don't, I hope I may—"

"Shut up," said Buck. "She's a-comin' back."

Timberline

The first great novel of the Old West—the Western novel, in many people's opinion, and a prototype for hundreds of others over the past eighty years—was Owen Wister's The Virginian, *first published in April of 1902. A bestseller for more than ten years, it led Wister (an easterner, curiously enough, educated at Harvard) to write other memorable Western adventures, among them the novel* Lin McLean *and numerous short stories collected under such titles as* Members of the Family *and* When the West Was West. *"Timberline," which first appeared in* The Saturday Evening Post *for March 7, 1908, is one of his (undeservedly) lesser known stories; it is a pleasure to reprint it here.*

JUST AS THE blaze of the sun seems to cast wild birds, when, by yielding themselves they invite it, into a sort of trance, so that they sit upon the ground tilted sidewise, their heads in the air, their beaks open, their wings hanging slack, their feathers ruffled and their eyes vacantly fixed, so must the spot of yellow at which I had sat staring steadily and idly have done something like this to me—given me a spell of torpor in which all thoughts and things receded far away from me. It was a yellow poster, still wet from rain.

A terrifying thunderstorm had left all space dumb and bruised, as it were, with the heavy blows of its noise. The damp seemed to make the yellow paper yellower, the black letters blacker. A dollar sign, figures and zeros, exclamation points and the two blackest words of all, *reward* and *murder,* were what stood out of the yellow.

Two feet from it, on the same shed, was another poster, white, concerning some stallion, his place of residence, and his pedigree. This also I had read, with equal inattention and idleness, but my eyes had been drawn to the yellow spot and held by it.

Not by its news; the news was now old, since at every cabin and station dotted along our lonely road the same poster had appeared. They had discussed it, and whether he would be caught, and how much money he had got from his victim.

The body hadn't been found on Owl Creek for a good many weeks. Funny his friend hadn't turned up. If they'd killed him, why wasn't his body on Owl Creek, too? If he'd got away, why didn't he turn up? Such comments, with many more, were they making at Lost Soldier, Bull Spring, Crook's Gap and Sweetwater Bridge.

I sat in the wagon waiting for Scipio Le Moyne to come out of the house; there in my nostrils was the smell of the wet sage brush and of the wet straw and manure, and there, against the gray sky, was an afterimage of the yellow poster, square, huge and blue. It moved with my eyes as I turned them to get rid of the annoying vision, and it only slowly dissolved away over the head of the figure sitting on the corral with its back to me, the stocktender of this stage section. He sang: *"If that I was where I would be Then should I be where I am not; Here am I where I must be, And where I would be I cannot."*

I could not see the figure's face, or that he moved. One boot was twisted between the bars of the corral to hold him steady, its trodden heel was worn to a slant; from one seat pocket a soiled rag protruded and through a hole below this a piece of his red shirt or drawers stuck out. A coat much too large for him hung from his neck rather than from his shoulders, and the damp, limp hat that he wore, with its spotted, unraveled hat band, somehow completed the suggestion that he was not alive at all, but had been tied together and stuffed and set out in joke. Certainly there were no birds, or crops to frighten birds from; the only thing man had sown the desert with at Rongis was empty bottles. These lay everywhere.

As he sat and repeated his song there came from his back and his hat and his voice an impression of loneliness, poignant and helpless. A windmill turned and turned and creaked near the corral, adding its note of forlornness to the song.

A man put his head out of the house. "Stop it," he said, and shut the door again.

The figure obediently climbed down and went over to the windmill, where he took hold of the rope hanging from its rudder and turned the contrivance slowly out of the wind, until the wheel ceased revolving.

The man put his head out of the house, this second time speaking louder: "I didn't say stop that. I said stop it; stop your damned singing." He withdrew his head immediately.

The boy—the mild, new yellow hair on his face was the unshaven growth of adolescence—stood a long while looking at the door in silence, with eyes and mouth expressing futile injury. Finally he thrust his hands into bunchy pockets, and said:

"I ain't no two-bit man."

He watched the door, as if daring it to deny this, then, as nothing happened, he slowly drew his hands from the bunchy pockets, climbed the corral at the spot nearest him, twisted the boot between the bars and sat as before only without singing.

Thus we sat waiting, I for Scipio to come out of the house with the information he had gone in for, while the boy waited for nothing. *Waiting for nothing* was stamped plain upon him from head to foot. This boy's eyebrows were insufficient, and his front was as ragged as his back. He just sat and waited.

Presently the same man put his head out of the door. "You after sheep?"

I nodded.

"I could a-showed you sheep. Rams. Horns as big as your thigh— bigger'n *your* thigh. That was before tenderfeet came in and spoiled this country. Counted seven thousand on that there butte one morning before breakfast. Seven thousand and twenty-three, if you want exact figgers. Quit your staring!" This was addressed to the boy on the corral. "Why, you're not a-going without another?" This convivial question was to Scipio, who now came out of the house and across to me with the news that he had failed on what he had went in for.

"I could a-showed you sheep—" resumed the man, but I was now attending to Scipio.

"He don't know anything," said Scipio, "nor any of 'em in there. But we haven't got this country rounded up yet. He's just come out of a week of snake fits, and, by the way it looks, he'll enter on another about tomorrow morning. But drink can't stop *him* lying."

"Bad weather," said the man, watching us make ready to continue our long drive. "Lot o' lightning loose in the air right now. Kind o' weather you're liable to see fire on the horns of the stock some night."

This sounded like such a good one that I encouraged him. "We have nothing like that in the East."

"Hm. Guess you've not. Guess you never seen sixteen thousand steers with a light at the end of every horn in the herd."

"Are they going to catch that man?" inquired Scipio, pointing to the yellow poster.

"Catch him? Them? No! But I could tell 'em where he's went. He's went to Idaho."

"Thought the '76 outfit had sold Auctioneer," Scipio continued conversationally.

"That stallion? No! But I could tell 'em they'd ought to." This was his good-bye to us; he removed himself and his alcoholic omniscience into the house.

"Wait," I said to Scipio as he got in and took the reins from me. "I'm going to deal some magic to you. Look at that poster. No, not the stallion, the yellow one. Keep looking at it hard." While he obeyed me I made solemn passes with my hands over his head. "Now look anywhere you please."

Scipio looked across the corral at the gray sky. A slight stiffening of figure ensued, and he knit his brows. Then he rubbed a hand over his eyes and looked again.

"You after sheep?" It was the boy sitting on the corral. We paid him no attention.

"It's about gone," said Scipio, rubbing his eyes again. "Did you do that to me? Of course you didn't! What did?"

I adopted the manner of the professor who lectured on light to me when I was nineteen. "The eye being normal in structure and focus, the color of an after-image of the negative variety is complementary to that of the object causing it. If, for instance, a yellow disk (or lozenge in this case) be attentively observed, the yellow-perceiving elements of the retina become fatigued. Hence, when the mixed rays which constitute white light fall upon that portion of the retina which has thus been fatigued, the rays which produce the sensation of yellow will cause less effect than the other rays for which the eye has not been fatigued. Therefore, white light to an eye fatigued for yellow will appear blue—blue being yellow's complementary color. Now, shall I go on?" I asked.

"Don't y'u!" Scipio begged. "I'd sooner believe y'u done it to me."

"I can show you sheep." It was the boy again. We had not noticed him come from the corral to our wagon, by which he now stood. His eyes were eagerly fixed upon me; as they looked into mine they seemed almost burning with some sort of appeal.

"Hello, Timberline!" said Scipio, not at all unkindly. "Still holding your job here? Well, you better stick to it. You're inclined to drift some."

He touched the horses and we left the boy standing and looking after us, lonely and baffled.

"Why Timberline?" I asked after several miles.

"Well, he came into this country the long, lanky innocent kid you saw him, and he'd always get too tall in the legs for his latest pair of pants. They'd be half up to his knees. So we called him that. Guess he's most forgot his real name."

"What is his real name?"

"I've quite forgot."

This much talk did for us for two or three miles more.

"Do you suppose the man really did go to Idaho?" I asked then.

"They do go there—and they go everywhere else that's convenient— Canada, San Francisco, some Indian reservation. He'll never get found. I expect like as not he killed the confederate along with the victims—it's claimed there was a cook along, too. He's never showed up. It's a bad proposition to get tangled up with a murderer."

I sat thinking of this and that and the other.

"That was a superior lie about the lights on the steers' horns," I remarked next.

Scipio shoved one hand under his hat and scratched his head. "They say that's so," he said. "I've heard it. Never seen it. But—tell y'u—he ain't got brains enough to invent a thing like that. And he's too conceited to tell another man's lie."

"There's St. Elmo's fire," I pondered. "That's genuine."

Scipio desired to know about this, and I told him of the lights that are seen at the ends of the yards and spars of ships at sea in atmospheric conditions of a certain kind. He let me also tell him of the old Breton sailor belief that these lights are the souls of dead sailor men come back to pray for the living in peril; but stopped me soon when I attempted to speak of charged thunder clouds, and the positive, and the negative, and conductors and Leyden jars.

"That's a heap worse than the other stuff about yellow and blue," he objected. "Here's Broke Axle. We'll camp here."

Scipio's sleep was superior to mine, coming sooner, burying him deeper from the world of wakefulness. Thus, he did not become aware of a figure sitting by our little fire of embers, whose presence penetrated my thinner sleep until my eyes opened and saw it. I lay still drawing my gun stealthily into a good position and thinking what were best to do; but he must have heard me.

"Lemme show you sheep."

"What's that?" It was Scipio starting to life and action.

"Don't shoot Timberline," I said. "He's come to show us sheep."

Scipio sat staring stupefied at the figure by the embers, and then he slowly turned his head around to me, and I thought he was going to pour out one of those long corrosive streams of comment that usually burst from him when he was enough surprised. But he was too much surprised.

"His name is Henry Hall," he said to me very mildly. "I've just remembered it."

The patient figure by the embers rose. "There's sheep in the Washakie Needles. Lots and lots and lots. I seen 'em myself in the spring. I can take you right to 'em. Don't make me go back and be stocktender." He recited all this in a sort of rising rhythm until the last sentence, in which the entreaty shook his voice.

"Washakie Needles is the nearest likely place," muttered Scipio.

"If you don't get any you needn't to pay me any," urged the boy; and he stretched out an arm to mark his words and his prayer.

We sat in our beds and he stood waiting by the embers to hear his fate, while nothing made a sound but Broke Axle.

"Why not?" I said. "We were talking a ways back of taking on a third man."

"A man," said Scipio. "Yes."

"I can cook, I can pack. I can cook good bread, and I can show you sheep, and if I don't you won't have to pay me a cent," stated the boy.

"He sure means what he says," Scipio commented. "It's your trip."

Thus it was I came to hire Timberline.

Dawn showed him in the same miserable rags he wore on my first sight of him at the corral, and these provided his sole visible property of any kind; he didn't possess a change of anything, he hadn't brought away from Rongis so much as a handkerchief tied up with things inside it. Most wonderful of all, he owned not even a horse—and in that country in those days five dollars' worth of horse was within the means of almost anybody.

But he was unclean, as I had feared. He washed his one set of rags, and his skin-and-bones body, by the light of that first sunrise on Broke Axle, and this proved a habit with him, which made all the more strange his neglect to throw the rags away and wear the new clothes I bought as we passed through Lander, and gave him.

"Timberline," said Scipio the next day, "If Anthony Comstock came up in this country he'd jail you."

"Who's he?" Timberline screamed sharply.

"He lives in New York and he's agin the nood. That costume of yours is getting close on to what they claim Venus and other Greek statuary used to wear."

After this Timberline put on the Lander clothes, but we found that he kept the rags next his skin. This clinging to such worthless things seemed probably the result of destitution, of having had nothing, day after day and month after month.

His help in camp was real, not merely well meant; the curious haze or blur in which his mind had seemed to be at the corral cleared away, and he was worth his wages. What he had said he could do he did, and more. And yet, when I looked at him he was somehow forever pitiful.

"Do you think anything is the matter with him?" I asked Scipio.

"Only just one thing. He'd oughtn't never have been born."

We continued along the trail, engrossed in our several thoughts, and I could hear Timberline, behind us with the pack-horses, singing: *"If that I was where I would be. Then should I be where I am not."*

OUR MODE of travel had changed at Fort Washakie: we had left the wagon and put ourselves and our baggage upon horses because we should presently be in a country where wagons could not go.

Once the vigorous words of some bypasser on a horse caused Scipio and me to discuss dropping the Washakie Needles for the country at the head of Green River. None of us had ever been in the Green River country, while Timberline evidently knew the Washakie Needles well, and this decided us. But Timberline had been thrown into the strangest agitation by our uncertainty. He had said nothing, but he walked about, coming near, going away, sitting down, getting up, instead of placidly watching his fire and cooking; until at last I told him not to worry, that I should keep him and pay him in any case. Then he spoke:

"I didn't hire to go to Green River."

"What have you got against Green River?"

"I hired to go to the Washakie Needles."

His agitation left him immediately upon our turning our faces in that direction. What had so disturbed him we could not guess; but, later that day, Scipio rode up to me, bursting with a solution. He had visited a freighter's camp, and the freighter, upon learning our destination, had said he supposed we were "after the reward."

It did not get through my head at once, but when Scipio reminded me of the yellow poster and the murder, it got through fast enough; the body had been found on Owl Creek, and the middle fork of Owl Creek headed among the Washakie Needles. There might be another body—the other Eastern man who had never been seen since—and there was a possible third, the confederate, the cook; many held it was the murderer's best policy to destroy him as well.

So now we had Timberline accounted for satisfactorily to ourselves: he was "after the reward." We never said this to him, but we worked out his steps from the start. As stocktender at Rongis he had seen that yellow poster pasted up, and had read it, day after day, with its promise of what to him was a fortune. My sheep hunt had dropped like a Providence into his hand.

We got across the hot country where rattlesnakes were thick, where neither man lived nor water ran, and came to the first lone habitation in this new part of the world—a new set of mountains, a new set of creeks. A man stood at the door, watching us come.

"Do you know him?" I asked Scipio.

"Well, I've heard of him," said Scipio. "He went and married a squaw."

We were now opposite the man's door. "You folks after the reward?" said he.

"After mountain sheep," I replied, somewhat angry.

We camped some ten miles beyond him, and the next day crossed a not high range, stopping near another cabin for noon. Two men were living here, cutting hay in a wild park. They gave us a quantity of berries they had picked, and we gave them some potatoes.

"After the reward?" said one of them as we rode away, and I contradicted him with temper.

"Lie to 'em," said Scipio. "Say yes."

Something had begun to weigh upon our cheerfulness in this new country. The reward dogged us, and we met strange actions of people, twice. We came upon some hot sulphur springs and camped near them, with a wide creek between us and another camp. Those people—two men and two women—emerged from their tent, surveyed us, nodded to us, and settled down again.

Next morning they had vanished; we could see empty bottles where they had been. And once, coming out of a little valley, we sighted close to us through cottonwoods a horseman leading a pack horse coming out of the next little valley. He did not nod to us, but pursued his parallel course some three hundred yards off, until a rise in the ground hid him for a while; when this was passed he was no longer where he should have been, abreast of us, but far to the front, galloping away. That was our last sight of him.

We spoke of these actions a little. Did these people suspect us, or were they afraid we suspected them? All we ever knew was that suspicion now closed down upon all things like a change of climate.

I DROVE UP the narrowing canyon of Owl Creek, a constant prey to such ill-ease, such distaste for continuing my sheep-hunt here, that shame alone prevented my giving it up and getting into another country out of sight and far away from these Washakie Needles, these twin spires of naked rock that rose in front of us now, high above the clustered mountaintops, closing the canyon in, shutting the setting sun away.

"He *can* talk when he wants to." This was Scipio, riding behind me.

"What has Timberline been telling you?"

"Nothing. But he's telling himself a heap of something." In the rear of our single-file party Timberline rode, and I could hear him. It was a relief to have a practical trouble threatening us; if the boy was going off his head we should have something real to deal with. But when I had chosen a camp and we were unsaddling and throwing the packs on the ground, Timberline was in his customary silence.

Next morning, the three of us left camp. It was warm summer in the valley by the streaming channel of our creek, and the quiet days smelled of the pines. By three o'clock we stood upon a lofty, wet, slippery ledge that fell away on three sides, sheer or broken, to the summer and the warmth thousands of feet below. Here it began to be very cold, and to the west the sky now clotted into advancing lumps of thick thunder cloud, black, weaving and merging heavily and swiftly in a fierce rising wind.

We got away from this promontory to follow a sheep trail, and as we went along the backbone of the mountain, two or three valleys off to the right long black streamers let down from the cloud. They hung and wavered mistily close over the pines that did not grow within a thousand feet of our high level. I gazed hard at the streamers and discerned water, or something pouring down in them. Above our heads the day was still serene, and we had a chance to make camp without a wetting.

"No! No!" said Timberline hoarsely. "See there! We can get them. We're above them. They don't see us."

I saw no sheep where he pointed but he insisted they had merely moved behind a point, and so we went on to a junction of the knife-ridges upon which a second storm was hastening from the southwest over deep valleys that we turned our backs on to creep near the Great Washakie Needle.

Below us there was a new valley like the bottom of a caldron; on the far side of the caldron the air, like a stroke of magic became thick white, and through it leaped the first lightning, a blinding violet. A sheet of the storm crossed over to us, the caldron sank from sight in its white sea, and the hail cut my face, so I bowed it down. On the ground I saw what looked like a tangle of old footprints in the hard-crusted mud.

These the pellets of the swarming hail soon filled. This tempest of flying ice struck my body, my horse, raced over the ground like spray on the crest of breaking waves, and drove me to dismount and sit under the horse, huddled together even as he was huddled against the fury and the biting pain of the hail.

From under the horse's belly I looked out upon a chaos of shooting, hissing white, through which, in every direction, lightning flashed and leaped, while the fearful crashes behind the curtain of the hail sounded as if I should see a destroyed world when the curtain lifted. The place was so flooded with electricity that I gave up the shelter of my horse, and left my rifle on the ground, and moved away from the vicinity of these points of attraction.

At length the hailstones fell more gently, the near view opened, revealing white winter on all save the steep, gray needles; the thick white curtain of hail departed slowly, the hail where I was fell more scantily still.

Something somewhere near my head set up a delicate sound. It seemed in my hat. I rose and began to wander, bewildered by this. The hail was now falling very fine and gentle, when suddenly I was aware of its stinging me behind my ear more sharply than it had done before. I turned my face in its direction and found its blows harmless, while the stinging in my ear grew sharper. The hissing continued close to my head wherever I walked. It resembled the little watery escape of gas from a charged bottle whose cork is being slowly drawn.

I was now more really disturbed than I had been during the storm's worst, and meeting Scipio, who was also wandering, I asked if he felt anything. He nodded uneasily, when, suddenly—I know not why—I snatched my hat off. The hissing was in the brim, and it died out as I looked at the leather binding and the stitches.

I expected to see some insect there, or some visible reason for the noise. I saw nothing, but the pricking behind my ear had also stopped. Then I knew my wet hat had been charged like a Leyden jar with electricity. Scipio, who had watched me, jerked his hat off also.

"Lights on steer horns are nothing to this," I began, when he cut me short with an exclamation.

Timberline, on his knees, with a frightful countenance, was tearing off his clothes. He had felt the prickling, but it caused him thought different from mine.

"Leave me go!" he screamed. "I didn't push you over! He made me push you. I never knowed his game. I was only the cook. I wish't I'd followed you. There! There! Take it back! There's your money! I never spent a cent of it!"

And from those rags he had cherished he tore the bills that had been sewed in them. But this confession seemed not to stop the stinging. He rose, stared wildly, and, screaming wildly, "You've got it all" plunged into the caldron from our sight. The fluttered money—some of the victim's, hush-money hapless Timberline had accepted from the murderer—was only five ten dollar bills; but it had been enough load of guilt to draw him to the spot of the crime.

We found the two bodies, the old and the new, and buried them both. But the true murderer was not caught, and no one ever claimed the reward.

JACK LONDON

All Gold Canyon

Jack London (1876–1916) was a master of the adventure story whose The Call of the Wild *will live forever. Somewhat of an adventurer himself, he knew of what he wrote, having spent parts of his early life living as a hobo, searching for gold in Alaska, and even serving time in prison for oyster pirating. Much of his work, such as his science fiction novel,* The Scarlet Plague, *contains considerable political content, a strange combination of Marxism and rugged individualism. But he also wrote knowingly of the frontier and the search for wealth, as in this powerful story.*

IT WAS THE GREEN HEART of the canyon, where the walls swerved back from the rigid plan and relieved their harshness of line by making a little sheltered nook and filling it to the brim with sweetness and roundness and softness. Here all things rested. Even the narrow stream ceased its turbulent down-rush long enough to form a quiet pool. Knee-deep in the water, with drooping head and half-shut eyes, drowsed a red-coated, many-antlered buck.

On one side, beginning at the very lip of the pool, was a tiny meadow, a cool, resilient surface of green that extended to the base of the frowning wall. Beyond the pool a gentle slope of earth ran up and up to meet the opposing wall. Fine grass covered the slope—grass that was spangled with flowers, with here-and-there patches of color, orange and purple and golden. Below, the canyon was shut in. There was no view. The walls leaned together abruptly, and the canyon ended in a chaos of rocks, moss-covered and hidden by a green screen of vines and creepers and boughs of trees. Up the canyon rose far hills and peaks, the big foothills, pine-covered and remote. And far beyond, like clouds upon the border of the sky, towered minarets of white, where the Sierra's eternal snows flashed austerely the blazes of the sun.

There was no dust in the canyon. The leaves and flowers were clean and virginal. The grass was young velvet. Over the pool three cottonwoods sent their snowy fluffs fluttering down the quiet air. On the slope the blossoms of the wine-wooded manzanita filled the air with springtime odors, while the leaves, wise with experience, were already beginning their vertical twist against the coming aridity of summer. In the open spaces on the slope, beyond the farthest shadow-reach of the manzanita, poised the mariposa lilies, like so many flights of jewelled moths suddenly arrested and on the verge of trembling into flight again. Here and there that woods harlequin, the madrone, permitting itself to be caught in the act of changing its pea green trunk to madder red, breathed its fragrance into the air from great clusters of waxen bells. Creamy white were these bells, shaped like lilies of the valley, with the sweetness of perfume that is of the springtime.

There was not a sigh of wind. The air was drowsy with its weight of perfume. It was a sweetness that would have been cloying had the air been heavy and humid. But the air was sharp and thin. It was as starlight transmuted into atmosphere, shot through and warmed by sunshine, and flower-drenched with sweetness.

An occasional butterfly drifted in and out through the patches of light and shade. And from all about rose the low and sleepy hum of mountain bees—feasting Sybarites that jostled one another good-naturedly at the board, nor found time for rough discourtesy. So quietly did the little stream drip and ripple its way through the canyon that it spoke only in faint and occasional gurgles. The voice of the stream was as a drowsy whisper, ever interrupted by dozings and silences, ever lifted again in the awakenings.

The motion of all things was a drifting in the heart of the canyon. Sunshine and butterflies drifted in and out among the trees. The hum of the bees and the whisper of the stream were a drifting of sound. And the drifting sound and drifting color seemed to weave together in the making of a delicate and intangible fabric which was the spirit of the place. It was a spirit of peace that was not of death, but of smooth-pulsing life, of quietude that was not silence, of movement that was not action, of repose that was quick with existence without being violent with struggle and travail. The spirit of the place was the spirit of the peace of the living, somnolent with the easement and content of prosperity, and undisturbed by rumors of far wars.

The red-coated, many-antlered buck acknowledged the lordship of the spirit of the place and dozed knee-deep in the cool, shaded pool. There seemed no flies to vex him and he was languid with rest. Sometimes his ears moved when the stream awoke and whispered; but they moved lazily, with foreknowledge that it was merely the stream grown garrulous at discovery that it had slept.

But there came a time when the buck's ears lifted and tensed with swift eagerness for sound. His head was turned down the canyon. His sensitive, quivering nostrils scented the air. His eyes could not pierce the green screen through which the stream rippled away, but to his ears came the voice of a man. It was a steady, monotonous, singsong voice. Once the buck heard the harsh clash of metal upon rock. At the sound he snorted with a sudden start that jerked him through the air from water to meadow, and his feet sank into the young velvet while he pricked his ears and again scented the air. Then he stole across the tiny meadow, pausing once and again to listen, and faded away out of the canyon like a wraith, soft-footed and without sound.

The clash of steel-shod soles against the rocks began to be heard, and the man's voice grew louder. It was raised in a sort of chant and became distinct with nearness, so that the words could be heard.

> "Tu'n around an' tu'n yo' face
> Untoe them sweet hills of grace
>   (D' pow'rs of sin yo' am scornin'!).
> Look about an' look aroun'
> Fling yo' sin-pack on d' groun'
>   (Yo' will meet wid d' Lord in d' mornin'!)."

A sound of scrambling accompanied the song, and the spirit of the place fled away on the heels of the red-coated buck. The green screen was burst asunder, and a man peered out at the meadow and the pool and the sloping side-hill. He was a deliberate sort of man. He took in the scene with one embracing glance, then ran his eyes over the details to verify the general impression. Then, and not until then, did he open his mouth in vivid and solemn approval.

"Smoke of life an' snakes of purgatory! Will you just look at that! Wood an' water an' grass an' a side-hill! A pocket-hunter's delight an' a cayuse's paradise! Cool green for tired eyes! Pink pills for pale people ain't in it. A secret pasture for prospectors and a resting-place for tired burros. It's just booful!"

He was a sandy-complexioned man in whose face geniality and humor seemed the salient characteristics. It was a mobile face, quick-changing to inward mood and thought. Thinking was in him a visible process. Ideas chased across his face like wind flaws across the surface of a lake. His hair, sparse and unkempt of growth, was as indeterminate and colorless as his complexion. It would seem that all the color of his frame had gone into his eyes, for they were startlingly blue. Also, they were laughing and merry eyes, within them much of the naiveté and wonder of the child; and yet, in an unassertive way, they contained much of calm self-reliance and strength of purpose founded upon self-experience and experience of the world.

From out the screen of vines and creepers, he flung ahead of him a miner's pick and shovel and gold-pan. Then he crawled out himself into the open. He was clad in faded overalls and black cotton shirt, with hobnailed brogans on his feet, and on his head a hat whose shapelessness and stains advertised the rough usage of wind and rain and sun and camp smoke. He stood erect, seeing wide-eyed the secrecy of the scene and sensuously inhaling the warm, sweet breath of the canyon garden through nostrils that dilated and quivered with delight. His eyes narrowed to laughing slits of blue, his face wreathed itself in joy, and his mouth curled in a smile as he cried aloud, "Jumping dandelions and happy hollyhocks, but that smells good to me! Talk about your attar o' roses an' cologne factories! They ain't in it!"

He had the habit of soliloquy. His quick-changing facial expressions might tell every thought and mood, but the tongue, perforce, ran hard after, repeating, like a second Boswell.

The man lay down on the lip of the pool and drank long and deep of its water. "Tastes good to me," he murmured, lifting his head and gazing across the pool at the side-hill, while he wiped his mouth with the back of his hand. The side-hill attracted his attention. Still lying on his stomach, he studied the hill formation long and carefully. It was a practiced eye that traveled up the slope to the crumbling canyon wall and back and down again to the edge of the pool. He scrambled to his feet and favored the side-hill with a second survey.

"Looks good to me," he concluded, picking up his pick and shovel and gold-pan.

He crossed the stream below the pool, stepping agilely from stone to stone. Where the side-hill touched the water he dug up a shovelful of dirt and put it into the gold-pan. He squatted down, holding the pan in his two hands, and partly immersing it in the stream. Then he imparted to the pan a deft circular motion that sent the water sluicing in and out through the dirt and gravel. The larger and the lighter particles worked to the surface, and these, by a skillful dipping movement of the pan, he spilled out and over the edge. Occasionally, to expedite matters, he rested the pan and with his fingers raked out the large pebbles and pieces of rock.

The contents of the pan diminished rapidly until only fine dirt and the smallest bits of gravel remained. At this stage he began to work very deliberately and carefully. It was fine washing, and he washed fine and finer, with a keen scrutiny and delicate and fastidious touch. At last the pan seemed empty of everything but water; but with a quick semicircular flirt that sent the water flying over the shallow rim into the stream, he disclosed a layer of black sand on the bottom of the pan. So thin was this layer that it was like a streak of paint. He examined it closely. In the midst of it was a tiny golden speck. He dribbled a little water in over the depressed edge of the pan. With a quick flirt he sent the water sluicing across the bottom, turning the grains of black sand over and over. A second tiny golden speck rewarded his effort.

The washing had now become very fine—fine beyond all need of ordinary placer mining. He worked the black sand, a small portion at a time, up the shallow rim of the pan. Each small portion he examined sharply, so that his eyes saw every grain of it before he allowed it to slide over the edge and away. Jealously, bit by bit, he let the black sand slip away. A golden speck, no larger than a pinpoint, appeared on the rim, and by his manipulation of the water it returned to the bottom of the pan. And in such fashion another speck was disclosed, and another. Great was his care of them. Like a shepherd he herded his flock of golden specks so that not one should be lost. At last, of the pan of dirt nothing remained but his golden herd. He counted it, and then, after all his labor, sent it flying out of the pan with one final swirl of water.

But his blue eyes were shining with desire as he rose to his feet. "Seven," he muttered aloud, asserting the sum of the specks for which he had toiled so hard and which he had so wantonly thrown away. "Seven," he repeated, with the emphasis of one trying to impress a number on his memory.

He stood still a long while, surveying the hillside. In his eyes was a curiosity, new-aroused and burning. There was an exultance about his bearing and a keenness like that of a hunting animal catching the fresh scent of game.

He moved down the stream a few steps and took a second panful of dirt.

Again came the careful washing, the jealous herding of the golden specks, and the wantonness with which he sent them flying into the stream. His golden herd diminished. "Four, five," he muttered, and repeated, "five."

He could not forbear another survey of the hill before filling the pan farther down the stream. His golden herds diminished. "Four, three, two, two, one," were his memory tabulations as he moved down the stream. When but one speck of gold rewarded his washing, he stopped and built a fire of dry twigs. Into this he thrust the gold-pan and burned it till it was blue black. He held up the pan and examined it critically. Then he nodded approbation. Against such a color-background he could defy the tiniest yellow speck to elude him.

Still moving down the stream, he panned again. A single speck was his reward. A third pan contained no gold at all. Not satisfied with this, he panned three times again, taking his shovels of dirt within a foot of one another. Each pan proved empty of gold, and the fact, instead of discouraging him, seemed to give him satisfaction. His elation increased with each barren washing, until he arose, exclaiming jubilantly:

"If it ain't the real thing, may God knock off my head with sour apples!"

Returning to where he had started operations, he began to pan up the stream. At first his golden herds increased—increased prodigiously. "Fourteen, eighteen, twenty-one, twenty-six," ran his memory tabulations. Just above the pool he struck his richest pan—thirty-five colors.

"Almost enough to save," he remarked regretfully as he allowed the water to sweep them away.

The sun climbed to the top of the sky. The man worked on. Pan by pan, he went up the stream, the tally of results steadily decreasing.

"It's just booful, the way it peters out," he exulted when a shovelful of dirt contained no more than a single speck of gold.

And when no specks at all were found in several pans, he straightened up and favored the hillside with a confident glance.

"Ah, ha! Mr. Pocket!" he cried out, as though to an auditor hidden somewhere above him beneath the surface of the slope.

"Ah, ha! Mr. Pocket! I'm a-comin', I'm a-comin', an' I'm shorely gwine to get yer! You heah me, Mr. Pocket? I'm gwine to get yer as shore as punkins ain't cauliflowers!"

He turned and flung a measuring glance at the sun poised above him in the azure of the cloudless sky. Then he went down the canyon, following the line of shovel holes he had made in filling the pans. He crossed the stream below the pool and disappeared through the green screen. There was little opportunity for the spirit of the place to return with its quietude and repose, for the man's voice, raised in ragtime song, still dominated the canyon with possession.

After a time, with a greater clashing of steel-shod feet on rock, he returned. The green screen was tremendously agitated. It surged back and forth in the throes of a struggle. There was a loud grating and clanging of metal. The man's voice leaped to a higher pitch and was sharp with imperativeness. A large body plunged and panted. There was a snapping and ripping and rending, and amid a shower of falling leaves a horse burst through the screen. On its back was a pack, and from this trailed broken vines and torn creepers. The animal gazed with astonished eyes at the scene into which it had been precipitated, then dropped its head to the grass and began contentedly to graze. A second horse scrambled into view, slipping once on the mossy rocks and regaining equilibrium when its hoofs sank into the yielding surface of the meadow. It was riderless, though on its back was a high-horned Mexican saddle, scarred and discolored by long usage.

The man brought up the rear. He threw off pack and saddle, with an eye to camp location, and gave the animals their freedom to graze. He unpacked his food and got out frying pan and coffeepot. He gathered an armful of dry wood, and with a few stones made a place for his fire.

"My!" he said, "but I've got an appetite. I could scoff ironfilings an' horseshoe nails an' thank you kindly, ma'am, for a second helpin'."

He straightened up, and while he reached for matches in the pocket of his overalls, his eyes traveled across the pool to the side-hill. His fingers had clutched the matchbox, but they relaxed their hold and the hand came out empty. The man wavered perceptibly. He looked at his preparations for cooking and he looked at the hill.

"Guess I'll take another whack at her," he concluded, starting to cross the stream.

"They ain't no sense in it, I know," he mumbled apologetically. "But keepin' grub back an hour ain't goin' to hurt none, I reckon."

A few feet back from his first of test pans he started a second line. The sun dropped down the western sky, the shadows lengthened, but the man worked on. He began a third line of test pans. He was crosscutting the hillside, line by line, as he ascended. The center of each line produced the richest pans, while the ends came where no colors showed in the pan. And as he ascended the hillside the lines grew perceptibly shorter. The regularity with which their length diminished served to indicate that somewhere up the slope the last line would be so short as to have scarcely length at all, and that beyond could come only a point. The design was growing into an inverted V. The converging sides of this V marked the boundaries of the gold-bearing dirt.

The apex of the V was evidently the man's goal. Often he ran his eye along the converging sides and on up the hill, trying to divine the apex, the point where the gold-bearing dirt must cease. Here resided Mr. Pocket—for so the man familiarly addressed the imaginary point above him on the slope, crying out, "Come down out o' that, Mr. Pocket! Be right smart an' agreeable, an' come down!

"All right," he would add later, in a voice resigned to determination. "All right, Mr. Pocket. It's plain to me I got to come right up an' snatch you out bald headed. An' I'll do it! I'll do it!" he would threaten still later.

Each pan he carried down to the water to wash, and as he went higher up the hill the pans grew richer, until he began to save the gold in an empty baking-powder can which he carried carelessly in his hip-pocket. So engrossed was he in his toil that he did not notice the long twilight of oncoming night. It was not until he tried vainly to see the gold colors in the bottom of the pan that he realized the passage of time. He straightened up abruptly. An expression of whimsical wonderment and awe overspread his face as he drawled, "Gosh darn my buttons! If I didn't plumb forget dinner!"

He stumbled across the stream in the darkness and lighted his long-delayed fire. Flapjacks and bacon and warmed-over beans constituted his supper. Then he smoked a pipe by the smoldering coals, listening to the night noises and watching the moonlight stream through the canyon. After that he unrolled his bed, took off his heavy shoes and pulled the blankets up to his chin. His face showed white in the moonlight, like the face of a corpse. But it was a corpse that knew its resurrection, for the man rose suddenly on one elbow and gazed across at his hillside.

"Good night, Mr. Pocket," he called sleepily. "Good night."

He slept through the early gray of morning until the direct rays of the sun smote his closed eyelids, when he awoke with a start and looked about him until he had established the continuity of his existence and identified his present self with the days previously lived.

To dress, he had merely to buckle on his shoes. He glanced at his fireplace and at his hillside, wavered, but fought down the temptation and started the fire.

"Keep yer shirt on, Bill; keep yer shirt on," he admonished himself. "What's the good of rushin'? No use in gettin' all het up an' sweaty. Mr. Pocket 'll wait for you. He ain't a-runnin' away before you can get your breakfast. Now, what you want, Bill, is something fresh in yer bill o' fare. So it's up to you to go an' get it."

He cut a short pole at the water's edge and drew from one of his pockets a bit of line and a draggled fly that had once been a royal coachman.

"Mebbe they'll bite in the early morning," he muttered, as he made his first cast into the pool. And a moment later he was gleefully crying, "What'd I tell you, eh? What 'd I tell you?"

He had no reel nor any inclination to waste time, and by main strength, and swiftly, he drew out of the water a flashing ten-inch trout. Three more, caught in rapid succession, furnished his breakfast. When he came to the stepping-stones on his way to his hillside, he was struck by a sudden thought, and paused.

"I'd just better take a hike downstream a ways," he said. "There's no tellin' who may be snoopin' around."

But he crossed over on the stones, and with a "I really oughter take that hike," the need of the precaution passed out of his mind, and he fell to work.

At nightfall he straightened up. The small of his back was stiff from stooping toil, and as he put his hand behind him to soothe the protesting muscles, he said; "Now what d'ye think of that? I clean forgot my dinner again! If I don't watch out, I'll sure be degeneratin' into a two-meal-a-day crank.

"Pockets is the hangedest things I ever see for makin' a man absent-minded," he communed that night, as he crawled into his blankets. Nor did he forget to call up the hillside, "Good night, Mr. Pocket! Good night!"

Rising with the sun, and snatching a hasty breakfast, he was early at work. A fever seemed to be growing in him, nor did the increasing richness of the test pans allay this fever. There was a flush in his cheek other than that made by the heat of the sun, and he was oblivious to fatigue and the passage of time. When he filled a pan with dirt, he ran down the hill to wash it; nor could he forbear running up the hill again, panting and stumbling profanely, to refill the pan.

He was now a hundred yards from the water, and the inverted V was assuming definite proportions. The width of the paydirt steadily decreased, and the man extended in his mind's eye the sides of the V to their meeting place far up the hill. This was his goal, the apex of the V, and he panned many times to locate it.

"Just about two yards above that manzanita bush an' a yard to the right," he finally concluded.

Then the temptation seized him. "As plain as the nose on your face," he said, as he abandoned his laborious crosscutting and climbed to the indicated apex. He filled a pan and carried it down the hill to wash. It contained no trace of gold. He dug deep, and he dug shallow, filling and washing a dozen pans, and was unrewarded even by the tiniest golden speck. He was enraged at having yielded to the temptation, and berated himself blasphemously and pridelessly. Then he went down the hill and took up the cross-cutting.

"Slow an' certain, Bill; slow an' certain," he crooned. "Shortcuts to fortune ain't in your line, an' it's about time you know it. Get wise, Bill; get wise. Slow an' certain's the only hand you can play; so get to it, an' keep to it, too."

As the crosscuts decreased, showing that the sides of the V were converging, the depth of the V increased. The gold trace was dipping into the hill. It was only at thirty inches beneath the surface that he could get colors in his pan. The dirt he found at twenty-five inches from the surface, and at thirty-five inches, yielded barren pans. At the base of the V, by the water's edge, he had found the gold colors at the grass roots. The higher he went up the hill, the deeper the gold dipped. To dig a hole three feet deep in order to get one test pan was a task of no mean magnitude; while between the man and the apex intervened an untold number of such holes to be dug. "An' there's no tellin' how much deeper it'll pitch," he sighed in a moment's pause while his fingers soothed his aching back.

Feverish with desire, with aching back and stiffening muscles, with pick and shovel gouging and mauling the soft brown earth, the man toiled up the hill. Before him was the smooth slope, spangled with flowers and made sweet with their breath. Behind him was devastation. It looked like some terrible eruption breaking out on the smooth skin of the hill. His slow progress was like that of a slug, befouling beauty with a monstrous trail.

Though the dipping gold trace increased the man's work, he found consolation in the increasing richness of the pans. Twenty cents, thirty cents, fifty cents, sixty cents, were the values of the gold found in the pans, and at nightfall he washed his banner pan, which gave him a dollar's worth of gold dust from a shovelful of dirt.

"I'll just bet it's my luck to have some inquisitive one come buttin' in here on my pasture," he mumbled sleepily that night as he pulled the blankets up to his chin.

Suddenly he sat upright. "Bill!" he called sharply. "Now, listen to me, Bill; d'ye hear! It's up to you, tomorrow mornin', to mosey round an' see what you can see. Understand? Tomorrow morning, an' don't you forget it!"

He yawned and glanced across at his side-hill. "Good night, Mr. Pocket," he called.

In the morning he stole a march on the sun, for he had finished breakfast when its first rays caught him, and he was climbing the wall of the canyon where it crumbled away and gave footing. From the outlook at the top he found himself in the midst of loneliness. As far as he could see, chain after chain of mountains heaved themselves into his vision. To the east his eyes, leaping the miles between range and range and between many ranges, brought up at last against the white-peaked Sierras—the main crest, where the backbone of the Western world reared itself against the sky! To the north and south he could see more distinctly the cross systems that broke through the main trend of the sea of mountains. To the west the ranges fell away, one behind the other, diminishing and fading into the gentle foothills that, in turn, descended into the great valley which he could not see.

And in all that mighty sweep of earth he saw no sign of man nor of the handiwork of man—save only the torn bosom of the hillside at his feet. The man looked long and carefully. Once, far down his own canyon, he thought he saw in the air a faint hint of smoke. He looked again and decided that it was the purple haze of the hills made dark by a convolution of the canyon wall at its back.

"Hey, you, Mr. Pocket!" he called down into the canyon. "Stand out from under! I'm a-comin', Mr. Pocket! I'm a-comin'!"

The heavy brogans on the man's feet made him appear clumsyfooted, but he swung down from the giddy height as lightly and airily as a mountain goat. A rock, turning under his foot on the edge of the precipice, did not disconcert him. He seemed to know the precise time required for the turn to culminate in disaster, and in the meantime he utilized the false footing itself for the momentary earth contact necessary to carry him on into safety. Where the earth sloped so steeply that it was impossible to stand for a second upright, the man did not hesitate. His foot pressed the impossible surface for but a fraction of the fatal second and gave him the bound that carried him onward. Again, where even the fraction of a second's footing was out of the question, he would swing his body past by a moment's handgrip on a jutting knob of rock, a crevice or a precariously rooted shrub. At last, with a wild leap and yell, he exchanged the face of the wall for an earthslide and finished the descent in the midst of several tons of sliding earth and gravel.

His first pan of the morning washed out over two dollars in coarse gold. It was from the center of the V. To either side the diminution in the values of the pans was swift. His lines of crosscutting holes were growing very short. The converging sides of the inverted V were only a few yards apart. Their meeting point was only a few yards above him. But the pay streak was dipping deeper and deeper into the earth. By early afternoon he was sinking the test holes five feet before the pans could show the gold trace.

For that matter, the gold trace had become something more than a trace; it was a placer mine in itself, and the man resolved to come back after he had found the pocket and work over the ground. But the increasing richness of the pans began to worry him. By late afternoon the worth of the pans had grown to three and four dollars. The man scratched his head perplexedly and looked a few feet up the hill at the manzanita bush that marked approximately the apex of the V. He nodded his head and said oracularly:

"It's one o' two things, Bill; one o' two things. Either Mr. Pocket's spilled himself all out an' down the hill, or else Mr. Pocket's so rich you maybe won't be able to carry him all away with you. And that'd be an awful shame, wouldn't it, now?" He chuckled at contemplation of so pleasant a dilemma.

Nightfall found him by the edge of the stream, his eyes wrestling with the gathering darkness over the washing of a five-dollar pan.

"Wisht I had an electric light to go on working," he said.

He found sleep difficult that night. Many times he composed himself and closed his eyes for slumber to overtake him; but his blood pounded with too strong desire, and as many times his eyes opened and he murmured wearily, "Wisht it was sunup."

Sleep came to him in the end, but his eyes were open with the first paling of the stars, and the gray of dawn caught him with breakfast finished and climbing the hillside in the direction of the secret abiding-place of Mr. Pocket.

The first crosscut the man made, there was space for only three holes, so narrow had become the pay streak and so close was he to the fountain-head of the golden stream he had been following for four days.

"Be ca'm, Bill; be ca'm," he admonished himself, as he broke ground for the final hole where the sides of the V had at last come together in a point.

"I've got the almighty cinch on you, Mr. Pocket, an' you can't lose me," he said many times as he sank the hole deeper and deeper.

Four feet, five feet, six feet, he dug his way down into the earth. The digging grew harder. His pick grated on broken rock. He examined the rock. "Rotten quartz" was his conclusion as, with the shovel, he cleared the bottom of the hole of loose dirt. He attacked the crumbling quartz with the pick, bursting the disintegrating rock asunder with every stroke.

He thrust his shovel into the loose mass. His eye caught a gleam of yellow. He dropped the shovel and squatted suddenly on his heels. As a farmer rubs the clinging earth from fresh-dug potatoes, so the man, a piece of rotten quartz held in both hands, rubbed the dirt away.

"Sufferin' Sardanopolis!" he cried. "Lumps an' chunks of it! Lumps an' chunks of it!"

It was only half rock he held in his hand. The other half was virgin gold. He dropped it into his pan and examined another piece. Little yellow was to be seen, but with his strong fingers he crumbled the rotten quartz away till both hands were filled with glowing yellow. He rubbed the dirt away from fragment after fragment, tossing them into the gold-pan. It was a treasure hole. So much had the quartz rotted away that there was less of it than there was of gold. Now and again he found a piece to which no rock clung—a piece that was all gold. A chunk where the pick had laid open the heart of the gold glittered like a handful of yellow jewels, and he cocked his head at it and slowly turned it around and over to observe the rich play of the light upon it.

"Talk about yer too-much-gold diggin's!" the man snorted contemptu-ously. "Why, this diggin' 'd make it look like thirty cents. This diggin' is all gold. An' right here an' now I name this yere canyon All Gold Canyon, b' gosh!"

Still squatting on his heels, he continued examining the fragments and tossing them into the pan. Suddenly there came to him a premonition of danger. It seemed a shadow had fallen upon him. But there was no shadow. His heart had given a great jump up into his throat and was choking him. Then his blood slowly chilled, and he felt the sweat of his shirt cold against his flesh.

He did not spring up nor look around. He did not move. He was considering the nature of the premonition he had received, trying to locate the source of the mysterious force that had warned him, striving to sense the imperative presence of the unseen thing that threatened him. There is an aura of things hostile, made manifest by messengers too refined for the senses to know; and this aura he felt, but knew not how he felt it. His was the feeling as when a cloud passes over the sun. It seemed that between him and life had passed something dark and smothering and meanacing; a gloom, as it were, that swallowed up life and made for death—his death.

Every force of his being impelled him to spring up and confront the unseen danger, but his soul dominated the panic, and he remained squatting on his heels, in his hands a chunk of gold. He did not dare to look around, but he knew by now that there was something behind him and above him. He made believe to be interested in the gold in his hand. He examined it critically, turned it over and over, and rubbed the dirt from it. And all the time he knew that something behind him was looking at the gold over his shoulder.

Still feigning interest in the chunk of gold in his hand, he listened intently and he heard the breathing of the thing behind him. His eyes searched the ground in front of him for a weapon, but they saw only the uprooted gold, worthless to him now in his extremity. There was his pick, a handy weapon on occasion; but this was not such an occasion. The man realized his predicament. He was in a narrow hole that was seven feet deep. His head did not come to the surface of the ground. He was in a trap.

He remained squatting on his heels. He was quite cool and collected; but his mind, considering every factor, showed him only his helplessness. He continued rubbing the dirt from the quartz fragments and throwing the gold into the pan. There was nothing else for him to do. Yet he knew that he would have to rise up, sooner or later, and face the danger that breathed at his back. The minutes passed, and with the passage of each minute he knew that by so much he was nearer the time when he must stand up, or else—and his wet shirt went cold against his flesh again at the thought—or else he might receive death as he stooped there over his treasure.

Still he squatted on his heels, rubbing dirt from gold and debating in just what manner he should rise up. He might rise up with a rush and claw his way out of the hole to meet whatever threatened on the even footing above ground. Or he might rise up slowly and carelessly, and feign casually to discover the thing that breathed at his back. His instinct and every fighting fiber of his body favored the mad, clawing rush to the surface. His intellect, and the craft thereof, favored the slow and cautious meeting with the thing that menaced and which he could not see. And while he debated, a loud, crashing noise burst on his ear. At the same instant he received a stunning blow on the left side of his back, and from the point of impact felt a rush of flame through his flesh. He sprang up in the air but, halfway to his feet, collapsed. His body crumpled in like a leaf withered in sudden heat, and he came down, his chest across his pan of gold, his face in the dirt and rock, his legs tangled and twisted because of the restricted space at the bottom of the hole. His legs twitched convulsively several times. His body was shaken with a mighty ague. There was a slow expansion of the lungs, accompanied by a deep sigh. Then the air was slowly, very slowly, exhaled, and his body as slowly flattened itself down into inertness.

Above, revolver in hand, a man was peering down over the edge of the hole. He peered for a long time at the prone and motionless body beneath him. After a while the stranger sat down on the edge of the hole so that he could see into it, and rested the revolver on his knee. Reaching his hand into a pocket, he drew out a wisp of brown paper. Into this he dropped a few crumbs of tobacco. The combination became a cigarette, brown and squat, with the ends turned in. Not once did he take his eyes from the body at the bottom of the hole. He lighted the cigarette and drew its smoke into his lungs with a caressing intake of the breath. He smoked slowly. Once the cigarette went out and he relighted it. And all the while he studied the body beneath him.

In the end he tossed the cigarette stub away and rose to his feet. He moved to the edge of the hole. Spanning it, a hand resting on each edge, and with the revolver still in the right hand, he muscled his body down into the hole. While his feet were yet a yard from the bottom, he released his hands and dropped down.

At the instant his feet struck bottom he saw the pocket-miner's arm leap out, and his own legs knew a swift, jerking grip that overthrew him. In the nature of the jump his revolver-hand was above his head. Swiftly as the grip had flashed about his legs, just as swiftly he brought the revolver down. He was still in the air, his fall in process of completion, when he pulled the trigger. The explosion was deafening in the confined space. The smoke filled the hole so that he could see nothing. He struck the bottom on his back, and like a cat's the pocket-miner's body was on top of him. Even as the miner's body passed on top, the stranger crooked in his right arm to fire; and even in that instant the miner, with a quick thrust of elbow, struck his wrist. The muzzle was thrown up and the bullet thudded into the dirt of the side of the hole.

The next instant the stranger felt the miner's hand grip his wrist. The struggle was now for the revolver. Each man strove to turn it against the other's body. The smoke in the hole was clearing. The stranger, lying on his back, was beginning to see dimly. But suddenly he was blinded by a handful of dirt deliberately flung into his eyes by his antagonist. In that moment of shock his grip on the revolver was broken. In the next moment he felt a smashing darkness descend upon his brain, and in the midst of the darkness even the darkness ceased.

But the pocket miner fired again and again, until the revolver was empty. Then he tossed it from him and, breathing heavily, sat down on the dead man's legs.

The miner was sobbing and struggling for breath. "Measly skunk!" he panted, "a-campin' on my trail an' lettin' me do the work, an' then shootin' me in the back!"

He was half crying from anger and exhaustion. He peered at the face of the dead man. It was sprinkled with loose dirt and gravel, and it was difficult to distinguish the features.

"Never laid eyes on him before," the miner concluded his scrutiny. "Just a common an' ordinary thief, hang him! An' he shot me in the back! He shot me in the back!"

He opened his shirt and felt himself, front and back, on his left side.

"Went clean through, and no harm done!" he cried jubilantly. "I'll bet he aimed all right; but he drew the gun over when he pulled the trigger —the cur! But I fixed 'm! Oh, I fixed 'm!"

His fingers were investigating the bullet hole in his side, and a shade of regret passed over his face. "It's goin' to be stiffer'n hell," he said. "An' it's up to me to get mended an' get out o' here."

He crawled out of the hole and went down the hill to his camp. Half an hour later he returned, leading his packhorse. His open shirt disclosed the rude bandages with which he had dressed his wound. He was slow and awkward with his left-hand movements, but that did not prevent his using the arm.

The bight of the pack rope under the dead man's shoulders enabled him to heave the body out of the hole. Then he set to work gathering up his gold. He worked steadily for several hours, pausing often to rest his stiffening shoulder and to exclaim, "He shot me in the back, the measly skunk! He shot me in the back!"

When his treasure was quite cleaned up and wrapped securely into a number of blanket-covered parcels, he made an estimate of its value.

"Four hundred pounds, or I'm a Hottentot," he concluded. "Say two hundred in quartz an' dirt—that leaves two hundred pounds of gold. Bill! Wake up! Two hundred pounds of gold! Forty thousand dollars! An' it's yourn—all yourn!"

He scratched his head delightedly and his fingers blundered into an unfamiliar groove. They quested along it for several inches. It was a crease through his scalp where the second bullet had ploughed.

He walked angrily over to the dead man.

"You would, would you?" he bullied. "You would, eh? Well, I fixed you good an' plenty, an' I'll give you a decent burial, too. That's more'n you'd have done for me."

He dragged the body to the edge of the hole and toppled it in. It struck the bottom with a dull crash, on its side, the face twisted up to the light. The miner peered down at it.

"An' you shot me in the back!" he said accusingly.

With pick and shovel he filled the hole. Then he loaded the gold on his horse. It was too great a load for the animal, and when he had gained his camp he transferred part of it to his saddle horse. Even so, he was compelled to abandon a portion of his outfit—pick and shovel and gold-pan, extra food and cooking utensils, and divers odds and ends.

The sun was at the zenith when the man forced the horses at the screen of vines and creepers. To climb the huge boulders the animals were compelled to uprear and struggle blindly through the tangled mass of vegetation. Once the saddle horse fell heavily and the man removed the pack to get the animal on its feet. After it started on its way again the man thrust his head out from among the leaves and peered up at the hillside.

"The measly skunk!" he said, and disappeared.

There was a ripping and tearing of vines and boughs. The trees surged back and forth, marking the passage of the animals through the midst of them. There was a clashing of steel-shod hoofs on stone, and now and again a sharp cry of command. Then the voice of the man was raised in song.

> "Tu'n around an' tu'n yo' face
> Untoe them sweet hills of grace
>   (D' pow'rs of sin you' am scornin'!).'
> Look about an' look aroun'
> Fling yo' sin-pack on d' groun'
>   (Yo' will meet wid d' Lord in d' mornin'!)."

The song grew faint and fainter, and through the silence crept back the spirit of the place. The stream once more drowsed and whispered; the hum of the mountain bees rose sleepily. Down through the perfume-weighted air fluttered the snowy fluffs of the cottonwoods. The butterflies drifted in and out among the trees, and over all blazed the quiet sunshine. Only remained the hoof marks in the meadow and the torn hillside to mark the boisterous trail of the life that had broken the peace of the place and passed on.

STEWART EDWARD WHITE

The Honk-Honk Breed

It has been said that Stewart Edward White was the first author to write of the West on its own terms from its own point of view, and that his body of work most fully represents all phases of pioneer America. His first novel, The Westerners, *appeared in 1901; more than fifty books followed, utilizing such settings as the plains, mountains, deserts and forests; such themes as Indian fighting, cattle ranching, logging, early exploration, gold rushes, land booms, and the exploits of mountain men, trappers, outlaws and lawmen. His most memorable work, perhaps, is* Arizona Nights *(1907), a cornerstone collection of Western short stories. And "The Honk-Honk Breed" is considered by many to be the finest tale in that book.*

IT WAS SUNDAY at the ranch. For a wonder the weather had been favourable; the windmills were all working, the bogs had dried up, the beef had lasted over, the remuda had not strayed—in short, there was nothing to do. Sang had given us a baked bread-pudding with raisins in it. We filled it in—a wash basin full of it—on top of a few incidental pounds of *chile con,* baked beans, soda biscuits, "air tights," and other delicacies. Then we adjourned with our pipes to the shady side of the blacksmith's shop where we could watch the ravens on top the adobe wall of the corral. Somebody told a story about ravens. They led to road-runners. This suggested rattlesnakes. They started Windy Bill.

"Speakin' of snakes," said Windy, "I mind when they catched the great-granddaddy of all the bullsnakes up at Lead in the Black Hills. I was only a kid then. This wasn't no such tur'ble long a snake, but he was more'n a foot thick. Looked just like a sahuaro stalk. Man name of Terwilliger Smith catched it. He named this yere bullsnake Clarence, and got it so plumb gentle it followed him everywhere. One day old P. T. Barnum come along and wanted to buy this Clarence snake—offered Terwilliger a thousand cold—but Smith wouldn't part with the snake nohow. So finally they fixed up a deal so Smith could go along with the show. They shoved Clarence in a box in the baggage car, but after a while Mr. Snake gets so lonesome he gnaws out and starts to crawl back to find his master. Just as he is half-way between the baggage car and the smoker, the couplin' give way—right on that heavy grade between Custer and Rocky Point. Well, sir, Clarence wound his head 'round one brake wheel and his tail around the other, and held that train together to the bottom of the grade. But it stretched him twenty-eight feet and they had to advertise him as a boa-constrictor."

Windy Bill's history of the faithful bullsnake aroused to reminiscence the grizzled stranger, who thereupon held forth as follows:

Well, I've see things and I've heard things, some of them ornery and some you'd love to believe, they was that gorgeous and improbable. Nat'-ral history was always my hobby and sportin' events my special pleasure—and this yarn of Windy's reminds me of the only chanst I ever had to ring in business and pleasure and hobby all in one grand merry-go-around of joy. It came about like this:

One day, a few years back, I was sittin' on the beach at Santa Barbara watchin' the sky stay up, and wonderin' what to do with my year's wages, when a little squinch-eye round-face with big bow spectacles came and plumped down beside me.

"Did you ever stop to think," says he, shovin' back his hat, "that if the horsepower delivered by them waves on this beach in one single hour could be concentrated behind washin' machines, it would be enough to wash all the shirts for a city of four hundred and fifty-one thousand one hundred and thirty-six people?"

"Can't say I ever did," says I, squintin' at him sideways.

"Fact," says he, "and did it ever occur to you that if all the food a man eats in the course of a natural life could be gathered together at one time, it would fill a wagon-train twelve miles long?"

"You make me hungry," says I.

"And ain't it interestin' to reflect," he goes on, "that if all the finger-nail parin's of the human race for one year was to be collected and subjected to hydraulic pressure it would equal in size the pyramid of Cheops?"

"Look yere," says I, sittin' up, "did you ever pause to excogitate that if all the hot air you is dispensin' was to be collected together it would fill a balloon big enough to waft you and me over that Bullyvard of Palms to yonder gin mill on the corner?"

He didn't say nothin' to that—just yanked me to my feet, faced me towards the gin mill above mentioned, and exerted considerable pressure on my arm in urgin' me forward.

"You ain't so much of a dreamer, after all," thinks I. "In important matters you are plumb decisive."

We sat down at little tables, and my friend ordered a beer and a chicken sandwich.

"Chickens," says he, gazin' at the sandwich, "is a dollar apiece in this country, and plumb scarce. Did you ever pause to ponder over the returns chickens would give on a small investment? Say you start with ten hens. Each hatches out thirteen aigs, of which allow a loss of say six for childish accidents. At the end of the year you has eighty chickens. At the end of two years that flock has increased to six hundred and twenty. At the end of the third year—"

He had the medicine tongue! Ten days later him and me was occupyin' of an old ranch fifty miles from anywhere. When they run stage-coaches this joint used to be a road-house. The outlook was on about a thousand little brown foothills. A road two miles four rods two foot eleven inches in sight run by in front of us. It come over one foothill and disappeared over another. I know just how long it was, for later in the game I measured it.

Out back was about a hundred little wire chicken corrals filled with chickens. We had two kinds. That was the doin's of Tuscarora. My pardner called himself Tuscarora Maxillary. I asked him once if that was his real name.

"It's the realest little old name you ever heard tell of," says he. "I know, for I made it myself—liked the sound of her. Parents ain't got no rights to name their children. Parents don't have to be called them names."

Well, these chickens, as I said, was of two kinds. The first was these low-set, heavy-weight propositions with feathers on their laigs, and not much laigs at that, called Cochin Chinys. The other was a tall ridiculous outfit made up entire of bulgin' breast and gangle laigs. They stood about two foot and a half tall, and when they went to peck the ground their tail feathers stuck straight up to the sky. Tusky called 'em Japanese Games.

"Which the chief advantage of them chickens is," says he, "that in weight about ninety per cent of 'em is breast meat. Now my idee is, that if we can cross 'em with these Cochin Chiny fowls we'll have a low-hung, heavy-weight chicken runnin' strong on breast meat. These Jap Games is too small, but if we can bring 'em up in size and shorten their laigs, we'll shore have a winner."

That looked good to me, so we started in on that idee. The theery was bully, but she didn't work out. The first broods we hatched growed up with big husky Cochin Chiny bodies and little short necks, perched up on laigs three foot long. Them chickens couldn't reach ground nohow. We had to build a table for 'em to eat off, and when they went out rustlin' for themselves they had to confine themselves to sidehills or flyin' insects. Their breasts was all right, though—"And think of them drumsticks for the boardin' house trade!" says Tusky.

So far things wasn't so bad. We had a good grubstake. Tusky and me used to feed them chickens twict a day, and then used to set around watchin' the playful critters chase grasshoppers up an' down the wire corrals, while Tusky figgered out what'd happen if somebody was dumfool enough to gather up somethin' and fix it in baskets or wagons or such. That was where we showed our ignorance of chickens.

One day in the spring I hitched up, rustled a dozen of the youngsters into coops, and druv over to the railroad to make our first sale. I couldn't fold them chickens up into them coops at first, but then I stuck the coops up on aidge and they worked all right, though I will admit they was a comical sight. At the railroad one of them towerist trains had just slowed down to a halt as I come up, and the towerists was paradin' up and down allowin' they was particular enjoyin' of the warm Californy sunshine. One old terrapin, with grey chin whiskers, projected over, with his wife, and took a peek through the slats of my coop. He straightened up like someone had touched him off with a red-hot poker.

"Stranger," said he, in a scared kind of whisper, "what's them?"

"Them's chickens," says I.

He took another long look.

"Marthy," says he to the old woman, "this will be about all! We come out from Ioway to see the Wonders of Californy, but I can't go nothin' stronger than this. If these is chickens, I don't want to see no Big Trees."

Well, I sold them chickens all right for a dollar and two bits, which was better than I expected, and got an order for more. About ten days later I got a letter from the commission house.

"We are returnin' a sample of your Arts and Crafts chickens with the lovin' marks of the teeth still onto him," says they. "Don't send any more till they stops pursuin' of the nimble grasshopper. Dentist bill will foller."

With the letter came the remains of one of the chickens. Tusky and I, very indignant, cooked her for supper. She was tough, all right. We thought she might do better biled, so we put her in the pot over night. Nary bit. Well, then we got interested. Tusky kep' the fire goin' and I rustled greasewood. We cooked her three days and three nights. At the end of that time she was sort of pale and frazzled, but still givin' points to three-year-old jerky on cohesion and other uncompromisin' forces of Nature. We buried her then, and went out back to recuperate.

There we could gaze on the smilin' landscape, dotted by about four hundred long-laigged chickens swoopin' here and there after grasshoppers.

"We got to stop that," says I.

"We can't," murmured Tusky, inspired. "We can't. It's born in 'em; it's a primal instinct, like the love of a mother for her young, and it can't be eradicated! Them chickens is constructed by a divine province for the express purpose of chasin' grasshoppers, jest as the beaver is made for buildin' dams, and the cowpuncher is made for whisky and faro-games. We can't keep 'em from it. If we was to shut 'em in a dark cellar, they'd flop after imaginary grasshoppers in their dreams, and die emaciated in the midst of plenty. Jimmy, we're up agin the Cosmos, the oversoul—" Oh, he had the medicine tongue, Tusky had, and risin' on the wings of eloquence that way, he had me faded in ten minutes. In fifteen I was wedded solid to the notion that the bottom had dropped out of the chicken business. I think now that if we'd shut them hens up, we might have—still, I don't know; they was a good deal in what Tusky said.

"Tuscarora Maxillary," says I, "did you ever stop to entertain that beautiful thought that if all the dumfoolishness possessed now by the human race could be gathered together, and lined up alongside of us, the first feller to come along would say to it 'Why, hello, Solomon!'"

We quit the notion of chickens for profit right then and there, but we couldn't quit the place. We hadn't much money, for one thing, and then we kind of liked loafin' around and raisin' a little garden truck, and—oh, well, I might as well say so, we had a notion about placers in the dry wash back of the house—you know how it is. So we stayed on, and kept a-raisin' these longlaigs for the fun of it. I used to like to watch 'em projectin' around, and I fed 'em twic't a day about as usual.

So Tusky and I lived alone there together, happy as ducks in Arizona. About onc't in a month somebody'd pike along the road. She wasn't much of a road, generally more chuck-holes than bumps, though sometimes it was the other way around. Unless it happened to be a man horseback or maybe a freighter without the fear of God in his soul, we didn't have no words with them; they was too busy cussin' the highways and generally too mad for social discourses.

One day early in the year, when the 'dobe mud made ruts to add to the bumps, one of these automobeels went past. It was the first Tusky and

me had seen in them parts, so we run out to view her. Owin' to the high
spots on the road, she looked like one of these movin' picters, as to blur
and wobble; sounded like a cyclone mingled with cuss-words, and smelt
like hell on housecleanin' day.

"Which them folks don't seem to be enjoyin' of the scenery," says I
to Tusky. "Do you reckon that there blue trail is smoke from the machine
or remarks from the inhabitants thereof?"

Tusky raised his head and sniffed long and inquirin'.

"It's langwidge," says he. "Did you ever stop to think that all the words
in the dictionary hitched end to end would reach—"

But at that minute I catched sight of somethin' brass lyin' in the road.
It proved to be a curled-up sort of horn with a rubber bulb on the end.
I squoze the bulb and jumped twenty foot over the remark she made.

"Jarred off the machine," says Tusky.

"Oh, did it?" says I, my nerves still wrong. "I thought maybe it had
growed up from the soil like a toadstool."

About this time we abolished the wire chicken corrals, because we
needed some of the wire. Them long-laigs thereupon scattered all over the
flat searchin' out their prey. When feed time come I had to screech my
lungs out gettin' of 'em im, and then sometimes they didn't all hear. It
was plumb discouragin', and I mighty nigh made up my mind to quit 'em,
but they had come to be sort of pets, and I hated to turn 'em down. It
used to tickle Tusky almost to death to see me out there hollerin' away
like an old bull-frog. He used to come out reg'lar, with his pipe lit, just
to enjoy me. Finally I got mad and opened up on him.

"Oh," he explains, "it just plumb amuses me to see the dumfool at his
childish work. Why don't you teach 'em to come to that brass horn, and
save your voice?"

"Tusky," says I, with feelin', "sometimes you do seem to get a glimmer
of real sense."

Well, first off them chickens used to throw back-sommersets over that
horn. You have no idea how slow chickens is to learn things. I could tell
you things about chickens—say, this yere bluff about roosters bein' gallant
is all wrong. I've watched 'em. When one finds a nice feed he gobbles it
so fast that the pieces foller down his throat like yearlin's through a hole
in the fence. It's only when he scratches up a measly one-grain quick-
lunch that he calls up the hens and stands noble and self-sacrificin' to one
side. That ain't the point, which is, that after two months I had them
long-laigs so they'd drop everythin' and come kitin' at the *honk-honk* of

that horn. It was a purty sight to see 'em, sailin' in from all directions twenty foot at a stride. I was proud of em, and named 'em the Honk-honk Breed. We didn't have no others, for by now the coyotes and bob-cats had nailed the straight-breds. There wasn't no wild cat or coyote could catch one of my Honkhonks, no, sir!

We made a little on our placer—just enough to keep interested. Then the supervisors decided to fix our road, and what's more, they done it! That's the only part in this yarn that's hard to believe, but, boys, you'll have to take it on faith. They ploughed her, and crowned her, and scraped her and rolled her, and when they moved on we had the fanciest highway in the State of Californy.

That noon—the day they called her a job—Tusky and I sat smokin' our pipes as per usual, when way over the foothills we seen a cloud of dust and faint to our ears was bore a whizzin' sound. The chickens was gathered under the cottonwood for the heat of the day, but they didn't pay no attention. Then faint, but clear, we heard another of them brass horns:

"Honk! Honk!" it says, and every one of them chickens woke up, and stood at attention.

"Honk! Honk!" It hollered clearer and nearer. Then over the hill come an automobeel, blowin' vigorous at every jump.

"My God!" I yells to Tusky, kickin' over my chair, as I springs to my feet. "Stop 'em! Stop 'em!"

But it was too late. Out the gate sprinted them poor devoted chickens, and up the road they trailed in vain pursuit. The last we seen of 'em was a minglin' of dust and dim figgers goin' thirty mile an hour after a disappearin' automobeel.

That was all we seen for the moment. About three o'clock the first straggler came limpin' in, his wings hanging', his mouth open, his eyes glazed with the heat. By sundown fourteen had returned. All the rest had disappeared utter; we never seen 'em again. I reckon they just naturally run themselves into a sunstroke and died on the road.

It takes a long time to learn a chicken thing, but a heap longer to unlearn him. After that two or three of these yere automobeeles went by every day, all a-blowin' of their horns, all kickin' up a hell of a dust. And every time them fourteen Honk-honks of mine took along after 'em, just as I'd taught 'em to do, layin' to get to their corn when they caught up. No more of 'em died, but that fourteen did get into elegant trainin'. After a while they got plumb to enjoyin' it. When you come right down to it, a chicken don't have many amusements and relaxations in this life. Searchin' for worms, chasin' grasshoppers, and wallerin' in the dust is about the limits of joys for chickens.

It was sure a fine sight to see 'em after they got well into the game. About nine o'clock every mornin' they would saunter down to the rise of the road where they would wait patient until a machine came along. Then it would warm your heart to see the enthusiasm of them. With exultant cackles of joy they'd trail in, reachin' out like quarter-horses, their wings half spread out, their eyes beamin' with delight. At the lower turn they'd quit. Then, after talkin' it over excited-like for a few minutes, they'd calm down and wait for another.

After a few months of this sort of trainin' they got purty good at it. I had one two-year-old rooster that made fifty-four mile an hour behind one of these sixty-horsepower Panhandles. When cars didn't come along often enough, they'd all turn out and chase jack-rabbits. They wasn't much fun at that. After a short, brief sprint the rabbit would crouch down plumb terrified, while the Honk-honks pulled off triumphal dances around his shrinkin' form.

Our ranch got to be purty well known them days among automobeel-ists. The strength of their cars was horse-power, of course, but the speed of them they got to ratin' by chicken-power. Some of them used to come way up from Los Angeles just to try out a new car along our road with the Honk-honks for pace-makers. We charged them a little somethin', and then, too, we opened up the road-house and the bar, so we did purty well. It wasn't necessary to work any longer at the bogus placer. Evenin's we sat around outside and swapped yarns, and I bragged on my chickens. The chickens would gather round close to listen. They liked to hear their praises sung, all right. You bet they *sabe!* The only reason a chicken, or any other critter, isn't intelligent is because he hasn't no chance to expand.

Why, we used to run races with 'em. Some of us would hold two or more chickens back of a chalk line, and the starter'd blow the horn from a hundred yards to a mile away, dependin' on whether it was a sprint or for distance. We had pools on the results, gave odds, made books, and kept records. After the thing got knowed we made money hand over fist.

The stranger broke off abruptly and began to roll a cigarette.

"What did you quit it for, then?" ventured Charley, out of the hushed silence.

"Pride," replied the stranger solemnly. "Haughtiness of spirit."

"How so?" urged Charley, after a pause.

"Them chickens," continued the stranger, after a moment, "stood around listenin' to me a-braggin' of what superior fowls they was until they got all puffed up. They wouldn't have nothin' whatever to do with the ordinary chickens we brought in for eatin' purposes, but stood around lookin' bored when there wasn't no sport doin'. They got to be just like that Four Hundred you read about in the papers. It was one continual round of grasshopper balls, race meets, and afternoon hen-parties. They got idle and haughty, just like folks. Then come race suicide. They got to feelin' so aristocratic the hens wouldn't have no eggs."

Nobody dared say a word.

"Windy Bill's snake—" began the narrator genially.

"Stranger," broke in Windy Bill, with great emphasis, "as to that snake, I want you to understand this: yereafter in my estimation that snake is nothin' but an ornery angle-worm!"

The Trouble Man

Every aficionado of Western fiction has his or her opinion as to the finest story ever written about the Old West. It is safe to say, though, that not a few of them would cast their votes for Eugene Manlove Rhodes's brilliant novella Pasó Por Aqui, *first published in 1927. Rhodes (1869–1934) has been called "the connoisseur's Western writer," and indeed his fiction is not only superb entertainment but of high literary merit as well. If* Pasó Por Aqui *is the standout among his longer works,* The Proud Sheriff, Stepsons of Light, *and* Copper Streak Trail *are not far behind; and of his shorter works, "The Trouble Man" certainly ranks as one of the best.*

BILLY BEEBE did not understand. There was no disguising the unpalatable fact: Rainbow treated him kindly. It galled him. Ballinger, his junior in Rainbow, was theme for ridicule and biting jest, target for contumely and abuse; while his own best efforts were met with grave, unfailing courtesy.

Yet the boys liked him; Billy was sure of that. And so far as the actual work was concerned, he was at least as good a roper and brand reader as Ballinger, quicker in action, a much better rider.

In irrelevant and extraneous matters—brains, principle, training, acquirements—Billy was conscious of unchallenged advantage. He was from Ohio, eligible to the Presidency, of family, rich, a college man; yet he had abandoned laudable moss-gathering, to become a rolling, bounding, riotous stone. He could not help feeling that it was rather noble of him. And then to be indulgently sheltered as an honored guest, how beloved soever! It hurt.

Not for himself alone was Billy grieved. Men paired on Rainbow. "One stick makes a poor fire"—so their word went. Billy sat at the feet of John Wesley Pringle—wrinkled, wind-brown Gamaliel. Ballinger was the disciple of Jeff Bransford, gay, willful, questionable man. Billy did not like him. His light banter, lapsing unexpectedly from Broad Doric to irreproachable New English, carried in solution audacious, glancing disrespect of convention, established institutions, authorities, axioms, "accepted theories of irregular verbs"—too elusive for disproof, too intolerably subversive to be ignored. That Ballinger, his shadow, was accepted man of action, while Billy was still an outsider, was, in some sense, a reflection on Pringle. Vicarious jealousy was added to the pangs of wounded self-love.

Billy was having ample time for reflection now, riding with Pringle up the Long Range to the Block roundup. Through the slow, dreamy days they threaded the mazed ridges and cañons falling eastward to the Pecos from Guadalupe, Sacramento and White Mountain. They drove their string of thirteen horses each; rough circlers, wise cutting horses, sedate night horses and patient old Steamboat, who, in the performance of pack duty, dropped his proper designation to be injuriously known as "the Wagon."

Their way lay through the heart of the Lincoln County War country —on winding trails, by glade and pine-clad mesa; by clear streams, bell-tinkling, beginning, with youth's eager haste, their journey to the far-off sea; by Seven Rivers, Bluewater, the Feliz, Penasco and Silver Spring.

Leisurely they rode, with shady halt at midday—leisurely, for an empire was to be worked. It would be months before they crossed the divide at Nogal, "threw in" with Bransford and Ballinger, now representing Rainbow with the Bar W, and drove home together down the west side.

While Billy pondered his problem Pringle sang or whistled tirelessly— old tunes of amazing variety, ranging from Nancy Lee and Auld Robin Gray to La Paloma Azul or the Nogal Waltz. But ever, by ranch house or brook or pass, he paused to tell of deeds there befallen in the years of old war, deeds violent and bloody, yet half redeemed by hardihood and unflinching courage.

Pringle's voice was low and unemphatic; his eyes were ever on the long horizon. Trojan nor Tyrian he favored, but as he told the Homeric tale of Buckshot Roberts, while they splashed through the broken waters of Ruidoso and held their winding way through the cutoff of Cedar Creek, Billy began dimly to understand.

Between him and Rainbow the difference was in kind, not in degree. The shadow of old names lay heavy on the land; these resolute ghosts yet shaped the acts of men. For Rainbow the Roman *virtus* was still the one virtue. Whenever these old names had been spoken, Billy remembered, men had listened. Horseshoers had listened at their shoeing; card-players had listened while the game went on; by campfires other speakers had ceased their talk to listen without comment. Not ill-doers, these listeners, but quiet men, kindly, generous; yet the tales to which they gave this tribute were too often of ill deeds. As if they asked not "Was this well done?" but rather "Was this done indeed—so that no man could have done more?" Were the deed good or evil, so it were done utterly it commanded admiration—therefore imitation.

Something of all this he got into words. Pringle nodded gravely. "You've got it sized up, my son," he said. "Rainbow ain't strictly up to date and still holds to them elder ethics, like Norval on the Grampian Hills, William Dhu Tell, and the rest of them neck-or-nothing boys. This Mr. Rolando, that Eusebio sings about, give our sentiment to a T-Y-ty. He was some scrappy and always blowin' his own horn, but, by jings, he delivered the goods as per invoice and could take a major league lickin' with no whimperin'. This Rolando he don't hold forth about gate money or individual percentages. 'Get results for your team,' he says. 'Don't flinch, don't foul, hit the line hard, here goes nothing!'

"That's a purty fair code. And it's all the one we got. Pioneerin' is troublesome—pioneer is all the same word as pawn, and you thrown away a pawn to gain a point. When we drive in a wild bunch, when we top off the boundin' bronco, it may look easy, but it's always a close thing. Even when we win we nearly lose; when we lose we nearly win. And that forms the stay-with-it-Bill-you're-doin'-well habit. See?

"So, we mostly size a fellow up by his abilities as a trouble man. Any kind of trouble—not necessarily the fightin' kind. If he goes the route, if he sets no limit, if he's enlisted for the war—why, you naturally depend on him.

"Now, take you and Jeff. Most ways you've got the edge on him. But you hold by rules and formulas and laws. There's things you must do or mustn't do—because somebody told you so. You go into a project with a mental reservation not to do anything indecorous or improper; also, to stop when you've taken a decent lickin'. But Jeff don't aim to stop while he can wiggle; and he makes up new rules as he goes along, to fit the situation. Naturally, when you get in a tight place you waste time rememberin' what the authorities prescribe as the neat thing. Now, Jeff consults only his own self, and he's mostly unanimous. Mebbe so you both do the same thing, mebbe not. But Jeff does it first. You're a good boy, Billy, but there's only one way to find out if you're a square peg or a round one."

"How's that?" demanded Billy, laughing, but half vexed.

"Get in the hole," said Pringle.

"Aw, stay all night! What's the matter with you fellows? I haven't seen a soul for a week. Everybody's gone to the round-up."

Wes' shook his head: "Can't do it, Jimmy. Got to go out to good grass. You're all eat out here."

"I'll side you," said Jimmy decisively. "I got a lot of stored-up talk I've got to get out of my system. I know a bully place to make camp. Box cañon to hobble your horses in, good grass, and a little tank of water in the rocks for cookin'. Bring along your little old Wagon, and I'll tie on a hunk of venison to feed your faces with. Get there by dark."

"How come you didn't go to the work your black self?" asked Wes', as Beebe tossed his rope on the Wagon and let him up.

Jimmy's twinkling eyes lit up his beardless face. "They left me here to play shinny-on-your-own-side," he explained.

"Shinny?" echoed Billy.

"With the Three Rivers sheep," said Jimmy. "I'm to keep them from crossing the mountain."

"Oh, I see. You've got an agreement that the east side is for cattle and the west side for sheep."

Jimmy's face puckered. "Agreement? H'm, yes, least ways, I'm agreed. I didn't ask them, but they've got the general idea. When I ketch 'em over here I drive them back. As I don't ever follow 'em beyond the summit they ought to savvy my the'ries by this time."

Pringle opened the gate. "Let's mosey along—they've got enough water. Which way, kid?"

"Left-hand trail," said Jimmy, falling in behind.

"But why don't you come to an understanding with them and fix on a dividing line?" insisted Beebe.

Jimmy lolled sidewise in his saddle, cocking an impish eye at his inquisitor. "Reckon ye don't have no sheep down Rainbow way? Thought not. Right there's the point exactly. They have a dividing line. They carry it with 'em wherever they go. For the cattle won't graze where sheep have been. Sheep pertects their own range, but we've got to look after ours or they'd drive us out. But the understanding's all right, all right. They don't speak no English, and I don't know no *paisano* talk, but I've fixed up a signal code they savvy as well's if they was all college aluminums."

"Oh, yes—sign talk," said Billy. "I've heard of that." Wes' turned his head aside.

"We-ell, not exactly. Sound talk'd be nearer. One shot means 'Git! two means 'Hurry up!' and three—"

"But you've no right to do that," protested Billy, warmly. "They've got just as much right here as your cattle, haven't they?"

"Surest thing they have—if they can make it stick," agreed Jimmy cordially. "And we've got just as much right to keep 'em off if we can. There ain't really no right to it. It's Uncle Sam's land we both graze on, and Unkie is some busy with conversation on natural resources, and keepin' republics up in South America and down in Asia, and selectin' texts for coins and infernal revenue stamps, and upbuildin' Pittsburgh, and keepin' up the price of wool and fightin' all the time to keep the laws from bein' better'n the Constitution, like a Bawston puncher trimmin' a growin' colt's foot down to fit last year's shoes. Shucks! *He* ain't got no time to look after us. We just got to do our own regulatin' or git out."

"How would you like it yourself?" demanded Billy.

Jimmy's eyes flashed. "If my brain was to leak out and I subsequent took to sheep herdin', I'd like to see any dern puncher drive me out," he declared belligerently.

"Then you can't complain if—"

"He don't," interrupted Pringle. "None of us complain—nary a murmur. If the sheep men want to go they go, an' a little shootin' up the contagious vicinity don't hurt 'em none. It's all over oncet the noise stops. Besides, I think they mostly sorter enjoy it. Sheep herdin' is mighty dull business, and a little excitement is mighty welcome. It gives 'em something to look forward to. But if they feel hostile they always get the first shot for keeps. That's a mighty big percentage in their favor, and the reports on file with the War Department shows that they generally get the best of it. Don't you worry none, my son. This ain't no new thing. It's been goin' on ever since Abraham's outfit and the LOT boys got to scrappin' on the Jordan range, and then some before that. After Abraham took to the hill country, I remember, somebody jumped one of his wells and two of Isaac's. It's been like that, in the shortgrass countries ever since. Human nature's not changed much. By Jings! There they be now!"

Through the twilight the winding trail climbed the side of a long ridge. To their left was a deep, impassable cañon; beyond that a parallel ridge; and from beyond that ridge came the throbbing, drumming clamor of a sheep herd.

"The son of a gun!" said Jimmy. "He means to camp in our box cañon. I'll show him!" He spurred by the grazing horses and clattered on in the cad, striking fire from the stony trail.

On the shoulder of the further ridge heaved a gray fog, spreading, rolling slowly down the hillside. The bleating, the sound of myriad trampling feet, the multiplication of bewildering echoes, swelled to a steady, unchanging, ubiquitous tumult. A dog suddenly topped the ridge; another; then a Mexican herder bearing a long rifle. With one glance at Jimmy beyond the blackshadowed gulf he began turning the herd back, shouting to the dogs. They ran in obedient haste to aid, sending the stragglers scurrying after the main bunch.

Jimmy reined up, black and gigantic against the skyline. He drew his gun. Once, twice, thrice, he shot. The fire streamed out against the growing dark. The bullets, striking the rocks, whined spitefully. The echoes took up the sound and sent it crashing to and fro. The sheep rushed huddling together, panic-stricken. Herder and dogs urged them on. The herder threw up a hand and shouted.

"That boy's shootin' might close to that *paisano*," muttered Pringle. "He orter quit now. Reckon he's showin' off a leetle." He raised his voice in warning. "Hi! You Jimmy!" he called. "He's agoin'! Let him be!"

"*Vamos! Hi-i!*" shrilled Jimmy gaily. He fired again. The Mexican clapped hand to his leg with an angry scream. With the one movement he sank to his knees, his long rifle fell to a level, cuddled to his shoulder, spitting fire. Jimmy's hand flew up. His gun dropped; he clutched at the saddle-horn, missed it, fell heavily to the ground. The Mexican dropped out of sight behind the ridge. It had been but a scant minute since he first appeared. The dogs followed with the remaining sheep. The ridge was bare. The dark fell fast.

Jimmy lay on his face. Pringle turned him over and opened his shirt. He was quite dead.

From Malagra to Willow Spring, the next available water, is the longest jump on the Bar W range. Working the "Long Lane" fenced by Malpais and White Mountain is easy enough. But after cutting out and branding there was the long wait for the slow day herd, the tedious holding to water from insufficient troughs. It was late when the day's "cut" was thrown in with the herd, sunset when the bobtail had caught their night horses and relieved the weary day herders.

The bobtail moves the herd to the bed ground—some distance from camp, to avoid mutual annoyance and alarm—and holds it while night horses are caught and supper eaten. A thankless job, missing the nightly joking and banter over the day's work. Then the first guard comes on and the bobtail goes, famished, to supper. It breakfasts by starlight, relieves the last guard, and holds cattle while breakfast is eaten, beds rolled and horses caught, turning them over to the day herders at sunup.

Bransford and Ballinger were two of the five bobtailers, hungry, tired, dusty and cross. With persuasive, soothing song they trotted around the restless cattle, with hasty, envious glances for the merry groups around the chuck wagon. The horse herd was coming in; four of the boys were butchering a yearling; beds were being dragged out and unrolled. Shouts of laughter arose; they were baiting the victim of some mishap by making public an exaggerated version of his discomfiture.

Turning his back on the camp, Jeff Bransford became aware of a man riding a big white horse down the old military road from Nogal way. The horse was trotting, but wearily; passing the herd he whinnied greeting, again wearily.

The cattle were slow to settle down. Jeff made several circlings before he had time for another campward glance. The horse herd was grazing off, and the boys were saddling and staking their night horses; but the stranger's horse, still saddled, was tied to a soapweed.

Jeff sniffed. "Oh, Solomon was sapient and Solomon was wise!" he crooned, keeping time with old Summersault's steady fox trot. "And Solomon was marvelously wide between the eyes!" He sniffed again, his nose wrinkled, one eyebrow arched, one corner of his mouth pulled down; he twisted his mustache and looked sharply down his nose for consultation, pursing his lips. "H'm! That's funny!" he said aloud. "That horse is some tired. Why don't he turn him loose? Bransford, you old fool, sit up and take notice! 'Eternal vigilance is the price of liberty.'"

He had been a tired and a hungry man. He put his weariness by as a garment, keyed up the slackened strings, and rode on with every faculty on the alert. It is to be feared that Jeff's conscience was not altogether void of offense toward his fellows.

A yearling pushed tentatively from the herd. Jeff let her go, fell in after her and circled her back to the bunch behind Clay Cooper. Not by chance. Clay was from beyond the divide.

"Know the new man, Clay?" Jeff asked casually, as he fell back to preserve the proper interval.

Clay turned his head. "Sure. Clem Littlefield, Bonita man."

When the first guard came at last Jeff was on the farther side and so the last to go in. A dim horseman overtook him and waved a sweeping arm in dismissal.

"We've got 'em! Light a rag, you hungry man!"

Jeff turned back slowly, so meeting all the relieving guard and noting that Squatty Robinson, of the V V, was not of them, Ollie Jackson taking his place.

He rode thoughtfully into camp. Staking his horse in the starlight he observed a significant fact. Squatty had not staked his regular night horse, but Alizan, his favorite. He made a swift investigation and found that not a man from the east side had caught his usual night horse. Clay Cooper's horse was not staked, but tied short to a mesquite, with the bridle still on.

Pete Johnson, the foreman, was just leaving the fire for bed. Beyond the fire the east-side men were gathered, speaking in subdued voices. Ballinger, with loaded plate, sat down near them. The talking ceased. It started again at once. This time their voices rose clear and distinct in customary bandiage.

"Why, this is face up," thought Jeff. "Trouble. Trouble from beyond the divide. They're going to hike shortly. They've told Pete that much, anyhow. Serious trouble—for they've kept it from the rest of them. Is it to my address? Likely. Old Wes' and Beebe are over there somewhere. If I had three guesses the first two'd be that them Rainbow chasers was in a tight."

He stumbled into the firelight, carrying his bridle, which he dropped by the wagon wheel. "This day's sure flown by like a week," he grumbled, fumbling around for cup and plate. "My stomach was just askin' was my throat cut."

As he bent over to spear a steak the tail of his eye took in the group beyond and intercepted a warning glance from Squatty to the stranger. There was an almost imperceptible thrusting motion of Squatty's chin and lips; a motion which included Jeff and the unconscious Ballinger. It was enough. Surmise, suspicion flamed to certainty. "My third guess," reflected Jeff sagely, "is just like the other two. Mr. John Wesley Pringle has been doing a running high jump or some such stunt, and has plumb neglected to come down."

He seated himself cross-legged and fell upon his supper vigorously, bandying quips and quirks with the bobtail as they ate. At last he jumped up, dropped his dishes clattering in the dishpan, and drew a long breath.

"I don't feel a bit hungry," he announced plaintively. "Gee! I'm glad I don't have to stand guard. I do hate to work between meals." He shouldered his roll of bedding. "Good-bye, old world—I'm going home!" he said, and melted into the darkness. Leo following, they unrolled their bed. But as Leo began pulling off his boots Jeff stopped him.

"Close that aperture in your face and keep it that way," he admonished guardedly. "You and me has got to do a ghost dance. Project around and help me find them Three Rivers men."

The Three Rivers men, Crosby and Os Hyde, were sound asleep. Awakened, they were disposed to peevish remonstrance.

"Keep quiet!" said Jeff. "Al, you slip on your boots and go tell Pete you and Os is goin' to Carrizo and that you'll be back in time to stand your guard. Tell him out loud. Then you come back here and you and Os crawl into our bed. I'll show him where it is while you're gone. You use our night horses. Me and Leo want to take yours."

"If there's anything else don't stand on ceremony," said Crosby. "Don't you want my tooth-brush?"

"You hurry up," responded Jeff. "D'ye think I'm doin' this for fun? We're It. We got to prove an alibi."

"Oh!" said Al.

A few minutes later, the Three Rivers men disappeared under the tarp of the Rainbow bed, while the Rainbow men, on Three Rivers horses, rode silently out of camp, avoiding the firelit circle.

Once over the ridge, well out of sight and hearing from camp, Jeff turned up the draw to the right and circled back toward the Nogal road on a long trot.

"Beautiful night," observed Leo after an interval. "I just love to ride. How far is it to the asylum?"

"Leo," said Jeff, "you're a good boy—a mighty good boy. But I don't believe you'd notice it if the sun didn't go down till after dark." He explained the situation. "Now, I'm going to leave you to hold the horses just this side of the Nogal road, while I go on afoot and eavesdrop. Them fellows'll be makin' big medicine when they come along here. I'll lay down by the road and get a line on their play. Don't you let them horses nicker."

Leo waited an interminable time before he heard the eastside men coming from camp. They passed by, talking, as Jeff had prophesied. After another small eternity Jeff joined him.

"I didn't get all the details," he reported. "But it seems that the Parsons City People has got it framed up to hang a sheepman some. Wes' is dead set against it—I didn't make out why. So there's a deadlock and we've got the casting vote. Call up your reserves, old man. We're due to ride around Nogal and beat that bunch to the divide."

It was midnight by the clock in the sky when they stood on Nogal divide. The air was chill. Clouds gathered blackly around Capitan, Nogal

Peak and White Mountain. There was steady, low muttering of thunder; the far lightnings flashed pale and green and rose.

"Hustle along to Lincoln, Leo," commanded Jeff, "and tell the sheriff they state, positive, that the hangin' takes place prompt after breakfast. Tell him to bring a big posse—and a couple of battleships if he's got 'em handy. Meantime, I'll go over and try what the gentle art of persuasion can do. So long! If I don't come back the mule's yours."

He turned up the right-hand road.

"Well?" said Pringle.

"Light up!" said Uncle Pete. "Nobody's goin' to shoot at ye from the dark. We don't do business that way. When we come we'll come in daylight, down the big middle of the road. Light up. I ain't got no gun. I come over for one last try to make you see reason. I knowed thar weren't use talkin' to you when you was fightin' mad. That's why I got the boys to put it off till mawnin'. And I wanted to send to Angus and Salado and the Bar W for Jimmy's friends. He ain't got no kinnery here. They've come. They all see it the same way. Chavez killed Jimmy, and they're goin' to hang him. And, since they've come, there's too many of us for you to fight."

Wes' lit the candle. "Set down. Talk all you want, but talk low and don't wake Billy," he said as the flame flared up.

That he did not want Billy waked up, that there was not even a passing glance to verify Uncle Pete's statement as to being unarmed, was, considering Uncle Pete's errand and his own position, a complete and voluminous commentary on the men and ethics of that time and place.

Pete Burleson carefully arranged his frame on a bench, and glanced around.

On his cot Billy tossed and moaned. His fevered sleep was tortured by a phantasmagoria of broken and hurried dreams, repeating with monstrous exaggeration the crowded hours of the past day. The brain-stunning shock and horror of sudden, bloody death, the rude litter, the night-long journey with their awful burden, the doubtful aisles of pine with star galaxies wheeling beyond, the gaunt, bare hill above, the steep zigzag to the sleeping town, the flaming wrath of violent men—in his dream they came and went. Again, hasty messengers flashed across the haggard dawn; again, he shared the pursuit and capture of the sheep-herder. Sudden clash of unyielding wills; black anger; wild voices for swift death, quickly backed by wild, strong hands; Pringle's cool and steady defiance; his own hot,

resolute protest; the prisoner's unflinching fatalism; the hard-won respite
—all these and more—the lights, the swaying crowd, fierce faces black
and bitter with inarticulate wrath—jumbled confusedly in shifting, un-
sequenced combinations leading ever to some incredible, unguessed catas-
trophe.

Beside him, peacefully asleep, lay the manslayer, so lately snatched from
death, unconscious of the chain that bound him, oblivious of the menace
of the coming day.

"He takes it pretty hard," observed Uncle Pete, nodding at Billy.

"Yes. He's never seen any sorrow. But he don't weaken one mite. I tried
every way I could think of to get him out of here. Told him to sidle off
down to Lincoln after the sheriff. But he was dead on to me."

"Yes? Well, he wouldn't 'a' got far, anyway," said Uncle Pete dryly.
"We're watching every move. Still, it's a pity he didn't try. We'd 'a' got
him without hurtin' him, and he'd 'a' been out o' this."

Wes' made no answer. Uncle Pete stroked his grizzled beard reflectively. He filled his pipe with cut plug and puffed deliberately.

"Now, look here," he said slowly: "Mr. Procopio Chavez killed Jimmy,
and Mr. Procopio Chavez is going to hang. It wa'n't no weakenin' or
doubt on my part that made me call the boys off yesterday evenin'. He's
got to hang. I just wanted to keep you fellers from gettin' killed. There
might 'a' been some sense in your fighting then, but there ain't now.
There's too many of us."

"Me and Billy see the whole thing," said Wes', unmoved. "It was too
bad Jimmy got killed, but he was certainly mighty brash. The sheep-
herder was goin' peaceable, but Jimmy kept shootin', and shootin' close.
When that splinter of rock hit the Mexican man he thought he was shot,
and he turned loose. Reckon it hurt like sin. There's a black-and-blue spot
on his leg big as the palm of your hand. You'd 'a' done just the same as
he did.

"I ain't much enthusiastic about sheep-herders. In fact, I jerked my gun
at the time; but I was way down the trail and he was out o' sight before
I could shoot. Thinkin' it over careful, I don't see where this Mexican's
got any hangin' comin'. You know, just as well as I do, no court's goin'
to hang him on the testimony me and Billy's got to give in."

"I do," said Uncle Pete. "That's exactly why we're goin' to hang him
ourselves. If we let him go it's just encouragin' the *pastores* to kill up some
more of the boys. So we'll just stretch his neck. This is the last friendly
warnin', my son. If you stick your fingers between the anvil and the

hammer you'll get 'em pinched. 'Tain't any of your business, anyway. This ain't Rainbow. This is the White Mountain and we're strictly home rulers. And, moresoever, that war talk you made yisterday made the boys plumb sore."

"That war talk goes as she lays," said Pringle steadily. "No hangin' till after the shootin'. That goes."

"Now, now—what's the use?" remonstrated Uncle Pete. "Ye'll just get yourself hurted and 'twon't do the greaser any good. You might mebbe so stand us off in a good, thick 'dobe house, but not in this old shanty. If you want to swell up and be stubborn about it, it just means a grave apiece for you all and likely for some few of us."

"It don't make no difference to me," said Pringle, "if it means diggin' a grave in a hole in the cellar under the bottomless pit. I'm goin' to make my word good and do what I think's right."

"So am I, by Jupiter! Mr. Also Ran Pringle, it is a privilege to have known you!" Billy, half awake, covered Uncle Pete with a gun held in a steady hand. "Let's keep him here for a hostage and shoot him if they attempt to carry out their lynching," he suggested.

"We can't, Billy. Put it down," said Pringle mildly. "He's here under flag of truce."

"I was tryin' to save your derned fool hides," said Uncle Pete benignantly.

"Well—'tain't no use. We're just talkin' round and round in a circle, Uncle Pete. Turn your wolf loose when you get ready. As I said before, I don't noways dote on sheepmen, but I seen this, and I've got to see that this poor devil gets a square deal. I got to!"

Uncle Pete sighed. "It's a pity!" he said; "a great pity! Well, we're comin' quiet and peaceful. If there's any shootin' done you all have got to fire the first shot. We'll have the last one."

"Did you ever stop to think that the Rainbow men may not like this?" inquired Pringle. "If they're anyways disatisfied they're liable to come up here and scratch your eyes out one by one."

"Jesso. That's why you're goin' to fire the first shot," explained Uncle Pete patiently. "Only for that—and likewise because it would be a sorter mean trick to do—we could get up on the hill and smoke you out with rifles at long range, out o' reach of your six-shooters. You all might get away, but the sheepherder's chained fast and we could shoot him to kingdom come, shack and all, in five minutes. But you've had fair warnin' and you'll get an even break. If you want to begin trouble it's your own lookout. That squares us with Rainbow."

"And you expect them to believe you?" demanded Billy.

"Believe us? Sure! Why shouldn't they?" said Uncle Pete simply. "Of course they'll believe us. It'll be so." He stood up and regarded them wistfully. "There don't seem to be any use o' sayin' any more, so I'll go. I hope there ain't no hard feelin's?"

"Not a bit!" said Pringle; but Billy threw his head back and laughed angrily. "Come, I like that! By Jove, if that isn't nerve for you! To wake a man up and announce that you're coming presently to kill him, and then to expect to part the best of friends!"

"Ain't I doin' the friendly part?" demanded Uncle Pete stiffly. He was both nettled and hurt. "If I hadn't thought well of you fellers and done all I could for you, you'd 'a' been dead and done forgot about it by now. I give you all credit for doin' what you think is right, and you might do as much for me."

"Great Caesar's ghost! Do you want us to wish you good luck?" said Billy, exasperated almost to tears. "Have it your own way, by all means —you gentle-hearted old assassin! For my part, I'm going to do my level best to shoot you right between the eyes, but there won't be any hard feeling about it. I'll just be doing what I think is right—a duty I owe to the world. Say! I should think a gentleman of your sportsmanlike instincts would send over a gun for our prisoner. Twenty to one is big odds."

"Twenty to one is a purty good reason why you could surrender without no disgrace," rejoined Uncle Pete earnestly. "You can't make nothin' by fightin', cause you lose your point, anyway. And then, a majority of twenty to one—ain't that a good proof that you're wrong?"

"Now, Billy, you can't get around that. That's your own argument," cried Pringle, delighted. "You've stuck to it right along that you Republicans was dead right because you always get seven votes to our six. *Nux vomica*, you know."

Uncle Pete rose with some haste. "Here's where I go. I never could talk politics without gettin' mad," he said.

"Billy, you're certainly making good. You're a square peg. All the same, I wish," said Wes' Pringle plaintively, as Uncle Pete crunched heavily through the gravel, "that I could hear my favorite tune now."

Billy stared at him. "Does your mind hurt your head?" he asked solicitiously.

"No, no—I'm not joking. It would do me good if I could only hear him sing it."

"Hear who sing what?"

"Why, hear Jeff Bransford sing The Little Eohippus—right now. Jeff's got the knack of doing the wrong thing at the right time. Hark! What's that?"

It was a firm footstep at the door, a serene voice low chanting:

> *There was once a little animal*
> *No bigger than a fox,*
> *And on five toes he scampered—*

"Good Lord!" said Billy. "It's the man himself."

Questionable Bransford stepped through the half-open door, closed it and set his back to it.

"That's my cue! Who was it said eavesdroppers never heard good of themselves?"

He was smiling, his step was light, his tones were cheerful, ringing. His eyes had looked on evil and terrible things. In this desperate pass they wrinkled to pleasant, sunny warmth. He was unhurried, collected, confident. Billy found himself wondering how he had found this man loud, arbitrary, distasteful.

Welcome, question, answer; daybreak paled the ineffectual candle. The Mexican still slept.

"I crawled around the opposition camp like a snake in the grass," said Jeff. "There's two things I observed there that's mightily in our favor. The first thing is, there's no whisky goin'. And the reason for that is the second thing—and our one best big chance. Mister Burleson won't let 'em. Fact! Pretty much the entire population of the Pecos and tributary streams had arrived. Them that I know are mostly bad actors, and the ones I don't know looked real horrid to me; but your Uncle Pete is the bell mare. 'No booze!' he says, liftin' one finger; and that settled it. I reckon that when Uncle Simon Peter says 'Thumbs up!' those digits'll be elevated accordingly. If I can get him to see the gate the rest will only need a little gentle persuasion."

"I see you persuading them now," said Billy. "This is a plain case of the irresistible force and the immovable body."

"You will," said Jeff confidently. "You don't know what a jollier I am when I get down to it. Watch me! I'll show you a regular triumph of mind over matter."

"They're coming now," announced Wes' placidly. "Two by two, like the animals out o' the ark. I'm glad of it. I never was good at waitin'. Mr. Bransford will now oblige with his monologue entitled 'Givin' a bull the stop signal with a red flag.' Ladies will kindly remove their hats."

It was a grim and silent cavalcade. Uncle Pete rode at the head. As they turned the corner Jeff walked briskly down the path, hopped lightly on the fence, seated himself on the gatepost and waved an amiable hand.

"Stop, look and listen!" said this cheerful apparition.

The procession stopped. A murmur, originating from the Bar W contingent, ran down the ranks. Uncle Pete reined up and demanded of him with marked disfavor: "Who in merry hell are you?"

Jeff's teeth flashed white under his brown mustache. "I'm Ali Baba," he said, and paused expectantly. But the allusion was wasted on Uncle Pete. Seeing that no introduction was forthcoming, Jeff went on:

"I've been laboring with my friends inside, and I've got a proposition to make. As I told Pringle just now, I don't see any sense of us gettin' killed, and killin' a lot of you won't bring us alive again. We'd put up a pretty fight—a very pretty fight. But you'd lay us out sooner or later. So what's the use?"

"I'm mighty glad to see some one with a leetle old horse sense," said Uncle Pete. "Your friends is dead game sports all right, but they got mighty little judgment. If they'd only been a few of us I wouldn't 'a' blamed 'em a might for not givin' up. But we got too much odds of 'em."

"This conversation is taking an unexpected turn," said Jeff, making his eyes round. "I ain't named giving up that I remember of. What I want to do is to rig up a compromise."

"If there's any halfway place between a hung Mexican and a live one," said Uncle Pete, "mebbe we can. And if not, not. This ain't no time for triflin', young fellow."

"Oh, shucks! I can think of half a dozen compromises," said Jeff blandly. "We might play seven-up and not count any turned-up jacks. But I was thinking of something different. I realize that you outnumber us, so I'll meet you a good deal more than half way. First, I want to show you something about my gun. Don't anybody shoot, 'cause I ain't going to. Hope I may die if I do!"

"You will if you do. Don't worry about that," said Uncle Pete. "And maybe so, anyhow. You're delayin' the game."

Jeff took this for permission. "Everybody please watch and see there is no deception."

Holding the gun, muzzle up, so all could see, he deliberately extracted all the cartridges but one. The audience exchanged puzzled looks.

Jeff twirled the cylinder and returned the gun to its scabbard. "Now!" he said, sparkling with enthusiasm. "You all see that I've only got one cartridge. I'm in no position to fight. If there's any fighting I'm already dead. What happens to me has no bearing on the discussion. I'm out of it.

"I realize that there's no use trying to intimidate you fellows. Any of you would take a bit chance with odds against you, and here the odds is for you. So, as far as I'm concerned, I substitute a certainty for chance. I don't want to kill up a lot of rank strangers—or friends, either. There's nothing in it.

"Neither can I go back on old Wes' and Billy. So I take a halfway course. Just to manifest my entire disapproval, if any one makes a move to go through that gate I'll use my one shot—and it won't be on the man goin' through the gate, either. Nor yet on you, Uncle Pete. You're the leader. So if you want to give the word, go it! I'm not goin' to shoot you. Nor I ain't goin' to shoot any of the Bar W push. They're free to start the ball rolling."

Uncle Pete, thus deprived of the initiatory power, looked helplessly around the Bar W push for confirmation. They nodded in concert. "He'll do whatever he says," said Clay Cooper.

"Thanks," said Jeff pleasantly, "for this unsolicited testimonial. Now, boys, there's no dare about this. Just cause and effect. All of you are plumb safe to make a break—but one. To show you that there's nothing personal about it, no dislike or anything like that, I'll tell you how I picked that one. I started at some place near both ends or the middle and counted backward, or forward, sayin' to myself, 'Intra, mintra, cutra, corn, apple seed and briar thorn,' and when I got to 'thorn' that man was stuck. That's all. Them's the rules."

That part of Uncle Pete's face visible between beard and hat was purple through the brown. He glared at Jeff, opened his mouth, shut it tightly, and breathed heavily through his nose. He looked at his horse's ears, he looked at the low sun, he looked at the distant hills; his gaze wandered disconsolately back to the twinkling indomitable eyes of the man on the gatepost. Uncle Pete sighed deeply.

"That's good! I'll just about make the wagon by noon," he remarked gently. He took his quirt from his saddlehorn. "Young man," he said gravely, flicking his horse's flank, "any time you're out of a job come over and see me." He waved his hand, nodded, and was gone.

Clay Cooper spurred up and took his place, his black eyes snapping. "I like a damned fool," he hissed; "but you suit me too well!"

The forty followed; some pausing for quip or jest, some in frowning silence. But each, as he passed that bright, audacious figure, touched his hat in salute to a gallant foe.

Squatty Robinson was the last. He rode close up and whispered confidentially:

"I want you should do me a favor, Jeff. Just throw down on me and take my gun away. I don't want to go back to camp with any such tale as this."

"You see, Billy," explained Jeff, "you mustn't dare the denizens—never! They dare. They're uncultured; their lives ain't noways valuable to society and they know it. If you notice, I took pains not to dare anybody. Quite otherhow. I merely stated annoyin' consequences to some other fellow, attractive as I could, but impersonal. Just like I'd tell you: 'Billy, I wouldn't set the oil can on the fire—it might boil over.'

"Now, if I'd said: 'Uncle Pete, if anybody makes a break I'll shoot your eye out, anyhow,' there'd 'a' been only one dignified course open to him. Him and me would now be dear Alphonsing each other about payin' the ferryman.

"S'pose I'd made oration to shoot the first man through the gate. Every man Jack would have come a-snuffin'—each one tryin' to be first. The way I put it up to 'em, to be first wasn't no graceful act—playin' safe at some one else's expense—and then they seen that some one else wouldn't be gettin' an equitable vibration. That's all there was to it. If there wasn't any first there couldn't conveniently be any second, so they went home. B-r-r! I'm sleepy. Let's go by-by. Wake that dern lazy Mexican up and make him keep watch till the sheriff comes!"

From Missouri

Zane Grey (1872–1939) was a bored dentist who turned to writing stories of the American West at the age of thirty-two. He proceeded to become a legend in his own time and a world-famous Western writer. Although he sold more than ten million copies of his books before the paperback era, he became even more popular after his death, and his works continue to sell in large numbers today. Among his sixty books are such classics as Riders of the Purple Sage *(1912),* Last of the Plainsmen *(1908), and* West of the Pecos *(1937).*

WITH JINGLING spurs a tall cowboy stalked out of the post office to confront three punchers who were just then crossing the wide street from the saloon opposite.

"Look heah," he said, shoving a letter under their noses. "Which one of you longhorns wrote her again?"

From a gay, careless trio his listeners suddenly looked blank, then intensely curious. They stared at the handwriting on the letter.

"Tex, I'm a son-of-a-gun if it ain't from Missouri!" exclaimed Andy Smith, his lean red face bursting into a smile.

"It shore is," declared Nevada.

"From Missouri!" echoed Panhandle Hanes.

"Well?" asked Tex, almost with a snort.

The three cowboys drew back to look from Tex to one another, and then back at Tex.

"It's from *her*," went on Tex, his voice hushing on the pronoun. "You all know that handwritin'. Now how about this deal? We swore none of us would write to this schoolmarm. But some one of you has double-crossed the outfit."

Loud and simultaneous protestations of innocence arose from them. But it was evident that Tex did not trust them, and that they did not trust him or each other.

"Say, boys," said Panhandle suddenly. "I see Beady Jones in here lookin' darn sharp at us. Let's get off in the woods somewhere."

"Back to the bar," said Nevada. "I reckon we'll all need bracers."

"Beady!" exclaimed Tex as they turned across the street. "He could be to blame as much as any of us. An' he was still at Stringer's when we wrote the first letter."

"Shore. It'd be more like Beady," said Nevada. "But Tex, your mind ain't workin'. Our lady friend from Missouri wrote before without gettin' any letter from us."

"How do we know thet?" asked Tex suspiciously. "Shore the boss' typewriter is a puzzle, but it could hide tracks. Savvy, pards?"

"Doggone it, Tex, you need a drink," said Panhandle peevishly.

They entered the saloon and strode up to the bar, where from all appearances Tex was not the only one to seek artificial strength. Then they repaired to a corner, where they took seats and stared at the letter Tex threw down before them.

"From Missouri, all right," said Panhandle, studying the postmark. "Kansas City, Missouri."

"It's her writin'," said Nevada, in awe. "Shore I'd know that out of a million letters."

"Ain't you goin' to read it to us?" asked Andy Smith.

"Mr. Frank Owens," said Tex, reading from the address on the letter. "Springer's Ranch, Beacon, Arizona. . . . Boys, this Frank Owens is all of us."

"Huh! Mebbe he's a darn sight more," added Andy.

"Looks like a lowdown trick we're to blame for," resumed Tex, seriously shaking his hawklike head. "Heah we reads in a Kansas City paper about a schoolteacher wantin' a job out in dry Arizona. An' we writes her an' gets her ararin' to come. Then when she writes and tells us she's *not over forty*—then we quits like yellow coyotes. An' we four anyhow shook hands on never writin' her agin. Well, somebody did, an' I reckon you all think me as big a liar as I think you are. But that ain't the point. Heah's another letter to Mr. Owens an' I'll bet my saddle it means trouble."

Tex impressively spread out the letter and read laboriously:

Kansas City, Mo.
June 15

Dear Mr. Owens:
   Your last letter has explained away much that was vague and per-
plexing in your other letters.
   It has inspired me with hope and anticipation. I shall not take time

*now to express my thanks, but hasten to get ready to go west. I shall
leave tomorrow and arrive at Beacon on June 19, at 4:30 P.M. You
see I have studied the timetable.*

*Yours very truly,
Jane Stacey*

Profound silence followed Tex's reading of the letter. The cowboys
were struck completely dumb. Then suddenly Nevada exploded:

"My Gawd, fellers, today's the nineteenth!"

"Well, Springer needs a schoolmarm at the ranch," finally spoke up the
more practical Andy. "There's half a dozen kids growin' up without
schoolin', not to talk about other ranches. I heard the boss say so himself."

Tex spoke up. "I've an idea. It's too late now to turn this poor schoolmarm back. An' somebody'll have to meet her. You all come with me. I'll
get a buckboard. I'll meet the lady and do the talkin'. I'll let her down
easy. And if I cain't head her back to Missouri we'll fetch her out to the
ranch an' then leave it up to Springer. Only we won't tell her or him or
anybody who's the real Frank Owens."

"Tex, that ain't so plumb bad," said Andy admiringly.

"What I want to know is who's goin' to do the talkin' to the boss,"
asked Panhandle. "It mightn't be so hard to explain now. But after drivin'
up to the ranch with a woman! You all know Springer's shy. Young an'
rich, like he is, an' a bachelor—he's been fussed over so he's plumb afraid
of girls. An' here you're fetchin' a middle-aged schoolmarm who's romantic an' mushy!—My Gawd; . . . I say send her home on the next train."

"Pan, you're wise as far as horses an' cattle goes, but you don't know
human nature, an' you're dead wrong about the boss," said Tex. "We're
in a bad fix, I'll admit. But I lean more to fetchin' the lady up than sendin'
her back. Somebody down Beacon way would get wise. Mebbe the schoolmarm might talk. She'd shore have cause. An' suppose Springer hears
about it—that some of us or all of us has played a lowdown trick on a
woman. He'd be madder at that than if we fetched her up.

"Likely he'll try to make amends. The boss may be shy on girls but he's
the squarest man in Arizona. My idea is that we'll deny any of us is Frank
Owens, and we'll meet Miss—Miss—what was her name?—Miss Jane
Stacey and fetch her up to the ranch, an' let her do the talkin' to
Springer."

During the next several hours while Tex searched the town for a
buckboard and team he could borrow, the other cowboys wandered from

the saloon to the post office and back again, and then to the store, the restaurant and back again, and finally settled in the saloon.

When they emerged some time later they were arm in arm, and far from steady on their feet. They paraded up the one main street of Beacon, not in the least conspicious on a Saturday afternoon. As they were neither hilarious nor dangerous, nobody paid any particular attention to them. Springer, their boss, met them, gazed at them casually, and passed by without sign of recognition. If he had studied the boys closely he might have received an impression that they were clinging to a secret, as well as to each other.

In due time the trio presented themselves at the railroad station. Tex was there, nervously striding up and down the platform, now and then looking at his watch. The afternoon train was nearly due. At the hitching rail below the platform stood a new buckboard and a rather spirited team of horses.

The boys, coming across the wide square, encountered this evidence of Tex's extremity, and struck a posture before it.

"Livery shtable outfit, my gosh," said Andy.

"Shon of a gun if it ain't," added Panhandle with a huge grin.

"This here Tex spendin' his money royal," agreed Nevada.

Then Tex saw them. He stared. Suddenly he jumped straight up. Striding to the edge of the platform, with face red as a beet, he began to curse them.

"Whash masher, ole pard?" asked Andy, who appeared a little less stable than his two comrades.

Tex's reply was another volley of expressive profanity. And he ended with: "—you all yellow quitters to get drunk and leave me in the lurch. But you gotta get away from here. I shore won't have you about when the train comes in."

"But pard, we jist want to shee you meet our Jane from Missouri," said Andy.

"If you all ain't a lot of fourflushers I'll eat my chaps!" burst out Tex hotly.

Just then a shrill whistle announced the arrival of the train.

"You can sneak off now," he went on, "an' leave me to face the music. I always knew I was the only gentleman in Springer's outfit."

The three cowboys did not act upon Tex's sarcastic suggestion, but they hung back, looking at once excited and sheepish and hugely delighted.

The long gray dusty train pulled into the station and stopped with a complaining of brakes. There was only one passenger for Springer—a woman—and she alighted from the coach near where the cowboys stood waiting. She wore a long linen coat and a brown veil that completely hid her face. She was not tall and she was much too slight for the heavy valise the porter handed down to her.

Tex strode swaggeringly toward her.

"Miss—Miss Stacey, ma'am?" he asked, removing his sombrero.

"Yes," she replied. "Are you Mr. Owens?"

Evidently the voice was not what Tex had expected and it disconcerted him.

"No, ma'am, I—I'm not Mister Owens," he said. "Please let me take your bag . . . I'm Tex Dillon, one of Springer's cowboys. An' I've come to meet you—and fetch you out to the ranch."

"Thank you, but I—I expected to be met by Mr. Owens," she replied.

"Ma'am, there's been a mistake—I've got to tell you—there ain't any Mister Owens," blurted out Tex manfully.

"Oh!" she said, with a little start.

"You see, it was this way," went on the confused cowboy. "One of Springer's cowboys—not *me*—wrote them letters to you, signin' his name Owens. There ain't no such named cowboy in this whole country. Your last letter—an' here it is—fell into my hands—all by accident, ma'am, it shore was. I took my three friends heah—I took them into my confidence. An' we all came down to meet you."

She moved her head and evidently looked at the strange trio of cowboys Tex pointed out as his friends. They shuffled forward, not too eagerly, and they still held on to each other. Their condition, not to consider their state of excitement, could not have been lost even upon a tenderfoot from Missouri.

"Please return my—my letter," she said, turning again to Tex, and she put out a small gloved hand to take it from him. "Then—there is no Mr. Frank Owens?"

"No ma'am, there shore ain't," said Tex miserably.

"Is there—no—no truth in his—is there no schoolteacher wanted here?" she faltered.

"I think so, ma'am," he replied. "Springer said he needed one. That's what started us answerin' the advertisement an' the letters to you. You can see the boss an'—an' explain. I'm shore it will be all right. He's one swell feller. He won't stand for no joke on a poor old schoolmarm."

In his bewilderment Tex had spoken his thoughts, and his last slip made him look more miserable than ever, and made the boys appear ready to burst.

"Poor old schoolmarm!" echoed Miss Stacey. "Perhaps the deceit has not been wholly on one side."

Whereupon she swept aside the enveloping veil to reveal a pale yet extremely pretty face. She was young. She had clear gray eyes and a sweet sensitive mouth. Little curls of chestnut hair straggled down from under her veil. And she had tiny freckles.

Tex stared at this lovely apparition.

"But you—you—the letter says she wasn't over forty," he exclaimed.

"She's not," rejoined Miss Stacey curtly.

Then there were visible and remarkable indication of a transformation in the attitude of the cowboy. But the approach of a stranger suddenly seemed to paralyze him. The newcomer was very tall. He strolled up to them. He was booted and spurred. He halted before the group and looked expectantly from the boys to the strange young woman and back again. But for the moment the four cowboys appeared dumb.

"Are—are you Mr. Springer?" asked Miss Stacey.

"Yes," he replied, and he took off his sombrero. He had a deeply tanned frank face and keen blue eyes.

"I am Jane Stacey," she explained hurriedly. "I'm a schoolteacher. I answered an advertisement. And I've come from Missouri because of letters I received from a Mr. Frank Owens, of Springer's Ranch. This young man met me. He has not been very—explicit. I gather there is no Mr. Owens—that I'm the victim of a cowboy joke . . . But he said that Mr. Springer wouldn't stand for a joke on a poor old schoolmarm."

"I sure am glad to meet you, Miss Stacey," said the rancher, with an easy Western courtesy that must have been comforting to her. "Please let me see the letters."

She opened a handbag, and searching in it, presently held out several letters. Springer never even glanced at his stricken cowboys. He took the letters.

"No, not that one," said Miss Stacey, blushing scarlet. "That's one I wrote to Mr. Owens, but didn't mail. It's—hardly necessary to read that."

While Springer read the others she looked at him. Presently he asked her for the letter she had taken back. Miss Stacey hesitated, then refused. He looked cool, serious, businesslike. Then his keen eyes swept over the four ill-at-ease cowboys.

"Tex, are you Mr. Frank Owens?" he asked sharply.

"I—shore—ain't," gasped Tex.

Springer asked each of the other boys the same question and received decidedly maudlin but negative answers. Then he turned to the girl.

"Miss Stacey, I regret to say that you are indeed the victim of a lowdown cowboy trick," he said. "I'd apologize for such heathen if I knew how. All I can say is I'm sorry."

"Then—then there isn't any school to teach—any place for me—out here?" she asked, and there were tears in her eyes.

"That's another matter," he said, with a pleasant smile. "Of course there's a place for you. I've wanted a schoolteacher for a long time. Some of the men out at the ranch have kids and they sure need a teacher badly."

"Oh, I'm—so glad," she murmured, in evident relief. "I was afraid I'd have to go all the way back. You see I'm not so strong as I used to be— and my doctor advised a change of climate—dry Western air."

"You don't look sick," he said, with his keen eyes on her. "You look very well to me."

"Oh, indeed, but I'm not very strong," she said quickly. "But I must confess I wasn't altogether truthful about my age."

"I was wondering about that," he said, gravely. There seemed just a glint of a twinkle in his eye. "Not over forty."

Again she blushed and this time with confusion.

"It wasn't altogether a lie. I was afraid to mention that I was only— young. And I wanted to get the position so much. . . . I'm a good—a competent teacher, unless the scholars are too grown up."

"The scholars you'll have at my ranch are children," he replied. "Well, we'd better be starting if we are to get there before dark. It's a long ride."

A few weeks altered many things at Springer's Ranch. There was a marvelous change in the dress and deportment of the cowboys when off duty. There were some clean and happy and interested children. There was a rather taciturn and lonely young rancher who was given to thoughtful dreams and whose keen blue eyes kept watch on the little adobe schoolhouse under the cottonwoods. And in Jane Stacey's face a rich bloom and tan had begun to drive out the city pallor.

It was not often that Jane left the schoolhouse without meeting one of Springer's cowboys. She met Tex most frequently, and according to Andy, that fact was because Tex was foreman and could send the boys off to the end of the range when he had the notion.

One afternoon Jane encountered the foreman. He was clean-shaven, bright and eager, a superb figure of a man. Tex had been lucky enough to have a gun with him one day when a rattlesnake had frightened the schoolteacher and he had shot the reptile. Miss Stacey had leaned against him in her fright; she had been grateful; she had admired his wonderful skill with a gun and had murmured that a woman always would be safe with such a man. Thereafter Tex packed his gun, unmindful of the ridicule of his rivals.

"Miss Stacey, come for a little ride, won't you?" he asked eagerly.

The cowboys had already taught her how to handle a horse and to ride; and if all they said of her appearance and accomplishment were true she was indeed worth watching.

"I'm sorry," said Jane. "I promised Nevada I'd ride with him today."

"I reckon Nevada is miles and miles up the valley by now," replied Tex. "He won't be back till long after dark."

"But he made an engagement with me," protested the schoolmistress.

"An' shore he has to work. He's ridin' for Springer, an' I'm foreman of this ranch," said Tex.

"You sent him off on some long chase," said Jane severely. "Now didn't you?"

"I shore did. He comes crowin' down to the bunkhouse—about how he's goin' to ride with you an' how we all are not in the runnin'."

"Oh! he did—And what did you say?"

"I says, 'Nevada, I reckon there's a steer mired in the sand up in Cedar Wash. You ride up there and pull him out.'"

"And then what did he say?" inquired Jane curiously.

"Why, Miss Stacey, shore I hate to tell you. I didn't think he was so —so bad. He just used the most awful language as was ever heard on this here ranch. Then he rode off."

"But was there a steer mired up in the wash?"

"I reckon so," replied Tex, rather shamefacedly. "Most always is one."

Jane let scornful eyes rest upon the foreman. "That was a mean trick," she said.

"There's been worse done to me by him, an' all of them. An' all's fair in love an' war . . . Will you ride with me?"

"No."

"Why not?"

"Because I think I'll ride off alone up Cedar Wash and help Nevada find that mired steer."

"Miss Stacey, you're shore not goin' to ride off alone. Savvy that."

"Who'll keep me from it?" demanded Jane with spirit.

"I will. Or any of the boys, for that matter, Springer's orders."

Jane started with surprise and then blushed rosy red. Tex, also, appeared confused at his disclosure.

"Miss Stacey, I oughtn't have said that. It slipped out. The boss said we needn't tell you, but you were to be watched an' taken care of. It's a wild range. You could get lost or thrown from a hoss."

"Mr. Springer is very kind and thoughtful," murmured Jane.

"The fact is, this ranch is a different place since you came," went on Tex as if suddenly emboldened. "An' this beatin' around the bush doesn't suit me. All the boys have lost their heads over you."

"Indeed? How flattering!" said Jane, with just a hint of mockery. She was fond of all her admirers, but there were four of them she had not yet forgiven.

The tall foreman was not without spirit. "It's true all right, as you'll find out pretty quick," he replied. "If you had any eyes you'd see that cattle raisin' on this ranch is about to halt till somethin' is decided. Why, even Springer himself is sweet on you!"

"How dare you!" flashed Jane, blushing furiously.

"I ain't afraid to tell the truth," said Tex stoutly. "He is. The boys all say so. He's grouchier than ever. He's jealous. Lord! he's jealous! He watches you—"

"Suppose I told him you had dared to say such things?" interrupted Jane, trembling on the verge of a strange emotion.

"Why, he'd be tickled to death. He hasn't got nerve enough to tell you himself."

Jane shook her head, but her face was still flushed. This cowboy, like all his comrades, was hopeless. She was about to change the topic of conversation when Tex suddenly took her into his arms. She struggled— and fought with all her might. But he succeeded in kissing her cheek and then the tip of her ear. Finally she broke away from him.

"Now—" she panted. "You've done it—you've insulted me! Now I'll never ride with you again—never even speak to you."

"Shore I didn't insult you," replied Tex. "Jane—won't you marry me?"

"No."

"Won't you be my sweetheart—till you care enough to—to—"

"No."

"But, Jane, you'll forgive me, an' be good friends with me again?"

"Never!"

Jane did not mean all she said. She had come to understand these men of the range—their loneliness—their hunger for love. But in spite of her sympathy and affection she needed sometimes to appear cold and severe with them.

"Jane, you owe me a great deal—more than you got any idea of," said Tex seriously.

"How so?"

"Didn't you ever guess about me?"

"My wildest flight at guessing would never make anything of you, Texas Jack."

"You'd never have been here but for me," he said solemnly.

Jane could only stare at him.

"I meant to tell you long ago. But I shore didn't have the nerve. Jane I—I was that there letter-writin' feller. I wrote them letters you got. I am Frank Owens."

"No!" exclaimed Jane.

She was startled. That matter of Frank Owens had never been cleared up to her satisfaction. It had ceased to rankle within her breast, but it had never been completely forgotten. She looked up earnestly into the big fellow's face. It was like a mask. But she saw through it. He was lying. He was brazen. Almost, she thought, she saw a laugh deep in his eyes.

"I shore am that lucky man who found you a job when you was sick an' needed a change . . . An' that you've grown so pretty an' so well you owe all to me."

"Tex, if you really were Frank Owens, *that* would make a great difference; indeed I do owe him everything, I would—but I don't believe you are he."

"It's shore honest Gospel fact," declared Tex. "I hope to die if it ain't!"

Jane shook her head sadly at his monstrous prevarication. "I don't believe you," she said, and left him standing there.

It might have been coincidence that the next few days both Nevada and Panhandle waylaid the pretty schoolteacher and conveyed to her intelligence by divers and pathetic arguments the astounding fact that each was none other than Mr. Frank Owens. More likely, however, was it attributable to the unerring instinct of lovers who had sensed the importance and significance of this mysterious correspondent's part in bringing health and happiness into Jane Stacey's life. She listened to them with both anger and amusement at their deceit, and she had the same answer for both. "I don't believe you."

Because of these clumsy machinations of the cowboys, Jane had begun to entertain some vague, sweet, and disturbing suspicions of her own as to the identity of that mysterious cowboy, Frank Owens.

It came about that a dance was to be held at Beacon during the late summer. The cowboys let Jane know that it was something she could not very well afford to miss. She had not attended either of the cowboy dances which had been given since her arrival. This next one, however, appeared to be an annual affair, at which all the ranching fraternity for miles around would be attending.

Jane, as a matter of fact, was wild to go. However, she felt that she could not accept the escort of any one of her cowboy admirers without alienating the others. And she began to have visions of this wonderful dance fading away without a chance of her attending, when Springer accosted her one day.

"Who's the lucky cowboy to take you to our dance?" he asked.

"He seems to be as mysterious and doubtful as Mr. Frank Owens," replied Jane.

"Oh, you still remember him," said the rancher, his keen dark eyes quizzically on her.

"Indeed I do," sighed Jane.

"Too bad! He was a villain . . . But you don't mean you haven't been asked to go?"

"They've all asked me. That's the trouble."

"I see. But you mustn't miss it. It'd be pleasant for you to meet some of the ranchers and their wives. Suppose you go with me?"

"Oh, Mr. Springer, I—I'd be delighted," replied Jane.

Jane's first sight of that dance hall astonished her. It was a big barnlike room, crudely raftered and sided, decorated with colored bunting which took away some of the bareness. The oil lamps were not bright, but there were plenty of them hung in brackets around the room. The volume of sound amazed her. Music and the trample of boots, gay laughter, the deep voices of men and the high-pitched voices of the children—all seemed to merge into a loud, confused uproar. A swaying, wheeling horde of dancers circled past her.

"Sure it's something pretty fine for old Bill Springer to have the prettiest girl here," her escort said.

"Than you—but, Mr. Springer—I can easily see that you were a cowboy before you became a rancher," she replied archly.

"Sure I was. And that you will be dead sure to find out," he laughed. "Of course I could never compete with—say—Frank Owens. But let's dance. I shall have little enough of you in this outfit."

So he swung her into the circle of dancers. Jane found him easy to dance with, though he was far from expert. It was a jostling mob, and she soon acquired a conviction that if her gown did outlast the entire dance her feet never would. Springer took his dancing seriously and had little to say. She felt strange and uncertain with him. Presently she became aware of the cessation of hum and movement. The music had stopped.

"That sure was the best dance I ever had," said Springer, with a glow of excitement on his dark face. "An' now I must lose you to this outfit just coming."

Manifestly he meant his cowboys, Tex, Nevada, Panhandle, and Andy, who were presenting themselves four abreast shiny of hair and face.

"Good luck," he whispered. "If you get into a jam, let me know."

What he meant quickly dawned upon Jane. Right then it began. She saw there was absolutely no use in trying to avoid or refuse these young men. The wisest and safest course was to surrender, which she did.

"Boys, don't all talk at once. I can dance with only one of you at a time. So I'll take you in alphabetical order. I'm a poor old schoolmarm from Missouri, you know. It'll be Andy, Nevada, Panhandle, and Tex."

Despite their protests she held rigidly to this rule. Each one of the cowboys took shameless advantage of his opportunity. Outrageously as they all hugged her, Tex was the worst offender. She tried to stop dancing, but he carried her along as if she had been a child. He was rapt, and yet there seemed a devil in him.

"Tex—how dare—you!" she panted, when at last the dance ended.

"Well, I reckon I'd about dare anythin' for you, Jane," he replied, towering over her.

"You ought to be—ashamed," she went on. "I'll not dance with you again."

"Aw, now," he pleaded.

"I won't, Tex, so there. You're no gentleman."

"Ahuh!" he retorted, drawing himself up stiffly. "All right I'll go out an' get drunk, an' when I come back I'll clean out this hall so quick that you'll get dizzy watchin'."

"Tex! Don't go," she called hurriedly, as he started to stride away. "I'll take that back. I will give you another dance—if you promise to—to behave."

With this hasty promise she got rid of him, and was carried off by Mrs. Hartwell to be introduced to the various ranchers and their wives, and to all the girls and their escorts. She found herself a center of admiring eyes. She promised more dances than she could ever hope to remember or keep.

Her next partner was a tall handsome cowboy named Jones. She did not know quite what to make of him. But he was an unusually good dancer, and he did not hold her in such a manner that she had difficulty in breathing. He talked all the time. He was witty and engaging, and he had a most subtly flattering tongue. Jane could not fail to grasp that he might even be more outrageous than Tex, but at least he did not make love to her with physical violence.

She enjoyed that dance and admitted to herself that the singular forceful charm about this Mr. Jones was appealing. If he was a little too bold of glance and somehow too primitively self-assured and debonair, she passed it by in the excitement and joy of the hour, and in the conviction that she was now a long way from Missouri. Jones demanded, rather than begged for, another dance, and though she laughingly explained her predicament in regard to partners he said he would come after her anyhow.

Then followed several dances with new partners, and Jane became more than ever the center of attraction. It all went to the schooleacher's head like wine. She was having a perfectly wonderful time. Jones claimed her again, in fact whirled her away from the man to whom she was talking and out on the floor. Twice again before the supper hour at midnight she found herself dancing with Jones. How he managed it she did not know. He just took her, carrying her off by storm.

She did not awaken to this unpardonable conduct of hers until she suddenly recalled that a little before she had promised Tex his second dance, and then she had given it to Jones, or at least had danced it with him. But, after all, what could she do when he had walked right off with her? It was a glimpse of Tex's face, as she whirled past in Jones' arms, that filled Jane with sudden remorse.

Then came the supper hour. It was a gala occasion, for which evidently the children had heroically kept awake. Jane enjoyed the children immensely. She sat with the numerous Hartwells, all of whom were most pleasantly attentive to her. Jane wondered why Mr. Springer did not put in an appearance, but considered his absence due to numerous duties on the dance committee!

When the supper hour ended and the people were stirring about the hall again, and the musicians were turning up, Jane caught sight of Andy. He looked rather pale and almost sick. Jane tried to catch his eye, but failing that she went to him.

"Andy, please find Tex for me. I owe him a dance, and I'll give him the very first, unless Mr. Springer comes for it."

Andy regarded her with an aloofness totally new to her.

"Well, I'll tell him. But I reckon Tex ain't presentable just now. An' all of us boys are through dancin' for tonight."

"What's happened?" asked Jane, swift to divine trouble.

"There's been a little fight."

"Oh, no!" cried Jane. "Who? Why?—Andy, please tell me."

"Well, when you cut Tex's dance for Beady Jones, you shore put our outfit in bad," replied Andy coldly. "At that there wouldn't have been anything come of it here if Beady Jones hadn't got to shootin' off his chin. Tex slapped his face an' that shore started a fight. Beady licked Tex, too, I'm sorry to say. He's a pretty bad hombre, Beady is, an' he's bigger'n Tex. Well, we had a hell of a time keepin' Nevada out of it. That would have been a worse fight. I'd like to have seen it. But we kept them apart till Springer come out. An' what the boss said to that outfit was sure aplenty.

"Beady Jones kept talkin' back, nastylike—you know he was once foreman for us—till Springer got good an' mad. An' he said: 'Jones, I fired you once because you were a little too slick for our outfit, an' I'll tell you this, if it come to a pinch I'll give you the damnedest thrashin' any smart-aleck cowboy ever got.' . . . Judas, the boss was riled. It sort of surprised me, an' tickled me pink. You can bet that shut Beady Jones's loud mouth and mighty quick!"

After his rather lengthy speech, Andy left her unceremoniously standing there alone. She was not alone long, but it was long enough for her to feel a rush of bitter dissatisfaction with herself.

Jane looked for Springer, hoping yet fearing he would come to her. But he did not. She had another uninterrupted dizzy round of dancing until her strength completely failed. By four o'clock she was scarcely able to walk. Her pretty dress was torn and mussed; her white stockings were no longer white; her slippers were worn ragged. And her feet were dead. She dragged herself to a chair where she sat looking on, and trying to keep awake. The wonderful dance that had begun so promisingly had ended sadly for her.

At length the exodus began, though Jane did not see many of the dancers leaving. She went out to be received by Springer, who had evidently made arrangements for their leaving. He seemed decidedly cool to the remorseful Jane.

All during the long ride to the ranch he never addressed her or looked toward her. Daylight came, appearing cold and gray to Jane. She felt as if she wanted to cry.

Springer's sister and the matronly housekeeper were waiting for them, with a cherry welcome, and an invitation to a hot breakfast.

Presently Jane found herself momentarily alone with the taciturn rancher.

"Miss Stacey," he said, in a voice she had never heard, "your crude flirting with Beady Jones made trouble for the Springer outfit last night."

"*Mr. Springer!*" she exclaimed, her head going up.

"Excuse me," he returned, in a cutting, dry tone that recalled Tex. After all, this Westerner was still a cowboy, just exactly like those who rode for him, only a little older, and therefore more reserved and careful of his speech. "If it wasn't that—then you sure appeared to be pretty much taken with Mr. Beady Jones."

"If that was anybody's business, it might have appeared so," she cried, tingling all over with some feeling which she could not control.

"Sure. But are you denying it?" he asked soberly, eyeing her with a grave frown and obvious disapproval. It was this more than his question that roused hot anger and contrariness in Jane.

"I admired Mr. Jones very much," she replied haughtily. "He was a splendid dancer. He did not maul me like a bear. I really had a chance to breathe during my dances with him. Then too he could talk. He was a gentleman."

Springer bowed with dignity. His dark face paled. It dawned upon Jane that the situation had become serious for everyone concerned. She began to repent her hasty pride.

"Thanks," he said. "Please excuse my impertinence. I see you have found your Mr. Frank Owens in this cowboy Jones, and it sure is not my place to say any more."

"But—but—Mr. Springer—" faltered Jane, quite unstrung by the rancher's amazing speech.

However, he merely bowed again and left her. Jane felt too miserable and weary for anything but rest and a good cry. She went to her room, and flinging off her hateful finery, she crawled into bed, and buried her head in her pillow.

About mid-afternoon Jane awakened greatly refreshed and relieved and strangely repentant. She invaded the kitchen, where the goodnatured housekeeper, who had become fond of her, gave her some wild-turkey sandwiches and cookies and sweet rich milk. While Jane appeased her hunger the woman gossiped about the cowboys and Springer, and the information she imparted renewed Jane's concern over the last night's affair.

From the kitchen Jane went out into the courtyard, and naturally, as always, gravitated toward the corrals and barns. Springer appeared in company with a rancher Jane did not know. She expected Springer to stop her for a few pleasant words as was his wont. This time, however, he merely touched his sombrero and passed on. Jane felt the incident almost as a slight. And it hurt.

As she went on down the land she became very thoughtful. A cloud suddenly had appeared above the horizon of her happy life there at the Springer ranch. It did not seem to her that what she had done deserved the change in everyone's attitude. The lane opened out onto a wide square, around which were the gates to the corrals, the entrances to several barns, the forge, granaries, and the commodious bunkhouse of the cowboys.

Jane's sharp eyes caught sight of the boys before they saw her. But when she looked up again every broad back was turned. They allowed her to pass without any apparent knowledge of her existence. This obvious snub was unprecedented. It offended her bitterly. She knew that she was being unreasonable, but could not or would not help it. She strolled on down to the pasture gate and watched the colts and calves.

Upon her return she passed even closer to the cowboys. But again they apparently did not see her. Jane added resentment to her wounded vanity and pride. Yet even then a still small voice tormented and accused her. She went back to her room, meaning to read or sew, or prepare school work. But instead she sat down in a chair and burst into tears.

Next day was Sunday. Heretofore every Sunday had been a full day for Jane. This one, however, bade fair to be an empty one. Company came as usual, neighbors from nearby ranches. The cowboys were off duty and other cowboys came over to visit them.

Jane's attention was attracted by sight of a superb horseman riding up the lane to the ranch house. He seemed familiar, somehow, but she could not place him. What a picture he made as he dismounted slick and shiny, booted and spurred, to doff his huge sombrero! Jane heard him ask for Miss Stacey. Then she recognized him. Beady Jones! She was at once horrified and yet attracted to this cowboy. She remembered how he had asked if he might call Sunday and she had certainly not refused to see him. But for him to come here after the fight with Tex and the bitter scene with Springer!

It seemed almost an unparalleled affront. What manner of man was this cowboy Jones? He certainly did not lack courage. But more to the point what idea he had of her? Jane rose to the occasion. She had let herself in for this, and she would see it through, come what might. Looming disaster stimulated her. She would show these indifferent, deceitful, fire-spirited, incomprehensible cowboys! She would let Springer see that she had indeed taken Beady Jones for Mr. Frank Owens.

With this thought in mind, Jane made her way down to the porch to greet her cowboy visitor. She made herself charming and gracious, and carried off the embarrassing situation—for Springer was present—just as if it were the most natural thing in the world. And she led Jones to one of the rustic benches farther down the porch.

Obvious, indeed, was it in all his actions that young Jones felt he had made a conquest. He was the most forceful and bold person Jane had ever met, quite incapable of appreciating her as a lady. It was not long before he was waxing ardent. Jane had become accustomed to the sentimental talk of cowboys, but this fellow was neither amusing nor interesting. He was dangerous. When she pulled her hand, by main force, free from his, and said she was not accustomed to allow men such privileges, he grinned at her like the handsome devil he was. Her conquest was only a matter of time.

"Sure, sweetheart, you have missed a heap of fun," Beady Jones said. "An' I reckon I'll have to break you in."

Jane could not really feel insulted at this brazen, conceited fool, but she certainly could feel enraged with herself. Her instant impulse was to excuse herself and abruptly leave him. But Springer was close by. She had caught his dark, speculative, covert glances. And the cowboys were at the other end of the long porch. Jane feared another fight. She had brought this situation upon herself, and she must stick it out. The ensuing hour was an increasing torment.

At last it seemed to her that she could not bear the false situation any longer. And when Jones again importuned her to meet him out on horseback some time, she stooped to deception to end the interview. She really did not concentrate her attention on his plan or really take stock of what she was agreeing to do, but she got rid of him with ease and dignity in the presence of Springer and the others. After that she did not have the courage to stay out there and face them, and stole off to the darkness and loneliness of her room.

The school teaching went on just the same, and the cowboys thawed out perceptibly, and Springer returned somewhat to his friendly manner, but Jane missed something from her work and in them, and her heart was sad the way everything was changed. Would it ever be the same again? What had happened? She had only been an emotional little tenderfoot, unused to Western ways. After all, she had not failed, at least in gratitude and affection, though now it seemed they would never know.

There came a day, when Jane rode off toward the hills. She forgot the risk and all of the admonitions of the cowboys. She wanted to be alone to think.

She rode fast until her horse was hot and she was out of breath. Then she slowed down. The foothills seemed so close now. But they were not really close. Still she could smell the fragrant dry cedar aroma on the air.

Then for the first time she looked back toward the ranch. It was a long way off—ten miles—a mere green spot in the gray. Suddenly she caught sight of a horseman coming. As usual, some one of the cowboys had observed her, let her think she had slipped away, and was now following her. Today it angered Jane. She wanted to be alone. She could take care of herself. And as was unusual with her, she used her quirt on the horse. He broke into a gallop.

She did not look back again for a long time. When she did it was to discover that the horseman had not only gained, but was now quite close to her. Jane looked intently, but she could not recognize the rider. Once she imagined it was Tex and again Andy. It did not make any difference which one of the cowboys it was. She was angry, and if he caught up with her he would be sorry.

Jane rode the longest and fastest race she had ever ridden. She reached the low foothills, and without heeding the fact that she might speedily become lost, she entered the cedars and began to climb.

What was her amazement when she heard a thud of hoofs and crackling of branches in the opposite direction from which she was expecting her pursuer, and saw a rider emerge from the cedars and trot his horse toward her. Jane needed only a second glance to recognize Beady Jones. Surely she had met him by chance. Suddenly she knew he was not the pursuer she had been so angrily aware of. Jones's horse was white. That checked her mounting anger.

Jones rode straight at her, and as he came close Jane saw his bold tanned face and gleaming eyes. Instantly she realized that she had been mad to ride so far into the wild country, to expose herself to something from which the cowboys on the ranch had always tried to save her.

"Howdy, sweetheart," sang out Jones, in his cool, devil-may-care way. "Reckon it took you a long time to make up your mind to meet me as you promised."

"I didn't ride out to meet you, Mr. Jones," said Jane spiritedly. "I know I agreed to something or other, but even then I didn't mean it."

"Yes, I had a hunch you were just playin' with me," he said darkly, riding his white mount right up against her horse.

He reached out a long gloved hand and grasped her arm.

"What do you mean, sir?" demanded Jane, trying to wrench her arm free.

"Shore I mean a lot," he said grimly. "You stood for the lovemakin' of that Springer outfit. Now you're goin' to get a taste of somethin' not quite so easy."

"Let go of me—you—you utter fool!" cried Jane, struggling fiercely. She was both furious and terrified. But she seemed to be a child in the grasp of a giant.

"Hell! Your fightin' will only make it more interestin'. Come here, you sassy little cat."

And he lifted her out of her saddle over onto his horse in front of him. Jane's mount, that had been frightened and plunging, ran away into the cedars. Then Jones proceeded to embrace Jane. She managed to keep her mouth from contact with his, but he kissed her face and neck, kisses that seemed to fill her with shame and disgust.

"Jane, I'm ridin' out of this country for good," he said. "An' I've just been waitin' for this chance. You bet you'll remember Beady Jones."

Jane realized that Jones would stop at nothing. Frantically she fought to get away from him, and to pitch herself to the ground. She screamed. She beat and tore at him. She scratched his face till the blood flowed. And as her struggles increased with her fright, she gradually slipped down between him and the pommel of his saddle, with head hanging down on one side and her feet on the other. This position was awkward and painful, but infinitely preferable to being crushed in his arms. He was riding off with her as if she had been a half-empty sack.

Suddenly Jane's hands, while trying to hold on to something to lessen the severe jolting her position was giving her, came in contact with Jones's gun. Dare she draw it and try to shoot him? Then all at once her ears filled with the approaching gallop of another horse. Inverted as she was, she was able to see and recognize Springer riding directly at Jones and yelling hoarsely.

Next she felt Jones's hard jerk at his gun. But Jane had hold of it, and suddenly her little hands had the strength of steel. The fierce energy with which Jones was wrestling to draw his gun threw Jane from the saddle. And when she dropped clear of the horse the gun came with her.

"Hands up, Beady!" she heard Springer call out, as she lay momentarily face down in the dust. Then she struggled to her knees, and crawled to get away from the danger of the horses' hoofs. She still clung to the heavy gun. And when breathless and almost collapsing she fell back on the ground, she saw Jones with his hands above his head and Springer on foot with leveled gun.

"Sit tight, cowboy," ordered the rancher, in a hard tone. "It'll take damn little more to make me bore you."

Then while still covering Jones, evidently ready for any sudden move, Springer spoke again.

"Jane, did you come out here to meet this cowboy?" he asked.

"Oh, no! How can you ask that?" cried Jane, almost sobbing.

"She's a liar, boss," spoke up Jones coolly. "She let me make love to her. An' she agreed to ride out an' meet me. Well it shore took her a spell, an' when she did come she was shy on the lovemakin'. I was packin' her off to scare some sense into her when you rode in."

"Beady, I know your way with women. You can save your breath, for I've a hunch you're going to need it."

"Mr. Springer," faltered Jane, getting to her knees. "I—I was foolishly attracted to this cowboy—at first. Then—that Sunday after the dance when he called on me at the ranch—I saw through him then. I heartily despised him. To get rid of him I did say I'd meet him. But I never meant to. Then I forgot all about it. Today I rode alone for the first time. I saw someone following me and thought it must be Tex or one of the boys. Finally I waited, and presently Jones rode up to me . . . And, Mr. Springer, he—he grabbed me off my horse—and handled me shamefully. I fought him with all my might, but what could I do?"

Springer's face changed markedly during Jane's long explanation. Then he threw his gun on the ground in front of Jane.

"Jones, I'm going to beat you within an inch of your life," he said grimly; and leaping at the cowboy, he jerked him out of the saddle and sent him sprawling on the ground. Next Springer threw aside his sombrero, his vest, his spurs. But he kept on his gloves. The cowboy rose to one knee, and he measured the distance between him and Springer, and then the gun that lay on the ground. Suddenly he sprang toward it. Springer intercepted him with a powerful kick that tripped Jones and laid him flat.

"Jones, you're sure about as lowdown as they come," he said, in a tone of disgust. "I've got to be satisfied with beating you when I ought to kill you!"

"Ahuh! Well, boss, it ain't any safe bet that you can do either," cried Beady Jones sullenly, as he got up.

As they rushed together Jane had wit enough to pick up the gun, and then with it and Jones's, to get back a safe distance. She wanted to run away out of sight. But she could not keep her fascinated gaze from the combatants. Even in her distraught condition she could see that the cowboy, young and active and strong as he was, could not hold his own with Springer. They fought all over the open space, and crashed into the cedars and out again. The time came when Jones was on the ground about as much as he was erect. Bloody, dishevelled, beaten, he kept on trying to stem the onslaught of blows.

Suddenly he broke off a dead branch of cedar, and brandishing it rushed at the rancher. Jane uttered a cry, closed her eyes, and sank to the ground. She heard fierce muttered imprecations and savage blows. When at length she opened her eyes again, fearing something dreadful, she saw Springer erect, wiping his face with the back of one hand and Jones lying on the ground.

Then Jane saw him go to his horse, untie a canteen from the saddle, remove his bloody gloves, and wash his face with a wet scarf. Next he poured some water on Jones's face.

"Come on, Jane," he called. "I reckon it's all over."

He tied the bridle of Jones's horse to a cedar, and leading his own animal turned to meet Jane.

"I want to compliment you on getting that cowboy's gun," he said warmly. "But for that there'd sure have been something bad. I'd have had to kill him, Jane. . . . Here, give me the guns. . . . You poor little tenderfoot from Missouri. No, not tenderfoot any longer. You became a Westerner today."

His face was bruised and cut, his clothes dirty and bloody, but he did not appear the worse for such a desperate fight. Jane found her legs scarcely able to support her, and she had apparently lost her voice.

"Let me put you on my saddle till we find your horse," he said, and lifted her lightly as a feather to a seat crosswise in the saddle. Then he walked with a hand on the bridle.

Jane saw him examining the ground, evidently searching for horse tracks. "Here we are." And he led off in another direction through the cedars. Soon Jane saw her horse, calmly nibbling at the bleached grass.

Springer stood beside her with a hand on her horse. He looked frankly into her face. The keen eyes were softer than usual. He looked so fine and strong and splendid that she found herself breathing with difficulty. She was afraid of her betraying eyes and looked away.

"When the boys found out that you were gone, they all saddled up to find you," he said. "But I asked them if they didn't think the boss ought to have one chance. So they let me come."

Right about then something completely unforeseen happened to Jane's heart. She was overwhelmed by a strange happiness that she knew she ought to hide, but could not. She could not speak. The silence grew. She felt Springer there, but she could not look at him.

"Do you like it out here in the West?" he asked presently.

"Oh, I love it! I'll never want to leave it," she replied impulsively.

"I reckon I'm glad to hear you say that."

Then there fell another silence. He pressed closer to her and seemed now to be leaning against the horse. She wondered if he heard the thunderous knocking of her heart against her side.

"Will you be my wife an' stay here always?" he asked simply. "I'm in love with you. I've been lonely since my mother died. . . . You'll sure have to marry some of us. Because, as Tex says, if you don't, ranchin' can't go on much longer. These boys don't seem to get anywhere with you. Have I any chance—Jane?"

He possessed himself of her gloved hand and gave her a gentle tug. Jane knew it was gentle because she scarcely felt it. Yet it had irresistible power. She was swayed by that gentle pull. She moved into his arms.

A little later he smiled at her and said, "Jane, they call me Bill for short. Same as they call me boss. But my two front names are Frank Owens."

"Oh!" cried Jane. "Then you—"

"Yes, I'm the guilty one," he said happily. "It happened this way. My bedroom, you know is next to my office. I often heard the boys pounding the typewriter. I had a hunch they were up to some trick. So I spied upon them—heard about Frank Owens and the letters to the little schoolmarm.

At Beacon I got the postmistress to give me your address. And, of course, I intercepted some of your letters. It sure has turned out great."

"I—I don't know about you or those terrible cowboys," said Jane dubiously. "How did *they* happen on the name Frank Owens?"

"That's sure a stumper. I reckon they put a job up on me."

"Frank—tell me—did *you* write the—the love letters?" she asked appealingly. "There were two kinds of letters. That's what I never could understand."

"Jane, I reckon I did," he confessed. "Something about your little notes made me fall in love with you clear back there in Missouri. Does that make it all right?"

"Yes, Frank, I reckon it does—now," she said.

"Let's ride back home and tell the boys," said Springer gayly. "The joke's sure on them. I've corralled the little 'under-forty schoolmarm from Missouri.' "

Ananias Green

With the publication of "Chip of the Flying U" in 1904, B.M. Bower established a different kind of Western story from those published to that time—the realistic, often humorous adventures of working cowboys on a large cattle ranch. Born on just such a Montana ranch in 1871, the author knew whereof she wrote; her books about the Flying U (as well as other Westerns, many of the later ones with mystery and spy elements) appeared regularly at the rate of two per year until her death in 1940. Until recent years, the fact that B.M. (for Bertha Muzzy) Bower was a woman was a well-kept secret for obvious, if unjust, reasons.

"Ananias Green," a Flying U story, was first published in 1910.

PINK, because he knew well the country and because Irish, who also knew it well, refused point-blank to go into it again, rode alone except for his horses down into the range of the Rocking R. General roundup was about to start, and there was stock bought by the Flying U which ranged north of the Bear Paws.

The owner of the Rocking R was entertaining a party of friends at the ranch; friends quite new to the West and its ways, and they were intensely interested in all pertaining thereto. Pink gathered that much from the crew.

Sherwood Branciforte was down in the blacksmith shop at the Rocking R, watching Andy Green hammer a spur-shank straight. Andy was a tamer of wild ones, and he was hard upon his riding gear. Sherwood had that morning watched with much admiration the bending of that same spur-shank, and his respect for Andy was beautiful to behold.

"Lord, but this is a big, wild country," he was saying enthusiastically.

"Wild," said Andy. "Yes, you've got us sized up correct." He went on hammering, and humming under his breath.

"Oh, but I didn't mean that," the young man protested. "What I meant was breezy and picturesque. Life and men don't run in grooves."

"No, nor horses," assented Andy. He was remembering how that spur-shank had become bent.

"You did some magnificent riding this morning, by Jove! Strange that one can come out here into a part of the country absolutely new and raw—"

"Oh, it ain't so raw as you might think," Andy defended jealously, "nor yet new."

"Of course it is new! You can't," he said, "point to anything man-made that existed a hundred years ago; scarcely fifty, either. Your civilization is yet in the cradle—a lusty infant." Sherwood Branciforte had given lectures before the YMCA of his home town, and young ladies had spoken of him as *"gifted."*

Andy Green squinted at the shank before he made reply. Andy, also, was "gifted," in his modest Western way. "A country that can now and then show the papers for a civilization old as the Phoenixes of Egypt," he said, in a drawling tone that was absolutely convincing, "ain't what I'd call raw."

Andy decided that a little more hammering right next the rowel was necessary, and bent over the anvil solicitously. Even the self-complacency of Sherwood Branciforte could not fail to note his utter indifference. Branciforte was not accustomed to indifference. He blinked.

"My dear fellow, do you realize what that statement might seem to imply?" he said.

Andy, being a cowpuncher of the brand known as a "real," objected strongly both to the term and the tone. He stood up and stared down at the other disapprovingly. "I don't as a general thing find myself guilty of talking in my sleep. We ain't no infant-in-the-cradle, mister. We had civilization here when the Pilgrim Fathers' rock wasn't nothing but a pebble to let fly at the birds!"

"Indeed!" sneered Sherwood Branciforte.

Andy clicked his teeth together, which was a symptom it were well for the other to recognize but did not. Then Andy smiled, which was another symptom. He fingered the spur absently, laid it down and reached for his papers and tobacco sack.

"Of course, you mean all right, and you ain't none to blame for what you don't know, but you're talking wild. When you tell me I can't point to nothing man-made that's fifty years old, you make me feel sorry for yuh. I can take you to something that's older than swearing; and I reckon that art goes back a long ways."

"Are you crazy, man?" Sherwood Branciforte exclaimed incredulously.

"Not what you can notice. You wait while I explain. Once last fall I

was riding by my high lonesome away down next the river, when my horse
went lame on me from slipping on a shale bank, and I was set afoot. Uh
course, you being plumb ignorant of our picturesque life, you don't half
know all that might signify to imply." This last in open imitation of
Branciforte. "It implies that I was in one hell of a fix, to put it elegant.
I was sixty miles from anywhere, and them sixty half the time standing
one end and lapping over on themselves.

"So there I was, and I wasn't in no mood to view the beauties uh nature.
I was high and dry and the walking was about as poor as I ever seen; and
my boots was highheel and rubbed blisters before I'd covered a mile of
that territory. I wanted water, and I wanted it bad. Before I got it I wanted
it a heap worse." He stopped, cupped his slim fingers around a match
blaze.

Branciforte sat closer. He almost forgot the point at issue in the adventure.

"Along about dark, I camped for the night under a big, bare-faced cliff,
made a bluff at sleeping and cussed my bum luck. At sunup I rose and
wandered around like a dogy when it's first turned loose on the range. All
that day I perambulated over them hills, and I will say I wasn't enjoying
the stroll none. You're right when you say things can happen, out here.
Getting lost and afoot in the Badlands is one.

"That afternoon I dragged myself up to the edge of a deep coulee and
looked over to see if there was any way of getting down. There was a bright
green streak down there that couldn't mean nothing but water. And over
beyond, I could see the river that I'd went and lost. I looked and looked,
but the walls looked straight as a Boston's man's pedigree. And then the
sun come out from behind a cloud and lit up a spot that made me forget
for a minute that I was thirsty as a dog and near starved besides.

"I was looking down on the ruins—and yet it was near perfect—of an
old castle. Every stone stood out that clear and distinct I could have
counted 'em. There was a tower at one end, partly fell to pieces but yet
enough left to easy tell what it was. I could see it had kind of loopholes
in it. There was an open place where I took it the main entrance had used
to be; what I'd call the official entrance. But there was other entrances
besides, and some of 'em was made by time and hard weather. There was
what looked like a ditch running around my side of it, and a bridge. Uh
course, it was all needing repairs bad.

"I laid there for quite a spell looking it over. It didn't look to me like
it ought to be there at all, but in a school geography or a history."

"The deuce! A castle in the Badlands!" said Branciforte.

"That's what it was, all right. I found a trail it would make a mountain sheep seasick to follow, and I got down into the coulee. It was lonesome as sin, and spooky; but there was a good spring close by, and a creek running from it, and you can gamble I filled up on it a-plenty. Then I shot a rabbit or two that was hanging out around the ruins, and camped there till next day, when I found a pass out, and got my bearings by the river and come on into camp. So when you throw slurs on our plumb newness, I've got the cards to call yuh. That castle wasn't built last summer, Mister. And whoever did build it was some civilized. So there yuh are."

Andy took a last, lingering pull at the cigarette stub, flung it into the blackened forge, and picked up the spur. He settled his hat on his head, and started for the door and the sunlight.

"Oh, but say! Didn't you find out anything about it afterwards? There must have been something—"

"If it's relics uh the dim and musty past yuh mean, there was; relics to burn. I kicked up specimens of ancient dishes, and truck like that, while I was prowling around for firewood. And inside the castle, in what I reckon was used for the main hall, I run acrost a skeleton. That is, part of one."

"But, man alive, why haven't you made use of a discovery like that?" Branciforte followed him out, lighting his pipe with fingers that trembled. "Don't you realize what a thing like that means?"

Andy turned and smiled lazily down at him. "At the time I was there, I was all took up with the idea uh getting home. I couldn't *eat* skeletons, Mister, nor yet the remains uh prehistoric dishes. A man could starve to death while he examined it thorough. And so far as I know there ain't any record of it. I never heard no one mention building it, anyhow."

Andy stooped and adjusted the spur to his heel to see if it were quite right, and went off to the stable humming under his breath.

Branciforte stood at the door of the blacksmith shop and gazed after him, puffing meditatively at his pipe. "Lord! the ignorance of these Western folk! To run upon a find like that, and to think it less important than getting home in time for supper. To let a discovery like that lie forgotten, a mere incident in a day's travel! That fellow thinks more, right now, about his horse going lame and himself raising blisters on his heels, than of—Jove, what ignorance!"

Branciforte knocked his pipe gently against the doorcasing, put it into his coat pocket and hurried into the house.

That night the roundup pulled in to the home ranch.

The visitors, headed by their host, swooped down upon the roundup wagons just when the boys were gathered together for a cigarette or two apiece and a little talk before rolling in. There was no night guarding to do. Sherwood Branciforte hunted out Andy Green where he lay at ease with head and shoulders propped against a wheel of the bedwagon and gossipped with Pink and a few others.

"Look here, Green," he said in a voice to arrest the attention of the whole camp, "I wish you'd tell the others that tale you told me this afternoon—about that ruined castle down in the hills. Mason, here, is a newspaper man; he scents a story for his paper. And the rest refuse to believe a word I say."

"I'd hate to have a rep like that, Mr. Branciforte," Andy said, and turned his big, honest gray eyes to where stood the women—two breezy young persons with sleeves rolled to tanned elbows and cowboy hats of the musical comedy brand. Also they had gay silk handkerchiefs knotted picturesquely around their throats. There was another, a giggly, gurgly lady with gray hair fluffed up.

"Do tell us, Mr. Green," this young-old lady urged. "It sounds so romantic."

"It's funny you never mentioned it to any of us," put in the "Old Man" suspiciously.

Andy pulled himself up into a more decorous position, and turned his eyes towards his boss. "I never knew yuh took any interest in relic hunting," he explained mildly.

"Sherwood says you found a skeleton!" said the young-old lady, shuddering pleasurably.

"Yes, I did find one—or part of one," Andy admitted reluctantly.

"What were the relics of pottery like?" demanded one of the cowboy-hatted girls, as if she meant to test him. "I do some collecting of that sort of thing."

Andy threw away his cigarette, and with it all compunction. "Well, I wasn't so much interested in the dishes as in getting something to eat," he said. "I saw several different kinds. One was a big, awkward looking thing and was pretty heavy, and had straight sides. Then I come across one or two more that was ornamented some. One had what looked like a fish on it, and the other I couldn't make out very well. They didn't look to be worth much, none of 'em."

"Green," said his employer steadily, "was there such a place?"

Andy returned his look honestly. "There was, and there is yet, I guess," he said. "I'll tell you how you can find it and what it's like—if yuh doubt my word."

Andy glanced around and found every man, including the cook, listening intently. He picked a blade of new grass and began splitting it into tiny threads. The host found boxes for the women to sit upon, and the men sat down upon the grass.

"Before I come here to work, I was riding for the Circle C. One day I was riding away down in the Badlands alone and my horse slipped in some shale rock and went lame; strained his shoulder so I couldn't ride him. That put me afoot, and climbing up and down them hills I lost my bearings and didn't know where I was at for a day or two. I wandered around aimless, and got into a strip uh country that was new to me and plumb lonesome and wild.

"That second day is when I happened across this ruin. I was looking down into a deep, shut-in coulee, hunting water, when the sun come out and shone straight on to this place. It was right down under me; a stone ruin, with a tower on one end and kinda tumbled down so it wasn't so awful high—the tower wasn't. There was a-a—"

"Moat," Branciforte suggested.

"That's the word—a moat around it, and a bridge that was just about gone to pieces. It had loopholes, like the pictures of castles, and a—"

"Battlement?" ventured one of the musical-comedy cowgirls.

Andy had not meant to say battlement; of a truth, his conception of battlements was extremely hazy, but he caught up the word and warmed to the subject. "Battlement? Well I should guess yes! There was about as elegant a battlement as I'd want to see anywhere. It was sure a peach. It was—" he hesitated for a fraction of a second. "It was high as the tower, and it had figures carved all over it; them kind that looks like kid drawing in school, with bows and arrows stuck out in front of 'em, threatening—"

"Not the old Greek!" exclaimed one of the girls.

"I couldn't say as to that," Andy made guarded reply. "I never made no special study of them things. But they was sure old."

"About how large was the castle?" put in the man who wrote things. "How many rooms, say?"

"I'd hate to give a guess at the size. I didn't step it off, and I'm a poor guesser. The rooms I didn't count. I only explored around in the main hall, like, a little. But it got dark early, down in there, and I didn't have no matches to waste. And next morning I started right out at sunup to find the way home. No, I never counted the rooms. I don't reckon, though, that there was so awful many. Anyway, not more than fifteen or twenty. Ruins don't interest me much, though I was kinda surprised to run acrost that one, all right, and I'm willing to gamble there was warm and exciting times down there when the place was in running order."

"A castle away out here! Just think, good people, what that means! Romance, adventure and scientific discoveries! We must go and explore the place. Why can't we start at once—in the morning? This gentleman can guide us there."

"It ain't easy going," Andy remarked, conscientiously. "It's pretty rough; some place, you'd have to walk and lead your horses."

They swept aside the discouragement.

"We'd need pick and shovels, and men to dig," cried one enthusiast. "Uncle Peter can lend us some of his men. There may be treasure to unearth. There may be *anything* that is wonderful and mysterious. Uncle Peter, get your outfit together; you've boasted that a roundup can beat the army in getting under way quickly. Now let us have a practical demonstration. We want to start by six o'clock—all of us, with a cook and four or five men to do the excavating." It was the voice of the girl whom her friends spoke of as "the life of the party"—the voice of the-girl-who-does-things.

"It's sixty-five miles from here, good and strong—and mostly up and down," put in Andy.

" 'Quoth the raven!' " mocked the-girl-who-does-things. "We are prepared to face the ups and downs. Do we start at six, Uncle Peter?"

Uncle Peter glanced sideways at the roundup boss. To bring it to pass, he would be obliged to impress the roundup cook and part of the crew. It was breaking an unwritten law of the rangeland, and worse, it was doing something unbusinesslike and foolish. But not even the owner of the Rocking R may withstand the pleading of a pretty woman. Uncle Peter squirmed, but he promised.

"We start at six; earlier if you say so."

The roundup boss gave his employer a look of disgust and walked away. The crew took it that he went off to some secluded place to swear.

Thereafter there was much discussion of ways and means, and much enthusiasm among the visitors from the East, equalled by the depression of the crew, for cowboys do not, as a rule, take kindly to pick and shovel, and the excavators had not yet been chosen from among them. They were uneasy, and they stole frequent, betraying glances at one another.

All of which amused Pink much. Pink would like to have gone along, and would certainly have offered his services, but for the fact that his work there was done and he would have to start back to the Flying U just as soon as one of his best saddlehorses, which had cut its foot, was able to travel. That would be in a few days, probably. So Pink sighed and watched the preparations enviously.

Since he was fairly committed into breaking all precedents, Uncle Peter plunged recklessly. He ordered the messwagon to be restocked and prepared for the trip, and he took the bed-tent and half the crew. The foreman he wisely left behind with the remnant of his outfit. They were all to eat at the house while the messwagon was away, and they were to spread their soogans—which is to say beds—where they might, if the bunkhouses proved too small or too hot.

The foreman, outraged beyond words, saddled at daybreak and rode to the nearest town, and the unchosen half turned out in a body to watch the departure of the explorers, which speaks eloquently of their interest; for off duty cowboys are prone to sleep long.

Andy Green, as guide, bolted ahead of the party that he might open the gate. Bolted is a good word, for his horse swerved and kept on running, swerved again, and came down in a heap. Andy did not get up, and the women screamed. Then Pink and some others hurried out and bore Andy, groaning, to the bunkhouse.

The visitors from the East gathered, perturbed, around the door, sympathetic and dismayed. It looked very much as if their exploration must end where it began, and the-girl-who-does-things looked about to weep, until Andy, still groaning, sent Pink out to comfort them.

"He says you needn't give up the trip on his account," Pink announced musically from the doorway. "He's drawing a map and marking the coulee where the ruin is. He says most any of the boys that know the country at all can find the place for yuh. And he isn't hurt permanent; he strained his back so he can't ride, is all." Pink dimpled at the young-old lady who was admiring him frankly, and withdrew.

Inside, Andy Green was making pencil marks and giving the chosen half-explicit directions. At last he folded the paper and handed it to one called Sandy.

"That's the best I can do for yuh," Andy finished. "I don't see how yuh can miss it if yuh follow that map close. And if them gay females make any kick on the trail, you just remind 'em that I said all along it was rough going. So long, and good luck."

So with high-keyed, feminine laughter and much dust, passed the exploring party from the Rocking R.

"Say," Pink began two days later to Andy, who was sitting on the shady side of the bunkhouse staring absently at the skyline. "There's a word uh praise I've been aiming to give yuh. I've seen riding, and I've done a trifle in that line myself and learned some uh the tricks. But I want to say I never did see a man flop his horse any neater than you done that morning. I'll bet there ain't another man in the outfit got next your play. I couldn't uh done it better myself. Where did you learn that? Ever ride in Wyoming?"

Andy turned his eyes, but not his head—which was a way he had—and regarded Pink slantwise for at least ten seconds.

"Yes, I've rode in Wyoming," he answered quietly. "What's the chance for a job, up your way? Is the Flying U open for good men and true?"

"It won't cost yuh a cent to try," Pink told him. "How's your back? Think you'll be able to ride by the time Skeeter is able to travel?"

Andy grinned. "Say," he confided suddenly, "if that hoss don't improve plumb speedy, I'll be riding on ahead. I reckon I'll be able to travel before them explorers get back, my friend."

"Why?" Pink asked boldly.

"Why? Well, the going is some rough, down that way. If they get them wagons half way to the coulee marked with a cross, they'll sure have to attach wings onto 'em. I've been kind of worried about that. I don't much believe Uncle Peter is going to enjoy that trip and he sure does get irritable by spells. I've got a notion to ride for some other outfit, this summer."

"Was that the reason you threwed your horse down and got hurt?" asked Pink, and Andy grinned again by way of reply. "They'll be gone a week, best they can do," he estimated aloud. "We ought to be able to make our getaway by then, easy."

Pink assured him that a week would see them headed for the Flying U.

It was the evening of the sixth day, and the two were packed and ready to leave in the morning, when Andy broke off humming and gave a snort of dismay.

"By gracious, there they come. My mother lives in Buffalo, Pink, in a little drab house with white trimmings. Write and tell her how her son —Oh, beloved! But they're hitting her up lively. If they made the whole trip in that there frame uh mind, they could uh gone clean to Miles City and back. How pretty the birds sing! Pink, you'll hear words, directly."

Directly Pink did.

"You're the biggest liar on earth," Sherwood Branciforte contributed to the recriminating wave that near engulfed Andy Green. "You sent us down there on a wild-goose chase, you fool."

"I never sent nobody," Andy defended. "You was all crazy to go."

"And nothing but an old stone hut some trapper had built!" came an indignant, female tone. "There never was any castle, nor—"

"A man's home is his castle," argued Andy, standing unabashed before them. "Putting it that way, it was a castle, all right."

There was babel, out of which—

"And the skeleton! Oh, you—it was a dead cow!" This from the young-old lady, who was looking very draggled and not at all young.

"I don't call to mind ever saying it was human," put in Andy, looking at her with surprised, gray eyes.

"And the battlements!" groaned the-girl-who-does-things.

"You wanted battlements," Andy flung mildly into the uproar. "I always aim to please." With that he edged away from them and made his escape to where the cook was profanely mixing biscuits for supper. All-day moves had put an edge to his temper. The cook growled an epithet, and Andy passed on. Down near the stable he met one of the chosen half, and the fellow greeted him with a grin. Andy stopped abruptly.

"Say, they don't seem none too agreeable," he said, jerking his thumb toward the buzzing group. "How about it, Sandy? Was they that petulant all the way?"

Sandy, the mapbearer, chuckled. "It's lucky you got hurt at the last minute! And yet it was worth the trip. Uh course we got stalled with the wagons the second day out, but them women was sure ambitious and made us go on with a packadero layout. I will say that, going down, they stood the hardships remarkable. It was coming back that frazzled the party.

"And when we found the place—say, but it was lucky you wasn't along! They sure went hogwild when they seen the ruins. The old party who acts young displayed temper and shed tears uh rage. When she looked into the cabin and seen the remains uh that cowcritter, there was language it wasn't polite to overhear. She said a lot uh things about you, Andy. One thing they couldn't seem to get over, and that was the smallness uh the blamed shack. Them fourteen or fifteen rooms laid heavy on their minds."

"I didn't say there was fourteen or fifteen rooms. I said I didn't count the rooms; I didn't either. I never heard of anybody counting one room. Did you, Pink?"

"No," Pink agreed, "I never did!"

Sandy became suddenly convulsed. "Oh, but the funniest thing was the ancient pottery," he gasped, the tears standing in his eyes. "That old dutch oven was bad enough; but when one uh the girls—that one who collects old dishes—happened across an old mackerel can and picked it up and saw the fish on the label, she was the maddest female person I ever saw in my life, bar none. If you'd been in reach about that time, she'd just about clawed your eyes out, Andy Green. Oh me, oh my!" Sandy slapped his thigh and had another spasm.

Sounds indicated that the wave of recrimination was rolling nearer. Andy turned to find himself within arm's length of Uncle Peter.

"Maybe this is your idea of a practical joke, Green," he said to Andy. "But anyway, it will cost you your job. I ought to charge you up with the time my outfit has spent gallivanting around the country on the strength of your wild yarn. The quicker you hit the trail, the better it will suit me. By the way, what's your first name?" he asked, pulling out a checkbook.

"Andy," answered the unrepentant one.

"Andy." Uncle Peter paused with a fountain pen between his fingers. He looked Andy up and down, and the frown left his face. He proceeded to write out the check, and when it was done he handed it over with a pleased smile. "What did you do it for, Green?" he asked in a friendlier tone.

"Self-defense," Andy told him laconically, and turned away.

Half an hour later, Andy and Pink trailed out of the coulee that sheltered the Rocking R. When they were out and away from the fence, and Pink's horses, knowing instinctively that they were homeward bound, were jogging straight west without need of guidance. Andy felt in his pocket for cigarette material. His fingers came in contact with the check Uncle Peter had given him, and he drew it forth and looked it over again.

"Well, by gracious!" he said. "Uncle Peter thinks we're even, I guess."

He handed the check to Pink, and rolled his cigarette; and Pink after one comprehending look at the slip of paper, doubled up over his saddlehorse and shouted with glee—for the check was written: "Pay to the order of Ananias Green."

"And I've got to sign myself a liar, or I don't collect no money," sighed Andy. "That's what I call tough luck, by gracious!"

CLARENCE E. MULFORD

The Hold-up

Hopalong Cassidy has become something of a legendary name in Western
fiction, owing as much (if not more) to the films and radio and TV shows
of the thirties, forties and fifties than to the novels and stories that first
featured him. Certainly the character is more famous than his creator,
Clarence E. Mulford (1883–1956), an easterner who possessed a lifelong
fascination with the West. Hoppy first appeared in Bar-20 Days *in 1907,*
and, along with the Bar-20 bunch, continued his fictional adventures for
more than forty years. Originally published in 1913, "The Hold-up" is a
rousing, salty tale of Hoppy and the boys versus a band of train robbers.

THE BAGGAGE smoking car reeked with strong tobacco, the clouds of
smoke shifting with the air currents, and dimly through the haze could
be seen several men. Three of these were playing cards near the baggage
room door, while two more lounged in a seat half way down the aisle and
on the other side of the car. Across from the cardplayers, reading a
magazine, was a fat man, and near the water cooler was a dyspeptic-
looking individual who was grumbling about the country through which
he was passing.

The first five, as their wearing apparel proclaimed, were not of the kind
usually found on trains. The Bar-20's Spring drive was over, and these—
Hopalong Cassidy, Lanky Smith, Skinny Thompson, Billy Williams and
Red Connors—had accompanied the herd in the cattle cars from Sandy
Springs to the city, and were now returning.

They had enjoyed their relaxation in the city and now were returning
to the station where their horses were waiting to carry them over the two
hundred miles which lay between their ranch and the nearest railroad.

The city had been pleasant, but after they had spent several days there
it lost its charm and would not have been acceptable to them even as a
place in which to die. They had spent their money, smoked "top-notcher"
cigars, seen the shows and feasted each as his fancy dictated, and as
behooved cowpunchers with money in their pockets. Now they were glad
that every hour reduced the time of their stay in the smoky, jolting,

rocking train, for they did not like trains, and this train was particularly bad. So they passed the hours as best they might and waited impatiently for the stop at Sandy Creek, where they had left their horses.

The baggage room door opened and the conductor looked down on the cardplayers and grinned. Skinny Thompson moved over in the seat to make room for the genial conductor.

"Sit down, Simms, an' take a hand," he invited. Laughter arose continually and the fat man joined in it, leaning forward more closely to watch the play.

Lanky Smith tossed his cards face down on the board and grinned at the onlooker.

"Billy shore bluffs more on a variegated flush than any man I ever saw."

"Call him once in a while and he'll get cured of it," laughed the fat man, bracing himself as the train swung around a sharp turn.

"He's too smart," growled Billy Williams. "He tried that an' found I didn't have no variegated flushes. Come on, Lanky. If you're playing cards, put up."

Farther down the car, their feet resting easily on the seat in front of them, Hopalong Cassidy and Red Connors puffed slowly at their black cigars and spoke infrequently, both tired and lazy from doing nothing but ride.

A startling, sudden increase in the roar of the train and a gust of hot, sulphurous smoke caused Hopalong to look up at the brakeman, who came down the swaying aisle as the door slammed shut.

"Phew!" he exclaimed, genially. "Why in thunder don't you fellows smoke up?"

Hopalong blew a heavy ring, stretched energetically and grinned: "Much farther to Sandy Creek?"

"Oh, you don't get off for three hours yet," laughed the brakeman.

"That's shore a long time to ride this train," Red complained as the singing began again. "She shore pitches a-plenty," he added.

The train-hand smiled and seated himself on the arm of the front seat. "Oh, it might be worse."

"Not this side of hades," replied Red Connors.

"Say, you must be a pretty nifty gang on the shoot, ain't you?" the brakeman said.

"Oh, some," answered Hopalong.

"I wish you fellers had been aboard with us one day about a month ago. We was the wrong end of a holdup, and we got cleaned out proper, too."

"An' how many of 'em did you get?" asked Hopalong quickly, sitting bolt upright.

The brakeman was surprised. "How many did we get! Gosh! we didn't get none! They was six to our five."

"You didn't get none?" cried Hopalong, doubting his ears.

"I should say not!"

"An' they owned th' whole train?"

"They did."

Red Connors laughed. "Th' cleaning up must have been sumptuous an' elevating."

"Every time I holds threes he always has better," growled Lanky to Simms.

"On th' level, we couldn't do a thing," the brakeman ran on. "There's a water tank a little farther on, and they must 'a' climbed aboard there when we stopped to connect. When we got into the gulch the train slowed down and stopped and I started to get up to go out and see what was the matter; but I saw *that* when I looked down a gun barrel. The man at the throttle end of it told me to put up my hands, but they were up as high then as I could get 'em without climbin' on the top of the seat."

"Can't you listen and play at th' same time?" Lanky asked Billy.

"I wasn't countin' on takin' the gun away from him," the brakeman went on, "for I was too busy watchin' for the slug to come out of the hole. Pretty soon somebody on the outside whistled and then another feller come in the car; he was the one that did the cleanin' up. All this time there had been a lot of shootin' outside, but now it got worse. Then I heard another whistle and the engine puffed up the track, and about five minutes later there was a big explosion, and then our two robbers backed out of the car among the rocks shootin' back regardless. They busted a lot of windows."

"An' you didn't get any," grumbled Hopalong regretfully.

"When we got to the express car, what had been pulled around the turn," continued the brakeman, not heeding the interruption, "we found a wreck. And we found the engineer and fireman standin' over the express messenger, too scared to know he wouldn't come back no more. The car had been blowed up with dynamite, and his fighting soul went with it. He never knowed he was licked."

"An' nobody tried to help him!" Hopalong exclaimed, wrathfully now.

"Nobody wanted to die with him," replied the brakeman.

"Well," cried the fat man, suddenly reaching for his valise, "I'd like to see anybody try to hold me up!" Saying which he brought forth a small revolver.

"You'd be praying out of your bald spot about that time," muttered the brakeman.

Hopalong and Red Connors turned, perceived the weapon, and then exchanged winks.

"That's a fine shootin' iron, stranger," Hopalong remarked.

"You bet it is!" said the owner, proudly. "I paid six dollars for that gun."

Lanky Smith smothered a laugh and his friend grinned broadly. "I reckon that'd kill a man—if you stuck it in his ear."

"Pshaw!" snorted the dyspeptic scornfully. "You wouldn't have time to get it out of that grip. Think a train robber is going to let you unpack? Why don't you carry it in your hip pocket, where you can get at it quickly?"

There were smiles at the stranger's belief in the hip-pocket fallacy but no one commented upon it.

"Wasn't there no passengers aboard when you was stuck up?" Lanky Smith asked the conductor.

"Yes, but you can't count passengers in on a deal like that."

Hopalong Cassidy looked around aggressively. "We're passengers, ain't we?"

"You certainly are."

"Well, if any misguided maverick gets it into his fool head to stick us up, you see what happens. Don't you know th' fellers outside have all th' worst o' th' deal?"

"They have not!" cried the brakeman.

"They've got all the best of it," said the conductor emphatically. "I've been inside, and I know."

"Best nothing!" cried Hopalong. "They are on th' ground, watching a dangerline over a hundred yards long, full of windows and doors. Then they brace th' door of a car full of people. While they climb up the steps they can't see inside, an' then they go an' stick their heads in plain sight. It's an even break who sees th' other first, with th' men inside training their guns on th' glass in th' door!"

"Darned if you ain't right!" cried the fat man.

Hopalong laughed. "It all depends on th' men inside. If they ain't used to handling guns, 'course they won't try to fight. We've been in so many gun festivals that we wouldn't stop to think. If any coincollector went an' stuck his ugly face against th' glass in that door he'd turn a back-flip off'n th' platform before he knowed he was hit. Is there any chance for a stickup today?"

"Can't tell," said the brakeman. "But this is about the time we have the section camps' pay on board," he said, going into the baggage end of the car.

Simms leaned over close to Skinny Thompson. "It's on this train now, and I'm worried to death about it. I wish we were at Sandy Creek."

"Don't you go to worryin' none, then," the puncher replied. "It'll get to Sandy Creek all right."

Hopalong looked out of the window again and saw that there was a gradual change in the nature of the scenery, for the plain was becoming more broken each succeeding mile. Small woods occasionally hurtled past and banks of cuts flashed by like mottled yellow curtains, shutting off the view. Scrub timber stretched away on both sides, a billowy sea of green, and miniature valleys lay under the increasing number of trestles twisting and winding toward a high horizon.

Hopalong yawned again. "Well, it's none o' our funeral. If they let us alone I don't reckon we'll take a hand."

Red Connors laughed derisively. "Oh, no! Why, you couldn't sit still nohow with a fight going on, an' you know it. An' if it's a stickup! Wow!"

"Who gave you any say in this?" said Cassidy. "Anyhow, you ain't no angel o' peace, not nohow!"

"Mebby they'll plug your new sombrero," laughed Red.

Hopalong felt of the article in question.

"If any two-laigged wolf plugs my war bonnet he'll be some sorry, an' so'll his folks," he asserted, rising and going down the aisle for a drink.

Red Connors turned to the brakeman, who had just returned:

"Say," he whispered, "get off at th' next stop, shoot off a gun, an' yell, just for fun. Go ahead. It'll be better'n a circus."

"Nix on the circus, says I," hastily replied the other. "I ain't looking for no excitement. I hope we don't even run over a tracktorpedo this side of Sandy Creek."

Hopalong returned, and as he came even with them the train slowed.

"What are we stopping for?" he asked, his hand going to his holster.

"To take on water. The tank's right ahead."

"What have you got?" asked Billy Williams, ruffling his cards.

"None of yore business," replied Lanky Smith. "You call when you gets any curious."

"Oh, th' devil!" yawned Hopalong, leaning back lazily. "I shore wish I was on my cayuse pounding leather on th' home trail."

"Me, too," grumbled Red, staring out of the window. "Well, we're moving again. It won't be long now before we get out of this."

The card game continued, the low-spoken terms being interspersed with casual comment; Hopalong exchanged infrequent remarks with Red Connors, while the brakeman and conductor stared out of the same window. There was noticeable an air of anxiety, and the fat man tried to read his magazine with his thoughts far from the printed page.

"We're there now," the conductor said, as the bank of a cut blanked out the view. "It was right here where it happened. The turn's farther on."

"How many cards did you draw, Skinny?" asked Lanky Smith.

"Three; drawin' to a straight flush," laughed the dealer.

"Here's the turn! We're through all right," exclaimed the brakeman.

Suddenly there was a rumbling bump, a screeching of airbrakes and the grinding and rattle of couplings and pins as the train slowed down and stopped with a suddenness that snapped the passengers forward and back. The conductor and brakeman leaped to their feet, where the latter stood quietly during a moment of indecision.

A shot was heard and the conductor's hand, raised quickly to the whistle rope, sent blast after blast shrieking over the land.

A babel of shouting burst from the other coaches and, as the whistle shrieked without pause, a shot was heard close at hand and the conductor reeled suddenly and sank into a seat, limp and silent.

At the first jerk of the train the cardplayers threw the board from across their knees, scattering the cards over the floor, and crouching, gained the center of the aisle, intently peering through the windows, their Colts ready for instant use.

Hopalong and Red Connors were also in the aisle, and when the conductor had reeled Hopalong's Colt exploded and the man outside threw up his arms and pitched forward.

"Good boy, Hopalong!" cried Skinny Thompson, who was fighting mad.

Hopalong wheeled and crouched, watching the door. It was not long before a masked face appeared on the farther side of the glass. Hopalong fired and a splotch of red stained the white mask as the robber fell against the door and slid to the platform.

"Hear that shooting?" cried the brakeman. "They're at the messenger. They'll blow him up!"

"Come on, fellers!" cried Hopalong, leaping toward the door, followed closely by his friends.

They stepped over the obstruction on the platform and jumped to the ground on the side of the car farthest from the robbers.

"Shoot under the cars for legs," whispered Skinny Thompson. "That'll bring 'em down where we can get 'em."

"Which is a good idea," replied Red Connors, dropping quickly and looking under the car.

"Somebody's going to be surprised, all right," Hopalong said.

The firing on the other side of the train was heavy, being for the purpose of terrifying the passengers and to forestall concerted resistance. The robbers could not distinguish between the many reports and did not know they were being opposed, or that two of their number were dead.

A whinny reached Hopalong's ears and he located it in a small grove ahead of him. "Well, we know where th' cayuses are in case they make a break."

A white, scared face peered out of the cab window and Hopalong stopped his finger just in time, for the inquisitive man wore the cap of a fireman.

"You idiot!" muttered Cassidy angrily. "Get back!" he ordered.

A pair of legs ran swiftly along the other side of the car and Red and Skinny Thompson fired instantly. The legs bent, their owner falling forward behind the rear truck, where he was screened from sight.

"They had it their own way before!" gritted Skinny. "Now we'll see if they can stand iron!"

By this time Hopalong and Red Connors were crawling under the express car and were so preoccupied that they did not notice the faint blue streak of smoke immediately over their heads. Then Red Connors glanced up, saw the glowing end of a three-inch fuse, and blanched. It was death not to dare and his hand shot up and back, and the dynamite cartridge sailed far behind him to the edge of the embankment, where it hung on a bush.

"Good!" panted Hopalong. "We'll pay 'em for that!"

"They're worse'n rustlers!"

They could hear the messenger running about over their heads, dragging and upending heavy objects against the doors of the car, and Hopalong laughed grimly.

"Luck's with this messenger, all right."

"It ought to be—he's a fighter."

"Where are they? Have they tumbled to our game?"

"They're waiting for the explosion, you chump."

"Stay where you are then. Wait till they come out to see what's th' matter with it."

Red snorted, "Wait nothing!"

"All right, then; I'm with you. Get out of my way."

"I've been in situations some peculiar, but this beats 'em all," Red Connors chuckled, crawling forward.

The robber by the car truck revived enough to realize that something was radically wrong, and shouted a warning as he raised himself on his elbow to fire at Skinny Thompson but the alert puncher shot first.

As Hopalong and Red Connors emerged from beneath the car and rose to their feet there was a terrific explosion and they were knocked to the ground, while a sudden, heavy shower of stones and earth rained down over everything. The two punchers were not hurt and they arose to their feet in time to see the engineer and fireman roll out of the cab and crawl along the track on their hands and knees, dazed and weakened by the concussion.

Suddenly, from one of the day coaches, a masked man looked out, saw the two punchers, and cried: "It's all up! Save yourselves!"

As Hopalong and Red Connors looked around, still dazed, he fired at them, the bullet singing past Hopalong's ear. Red smothered a curse and reeled as his friend grasped him. A wound over his right eye was bleeding profusely and Hopalong's face cleared of its look of anxiety when he realized that it was not serious.

"They creased you! Blamed near got you for keeps!" he cried, wiping away the blood with his sleeve.

Red Connors, slightly stunned, opened his eyes and looked about confusedly. "Who done that? Where is he?"

"Don't know, but I'll shore find out," Hopalong replied. "Can you stand alone?"

Red pushed himself free and leaned against the car for support: "Course I can! Get that cuss!"

When Skinny Thompson heard the robber shout the warning he wheeled and ran back, intently watching the windows and doors of the car for trouble.

"We'll finish yore tally right here!" he muttered.

When he reached the smoker he turned and went towards the rear, where he found Lanky Smith and Billy Williams lying under the platform.

Billy was looking back and guarding their rear, while his companion watched the clump of trees where the second herd of horses was known to be.

Just as they were joined by their foreman, they saw two men run across the track, fifty yards distant and into the grove, both going so rapidly as to give no chance for a shot at them.

"There they are!" shouted Skinny, opening fire on the grove.

At that instant Hopalong turned the rear platform and saw the brakeman leap out of the door with a Winchester in his hands. The puncher sprang up the steps, wrenched the rifle from its owner, and, tossing it to Skinny Thompson, cried: "Here, this is better!"

"Too late," grunted the puncher, looking up, but Hopalong had become lost to sight among the rocks along the right of way. "If I only had this a minute ago!" he grumbled.

The men in the grove, now in the saddle, turned and opened fire on the group by the train, driving them back to shelter. Skinny, taking advantage of the cover afforded, ran towards the grove, ordering his friends to spread out and surround it; but it was too late, for at that minute galloping was heard and it grew rapidly fainter.

Red Connors appeared at the end of the train. "Where's th' rest of the coyotes?"

"Two of 'em got away," Lanky Smith replied.

"Ya-ho!" shouted Hopalong from the grove. "Don't none of you fools shoot! I'm coming out. They plumb got away!"

"They near got *you*, Red," Skinny cried.

"Nears don't count," Red Connors laughed.

"Did you ever notice Hopalong when he's fighting mad?" asked Lanky, grinning at the man who was leaving the woods. "He always wears his sombrero hanging on one ear. Look at it now!"

"Who touched off that cannon some time back?" asked Billy Williams.

"I did. It was an anti-gravity cartridge what I found sizzling on a rod under th' floor of th' express car," replied Red.

"Why didn't you pinch out th' fuse 'stead of blowing everything up, you half-breed?" Lanky asked.

"I reckon I was some hasty," grinned Red.

"It blowed me under th' car an' my lid through a windy," cried Billy. "An' Skinny, he went up in th' air like a shore-'nough grasshopper."

Hopalong joined them, grinning broadly "Hey, reckon ridin' in th' cars ain't so bad after all, is it?"

"Holy smoke!" cried Skinny. "What's that a-popping?"

Hopalong, Colt in hand, leaped to the side of the train and looked along it, the others close behind him, and saw the fat man with his head and arm out of the window, blazing away into the air, which increased the panic in the coaches. Hopalong grinned and fired into the ground, and the fat man nearly dislocated parts of his anatomy by his hasty disappearance.

"Reckon he plumb forgot all about his fine six-dollar gun till just now," Skinny Thompson laughed.

"Oh, he's making good," Red Connors replied. "He said he'd take a hand if anything busted loose. It's a good thing he didn't come to life while me an' Hoppy was under his window looking for legs."

"Reckon some of us better go in th' cars an' quiet th' stampede," Skinny Thompson remarked, mounting the steps, followed by Hopalong. "They're shore *loco.*"

The uproar in the coach ceased abruptly when the two punchers stepped through the door, the inmates shrinking into their seats, frightened into silence.

Skinny and his companion did not make a reassuring sight, for they were grimy with burned powder and dust, and Hopalong's sleeve was stained with Red's blood.

"Oh, my jewels," sobbed a woman, staring at Skinny and wringing her hands.

"Ma'am, we shore don't want your jewelry," replied Skinny, earnestly. "Calm yoreself; we don't want nothin'."

"*I* don't want that!" growled Hopalong, pushing a wallet from him. "How many times do you want us to tell you we don't want nothin'? We ain't robbers, we licked th' robbers."

Suddenly he stopped and, grasping a pair of legs which protruded into the aisle obstructing the passage, straightened up and backed towards Red Connors, who had just entered the car, dragging into sight a portly gentleman, who kicked and struggled and squealed, as he grabbed at the stanchions of seats to stay his progress. Connors stepped aside between two seats and let his friend pass, and then leaned over and grasped the portly gentleman's coat collar. He tugged energetically and lifted the frightened man clear of the aisle and deposited him across the back of a seat, face down, where he hung balanced, yelling and kicking.

"Shut your face, you cave hunter!" cried Red Connors in disgust. "Stop that infernal noise! You fat fellers make all your noise after th' fighting is all over!"

The man on the seat, suddenly realizing what a sight he made, rolled off his perch and sat up, now more angry than frightened. He glared at Red's grinning face and sputtered: "It's an outrage! It's an outrage! I'll have you hung for this day's work, young man!"

"That's right," grinned Hopalong. "He shore deserves it. I told him more'n once that he'd get strung up some day."

"Yes, and you, too!"

"Please don't," begged Hopalong. "I don't want t' die!"

Fuming impotently, the portly gentleman fled into the smoker.

"I'll bet he had a six-dollar gun, too," laughed Red.

"I'll bet he's calling himself names right about now," Hopalong replied.

Then he turned to reply to a woman. "Yes, ma'am, we did. But they wasn't real badmen."

At this a pretty young woman arose and ran to Hopalong Cassidy and, impulsively throwing her arms around his neck, cried: "You brave man! You hero! You dear!"

He made frantic efforts to keep his head back. "Ma'am!" he cried, desperately. "Leggo, ma'am! Leggo!"

Just then the brakeman entered the car, grinning, and Skinny Thompson asked about the condition of the conductor.

"Oh, he's all right now," the brakeman replied. "They shot him throught the arm, but he's repaired and out bossin' the job of clearin' the rocks off the track. He's a little shaky yet, but he'll come around all right."

"That's good. I'm shore glad to hear it."

"Won't you wear this pin as a small token of my gratitude?" asked a voice at Skinny's shoulder.

He wheeled and raised his sombrero, a flush stealing over his face: "Thank you, ma'am, but I don't want no pay. We was plumb glad to do it."

"But this is not pay! It's just a trifling token of my appreciation of your courage, just something to remind you of it. I shall feel hurt if you refuse."

Her quick fingers had pinned it to Thompson's shirt while she spoke and he thanked her as well as his embarrassment would permit. Then there was a rush toward him and, having visions of a shirt looking like a jeweler's window, he turned and fled from the car, crying: "Pin 'em on th' brakeman!"

He found the outfit working at a pile of rocks on the track, under the supervision of the conductor, and Hopalong looked up apprehensively at Skinny's approach.

"Lord!" Thompson ejaculated, grinning sheepishly, "I was some scairt you was a woman." Then, turning to the conductor: "How do you feel, Simms?"

"Oh, I'm all right, but it took the starch out of me for a while."

"Well, I don't wonder, not a bit."

"You fellows certainly don't waste any time getting busy," Simms laughed.

"That's the secret of gun fightin'," replied Skinny Thompson.

"Well, you're a fine crowd all right. Any time you want to go any place when you're broke, climb aboard my train and I'll see't you get there."

"Much obliged."

Simms turned to the express car. "Hey, Jackson! You can open up now if you want to."

But the express messenger was suspicious, fearing that the conductor was talking with a gun at his head.

"You go to hell!" he called back.

"Honest!" laughed Simms. "Some cowboy friends o' mine licked the gang. Didn't you hear that dynamite go off? If they hadn't fished it out from under your feet you'd be communing with the angels 'bout now."

For a moment there was no response, and then Jackson could be heard dragging things away from the door. When he was told of the cartridge and Red Connors had been pointed out to him as the man who had saved his life, he leaped to the ground and ran to where that puncher was engaged in carrying the ever-silenced robbers to the baggage car. He shook hands with Red Connors, who laughed deprecatingly, and then turned and assisted him.

Hopalong came up and grinned. "Say, there's some cayuses in that grove up th' track. Shall I go up an' get 'em?"

"Shore! I'll go an' get 'em with you," replied Skinny Thompson.

In the grove they found seven horses picketed, two of them being pack animals, and they led them forth and reached the train as the others came up.

"Well, here's five saddled cayuses an' two others," Skinny grinned.

"Then we can ride th' rest of th' way in th' saddle instead of in that blamed train," Red Connors eagerly suggested.

"That's just what we can do," replied Skinny. "Leather beats car seats any time. How far are we from Sandy Creek, Simms?"

"About twenty miles."

"An' we can ride along th' track, too," said Hopalong.

Hopalong and the others had mounted and were busy waving their sombreros and bowing to the heads and handkerchiefs which were decorating the car windows.

"All aboard!" shouted the conductor, and cheers and good wishes rang out and were replied to by bows and waving of sombreros.

Then Hopalong jerked his gun loose and emptied it into the air, his companions doing likewise. Suddenly five reports rang out from the smoker and they cheered the fat man as he waved at them. They sat quietly and watched the train until the last handkerchief became lost to sight around curve, but the screeching whistle could be heard for a long time.

"Gee!" laughed Hopalong Cassidy as they rode on after the train, "won't the fellers home on the ranch be a whole lot sore when they hear about the good time what they missed!"

EMERSON HOUGH

Science at Heart's Desire

Emerson Hough (1857–1923) was one of the great early masters of the Western story. Trained as a lawyer, he rarely practiced this trade, concentrating instead on editing positions with such journals as Field and Stream *and* The Saturday Evening Post. *Primarily, though, he was a writer of the west, and left us such wonderful works as* The Singing Mouse Stories, *the nonfiction* The Story of the Cowboy, *and excellent historical westerns like* North of Thirty-six. *But his masterpiece remains his novel,* The Covered Wagon, *one of the great works on the movement west and the basis for the famous silent film of the same name.*

"THAT OLD RAILROAD'LL shore bust me up a heap if it ever does git in here," remarked Tom Osby one morning in the forum of Whiteman's corral, where the accustomed group was sitting in the sun, waiting for some one to volunteer as Homer for the day.

There was little to do but listen to story telling, for Tom Osby dwelt in the tents of Kedar, delaying departure on his accustomed trip to Vegas.

"A feller down there to Sky Top," he went on, arousing only the most indolent interest, "one of them spy-glass ingineers—tenderfoot, with his six-shooter belt buckled so tight he couldn't get his feet to the ground— he says to me I might as well trade my old grays for a nice new checkerboard, or a deck of author cards, for I won't have nothing to do but just amuse myself when the railroad cars gets here."

No one spoke. All present were trying to imagine how Heart's Desire would seem with a railroad train each day.

"Things'll be some different in them days, mebbe *so.*" Tom recrossed his legs with well-considered deliberation.

"There's a heap of things different already from what they used to be when I first hit the cow range," said Curly. "The whole country's changed, and it ain't changed for the better, either. Grass is longer, and horns is shorter, and men is triflin'er. Since the Yankees has got west of the Missouri River, a ranch foreman ain't allowed to run his own brandin' iron any more, and that takes more'n half the poetry out of the cow business, don't it, Mac?" This to McKinney, who was nearly asleep.

"Everything else is changin', too," Curly continued, gathering fluency as memories began to crowd upon him. "Look at the lawyers and doctors there is in the Territory now—and this country used to be respectable. Why, when I first come here, there wasn't a doctor within a thousand miles, and no need for one. If one of the boys got shot up much, we always found some way to laundry him and sew him together again without no need of a diplomy. No one ever got sick; and, of course, no one ever did die of his own accord, the way they do back in the States."

"What's it all about, Curly?" drawled Dan Anderson. "You can't tell a story worth a cent." Curly paid no attention to him.

"The first doctor that ever come out here for to alleviate us fellers," he went on, "why, he settled over on the Sweetwater. He was a allopath from Bitter Creek. What medicine that feller did give! He gradual drifted into the vet'inary line.

"Then there come a homeopath—that was after a good many women-folk had settled in along the railroad over west. Still, there wasn't much sickness, and I don't reckon the homeopath ever did winter through. I was livin' with the Bar-T outfit on the Oscura range, at that time.

"Next doctor that come along was a ostypath." Curly took a chew of tobacco, and paused a moment reflectively.

"I said the first feller drifted into vet'inary lines, didn't I?" he resumed. "Well, the ostypath did, too. Didn't you never hear about that? Why, he ostypathed a horse!"

"Did *what?*" asked Tom Osby, sitting up; for hitherto there had seemed no need to listen attentively.

"Yes, sir," he went on, "he ostypathed a horse for us. The boys they gambled about two thousand dollars on that horse over at Socorro. It was a cross-eyed horse, too."

"What's that?" Doc Tomlinson objected. "There never was such a thing as a cross-eyed horse."

"Oh, there wasn't, wasn't there?" said Curly. "Well, now, my friend, when you talk that-a-way, you simply show me how much you don't know about horses. This here Bar-T horse was as cross-eyed as a sawhorse, until we got him ostypathed. But, of course, if you don't believe what I say, there's no use tellin' you this story at all."

"Oh, go on, go on," McKinney spoke up, "don't pay no attention to doc."

"Well," Curly resumed, "that there horse was knowed constant on this range for over three years. He was a outlaw, with cream mane and tail, and a *pinto* map of Europe, Asia and Africa wrote all over his ribs. Run? Why, that horse could run down a coyote as a moral pastime. We used him to catch jackrabbits with, between meals. It wasn't no trouble for him to *run*. The trouble was to tell when he was goin' to *stop* runnin'. Sometimes it was a good while before the feller ridin' him could get him around to where he begun to run. He run in curves natural, and he handed out a right curve or a left one, just as he happened to feel, same as the feller dealin' faro, and just as easy.

"Tom Redmond, on the Bar T, he got this horse from a feller by the name of Hasenberg, that brought in a bunch of a has-beens and outlaws, and allowed to distribute 'em in this country. Hasenberg was a foreign gent that looked a good deal like Whiteman, our distinguished feller citizen here. He was cross-eyed hisself, body and soul. There wasn't a straight thing about him. We allowed that maybe this pinto *caballo* got cross-eyed from associatin' with old Hasenberg, who was strictly on the bias, any way you figured."

"You ain't so bad, after all, Curly," said Dan Anderson, sitting up. "You're beginning now to hit the human interest part. You ought to be a reg'lar contributor."

"Shut up!" said Curly. "Now Tom Redmond, he took to this here pinto horse from havin' seen him jump the corral fence several times, and start floatin' off across the country for a eight or ten mile sashay without no special encouragement. He hired three Castilian busters to operate on pinto, and he got so he could be rode occasional, but every one allowed they never did see any horse just like him. He was the most aggravatinest thing we ever did have on this range. He had a sort of odd-lookin' white eye, but a heap of them pintos has got glass eyes, and so no one thought to examine his lookers very close, though it was noticed early in the game that pinto might be lookin' one way and goin' the other, at the same time. He'd be goin' on a keen lope, and then something or other might get on his mind, and he'd stop and untangle hisself from all kinds of ridin'. Sometimes he'd jump and snort like he was seein' ghosts. A feller on that horse could have roped antelopes as easy as yearlin' calves, if he could just have told which way Mr. Pinto was goin'.; but he was a shore hard one to estermate.

"At last Tom, why, he suspected somethin' wasn't right with pinto's lamps. If you stuck out a bunch of hay at him, he couldn't bite it by about five feet. When you led him down to water, you had to go sideways; and if you wanted to get him in through the corral gate, you had to push him in backward. We discovered right soon that he was born with his parallax or something out of gear. His graduated scale of seein' things was different from our'n. I don't reckon anybody ever will know what all pinto saw with them glass lamps of his, but all the time we knowed that if we could ever onct get his lookin' outfit turned up proper, we had the whole country skinned in a horse race; for he could shore run copious.

"That was why he had the whole Bar-T outfit guessin' all the time. We all wanted to bet on him, and we was all scared to. Sometimes we'd make up a purse among us, and we'd go over to some social gatherin' or other and win a thousand dollars. Old pinto could run all day; he can yet, for that matter. Didn't make no difference to him how often we raced him; and natural, after we'd won one hatful of money with him, we'd want to win another. That was where our judgment was weak.

"You never could tell whether pinto was goin' to finish under the wire, or out in the landscape. His eyes seemed to be sort of moverable, but like enough they'd get sot when he went to runnin'. Then he'd run whichever way he was lookin' at the time, or happened to think he was lookin'; and dependin' additional on what he thought he saw. And law! A whole board of supervisors and school commissioners couldn't have looked that horse in the face, and guessed on their sacred honor whether he was goin' to jump the fence to the left or take to the high sage on the outside of the track.

"Oncet in a while we'd git pinto's left eye set at a angle, and he'd come around the track and under the wire before she wobbled out of place. On them occasions we made money a heap easier than I ever did a-gettin' it from home. But, owin' to the looseness of them eyes, I don't reckon there never was no horse racin' as uncertain as this here; and like enough you may have observed it's uncertain enough even when things is fixed in the most comf'terble way possible."

A deep sigh greeted this, which showed that Curly's audience was in full sympathy.

"You always felt like puttin' the saddle on to pinto hind end to, he was so cross-eyed," he resumed ruminatingly, "but still you couldn't help feelin' sorry for him, neither. Now, he had a right pained and grieved look in his face all the time. I reckon he thought this was a hard sort of a world to get along in. It is. A cross-eyed man has a hard enough time, but a cross-eyed *horse*—well, you don't know how much trouble he can be for hisself and every one else around him.

"Now, here we was, fixed up like I told you. Mr. Allopath is over on Sweetwater creek, Mr. Homeopath is maybe in the last stages of starvation. Old pinto looks plumb hopeless, and all us fellers is mostly hopeless too, owin' to his uncertain habits in a horse race, yet knowin' that it ain't perfessional for us not to back a Bar-T horse that can run as fast as this one can.

"About then along come Mr. Ostypath. This was just about thirty days before the county fair at Socorro, and there was money hung up for horse races over there that made us feel sick to think of. We knew we could go out of the cowpunchin' business for good if we could just only onct get pinto over there, and get him to run the right way for a few brief moments.

"Was he game? I don't know. There never was no horse ever got clost enough to him in a horse race to tell whether he was game or not. He might not get back home in time for supper, but he would shore run industrious. Say, I talked in a telyphome onct. The book hung on the box said the telyphome was instantaneous. It ain't. But now this pinto, he was a heap more instantaneous than a telyphome.

"As I was sayin', it was long about now Mr. Ostypath comes in. He talks with the boss about locatin' around in here. Boss studies him over a while, and as there ain't been anybody sick for over ten years, he tries to break it to Mr. Ostypath gentle that the Bar T ain't a good place for a doctor. They have some conversation along in there, that-a-way, and Mr. Ostypath before long gets the boss interested deep and plenty. He says there ain't no such a thing as gettin' sick. We all knew that before; but he certainly floors the lot when he allows that the reason a feller don't feel good, so as he can eat tenpenny nails, and make a million dollars a year, is always because there is something wrong with his osshus structure.

"He says the only thing that makes a feller have rheumatism, or dyspepsia, or headache, or nosebleed, or red hair, or any other sickness, is that something is wrong with his nervous system. Now, it's this-a-way. He allows them nerves is like a bunch of garden hose. If you put your foot on the hose, the water can't run right free. If you take it off, everything's lovely. 'Now,' says Mr. Ostypath, "if, owin' to some luxation, some lee-shun, some temporary mechanical disarrangement of your osshus structure, due to a oversight of a All-wise Providence, or maybe a fall off'n a buckin' horse, one of them bones of yours gets to pressin' on a nerve, why, it ain't natural you *ought* to feel good. Now, *is* it?' says he.

"He goes on and shows how all up and down a feller's backbone there is plenty of soft spots, and he shows likewise that there is scattered around in different parts of a feller's territory something like two hundred and four and a half bones, any one of which is likely any minute to jar loose and go to pressin' on a soft spot; 'In which case,' says he, 'there is need of a ostypath immediate.'

" 'For instance,' he says to me, 'I could make quite a man out of you in a couple of years if I had the chanct.' I ast him what his price would be for that, and he said he was willin' to tackle it for about fifty dollars a month. That bein' just five dollars a month more than the boss was allowin' me at the time, and me seein' I'd have to go about two years without anything to wear or eat—let alone anything to drink—I had to let this chanct go by. I been strugglin' along, as you know, ever since, just like this, some shopworn, but so's to set up. There was one while, I admit, when the doc made me some nervous, when I thought of all them soft spots in my spine, and all them bones liable to get loose any minute and go to pressin' on them. But I had to take my chances, like any other cow puncher at forty-five a month."

"You ought to raise his wages, Mac," said Doc Tomlinson to McKinney, the ranch foreman, but the latter only grunted.

"Mr. Ostypath, he stayed around the Bar T quite a while," began Curly again, "and we got to talkin' to him a heap about modern science. Says he, one evenin', this-a-way to us fellers, says he, 'Why, a great many things goes wrong because the nervous system is interfered with, along of your osshus structure. You think your stomach is out of whack,' says he. 'It ain't. All it needs is more nerve supply. I git that by loosenin' up the bones in your back. Why, I've cured a heap of rheumatism, and paralysis, and cross-eyes, and—'

" 'What's that?' says Tom Redmond, right sudden.

" 'You heard me, sir,' says the doc, severe.

"Tom, he couldn't hardly wait, he was so bad struck with the idea he had. 'Come here, doc,' says he. And then him and doc walked off a little ways and begun to talk. When they come up toward us again, we heard the doc sayin': 'Of course I could cure him. Straybismus is dead easy. I never did operate on no horse, but I've got to eat, and if this here is the only patient in this whole blamed country, why I'll have to go you, if it's only for the sake of science,' says he. Then we all bunched in together and drifted off toward the corral, where old pinto was standin', lookin' hopeless and thoughtful. 'Is this the patient?' says the doc, sort of sighin'.

" 'It are,' says Tom Redmond.

"Doc he walks up to old pinto, and has a look at him, frontways, sideways and all around. Pinto raises his head up, snorts, and looks doc full in the face; leastwise, if he'd 'a' been any other horse, he'd 'a' been lookin' him full in the face. Doc he stands thoughtful for quite a while, and then he goes and kind of runs his hand up and down along pinto's spine. He growed plumb enthusiastic then. 'Beautiful subject,' says he. 'Be-*yoo*-tiful ostypathic subject! Whole osshus structure exposed!' And pinto shore was a dream if bones was needful in the game."

Curly paused for another chew of tobacco, then went on again.

"Well, it's like this, you see; the backbone of a man or a horse is full of little humps—you can see that easy in the springtime. Now old pinto's back, it looked liked a topygraphical survey of the whole Rocky Mountain range.

"Doc he runs his hand up and down along this high divide, and says he, 'Just like I thought,' says he. 'The patient has suffered a distinct leeshun in the immediate vicinity of his vaseline motor centers.' "

"You mean the vasomotor centers," suggested Dan Anderson.

"That's what I said," said Curly, aggressively.

"Now, when we all heard doc say them words, we knowed he was shore scientific, and we come up clost while the examination was progressin'.

" 'Most extraordinary,' says doc, feelin' some more. 'Now, here is a distant luxation in the lumber regions.' He talked like pinto had a wooden leg.

" 'I should diagnose great cerebral excitation, along with pernounced ocular hesitation,' says doc at last.

" 'Now look here, doc,' says Tom Redmond to him then. 'You go careful. We all know there's something strange about this here horse; but now, if he's got any bone pressin' on him anywhere that makes him *run* the way he does, why, you be blamed careful not to monkey with that there particular bone. Don't you touch his *runnin'* bone, because *that's* all right the way it is.'

" 'Don't you worry any,' says the doc. 'All I should do would only increase his nerve supply. In time I could remedy his ocular defecks, too,' says he. He allows that if we will give him time, he can make pinto's eyes straighten out so's he'll look like a new rockin' horse Christmas mornin' at a church festerval. Incidentally he suggests that we get a tall leather blinder and run it down pinto's nose, right between his eyes.

"This last was what caught us most of all. 'This here blinder idea,' says Tom Redmond, 'is plumb scientific. The trouble with us cowpunchers is we ain't got no brains—or we wouldn't be cowpunchers! Now look here, pinto's right eye looks off to the left, and his left eye looks off to the right. Like enough he sees all sorts of things on both sides of him, and gets 'em mixed. Now, you put this here harness leather between his eyes, and his right eye looks plumb into it on one side, and his left eye looks into it on the other. Result is, he can't see nothing at *all!* Now, if he'll only run when he's *blind,* why, we can skin them Socorro people till it seems like a shame.'

"Well, right then we all felt money in our pockets. We seemed most too good to be out ridin' sign, or pullin' old cows out of mudholes. 'You leave all that to me,' says doc. 'By the time I've worked on this patient's nerve centers for a while, I'll make a new horse out of him. You watch me,' says he. That made us all feel cheerful. We thought this wasn't such a bad world, after all.

"We passed the hat in the interest of modern science, and we fenced off a place in the corral and set up a school of ostypathy in our midst. Doc, he done some things that seemed to us right strange at first. He gets pinto up in one corner and takes him by the ear, and tries to break his neck, with his foot in the middle of his back. Then he goes around on the other side and does the same thing. He hammers him up one side and down the other, and works him and wiggles him till us cowpunchers thought he was goin' to scatter him around worse than Cassybianca on the burnin' deck after the exploshun. My experience, though, is that it's right hard to shake a horse to pieces. Pinto, he stood it all right. And say, he got so gentle, with that tall blinder between his eyes, that he'd 'a' followed off a sheepherder.

"All this time we was throwin' oats a-plenty into pinto, rubbin' his legs down, and gettin' him used to a saddle a little bit lighter than a regular cow saddle. Doc, he allows he can see his eyes straightenin' out every day. 'I ought to have a year on this job,' says he; 'but these here is urgent times.'

"I should say they was urgent. The time for the county fair at Socorro was comin' right clost.

"At last we takes the old Hasenberg pinto over to Socorro to the fair, and there we enters him in everything from the front to the back of the racin' book. My friends, you would 'a' shed tears of pity to see them folks fall down over theirselves tryin' to hand us their money against old pinto. There was horses there from Montanny to Arizony, all kinds of fancy riders, and money—oh, law! Us Bar-T fellers, we took everything offered —put up everything we had, down to our spurs. Then we'd go off by ourselves and look at each other solemn. We was gettin' rich so quick we felt almost scared.

"There come nigh to bein' a little shootin' just before the horses was gettin' ready for the first race, which was for a mile and a half. We led old pinto out, and some feller standin' by, he says sarcastic like, "What's that I see comin'; a snowplow?' Him alludin' to the single blinder on pinto's nose.

" 'I reckon you'll think it's been snowin' when we get through,' says Tom Redmond to him, scornful. 'The best thing you can do is to shut up, unless you've got a little money you want to contribute to the Bar-T festerval.' But about then they hollered for the horses to go to the post, and there wasn't no more talk.

"Pinto, he acted meek and humble, just like a glass-eyed angel, and the starter didn't have no trouble with him at all. At last he got them all off, so clost together one saddle blanket would have done for the whole bunch. Say, man, that was a fine start.

"Along with oats and ostypathy, old pinto he'd come out on the track that day just standin' on the edges of his feet, he was feelin' that fine. We put José Santa Maria Trujillo, one of our lightest boys, up on pinto for to ride him. Now a greaser ain't got no sense. It was that fool boy José that busted up modern science on the Bar T.

"I was tellin' you that there horse was ostypathed, so to speak, plumb to a razor edge, and I was sayin' that he went off on a even start. Then what did he do? Run? No, he didn't run. He just sort of passed *away* from the place where he started at. Our greaser, he sees the race is all over, and like any fool cowpuncher, he must get frisky. Comin' down the home-stretch, only needin' about one more jump—for it ain't above a quarter of a mile—José, he stands up in his stirrups and pulls off his hat, and just whangs old pinto over the head with it, friendlylike, to show him there ain't no coldness.

"We never did rightly know what happened at that time. The greaser admits he may have busted off the fastenin' of that single blinder down pinto's nose. Anyhow, pinto runs a few short jumps, and then stops, lookin' troubled. The next minute he hides his face on the greaser and there is a glimpse of bright, glad sunlight on the bottom of José's moccasins. Next minute after that pinto is up in the grandstand among the ladies, and there he sits down in the lap of the governor's wife, which was among them present.

"There was time, even then, to lead him down and over the line, but before we could think of that he falls to buckin' sincere and conscientious, up there among the benches, and if he didn't jar his osshus structure a heap *then*, it wasn't no fault of his'n. We all run up in front of the grandstand, and stood lookin' up at pinto, and him the maddest, scaredest, cross-eyedest horse I ever did see in all my life. His single blinder was swingin' loose under his neck. His eyes were right mean and white, and the Mexican saints only knows which way he *was* a-lookin'.

"So there we was," went on Curly, with another sigh, "all Socorro sayin' bright and cheerful things to the Bar T, and us plumb broke, and far, far from home.

"We roped pinto, and led him home behind the wagon, forty miles over the sand, by the soft, silver light of the moon. There wasn't a horse or saddle left in our *rodeo*, and we had to ride on the grub wagon, which you know is a disgrace to any gentleman that wears spurs. Pinto, he was the gayest one in the lot. I reckon he allowed he'd been Queen of the May. Every time he saw a jackrabbit or a bunch of sage brush, he'd snort and take a *pasear* sideways as far as the rope would let him go.

" 'The patient seems to be still laborin' under great cerebral excitation,' says the doc, which was likewise on the wagon. 'I ought to have had a year on him,' says he, despondentlike.

" 'Shut up,' says Tom Redmond to the doc. 'I'd shoot up your own osshus structure plenty,' he says, 'if I hadn't bet my gun on that horse race.'

"Well, we got home, the wagonload of us, in the mornin' sometime, every one of us ashamed to look the cook in the face, and hopin' the boss was away from home. But he wasn't. He looks at us, and says he, "Is this a sheep outfit I see before me, or is it the remnants of the former cow camp on the Bar T?' He was right sarcastic. 'Doc,' says he, 'explain this here to me.' But the doc, he couldn't. Says the boss to him at last, 'The *right* time to do the explainin' is before the hoss race is over, and not after,' says he. 'That's the only kind of science that goes hereafter on the Bar T,' says he.

"I reckon the boss was feelin' a little riled, because he had two hundred on pinto hisself. A cross-eyed horse shore can make a sight of trouble," Curly sighed in conclusion, "yet I bought pinto for four dollars, and— sometimes, anyway—he's the best horse in my string down at Carrizosy, ain't he, Mac?"

In the thoughtful silence following this tale, Tom Osby knocked his pipe reflectively against a cedar log. "That's the way with the railroad," he said. "It's goin' to come in here with one eye on the gold mines and the other on the town—and there won't be no blind-bridle up in front of Mr. Ingine, neither. If we got as much sense as the Bar-T feller, we'll do our explainin' before, and not after, the hoss race is over. Before I leave for Vegas, I want to see one of you ostypothetic lawyers about that there railroad outfit."

WILLIAM MacLEOD RAINE

Last Warning

A prolific novelist and historian, author of close to one hundred books, William MacLeod Raine was one of the biggest names in the popular Western field during the first half of this century. Although English-born, he was raised in the West and numbered rustlers, lawmen and gamblers among his acquaintances when the country was still wild; his fiction—such novels as his first, Wyoming *(1908),* Trail's End, Mavericks, *and* Ranger's Luck, *and such stories as "Last Warning"—have an authentic ring to them as a result. He also wrote notable works of Western history, the best known of which is* Famous Sheriffs and Western Outlaws *(1929).*

ALL DAY John Muir had been stringing wire for the south pasture. Dust and sand had sifted into every crease of his clothes. He was hot and tired and dirty. Yet the sweat and toil under a broiling sun had not obscured a certain gallant grace in this slender black-haired man. He sat lightly in the saddle, a figure to draw the eyes of men as well as women.

He topped a rise and rode into a park knee deep with grass and flowers. Not in a dozen years had there been such spring rains as in the past few months, and among the aspen were strewn abundantly gentian and bluebell, Indian paintbrush, fireweed, and columbine. It was a goodly spread, this mountain Eden he had homesteaded, but its beauty could not drive away the frown that furrowed his brow. Though he held legal title to the demesne, a bullet might at any hour terminate his ownership. Might and indeed probably would, unless he could bend his stubborn pride to make terms with the enemy.

Riding across the floor of the park toward his cabin in the pines was one who made him forget his fears and his weariness. Even at a distance he recognized that slender erect body. Above it was a bare head, golden in the sunset, and he knew that when he drew nearer he would see a face of lovely planes and eager sparkling eyes. She was of the house of his foe, but between them was a tie on his side at least closer than friendship.

She saw him and flung up a hand in greeting, pulling up her pony to wait for him. To see her there surprised him. They had met at dances, once at a rodeo, and twice in town—six times in all. No word of love had they spoken, but it had been in the background of both their thoughts. Never had she been on his land since he had filed claim to it. Now she had come, he was sure, for a reason that soon would be explained, an important and not a trivial one.

He lifted the dusty sombrero from his dark head. "Welcome to Sweet Springs park," he said.

She let her gaze sweep over the grass-carpeted valley bright with flowers, across the busy brook to the gentle slope leading to the small house that nestled in the cool evergreens. "You've chosen a lovely spot for a home," she replied.

"No place is home where a man lives alone," he told her, and a moment later regretted the impulsive confession.

The girl blushed pink, from throat to cheek. "I must send you a paper I saw one of our men reading yesterday," she answered lightly. "You write to a lady, object matrimony, exchange photographs, and she comes to you sight unseen to live happily with you ever after."

His dark eyes rested on her, bitterness in them. "I would have a lot to offer her—a homestead right, a cabin, a few cattle, and a feud."

She held her bright head proudly, her brave look direct and unashamed. "Does a woman marry a man for the things he owns?" she asked.

Neither of them had meant to lay bare the hidden emotions that had leaped out, to speak of the frustrations and barriers that held them apart. But one revealing second had brushed aside their guards.

He shook his head. "A nester doesn't marry the daughter of a cattle king with whom he is at war."

In her answer there was a touch of scorn. "Not if he is humble and timid and wants above all to nurse his grudge." She gave him no time for a reply. Already she had gone too far, had said more than any modest girl might with propriety reveal. If he did not choose to follow the offered lead she could not help it. "I came because I overheard two of our men talking and what they said worried me. I don't suppose there is anything in it. There can't be. But it was disturbing. Father was away from home. So I came to you. Maybe I was silly. I caught your name and listened. One of them said it would be with you the way it was with Barry and the other added, 'Unless he lights out sudden.' When I came out from the stable and surprised them they said they had just been fooling. But I know better." She flung a sharp question at Muir. "What did they mean about Barry? I know he left suddenly."

The homesteader's smile was thin and grim. "Nobody knows for sure what happened to Barry."

Her blue startled eyes held fast to his. "Do you mean—he didn't leave?"

"He didn't take his team. The horses were found in the pasture after he was missed. He did not go by train."

"Perhaps he met with an accident."

"Or was dry-gulched. He had been warned to get out or take the consequences."

"Who warned him?"

"The fellow didn't leave his name," Muir answered dryly.

The girl felt a cold sinking at the stomach. They had turned and were riding up the slope toward the house. "Did he have an enemy?" she asked, almost in a whisper.

"He was in somebody's way." Muir spoke with stiff reserve.

On the closed door of the house a bit of yellow paper was tacked. "A message for you," she suggested, her mind still groping with the shadowy horror drawing close.

"Yes." He looked at her strangely as he slipped from the saddle to get the paper before she could read it. What he would find on that torn sheet of paper he knew.

Rose Durbin caught his swift glance and moved her horse forward to anticipate his intention. She read:

> Get out, you damned rustler, before 24 hours. This is your last warning.

There was no signature. Muir did not need one to know who was responsible for the notice. It came from Hank Durbin of the Bar Double S, though he had not nailed it there himself.

"But you're not a rustler," Rose cried. "What do they mean?"

"Even a killer needs some excuse to justify himself," Muir explained. "So he has trumped up this one."

"If you know who he is—"

He lifted his hands in a little gesture of hopelessness. "Nothing I can do about it. He's protected."

"Are you going to leave?"

"No."

"Then what are you going to do?"

"I don't know."

As she looked into the lean brown boyish face, a sickness ran through her. Fear tightened her chest. She felt the quick pounding of her heart, the terror crawling up her spine. Swinging down from the saddle, she caught him by the lapels of his coat and looked up into his eyes. All the color had washed out of her cheeks and left her ashen.

"You are not just going to stay and let them—kill you?" she asked.

"Not if I can help it."

"This all sounds crazy," she cried. "There's a law against murder. If you know somebody means to kill you, it's not necessary to let him do it. Come to the Bar Double S and stay with us until the danger is over. Father will give you a job if you want to work."

Her suggestion was as fantastic as anything else in this impossible situation. In the first place there was no law in this far-flung range country that would protect him against a big outfit intent on his destruction. Nor could he run to Hank Durbin for help against his own killer Frenault, a man who was reported to have rubbed out eight victims, most of them for pay and from ambush. Durbin meant to hold the grass and the water holes of this district for his stock against homesteaders. The gunman was only a tool who obeyed orders.

"No," Muir told her harshly. "I have to play my own hand."

"But how? This is no time to be stubborn, John."

He did not know how. But there was in him a stiff sense of justice, of self-respect, that would not let him be driven from the property that was lawfully his. Neither argument nor pleading moved him. The girl realized at last despairingly that not even his love for her could make him alter his decision.

After she had gone Muir lit a fire, washed himself, and prepared supper. He did not want food, but he had to carry on the routine of life. Mechanically he ate, washing a few mouthfuls of bread and bacon down with coffee. His shoulders sagged wearily. In the pit of his stomach was a lump of ice. No illusions buoyed him up. Frenault would shoot him from ambush, though the gunfighter could meet him in the open with small risk. The Bar Double S warrior was a dead shot, cool and wary. Muir had never fired a gun at a man. An emergency like this was one that preyed on his imagination. Even if he were given a chance he might be weak and unnerved at the critical moment.

He curtained the windows, bolted the door, and smoked an unsatisfying pipe. It was long before he slept. Troubled dreams disturbed his rest.

Before daylight he rose, saddled a horse, and started for River Fork. There were a few loose ends of business he wanted to clear up while he could.

Rose did not mean to give up because John Muir had proved so obstinate. She found her father in the little room he used as an office. He was figuring out some costs on the back of an old envelope with the stub of a pencil.

Hank Durbin was a gross paunchy man with heavy rounded shoulders and shapeless body. He had small gray green eyes, sly and mocking, lit at times by an evil ironic mirth. His clothes were cheap and outworn, his boots run down at the heels. To those who knew both father and daughter it was a continuous surprise that Rose should have sprung from such a source. Of her sweet and dainty grace there was no suggestion in his thick bulky torso or his heavy-footed clumping gait.

"Somebody is planning to kill John Muir," she flung out.

Hank squinted up at her. "Who told you that?" he squeaked in a high falsetto voice that sounded strange coming from such a mountain of flesh.

"I saw a notice on the door of his cabin."

"What were you doing on his place?" Hank snapped.

"I heard two men talking, and when I couldn't find you I went to warn him."

"You keep outa this. It's none of yore business," he snarled. Swiftly he added: "What two men?"

Some instinct cautioned her to be careful. "I couldn't see who they were."

"If I find out, I'll learn the fools." He slammed a heavy fist on the table.

"I told John Muir to come and stay with us till the danger was past. He wouldn't come. You must do something about it, Father."

"So he wouldn't come." Hank tittered. "Give any reason?"

"Said he would have to play his own hand. Who is it wants to kill him?"

Durbin stroked his unshaven chin to conceal a grin. "I don't reckon anybody wants to kill him, honey. It must be some of the boys' monkey shines."

"No." She had always been afraid of something secret and sinister in him, but now she faced him resolutely, a challenge in her fear-filled eyes. "He's going to be killed unless we stop it. I know you don't like him and resent anyone homesteading your range. But you can't stand back and let him be murdered. It's too—horrible."

"I didn't invite him here to fence my water holes. He's made his own bed. If he's got a lick of sense he can still get out. I've offered to buy his spread. But he won't have it that way. I won't lift a hand for the stubborn fool."

He had come out into the open, practically admitting that what she feared was true. His little eyes glittered with malice. An appalling conviction flashed to her mind. He was the enemy who threatened John Muir's destruction. That was why John had said he was protected. Thirty Bar Double S riders fenced Hank Durbin from danger.

She drew back, as one does from a venomous reptile. A strangled sob came from her throat. She turned and ran from the room.

Rose too had an unhappy night. She rose early, in time to see her father and Frenault riding down the road that led to town. It was a relief to know that they were not traveling toward Sweet Springs park. After a hurried breakfast she had a horse saddled and set out to have another talk with John Muir. An idea was simmering in her mind. She knew he cared for her. If she could persuade him to marry her at once her father might spare her lover. Bad though he was, Rose knew he had a soft spot in his tough heart for her.

The girl found the homestead deserted. John had told her he would probably go to town to settle some accounts. Very likely he would meet her father and Frenault there. On the way home he might be waylaid. As she turned to strike the trail for River Fork she felt her heart thumping against her ribs.

John Muir knew that he was safer in River Fork than on his own land. His enemies would not dare shoot him down from ambush in the sight of men. They would have to give him a chance for his white alley. Out in the hills the law of the frontier could be ignored, since there would be no witness to prove who had violated it. Yet heavy heavy hung over the head of the homesteader. In a few hours he would be back within reach of the Bar Double S killer's rifle.

It was a day of warm and pleasant sunshine. Billowy clouds, with little white islands clinging close to their indented edges, floated lazily across the bluest possible sky. He wondered if he would see that sky tomorrow —if his eyes would not be forever closed.

He called at the office of Jim Baylor, lawyer, and made his will. Jim joked with him a little about it. Brown young riders rarely bothered about the future. From the attorney's office he went to the livery stable and settled a bill. Presently he was at a general store cleaning up what he owed there. It was while he was doing this that a lounger dropped in and mentioned casually having seen Durbin and Frenault at the Cowman's Rest.

Muir gave no sign of interest. He put the change handed him by the storekeeper in his pocket and wandered out of the building. An acquaintance passed him on the sidewalk and he nodded a greeting. But the undercurrent of his mind was busy with the implications of what he had just heard. There might still be a chance if he tried to talk Durbin into a compromise. For a full minute he hesitated, then walked down the street to the Cowman's Rest. He moved swiftly, afraid his resolution might give way if he lingered.

Durbin and Frenault were at the bar drinking. Hank caught sight of Muir in the doorway. His heavy lids narrowed, and into the gray-green eyes a cruel mirth leaped.

He called to the nester. "I hear you're leaving. Come in and have a drink with us before you go."

Muir could not draw back now. He came forward slowly setting his back teeth to choke down the fear that rose in his throat at sight of these two men together.

"I'm not leaving," he answered quietly.

"My mistake." Durbin's great midriff shook like a jelly. This was the kind of situation he enjoyed, to play cat and mouse with some poor devil he had in his power. "I heard the climate didn't agree with you."

"I'd like to talk with you, Mr. Durbin."

"Fine. Neighbors ought to have a pow-wow onct in a while. How's yore fencing going?"

"Three nights ago the wires were cut to pieces in fifty places."

Hank showed elaborate concern. "You don't say. Now who in time could have done that."

Muir moistened dry lips with his tongue. "I thought if I talked over our difficulties with you—"

"What difficulties?" the Bar Double S owner inquired blandly. "Didn't know I had any difficulties."

The homesteader went on, his voice low and pleading, "I'm running only a two-by-four spread, Mr. Durbin, and I've fenced just one water hole. That won't interfere with your stock. There's feed and water enough for both of us."

"Another glass, Mike," the cattleman told the bartender. "Mr. Muir is having a last drink with us—before leaving." Durbin turned to the nester. He too spoke low, but with a thread of suave cruelty in his spaced words. "That's where you're wrong. I had the Sweet Springs range before you ever saw this country. I aim to hold it against any two-bit drifter who tries to fence off my water holes."

"Only one, Mr. Durbin, and your cattle can get water just below my south fence."

"I don't give a tinker's damn whether it's one or twenty. I'll fight for my rights. If I let you get away with this some other guy will try it."

Mike had pushed the bottle and another glass toward Muir, but the young man paid no attention to them. "I'm not looking for trouble," he said, his forehead creased with anxious thought. "You know that, Mr. Durbin. But I have rights too. The law says . . ."

"Who the hell cares about law?" The cattleman brushed it aside with a sweep of his plump hand. "A bunch of nincompoops sit in Washington on their behinds and make laws that have no sense for a range country they have never seen and know nothing about. This is cow territory—no good for anything else. It belongs to the man who uses it first. The Sweet Springs water and grass are mine. Get that in your thick skull while there is time."

Durbin's voice was losing its smoothness and getting shrill. He pounded on the bar with his hamlike fist.

A man who had come in and ordered a bottle of beer became aware of the tensity. He had spoken to Muir and Durbin with only a scant nod of greeting. Hurriedly he drank his beer and departed without paying for it. Mike did not remind him of the obligation. His mind too was preoccupied. Maybe he had better make some excuse to beat it into the back room and escape by way of the rear door. He did not like the cold intent look Frenault held fixed on Muir.

Since the homesteader had come into the room Frenault had not spoken a word. He was slightly below middle height, tight-lipped, with a colorless face of strong bony conformation. His eyes were as cold and expressionless as those of a dead mackerel. Their wary stillness was a threat. When he changed his position, to leave his right arm freer, there was a catlike rhythm in the movement.

Muir had come in to make peace if he could, but anger at Durbin's domineering arrogance began to smolder in him. "The United States government says different," he insisted stubbornly. "I have a paper from it that tells me Sweet Springs park is mine."

"Better write to yore congressman and have him send a troop of soldiers to help you hold it," Durbin warned. "Don't go crazy with the heat, you lunkhead. I've offered to buy. Last chance, Muir."

"You didn't offer me one-fourth of what my spread is worth."

"I offered you all it's worth to me. I don't give a cuss whether you accept or don't. I'll get it anyhow."

The homesteader felt a cold wind blowing over him. He was convinced that Frenault was waiting for his chief to give the word. He ought to knuckle under and give way. Not to do so was suicidal. He heard the clock on the wall ticking away the seconds between him and eternity. A chill sweat broke out on his forehead. But he could not throw up his hands and quit. He wanted to, and did not find it possible. A man could not run like a rabbit.

"I'm not going to let anybody rob me," he said thickly.

The eyes of the cattleman and his killer met. A message passed from one to the other. Without another word Durbin turned and clumped out of the building. Muir knew the showdown had come.

Before the swing doors had settled to rest somebody from outside pushed through them. He was a short thick-set man in chaps and checked shirt.

" 'Lo, Frenault," he said. "Heard you were in town and brought the twenty bucks I owe you."

The gunfighter turned his head to the newcomer. "Hand it to Mike," he said. "I'm busy right now."

Muir picked up the empty beer bottle and pressed the rim of the narrow end against the back of the desperado's neck. "Don't move," he warned.

The homesteader was surprised to find that his voice was cool and firm. Now that the moment for action had come the fear had dropped from him like a discarded coat.

Frenault stood rigid. He did not move while Muir slipped the .45 from the scabbard at the man's side.

"Goddlemighty!" the cowpuncher at the door gasped.

"Keep your hands at your sides, Frenault," Muir warned. "You may turn now."

Frenault turned, a blazing passion in his bleak eyes. His right arm moved upward swiftly. It brushed under his coat and continued to lift without stopping.

With his left hand Muir slapped down the barrel of the revolver and at the same time fired. The bullet from Frenault's second gun crashed through the floor.

The hired killer caught at his heart. From his slack fingers the .45

clattered to the ground. He swayed, took a step forward, and plunged down beside his gun. The body twitched and lay motionless.

Muir stared down at the still huddled figure. He was amazed and shocked at what he had done. With the touch of a finger he had blasted life from a desperado of whom he had walked in terror.

The man in the doorway slapped a hand against his shiny chaps. "I never saw the beat of it," he yelped. "All his life Frenault played to get the breaks. He slips once, and—curtain, gents."

A thin film of smoke still trickled from the barrel of the revolver in Muir's hand. He fought down the sickness that ran through him and said in a low voice, "I wasn't armed."

"Not armed?" Mike looked at him in wonder. "And with a beer bottle you rubbed out the worst killer ever in this part of the country."

"If he hadn't carried two guns he might still have been alive," Muir said. "I had to do it."

The man in chaps straddled forward. "You bet you had. It was him or you, one." His eyes dropped to the body of the Bar Double S gunfighter. "No regrets. Quite a bunch of guys will breathe freer now he's gone."

There was not enough air in the room for Muir. He pushed through the swing doors and stood outside. What he wanted was to be alone in order to quiet the tumult within him.

A big man with a lumbering body was clumping up the street toward the Cowman's Rest. He pulled up abruptly, startled surprise in his little gray green eyes. The man at the entrance to the saloon with the gun in his hand was not the one he had expected to see there. He had been hurrying back to explain to the bartender and others present how much he regretted that the homesteader had forced Frenault to kill him.

At sight of Durbin all of Muir's agitation was sloughed away. He said quietly, "We'll settle this business now."

Already a crowd was beginning to gather. From stores and offices men came running.

The cattleman lifted a fat hand in frightened protest. "Lemme explain, Muir. Don't rush this. We can fix it up all right. Whatever you say."

Durbin had been the big man in this district for twenty years. He had overridden other men's rights without compunction. It had become a tradition that nobody could safely stand up against him. A dozen men saw this legend being shattered before their eyes.

"Come here, Durbin," ordered Muir.

The ranch owner shambled reluctantly closer, terror in the fascinated eyes that clung to the grim ones dragging him forward. "Don't shoot," he begged. "You got me all wrong. We'll be good neighbors, John."

"You're through running this country," Muir told him. "Do you understand that?"

"That's all right, if you feel that way. I always was yore friend. Fact is, I was about ready to give Frenault his time."

"Some of your men burned my barn two weeks ago. You'll build me a new one."

"Sure," agreed Durbin eagerly. "If any of my boys did that, I don't know anything about it. But that's fine. I'll certainly build you a better one."

"And you'll never interfere again with any homesteader who wants to take up government land."

"Why no, I wouldn't do that. I'm a law-abiding citizen. I expect some of my boys have been a little bossy. I'll ride herd on them closer."

"Better start at once. Fork your horse and get out of town."

Durbin hesitated. He wanted to save face if he could. His furtive glance slid round, to meet a circle of unfriendly eyes. They told him that his reign was over. Plodding across the street to the hitch rack where his horse was tied, he swung heavily to the saddle and rode away.

Through the crowd a girl pushed her way to Muir.

"You here?" he cried.

"I was afraid I would be too late." Rose was trembling from the reaction to the fear that had driven her all through her long ride.

He took both her hands in his and looked down into her eyes. "You're just in time," he told her.

The Weight of Obligation

*Like Jack London, Rex Beach (1877–1949) was lured by the excitement
and adventure of the 1898 Yukon Gold Rush and subsequently spent a
number of years prospecting in the Yukon and later in Alaska. Also like
London, he wrote often and well of the "Land of the Midnight Sun" (as
well as of the American West, South America and other exotic locales).
His first book, a collection of "Northern" and Western stories,* Pardners,
was published in 1905; his best novel, The Spoilers, *appeared a year later
and was a runaway bestseller. Beach's work is little known among modern
readers, a regrettable fact. "The Weight of Obligation," a harrowing tale
of the Frozen North and of the test of a friendship, is one example of how
it remains as fresh and vital as when it was initially published.*

THIS IS THE STORY of a burden, the tale of a load that irked a strong
man's shoulders. To those who do not know the North it may seem
strange, but to those who understand the humors of men in solitude, and
the extravagant vagaries that steal in upon their minds, as fog drifts with
the night, it will not appear unusual. There are spirits in the wilderness,
eerie forces which play pranks; some droll or whimsical, others grim.

Johnny Cantwell and Mortimer Grant were partners, trail-mates,
brothers in soul if not in blood. The ebb and flow of frontier life had
brought them together, its hardships had united them until they were as
one. They were something of a mystery to each other, neither having
surrendered all his confidence, and because of this they retained their
mutual attraction. Had they known each other fully, had they thoroughly
sounded each other's depths, they would have lost interest, just like
husbands and wives who give themselves too freely and reserve nothing.

They had met by accident, but they remained together by desire, and
so satisfactory was the union that not even the jealousy of women had
come between them. There had been women, of course, just as there had
been adventures of other sorts, but the love of the partners was larger and
finer than anything else they had experienced. It was so true and fine and
unselfish, in fact, that either would have smilingly relinquished the woman

of his desires had the other wished to possess her. They were young, strong men, and the world was full of sweethearts, but where was there a partnership like theirs, they asked themselves.

The spirit of adventure bubbled merrily within them, too, and it led them into curious byways. It was this which sent them northward from the States in the dead of winter, on the heels of the Stony River strike; it was this which induced them to land at Katmai instead of Illiamna, whither their land journey should have commenced.

"There are two routes over the coast range," the captain of the *Dora* told them, "and only two. Illiamna Pass is low and easy, but the distance is longer than by way of Katmai. I can land you at either place."

"Katmai is pretty tough, isn't it?" Grant inquired.

"We've understood it's the worst pass in Alaska." Cantwell's eyes were eager.

"It's a heller! Nobody travels it except natives, and they don't like it. Now, Illiamna—"

"We'll try Katmai. Eh, Mort?"

"Sure! They don't come hard enough for us, Cap. We'll see if it's as bad as it's painted."

So, one gray January morning they were landed on a frozen beach, their outfit was flung ashore through the surf, the life-boat pulled away, and the *Dora* disappeared after a farewell toot of her whistle. Their last glimpse of her showed the captain waving good-by and the purser flapping a red table-cloth at them from the after-deck.

"Cheerful place, this," Grant remarked, as he noted the desolate surroundings of dune and hillside.

The beach itself was black and raw where the surf washed it, but elsewhere all was white, save for the thickets of alder and willow which protruded nakedly. The bay was little more than a hollow scooped out of the Alaskan range; along the foot-hills behind there was a belt of spruce and cottonwood and birch. It was a lonely and apparently unpeopled wilderness in which they had been set down.

"Seems good to be back in the North again, doesn't it?" said Cantwell, cheerily. "I'm tired of the booze, and the streetcars, and the dames, and all that civilized stuff. I'd rather be broken in Alaska—with you—than a banker's son, back home."

Soon a globular Russian half-breed, the Katmai trader, appeared among the dunes, and with him were some native villagers. That night the partners slept in a snug log cabin, the roof of which was chained down with old ships' cables. Petellin, the fat little trader, explained that roofs in Katmai had a way of sailing off to seaward when the wind blew. He listened to their plan of crossing the divide and nodded.

It could be done, of course, he agreed, but they were foolish to try it, when the Illiamna route was open. Still, now that they were here, he would find dogs for them, and a guide. The village hunters were out after meat, however, and until they returned the white men would need to wait in patience.

There followed several days of idleness, during which Cantwell and Grant amused themselves around the village, teasing the squaws, playing games with the boys, and flirting harmlessly with the girls, one of whom, in particular, was not unattractive. She was perhaps three-quarters Aleut, the other quarter being plain coquette, and, having been educated at the town of Kodiak, she knews the ways and the wiles of the white man.

Cantwell approached her, and she met his extravagant advances more than halfway. They were getting along nicely together when Grant, in a spirit of fun, entered the game and won her fickle smiles for himself. He joked his partner unmercifully, and Johnny accepted defeat gracefully, never giving the matter a second thought.

When the hunters returned, dogs were bought, a guide was hired, and, a week after landing, the friends were camped at timber-line awaiting a favorable moment for their dash across the range. Above them white hillsides rose in irregular leaps to the gash in the saw-toothed barrier which formed the pass; below them a short valley led down to Katmai and the sea. The day was bright, the air clear, nevertheless after the guide had stared up at the peaks for a time he shook his head, then re-entered the tent and lay down. The mountains were "smoking"; from their tops streamed a gossamer veil which the travellers knew to be drifting snow-clouds carried by the wind. It meant delay, but they were patient.

They were up and going on the following morning, however, with the Indian in the lead. There was no trail; the hills were steep; in places they were forced to unload the sled and hoist their outfit by means of ropes, and as they mounted higher the snow deepened. It lay like loose sand, only lighter; it shoved ahead of the sled in a feathery mass; the dogs wallowed in it and were unable to pull, hence the greater part of the work devolved upon the men. Once above the foot-hills and into the range proper, the going became more level, but the snow remained knee-deep.

The Indian broke trail stolidly; the partners strained at the sled, which hung back like a leaden thing. By afternoon the dogs had become disheartened and refused to heed the whip. There was neither fuel nor running water, and therefore the party did not pause for luncheon. The men were sweating profusely from their exertions and had long since become parched with thirst, but the dry snow was like chalk and scoured their throats.

Cantwell was the first to show the effects of his unusual exertions, for not only had he assumed a lion's share of the work, but the last few months of easy living had softened his muscles, and in consequence his vitality was quickly spent. His undergarments were drenched; he was fearfully dry inside; a terrible thirst seemed to penetrate his whole body; he was forced to rest frequently.

Grant eyed him with some concern, finally inquiring, "Feel bad, Johnny?"

Cantwell nodded. Their fatigue made both men economical of language.

"What's the matter?"

"Thirsty!" The former could barely speak.

"There won't be any water till we get across. You'll have to stand it."

They resumed their duties; the Indian "swish-swished" ahead, as if wading through a sea of swan's-down; the dogs followed listlessly; the partners leaned against the stubborn load.

A faint breath finally came out of the north, causing Grant and the guide to study the sky anxiously. Cantwell was too weary to heed the increasing cold. The snow on the slopes above began to move; here and there, on exposed ridges, it rose in clouds and puffs; the cleancut outlines of the hills became obscured as by a fog; the languid wind bit cruelly.

After a time Johnny fell back upon the sled and exclaimed: "I'm—all in, Mort. Don't seem to have the—guts." He was pale, his eyes were tortured. He scooped a mitten full of snow and raised it to his lips, then spat it out, still dry.

"Here! Brace up!" In a panic of apprehension at this collapse Grant shook him; he had never known Johnny to fail like this. "Take a drink of booze; it'll do you good." He drew a bottle of brandy from one of the dunnage bags and Cantwell seized it avidly. It was wet; it would quench his thirst, he thought. Before Mort could check him he had drunk a third of the contents.

The effect was almost instantaneous, for Cantwell's stomach was empty and his tissues seemed to absorb the liquor like a dry sponge; his fatigue fell away, he became suddenly strong and vigorous again. But before he had gone a hundred yards the reaction followed. First his mind grew thick, then his limbs became unmanageable and his muscles flabby. He was drunk. Yet it was a strange and dangerous intoxication, against which he struggled desperately. He fought it for perhaps a quarter of a mile before it mastered him; then he gave up.

Both men knew that stimulants are never taken on the trail, but they had never stopped to reason why, and even now they did not attribute Johnny's breakdown to the brandy. After a while he stumbled and fell, then, the cool snow being grateful to his face, he sprawled there motionless until Mort dragged him to the sled. He stared at his partner in perplexity and laughed foolishly. The wind was increasing, darkness was near, they had not yet reached the Bering slope.

Something in the drunken man's face frightened Grant and, extracting a ship's biscuit from the grub-box, he said, hurriedly: "Here, Johnny. Get something under your belt, quick."

Cantwell obediently munched the hard cracker, but there was no moisture on his tongue; his throat was paralyzed; the crumbs crowded themselves from the corners of his lips. He tried with limber fingers to stuff them down, or to assist the muscular action of swallowing, but finally expelled them in a cloud. Mort drew the parka hood over his partner's head, for the wind cut like a scythe and the dogs were turning tail to it, digging holes in the snow for protection. The air about them was like yeast; the light was fading.

The Indian snow-shoed his way back, advising a quick camp until the storm abated, but to this suggestion Grant refused to listen, knowing only too well the peril of such a course. Nor did he dare take Johnny on the sled, since the fellow was half asleep already, but instead whipped up the dogs and urged his companion to follow as best he could.

When Cantwell fell, for a second time, he returned, dragged him forward, and tied his wrists firmly, yet loosely, to the load.

The storm was pouring over them now, like water out of a spout; it seared and blinded them; its touch was like that of a flame. Nevertheless they struggled on into the smother, making what headway they could. The Indian led, pulling at the end of a rope; Grant strained at the sled and hoarsely encouraged the dogs; Cantwell stumbled and lurched in the rear like an unwilling prisoner. When he fell his companion lifted him, then beat him, cursed him, tried in every way to rouse him from his lethargy.

After an interminable time they found they were descending and this gave them heart to plunge ahead more rapidly. The dogs began to trot as the sled overran them; they rushed blindly into gullies, fetching up at the bottom in a tangle, and Johnny followed in a nerveless, stupefied condition. He was dragged like a sack of flour, for his legs were limp and he lacked muscular control, but every dash, every fall, every quick descent drove the sluggish blood through his veins and cleared his brain momentarily. Such moments were fleeting, however; much of the time his mind was a blank, and it was only by a mechanical effort that he fought off unconsciousness.

He had vague memories of many beatings at Mort's hands, of the slippery clean-swept ice of a stream over which he limply skidded, of being carried into a tent where a candle flickered and a stove roared. Grant was holding something hot to his lips, and then—

It was morning. He was weak and sick; he felt as if he had awakened from a hideous dream. "I played out, didn't I?" he queried, wonderingly.

"You sure did," Grant laughed. "It was a tight squeak, old boy. I never thought I'd get you through."

"Played out! I—can't understand it." Cantwell prided himself on his strength and stamina, therefore the truth was unbelievable. He and Mort had long been partners, they had given and taken much at each other's hands, but this was something altogether different. Grant had saved his life, at risk of his own; the older man's endurance had been the greater and he had used it to good advantage. It embarrassed Johnny tremendously to realize that he had proven unequal to his share of the work, for he had never before experienced such an obligation. He apologized repeatedly during the few days he lay sick, and meanwhile Mort waited upon him like a mother.

Cantwell was relieved when at last they had abandoned camp, changed guides at the next village, and were on their way along the coast, for somehow he felt very sensitive about his collapse. He was, in fact, extremely ashamed of himself.

Once he had fully recovered he had no further trouble, but soon rounded into fit condition and showed no effects of his ordeal. Day after day he and Mort travelled through the solitudes, their isolation broken only by occasional glimpses of native villages, where they rested briefly and renewed their supply of dog feed.

But although the younger man was now as well and strong as ever, he was uncomfortably conscious that his trailmate regarded him as the weaker of the two and shielded him in many ways. Grant performed most of the unpleasant tasks, and occasionally cautioned Johnny about overdoing. This protective attitude at first amused, then offended Cantwell; it galled him until he was upon the point of voicing his resentment, but reflected that he had no right to object, for, judging by past performances, he had proven his inferiority. This uncomfortable realization forever arose to prevent open rebellion, but he asserted himself secretly by robbing Grant of his self-appointed tasks. He rose first in the mornings, he did the cooking, he lengthened his turns ahead of the dogs, he mended harness after the day's hike had ended. Of course the older man objected, and for a time they had a good-natured rivalry as to who should work and who should rest—only it was not quite so good-natured on Cantwell's part as he made it appear.

Mort broke out in friendly irritation one day: "Don't try to do everything, Johnny. Remember I'm no cripple."

"Humph! You proved that. I guess it's up to me to do your work."

"Oh, forget that day on the pass, can't you?"

Johnny grunted a second time, and from his tone it was evident that he would never forget, unpleasant though the memory remained. Sensing his sullen resentment, the other tried to rally him, but made a bad job of it. The humor of men in the open is not delicate; their wit and their words become coarsened in direct proportion as they revert to the primitive; it is one effect of the solitudes.

Grant spoke extravagantly, mockingly, of his own superiority in a way which ordinarily would have brought a smile to Cantwell's lips, but the latter did not smile. He taunted Johnny humorously on his lack of physical prowess, his lack of good looks and manly qualities—something which had never failed to result in a friendly exchange of badinage; he even teased him about his defeat with the Katmai girl.

Cantwell did respond finally, but afterward he found himself wondering if Mort could have been in earnest. He dismissed the thought with some impatience. But men on the trail have too much time for their thoughts; there is nothing in the monotonous routine of the day's work to distract them, so the partner who had played out dwelt more and more upon his debt and upon his friend's easy assumption of pre-eminence. The weight of obligation began to chafe him, lightly at first, but with ever-increasing discomfort. He began to think that Grant honestly considered himself the better man, merely because chance had played into his hands.

It was silly, even childish, to dwell on the subject, he reflected, and yet he could not banish it from his mind. It was always before him, in one form or another. He felt the strength in his lean muscles, and sneered at the thought that Mort should be deceived. If it came to a physical test he felt sure he could break his slighter partner with his bare hands, and as for endurance—well, he was hungry for a chance to demonstrate it.

They talked little; men seldom converse in the wastes, for there is something about the silence of the wilderness which discourages speech. And no land is so grimly silent, so hushed and soundless, as the frozen North. For days they marched through desolation, without glimpse of human habitation, without sight of track or trail, without sound of a human voice to break the monotony. There was no game in the country, with the exception of an occasional bird or rabbit, nothing but the white hills, the fringe of aldertops along the watercourses, and the thickets of gnarled, unhealthy spruce in the smothered valleys.

Their destination was a mysterious stream at the headwaters of the unmapped Kuskokwim, where rumor said there was gold, and whither they feared other men were hastening from the mining country far to the north.

Now it is a penalty of the White Country that men shall think of women. The open life brings health and vigor, strength and animal vitality, and these clamor for play. The cold of the still, clear days is no more biting than the fierce memories and appetites which charge through the brain at night. Passions intensify with imprisonment, recollections come to life, longings grow vivid and wild. Thoughts change to realities, the past creeps close, and dream figures are filled with blood and fire. One remembers pleasures and excesses, women's smiles, women's kisses, the invitation of outstretched arms. Wasted opportunities mock at one.

Cantwell began to brood upon the Katmai girl, for she was the last; her eyes were haunting and distance had worked its usual enchantment. He reflected that Mort had shouldered him aside and won her favor, then boasted of it. Johnny awoke one night with a dream of her, and lay quivering.

"Hell! She was only a squaw," he said, half aloud. "If I'd really tried—"

Grant lay beside him, snoring; the heat of their bodies intermingled. The waking man tried to compose himself, but his partner's stertorous breathing irritated him beyond measure; for a long time he remained motionless, staring into the gray blur of the tent-top. He had played out. He owed his life to the man who had cheated him of the Katmai girl, and that man knew it. He had become a weak, helpless thing, dependent upon another's strength, and that other now accepted his superiority as

a matter of course. The obligation was insufferable, and—it was unjust.
The North had played him a devilish trick, it had betrayed him, it had
bound him to his benefactor with chains of gratitude which were irksome.
Had they been real chains they could have galled him no more than at
this moment.

As time passed the men spoke less frequently to each other. Grant
joshed his mate roughly, once or twice, masking beneath an assumption
of jocularity his own vague irritation at the change that had come over
them. It was as if he had probed at an open wound with clumsy fingers.

Cantwell had by this time assumed most of those petty camp tasks
which provoke tired trailers, those humdrum duties which are so trying
to exhausted nerves, and of course they wore upon him as they wear upon
every man. But, once he had taken them over, he began to resent Grant's
easy relinquishment; it rankled him to realize how willingly the other
allowed him to do the cooking, the dishwashing, the fire-building, the
bed-making. Little monotonies of this kind form the hardest part of
winter travel, they are the rocks upon which friendships founder and
partnerships are wrecked. Out on the trail, nature equalizes the work to
a great extent, and no man can shirk unduly, but in camp, inside the
cramped confines of a tent pitched on boughs laid over the snow, it is very
different. There one must busy himself while the other rests and keeps
his legs out of the way if possible. One man sits on the bedding at the
rear of the shelter, and shivers, while the other squats over a tantalizing
fire of green wood, blistering his face and parboiling his limbs inside his
sweaty clothing. Dishes must be passed, food divided, and it is poor food,
poorly prepared at best. Sometimes men criticize and voice longings for
better grub and better cooking. Remarks of this kind have been known
to result in tragedies, bitter words and flaming curses—then, perhaps, wild
actions, memories of which the later years can never erase.

It is but one prank of the wilderness, one grim manifestation of its silent
forces.

Had Grant been unable to do his part Cantwell would have willingly
accepted the added burden, but Mort was able, he was nimble and
"handy," he was the better cook of the two; in fact, he was the better man
in every way—or so he believed. Cantwell sneered at the last thought, and
the memory of his debt was like bitter medicine.

His resentment—in reality nothing more than a phase of insanity begot
of isolation and silence—could not help but communicate itself to his
companion, and there resulted a mutual antagonism, which grew into a

dislike, then festered into something more, something strange, reasonless, yet terribly vivid and amazingly potent for evil. Neither man ever mentioned it—their tongues were clenched between their teeth and they held themselves in check with harsh hands—but it was constantly in their minds, nevertheless. No man who has not suffered the manifold irritations of such an intimate association can appreciate the gnawing canker of animosity like this. It was dangerous because there was no relief from it: the two were bound together as by gyves; they shared each other's every action and every plan; they trod in each other's tracks, slept in the same bed, ate from the same plate. They were like prisoners ironed to the same staple.

Each fought the obsession in his own way, but it is hard to fight the impalpable, hence their sick fancies grew in spite of themselves. Their minds needed food to prey upon, but found none. Each began to criticize the other silently, to sneer at his weaknesses, to meditate derisively upon his peculiarities. After a time they no longer resisted the advance of these poisonous thoughts, but welcomed it.

On more than one occasion the embers of their wrath were upon the point of bursting into flame, but each realized that the first ill-considered word would serve to slip the leash from those demons that were straining to go free, and so managed to restrain himself.

The crisis came one crisp morning when a dog-team whirled around a bend in the river and a white man hailed them. He was the mail-carrier, on his way out from Nome, and he brought news of the "inside."

"Where are you boys bound for?" he inquired when greetings were over and gossip of the trail had passed.

"We're going to the Stony River strike," Grant told him.

"Stony River? Up the Kuskokwim?"

"Yes!"

The mailman laughed. "Can you beat that? Ain't you heard about Stony River?"

"No!"

"Why, it's a fake—no such place."

There was a silence; the partners avoided each other's eyes.

"MacDonald, the fellow that started it, is on his way to Dawson. There's a gang after him, too, and if he's caught it'll go hard with him. He wrote the letters—to himself—and spread the news just to raise a grub-stake. He cleaned up big before they got onto him. He peddled his tips for real money."

"Yes!" Grant spoke quietly. "Johnny bought one. That's what brought us from Seattle. We went out on the last boat and figured we'd come in from this side before the breakup. So—fake! By God!"

"Gee! You fellers bit good." The mail carrier shook his head. "Well! You'd better keep going now; you'll get to Nome before the season opens. Better take dog-fish from Bethel—it's four bits a pound on the Yukon. Sorry I didn't hit your camp last night; we'd 'a' had a visit. Tell the gang that you saw me." He shook hands ceremoniously, yelled at his panting dogs, and went swiftly on his way, waving a mitten on high as he vanished around the next bend.

The partners watched him go, then Grant turned to Johnny, and repeated: "Fake! By God! MacDonald stung you."

Cantwell's face went as white as the snow behind him, his eyes blazed. "Why did you tell him I bit?" he demanded, harshly.

"Hunh! *Didn't* you bite? Two thousand miles afoot; three months of hell; for nothing. That's biting some."

"*Well!*" The speaker's face was convulsed, and Grant's flamed with an answering anger. They glared at each other for a moment. "Don't blame me. You fell for it, too."

"I—" Mort checked his rushing words.

"Yes, *you!* Now, what are you going to do about it? Welch?"

"I'm going through to Nome." The sight of his partner's rage had set Mort to shaking with a furious desire to fly at his throat, but, fortunately, he retained a spark of sanity.

"Then shut up, and quit chewing the rag. You—talk too damned much."

Mort's eyes were bloodshot; they fell upon the carbine under the sled lashings, and lingered there, then wavered. He opened his lips, reconsidered, spoke softly to the team, then lifted the heavy dog whip and smote the malamutes with all his strength.

The men resumed their journey without further words, but each was cursing inwardly.

"So! I talk too much," Grant thought. The accusation stuck in his mind and he determined to speak no more.

"He blames me," Cantwell reflected, bitterly. "I'm in wrong again and he couldn't keep his mouth shut. A hell of a partner, he is!"

All day they plodded on, neither trusting himself to speak. They ate their evening meal like mutes; they avoided each other's eyes. Even the guide noticed the change and looked on curiously.

There were two robes and these the partners shared nightly, but their hatred had grown so during the past few hours that the thought of lying side by side, limb to limb, was distasteful. Yet neither dared suggest a division of the bedding, for that would have brought further words and resulted in the crash which they longed for, but feared. They stripped off their furs, and lay down beside each other with the same repugnance they would have felt had there been a serpent in the couch.

This unending malevolent silence became terrible. The strain of it increased, for each man now had something definite to cherish in the words and the looks that had passed. They divided the camp work with scrupulous nicety, each man waited upon himself and asked no favors. The knowledge of his debt forever chafed Cantwell; Grant resented his companion's lack of gratitude.

Of course they spoke occasionally—it was beyond human endurance to remain entirely dumb—but they conversed in monosyllables, about trivial things, and their voices were throaty, as if the effort choked them. Meanwhile they continued to glow inwardly at a white heat.

Cantwell no longer felt the desire to merely match his strength against Grant's; the estrangement had become too wide for that; a physical victory would have been flat and tasteless; he craved some deeper satisfaction. He began to think of the ax—just how or when or why he never knew. It was a thin-bladed, polished thing of frosty steel, and the more he thought of it the stronger grew his impulse to rid himself once and for all of that presence which exasperated him. It would be very easy, he reasoned; a sudden blow, with the weight of his shoulders behind it—he fancied he could feel the bit sink into Grant's flesh, cleaving bone and cartilage in its course—a slanting downward stroke, aimed at the neck where it joined the body, and he would be forever satisfied. It would be ridiculously simple. He practiced in the gloom of evening as he felled sprucetrees for firewood; he guarded the ax religiously; it became a living thing which urged him on to violence. He saw it standing by the tent fly when he closed his eyes to sleep; he dreamed of it; he sought it out with his eyes when he first awoke. He slid it loosely under the sled lashings every morning, thinking that its use could not long be delayed.

As for Grant, the carbine dwelt forever in his mind, and his fingers itched for it. He secretly slipped a cartridge into the chamber, and when an occasional ptarmigan offered itself for a target he saw the white spot on the breast of Johnny's reindeer parkas, dancing ahead of the Lyman bead.

The solitude had done its work; the North had played its grim comedy to the final curtain, making sport of men's affections and turning love to rankling hate. But into the mind of each man crept a certain craftiness. Each longed to strike, but feared to face the consequences. It was lonesome, here among the white hills and the deathly silences, yet they reflected that it would be still more lonesome if they were left to keep step with nothing more substantial than a memory. They determined, therefore, to wait until civilization was nearer, meanwhile rehearsing the moment they knew was inevitable. Over and over in their thoughts each of them enacted the scene, ending it always with the picture of a prostrate man in a patch of trampled snow which grew crimson as the other gloated.

They paused at Bethel Mission long enough to load with dried salmon, then made the ninety-mile portage over lake and tundra to the Yukon. There they got their first touch of the "inside" world. They camped in a barabara where white men had slept a few nights before, and heard their own language spoken by native tongues. The time was growing short now, and they purposely dismissed their guide, knowing that the trail was plain from there on. When they hitched up, on the next morning, Cantwell placed the ax, bit down, between the tarpaulin and the sled rail, leaving the helve projecting where his hand could reach it. Grant thrust the barrel of the rifle beneath a lashing, with the butt close by the handle-bars, and it was loaded.

A mile from the village they were overtaken by an Indian and his squaw, travelling light behind hungry dogs. The natives attached themselves to the white men and hung stubbornly to their heels, taking advantage of their tracks. When night came they camped alongside, in the hope of food. They announced that they were bound for St. Michaels, and in spite of every effort to shake them off they remained close behind the partners until that point was reached.

At St. Michaels there were white men, practically the first Johnny and Mort had encountered since landing at Katmai, and for a day at least they were sane. But there were still three hundred miles to be travelled, three hundred miles of solitude and haunting thoughts. Just as they were about to start, Cantwell came upon Grant and the A. C. agent, and heard his name pronounced, also the word "Katmai." He noted that Mort fell silent at his approach, and instantly his anger blazed afresh. He decided that the latter had been telling the story of their experience on the pass and boasting of his service. So much the better, he thought, in a blind rage;

that which he planned doing would appear all the more like an accident, for who would dream that a man could kill the person to whom he owed his life?

That night he waited for a chance.

They were camped in a dismal hut on a wind-swept shore; they were alone. But Grant was waiting also, it seemed. They lay down beside each other, ostensibly to sleep; their limbs touched; the warmth from their bodies intermingled, but they did not close their eyes.

They were up and away early, with Nome drawing rapidly nearer. They had skirted an ocean, foot by foot; Bering Sea lay behind them, now, and its northern shore swung westward to their goal. For two months they had lived in silent animosity, feeding on bitter food while their elbows rubbed.

Noon found them floundering through one of those unheralded storms which make coast travel so hazardous. The morning had turned off gray, the sky was of a leaden hue which blended perfectly with the snow underfoot, there was no horizon, it was impossible to see more than a few yards in any direction. The trail soon became obliterated and their eyes began to play tricks. For all they could distinguish, they might have been suspended in space; they seemed to be treading the measures of an endless dance in the center of a whirling cloud. Of course it was cold, for the wind off the open sea was damp, but they were not men to turn back.

They soon discovered that their difficulty lay not in facing the storm, but in holding to the trail. That narrow, two-foot causeway, packed by a winter's travel and frozen into a ribbon of ice by a winter's frosts, afforded their only avenue of progress, for the moment they left it the sled plowed into the loose snow, well-nigh disappearing and bringing the dogs to a standstill. It was the duty of the driver, in such case, to wallow forward, right the load if necessary, and lift it back into place. These mishaps were forever occurring, for it was impossible to distinguish the trail beneath its soft covering. However, if the driver's task was hard it was no more trying than that of the man ahead, who was compelled to feel out and explore the ridge of hardened snow and ice with his feet, after the fashion of a man walking a plank in the dark. Frequently he lunged into the drifts with one foot, or both; his glazed mukluk soles slid about, causing him to bestride the invisible hogback, or again his legs crossed awkwardly, throwing him off his balance. At times he wandered away from the path entirely and had to search it out again. These exertions were very wearing and they were dangerous, also, for joints are easily dislocated, muscles twisted and tendons strained.

Hour after hour the march continued, unrelieved by any change, unbroken by any speck or spot of color. The nerves of their eyes, wearied by constant near-sighted peering at the snow, began to jump so that vision became untrustworthy. Both travellers appreciated the necessity of clinging to the trail, for, once they lost it, they knew they might wander about indefinitely until they chanced to regain it or found their way to the shore, while always to seaward was the menace of open water, of air-holes, or cracks which might gape beneath their feet like jaws. Immersion in this temperature, no matter how brief, meant death.

The monotony of progress through this unreal, leaden world became almost unbearable. The repeated strainings and twistings they suffered in walking the slippery ridge reduced the men to weariness; their legs grew clumsy and their feet uncertain. Had they found a camping-place they would have stopped, but they dared not forsake the thin thread that linked them with safety to go and look for one, not knowing where the shore lay. In storms of this kind men have lain in their sleeping bags for days within a stone's throw of a road-house or village. Bodies had been found within a hundred yards of shelter after blizzards have abated.

Cantwell and Grant had no choice, therefore, except to bore into the welter of drifting flakes.

It was late in the afternoon when the latter met with an accident. Johnny, who had taken a spell at the rear, heard him cry out, saw him stagger, struggle to hold his footing, then sink into the snow. The dogs paused instantly, lay down, and began to strip the ice pellets from between their toes.

Cantwell spoke harshly, leaning upon the handlebars: "Well! What's the idea?"

It was the longest sentence of the day.

"I've—hurt myself." Mort's voice was thin and strange; he raised himself to a sitting posture, and reached beneath his parka, then lay back weakly. He writhed, his face was twisted with pain. He continued to lie there, doubled into a knot of suffering. A groan was wrenched from between his teeth.

"Hurt? How?" Johnny inquired, dully.

It seemed very ridiculous to see that strong man kicking around in the snow.

"I've ripped something loose—here." Mort's palms were pressed in upon his groin, his fingers were clutching something. "Ruptured—I guess." He tried again to rise, but sank back. His cap had fallen off and his forehead glistened with sweat.

Cantwell went forward and lifted him. It was the first time in many days that their hands had touched, and the sensation affected him strangely. He struggled to repress a devilish mirth at the thought that Grant had played out—it amounted to that and nothing less; the trail had delivered him into his enemy's hands, his hour had struck. Johnny determined to square the debt now, once for all, and wipe his own mind clean of that poison which corroded it. His muscles were strong, his brain clear, he had never felt his strength so irresistible as at this moment, while Mort, for all his boasted superiority, was nothing but a nerveless thing hanging limp against his breast. Providence had arranged it all. The younger man was impelled to give raucous voice to his glee, and yet—his helpless burden exerted an odd effect upon him.

He deposited his foe upon the sled and stared at the face he had not met for many days. He saw how white it was, how wet and cold, how weak and dazed, then as he looked he cursed inwardly, for the triumph of his moment was spoiled.

The ax was there, its polished bit showed like a piece of ice, its helve protruded handily, but there was no need of it now; his fingers were all the weapons Johnny needed; they were more than sufficient, in fact, for Mort was like a child.

Cantwell was a strong man, and, although the North had coarsened him, yet underneath the surface was a chivalrous regard for all things weak, and this the trail-madness had not affected. He had longed for this instant, but now that it had come he felt no enjoyment, since he could not harm a sick man and waged no war on cripples. Perhaps, when Mort had rested, they could settle their quarrel; this was as good a place as any. The storm hid them, they would leave no traces, there could be no interruption.

But Mort did not rest. He could not walk; movement brought excruciating pain.

Finally Cantwell heard himself saying: "Better wrap up and lie still for a while. I'll get the dogs under way." His words amazed him dully. They were not at all what he had intended to say.

The injured man demurred, but the other insisted gruffly, then brought him his mittens and cap, slapping the snow out of them before rousing the team to motion. The load was very heavy now, the dogs had no footprints to guide them, and it required all of Cantwell's efforts to prevent capsizing. Night approached swiftly, the whirling snow particles continued to flow past upon the wind, shrouding the earth in an impenetrable pall.

The journey soon became a terrible ordeal, a slow, halting progress that led nowhere and was accomplished at the cost of tremendous exertion. Time after time Johnny broke trail, then returned and urged the huskies forward to the end of his tracks. When he lost the path he sought it out, laboriously hoisted the sledge back into place, and coaxed his four-footed helpers to renewed effort. He was drenched with perspiration, his inner garments were steaming, his outer ones were frozen into a coat of armor; when he paused he chilled rapidly. His vision was untrustworthy, also, and he felt snow-blindness coming on. Grant begged him more than once to unroll the bedding and prepare to sleep out the storm; he even urged Johnny to leave him and make a dash for his own safety, but at this the younger man cursed and bade him hold his tongue.

Night found the lone driver slipping, plunging, lurching ahead of the dogs, or shoving at the handle-bars and shouting at the dogs. Finally during a pause for rest he heard a sound which roused him. Out of the gloom to the right came the faint, complaining howl of a malamute; it was answered by his own dogs, and the next moment they had caught a scent which swerved them shoreward and led them scrambling through the drifts. Two hundred yards, and a steep bank loomed above, up and over which they rushed, with Cantwell yelling encouragement; then a light showed, and they were in the lee of a low-roofed hut.

A sick native, huddled over a Yukon stove, made them welcome to his mean abode, explaining that his wife and son had gone to Unalaklik for supplies.

Johnny carried his partner to the one unoccupied bunk and stripped his clothes from him. With his own hands he rubbed the warmth back into Mortimer's limbs, then swiftly prepared hot food, and, holding him in the hollow of his aching arm, fed him, a little at a time. He was like to drop from exhaustion, but he made no complaint. With one folded robe he made the hard boards comfortable, then spread the other as a covering. For himself he sat beside the fire and fought his weariness. When he dozed off and the cold awakened him, he renewed the fire; he heated beeftea, and, rousing Mort, fed it to him with a teaspoon. All night long, at intervals, he tended the sick man, and Grant's eyes followed him with an expression that brought a fierce pain to Cantwell's throat.

"You're mighty good—after the rotten way I acted," the former whispered once.

And Johnny's big hand trembled so that he spilled the broth.

His voice was low and tender as he inquired, "Are you resting easier now?"

The other nodded.

"Maybe you're not hurt badly, after—all. God! That would be awful —" Cantwell choked, turned away, and, raising his arms against the log wall, buried his face in them.

The morning broke clear; Grant was sleeping. As Johnny stiffly mounted the creek bank with a bucket of water he heard a jingle of sleigh-bells and saw a sled with two white men swing in toward the cabin.

"Hello!" he called, then heard his own name pronounced.

"Johnny Cantwell, by all that's holy!"

The next moment he was shaking hands vigorously with two old friends from Nome.

"Martin and me are bound for Saint Mike's," one of them explained. "Where the deuce did you come from, Johnny?"

"The 'outside,' started for Stony River, but—"

"Stony River!" The newcomers began to laugh loudly and Cantwell joined them. It was the first time he had laughed for weeks. He realized the fact with a start, then recollected also his sleeping partner, and said, "Sh-h! Mort's inside, asleep!"

During the night everything had changed for Johnny Cantwell; his mental attitude, his hatred, his whole reasonless insanity. Everything was different now, even his debt was cancelled, the weight of obligation was removed, and his diseased fancies were completely cured.

"Yes! Stony River," he repeated, grinning broadly. "I bit!"

Martin burst forth gleefully, "They caught MacDonald at Holy Cross and ran him out on a limb. He'll never start another stampede. Old Man Baker gun-branded him."

"What's the matter with Mort?" inquired the second traveller.

"He's resting up. Yesterday, during the storm, he—" Johnny was upon the point of saying "played out," but changed it to "had an accident. We thought it was serious, but a few days' rest'll bring him around all right. He saved me at Katmai, coming in. I petered out and threw up my tail, but he got me through. Come inside and tell him the news."

"Sure thing."

"Well, well!" Martin said. "So you and Mort are still partners, eh?"

"*Still* partners!" Johnny took up the pail of water. "Well, rather! We'll always be partners." His voice was young and full and hearty as he continued: "Why, Mort's the best damned fellow in the world. I'd lay down my life for him."

Dust Storm

Max Brand was one of many pseudonyms used by Frederick Faust (1892–1944), one of the most amazing giants of the pulp fiction field. Faust produced about one hundred twenty-five novels and more than three hundred thirty stories in many fields (among other things, he was the creator of "Dr. Kildare"), but it was as a Western writer that he achieved his greatest fame. His stories were well-plotted, reasonably true to historical fact and always fast-moving and involving for the reader. He was so prolific that he often had three or four stories in the same magazine issue, each under a different name. He tragically died in action as a war correspondent for Harper's during World War II.

"Dust Storm," one of his best stories, captures all of the qualities that made him so popular, a popularity that continues today.

FOR SEVEN DAYS the wind came out of the northeast over the Powder Mountains and blew the skirts of a dust storm between Digger Hill and Bender Hill into the hollow where Lindsay was living in his shack. During that week Lindsay waked and slept with a piece of black coat-lining worn across his mouth and nostrils, but the dust penetrated like cosmic rays through the chinks in the walls of the cabin, through the mask and to the bottom of his lungs, so that every night he roused from sleep gasping for breath with a nightmare of being buried alive. Even lamplight could not drive that bad dream farther away than the misty corners of the room.

The blow began on a Tuesday morning, and by twilight of that day he knew what he was in for, so he went out through the whistling murk and led Jenny and Lind, his two mules, and Mustard, his old cream-colored mustang, from the pasture into the barn. There he had in the mow a good heap of the volunteer hay which he had cut last May on the southeast forty, but the thin silt of the storm soon whitened the hay to such a degree that he had to shake it thoroughly before he fed the stock. Every two hours during that week, he roused himself by an alarm-clock instinct and went out to wash the nostrils and mouths of the stock, prying their teeth open and reaching right in to swab the black off their tongues. On Wednesday,

Jenny, like the fool and villainess that she was, closed on his right forearm and raked off eight inches of skin.

Monotony of diet was more terrible to Lindsay than the storm. He had been on the point of riding to town and borrowing money from the bank on his growing crop so as to lay in a stock of provisions, but now he was confined with a bushel of potatoes and the heel of a side of bacon.

Only labor like that of the harvest field could make such food palatable and, in confinement as he was, never thoroughly stretching his muscles once a day, Lindsay began to revolt in belly and then in spirit. He even lacked coffee to give savor to the menu; he could not force himself more than once a day to eat potatoes, boiled or fried in bacon fat, with the dust gritting continually between his teeth.

He had no comfort whatever except for Caesar, his mongrel dog, and half a bottle of whisky, from which he gave himself a nip once a day. Then in the night of the seventh day, there came to Lindsay a dream of a country where rolling waves of grass washed from horizon to horizon and all the winds of the earth could not blow a single breath of dust into the blue of the sky. He wakened with the dawn visible through the cracks in the shanty walls and a strange expectancy in his mind.

That singular expectation remained in him when he threw the door open and looked across the black of the hills toward the green light that was opening like a fan in the east; then he realized that it was the silence after the storm that seemed more enormous than all the stretch of landscape between him and the Powder Mountains. Caesar ran out past his legs to leap and bark and sneeze until something overawed him, in turn, and sent him skulking here and there with his nose to the ground as though he were following invisible bird trails. It was true that the face of the land was changed.

As the light grew Lindsay saw that the water hole in the hollow was a black wallow of mud and against the woodshed leaned a sloping mass of dust like a drift of snow. The sight of this started him on the run for his eighty acres of winter-sown summer fallow. From a distance he saw the disaster but could not believe it until his feet were wading deep in the dust. Except for a few marginal strips, the whole swale of the plowed land was covered with wind-filtered soil, a yard thick in the deepest places.

Two thirds of his farm was wiped out, two thirds of it was erased into permanent sterility; and the work of nearly ten years was entombed. He glanced down at the palms of his hands, for he was thinking of the burning, pulpy blisters that had covered them day after day when he was digging holes with the blunt post auger.

He looked up, then, at the distant ridges of the Powder Mountains. Ten years before in the morning light he had been able almost to count the great pines that walked up the slopes and stood on the mountains' crests, but the whole range had been cut over in the interim and the thick coat of forest which bound with its roots the accumulated soil of a million years had been mowed down. That was why the teeth of the wind had found substance they could eat into.

The entire burden of precious loam that dressed the mountains had been blown adrift in recent years and now the worthless underclay, made friable by a dry season, was laid in a stifling coat of silt across the farmlands of the lower valleys and the upper pastures of the range.

Lindsay did not think about anything for a time. His feet, and an automatic impulse that made him turn always to the stock first, took him to the barn, where he turned loose the confined animals. Even the mules were glad enough to kick up their heels a few times, and fifteen years of hard living could not keep Mustard from exploding like a bomb all over the pasture, bucking as though a ghost were on his back and knocking up a puff of dust every time he hit the ground.

Lindsay, standing with feet spread and folded arms, a huge figure in the door of the barn, watched the antics of his old horse with a vacant smile, for he was trying to rouse himself and failing wretchedly. Instead, he could see himself standing in line with signed application slips in his hand, and then in front of a desk where some hired clerk with an insolent face put sharp questions to him. A month hence, when people asked him how things went, he would have to say, "I'm on the county."

When he had gone that far in his thinking, his soul at last rose in him but to such a cold, swift altitude that he was filled with fear, and he found his lips repeating words, stiffly, whispering them aloud, "I'll be damned and dead, first!" The fear of what he would do with his own hands grew stronger and stronger, for he felt that he had made a promise which would be heard and recorded by that living, inmost god of all honest men, his higher self.

Once more, automatically, his feet took him on to the next step in the day: breakfast. Back in the shanty, his lips twitched with disgust as he started frying potatoes; the rank smell of the bacon grease mounted to his brain and gathered in clouds there, but his unthinking hands finished the cookery and dumped the fried potatoes into a tin plate.

A faint chorus came down to him then out of the windless sky. He snatched the loaded pistol from the holster that hung against the wall and ran outside, for sometimes the wild geese, flying north, came very low over the hill as they rose from the marsh south of it, but now he found himself agape like a schoolboy, staring up.

He should have known by the dimness of the honking and by the melancholy harmony which distance added to it that the geese were half a mile up in the sky. Thousands of them were streaming north in a great wedge that kept shuffling and reshuffling at the open ends; ten tons of meat on the wing.

A tin pan crashed inside the shack and Caesar came out on wings with his tail between his legs; Lindsay went inside and found the plate of potatoes overturned on the floor. He called, "Come in here, Caesar, you damned old thief. Come in here and get it, if you want the stuff. I'm better without."

The dog came back, skulking. From the doorway he prospected the face of his master for a moment, slavering with greed: then he sneaked to the food on the floor and began to eat guiltily, but Lindsay already had forgotten him. All through the hollow, which a week before had been a shining tremor of yellow green wheat stalks, the rising wind of the morning was now stirring little airy whirlpools and walking ghosts of dust that made a step or two and vanished.

It seemed to Lindsay that he had endured long enough. He was thirty-five. He had twenty years of hard work behind him. And he would not —by God, he would not—be a government pensioner! The wild geese had called the gun into his hand; he felt, suddenly, that it must be used for one last shot anyway. As for life, there was a stinking savor of bacon that clung inevitably to it. He looked with fearless eyes into the big muzzle of the gun.

Then Mustard whinnied not far from the house and Lindsay lifted his head with a faint smile, for there was a stallion's trumpet sound in the neigh of the old gelding, always, just as there was always an active devil in his heels and his teeth. He combined the savage instincts of a wildcat with the intellectual, patient malevolence of a mule, but Lindsay loved the brute because no winter cold was sharp enough to freeze the big heart in him and no dry summer march was long enough to wither it. At fifteen, the old fellow still could put fifty miles of hard country behind him between dawn and dark. For years Lindsay had felt that those long, mulish ears must eventually point the way to some great destiny.

He stepped into the doorway now and saw that Mustard was whinnying a challenge to a horseman who jogged up the Gavvigan Trail with a telltale dust cloud boiling up behind. Mechanical instinct, again, made Lindsay drop the gun into the old leather holster that hung on the wall. Then he stepped outside to wait.

Half a mile off, the approaching rider put his horse into a lope and Lindsay recognized, by his slant in the saddle, that inveterate range tramp and worthless roustabout Gypsy Renner. He reined in at the door of the shack, lifted his bandanna from nose and mouth, and spat black.

"Got a drink, Bob?" he asked without other greeting.

"I've got a drink for you," said Lindsay.

"I'll get off a minute, then," replied Renner, and swung out of the saddle.

Lindsay poured some whisky into a tin cup and Renner received it without thanks. Dust was still rising like thick smoke from his shoulders.

"You been far?" asked Lindsay.

"From Boulder," said Renner.

"Much of the range like out yonder?"

"Mostly," said Renner.

He finished the whisky and held out the cup. Lindsay poured the rest of the bottle.

"If much of the range is like this," said Lindsay, "it's gonna be hell."

"It's gonna be and it is," said Renner. "It's hell already over on the Oliver Range."

"Wait a minute. That's where Andy Barnes and John Strect run their cows. What you mean it's hell up there?"

"That's where I'm bound," said Renner. "They're hiring men and guns on both sides. Most of the water holes and tanks on Andy Barnes's place are filled up with mud, right to the ridge of the Oliver Hills, and his cows are choking. And John Street, his land is clean because the wind kind of funneled the dust up over the hills and it landed beyond him. Andy has to water those cows and Street wants to charge ten cents a head. Andy says he'll be damned if he pays money for the water that God put free on earth. So there's gonna be a fight."

Lindsay looked through the door at that lumpheaded mustang of his and saw, between his mind and the world, a moonlight night with five thousand head of cattle, market-fat and full of beans, stampeding into the northeast with a thunder and rattle of split hoofs and a swordlike clashing of horns. He saw riders galloping ahead, vainly shooting into the face of the herd in the vain hope of turning it, until two of those cowpunchers, going it blind, clapped together and went down, head over heels.

"They used to be friends," said Lindsay. "They come so close to dying together, one night, that they been living side by side ever since; and they used to be friends."

"They got too damn rich," suggested Renner. "A rich man ain't nobody's friend. . . . It was you that saved the two hides of them one night in a stampede, ten, twelve years ago, wasn't it?"

Lindsay pointed to Mustard.

"Now I'm gonna tell you something about that," he said. "The fact is that those cows would've washed right over the whole three of us, but I was riding that Mustard horse, and when I turned him back and pointed him at the herd, he just went off like a roman candle and scattered sparks right up to the Milky Way. He pitched so damn hard that he pretty near snapped my head off and he made himself look so big that those steers doggone near fainted and pushed aside from that spot."

Renner looked at the mustang with his natural sneer. Then he said, "Anyway, there's gonna be a fight up there, and it's gonna be paid for."

"There oughtn't be no fight," answered big Bob Lindsay, frowning.

"They're mean enough to fight," said Renner. "Didn't you save their scalps? And ain't they left you to starve here on a hundred and twenty acres of blowsand that can't raise enough to keep a dog fat?"

"Yeah?" said Lindsay. "Maybe you better be vamoosing along."

Renner looked at him, left the shack and swung into the saddle. When he was safely there he muttered, "Ah, to hell with you!" and jogged away.

Lindsay, with a troubled mind, watched him out of sight. An hour later he saddled Mustard and took the way toward the Oliver Hills.

The Oliver Hills lie west of the Powder Mountains, their sides fat with grasslands all the way to the ridge, and right over the crest walked the posts of the fence that separated the holdings of Andy Barnes from those of John Street. Lindsay, as he came up the old Mexican Trail, stopped on a hilltop and took a careful view of the picture.

He had to strain his eyes a little because dust was blowing like battle smoke off the whitened acres of Andy Barnes and over the ridge, and that dust was stirred up by thousands of cattle which milled close to the fence line, drawn by the smell of water. Down the eastern hollows some of the beefs were wallowing in the holes where water once had been and where there was only mud now. But west of the ridge the lands of John Street were clean as green velvet under the noonday sun.

Scattered down the Street side of the fence, a score of riders wandered up and down with significant lines of light balancing across the pommels of the saddles. Those were the rifles. As many more cowpunchers headed the milling cattle of Andy Barnes with difficulty, for in clear view of the cows, but on Street's side of the fence ran a knee-deep stream of silver water that spread out into a quiet blue lake, halfway down the slope.

He found a gate onto the Street land and went through it. Two or three of the line-riders hailed him with waving hats. One of them sang out, "Where's your rifle, brother? Men ain't worth a damn here without they got rifles."

He found John Street sitting on a spectacular black horse just west of a hilltop where the rise of land gave him shelter from ambitious sharp-shooters. When he saw Lindsay, he grabbed him by the shoulders and bellowed like a bull in spring, "I knew you'd be over and I knew you'd be on the right side. By God, it's been eleven years since I was as glad to see you as I am today. . . . Boys, I wanta tell you what Bob Lindsay here done for me when I got caught in—"

"Shut up, will you?" said Lindsay. "Looks like Andy has got some pretty dry cows, over yonder."

"I hope they dry up till there's nothing but wind in their bellies," said John Street.

"I thought you and Andy been pretty good friends," said Lindsay.

"If he was my brother—if he was two brothers—if he was my son and daughter and my pa and ma, he's so damn mean that I'd see him in hellfire before I'd give him a cup of water to wash the hellfire cinders out of his throat," said John Street, in part.

So Lindsay rode back to the gate and around to the party of Andy Barnes, passing steers with caked, dry mud of the choked water holes layered around their muzzles. They were red-eyed with thirst and their bellowing seemed to rise like an unnatural thunder out of the ground instead of booming from the skies. Yearlings, already knock-kneed with weakness, were shouldered to the ground by the heavier stock and lay there, surrendering.

Andy Barnes sat cross-legged on the ground inside the rock circle of an old Indian camp on a hilltop, picking the grass, chewing it, spitting it out.

He had grown much fatter and redder of face and the fat had got into his eyes, leaving them a little dull and staring.

Lindsay sat down beside him.

"You know something, Bob?" said Andy.

"Know what?" asked Lindsay.

"My wife's kid sister is over to the house," said Andy. "She's just turned twenty-three and she's got enough sense to cook a man and steak and onions. As tall as your shoulder and the bluest damn' pair of eyes you ever seen outside a blind horse. Never had bridle or saddle on her and I dunno how she'd go in harness, but you got a pair of hands. What you say? She's heard about Bob Lindsay for ten years, and she don't believe that there's that much man outside of a fairy story."

"Shut up, will you?" said Lindsay. "Seems like ten cents ain't much to pay for the difference between two thousand dead steers and two thousand dogies, all picking grass and fat and happy."

"Look up at that sky," said Andy.

"I'm looking," said Lindsay.

"Look blue?"

"Yeah. Kind of."

"Who put the blue in it?"

"God, maybe."

"Anybody ever pay him for it? And who put the water in the ground and made it leak out again? And why should I pay for *that?*"

"There's a lot of difference," said Lindsay, "between a dead steer on the range and a live steer in Chicago."

"Maybe," dreamed Andy, "but I guess they won't all be dead. You see that yearling over yonder, standing kind of spray-legged, with its nose pretty near on the ground?"

"I see it," said Lindsay.

"When that yearling kneels down," said Andy, "ther's gonna be something happen. . . . Ain't that old Mustard?"

"Yeah, that's Mustard," said Lindsay, rising.

"If you ever get through with him," said Andy, "I got a lot of pasture land nothing ain't using where he could just range around and laugh himself to death. I ain't forgot when he was bucking the saddle off his back and knocking splinters out of the stars that night. He must've looked like a mountain to them steers, eh?"

Lindsay got on Mustard and rode over the hill. He went straight up to the fence which divided the two estates and dismounted before it with a wire pincers in his hand. He felt scorn and uttermost detestation for the thing he was about to do. Men who cut fences are dirty rustlers and horse thieves and every man jack of them ought to be strung up as high as the top of the Powder Mountains; but the thirsty uproar of the cattle drove him on to what he felt was both a crime and a sin.

It had been a far easier thing, eleven years ago, to save Barnes and Street from the stampeding herd than it was to save them now from the petty hatred that had grown up between them without cause, without reason. The posts stood at such distance apart that the wires were strung with an extra heavy tension. When the steel edges cut through the topmost strand, it parted with a twang and leaped back to either side, coiling and tangling like thin, bright metallic snakes around the posts.

Yelling voices of protest came shouting through the dusty wind. Lindsay could see men dropping off their horses and lying prone to level their rifles at him; and all at once it seemed to him that the odor of frying bacon grease was thickening in his nostrils again and that this was the true savor of existence.

He saw the Powder Mountains lifting their sides from brown to blue in the distant sky with a promise of better lands beyond that horizon but the promise was a lie, he knew. No matter what he did, he felt assured· that ten years hence he would be as now, a poor unrespected squatter on the range, slaving endlessly, not even for a monthly pay check, but merely to fill his larder with—bacon and Irish potatoes! Hope, as vital to the soul as breath to the nostrils, had been subtracted from him, and therefore what he did with his life was of no importance whatever. He leaned a little and snapped the pincers through the second wire of the fence.

He did not hear the sharp twanging sound of the parting strand, for a louder noise struck at his ear, a ringing rifle report full of resonance, like two heavy sledge hammers struck face to face. At his feet a riffle of dust lifted; he heard the bullet hiss like a snake through the grass. Then a whole volley crashed. Bullets went by him on rising notes of inquiry; and just behind him a slug spatted into the flesh of Mustard. Sometimes an ax makes a sound like that when it sinks into green wood.

He turned and saw Mustard sitting down like a dog, with his long, mulish ears pointing straight ahead and a look of pleased expectancy in his eyes. Out of a hole in his breast blood was pumping in long, thin jets.

Lindsay leaned and cut the third and last wire.

When he straightened again he heard the body of Mustard slump down against the ground with a squeaking, jouncing noise of liquids inside his belly. He did not lie on his side but with his head outstretched and his legs doubled under him as though he were playing a game and would spring up again in a moment.

Lindsay looked toward the guns. They never should have missed him the first time except that something like buck fever must have shaken the marksmen. He walked right through the open gap in the fence to meet the fire with a feeling that the wire clipper in his hand was marking him down like a cattle thief for the lowest sort of a death.

Then someone began to scream in a shrill falsetto. He recognized the voice of Big John Street, transformed by hysterical emotion. Street himself broke over the top of the hill with the black horse at a full gallop, yelling for his men to stop firing.

The wind of the gallop furled up the wide brim of his sombrero and he made a noble picture, considering the rifles of Andy Barnes, which must be sighting curiously at him by this time; then a hammer stroke clipped Lindsay on the side of the head. The Powder Mountains whirled into a mist of brown and blue; the grass spun before him like running water; he dropped to his knees, and down his face ran a soft, warm stream.

Into his dizzy view came the legs and the sliding hoofs of the black horse, cutting shallow furrows in the grass as it slid to a halt, and he heard the voice of John Street, dismounted beside him, yelling terrible oaths. He was grabbed beneath the armpits and lifted.

"Are you dead, Bob?" yelled Street.

"I'm gonna be all right," said Lindsay. He ran a finger tip through the bullet furrow in his scalp and felt the hard bone of the skull all the way. "I'm gonna be fine," he stated, and turned toward the uproar that was pouring through the gap he had cut in the fence.

For the outburst of rifle fire had taken the attention of Barnes's men from their herding and the cattle had surged past them toward water. Nothing now could stop that hungry stampede as they crowded through the gap with rattling hooves and the steady clashing of horns. Inside the fence the stream divided right and left and rushed on toward water, some to the noisy, white cataract, some to the wide blue pool.

"I'm sorry, John," said Lindsay, "but those cows looked kind of dry to me."

Then a nausea of body and a whirling dimness of mind overtook him and did not clear away again until he found himself lying with a bandaged head on the broad top of a hill. John Street was on one side of him and Andy Barnes on the other. They were holding hands like children and peering down at him anxiously.

"How are you, Bob, old son?" asked Andy.

"Fine," said Lindsay, sitting up. "Fine as a fiddle," he added, rising to his feet.

Street supported him hastily by one arm and Barnes by the other. Below him he could see the Barnes cattle thronging into the shallow water of the creek.

"About that ten cents a head," said Andy, "it's all right with me."

"Damn the money," said Street. "I wouldn't take money from you if you were made of gold. . . . I guess Bob has paid for the water like he paid for our two hides eleven years ago. Bob, don't you give a hang about nothing? Don't you care nothing about your life?"

"The cows seemed kind of dry to me," said Lindsay, helplessly.

"You're comin' home with me," said Street.

"I got *two* females in my place to look after him," pointed out Andy Barnes.

"I got a cook that's a doggone sight better than a doctor," said Street.

"I don't need any doctor," said Lindsay. "You two just shut up and say good-bye to me, will you? I'm going home. I got work to do tomorrow."

This remark produced a silence out of which Lindsay heard, from the surrounding circle of cowmen, a voice that murmured, "He's gonna go home!" And another said, "He's got the chores to do, I guess."

Andy looked at John Street.

"He's gonna go, John," he said.

"There ain't any changing him," said John Street sadly. "Hey, Bob, take this here horse of mine, will you?"

"Doncha do it!" shouted Barnes. "Hey, Mickie, bring up that gray, will you? . . . Look at that piece of gray sky and wind, Bob, will you?"

"They're a mighty slick pair," said Lindsay. "I never seen a more upstanding pair of hellcats in my life. It would take a lot of barley and oats to keep them sleeked up so's they shine like this. . . . But if you wanta wish a horse onto me, how about that down-headed, wise-lookin' cayuse over there? He's got some bottom to him and the hellfire is kind of worked out of his eyes."

He pointed to a brown gelding which seemed to have fallen half asleep.

Another silence was spread by this remark. Then someone said: "He's picked out Slim's cuttin' horse. . . . He's gone and picked out old Dick."

"Give them reins to Bob, Slim!" commanded Andy Barnes, "and leave the horse tied right onto the reins, too."

Lindsay said, "Am I parting you from something, Slim?"

Slim screwed up his face and looked at the sky.

"Why, I've heard about you, Lindsay," he said, "and today I've seen you. I guess when a horse goes to you, he's just going home; and this Dick horse of mine, I had the making of him and he sure rates a home. . . . If you just ease him along the first half hour, he'll be ready to die for you all the rest of the day."

"Thanks," said Lindsay, shaking hands. "I'm gonna value him, brother."

He swung into the saddle and waved his adieu. John Street followed him a few steps, and so did Andy Barnes.

"Are you gonna be comin' over? Are you gonna be comin' back, Bob?" they asked him.

"Are you two gonna stop being damn fools?" he replied.

They laughed and waved a cheerful agreement and they were still waving as he jogged Dick down the hill. The pain in his head burned him to the brain with every pulse of his blood but a strange feeling of triumph rose in his heart. He felt he never would be impatient again, for he could see that he was enriched forever.

The twilight found him close to home and planning the work of the next days. If he put a drag behind the two mules he could sweep back the dust where it thinned out at the margin and so redeem from total loss a few more acres. With any luck, he would get seed for the next year; and as for food, he could do what he had scorned all his days—he could make a kitchen garden and irrigate it from the windmill.

It was dark when he came up the last slope and the stars rose like fireflies over the edge of the hill. Against them he made out Jenny and Lind waiting for him beside the door of the shack. He paused to stare at the vague silhouettes and remembered poor Mustard with a great stroke in his heart.

Caesar came with a shrill howl of delight to leap about his master and bark at the new horse, but Dick merely pricked his ears with patient understanding as though he knew he had come home indeed.

Inside the shanty the hand of Lindsay found the lantern. Lighting it brought a suffocating odor of kerosene fumes, but even through this Lindsay could detect the smell of fried bacon and potatoes in the air. He took a deep breath of it for it seemed to him the most delicious savor in the world.

THE SECOND FIFTY YEARS

Top Hand

With the exception of Louis L'Amour, no writer of popular Westerns attracted a larger and more faithful audience in the fifties, sixties, and seventies than Luke Short (Frederick D. Glidden). From 1936, when his first novel, The Feud at Single Shot, *was published, until his death in 1975, he wrote more than fifty novels whose aggregate sales in hardcover and paperback exceeded thirty million copies. Among his most memorable titles are* Fiddlefoot, Saddle by Starlight, High Vermilion, Silver Rock, *and* King Colt. *Many of his short stories, and many of his longer works as well, appeared in such magazines as* Collier's *and* The Saturday Evening Post. *It was in the pages of the latter that "Top Hand," considered by many to be the finest of his short tales, first saw print in 1943.*

GUS IRBY was out on the boardwalk in front of the Elite, giving his swamper hell for staving in an empty beer barrel, when the kid passed on his way to the feed stable. His horse was a good one and it was tired, Gus saw, and the kid had a little hump in his back from the cold of a mountain October morning. In spite of the ample layer of flesh that Gus wore carefully like an uncomfortable shroud, he shivered in his shirt sleeves and turned into the saloon, thinking without much interest *Another fiddlefooted dry-country kid that's been paid off after round-up.*

Later, while he was taking out the cash for the day and opening up some fresh cigars, Gus saw the kid go into the Pride Café for breakfast, and afterward come out, toothpick in mouth, and cruise both sides of Wagon Mound's main street in aimless curiosity.

After that, Gus wasn't surprised when he looked around at the sound of the door opening, and saw the kid coming toward the bar. He was in a clean and faded shirt and looked as if he'd been cold for a good many hours. Gus said good morning and took down his best whisky and a glass and put them in front of the kid.

"First customer in the morning gets a drink on the house," Gus announced.

"Now I know why I rode all night," the kid said, and he grinned at Gus.

He was a pleasant-faced kid with pale eyes that weren't shy or sullen or bold, and maybe because of this he didn't fit readily into any of Gus' handy character pigeonholes. Gus had seen them young and fiddlefooted before, but they were the tough kids, and for a man with no truculence in him, like Gus, talking with them was like trying to pet a tiger.

Gus leaned against the back bar and watched the kid take his whisky and wipe his mouth on his sleeve, and Gus found himself getting curious. Half a lifetime of asking skillful questions that didn't seem like questions at all, prompted Gus to observe now, "If you're goin' on through you better pick up a coat. This high country's cold now."

"I figure this is far enough," the kid said.

"Oh, well, if somebody sent for you, that's different." Gus reached around lazily for a cigar.

The kid pulled out a silver dollar from his pocket and put it on the bar top, and then poured himself another whisky, which Gus was sure he didn't want, but which courtesy dictated he should buy. "Nobody sent for me, either," the kid observed. "I ain't got any money."

Gus picked up the dollar and got change from the cash drawer and put it in front of the kid, afterward lighting his cigar. This was when the announcement came.

"I'm a top hand," the kid said quietly, looking levelly at Gus. "Who's lookin' for one?"

Gus was glad he was still lighting his cigar, else he might have smiled. If there had been a third man here, Gus would have winked at him surreptitiously; but since there wasn't, Gus kept his face expressionless, drew on his cigar a moment, and then observed gently, "You look pretty young for a top hand."

"The best cow pony I ever saw was four years old," the kid answered pointedly.

Gus smiled faintly and shook his head. "You picked a bad time. Round-up's over."

The kid nodded, and drank down his second whisky quickly, waited for his breath to come normally. Then he said, "Much obliged. I'll see you again," and turned toward the door.

A mild cussedness stirred within Gus, and after a moment's hesitation he called out, "Wait a minute."

The kid hauled up and came back to the bar. He moved with an easy grace that suggested quickness and work-hardened muscle, and for a moment Gus, a careful man, was undecided. But the kid's face, so young and without caution, reassured him, and he folded his heavy arms on the bar top and pulled his nose thoughtfully. "You figure to hit all the outfits, one by one, don't you?"

The kid nodded, and Gus frowned and was silent a moment, and then he murmured, almost to himself, "I had a notion—oh, hell, I don't know."

"Go ahead," the kid said, and then his swift grin came again. "I'll try anything once."

"Look," Gus said, as if his mind were made up. "We got a newspaper here—the Wickford County Free Press. Comes out every Thursday, that's today." He looked soberly at the kid. "Whyn't you put a piece in there and say 'Top hand wants a job at forty dollars a month'? Tell 'em what you can do and tell 'em to come see you here if they want a hand. They'll all get it in a couple days. That way you'll save yourself a hundred miles of ridin'. Won't cost much either."

The kid thought awhile and then asked, without smiling, "Where's this newspaper at?"

Gus told him and the kid went out. Gus put the bottle away and doused the glass in water, and he was smiling slyly at his thoughts. Wait till the boys read that in the Free Press. They were going to have some fun with that kid, Gus reflected.

Johnny McSorley stepped out into the chill thin sunshine. The last silver dollar in his pants pocket was a solid weight against his leg, and he was aware that he'd probably spend it in the next few minutes on the newspaper piece. He wondered about that, and figured shrewdly it had an off chance of working.

Four riders dismounted at a tie rail ahead and paused a moment, talking. Johnny looked them over and picked out their leader, a tall, heavy, scowling man in his middle thirties who was wearing a mackinaw unbuttoned.

Johnny stopped and said, "You know anybody lookin' for a top hand?" and grinned pleasantly at the big man.

For a second Johnny thought he was going to smile. He didn't think he'd have liked the smile, once he saw it, but the man's face settled into the scowl again. "I never saw a top hand that couldn't vote," he said.

Johnny looked at him carefully, not smiling, and said, "Look at one now, then," and went on, and by the time he'd taken two steps he thought, *Voted, huh? A man must grow pretty slow in this high country.*

He crossed the street and paused before a window marked WICKFORD COUNTY FREE PRESS. JOB PRINTING. D. MELAVEN, ED. AND PROP. He went inside, then. A girl was seated at a cluttered desk, staring at the street, tapping a pencil against her teeth. Johnny tramped over to her, noting the infernal racket made by one of two men at a small press under the lamp behind the railed-off office space.

Johnny said "Hello," and the girl turned tiredly and said, "Hello, bub." She had on a plain blue dress with a high bodice and a narrow lace collar, and she was a very pretty girl, but tired, Johnny noticed. Her long yellow hair was worn in braids that crossed almost atop her head, and she looked, Johnny thought, like a small kid who has pinned her hair up out of the way for her Saturday night bath. He thought all this and then remembered her greeting, and he reflected without rancor, *Damn, that's twice,* and he said, "I got a piece for the paper, sis."

"Don't call me sis," the girl said. "Anybody's name I don't know, I call him bub. No offense. I got that from pa, I guess."

That's likely, Johnny thought, and he said amiably, "Any girl's name I don't know, I call her sis. I got that from ma."

The cheerful effrontery of the remark widened the girl's eyes. She held out her hand now and said with dignity, "Give it to me. I'll see it gets in next week."

"That's too late," Johnny said. "I got to get it in this week."

"Why?"

"I ain't got money enough to hang around another week."

The girl stared carefully at him. "What is it?"

"I want to put a piece in about myself. I'm a top hand, and I'm lookin' for work. The fella over there at the saloon says why don't I put a piece in the paper about wantin' work, instead of ridin' out lookin' for it."

The girl was silent a full five seconds and then said, "You don't look that simple. Gus was having fun with you."

"I figured that," Johnny agreed. "Still, it might work. If you're caught short-handed, you take anything."

The girl shook her head. "It's too late. The paper's made up." Her voice was meant to hold a note of finality, but Johnny regarded her curiously, with a maddening placidity.

"You D. Melaven?" he asked.

"No. That's pa."

"Where's he?"

"Back there. Busy."

Johnny saw the gate in the rail that separated the office from the shop and he headed toward it. He heard the girl's chair scrape on the floor and her urgent command, "Don't go back there. It's not allowed."

Johnny looked over his shoulder and grinned and said, "I'll try anything once," and went on through the gate, hearing the girl's swift steps behind him. He halted alongside a square-built and solid man with a thatch of stiff hair more gray than black, and said, "You D. Melaven?"

"Dan Melaven, bub. What can I do for you?"

That's three times, Johnny thought, and he regarded Melaven's square face without anger. He liked the face; it was homely and stubborn and intelligent, and the eyes were both sharp and kindly. Hearing the girl stop beside him, Johnny said, "I got a piece for the paper today."

The girl put in quickly, "I told him it was too late, pa. Now you tell him, and maybe he'll get out."

"Cassie," Melaven said in surprised protest.

"I don't care. We can't unlock the forms for every out-at-the-pants puncher that asks us. Besides, I think he's one of Alec Barr's bunch." She spoke vehemently, angrily, and Johnny listened to her with growing amazement.

"Alec who?" he asked.

"I saw you talking to him, and then you came straight over here from him," Cassie said hotly.

"I hit him for work."

"I don't believe it."

"Cassie," Melaven said grimly, "come back here a minute." He took her by the arm and led her toward the back of the shop, where they halted and engaged in a quiet, earnest conversation.

Johnny shook his head in bewilderment, and then looked around him. The biggest press, he observed, was idle. And on a stone-topped table where Melaven had been working was a metal form almost filled with lines of type and gray metal pieces of assorted sizes and shapes. Now, Johnny McSorley did not know any more than the average person about the workings of a newspaper, but his common sense told him that Cassie had lied to him when she said it was too late to accept his advertisement. Why, there was space and to spare in that form for the few lines of type his message would need. Turning this over in his mind, he wondered what was behind her refusal.

Presently, the argument settled, Melaven and Cassie came back to him, and Johnny observed that Cassie, while chastened, was still mad.

"All right, what do you want printed, bub?" Melaven asked.

Johnny told him and Melaven nodded when he was finished, said, "Pay her," and went over to the type case.

Cassie went back to the desk and Johnny followed her, and when she was seated he said, "What do I owe you?"

Cassie looked speculatively at him, her face still flushed with anger. "How much money have you got?"

"A dollar some."

"It'll be two dollars," Cassie said.

Johnny pulled out his lone silver dollar and put it on the desk. "You print it just the same; I'll be back with the rest later."

Cassie said with open malice, "You'd have it now, bub, if you hadn't been drinking before ten o'clock."

Johnny didn't do anything for a moment, and then he put both hands on the desk and leaned close to her. "How old are you?" he asked quietly.

"Seventeen."

"I'm older'n you," Johnny murmured. "So the next time you call me 'bub' I'm goin' to take down your pigtails and pull 'em. I'll try anything once."

Once he was in the sunlight, crossing toward the Elite, he felt better. He smiled—partly at himself but mostly at Cassie. She was a real spitfire, kind of pretty and kind of nice, and he wished he knew what her father said to her that made her so mad, and why she'd been mad in the first place.

Gus was breaking out a new case of whisky and stacking bottles against the back mirror as Johnny came in and went up to the bar. Neither of them spoke while Gus finished, and Johnny gazed absently at the poker game at one of the tables and now yawned sleepily.

Gus said finally, "You get it in all right?"

Johnny nodded thoughtfully and said, "She mad like that at every-body?"

"Who? Cassie?"

"First she didn't want to take the piece, but her old man made her. Then she charges me more for it than I got in my pocket. Then she combs me over like I got my head stuck in the cookie crock for drinkin' in the morning. She calls me bub, to boot."

"She calls everybody bub."

"Not me no more," Johnny said firmly, and yawned again.

Gus grinned and sauntered over to the cash box. When he came back he put ten silver dollars on the bar top and said, "Pay me back when you get your job. And I got rooms upstairs if you want to sleep."

Johnny grinned. "Sleep, hunh? I'll try anything once." He took the money, said "Much obliged" and started away from the bar and then paused. "Say, who's this Alec Barr?"

Johnny saw Gus's eyes shift swiftly to the poker game and then shuttle back to him. Gus didn't say anything.

"See you later," Johnny said.

He climbed the stairs whose entrance was at the end of the bar, wondering why Gus was so careful about Alec Barr.

A gunshot somewhere out in the street woke him. The sun was gone from the room, so it must be afternoon, he thought. He pulled on his boots, slopped some water into the washbowl and washed up, pulled hand across his cheek and decided he should shave, and went downstairs. There wasn't anybody in the saloon, not even behind the bar. On the tables and on the bar top, however, were several newspapers, all fresh. He was reminded at once that he was in debt to the Wickford County Free Press for the sum of one dollar. He pulled one of the newspapers toward him and turned to the page where all the advertisements were.

When, after some minutes, he finished, he saw that his advertisement was not there. A slow wrath grew in him as he thought of the girl and her father taking his money, and when it had come to full flower, he went out of the Elite and cut across toward the newspaper office. He saw, without really noticing it, the group of men clustered in front of the store across from the newspaper office. He swung under the tie rail and reached the opposite boardwalk just this side of the newspaper office and a man who was lounging against the building. He was a puncher and when he saw Johnny heading up the walk he said, "Don't go across there."

Johnny said grimly, "You stop me," and went on, and he heard the puncher say, "All right, getcher head blown off."

His boots crunched broken glass in front of the office and he came to a gingerly halt, looking down at his feet. His glance raised to the window, and he saw where there was a big jag of glass out of the window, neatly wiping out the Wickford except for the W on the sign and ribboning cracks to all four corners of the frame. His surprise held him motionless for a moment, and then he heard a voice calling from across the street, "Clear out of there, son."

That makes four times, Johnny thought resignedly, and he glanced across the street and saw Alec Barr, several men clotted around him, looking his way.

Johnny went on and turned into the newspaper office and pit was like walking into a dark cave. The lamp was extinguished.

And then he saw the dim forms of Cassie Melaven and her father back of the railing beside the job press, and the reason for his errand came back to him with a rush. Walking through the gate, he began firmly, "I got a dollar owed—" and ceased talking and halted abruptly. There was a six-shooter in Dan Melaven's hand hanging at his side. Johnny looked at it, and then raised his glance to Melaven's face and found the man watching him with a bitter amusement in his eyes. His glance shuttled to Cassie, and she was looking at him as if she didn't see him, and her face seemed very pale in that gloom. He half gestured toward the gun and said, "What's that for?"

"A little trouble, bub," Melaven said mildly. "Come back for your money?"

"Yeah," Johnny said slowly.

Suddenly it came to him, and he wheeled and looked out through the broken window and saw Alec Barr across the street in conversation with two men, his own hands, Johnny supposed. That explained the shot that wakened him. A little trouble.

He looked back at Melaven now in time to hear him say to Cassie, "Give him his money."

Cassie came past him to the desk and pulled open a drawer and opened the cash box. While she was doing it, Johnny strolled soberly over to the desk. She gave him the dollar and he took it, and their glances met. She's been crying, he thought, with a strange distress.

"That's what I tried to tell you," Cassie said. "We didn't want to take your money, but you wouldn't have it. That's why I was so mean."

"What's it all about?" Johnny asked soberly.

"Didn't you read the paper?"

Johnny shook his head in negation, and Cassie said dully, "It's right there on page one. There's a big chunk of Government land out on Artillery Creek coming up for sale. Alec Barr wanted it, but he didn't want anybody bidding against him. He knew pa would have to publish a notice of sale. He tried to get pa to hold off publication of the date of sale until it would be too late for other bidders to make it. Pa was to get a piece of the land in return for the favor, or money. I guess we needed it all right, but pa told him no."

Johnny looked over at Melaven, who had come up to the rail now and was listening. Melaven said, "I knew Barr'd be in today with his bunch, and they'd want a look at a pull sheet before the press got busy, just to make sure the notice wasn't there. Well, Cassie and Dad Hopper worked with me all last night to turn out the real paper, with the notice of sale and a front-page editorial about Barr's proposition to me, to boot."

"We got it printed and hid it out in the shed early this morning," Cassie explained.

Melaven grinned faintly at Cassie, and there was a kind of open admiration for the job in the way he smiled. He said to Johnny now, "So what you saw in the forms this mornin' was a fake, bub. That's why Cassie didn't want your money. The paper was already printed." He smiled again, that rather proud smile. "After you'd gone, Barr came in. He wanted a pull sheet and we gave it to him, and he had a man out front watching us most of the morning. But he pulled him off later. We got the real paper out of the shed onto the Willow Valley stage, and we got it delivered all over town before Barr saw it."

Johnny was silent a moment, thinking this over. Then he nodded toward the window. "Barr do that?"

"I did," Melaven said quietly. "I reckon I can keep him out until someone in this town gets the guts to run him off."

Johnny looked down at the dollar in his hand and stared at it a moment and put it in his pocket. When he looked up at Cassie, he surprised her watching him, and she smiled a little, as if to ask forgiveness.

Johnny said, "Want any help?" to Melaven, and the man looked at him thoughtfully and then nodded. "Yes. You can take Cassie home."

"Oh, no," Cassie said. She backed away from the desk and put her back against the wall, looking from one to the other. "I don't go. As long as I'm here, he'll stay there."

"Sooner or later, he'll come in," Melaven said grimly. "I don't want you hurt."

"Let him come," Cassie said stubbornly. "I can swing a wrench better than some of his crew can shoot."

"Please go with him."

Cassie shook her head. "No, pa. There's some men left in this town. They'll turn up."

Melaven said "Hell," quietly, angrily, and went back into the shop. Johnny and the girl looked at each other for a long moment, and Johnny saw the fear in her eyes. She was fighting it, but she didn't have it licked, and he couldn't blame her. He said, "If I'd had a gun on me, I don't reckon they'd of let me in here, would they?"

"Don't try it again," Cassie said. "Don't try the back either. They're out there."

Johnny said, "Sure you won't come with me?"

"I'm sure."

"Good," Johnny said quietly. He stepped outside and turned upstreet, glancing over at Barr and the three men with him, who were watching him wordlessly. The man leaning against the building straightened up and asked, "She comin' out?"

"She's thinkin' it over," Johnny said.

The man called across the street to Barr, "She's thinkin' it over," and Johnny headed obliquely across the wide street toward the Elite. *What kind of a town is this, where they'd let this happen?* he thought angrily, and then he caught sight of Gus Irby standing under the wooden awning in front of the Elite, watching the show. Everybody else was doing the same thing. A man behind Johnny yelled, "Send her out, Melaven," and Johnny vaulted up onto the boardwalk and halted in front of Gus.

"What do you aim to do?" he asked Gus.

"Mind my own business, same as you," Gus growled, but he couldn't hold Johnny's gaze.

There was shame in his face, and when Johnny saw it his mind was made up. He shouldered past him and went into the Elite and saw it was empty. He stepped behind the bar now and, bent over so he could look under it, slowly traveled down it. Right beside the beer taps he found what he was looking for. It was a sawed-off shotgun and he lifted it up and broke it and saw that both barrels were loaded. Standing motionless, he thought about this now, and presently he moved on toward the back and went out the rear door. It opened onto an alley, and he turned left and went up it, thinking, *It was brick, and the one next to it was painted brown, at least in front.* And then he saw it up ahead, a low brick store with a big loading platform running across its rear.

He went up to it, and looked down the narrow passageway he'd remembered was between this building and the brown one beside it. There was a small areaway here, this end cluttered with weeds and bottles and tin cans. Looking through it he could see a man's elbow and segment of leg at the boardwalk, and he stepped as noiselessly as he could over the trash and worked forward to the boardwalk.

At the end of the areaway, he hauled up and looked out and saw Alec

Barr some ten feet to his right and teetering on the edge of the high boardwalk, gun in hand. He was engaged in low conversation with three other men on either side of him. There was a supreme insolence in the way he exposed himself, as if he knew Melaven would not shoot at him and could not hit him if he did.

Johnny raised the shotgun hip high and stepped out and said quietly, "Barr, you goin' to throw away that gun and get on your horse or am I goin' to burn you down?"

The four men turned slowly, not moving anything except their heads. It was Barr whom Johnny watched, and he saw the man's bold baleful eyes gauge his chances and decline the risk, and Johnny smiled. The three other men were watching Barr for a clue to their moves.

Johnny said "Now," and on the heel of it he heard the faint clatter of a kicked tin can in the areaway behind him. He lunged out of the areaway just as a pistol shot erupted with a savage roar between the two buildings.

Barr half turned now with the swiftness with which he lifted his gun across his front, and Johnny, watching him, didn't even raise the shotgun in his haste; he let go from the hip. He saw Barr rammed off the high boardwalk into the tie rail, and heard it crack and splinter and break with the big man's weight, and then Barr fell in the street out of sight.

The three other men scattered into the street, running blindly for the opposite sidewalk. And at the same time, the men who had been standing in front of the buildings watching this now ran toward Barr, and Gus Irby was in the van. Johnny poked the shotgun into the areaway and without even taking sight he pulled the trigger and listened to the bellow of the explosion and the rattling raking of the buckshot as it caromed between the two buildings. Afterward, he turned down the street and let Gus and the others run past him, and he went into the Elite.

It was empty, and he put the shotgun on the bar and got himself a glass of water and stood there drinking it, thinking, *I feel some different, but not much.*

He was still drinking water when Gus came in later. Gus looked at him long and hard, as he poured himself a stout glass of whisky and downed it. Finally, Gus said, "There ain't a right thing about it, but they won't pay you a bounty for him. They should."

Johnny didn't say anything, only rinsed out his glass.

"Melaven wants to see you," Gus said then.

"All right." Johnny walked past him and Gus let him get past him ten feet, and then said, "Kid, look."

Johnny halted and turned around and Gus, looking sheepish, said, "About that there newspaper piece. That was meant to be a rawhide, but damned if it didn't backfire on me."

Johnny just waited, and Gus went on. "You remember the man that was standing this side of Barr? He works for me, runs some cows for me. Did, I mean, because he stood there all afternoon sickin' Barr on Melaven. You want his job? Forty a month, top hand."

"Sure," Johnny said promptly.

Gus smiled expansively and said, "Let's have a drink on it."

"Tomorrow," Johnny said. "I don't aim to get a reputation for drinkin' all day long."

Gus looked puzzled, and then laughed. "Reputation? Who with? Who knows—" His talk faded off, and then he said quietly, "Oh."

Johnny waited long enough to see if Gus would smile, and when Gus didn't, he went out. Gus didn't smile after he'd gone either.

ERNEST HAYCOX

High Wind

No one, it has been said, wrote the traditional Western story better than Ernest Haycox. Such novels as The Earth-breakers, Alder Gulch, Long Storm *and* Bugles in the Afternoon, *and such collections as* Murder on the Frontier, Pioneer Loves, By Rope and Lead *and* Rough Justice, *offer eloquent testimony in support of that claim. In Haycox's hands, the simplest (and sometimes most conventional) theme became something moving, powerful, memorable. "High Wind" is a perfect case in point—a story so good it captures the true essence of life in frontier towns like Abilene.*

WHEN ABBIE saw his big, easygoing shape press through the crowd on the platform, she stepped down from the car vestibule and went directly to him, excitement turning her dark and definite New England face quite lovely. He was enormously smiling; he simply absorbed her inside his arms. They were not particularly demonstrative people, but this was the climax of two years' waiting and two thousand miles of westward travel and it made them quite indifferent to the crowd round about.

Buck LaGrange said, "It's been a long time, Abbie," and kissed her in a way that erased for a moment her faint dread. Afterward he stepped back, his deeply pleased glance absorbing this girl who had come from their common home in Connecticut to marry him.

"You've changed," she said.

"Better or worse?"

"You're bigger—you're different."

The train porter had piled her luggage on the platform. Buck LaGrange said to a nearby man, "Put this stuff in my buggy, Pete," and drew Abbie over the platform.

Across the way Abilene's frame buildings made a raw, ragged line. There was a high wind blowing up from the south, dust-laden, hot, steady. When they left the lee shelter of the depot, it threw her against Buck LaGrange and at once smothered her breathing.

She put a hand on her hat, gasping, "It's been like this all the way from Omaha. Does it never stop?"

He had to shout his answer against the wind. "Can't tell about a dust storm."

They beat across the street, following a weather-warped boardwalk as far as a small building on a corner; Buck LaGrange opened its door and pushed her in and closed the door again. Two men were standing in the narrow room, and a third man rose from a plain pine table. Buck La-Grange's amusement rolled out of his throat. "She's getting an immediate introduction to our prairie zephyr. Abbie, this is Mayor Henry, and Steve Gearin—and Wild Bill Hickok."

She acknowledged their slow nods with the briefest tilt of her own dark head, knowing nothing better to do. The wind shouldered against the walls and set up a squeezing protest of the boards. Something outside cracked like a pistol's shot. A man's yell whipped down the street, and suddenly she remembered Wild Bill Hickok's name with a start. Even in Connecticut, where the reports of the world seemed to be heard only as muffled echoes, this man's reputation had penetrated, and his deeds had become a legend out of the Wild West.

She recalled one thing she had read about him in a magazine—that he had killed nine men single-handed in one bloody fight. It caused her to draw faintly back against Buck LaGrange, but she made her eyes remain on Wild Bill. He was very tall and symmetrical, with light hair falling full length to his shoulders and a stringy mustache bordering full, broad lips. All his features were big and bold; yet they were soft, almost as soft as a woman's.

Buck LaGrange's deeply pleased words broke in, "Theodore"—pointing to Mayor Henry—"is a justice of the peace and can perform the ceremony. I asked Bill and Steve to be witnesses. These are my best friends. Well, I left Connecticut and this girl two years ago. It has been a long wait for both of us. Go ahead, Theodore."

The drumming of the wind, the eerie yellow color of the daylight, the strangeness of the town—these things confused her. Buck took her hand, and Mayor Henry, not much more than a boy behind his beard, said something about the authority of the state of Kansas. She heard herself whisper, "Yes." Then Buck turned her about in his big arms and kissed her. Wild Bill was watching all this with his heavy, winkless glance. His voice was musical and infinitely courteous. "It is not an easy country on women. Use your friends, Mrs. LaGrange, when you need them. Buck is to be congratulated."

The other two men shook hands with her, but it was all hazy and hurried, with Buck guiding her through the door. Somebody had brought the buggy around, and she climbed to the seat and felt the blast of the wind. A square sheet of paper curled through the half gale, so weirdly that the nervous horses began bucking. Buck's voice lifted. "Steady—steady." He was laughing. He bent over, shouting, "Write and tell your people the greatest gunman in the West was a witness at the ceremony!"

"A desperado!"

He didn't hear. He said, "What?" She didn't answer. They were careening around a corner, enveloped by a whirling wave of dust and sand. A row of houses, all unpainted and angular, sat along the short street; and beyond lay the howling open country, lost behind the dust. They stopped. Buck tied the reins and got down, handing her out. He led her across a yard faintly marked by tufts of scorched buffalo grass to a house standing square and uncompromising in the yellow light. Nothing distinguished it from the other houses, nothing relieved its barren outline. Buck opened the door quickly.

A hot, trapped air rolled into her face. The smell of dust and baked lumber was overpowering. It moved her backward against him, and he had to propel her gently across the threshold. When he closed the door, the eternal rush of the wind died to a groaning, rubbing sibilance. A few pieces of furniture partially relieved the gauntness of the room. There was a white cloth on a center table, slowly turning gray.

"This is our home?"

"This is it," he said.

She turned toward him, and the sight of her eyes instantly sobered him. He delayed speaking a moment, seeking the right words. He said, "I tried not to lead you to expect too much in my letters. It isn't the sort of house you came from. There are no such houses in Abilene. This town's only four years old. About all I can say is that nobody else here lives in any better house."

She came against him, putting her head down. He steadied her. "The zephyr's on your nerves, honey."

"Does it never stop?"

"Maybe tonight. Maybe a month from tonight. Nobody knows."

He went out for her luggage, making several trips of it, and afterward stabled his horses and rig in the barn behind the house. When he came back he found her in the kitchen, staring darkly at the stove. Wind gushed down the pipe, throwing ashes out through the grating. There was a mat of ashes on the floor.

He said, inexpressibly gentle, "One thing all of us have been forced to learn out here. We haven't the time nor the strength yet to fight the temper of the weather. The land won't change for us. We have to change with the land."

She was still watching the stove. "You have changed, Buck."

"In Connecticut I was a grocery clerk. I never would have been anything better. There's a chance for everybody out here. I mean to take my chance—and make a go of it."

She turned then. His deep pleasure was gone, and a shadow hovered faintly across his eyes. She knew what that was—it was the reflection of the doubt he had seen on her face. She had disappointed him. In this first hour of hope and happiness, her faint withdrawing had made it less than perfect; and because he was a New Englander, she knew the flaw would lie in his memory. The situation had slipped out of her hands. She didn't know how to set the shadow aside.

She said, with a faint laconic drawl, "I had better begin to work."

It continued to lie between them and to chill the intimacy which should have been theirs—the memory of that single instant in which her faith had wavered. Across the breakfast table she felt how easy it would be to bridge that gap with one warm word—and could not find the word; at night she knew he had only to put his arms around her in the rough, hot way of a man and kill the coldness forever. But he did not. In his slow, quiet talk was a perception of her reserve and a memory of his hurt.

This was the fourth day of their marriage; this was the fourth day of the wind. Walking with him toward the stores of Abilene, holding her skirts resolutely against the gusty plucking of that southern blast, she stared at the smoldering yellow sky and the sand-shot air with a feeling of unreality. It was as though she had been transplanted from a familiar world to the howling vacuum of another planet. The train was in from Omaha, spilling out its load of settlers and increasing the confusion in this bustling town. Men on the street spoke cordially to Buck. Everybody knew him; everybody seemed glad to see him. It reminded her more sharply of the fact that this genial, chuckling man was not the diffident Connecticut youth she once had known.

At Herrick's store he stopped. "I'm taking a couple of Dutchmen out to see some land. It looks like a sale. Real estate is on the boom, Abbie. I knew it would come some day." Then his solid pleasure broadened. "Land is our wealth."

Wild Bill came by and spoke. It was morning, with the dust rolling against all the building fronts. Up and down the uneven sidewalks cruised cattle hands in from the Texas trail, restless and reckless in their brief stay here. Steady traffic rolled through the saloon doors studding this street, and men's voices were high and rough against the wail of the wind. The smell of the stockyards on the southern edge of town covered everything unpleasantly.

"Just one thing, Abbie. We make our money from cattle driven here, and from the cowhands that come along. They're free spenders—and they're all wild. It's a rule that decent women stay out of this district after dark. But you're safe enough by daylight. No cowhand will presume to speak to you."

He lifted his hat and walked away; she turned into the grateful shelter of the store. She knew some of the women already there and acknowledged their greetings. Flora Gearin, the wife of that Steve Gearin who had been a witness at the mayor's office, came over to talk. She was a comfortably plump woman full of aimless gossip. In a little while Abbie went out, her arms full. Three cowhands rolled toward her and for a moment she felt fear; but it was strange how all of them instantly left the walk and passed by her without looking. Crossing the tracks, she saw Buck standing with a party of new settlers, his big shape rising above them. She had a doormat rolled under her arm. It dropped, and she struggled with her skirts and got it again and went on, the wind-driven sand stinging her fresh cheeks. Dust lay thick along her porch. It rose in powdery waves when she arranged the mat in front of the door; it clung to her shoes and left prints across the bare boards of the living room.

Coming home late in the afternoon, Buck LaGrange found her on her knees with a scrub brush and a bucket of water. She had a towel tied around her head, and against its whiteness her face was very dark, very slim. She looked at him, not stopping her work. "Please brush your shoes on the mat before coming in."

He obeyed and closed the door and stood against it, observing the flush of her cheeks, the fire of energy that glowed through her. He didn't protest. He understood the driving zeal for order and cleanliness that impelled this New England girl to toil on her knees. But he said quietly, "Don't try to do it all at once, Abbie."

She sat back on her legs, small and indomitable in the center of the floor. "The Gearins are coming tonight. I won't receive them in a dirty house."

"There are no clean houses in Abilene. You'll have to compromise with the dust. It will creep back as soon as you scrub it away. It will be in your clothes and your hair and in your food."

Her shoulders suddenly sloped, bereft of vigor. Her voice ran low. "Always?"

"No. In twenty years we'll have trees around Abilene to break this wind."

She murmured, "We'll be old people in twenty years, Buck."

He dissented cheerfully. "It will be a grown town in a settled country then. Such riches and comforts as there are, we shall share." He stopped, waiting for an answer that didn't come, then added gently, "The first years are hardest. Don't make them harder than necessary."

She rose and went into the kitchen, not speaking.

After supper the Gearins came. Hands folded across a fresh dress, Abbie sat quietly in her chair and could not make her words seem more than civil. Faint antagonism stirred in her, though she did not know exactly why. Nothing, it seemed, would ever disturb Flora Gearin's placid acceptance of things; her nerves were buried in her large, untidy body and her enigmatic smile repulsed all trouble. There was an indifference to what came along in both Flora and the bony, sprawling Steve that was to Abbie unforgivably close to laziness. Gearin seemed to possess a secret amusement at the world; and his talk was consistently ironical. "Heard you sold a Dutchman some land today, Buck."

"Part of Mike Olin's ranch."

"Another poor devil comes out here to starve."

"Someday you'll see all that section filled with big red barns," Buck drawled. He was in his shirt sleeves; his body comfortably filled the chair. Abbie watched him closely, this stranger she had married.

"If the wind don't blow the barns away," said Gearin.

"It will pass. It always has." His glance touched his wife and dropped. "I bought the rest of Olin's place for myself. Mitch Sullivan's stringing fence wire around it today. There's a brand of winter wheat being worked out in Minnesota. I'm seeding a hundred acres of it this fall."

Gearin leaned forward. "That's on the trail. You fenced across the trail?"

There was something here, unsaid but expressive. Abbie watched her husband's face tighten. "I know the trail drivers hate fences. But Abilene will outgrow the trail soon enough. When the herds quit coming from Texas, we'll have something else better—farms."

"They'll tear out your fence—the first outfit that runs into it."

"I'll have something to say about that."

The Gearins left after an hour. Abbie said, formally, "It was very kind of you to call," and there was a moment then in which the Gearins looked quietly at her and Buck LaGrange stared solemnly at the floor. Mrs. Gearin said, "Come over to our place any time," and turned into the thick, swirling dark. Abbie watched them bend against the rising wind. Dust beat into the room; Buck LaGrange closed the door and filled his pipe, eyes striking across the bowl to his wife, poised rigidly by the table. Her head came around, and she thrust a still, questioning glance at him.

"You need all the friends you can get out here, Abbie. Don't lose any."

Her lips barely moved. "Why do you say that?"

"You froze the Gearins out, honey. They won't come again."

She said, "I'm—" and closed her mouth definitely. Her shoulders were very straight; yellow lamplight ran smoothly across her black head. Gunshots raced out of the dark, a half dozen explosions running together, dying together. Buck saw her flinch. "Texas cowhands," he said. "They're a wild bunch. But," he added patiently, "they will never touch you."

Her hands slowly reached the table's edge and gripped it. "Doesn't anybody care?"

"The house covers us. We're where we want to be. Those men out on the street are where they want to be. A man's his own master. He can take that gamble if he wants to. If he suffers, it is his own fault."

"You've changed. You're gambling, too. In other things. In land and a new kind of wheat—and trees that may or may not grow in twenty years. With the dust and the wind. With your whole life to come, and mine." She pulled up her head. Her arms pushed against the table. "Isn't there anything certain at all here?"

He drew his pipe from his mouth, fist closing around the hot bowl. He scrubbed a broad palm across his jet, unruly hair. He dropped his chin, and the light of his eyes was ruffled and harassed. The calmness of his voice minutely broke.

"Well, there is one thing between a husband and wife that ought to be certain. One thing, Abbie—in spite of hell and high wind." His tone had turned harder. He stopped himself instantly and put the pipe between his teeth. She hadn't moved; her lips were set as though against pain. He said very quietly, "Don't let things ride you too hard."

She went through the bedroom door and closed it. Undressing in the dark, she crept between the sheets and lay straight and unyielding on the far edge of the bed, against the house wall. The wind struck the boards solidly, the sound of it like the rush of water. All the corners of the house were howling, and above her and around her was the moan of a terrific and overwhelming emptiness—the insane laughter of space. She closed her eyes and pressed her hands against her ears, but the reverberations of the wall came through the bed and into her body and scraped across her nerves. She clenched her teeth together, thinking of the soft, still twilight of Connecticut.

Buck came quietly in, and she pulled her hands from her ears and remained still. When he laid himself beside her, he was careful not to touch her. Her fingernails bit into her palms; she cried silently, and her tremors shook the bed a little. But the frenzy of the mad world outside overbore this small disturbance, and he wasn't hearing her. She stared at the black ceiling. "I have failed him," she told herself. None of his warmth reached across the distance between them.

It was the fourteenth day of the wind. Going toward Herrick's store, she bowed her head against this insistent misery and tried to remember how it felt not to have that sullen crying in her ears.

It was a relief to be in Herrick's store, but only a momentary relief. Coming up on the women gathered there for the morning's shopping, she felt a dread at their reserve. In the beginning she had not known how to meet their friendliness; now she had no way of overcoming their chilling judgment. They thought her cold and proud. There was some polite talk, yet it was only by effort that she could relax the tight set of her lips to answer. Watching them, she was suddenly aware of a weariness, a premature oldness in each. The storm had done something to their faces.

She made her purchases and went out again into the driving smother. At the corner of the Alamo saloon, partially sheltered against the blast racing down the railroad tracks, she stopped to grip her bundles more securely. Men were swinging the Alamo's doors wide as they moved through, letting out the strong stench of tobacco and whiskey. Her glance traveled in a moment—and identified the tall figure of Buck standing by the bar, surrounded by a group of settlers. A high gust of laughter rushed at her; the doors swung shut. Abbie's teeth bit into her lower lip. She hurried on home. Somebody was moving into the adjoining house, for there was a clutter of furniture in the yard and five children running around the yard while a man, violently swearing, tried to move a heavy bureau through the front door. A woman stood in the flailing dust of the street and held the heads of a nervous team, the loose shape of her body describing an unutterable weariness.

Coming home in the premature six-o'clock darkness, Buck LaGrange found his wife standing at the stove, pouring jelly into glasses. The room was filled with a stifling heat; Abbie's cheeks were flushed and wet. She didn't look at him. "Supper's late. The wind comes down the chimney, and the oven won't heat."

"Never mind. Let's go over to the Drover's Rest and have supper."

Her voice was flat, stubborn. "I won't spend your money that way."

"Don't drive yourself so hard, Abbie."

She said, "Do you drink?"

"You'll never need worry about that. I do my business where I find men. The saloon is a good place to find them."

Lamplight shone against a window turned black by the weird night. Out of the steady, beating tempo of the storm rushed a sudden furious attack. It smote the house wall with a long, hollow booming and shuddered every board. The walls definitely swayed. Abbie stepped back from the stove. She looked at Buck, alarm widening her eyes. Her lips moved.

"In the center of it now," he said, and watched the elbow of the stove pipe bend from the wall. Soot gushed down the wall, its fine powder spreading darkly. Above the roar lifted the passionate yelling of a woman, the frightened cry of children. Then a man's outraged voice rode over this.

Abbie said, "They've been quarreling all afternoon. The words have been horrible."

"They're settlers, without any money. It's tough on them."

"They're vulgar!"

He looked at her carefully. "People like that can't afford to be polite and repressed." His words struck her more pronouncedly. "Maybe it's a good idea to quarrel and get it out of your system."

On the third Sunday she sat in the gaunt little room that was Abilene's church and bowed her head and remembered the lost gentleness of her Connecticut home. She could have cried then, had the bitter wind left any tears in her. Beside her, Buck stirred his big brown hands restlessly on his knees while the man in the pulpit shook a fist at the sparse congregation and spoke of the hellfire and damnation to come. His voice was as strident as an auctioneer's. He had no pity and no gentleness in him, and his long, hungry face seemed to exult in the misery he pictured for them. When he had finished, he strode down the narrow aisle, blotting the sweat from his face. Abbie was glad to leave. All the faces around her were tired, all talk was low.

She brought up her handkerchief and held it against her nose. The rank odor of the stockyards came on with the wind again, and all the sidewalk sweepings from the nearby saloons were whipping up into the air. A little beyond the church three narrow buildings sat side by side with drawn blinds; abreast them, Buck LaGrange moved around, placing himself between Abbie and the buildings. Nearby stood the school.

"Must the school and the church be here—beside *those?*" murmured Abbie.

"We do the best we can."

But she shook her head, speaking with suppressed vehemence. "Never —never!"

Buck said, "Hello, Bill." Abbie raised her head and found Wild Bill Hickok, hat lifted, standing in the dust to let them pass, his long locks flung out behind his shoulders. She nodded only, made afraid again by that bold, womanish face. Above her the hidden sun made a round orange stain in the clogged air. In her own house once more, she put away her bonnet and stood a moment in the bedroom, feeling the tremble of her nerves. When Buck spoke, directly behind her, she started. She wheeled about, her fists doubled, her hands rising.

He said, concerned, "Didn't mean to scare you."

"I hate that man. Why do all of you go out of your way to show him your respect?"

"Wild Bill? He's my friend. Whatever else he is, he's that."

"A killer," she breathed in a minutely uncontrolled voice.

It brought his head down. "In the East," he said, "we'd be showing respect to the banker—for his money. Here we show our respect to Bill —for his courage. It's the thing we look up to. It's the thing we've all got to have. Just courage."

"Do you think I'd tell anybody at home he was at our wedding? Do you think I'd even tell them the kind of a wedding I had? I'm ashamed of it!"

"You're upset."

"Won't the wind ever stop?"

He scrubbed his hand along the sudden dampness of his face; worry cut quick lines across his brow. His eyes showed a ragged light. "Abbie," he said, "you're not happy."

"How can I be?"

He turned away from her. He went into the front room. His voice came back after a while, without emotion. "I had better send you home."

She came after him; she stood across the table from him, white and small. "You wouldn't go back with me?"

"I should be nothing but a clerk there. It isn't enough. I can't live that sort of a life any more. I'm not that sort of a man any more."

"Ambition has made you wild."

He said in a careful, dull voice, "The time to correct this mistake is now. I should be no happier there than you are here."

"There's something between us. There has been since the first day."

"Yes," he said.

Her lips stiffened. "I hate to think I can't be a good wife. Let's go back."

He spoke bleakly. "We'd carry this back with us. It would be in your head and in mine. Twenty years from now we'd be middle-aged people living in a house that had no warmth, no hope in it. That sort of starvation is worse than hunger for food."

She said, "Why do you—?"

Someone knocked rapidly on the door; someone said, in an excited voice, "Buck!" Abbie's lips went narrow and still again. She stood defensively in the center of the room, chin up and shoulders lifted. Buck's big frame blocked a half-open doorway, and a man outside was speaking in swift phrases rendered unintelligible by the pound of the wind. In a moment he was gone. Buck closed the door. He stood with his hand on the knob, staring at the panel; when he swung about she saw the change in his face. It was darker, with a rising anger whipping up in his eyes. She said, "What is it, Buck?"

He crossed the room to a closet, reaching into it with an abrupt twist of his shoulders. Inexpressibly startled, she found he had a rifle in his hand when he turned again. Her voice lifted; it was breathless and peremptory: "Buck!"

"Well," he said evenly, "this had to come sometime. There's a trail herd coming toward my fence. They could travel another mile and go around it, but they're Texans and they hate fences. They intend to cut my wire." He stopped speaking and stared at the strangeness on her pale cheeks. He said, spuriously quiet, "I didn't put up that fence just for fun," and left the room. A little later, rooted to her place by the table, she saw him carried past a window in a buckboard driven by another man, who had whipped the horses to a run.

Something in that haste struck fear entirely through her. She moved over to the window and watched the buckboard swing at the railroad track and continue at a dead gallop on down toward the livestock yards, toward Buck's ranch two miles beyond town; she watched it fade into the yellow pall of dust. Afterward, for perhaps ten minutes, she remained in this position, her hands on the sill, the steady pounding of the storm vibrating through her arms. Her heart beat small and fast, and her lungs began to oppress her; and she thought in sudden despair she would never get enough air. There was some malignant, cruel force squeezing the breath out of her.

She turned and went into the kitchen. The stove had gone cold, and there was a roast half cooked in the oven; she rekindled the fire stolidly, matching her bitter anger against a draught which poured down the chimney and blew smoke out of the stove into her face. Her eyes, heavy with the constant dust, smarted unbearably. She gasped, "Won't it ever stop?" She held the stove-lid lifted in her hand. Suddenly she threw it blindly from her and went into the bedroom to change out of her Sunday clothes.

But she didn't change. Seated on the edge of the bed, she closed her eyes and put her hands over her face. Dust smell poured through the room. She got up and closed the bedroom door, hoping to shut off the strong current of wind leaking around her. It was no better. She said, on the edge of screaming, "Won't it ever stop?" There was a hard, long report sailing over her house; it dragged her back to a front window. All her muscles were taut, and her nerves were thin and raw, yet nothing was to be seen on the windy street beyond the railroad track, nothing but one humped-over figure beating his way against the wind into the clouded emptiness surrounding farther Abilene.

She let out a quick, gasping sound and ran across the room and left the house, bareheaded. She had to support herself for a little while against the picket fence; and then pushed on toward the center of town. Past the railroad tracks it occurred to her that Wild Bill would be in his saloon, where she couldn't go. But she could go to Theodore Henry, who would fetch him. Beyond the shanty depot the wind, racing up the open length of the street, struck her fully and wickedly. She had to push herself against it; she had to cover her nose to breathe. Over against the wall of the Alamo, she stopped to catch her wind. Theodore Henry's real-estate office was a few doors farther along a walk swept bare of life.

She pushed on; and then was halted by a voice coming curiously at her.

Lifting her head she saw the buckboard coming back, veering to the walk's edge. Buck got out, holding to his rifle. The other man stayed up on the seat and turned to look behind.

"What have you done?" said Abbie.

He had done something, she knew. His face had no warmth in it. "They'll go around the fence. I shot one of them. Go home, Abbie—"

The man on the buckboard yelled. "Hey—"

Buck LaGrange pushed his wife away. He wheeled slowly, and the snout of his rifle lifted. "Go home, Abbie—"

A column of cowhands rode out of vagueness into the walk. Dust rolled enormously up. They were dismounting; and they were coming along the walk at a set and deliberate stride—one heavy man leading them. She had her fingers around Buck's arm; she felt his muscles go tight. That leading man stopped a pace away, his crew collecting around him. She knew they meant to kill Buck. Violence was in them, hatred poured out of them. The man said in a lashing voice, "Put your woman aside! Put your gun down! We'll settle this fence business in a hurry. You'll shoot no more trail hands!"

Buck's arm swept out. It threw her across the walk into the side of the buckboard against the feet of the driver, who had never moved. There was a shout behind her, a scuffling of feet, and a deep cursing. She turned her head and saw a man drop under Buck's fist; she saw them coming on, smothering him. The man in the wagon yelled, "My God, lady, get out of here!" Her eyes went up to him and knew he wouldn't be any good. But there was a whip standing in his holder. She saw it and seized it and whirled back. Buck's shoulders rose in the middle of the mass bearing against him; he was silent in this pack which howled and struck and tried to bear him down. She raised the whip, slashing blindly out. She walked on, felt it strike them; she closed her eyes and kept striking and opened her eyes and saw men cringing away.

Behind her a cold voice commanded, "Stop that, boys!"

She was exhausted; and one of the crew had snatched the whip away. But there was no further need of it. For the cowhands had sprung back from Buck LaGrange, who was still on his feet, whose big arms swung and were ready to hit again. One man lay on the walk with blood dripping from his face. The voice behind her spoke again, chilly and monotonous.

"Looking for a little trouble, boys?" Turning, then, Abbie found Wild Bill standing behind her. His big body made an indolent shape in the mealy yellow light. One half-risen hand poised a burning cigar. But there was something greedy and deadly in the man's round, winkless eyes. He said, never changing his level tone, "Get out of Abilene."

The silence behind her was absolute; it was strange to her. She swung around—and witnessed then the power that belonged to one man and the fear he placed in other men's hearts. The cowhand struck down by Buck's fists got awkwardly to his feet, saying nothing. He simply turned and lifted an arm at his crew, and they all walked back to their horses. Her glance followed them until Buck's voice broke in. He was standing beside her, looking down with an intent interest. Wild Bill said, "What are friends for, Buck? If you had a fight on your hands, why didn't you call me?"

He had taken off his hat, the wind whipping his long hair around his shoulders. He had put the cigar between his big lips and he was remotely smiling. "You're a fighter, ma'am. I admire courage. If there is anything you want me to do for you—"

The power of speech was out of her; she had nothing to say. Buck's hand took her arm and swayed her gently forward. They went out into the street and across the tracks toward home. He said something she didn't hear and braced her against the risen relentlessness of the wind. On the porch he opened the door for her. But he wasn't following. He had stopped at the threshold and was slowly brushing his boot against the mat. Weariness pulled his shoulders down and he braced one arm against the doorway.

Abbie's voice was stony; it was vehement; it was outraged. "Never mind, Buck. Come in here!"

His heavy eyes stared at her. She had to reach out and pull him forward; she had to close the door behind him. He seemed to have no strength left in him. There was a quickness in her breathing, a sudden graphic emotion across her dark face.

"You think I'm cold—everybody thinks I'm cold! I'm not—I never was! I have been a poor wife, Buck! But I love you!"

There was in his eyes the quick burst of hope. He reached out and he brought her against him, heavy arms pressing her hard. A flicker of humor loosened his lips. She felt the soft stir of his chuckle.

"I thought you'd never change, Abbie. It's been tough for us all. But the wind will stop. It will stop—and it doesn't matter any more."

LOUIS L'AMOUR

The Gift of Cochise

Now in his seventies. Louis L'Amour is the bestselling Western writer in the world today—indeed, he is one of the bestselling writers of any type of fiction. A self-educated man, he held a wide variety of jobs before becoming a full-time writer. His sales, which are now approaching one hundred million copies, continue to grow due to his unparalleled commitment to historical accuracy, the authentic feel of his books and his enormous capabilities as a storyteller. His most famous novels are those that have been filmed, including Hondo, How the West Was Won, Shalako, *and* Heller with a Gun.

TENSE, AND white to the lips, Angie Lowe stood in the door of her cabin with a double-barreled shotgun in her hands. Beside the door was a Winchester '73, and on the table inside the house were two Walker Colts.

Facing the cabin were twelve Apaches on ragged calico ponies, and one of the Indians had lifted his hand palm outward. The Apache sitting the white-splashed bay pony was Cochise.

Beside Angie were her seven-year-old son Jimmy and her five-year-old daughter Jane.

Cochise sat his pony in silence, his black, unreadable eyes studied the woman, the children, the cabin, and the small garden. He looked at the two ponies in the corral and the three cows. His eyes strayed to the small stack of hay cut from the meadow, and to the few steers farther up the canyon.

Three times the warriors of Cochise had attacked this solitary cabin and three times they had been turned back. In all, they had lost seven men, and three had been wounded. Four ponies had been killed. His braves reported that there was no man in the house, only a woman and two children, so Cochise had come to see for himself this woman who was so certain a shot with a rifle and who killed his fighting men.

These were some of the same fighting men who had outfought, outguessed and outrun the finest American army on record, an army outnumbering the Apaches by a hundred to one. Yet a lone woman with two small children had fought them off, and the woman was scarcely more than a girl. And she was prepared to fight now. There was a glint of admiration in the old eyes that appraised her. The Apache was a fighting man, and he respected fighting blood.

"Where is your man?"

"He has gone to El Paso." Angie's voice was steady, but she was frightened as she had never been before. She recognized Cochise from descriptions, and she knew that if he decided to kill or capture her it would be done. Until now, the sporadic attacks she had fought off had been those of casual bands of warriors who raided her in passing.

"He has been gone a long time. How long?"

Angie hesitated, but it was not in her to lie. "He has been gone four months."

Cochise considered that. No one but a fool would leave such a woman, or such fine children. Only one thing could have prevented his return. "Your man is dead," he said.

Angie waited, her heart pounding with heavy, measured beats. She had guessed long ago that Ed had been killed but the way Cochise spoke did not imply that Apaches had killed him, only that he must be dead or he would have returned.

"You fight well," Cochise said. "You have killed my young men."

"Your young men attacked me." She hesitated then added, "They stole my horses."

"Your man is gone. Why do you not leave?"

Angie looked at him with surprise. "Leave? Why, this is my home. This land is mine. This spring is mine. I shall not leave."

"This was an Apache spring," Cochise reminded her reasonably.

"The Apache lives in the mountains," Angie replied. "He does not need this spring. I have two children, and I do need it."

"But when the Apache comes this way, where shall he drink? His throat is dry and you keep him from water."

The very fact that Cochise was willing to talk raised her hopes. There had been a time when the Apache made no war on the white man. "Cochise speaks with a forked tongue," she said. "There is water yonder." She gestured toward the hills, where Ed had told her there were springs. "But if the people of Cochise come in peace they may drink at this spring."

The Apache leader smiled faintly. Such a woman would rear a nation of warriors. He nodded at Jimmy. "The small one—does he also shoot?"

"He does," Angie said proudly, "and well, too!" She pointed at an upthrust leaf of prickly pear. "Show them, Jimmy."

The prickly pear was an easy two hundred yards away, and the Winchester was long and heavy, but he lifted it eagerly and steadied it against the doorjamb as his father had taught him, held his sight an instant, then fired. The bud on top of the prickly pear disintegrated.

There were grunts of appreciation from the dark-faced warriors. Cochise chuckled.

"The little warrior shoots well. It is well you have no man. You might raise an army of little warriors to fight my people."

"I have no wish to fight your people," Angie said quietly. "Your people have your ways, and I have mine. I live in peace when I am left in peace. I did not think," she added with dignity, "that the great Cochise made war on women!"

The Apache looked at her, then turned his pony away. "My people will trouble you no longer," he said. "You are the mother of a strong son."

"What about my two ponies?" she called after him. "Your young men took them from me."

Cochise did not turn or look back, and the little cavalcade of riders followed him away. Angie stepped back into the cabin and closed the door. Then she sat down abruptly, her face white, the muscles in her legs trembling.

When morning came, she went cautiously to the spring for water. Her ponies were back in the corral. They had been returned during the night.

Slowly, the days drew on. Angie broke a small piece of the meadow and planted it. Alone, she cut hay in the meadow and built another stack. She saw Indians several times, but they did not bother her. One morning, when she opened her door, a quarter of antelope lay on the step, but no Indian was in sight. Several times, during the weeks that followed, she saw moccasin tracks near the spring.

Once, going out at daybreak, she saw an Indian girl dipping water from the spring. Angie called to her, and the girl turned quickly, facing her. Angie walked toward her, offering a bright red silk ribbon. Pleased at the gift, the Apache girl left.

And the following morning there was another quarter of antelope on her step—but she saw no Indian.

Ed Lowe had built the cabin in West Dog Canyon in the spring of 1871, but it was Angie who chose the spot, not Ed. In Santa Fe they would have told you that Ed Lowe was good-looking, shiftless and agreeable. He was, also, unfortunately handy with a pistol.

Angie's father had come from County Mayo to New York and from New York to the Mississippi, where he became a tough, brawling river boatman. In New Orleans, he met a beautiful Cajun girl and married her. Together, they started west for Santa Fe, and Angie was born en route. Both parents died of cholera when Angie was fourteen. She lived with an Irish family for the following three years, then married Ed Lowe when she was seventeen.

Santa Fe was not good for Ed, and Angie kept after him until they started south. It was Apache country, but they kept on until they reached the old Spanish ruin in West Dog. Here there were grass, water, and shelter from the wind.

There was fuel, and there were pinons and game. And Angie, with an Irish eye for the land, saw that it would grow crops.

The house itself was built on the ruins of the old Spanish building, using the thick walls and the floor. The location had been admirably chosen for defense. The house was built in a corner of the cliff, under the sheltering overhang, so that approach was possible from only two directions, both covered by an easy field of fire from the door and windows.

For seven months, Ed worked hard and steadily. He put in the first crop, he built the house, and proved himself a handy man with tools. He repaired the old plow they had bought, cleaned out the spring, and paved and walled it with slabs of stone. If he was lonely for the carefree companions of Santa Fe, he gave no indication of it. Provisions were low, and when he finally started off to the south, Angie watched him go with an ache in her heart.

She did not know whether she loved Ed. The first flush of enthusiasm had passed, and Ed Lowe had proved something less than she had believed. But he had tried, she admitted. And it had not been easy for him. He was an amiable soul, given to whittling and idle talk, all of which he missed in the loneliness of the Apache country. And when he rode away, she had no idea whether she would ever see him again. She never did.

Santa Fe was far and away to the north, but the growing village of El Paso was less than a hundred miles to the west, and it was there Ed Lowe rode for supplies and seed.

He had several drinks—his first in months—in one of the saloons. As the liquor warmed his stomach, Ed Lowe looked around agreeably. For a moment, his eyes clouded with worry as he thought of his wife and children back in Apache country, but it was not in Ed Lowe to worry for long. He had another drink and leaned on the bar, talking to the bartender. All Ed had ever asked of life was enough to eat, a horse to ride, an occasional drink, and companions to talk with. Not that he had anything important to say. He just liked to talk.

Suddenly a chair grated on the floor, and Ed turned. A lean, powerful man with a shock of uncut black hair and a torn, weather-faded shirt stood at bay. Facing him across the table were three hard-faced young men, obviously brothers.

Ches Lane did not notice Ed Lowe watching from the bar. He had eyes only for the men facing him. "You done that deliberate!" The statement was a challenge.

The broad-chested man on the left grinned through broken teeth. "That's right, Ches. I done it deliberate. You killed Dan Tolliver on the Brazos."

"He made the quarrel." Comprehension came to Ches. He was boxed, and by three of the fighting, blood-hungry Tollivers.

"Don't make no difference," the broad-chested Tolliver said. " 'Who sheds a Tolliver's blood, by a Tolliver's hand must die!' "

Ed Lowe moved suddenly from the bar. "Three to one is long odds," he said, his voice low and friendly. "If the gent in the corner is willin', I'll side him."

Two Tollivers turned toward him. Ed Lowe was smiling easily, his hand hovering near his gun. "You stay out of this!" one of the brothers said harshly.

"I'm in," Ed replied. "Why don't you boys light a shuck?"

"No, by—!" The man's hand dropped for his gun, and the room thundered with sound.

Ed was smiling easily, unworried as always. His gun flashed up. He felt it leap in his hand, saw the nearest Tolliver smashed back, and he shot him again as he dropped. He had only time to see Ches Lane with two guns out and another Tolliver down when something struck him through the stomach and he stepped back against the bar, suddenly sick.

The sound stopped, and the room was quiet, and there was the acrid smell of powder smoke. Three Tollivers were down and dead, and Ed Lowe was dying. Ches Lane crossed to him.

"We got 'em," Ed said, "we sure did. But they got me."

Suddenly his face changed. "Oh Lord in heaven, what'll Angie do?" And then he crumpled over on the floor and lay still, the blood staining his shirt and mingling with the sawdust.

Stiff-faced, Ches looked up. "Who was Angie?" he asked.

"His wife," the bartender told him. "She's up northeast somewhere, in Apache country. He was tellin' me about her. Two kids, too."

Ches Lane stared down at the crumpled, used-up body of Ed Lowe. The man had saved his life.

One he could have beaten, two he might have beaten; three would have killed him. Ed Lowe, stepping in when he did, had saved the life of Ches Lane.

"He didn't say where?"

"No."

Ches Lane shoved his hat back on his head. "What's northeast of here?"

The bartender rested his hands on the bar. "Cochise," he said. . . .

For more than three months, whenever he could rustle the grub, Ches Lane quartered the country over and back. The trouble was, he had no lead to the location of Ed Lowe's homestead. An examination of Ed's horse revealed nothing. Lowe had bought seed and ammunition, and the seed indicated a good water supply, and the ammunition implied trouble. But in the country there was always trouble.

A man had died to save his life, and Ches Lane had a deep sense of obligation. Somewhere that wife waited, if she was still alive, and it was up to him to find her and look out for her. He rode northeast, cutting for sign, but found none. Sandstorms had wiped out any hope of back-trailing Lowe. Actually, West Dog Canyon was more east than north, but this he had no way of knowing.

North he went, skirting the rugged San Andreas Mountains. Heat baked him hot, dry winds parched his skin. His hair grew dry and stiff and alkali-whitened. He rode north, and soon the Apaches knew of him. He fought them at a lonely water hole, and he fought them on the run. They killed his horse, and he switched his saddle to the spare and rode on. They cornered him in the rocks, and he killed two of them and escaped by night.

They trailed him through the White Sands, and he left two more for dead. He fought fiercely and bitterly, and would not be turned from his quest. He turned east through the lava beds and still more east to the Pecos. He saw only two white men, and neither knew of a white woman.

The bearded man laughed harshly. "A woman alone? She wouldn't last a month! By now the Apaches got her, or she's dead. Don't be a fool! Leave this country before you die here."

Lean, wind-whipped and savage, Ches Lane pushed on. The Mescaleros concerned him in Rawhide Draw and he fought them to a standstill. Grimly, the Apaches clung to his trail.

The sheer determination of the man fascinated them. Bred and born in a rugged and lonely land, the Apaches knew the difficulties of survival; they knew how a man could live, how he must live. Even as they tried to kill this man, they loved him, for he was one of their own.

Lane's jeans grew ragged. Two bullet holes were added to the old black hat. The slicker was torn; the saddle, so carefully kept until now, was scratched by gravel and brush. At night he cleaned his guns and by day he scouted the trails. Three times he found lonely ranch houses burned to the ground, the buzzard- and coyote-stripped bones of their owners lying nearby.

Once he found a covered wagon, its canvas flopping in the wind, a man lying sprawled on the seat with a pistol near his hand. He was dead and his wife was dead, and their canteens rattled like empty skulls.

Leaner every day, Ches Lane pushed on. He camped one night in a canyon near some white oaks. He heard a hoof click on stone and he backed away from his tiny fire, gun in hand.

The riders were white men, and there were two of them. Joe Tompkins and Wiley Lynn were headed west, and Ches Lane could have guessed why. They were men he had known before, and he told them what he was doing.

Lynn chuckled. He was a thin-faced man with lank yellow hair and dirty fingers. "Seems a mighty strange way to get a woman. There's some as comes easier."

"This ain't for fun," Ches replied shortly. "I got to find her."

Tompkins stared at him. "Ches, you're crazy! That gent declared himself in of his own wish and desire. Far's that goes, the gal's dead. No woman could last this long in Apache country."

At daylight, the two men headed west, and Ches Lane turned south.

Antelope and deer are curious creatures, often led to their death by curiosity. The longhorn, soon going wild on the plains, acquires the same characteristic. He is essentially curious. Any new thing or strange action will bring his head up and his ears alert. Often a longhorn, like a deer, can be lured within a stone's throw by some queer antic, by a handkerchief waving, by a man under a hide, by a man on foot.

This character of the wild things holds true of the Indian. The lonely rider who fought so desperately and knew the desert so well soon became a subject of gossip among the Apaches. Over the fires of many a rancheria they discussed this strange rider who seemed to be going nowhere, but always riding, like a lean wolf dog on a trail. He rode across the mesas and down the canyons; he studied sign at every water hole; he looked long from every ridge. It was obvious to the Indians that he searched for something—but what?

Cochise had come again to the cabin in West Dog Canyon. "Little warrior too small," he said, "too small for hunt. You join my people. Take Apache for man."

"No." Angie shook her head. "Apache ways are good for the Apache, and the white man's ways are good for white men—and women."

They rode away and said no more, but that night, as she had on many other nights after the children were asleep, Angie cried. She wept silently, her head pillowed on her arms. She was as pretty as ever, but her face was thin, showing the worry and struggle of the months gone by, the weeks and months without hope.

The crops were small but good. Little Jimmy worked beside her. At night, Angie sat alone on the steps and watched the shadows gather down the long canyon, listening to the coyotes yapping from the rim of the Guadalupes, hearing the horses blowing in the corral. She watched, still hopeful, but now she knew that Cochise was right: Ed would not return.

But even if she had been ready to give up this, the first home she had known, there could be no escape. Here she was protected by Cochise. Other Apaches from other tribes would not so willingly grant her peace.

At daylight she was up. The morning air was bright and balmy, but soon it would be hot again. Jimmy went to the spring for water, and when breakfast was over, the children played while Angie sat in the shade of a huge old cottonwood and sewed. It was a Sunday, warm and lovely. From time to time, she lifted her eyes to look down the canyon, half smiling at her own foolishness.

The hard-packed earth of the yard was swept clean of dust; the pans hanging on the kitchen wall were neat and shining. The children's hair had been clipped, and there was a small bouquet on the kitchen table.

After a while, Angie put aside her sewing and changed her dress. She did her hair carefully, and then, looking in her mirror, she reflected with sudden pain that she *was* pretty, and that she was only a girl.

Resolutely, she turned from the mirror and, taking up her Bible, went back to the seat under the cottonwood. The children left their playing and came to her, for this was a Sunday ritual, their only one. Opening the Bible, she read slowly,

". . . though I walk through the valley of the shadow of death, I will fear no evil; for thou art with me; thy rod and thy staff, they comfort me. Thou preparest a table before me in the presence of mine enemies: thou . . ."

"Mommy." Jimmy tugged at her sleeve. "Look!"

Ches Lane had reached a narrow canyon by midafternoon and decided to make camp. There was small possibility he would find another such spot, and he was dead tired, his muscles sodden with fatigue. The canyon was one of those unexpected gashes in the cap rock that gave no indication of its presence until you came right on it. After some searching, Ches found a route to the bottom and made camp under a wind-hollowed overhang. There was water, and there was a small patch of grass.

After his horse had a drink and a roll on the ground, it began cropping eagerly at the rich, green grass, and Ches built a smokeless fire of some ancient driftwood in the canyon bottom. It was his first hot meal in days, and when he had finished he put out his fire, rolled a smoke, and leaned back contentedly.

Before darkness settled, he climbed to the rim and looked over the country. The sun had gone down, and the shadows were growing long. After a half hour of study, he decided there was no living thing within miles, except for the usual desert life. Returning to the bottom, he moved his horse to fresh grass, then rolled in his blanket. For the first time in a month, he slept without fear.

He woke up suddenly in the broad daylight. The horse was listening to something, his head up. Swiftly, Ches went to the horse and led it back under the overhang. Then he drew on his boots, rolled his blankets, and saddled the horse. Still he heard no sound.

Climbing the rim again, he studied the desert and found nothing. Returning to his horse, he mounted up and rode down the canyon toward the flatland beyond. Coming out of the canyon mouth, he rode right into the middle of a war party of more than twenty Apaches—invisible until suddenly they stood up behind rocks, their rifles leveled. And he didn't have a chance.

Swiftly, they bound his wrists to the saddle horn and tied his feet. Only then did he see the man who led the party. It was Cochise.

He was a lean, wiry Indian of past fifty, his black hair streaked with gray, his features strong and clean-cut. He stared at Lane, and there was nothing in his face to reveal what he might be thinking.

Several of the younger warriors pushed forward, talking excitedly and waving their arms. Ches Lane understood some of it, but he sat straight in the saddle, his head up, waiting. Then Cochise spoke and the party turned, and, leading his horse, they rode away.

The miles grew long and the sun was hot. He was offered no water and he asked for none. The Indians ignored him. Once a young brave rode near and struck him viciously. Lane made no sound, gave no indication of pain. When they finally stopped, it was beside a huge anthill swarming with big red desert ants.

Roughly, they quickly untied him and jerked him from his horse. He dug in his heels and shouted at them in Spanish: "The Apaches are women! They tie me to the ants because they are afraid to fight me!"

An Indian struck him, and Ches glared at the man. If he must die, he would show them how it should be done. Yet he knew the unpredictable nature of the Indian, of his great respect for courage.

"Give me a knife, and I'll kill any of your warriors!"

They stared at him, and one powerfully built Apache angrily ordered them to get on with it. Cochise spoke, and the big warrior replied angrily.

Ches Lane nodded at the anthill. "Is this the death for a fighting man? I have fought your strong men and beaten them. I have left no trail for them to follow, and for months I have lived among you, and now only by accident have you captured me. Give me a knife," he added grimly, "and I will fight *him!*" He indicated the big, black-faced Apache.

The warrior's cruel mouth hardened, and he struck Ches across the face.

The white man tasted blood and fury. "Woman!" Ches said. "Coyote! You are afraid!" Ches turned on Cochise, as the Indians stood irresolute. "Free my hands and let me fight!" he demanded. "If I win, let me go free."

Cochise said something to the big Indian. Instantly, there was stillness. Then an Apache sprang forward and, with a slash of his knife, freed Lane's hands. Shaking loose the thongs, Ches Lane chafed his wrists to bring back the circulation. An Indian threw a knife at his feet. It was his own bowie knife.

Ches took off his riding boots. In sock feet, his knife gripped low in his hand, its cutting edge up, he looked at the big warrior.

"I promise you nothing," Cochise said in Spanish, "but an honorable death."

The big warrior came at him on cat feet. Warily, Ches circled. He had not only to defeat this Apache but to escape. He permitted himself a side glance toward his horse. It stood alone. No Indian held it.

The Apache closed swiftly, thrusting wickedly with the knife. Ches, who had learned knife-fighting in the bayou country of Louisiana, turned his hip sharply, and the blade slid past him. He struck swiftly, but the Apache's forward movement deflected the blade, and it failed to penetrate. However, as it swept up between the Indian's body and arm, it cut a deep gash in the warrior's left armpit.

The Indian sprang again, like a clawing cat, streaming blood. Ches moved aside, but a backhand sweep nicked him, and he felt the sharp bite of the blade. Turning, he paused on the balls of his feet.

He had had no water in hours. His lips were cracked. Yet he sweated now, and the salt of it stung his eyes. He stared into the malevolent black eyes of the Apache, then moved to meet him. The Indian lunged, and Ches sidestepped like a boxer and spun on the ball of his foot.

The sudden side step threw the Indian past him, but Ches failed to drive the knife into the Apache's kidney when his foot rolled on a stone. The point left a thin red line across the Indian's back. The Indian was quick. Before Ches could recover his balance, he grasped the white man's knife wrist. Desperately, Ches grabbed for the Indian's knife hand and got the wrist, and they stood there straining, chest to chest.

Seeing his chance, Ches suddenly let his knees buckle, then brought up his knee and fell back, throwing the Apache over his head to the sand. Instantly, he whirled and was on his feet, standing over the Apache. The warrior had lost his knife, and he lay there, staring up, his eyes black with hatred.

Coolly, Ches stepped back, picked up the Indian's knife, and tossed it to him contemptuously. There was a grunt from the watching Indians, and then his antagonist rushed. But loss of blood had weakened the warrior, and Ches stepped in swiftly, struck the blade aside, then thrust the point of his blade hard against the Indian's belly.

Black eyes glared into his without yielding. A thrust, and the man would be disemboweled, but Ches stepped back. "He is a strong man," Ches said in Spanish. "It is enough that I have won."

Deliberately, he walked to his horse and swung into the saddle. He looked around, and every rifle covered him.

So he had gained nothing. He had hoped that mercy might lead to mercy, that the Apache's respect for a fighting man would win his freedom. He had failed. Again they bound him to his horse, but they did not take his knife from him.

When they camped at last, he was given food and drink. He was bound again, and a blanket was thrown over him. At daylight they were again in the saddle. In Spanish he asked where they were taking him, but they gave no indication of hearing. When they stopped again, it was beside a pole corral, near a stone cabin.

When Jimmy spoke, Angie got quickly to her feet. She recognized Cochise with a start of relief, but she saw instantly that this was a war party. And then she saw the prisoner.

Their eyes met and she felt a distinct shock. He was a white man, a big, unshaven man who badly needed both a bath and a haircut, his clothes ragged and bloody. Cochise gestured at the prisoner.

"No take Apache man, you take white man. This man good for hunt, good for fight. He strong warrior. You take 'em."

Flushed and startled, Angie stared at the prisoner and caught a faint glint of humor in his dark eyes.

"Is this here the fate worse than death I hear tell of?" he inquired gently.

"Who are you?" she asked, and was immediately conscious that it was an extremely silly question.

The Apaches had drawn back and were watching curiously. She could do nothing for the present but accept the situation. Obviously they intended to do her a kindness, and it would not do to offend them. If they had not brought this man to her, he might have been killed.

"Name's Ches Lane, ma'am," he said. "Will you untie me? I'd feel a lot safer."

"Of course." Still flustered, she went to him and untied his hands. One Indian said something, and the others chuckled; then, with a whoop, they swung their horses and galloped off down the canyon.

Their departure left her suddenly helpless, the shadowy globe of her loneliness shattered by this utterly strange man standing before her, this big, bearded man brought to her out of the desert.

She smoothed her apron, suddenly pale as she realized what his delivery to her implied. What must he think of her? She turned away quickly.

"There's hot water," she said hastily, to prevent his speaking. "Dinner is almost ready."

She walked quickly into the house and stopped before the stove, her mind a blank. She looked around her as if she had suddenly waked up in a strange place. She heard water being poured into the basin by the door, and heard him take Ed's razor. She had never moved the box. To have moved it would—

"Sight of work done here, ma'am."

She hesitated, then turned with determination and stepped into the doorway. "Yes, Ed—"

"You're Angie Lowe."

Surprised, she turned toward him, and recognized his own startled awareness of her. As he shaved, he told her about Ed, and what had happened that day in the saloon.

"He—Ed was like that. He never considered consequences until it was too late."

"Lucky for me he didn't."

He was younger looking with his beard gone. There was a certain quiet dignity in his face. She went back inside and began putting plates on the table. She was conscious that he had moved to the door and was watching her.

"You don't have to stay," she said. "You owe me nothing. Whatever Ed did, he did because he was that kind of person. You aren't responsible."

He did not answer, and when she turned again to the stove, she glanced swiftly at him. He was looking across the valley.

There was a studied deference about him when he moved to a place at the table. The children stared, wide-eyed and silent; it had been so long since a man sat at this table.

Angie could not remember when she had felt like this. She was awkwardly conscious of her hands, which never seemed to be in the right place or doing the right things. She scarcely tasted her food, nor did the children.

Ches Lane had no such inhibitions. For the first time, he realized how hungry he was. After the half-cooked meat of lonely, trailside fires, this was tender and flavored. Hot biscuits, desert honey . . . Suddenly he looked up, embarrassed at his appetite.

"You were really hungry," she said.

"Man can't fix much, out on the trail."

Later, after he'd got his bedroll from his saddle and unrolled it on the hay in the barn, he walked back to the house and sat on the lowest step. The sun was gone, and they watched the cliffs stretch their red shadows across the valley. A quail called plaintively, a mellow sound of twilight.

"You needn't worry about Cochise," she said. "He'll soon be crossing into Mexico."

"I wasn't thinking about Cochise."

That left her with nothing to say, and she listened again to the quail and watched a lone bright star in the sky.

"A man could get to like it here," he said quietly.

A.B. GUTHRIE, JR.

First Principal

A.B. Guthrie, Jr., is indisputably one of the giants of Western literature. His novel The Big Sky *has been called "a monument of a book" and is on most everyone's list of the ten best Western novels; it and its sequels,* The Way West, These Thousand Hills, Arfive *and* The Last Valley, *comprise a masterful chronicle of Western history. Mr. Guthrie is also an accomplished writer of mystery novels* (Wild Pitch, The Genuine Article); *and of short stories, as "First Principal" (and his superior collection* The Big It and Other Stories) *amply demonstrates.*

THE FIRST MAN Lonnie Ellenwood saw to remember after the stage arrived at Moon Dance was Mr. Ross, the chairman of the school board.

The second was the man with the yellow eyes.

The first one stepped out and stood by the wheel as the driver checked the horses. His voice boomed up at Lonnie's father before they could get down. "Howdy there, professor. I'm Ross. Glad to see you."

The man stood as high as a high-headed horse. He had a red face and bright blue eyes. "Howdy, Mrs. Ellenwood. How's Ohio?" He offered a hand to match the voice. "Hope you're going to like it here."

He stooped to shake hands with Lonnie. "Howdy there. Guess you're too young for your dad's new high school. Like to fish, bub?" Lonnie smelled the evil smell of whisky on his breath. The man straightened and turned to Mr. Ellenwood. "We can go, soon's we get your plunder."

They stood in front of a frame hotel—Lonnie and his parents and Mr. Ross in a little group—and the grown people talked while they waited for the driver to hand down the baggage. A sign across the hotel said Herren House. Another, below it, said Bar. The other buildings along the street were wooden, too, and mostly one story. The dust that the stage had raised was settling back.

A line of men leaned against the front of the hotel, watching from under wide hats. Lonnie saw curiosity in their faces, and doubt and maybe dislike for the new principal and his wife and boy. At first he thought the men all looked alike—weathered cheeks, blue or black shirts, faded pants

—and then he saw the man with the yellow eyes. They weren't exactly yellow, though, but pale brown, pale enough to look yellow, yellow and cold like a cat's. Under his nose was a cat's draggle of mustache.

The eyes caught Lonnie's and held them, and Lonnie felt a quick alarm, seeing bold and rude in them the veiled suspicions of the rest.

"Kind of raw country to you, I guess, prof," Mr. Ross was saying, "but you'll get along." He took a cigar from the pocket of his unbuttoned vest and bit the end off it and spit it out. "Great country, Montana is, and bound to be better. We got a church already, like I told you in my letter, and now we'll have a high school. Yep, you'll get along."

Two of the men who lounged against the hotel were chewing tobacco, staining the plank sidewalk with thoughtful spurts of spit. A swinging door divided them, and a sweet-sour smell came from inside.

"Preacher's a fine man, or so they tell me," Mr. Ross went on. "He figured to be here, only a funeral came up."

Beside Mr. Ross, beside the shirt sleeves and the open vest, Mr. Ellenwood looked small and pale, and too proper in the new suit he'd bought in Cincinnati.

Lonnie's mother wasn't paying any attention to the watching men. She looked up and down the dusty street, at the board buildings that fronted up to it, and at the sky that arched over. She smiled down at Lonnie and touched him on the shoulder. "This is our new home, son."

He didn't answer. He wished he were back in Ohio, screened in the friendly woods and hills, away from this bare, flat land where even the sun seemed to stare at him.

Mr. Ross was still talking. "I got a team hitched around the corner. I'll ride you over. Hope you like the house we got for you."

The stage driver had set the baggage down. Mr. Ross grabbed hold of a bag and suitcase and an old telescope and began walking along with Mrs. Ellenwood.

As Lonnie's father started to follow, carrying a box in one hand and a straw suitcase in the other, a man lurched from the door of the hotel and fell against him and caught his balance and went swaying up the street talking to himself.

When Lonnie brought his gaze back from the man, he saw his father leaning over. The suitcase had broken open and spilled towels and cold cream and powder and one of his mother's petticoats on the walk. Father was stuffing them back in, stuffing them in slowly, one by one, while blood colored his neck.

The men were laughing, not very loud but inside themselves while they tried to keep their mouths straight. Only the man with the yellow eyes really let his laughs come out. He was angled against the wall of the hotel, one booted foot laid across the other. His voice sounded in little jeering explosions.

Mr. Ellenwood didn't say anything. He went ahead stuffing things back into the suitcase and trying to make the lock catch afterwards.

Mr. Ross looked back and saw what had happened and turned around and returned. His face got redder than ever. To the one man he said, "Funny, ain't it, Chilter!"

"To me it is," the man answered and laughed again.

Mrs. Ellenwood was standing where Mr. Ross had left her. Lonnie saw an anxious look on her face.

Mr. Ellenwood finally got the lock to catch. He picked up the suitcase, and they started off again, the eyes following them and then being lost around a corner. Mr. Ross didn't speak until they had put the baggage in the buggy, and then all he said was, "Sorry, prof."

Lonnie's father sat quietly while Mr. Ross cramped the wheel around and got straightened out. "It's all right." His voice was even. "It doesn't matter."

Mrs. Ellenwood smiled at Lonnie. "I guess it was funny to everybody but us."

Mr. Ross grunted as if he didn't think so.

He came around the next day, the day before school was to open. "Like I told you," he promised Mr. Ellenwood, "next year we'll have a building, but the old hall'll have to do until then. You seen it? Everything ship-shape?" He stood half a foot higher than Mr. Ellenwood. He was bigger, thicker, stronger, more assured. When he laughed, he rattled the china that Lonnie's mother hadn't found a place for yet. He turned to Lonnie. "Your school don't start till next week, eh, bub?"

He bit off the end of a cigar and lighted up and settled back in the rocking chair. "You're going to like it here, prof. It ain't much, in a way, but in a way it is, too. Best damn people—excuse me—that ever lived, most of 'em. You'll see."

Mr. Ellenwood was nodding politely.

"Kind of rough, but you'll get on."

"Yes," Mr. Ellenwood said and waited for Mr. Ross to say more.

Mr. Ross took his cigar out and rolled it between his fingers. He studied it for a long time. "People'll take to you," he said slowly as if reading the words from the cigar, "soon as they learn you ain't being buffaloed."

"I don't know that I know what you mean."

"It's just a word, is all. Comes, I guess, because buffalo scare kind of easy."

"I see."

Mr. Ross squirmed in the rocker. He rolled the cigar some more, and then chewed on it and pulled and let out a plume of smoke. "Some maybe ain't used to a man teaching school," he said, not looking at Mr. Ellenwood.

"I see."

"You'll get on. Mostly it's women who teach in this country."

"I see."

Mrs. Ellenwood came from the kitchen. She said, "Good morning."

Mr. Ross lifted himself from the rocker. "Howdy, ma'am. Preacher been around yet, and Mrs. Rozzell?"

Mrs. Ellenwood nodded. "Yesterday."

"We liked them," Mr. Ellenwood said.

Lonnie's mother put her hand on his father's shoulder. "They insist Tom has to be superintendent of the Sunday school."

Mr. Ross nodded and smoked some more on his cigar. When he got up to go, Mr. Ellenwood stepped to the door with him. "We'll get on, as you say."

For what seemed a long time, Mr. Ross looked him up and down. Lonnie wondered if he saw a kind of chunky man, not very tall, with a pale complexion and sandy hair and the look of books and church about him, a man firm in the right but not forward, not hearty and sure like Mr. Ross himself.

"O' course," Mr. Ross said, "you'll get on." He put his cigar back in his mouth and closed the door.

It rained the next day, a cold misty rain that sifted out of the north. The air was still wet with drizzle that afternoon as Lonnie started out to meet his father on his return from school. The dirt trails that passed for streets were sticky with mud. At the crossings Lonnie hopped and skipped until he reached the plank sidewalk again, but even so, he got mud on his shoes.

A little bunch of cattle was being herded down the street. Lonnie could see the horseman behind them, reining to and fro to bring up the poky ones and flicking at them with his quirt. The cattle had their heads stuck out, their eyes big with the strangeness of town, their mouths opening to a lost mooing. The voice of the driver as he herded them along came to Lonnie like a snarl.

For a minute he was frightened, seeing the cattle coming his way and the long horns gleaming white, and then he saw his father and felt safe and hurried along to meet him. Mr. Ellenwood was walking with half a dozen boys and girls. They were students, Lonnie guessed. He saw his father lift his head and turn his face toward the horseman. The boys and girls stopped. The rider pulled up, held his horse for a moment, and then reined over.

Lonnie had got close enough to hear. The rider said, "How was that, schoolteacher?"

Even before he saw for sure, Lonnie felt his insides tighten. The man was Chilter, of the almost yellow eyes and the cat's mustache beneath.

"I asked you to stop that cursing."

Chilter spit, then asked, "Why so?"

Mr. Ellenwood made a little motion toward the boys and girls. "You can see why."

For a while the man didn't say anything. He sat his horse, curbing it as it tried to step around, and let his gaze go over Mr. Ellenwood. He looked big, sitting there over everybody. "Why," he said, "I heard this was a free country."

Mr. Ellenwood stepped out into the mud. He didn't speak; he just stepped out into the mud, his face lifted and his gaze steady.

The cat-eyes looked him over. They traveled down the street to the cattle. Lonnie saw that the bunch was loosening. Some had poked through the open gate of a front yard. Some had started up an alley. A man came out of a door and called from the front yard. "Hey, you, haze these steers away, will you?"

Mr. Ellenwood said, "These are just children."

The eyes came back to him. They looked him over again, slowly, yellow and cold and scornful. The man spit and dug his spurs into his horse. It threw some mud on Mr. Ellenwood as it lunged. When it had run a little way, Chilter jerked it up and turned in his saddle and lifted his hat and bobbed his head at Mr. Ellenwood as if speaking to a lady.

Mr. Ellenwood pulled back from the mud. He kept silent, walking home, even after the high schoolers had dropped away one by one. Lonnie wanted to question him but felt closed off. And when finally the words came to his mouth, he would see the man turning and lifting his hat, like saying "Excuse me, ma'am," and anger or shame or the fear in his stomach kept them unsaid. All he managed was, "Mother said to tell you she was meeting with the ladies of the church."

At home Mr. Ellenwood changed clothes and went out into the back yard and began to split wood for the kitchen range. Lonnie sat on the steps and watched.

It had quit drizzling. In the west the sun showed red through black clouds. The sharp smell of fall was in the air, the smell of summer done and things dying, of cold to come, of leaves that someone was trying to make into a bonfire.

Lonnie's father was still chopping wood when Mr. Ross came clattering down the back steps. "Couldn't rouse anyone," Mr. Ross explained, "so I come on through, figuring you might be out here in back."

Mr. Ellenwood anchored the ax in the chopping block and turned to talk.

Mr. Ross bobbed his head toward Lonnie, and Mr. Ellenwood said, "You run in the house, son."

Lonnie backed up and lagged up the steps, but he didn't go in. He sat down on the porch, behind the low wall of it, and listened and now and then dared a look.

"Might as well tell you, prof," Mr. Ross said, "that man Chilter's up to the saloon, making big medicine against you."

Mr. Ellenwood nodded, as if he expected it all the time.

"I don't know what to tell you."

"Nothing. It's all right."

"He's got a kind of a reputation as a bad actor."

"Oh."

"You got a gun or something?"

"I wouldn't want a gun."

"No?"

"No."

"You can't just hold quiet, and let him do whatever he figures on!"

"I'll just have to wait and see."

"I could stay with you, I guess." It was as if the words were being pulled out of Mr. Ross.

Mr. Ellenwood looked him in the eye. "Mr. Ross," he said, "a man has to hoe his own row, here or in Ohio."

"Good for you. I wasn't so sure about Ohio. I kind of wish you'd let me give you a six-shooter. I brought one along for you, just in case."

"No. Thanks."

"He ain't likely to use one. More likely to be fist fighting or wrastling, no holds barred."

"Anyhow, you go on."

"I might hang around, kind of out of sight."

"You go on."

Mr. Ross rolled his lower lip with his thumb and forefinger. "Damn if I ain't acting like a mother hen." He laughed without humor. "Good luck, prof." He turned and walked away. Lonnie could see, before he rounded the corner of the house, that his face was troubled.

Later, out of the beginning dusk, the man came riding. Far off, before he could see him, Lonnie heard the quick suck of horse's hoofs in the mud. They might have been meaningless at first, just sounds that went along with other sounds like the creak of an axle and the cry of children and the whisper of wind, except that already Lonnie knew, and his stomach sickened and the blood raced in him.

He wanted to cry out, wanted to shout the man was coming, wanted to scream that here he was, forever identifiable now by the mere turn of a shoulder and the set of his head.

The man didn't speak. He just kept coming, his horse's feet dancing fancy in the mud.

Mr. Ellenwood raised his ax and saw him and tapped the ax head into the block and stood straight.

The man rode from the alley into the unfenced back yard, and for a minute Lonnie thought he meant to ride his father down. Then he saw the hand leap up and the butt of the quirt arching from it. The quirt came down to the sound of torn air.

A weal sprang out on Mr. Ellenwood's face. One second it wasn't there, and the next it was, like something magical, a red and purple weal swollen high as half a rope. It ran from the temple across the cheek and down the line of the jaw.

For one breath it was like looking at a picture, the horse pulled up, the quirt downswept from the hand, the weal hot and angry, and nothing moving, everything caught up and held by the violence that had gone before.

The picture broke into sound and fury, father's hand shooting out and catching the man's arm and tearing him from his horse and the horse snorting and shying away and the man landing sprawled and gathering himself like a cat and raising the quirt high again while swear words streamed from his mouth.

Mr. Ellenwood was stepping, stepping forward, not back, stepping into the wicked whistle and cut of the quirt, his head up and his eyes fixed. There was a terrible rightness about him, a rightness so terrible and so fated that for a minute Lonnie couldn't bear to look, thinking of Stephen stoned and Christ dying on the cross—of all the pale, good, thoughtful men foredoomed before the hearty.

He heard the whine of the quirt and the two men grunting and the whine of the quirt and feet slipping in the wet grass and breaths hoarse in the throat and the sound of the quirt again.

He heard the grunting and the slipping and the hoarse breathing, and all at once he remembered he didn't hear the quirt now, and he looked and saw it looping away, thrown by his father's hand. He saw his father's fists begin to work and heard the flat smacks of bone against flesh and saw the man try to shield himself and go down and get up and go down again. His eyes ran from side to side like a cornered animal's. He began crawling away. Rather than meet those fists again, he crawled away, beaten and silent, and climbed his horse and rode off.

Mr. Ellenwood watched him, then turned and saw Lonnie, who had come off the porch and down the steps. "Son," he said sternly, still panting, "I thought I told you to go inside."

From a distance Mr. Ross's voice, raised in a great whoop, came to Lonnie's ears.

"I did—I mean I couldn't. I just couldn't."

Lonnie watched his father's face, wanting, now that he had won, to see it loosen and light up and the weal bend to a smile.

"You're pale as paper, son."

"I didn't know if you could fight. I didn't know if you would think it was right to fight."

Mr. Ross's voice drowned out the answer. From across the street it boomed at them, the words sounding almost like hurrahs. "By God, prof, you're all right!"

Mr. Ellenwood straightened and turned in the direction of the voice, and then turned back and looked at Lonnie and abruptly sat down on the step by him. "If a man has to fight, he has to fight, Lonnie."

Mr. Ross came marching through the mud, his big mouth open in a smile. "I saw it, prof. I hung around. Damn me, if that ain't a bridge crossed!" He stuck out his hand.

Mr. Ellenwood took the hand and answered, "Thanks," but he didn't smile back. He looked at Mr. Ross and then looked off into space.

Mr. Ross said, "There's one man ain't going to be thinking education's so sissified."

Father nodded at the space he was looking into. "One," he said.

DOROTHY M. JOHNSON

I Woke Up Wicked

In reviewing Dorothy Johnson's 1958 collection, The Hanging Tree *(from which "I Woke Up Wicked" is taken),* Time *magazine said, "The best of these tales of a lost frontier echo Bret Harte or Mark Twain in the West." No finer compliment can be paid to the first lady of Western fiction whose work has found great favor not only with readers and reviewers, but with Hollywood moviemakers who have transformed three of her best stories— "The Man Who Shot Liberty Valance," "The Hanging Tree" and "A Man Called Horse"—into equally first-rate films.*

I USED TO RIDE with the Rough String, but not any more. They were tough outlaws, the Rough String; and the lawmen that chased them— from a safe distance—were hard cases too. In fact, everybody around was plumb dangerous except me.

I was just a poor innocent cowboy, broke but not otherwise wicked. I didn't want to join them outlaws, but I was running away from justice— the crookedest justice a man ever did see.

I was twenty-two years old when I rode into Durkee, a cow town in Montana, after helping eight other fellows deliver a trail herd of steers.

"Meet me at the bank in an hour, boys," says the wagon boss. "I'll pay you off there."

We scattered and started strutting the streets, all ragged and dusty. We was too broke to do anything but strut. Anyhow, while I was strutting, I see this fellow behind a lawman's badge; he's leaning against a wall and looking at me with his eyes narrow. It made me kind of mad, and my heart was pure, so I says, "See anything green? Well, by gosh, if it ain't Cousin Cuthbert! Cuthbert, you shouldn't of ever run off. Your ma's been real upset. . . ."

This fellow's eyes got so narrow I doubt if he could see out of 'em. "I am Buck Sanderson, deputy sheriff of this county, stranger," he said. And then, looking around, he whispers, "How are you, Willie?"

"My name is Duke Jackson," I says, huffy. "Seems like I made a mistake."

"You are a likely looking young fellow," he says, "and you remind me of somebody." He grinned, and I knew that he had got the idea—when I mentioned a mistake—that I meant I was on the run. But I wasn't, not then.

"You got any plans?" he says.

"The crew is gonna get paid off at the bank pretty quick," I says. "After that, I don't know what I'm going to do."

"Well, come have a drink," Cuthbert says. I should have known better than to drink with Cuthbert; he'd been a mean one as far back as anyone could remember. But I had a beer and he had red-eye, and then he says, "I'll mosey along with you to the bank."

"I can find it," I says, but he come anyway.

On the way he stopped by a hitch rack and squinted at a sorrel gelding with a fancy saddle on it. "Now what's the sheriff's horse doing there?" Cuthbert says. "It was supposed to be took to the livery stable, but I guess the hostler forgot. Here, you lead him. I got to keep my gun-hand free. This is a tough town."

So I led the sheriff's horse, rather than argue with him. There was some fellas standing in front of the bank, but none of them was from our crew, and there was some horses standing around.

"I'll go see if they're paying off yet," Cuthbert says. "You hold the horse."

"You hold him," I says. "It's me that's getting paid off."

"Hold the horse," he says, and walked into the bank.

So I was standing there, getting mad, when three or four shots blasted out. And then men came boiling out of the bank like hornets and leaped onto those horses that were waiting. Cuthbert came running out with them and after he'd let the men get a start, he began shooting after them but up in the air. Well, I saw that Cuthbert hadn't changed any, and so I did the obvious thing. I jumped on the sheriff's horse and galloped him out of town.

Ten miles out, I stopped to see if any bullets had hit me. They hadn't.

There I was, a refugee from justice. I'd stolen the sheriff's horse, and the bank had been robbed with me standing there looking like I was part of the gang; and I was a witness to the fact that Cuthbert was in on the holdup.

I sat down in some bushes and wished for a smoke and thought what a perfidious villain Cuthbert was. I decided to go back and tell the sheriff so, but not just then. Some other year would do. If I went riding back to

Durkee that day, on the sheriff's horse, people might misunderstand.

So I rode another ten miles farther away. It was getting dark then, so I unsaddled and went to bed in the brush, wishing I could eat grass like the sorrel.

I woke up in the dark, only it wasn't as dark as it should have been. Somebody had a fire going, and I could hear voices. Couldn't even get a good night's sleep. I sat up, and somebody says, "That you, Larry?"

"Never heard of him," I says, "and can't you guys shut up?" That just goes to show what a pure heart I had, and how little brains. All of a sudden I recalled that I was a wanted man.

"Got a rifle on you, mister," a man says. "Come into the light with your hands up."

Well, I didn't even stop to pull my boots on.

"How long you been there?" says a man with a black mustache. There was four of them, all with guns.

"How long don't matter," says a man with a beard. "Either he's on our side or he's dead."

"I'm on your side," I says. "Which side is it?"

The man with the beard scowled. "You ever drive cattle on shares?"

"Just for wages," I says. "I'm a hard-working cowpuncher looking for opportunity."

"It has found you," he says. "What name do you go by?"

"Duke," I says.

"No you don't," he says. "I'm Duke." He glared at me in the firelight and says, "You're Leather."

"Why, no such thing," I says. "I'm just ordinary skin like anybody else." Then it dawned on me who Duke was. Everybody knew the name Duke—he was one of the head men of the Rough String. Fact was, I took the name Duke not long before just because a reputation went with it. "If you say so," I says politely, "I'm Leather."

"Go bring Leather his boots," says Duke. "Give Leather a cup of coffee."

So that was how my name changed to Leather. And that was how I turned outlaw. No trouble at all. Went to bed honest and broke, woke up wicked and still broke, and misunderstood by everybody.

"We'll use you in our cattle business," Duke says. I didn't have to make any decisions at all. Seemed like I was cut out to be an outlaw.

You might think driving stolen cattle was exciting, but it wasn't. They didn't look any different, viewed from the dust of the drags, than they had when I pushed 'em along as a law-abiding citizen. Why should they look any different? They were some of the very same cattle.

After they became rustled cattle, they were easier to move. When they were an honest herd, the trail crew was always running into officious lawmen and nesters that said "You can't bring that herd through here" or "You can't cross this line." But when the Rough String moved them steers, the lawmen were somewheres else on urgent business, and the nesters waited for the Rough String with open arms.

This is the life, I began to think. It's safer and quieter than being an honest cowboy. Nobody gets close enough to point a gun at you.

I could even have enjoyed it if all them outlaws hadn't made me so nervous. Duke and the boys looked like cowboys anywhere, dusty and needing a shave, and red-eyed because with a trail herd you never get enough sleep. But just knowing they were the Rough String made me shiver. I tried being real polite and they glared at me. So I glared back and showed my teeth, and after that we got along pretty good. Being an outlaw is awful tiring on your facial muscles.

We moved them cattle right along because the former owner had men on our trail. When the men got too close, they slowed up and waited for a prudent length of time. Their boss was even safer—he was home on the ranch.

One day we pushed them cattle up to the top of a ridge of rimrock, and Duke says with a happy sigh, "Well, there it is. Eagle Nest."

The boys sat their horses, and we looked down into the prettiest green valley I ever saw. The steers went snorting down the trail to water and that good green grass, and most of the boys went "Yippee!" and spurred their horses down that way too.

"Got girls waiting down there," says Duke, explaining to me. "Now there is a settlement no lawman ever laid eyes on, boy. Eagle Nest. Not that they don't know where it is." He chuckled fondly. "We got a nice layout there. Families, kids. Even had a school till the teacher got married."

Then he yelled, "Yippee!" and off he went.

"I am Leather Jackson," I says out loud to myself. "One of the Rough String. I am a real bad fellow." But I wished my teeth wouldn't chatter.

I yelled, "Yippee!" and spurred my horse down the trail to Eagle Nest. Down there they would protect me. I flung out of the saddle in front of a log building with a hitch rack. I started to swagger in. A dark-skinned girl with long earrings came out, grinned at me.

"You are Leath-air Jackson," she says to me.

I swept off my hat and says, "Yes, ma'am, I sure am, and what might your name be?" Not that I gave a hang, but it occurred to me that the Rough String's women folk might be even more dangerous than the outlaws themselves, and one thing you can always do when you meet a strange woman, dangerous or not, is be awful polite.

"My name ees Carmen," she says. She would have been kind of pretty if she hadn't had a front tooth missing.

Just then Duke came, glaring at me and her, so I says, "Pleased to meet you, ma'am," and, "Boss, where do I bunk? Because it's a long, long time since I had a solid night's sleep."

"The big cabin is for the single men," Duke says. "The little shacks is for those of us that's got our own housekeeping arrangements. Carmen, you git along home and don't dally."

She dallied long enough to wave her eyelashes at me, and that raised a chill along the back of my neck.

"Your credit's good at the store here," Duke says, motioning.

That was a relief, because being an outlaw hadn't made me any more prosperous than I was while honest.

The storekeeper squinted at me and says, "I reckon you're Leather Jackson. What'll you have?"

"Soap to get the dust off the outside," I says. "And a can of peaches to cut it on the inside, and some smoking tobacco to relax with before I go to sleep for four or five days." I was a real tough rustler, I was. Still wanted the same old comforts.

While I was drinking the peach juice, my eyes got used to the dim light, and I see there was a woman about ten feet away. I put a little more distance between us, and she says in a ladylike voice, "Mr. Frasier, would you introduce us?"

"Oh, gosh, excuse me," the storekeeper says. "Miz Pickett, meet Leather Jackson, the new man."

I grabbed off my hat and bowed, and she says, "How do you do."

She was a pretty lady, real young, had all her teeth too, but she looked prim and wore a black dress. Now if there was anything you didn't expect to see in Eagle Nest, it was a prim lady.

"I hope we shall become better acquainted," she says, and went out.

"Yes, sir," I says, baffled. "Yes, ma'am, I do too."

Mr. Frasier leaned on the counter and says, "The widow there, she came in here to teach school and married Ed Pickett. He got shot a while back. The other women say she's a snob because she keeps her marriage certificate up on the wall. They're just jealous."

"A very nice lady," I says.

"You bet she is," says Mr. Frasier. "And if you ever find out whether she really did ride with the String when they took the express car at Middle Fork, I sure wish you'd tell me."

I didn't say anything. My teeth were chattering on the rim of the peach can.

Then I could see it all—the poor orphan girl with no folks, lured into that nest of thieves to teach school, falling in love with this bandit, Pickett, then widowed when he was shot. Poor girl.

I put down the empty peach can and throwed my shoulders back and says, "If you want trouble with Leather Jackson, mister, just let me hear you say one evil word about that little lady."

He cringed. "I wouldn't, Leather, I sure wouldn't! I bet it's all a vicious rumor, about her riding with the—"

"That's the kind of evil word I mean," I grated at him, getting my gun out after only one fumble.

He backed off with his hands hovering level with his shoulders. "Just a vicious rumor," he repeated, "and to show you my heart's in the right place, I won't even charge you for that merchandise you just bought."

"I'll let the slander pass this time," I says through my teeth.

I found the bunkhouse, swaggered in like I owned it, growled at the boys and laid down in a bunk. I slept thirty-six hours and would have stretched it longer except I got hungry.

I woke up mad—and scared—and laid there with my eyes shut, figuring. William Jackson, I says to myself. Duke Jackson. Leather Jackson— now I know you, boy. What you going to do about the jam you're in? You're not the best shot in the world, and your hide's not made of cast iron.

Then I figured out why I was mad, and I was ashamed of being so selfish when there was that unprotected little widow marooned among that bunch of outlaws.

She dassent leave, I figured, because probably the hardhearted lawmen would get her on account of her associations. She wouldn't have no money to live on if she could escape. And them saying she held up a train!

Well, I worked up such a mad that I wasn't scared no more. I marched out of there in a towering rage, clean forgetting to put on my gun belt, which was in my war sack. Outside I met two or three of the Rough String and glared 'em down. They glanced at my hip—no holster there—and my murderous expression, and they seen a cold-blooded killer who didn't need firearms. Why, Leather Jackson was the type that would throttle an innocent grizzly bear with his raw hands.

They stepped aside for me, they did, and made me welcome.

I never did so much loafing since I got out of my cradle. There was nothing to do but lounge around and gossip and play cards and get drunk. But I didn't wish to drink in that company and was scared to win at cards and was not willing to lose, even if I'd had any money. So I listened, and that got monotonous too. My face got tired from keeping that tough look on it, just waiting for somebody to drop an evil word about poor little Miz Pickett.

They gabbed about old holdups till hell wouldn't have it. Miz Pickett's late husband was horse-holder when they robbed a bank, I learned, and some kid shot him from an upstairs window when they came out with the money.

About once an hour somebody would say with a long face, "I never did believe that nonsense about the widow riding with the boys when they took that train, though," and the rest of them, carefully not looking my way, would chime in, "No, no!" like the Ladies Aid fighting off the idea that the preacher had been seen staggering out of a saloon.

After three or four days one of Duke's boys gave me the word I was on guard duty that night.

"Take your rifle up to the rim," he says, "and keep it ready. Nobody's tried to bust into Eagle Nest yet, but some lawman out to make a reputation might try it.

"One shot from up there, and we'll all be with you. But don't go shooting just to hear the echo. There's few things make the boys madder than to get routed out of a quiet night's sleep because some green guard gets jumpy and shoots the blazes out of a friendly juniper.

"In fact," he says, "one fellow that done it ain't been seen since."

There was even a password. It was Twenty Dollars.

Night-herding rimrock and juniper trees is even duller than riding around bedded-down cattle. I hummed and whistled and sang and practiced cussing. Then I dozed, setting on a rock with the rifle on my knees.

I woke up with an awful start, hearing horses coming up the trail from the outside. I rolled down behind the rock and yelped, "Who's there?"

A deep voice says, "Who the hell do you think it is? And who are you?"

See, no password. So if he didn't want to give it, I was willing. Nobody told me who was supposed to deal.

"For twenty dollars I'd bore a hole clean through you," I says, big and rough, but protected by that rock. Anyhow I hoped I was.

He says, "Oh, hell, I forgot that. We got lots more than twenty dollars on a led horse here."

So we got acquainted. There was five of them, and they had eighteen thousand dollars in gold coin on a pack horse. We shook hands and had a smoke and then they went on down to Eagle Nest.

I set there shaking like a leaf, because I found out, hiding behind that rock, that I wasn't going to shoot nobody no matter how big I talked about it. Even if they'd all been Cuthbert, I wouldn't have fired. I'd shot lots of game and butchered yearlings that wasn't mine, like any cowboy when the grub's short. I'd even shot a horse once. But I never had shot any people. And damned if I was going to start then, just to protect that bunch of bandits down in Eagle Nest.

It was quite a surprise to find that out, let me tell you. Made me stop and think.

Well, I wasn't hobbled on that rimrock. What's to stop me, I says to myself, from getting on my horse and going down over the side to where the rest of the world is?

Several things stopped me. The Rough String wouldn't like it, though I hadn't taken no blood oath or anything. The law might not like it too well because I still had the sheriff's horse. And if I left, who was going to look out for Miz Pickett? No, I wasn't hobbled. But I was sure ground-tied.

So there I was, a stout young fellow with no bad habits, stuck with them outlaws and helpless to protect the lady. Rustling cattle was no habit with me. I never did drink much, I'd quit gambling and I was scared of the girls in Eagle Nest—they carried little knives in their garters. All in all, I was a nicer fellow since turning badman. I was way too good for Eagle Nest, but I was scared to pull out.

When I rode down at sunup, Miz Pickett was lugging a couple of buckets of water to her cabin, so I stopped to help. Delicate-looking little thing, she was.

"I'd ask you in to breakfast," she says, "but you know how people talk."

"Ma'am, I would gladly go hungry to protect your good name," I says gallantly, setting down the buckets on her doorsill.

She gave me an approving look, and I noticed something funny. She was such a prim little lady, and she looked at me like my aunt used to, over her glasses. But Miz Pickett didn't have any glasses on.

"Leather," says she, "have you ever thought of quitting this life of banditry?"

Of course, I hadn't thought of much else since I got into it, but I was cautious. Anyhow, if she wanted to reform me, I wanted to give her the satisfaction of having a job to do. "A fellow thinks about a lot of things," I says.

"Crime brings nobody any good. There was my husband, shot down in a bank robbery. Are you any better off since you joined the Rough String?"

"Well, yes," I says. "I've got credit at Mr. Frasier's store."

"But no cash. Not until those steers you brought in are fattened up and sold. And what if the nesters who usually buy them get cold feet? The price on stolen beef goes pretty low."

"Was you thinking of getting out of here, ma'am?" I asked in a whisper. "Not that I want to inquire into your private business."

She looked droopy and pitiful. "I could go back to teaching. But would the Rough String dare to let me leave?"

"Any time you want help, ma'am," I says, big and bold. "Any time you want to go. . . ."

She smiled, sad and sweet. "Thank you, Leather. Thank you for carrying the water."

Less than a week later Duke said it was my turn on guard again. For a minute—or less, probably—I thought of asking him what those other lazy loafers were going to do with their time and why should I get night duty so soon, but it seemed smarter to show my teeth and answer, "Fine. Maybe a posse will try coming in tonight."

So I went up there again on the rimrock, but this time it was some different. Miz Pickett had fixed up a nice lunch for me. I ate away at it in the dark, mourning my misspent past and cloudy future, and yawning and fretting. Then I sat up with a jerk.

There was the sound of a horse down below, on the Eagle Nest side of the rim. No horse in his right mind would be up there in the rocks and brush of his own choice. The Rough String prided itself on good horses; there wasn't a halfwit in the lot. So that horse wasn't there by accident.

Maybe Duke or somebody was testing me out, I thought. I hollered,

"Who's there? Come up and lemme look at you or I shoot!" My, I sounded mean. Even scared myself.

A woman's voice says, "Oh, please don't!"

If there was anything I didn't want up there, it was a visit from one of those Eagle Nest girls. I grabbed the sheriff's horse's reins, ready to ride down to the outside into the arms of the law, if I could find any.

Then the voice said, "Leather, please help me. Can you change twenty dollars?" and I went plunging through the brush toward it, because it was Miz Pickett. For her I wouldn't even have needed the password.

She had a saddle horse and a pack horse, and one of them had a hoof caught between two logs. She had come up through the brush instead of on the trail. I yanked him out. I felt so big and strong I could have picked him up and lifted him out if necessary.

"This is the night I'm leaving," Miz Pickett says. "The String is having a big meeting down in the saloon, planning something."

"Let's ride," I says, with my chest puffed up like a balloon. And that was how I left Eagle Nest. Easy enough, once somebody gave me a push.

We could have gone faster if she hadn't brought so much stuff on that pack horse. I didn't even have my war sack, what cowboys used to call their forty years' gatherings, but Miz Pickett had everything—grub and blankets and a couple of wooden boxes roped on. A neater job of packing stuff on a horse I never saw.

"Those are my books in there," she explained when I glanced at the boxes at our first camp stop.

But when I stepped toward the pack horse to start unloading, she says, "Never mind. Get the fire going."

"Sure, I'll get the fire going," I says, "but I wouldn't want you to lift that heavy stuff off the pack saddle."

"Leather," she says, and I turned around. She still looked prim, in a black dress with a divided skirt for riding, but do you know what? She had a gun in her hand, pointed right at me.

"There's some good firewood over there to the left," I says, marching that way in a hurry. Right then I got a strong suspicion there was mighty few books in them boxes.

Officially, we took turns sleeping, with one awake staying on guard, not necessarily against wandering lawmen. The Eagle Nest boys were going to miss that gold any minute. But Miz Pickett didn't seem to sleep at all. We camped four nights, and every time I moved a muscle while I was on guard, I could feel that she was watching me from where she was supposed to be asleep.

One morning she says, "Another forty miles to the railroad."

"Fine," I says, wondering if she'd dry-gulch me before we got there.

"Ever been in the cattle business on your own?" she asks during coffee by the breakfast fire.

"Never have," I says.

"I think I'll give up schoolteaching," she says, "and raise beef instead. I'll need a foreman."

That girl didn't need a foreman. Everything she needed she already had. But I was in no position to refuse.

"Expect you will, ma'am," I says, and she nodded as if it was all settled.

"I'm going to take the train," she says. "You can come along a week later. I'm your sister, Mary Smith."

"Pleased to meet you, sis," I says. "And where should I meet you later?" Not that I was going to, but it seemed wise to act interested.

She wrote down the address, and I put the paper in my shirt pocket.

She smiled her prim little smile and says, "We're going to get along all right in the cattle business, Leather."

I hoped we were, with a thousand miles between us as soon as I could arrange it.

"You'd better hide out," she suggested. "The Rough String must be getting pretty close by now."

"Reckon so," I agreed. She didn't recommend any place for me to hide. With the law ahead, and the String hot on the trail behind, what was a poor cowboy to do that was wanted for bank robbery, cattle rustling and stealing the sheriff's sorrel horse?

"By the way," I says, "where do you figure to catch your train?"

"Durkee," she says.

I jumped a foot. "Durkee! Hell—excuse me, ma'am—shucks, I can't go to Durkee! That's where the bank was held up while I was holding this horse right in front of it, and this horse belongs to the sheriff."

She looked annoyed. I sure hated to annoy Miz Pickett.

"Durkee is where I intend to get the train," she says. "My goodness, do you think you're so outstanding that anybody's going to recognize you?"

She had a sound argument there. I did look like an ordinary feller now I'd stopped scowling at the Rough String and let my face hang loose. And if Cuthbert was around, was he going to identify me? He certainly was not. I'd identify him right back.

"There's a man in Durkee I'd like to meet sometime," she says thoughtfully. "I don't know for sure who he is, but he's a cunning wretch. He engineered a bank holdup there that the Rough String got the blame for. The String didn't hold up that bank."

"No, ma'am, they didn't," I says. "They were rustling cattle."

We made it to the depot just ahead of the train. As I was snatching at the ropes on the pack saddle, I glanced at the loafers by the depot, and cold chills went up my spine, because there was Cuthbert behind his nickel-plated star. But I preferred his company to Miz Pickett's. Also to the Rough String, and they might catch up with me any time, now she was going to leave me with no protection but my own wits.

"Good-bye, Harry, take care of yourself," says Little Rattlesnake, and I histed her boxes on the train.

"My books," I heard her tell the conductor.

The train started chugging, and I heard my second cousin say behind me, "Hello, Duke."

Cuthbert has got a nice safe jail, I says to myself. That's one place the Rough String won't come looking for me. I says, "Hello, Buck."

"Who's the girl?" he says.

"My sister," I says.

"I know your sisters, Willie, and she ain't one of 'em," he says. "You always were a liar."

So I hit him, but not very hard. He grappled me, and I fought just a bit.

"Resisting an officer, eh?" he says, yanking his gun out and relieving me of mine. "March right along, Willie, and if you tell anyone we're related, I'll shoot you."

"I'd rather be shot than admit it," I says, marching so fast he had to trot to keep up with me.

I was sure glad to get in that jail.

"Now we'll see what you got in your pockets," says Cuthbert. "H'm, broke, of course. What's this piece of paper here in your shirt pocket? I bet that's the address of the girl you put on the train."

"Don't take that!" I says. "I'll never remember where I'm to meet her."

He backed off, grinning, with the paper in his hand. "And why should she want you to meet her?" he says.

"Don't know as she does," I says, "but she's my golden future. She's not only pretty, she's also rich and wants a foreman for her ranch."

"Shouldn't be hard to find her a good man," says Cuthbert, tilting his hat.

"She said she'd sure like to meet you," I says, "but if you was to go climb on that train, it would be just plain dirty of you, because I seen her first." The train tooted and Cuthbert grinned.

"Stay here, Willie boy," he says.

He plumb forgot to lock the door, but I stayed in the cell. I stayed and stayed and stayed.

Around suppertime an older man came in. "What you doing here?"

"Was put here by a fellow with a star on," I says.

"Ain't nothing wrote down in the book," he says. "What you in for?"

"Hitting him, I guess," I says.

"Often wanted to do it myself," says the man. "You can go, for all I care."

Was there no refuge for Willie Jackson, the reformed outlaw?

"I'm wanted in nine states and some territories," I says. "Robbing banks, rustling cattle, forgery, arson—and stealing horses! Why, I've got a horse that belongs to the sheriff right now!"

"You have!" he says, grinning. "Why, boy, I'm so glad to find that horse, you know what I'm going to do? I'm going to make you a deputy. Somebody said they seen Buck get on the train, so I'm going to need a new deputy. We got some big game coming in here. You know who's coming? Eight members of the Rough String, that's who. Got fourteen more of 'em divided up among two other counties, and we get the overflow. Telegram just came in about how they run into a posse that was looking for somebody else. You want to work for me?"

"My health ain't good," I says. "I get the leaping flitters."

He yelled down the street after me, "Hey, you forgot your gun and your hat," so I had to delay long enough to go back and get them.

"Yes, sir," the sheriff says, "they got just about all the Rough String except the little lady that was boss of the whole shebang. Five thousand dollars' reward for her, but nobody outside the outlaws knows what she looks like."

"Five feet two," I says, "dark hair, looks like the president of the Ladies Aid. She took the same train out as your deputy. That's why he was on it."

"Whoof!" says the sheriff and left without warning. I was right behind him, but I passed him when he swung into the telegraph office. His horse was ten yards farther on.

It was a year or so, I guess, before they stopped looking for me, the unidentified cowboy riding the sheriff's horse who set the law on Miz Pickett and perfidious Cuthbert. If I'd turned myself in to be a witness, I could have been a hero. But I always felt kind of guilty about Cuthbert, and anyhow, you never knew which ones of the Rough String would break out of the penitentiary next.

Miz Pickett broke out and got away to South America. I was sure relieved to read about it in a newspaper, though I never had nothing against the South Americans. But they saved me from having to run off to some heathen place like China to stay clear of Miz Pickett. I went home to Pennsylvania and took up plowing.

Sergeant Houck

With the publication of his classic short novel, Shane, *in 1949, Jack Schaefer established himself as one of the premier Western writers of all time. The books which followed—*First Blood, The Canyon, Company of Cowards, Monte Walsh, *and such collections as* The Big Range, The Kean Land and Other Stories, *and* The Collected Stories of Jack Schaefer *—firmly cemented that reputation. Nowhere has his talent been better displayed than in his short stories, and no short story of his is better than "Sergeant Houck"—a realistic and moving tale of what happens when a young woman, captured by Indians and forced to mate with and bear the child of one of the tribe, is rescued by a cavalry troop.*

SERGEANT HOUCK stopped his horse just below the top of the ridge ahead. The upper part of his body was silhouetted against the sky line as he rose in his stirrups to peer over the crest. He urged the horse on up and the two of them, the man and the horse, were sharp and distinct against the copper sky. After a moment he turned and rode down to the small troop waiting. He reined beside Lieutenant Imler.

"It's there, sir. Alongside a creek in the next hollow. Maybe a third of a mile."

Lieutenant Imler looked at him coldly. "You took your time, sergeant. Smack on the top, too."

"Couldn't see plain, sir. Sun was in my eyes."

"Wanted them to spot you, eh, sergeant?"

"No, sir. Sun was bothering me. I don't think—"

"Forget it, sergeant. I don't like this either."

Lieutenant Imler was in no hurry. He led the troop slowly up the hill. The real fuss was fifty-some miles away. Captain McKay was hogging the honors there. Here he was, tied to this sideline detail. Twenty men. Ten would have been enough. Ten and an old hand like Sergeant Houck.

With his drawn saber pointing forward, Lieutenant Imler led the charge up and over the crest and down the long slope to the Indian village. There were some scattered shots from bushes by the creek, ragged pops indicating poor powder and poorer weapons, probably fired by the last of the old men left behind when the young braves departed in war paint ten days before. The village was silent and deserted.

Lieutenant Imler surveyed the ground they'd taken. "Spectacular achievement," he muttered to himself. He beckoned Sergeant Houck to him.

"Your redskin friend was right, sergeant. This is it."

"Knew he could be trusted, sir."

"Our orders are to destroy the village. Send a squad out to round up any stock. There might be some horses around. We're to take them in." Lieutenant Imler waved an arm at the thirty-odd skin-and-pole huts. "Set the others to pulling those down. Burn what you can and smash everything else."

"Right, sir."

Lieutenant Imler rode into the slight shade of the cottonwoods along the creek. He wiped the dust from his face and set his campaign hat at a fresh angle to ease the crease the band had made on his forehead. Here he was, hot and tired and way out at the end of nowhere with another long ride ahead, while Captain McKay was having it out at last with Grey Otter and his renegade warriors somewhere between the Turkey Foot and the Washakie. He relaxed to wait in the saddle, beginning to frame his report in his mind.

"Pardon, sir."

Lieutenant Imler looked around. Sergeant Houck was standing nearby with something in his arms, something that squirmed and seemed to have dozens of legs and arms.

"What the devil is that, sergeant?"

"A baby, sir. Or rather, a boy. Two years old, sir."

"How the devil do you know? By his teeth?"

"His mother told me, sir."

"His mother?"

"Certainly, sir. She's right here."

Lieutenant Imler saw her then, standing beside a neighboring tree, shrinking into the shadow and staring at Sergeant Houck and the squirming child. He leaned to look closer. She wore a shapeless, sacklike covering with slits for her arms and head. She was sun- and-windburned dark yet not as dark as he expected. And there was no mistaking the color of her hair. It was light brown and long and coiled in a bun on her neck.

"Sergeant! It's a white woman!"

"Right, sir. Her name's Cora Sutliff. The wagon train she was with was wiped out by a raiding party. She and another woman were taken along. The other woman died. She didn't. The village bought her. She's been in Grey Otter's lodge." Sergeant Houck smacked the squirming boy briskly and tucked him under one arm. He looked straight at Lieutenant Imler. "That was three years ago, sir."

"Three years? Then that boy—"

"That's right, sir."

Captain McKay looked up from his desk to see Sergeant Houck stiff at attention before him. It always gave him a feeling of satisfaction to see this great, granite man. The replacements they were sending these days, raw and unseasoned, were enough to shake his faith in the service. But as long as there remained a sprinkling of these case-hardened old-time regulars, the army would still be the army.

"At ease, sergeant."

"Thank you, sir."

Captain McKay drummed his fingers on the desk. This was a ridiculous situation and the solid, impassive bulk of Sergeant Houck made it seem even more so.

"That woman, sergeant. She's married. The husband's alive—wasn't with the train when it was attacked. He's been located. Has a place about twenty miles out of Laramie. The name's right and everything checks. You're to take her there and turn her over with the troop's compliments."

"Me, sir?"

"She asked for you. The big man who found her. Lieutenant Imler says that's you."

Sergeant Houck considered this expressionlessly. "And about the boy, sir?"

"He goes with her." Captain McKay drummed on the desk again. "Speaking frankly, sergeant, I think she's making a mistake. I suggested she let us see that the boy got back to the tribe. Grey Otter's dead and after that affair two weeks ago there's not many of the men left. But they'll be on the reservation now and he'd be taken care of. She wouldn't hear of it; said if he had to go she would, too." Captain McKay felt his former indignation rising again. "I say she's playing the fool. You agree with me, of course."

"No, sir. I don't."

"And why the devil not?"

"He's her son, sir."

"But he's—Well, that's neither here nor there, sergeant. It's not our affair. We deliver her and there's an end to it. You'll draw expense money and start within the hour."

"Right, sir." Sergeant Houck straightened up and started for the door.

"Houck."

"Yes, sir."

"Take good care of her—and that damn' kid."

"Right, sir."

Captain McKay stood by the window and watched the small cavalcade go past toward the post gateway. Lucky that his wife had come with him to this godforsaken station lost in the prairie wasteland. Without her they would have been in a fix with the woman. As it was, the woman looked like a woman now. And why shouldn't she, wearing his wife's third-best crinoline dress? It was a bit large, but it gave her a proper feminine appearance. His wife had enjoyed fitting her, from the skin out, everything except shoes. Those were too small. The woman seemed to prefer her worn moccasins anyway. And she was uncomfortable in the clothes. But she was decently grateful for them, insisting she would have them returned or would pay for them somehow. She was riding past the window, sidesaddle on his wife's horse, still with that strange shrinking air about her, not so much frightened as remote, as if she could not quite connect with what was happening to her, what was going on around her.

Behind her was Private Lakin, neat and spruce in his uniform, with the boy in front of him on the horse. The boy's legs stuck out on each side of the small, improvised pillow tied to the forward arch of the saddle to give him a better seat. He looked like a weird, dark-haired doll bobbing with the movements of the horse.

And there beside the woman, shadowing her in the midmorning, was that extra incongruous touch, the great hulk of Sergeant Houck, straight in his saddle, taking this as he took everything, with no excitement and no show of any emotion, a job to be done.

They went past and Captain McKay watched them ride out through the gateway. It was not quite so incongruous after all. As he had discovered on many a tight occasion, there was something comforting in the presence of that big man. Nothing ever shook him. You might never know exactly what went on inside his close-cropped skull, but you could be certain that what needed to be done he would do.

They were scarcely out of sight of the post when the boy began squirming. Private Lakin clamped him to the pillow with a capable right hand. The squirming persisted. The boy seemed determined to escape from what he regarded as an alien captor. Silent, intent, he writhed on the pillow. Private Lakin's hand and arm grew weary. He tickled his horse forward with his heels until he was close behind the others.

"Beg pardon, sir."

Sergeant Houck shifted in his saddle and looked around. "Yes?"

"He's trying to get away, sir. It'd be easier if I tied him down. Could I use my belt, sir?"

Sergeant Houck held in his horse to drop back alongside Private Lakin. "Kids don't need tying," he said. He reached out and plucked the boy from in front of Private Lakin and laid him, face down, across the withers of his own horse and smacked him sharply. Then he set him back on the pillow. The boy sat still, very still. Sergeant Houck pushed his left hand into his left side pocket and pulled out a fistful of small hard biscuits. He passed these to Private Lakin. "Stick one of these in his mouth when he gets restless."

Sergeant Houck urged his horse forward until he was beside the woman once more. She had turned her head to watch and she stared sidewise at him for a long moment, then looked straight forward again.

They came to the settlement in the same order: the woman and Sergeant Houck side by side in the lead, Private Lakin and the boy tagging behind at a respectful distance. Sergeant Houck dismounted and helped the woman down and handed the boy to her. He saw Private Lakin looking wistfully at the painted front of the settlement's one saloon and tapped him on one knee. "Scat," he said and watched Private Lakin turn his horse and ride off, leading the other two horses.

Then he led the woman into the squat frame building that served as general store and post office and stage stop. He settled the woman and her child on a preserved-goods box and went to the counter to arrange for their fares. When he came back to sit on another box near her, the entire permanent male population of the settlement was assembled just inside the door, all eleven of them staring at the woman.

". . . that's the one . . ."

". . . an Indian had her . . ."

". . . shows in the kid . . ."

Sergeant Houck looked at the woman. She was staring at the floor and the blood was leaving her face. He started to rise and felt her hand on his arm. She had leaned over quickly and clutched his sleeve.

"Please," she said. "Don't make trouble account of me."

"Trouble?" said Sergeant Houck. "No trouble." He stood up and confronted the fidgeting men by the door. "I've seen kids around this place. Some of them small. This one needs decent clothes and the store here doesn't stock them."

The men stared at him, startled, and then at the wide-eyed boy in his clean but patched skimpy cloth covering. Five or six of them went out through the door and disappeared in various directions. The others scattered through the store. Sergeant Houck stood sentinel, relaxed and quiet, by his box, and those who had gone out straggled back, several embarrassed and empty-handed, the rest proud with their offerings. Sergeant took the boy from the woman's lap and stood him on his box. He measured the offerings against the small body and chose a small red-checked shirt and a small pair of overalls. He set the one pair of small scuffed shoes aside. "Kids don't need shoes," he said. "Only in winter."

When the coach rolled in, it was empty, and they had it to themselves for the first hours. Dust drifted steadily through the windows and the silence inside was a persistent thing. The woman did not want to talk. She had lost all liking for it and would speak only when necessary. And Sergeant Houck used words with a natural economy, for the sole simple purpose of conveying or obtaining information that he regarded as pertinent to the business immediately in hand. Only once did he speak during these hours and then only to set a fact straight in his mind. He kept his eyes fixed on the scenery outside as he spoke.

"Did he treat you all right?"

The woman made no pretense of misunderstanding him. "Yes," she said.

The coach rolled on and the dust drifted. "He beat me once," she said and four full minutes passed before she finished the thought. "Maybe it was right. I wouldn't work."

They stopped for a quick meal at a lonely ranch house and ate in silence while the man there helped the driver change horses. It was two mail stops later, at the next change, that another passenger climbed in and plopped his battered suitcase and himself on the front seat opposite them. He was of medium height and plump. He wore city clothes and had quick eyes and features that seemed small in the plumpness of his face. He took out a handkerchief and wiped his face and took off his hat to wipe all the way up his forehead. He laid the hat on top of the suitcase and moved restlessly on the seat, trying to find a comfortable position.

"You three together?"

"Yes," said Sergeant Houck.

"Your wife then?"

"No," said Sergeant Houck. He looked out the window on his side and studied the far horizon.

The coach rolled on and the man's quick eyes examined the three of them and came to rest on the woman's feet.

"Begging your pardon, lady, but why do you wear those things? Moccasins, aren't they? They more comfortable?"

She shrank back further in the seat and the blood began to leave her face.

"No offense, lady," said the man. "I just wondered—" He stopped. Sergeant Houck was looking at him.

"Dust's bad," said Sergeant Houck. "And the flies this time of year. Best to keep your mouth closed." He looked out the window again, and the only sounds were the running beat of the hoofs and the creakings of the old coach.

A front wheel struck a stone and the coach jolted up at an angle and lurched sideways and the boy gave a small whimper. The woman pulled him onto her lap.

"Say," said the man. "Where'd you ever pick up that kid? Looks like —" He stopped. Sergeant Houck was reaching up and rapping against the top of the coach. The driver's voice could be heard shouting at the horses, and the coach stopped. One of the doors opened and the driver peered in. Instinctively he picked Sergeant Houck.

"What's the trouble, soldier?"

"No trouble," said Sergeant Houck. "Our friend here wants to ride up with you." He looked at the plump man. "Less dust up there. It's healthy and gives a good view."

"Now, wait a minute," said the man. "Where'd you get the idea—"

"Healthy," said Sergeant Houck.

The driver looked at the bleak, impassive hardness of Sergeant Houck and at the twitching softness of the plump man. "Reckon it would be," he said. "Come along. I'll boost you up."

The coach rolled along the false-fronted one street of a mushroom town and stopped before a frame building tagged Hotel. One of the coach doors opened, and the plump man retrieved his hat and suitcase and scuttled into the building. The driver appeared at the coach door. "Last meal here before the night run," he said.

When they came out, the shadows were long, and fresh horses had been harnessed. As they settled themselves again, a new driver, whip in hand, climbed up to the high seat and gathered the reins into his left hand. The whip cracked and the coach lurched forward and a young man ran out of the low building across the street carrying a saddle. He ran alongside and heaved the saddle up on the roof inside the guardrail. He pulled at the door and managed to scramble in as the coach picked up speed. He dropped onto the front seat, puffing deeply. "Evening, ma'am," he said between puffs. "And you, general." He leaned forward to slap the boy gently along the jaw. "And you too, bub."

Sergeant Houck looked at the lean young man, at the faded Levis tucked into high-heeled boots, the plaid shirt, the amiable competent young face. He grunted a greeting, unintelligible but a pleasant sound.

"A man's legs ain't made for running," said the young man. "Just to fork a horse. That last drink was near too long."

"The army'd put some starch in those legs," said Sergeant Houck.

"Maybe. Maybe that's why I ain't in the army." The young man sat quietly, relaxed to the jolting of the coach. "Is there some other topic of genteel conversation you folks'd want to worry some?"

"No," said Sergeant Houck.

"Then maybe you'll pardon me," said the young man. "I hoofed it a lot of miles today." He worked hard at his boots and at last got them off and tucked them out of the way on the floor. He hitched himself up and over on the seat until he was resting on one hip. He put an arm on the windowsill and cradled his head on it. His head dropped down and he was asleep.

Sergeant Houck felt a small bump on his left side. The boy had toppled against him. Sergeant Houck set the small body across his lap with the head nestled into the crook of his right arm. He leaned his head down and heard the soft little last sigh as drowsiness overcame the boy. He looked sidewise at the woman and dimly made out the outline of her head falling forward and jerking back up and he reached his left arm along the top of the seat until his hand touched her far shoulder. He felt her shoulder stiffen and then relax as she moved closer and leaned toward him. He slipped down lower in the seat so that her head could reach his shoulder and he felt the gentle touch of her brown hair on his neck above his shirt collar. He waited patiently and at last he could tell by her steady deep breathing that all fright had left her and all her thoughts were stilled.

The coach reached a rutted stretch and began to sway and the young man stirred and began to slide on the smooth leather of his seat. Sergeant Houck put up a foot and braced it against the seat edge and the young man's body rested against it. Sergeant Houck leaned his head back on the top of the seat. The stars came out in the clear sky and the running beat of the hoofs had the rhythm of a cavalry squad at a steady trot and gradually Sergeant Houck softened slightly into sleep.

Sergeant Houck awoke, as always, all at once and aware. The coach had stopped. From the sounds outside, fresh horses were being buckled into the traces. The first light of dawn was creeping into the coach. He raised his head and he realized that he was stiff.

The young man was awake. He was inspecting the vast leather sole of Sergeant Houck's shoe. His eyes flicked up and met Sergeant Houck's eyes and he grinned.

"That's impressive footwear," he whispered. "You'd need starch in the legs with hoofs like that." He sat up and stretched, long and reaching, like a lazy young animal. "Hell," he whispered again. "You must be stiff as a branding iron." He took hold of Sergeant Houck's leg at the knee and hoisted it slightly so that Sergeant Houck could bend it and ease the foot down to the floor without disturbing the sleeping woman leaning against him. He stretched out both hands and gently lifted the sleeping boy from Sergeant Houck's lap and sat back with the boy in his arms. The young man studied the boy's face. "Can't be yours," he whispered.

"No," whispered Sergeant Houck.

"Must have some Indian strain."

"Yes."

The young man whispered down at the sleeping boy. "You can't help that, can you, bub?"

"No," said Sergeant Houck suddenly, out loud. "He can't."

The woman jerked upright and pulled over to the window on her side, rubbing at her eyes. The boy woke up, wide awake on the instant and saw the unfamiliar face above him and began to squirm violently. The young man clamped his arms tighter. "Morning, ma'am," he said. "Looks like I ain't such a good nursemaid."

Sergeant Houck reached out a hand and picked up the boy by a grip on the small overalls and deposited him in a sitting position on the seat beside the young man. The boy sat very still.

The sun climbed into plain view and now the coach was stirring the dust of a well-worn road. It stopped where another road crossed and the young man inside pulled on his boots. He bobbed his head in the direction of a group of low buildings up the side road. "Think I'll try it there. They'll be peeling broncs about now and the foreman knows I can sit a saddle." He opened a door and jumped to the ground and turned to poke his head in. "Hope you make it right," he said. "Wherever you're heading." The door closed and he could be heard scrambling up the back of the coach to get his saddle. There was a thump as he and the saddle hit the ground and then voices began outside, rising in tone.

Sergeant Houck pushed his head through the window beside him. The young man and the driver were facing each other over the saddle. The young man was pulling the pockets of his Levis inside out. "Lookahere, Will," he said. "You know I'll kick in soon as I have some cash. Hell, I've hooked rides with you before."

"Not now no more," said the driver. "The company's sore. They hear of this they'd have my job. I'll have to hold the saddle."

"You touch that saddle and they'll pick you up in pieces from here to breakfast."

Sergeant Houck fumbled for his inside jacket pocket. He whistled. The two men turned. He looked hard at the young man. "There's something on the seat in here. Must have slipped out of your pocket."

The young man leaned in and saw the two silver dollars on the hard seat and looked up at Sergeant Houck. "You've been in spots yourself," he said.

"Yes," said Sergeant Houck.

The young man grinned. He picked up the two coins in one hand and swung the other to slap Sergeant Houck's leg, sharp and stinging and grateful. "Age ain't hurting you any, general," he said.

The coach started up and the woman looked at Sergeant Houck. The minutes passed and still she looked at him.

"If I'd had brains enough to get married," he said, "might be I'd have had a son. Might have been one like that."

The woman looked away, out her window. She reached up to pat at her hair and the firm line of her lips softened in the tiny imperceptible beginnings of a smile. The minutes passed and Sergeant Houck stirred again. "It's the upbringing that counts," he said and settled into silent immobility, watching the miles go by.

It was near noon when they stopped in Laramie and Sergeant Houck handed the woman out and tucked the boy under one arm and led the way to the waiting room. He settled the woman and the boy in two chairs and left them. He was back soon, driving a light buckboard wagon drawn by a pair of deep-barreled chestnuts. The wagon bed was well padded with layers of empty burlap bags. He went into the waiting room and picked up the boy and beckoned to the woman to follow. He put the boy down on the burlap bags and helped the woman up on the driving seat.

"Straight out the road, they tell me," he said. "About fifteen miles. Then right along the creek. Can't miss it."

He stood by the wagon, staring along the road. The woman leaned from the seat and clutched at his shoulder. Her voice was high and frightened. "You're going with me?" Her fingers clung to his service jacket. "Please! You've got to!"

Sergeant Houck put a hand over hers on his shoulder and released her fingers. "Yes. I'm going." He put the child in her lap and stepped to the seat and took the reins. The wagon moved forward.

"You're afraid," he said.

"They haven't told him," she said, "about the boy."

Sergeant Houck's hands tightened on the reins and the horses slowed to a walk. He clucked sharply to them and slapped the reins on their backs and they quickened again into a trot. The wagon topped a slight rise and the road sloped downward for a long stretch to where the green of trees and tall bushes showed in the distance. A jackrabbit started from the scrub growth by the roadside and leaped high and leveled out, a gray brown streak. The horses shied and broke rhythm and quieted to a walk under the firm pressure of the reins. Sergeant Houck kept them at a walk, easing the heat out of their muscles, down the long slope to the trees. He let them step into the creek up to their knees and dip their muzzles in the clear running water. The front wheels of the wagon were in the creek and he reached behind him to find a tin dipper tucked among the burlap bags and leaned far out to dip up water for the woman and the boy and himself. He backed the team out of the creek and swung them into the wagon ruts leading along the bank to the right.

The creek was on their left and the sun was behind them, warm on their backs, and the shadows of the horses pushed ahead. The shadows were

longer, stretching farther ahead, when they rounded a bend along the
creek and the buildings came in sight, the two-room cabin and the several
lean-to sheds and the rickety pole corral. A man was standing by one of
the sheds and when Sergeant Houck stopped the team he came toward
them and stopped about twenty feet away. He was not young, perhaps in
his middle thirties, but with the young look of a man on whom the years
have made no mark except that of the simple passing of time. He was tall,
soft and loose-jointed in build, and indecisive in manner and movement.
His eyes wavered as he looked at the woman, and the fingers of his hands
hanging limp at his sides twitched as he waited for her to speak.

She climbed down her side of the wagon and faced him. She stood
straight and the sun behind her shone on her hair. "Well, Fred," she said.
"I'm here."

"Cora," he said. "It's been a long time, Cora. I didn't know you'd come
so soon."

"Why didn't you come get me? Why didn't you, Fred?"

"I didn't rightly know what to do, Cora. It was all so mixed up.
Thinking you were dead. Then hearing about you. And what happened.
I had to think about things. And I couldn't get away easy. I was going
to try maybe next week."

"I hoped you'd come. Right away when you heard."

His body twisted uneasily while his feet remained flat and motionless
on the ground. "Your hair's still pretty," he said. "The way it used to be."

Something like a sob caught in her throat and she started toward him.
Sergeant Houck stepped down on the other side of the wagon and walked
off to the creek and knelt to bend and wash the dust from his face. He
stood drying his face with a handkerchief and watching the little eddies
of the current around several stones in the creek. He heard the voices
behind him.

"Wait, Fred. There's something you have to know."

"That kid? What's it doing here with you?"

"It's mine, Fred."

"Yours? Where'd you get it?"

"It's my child. Mine."

There was silence and then the man's voice, bewildered, hurt. "So it's
really true what they said. About that Indian."

"Yes. He bought me. By their rules I belonged to him. I wouldn't be
alive and here now, any other way. I didn't have any say about it."

There was silence again and then the man spoke, self-pity creeping into his tone. "I didn't count on anything like this."

Sergeant Houck walked back to the wagon. The woman seemed relieved at the interruption. "This is Sergeant Houck," she said. "He brought me all the way."

The man nodded his head and raised a hand to shove back the sandy hair that kept falling forward on his forehead. "I suppose I ought to thank you, soldier. All that trouble."

"No trouble," said Sergeant Houck.

The man pushed at the ground in front of him with one shoe, poking the toe into the dirt and studying it. "I suppose we ought to go inside. It's near suppertime. I guess you'll be taking a meal here, soldier, before you start back to town."

"Right," said Sergeant Houck. "And I'm tired. I'll stay the night, too. Start in the morning. Sleep in one of those sheds."

The man pushed at the ground more vigorously. The little pile of dirt in front of his shoe seemed to interest him a great deal. "All right, soldier. Sorry there's no quarters inside." He turned quickly and started for the cabin.

The woman took the boy from the wagon and followed him. Sergeant Houck unharnessed the horses and led them to the creek for a drink and to the corral and let them through the gate. He walked quietly to the cabin doorway and stopped just outside.

"For God's sake, Cora," the man was saying, "I don't see why you had to bring that kid with you. You could have told me about it. I didn't have to see him."

"What do you mean?"

"Why, now we've got the problem of how to get rid of him. Have to find a mission or some place that'll take him. Why didn't you leave him where he came from?"

"No! He's mine!"

"Good God, Cora! Are you crazy? Think you can foist off a thing like that on me?"

Sergeant Houck stepped through the doorway. "Thought I heard something about supper," he said. He looked around the small room, then let his eyes rest on the man. "I see the makings on those shelves. Come along, Mr. Sutliff. A woman doesn't want men cluttering about when she's getting a meal. Show me your place before it gets dark."

He stood, waiting, and the man scraped at the floor with one foot and slowly stood up and went with him.

They were well beyond earshot of the cabin when Sergeant Houck spoke again. "How long were you married? Before it happened?"

"Six years," said the man. "No, seven. It was seven when we lost the last place and headed this way with the train."

"Seven years," said Sergeant Houck. "And no child."

"It just didn't happen. I don't know why." The man stopped and looked sharply at Sergeant Houck. "Oh. So that's the way you're looking at it."

"Yes," said Sergeant Houck. "Now you've got one. A son."

"Not mine," said the man. "You can talk. It's not *your* wife. It's bad enough thinking of taking an Indian's leavings." He wiped his lips on his sleeve and spat in disgust. "I'll be damned if I'll take his kid."

"Not his any more. He's dead."

"Look, man. Look how it'd be. A damn little half-breed. Around all the time to make me remember what she did. A reminder of things I'd want to forget."

"Could be a reminder that she had some mighty hard going. And maybe come through the better for it."

"*She* had hard going! What about me? Thinking she was dead. Getting used to that. Maybe thinking of another woman. Then she comes back —and an Indian kid with her. What does that make me?"

"Could make you a man," said Sergeant Houck. "Think it over." He turned away and went to the corral and leaned on the rail, watching the horses roll the sweat-itches out of the dry sod. The man went slowly down by the creek and stood on the bank, pushing at the dirt with one shoe and kicking small pebbles into the water. The sun, holding to the horizon rim, dropped suddenly out of sight and dusk came swiftly to blur the outlines of the buildings. The woman appeared in the doorway and called and they went in. There was simple food on the table and the woman stood beside it. "I've already fed him," she said and moved her head toward the door to the inner room.

Sergeant Houck ate steadily and reached to refill his plate. The man picked briefly at the food before him and stopped, and the woman ate nothing at all. The man put his hands on the table edge and pushed back and stood up. He went to a side shelf and took a bottle and two thick cups and set them by his plate. He filled the cups a third full from the bottle and shoved one along the table boards toward Sergeant Houck. He lifted the other. His voice was bitter. "Happy homecoming," he said. He waited and Sergeant Houck took the other cup and they drank. The man lifted the bottle and poured himself another drink.

The woman looked quickly at him and away. "Please, Fred."

The man paid no attention. He reached with the bottle toward the other cup.

"No," said Sergeant Houck.

The man shrugged. "You can think better on whisky. Sharpens the mind." He set the bottle down and took his cup and drained it. Sergeant Houck fumbled in his right side pocket and found a short straight straw there and pulled it out and put one end in his mouth and chewed slowly on it. The man and the woman sat still, opposite each other at the table, and seemed to forget his quiet presence. They stared everywhere except at each other. Yet their attention was plainly concentrated on each other. The man spoke first. His voice was restrained, carrying conscious patience.

"Look, Cora. You wouldn't want to do that to me. You can't mean what you said before."

Her voice was determined. "He's mine."

"Now, Cora. You don't want to push it too far. A man can take just so much. I didn't know what to do after I heard about you. But I was all ready to forgive you. And now you—"

"Forgive me!" She knocked against her chair rising to her feet. Hurt and bewilderment made her voice ragged as she repeated the words. "Forgive me?" She turned and ran into the inner room. The handleless door banged shut behind her.

The man stared after her and shook his head and reached again for the bottle.

"Enough's enough," said Sergeant Houck.

The man shrugged in quick irritation, "For you maybe," he said and poured himself another drink. "Is there any reason you should be nosying in on this?"

"My orders," said Sergeant Houck, "were to deliver them safely. Both of them."

"You've done that," said the man. He lifted the cup and drained it and set it down carefully. "They're here."

"Yes," said Sergeant Houck. "They're here." He stood up and stepped to the outside door and looked into the night. He waited a moment until his eyes were accustomed to the darkness and could distinguish objects faintly in the starlight. He stepped out and went to the pile of straw behind one of the sheds and took an armload and carried it back by the cabin and dropped it at the foot of a tree by one corner. He sat on it, his legs stretched out, his shoulders against the tree, and broke off a straw stem and chewed slowly on it. After a while his jaws stopped their slow slight movement and his head sank forward and his eyes closed.

Sergeant Houck woke up abruptly. He was on his feet in a moment, and listening. He heard the faint sound of voices in the cabin, indistinct but rising as the tension rose in them. He went toward the doorway and stopped just short of the rectangle of light from the lamp.

"You're not going to have anything to do with me!" The woman's voice was harsh with stubborn anger. "Not until this has been settled right!"

"Aw, come on, Cora." The man's voice was fuzzy, slow-paced. "We'll talk about that in the morning."

"No!"

"All right!" Sudden fury made the man's voice shake. "You want it settled now! Well, it's settled! We're getting rid of that damn kid first thing tomorrow!"

"No!"

"What gave you the idea you've got any say around here after what you did? I'm the one to say what's to be done. You don't be careful, maybe I won't take you back."

"Maybe I don't want you to!"

"So damn finicky all of a sudden! After being with that Indian and maybe a lot more!"

Sergeant Houck stepped through the doorway. The man's back was to him, and he spun him around and his right hand smacked against the side of the man's face and sent him staggering against the wall.

"Forgetting your manners won't help," said Sergeant Houck. He looked around, and the woman had disappeared into the inner room. The man leaned against the wall, rubbing his cheek, and she came out, the boy in her arms, and ran toward the outer door.

"Cora!" the man shouted. "Cora!"

She stopped, a brief hesitation in flight. "I don't belong to you," she said and was gone through the doorway. The man pushed out from the wall and started after her and the great bulk of Sergeant Houck blocked the way.

"You heard her," said Sergeant Houck. "She doesn't belong to anybody now. Nobody but that boy."

The man stared at him and some of the fury went out of his eyes and he stumbled to his chair at the table and reached for the bottle. Sergeant Houck watched him a moment, then turned and quietly went outside. He walked toward the corral and as he passed the second shed, she came out of the darker shadows and her voice, low and intense, whispered at him.

"I've got to go. I can't stay here."

Sergeant Houck nodded and went on to the corral. He harnessed the horses quickly and with a minimum of sound. He finished buckling the traces and stood straight and looked toward the cabin. He walked to the doorway and stepped inside. The man was leaning forward in his chair, his elbows on the table, staring at the empty bottle.

"It's finished," said Sergeant Houck. "She's leaving now."

The man shook his head and pushed at the bottle with one forefinger. "She can't do that." He looked up at Sergeant Houck and sudden rage began to show in his eyes. "She can't do that! She's my wife!"

"Not any more," said Sergeant Houck. "Best forget she ever came back." He started toward the door and heard the sharp sound of the chair scraping on the floor behind him. The man's voice rose, shrilling up almost into a shriek.

"Stop!" The man rushed to the wall rack and grabbed the rifle there and held it low and aimed it at Sergeant Houck. "Stop!" He was breathing deeply and he fought for control of his voice. "You're not going to take her away!"

Sergeant Houck turned slowly. He stood still, a motionless granite shape in the lamplight.

"Threatening an army man," said Sergeant Houck. "And with an empty gun."

The man wavered and his eyes flicked down at the rifle. In the second of indecision Sergeant Houck plunged toward him and one huge hand grasped the gun barrel and pushed it aside and the shot thudded harmlessly into the cabin wall. He wrenched the gun from the man's grasp and his other hand took the man by the shirtfront and pushed him down into the chair.

"No more of that," said Sergeant Houck. "Best sit quiet." He looked around the room and found the box of cartridges on a shelf and he took this with the rifle and went to the door. "Look around in the morning and you'll find these." He went outside and tossed the gun up on the roof of one of the sheds and dropped the little box by the pile of straw and kicked some straw over it. He went to the wagon and stood by it and the woman came out of the darkness, carrying the boy.

The wagon wheels rolled silently. The small creakings of the wagon body and the thudding rhythm of the horses' hooves were distinct, isolated sounds in the night. The creek was on their right and they followed the road back the way they had come. The woman moved on the seat, shifting the boy's weight from one arm to the other, until Sergeant Houck took him by the overalls and lifted him and reached behind to lay him on the burlap bags. "A good boy," he said. "Has the Indian way of taking things without yapping. A good way."

The thin new tracks in the dust unwound endlessly under the wheels and the waning moon climbed through the scattered bushes and trees along the creek.

"I have relatives in Missouri," said the woman. "I could go there."

Sergeant Houck fumbled in his side pocket and found a straw and put this in his mouth and chewed slowly on it. "Is that what you want?"

"No."

They came to the main-road crossing and swung left and the dust thickened under the horses' hooves. The lean dark shape of a coyote slipped from the brush on one side and bounded along the road and disappeared on the other side.

"I'm forty-seven," said Sergeant Houck. "Nearly thirty of that in the army. Makes a man rough."

The woman looked straight ahead and a small smile showed in the corners of her mouth.

"Four months," said Sergeant Houck, "and this last hitch's done. I'm thinking of homesteading on out in the Territory." He chewed on the straw and took it between a thumb and forefinger and flipped it away. "You could get a room at the settlement."

"I could," said the woman. The horses slowed to a walk, breathing deeply, and he let them hold the steady, plodding pace. Far off a coyote howled and others caught the signal and the sounds echoed back and forth in the distance and died away into the night silence.

"Four months," said Sergeant Houck. "That's not so long."

"No," said the woman. "Not too long."

A breeze stirred across the brush and she put out a hand and touched his shoulder. Her fingers moved down along his upper arm and curved over the big muscles there and the warmth of them sank through the cloth of his worn service jacket. She dropped her hand in her lap again and looked ahead along the ribbon of the road. He clucked to the horses and urged them again into a trot and the small creakings of the wagon body and the dulled rhythm of the hoofs were gentle sounds in the night.

The late moon climbed and its pale light shone slantwise down on the moving wagon, on the sleeping boy and the woman looking straight ahead, and on the great solid figure of Sergeant Houck.

JOHN JAKES

The Woman at Apache Wells

John Jakes is one of the bestselling of contemporary novelists—his American Bicentennial Series, a group of eight novels tracing the evolution of one American family from the American Revolution to the present has been tremendously popular, as has his recent bestselling novel, North and South. *But before the fame and the commercial success, John Jakes was a regular contributor in a variety of genres: fantasy, science fiction, historical romance and the thriller—he worked them all and he worked them well in over fifty novels and two hundred short stories. He also wrote Westerns, more than twenty of them, the best of which is the present selection, which first appeared in* Max Brand's Western Magazine *in 1952.*

TRACY RODE DOWN from the rimrock with the seed of the plan already in mind. It was four days since they had blown up the safe in the bank at Wagon Bow and ridden off with almost fifty thousand dollars in Pawker's brown leather satchel. They had split up, taking three different directions, with Jacknife, the most trustworthy of the lot, carrying the satchel. Now, after four days of riding and sleeping out, Tracy saw no reason why he should split the money with the other two men.

His horse moved slowly along the valley floor beneath the sheet of blue sky. Rags of clouds scudded before the wind, disappearing past the craggy tops of the mountains to the west. Beyond those mountains lay California. Fifty thousand dollars in California would go a long way toward setting a man up for the rest of his life.

Tracy was a big man, with heavy capable hands and peaceful blue eyes looking out at the world from under a shock of sandy hair. He was by nature a man of the earth, and if the war hadn't come along, culminating in the frantic breakup at Petersburg, he knew he would still be working the rich Georgia soil. But his farm, like many others, had been put to the torch by Sherman, and the old way of life had been wiped out. The restless postwar tide had caught him and pushed him westward to a meeting with Pawker and Jacknife, also ex-Confederates, and the robbery of the bank filled with Yankee money.

Tracy approached the huddle of rundown wooden buildings. The valley was deserted now that the stage had been rerouted, and the Apache Wells Station was slowly sagging into ruin. Tracy pushed his hat down over his eyes, shielding his face from the sun.

Jacknife stood in the door of the main building, hand close to his holster. The old man's eyes were poor, and when he finally recognized Tracy, he let out a loud whoop and ran toward him. Tracy kicked his mount and clattered to a stop before the long ramshackle building. He climbed down, grinning. He didn't want Jacknife to become suspicious.

"By jingoes," Jacknife crowed, "it sure as hell is good to see you, boy. This's been four days of pure murder, with all that cash just waitin' for us." He scratched his incredibly tangled beard, unmindful of the dirt on his face or the stink on his clothes.

Tracy looked toward the open door. The interior of the building was in shadows. "Pawker here yet?" he asked.

"Nope. He's due in by sundown, though. Least, that's what he said."

"You got the money?" Tracy spoke sharply.

"Sure, boy, I got it." Jacknife laughed. "Don't get so worried. It's inside, safe as can be."

Tracy thought about shoving a gun into Jacknife's ribs and taking off with the bag right away. But he rejected the idea. He didn't have any grudge against the oldster. It was Pawker he disliked, with his boyish yellow beard and somehow nasty smile. He wanted the satisfaction of taking the money away from Pawker himself. He would wait.

Then Tracy noticed Jacknife's face was clouded with anxiety. He stared hard at the old man. "What's the trouble? You look like you got kicked in the teeth by a Yankee."

"Almost," Jacknife admitted. "We're right smack in the middle of a sitcheation which just aint healthy. A woman rode in here this morning."

Tracy nearly fell over. "A woman! What the hell you trying to pull?"

"Nothin', Tracy. She said she's Pawker's woman and he told her to meet him here. You know what a killer he is with the ladies."

"Of all the damn fool things," Tracy growled. "With cash to split up and every lawman around here just itching to catch us, Pawker's got to bring a woman along. Where is she?"

"Right inside," Jacknife repeated, jerking a thumb at the doorway.

"I got to see this."

He strode through the door into the cool shadowy interior. The only light in the room came from a window in the west wall. The mountains and the broken panes made a double line of ragged teeth against the cloud-dotted sky.

She sat on top of an old wooden table, whittling a piece of wood. Her clothes were rough, denim pants and a work shirt. Her body, Tracy could see, was womanly all over, and her lips were full. The eyes that looked up at him were large and gray, filled with a strange light that seemed, at succeeding moments, girlishly innocent and fiercely hungry for excitement. Just Pawker's type, he decided. A fast word, and they came tagging along. The baby-faced Confederate angered him more than ever.

"I hear you joined the party," Tracy said, a bit nastily.

"That's right." She didn't flinch from his stare. The knife hovered over the whittled stick. "My name's Lola."

"Tracy's mine. That doesn't change the fact that I don't like a woman hanging around on a deal like this."

"Pawker told me to come," she said defiantly. From her accent he could tell she was a Yankee.

"Pawker tells a lot of them to come. I been riding with him for a couple of months. That's long enough to see how he operates. Only a few of them are sucker enough to fall."

Her face wore a puzzled expression for a minute, as if she were not quite certain she believed what she said next. "He told me we were going to California with the money he stole from the bank."

"That's right," Tracy said. "Did he tell you there were two more of us?"

"No."

Tracy laughed, seating himself on a bench. "I thought so." Inwardly he felt even more justified at taking the money for himself. Pawker was probably planning to do the same thing. He wouldn't be expecting Tracy to try it.

"If I were you, miss, I'd ride back to where I came from and forget about Pawker. I worked with him at Wagon Bow, but I don't like him. He's a thief and a killer."

Her eyes flared with contempt. She cut a slice from the stick. "You're a fine one to talk, Mister Tracy. You were there too. You just said so. I suppose you've never robbed anybody in your life before."

"No, I haven't."

"Or killed anybody?"

"No. I didn't do any shooting at Wagon Bow. Pawker killed the teller. Jacknife outside didn't use his gun either. Pawker likes to use his gun. You ought to know that. Anybody can tell what kind of a man he is after about ten minutes."

Lola threw down the knife and the stick and stormed to the window. "I don't see what call you've got to be so righteous. You took the money, just like Pawker."

"Pawker's done it before. I figured this was payment for my farm in Georgia. Your soldiers burned me out. I figured I could collect this way and get a new start in California."

She turned suddenly, staring. "You were in the war?"

"I was. But that's not important. The important thing is for you to get home to your people before Pawker gets here. Believe me, he isn't worth it."

"I haven't got any people," she said. Her eyes suddenly closed a bit. "And I don't have a nice clean town to go back to. They don't want me back there. I had a baby, about a month ago. It died when it was born. The baby's father never came home from the war—" She looked away for a moment. "Anyway—Pawker came into the restaurant where I was working and offered to take me West."

"Somebody in the town ought to be willing to help you."

Lola shook her head, staring at the blue morning sky. Jacknife's whistle sounded busily from the broken-down corral. "No," she said. "The baby's father and I were never married."

Tracy walked over to her and stood behind her, looking down at her hair. He suddenly felt very sorry for this girl, for the life lying behind her. He had never felt particularly attached to any woman, except perhaps Elaine, dead and burned now, a victim of Sherman's bummers back in Georgia. He could justify the Wagon Bow robbery to himself. Not completely, but enough. But he coudn't justify Pawker or Pawker's love of killing or the taking of the girl.

"Look, Lola," he said. "You don't know me very well, but I'm willing to make you an offer. If you help me get the money, I'll take you with me. It'd be better than going with Pawker."

She didn't answer him immediately. "How do I know you're not just like him?"

"You don't. You'll have to trust me."

She studied him a minute. Then she said, "All right."

She stood very close to Tracy, her face uplifted, her breasts pushing out against the cloth of her shirt. A kind of resigned expectancy lay on her face. Tracy took her shoulders in his hands, pulled her to him and kissed her cheek lightly. When she moved away, the expectancy had changed to amazement.

"You don't need to think that's any part of the bargain," he said.

She looked into his eyes. "Thanks."

Tracy walked back to the table and sat down on the edge. He couldn't understand her, or know her motives, and yet he felt a respect for her and for the clear, steady expression of her eyes. Something in them almost made him ashamed of his part in the Wagon Bow holdup.

Jacknife stuck his head in the door, his watery eyes excited. A big glob of tobacco distended one cheek. "Hey, Tracy. Pawker's coming in."

Tracy headed outside without looking at Lola. A big roan stallion with Pawker bobbing in the saddle was pounding toward the buildings over the valley floor from the north, sending a cloud of tan dust into the sky. Tracy climbed the rail fence at a spot where it wasn't collapsing and from there watched Pawker ride into the yard.

Pawker climbed down. He was a slender man, but his chest was large and muscled under the torn Union cavalry coat. He wore two pistols, butts forward, and cartridge belts across his shirtfront under the coat. Large silver Spanish spurs jingled loudly when he moved. His flat-crowned black hat was tilted at a rakish angle over his boyish blond-whiskered face. Tracy had always disliked the effect Pawker tried to create, the effect of the careless guerrilla still fighting the war, the romantic desperado laughing and crinkling his childish blue eyes when his guns exploded. Right now, the careless guerrilla was drunk.

He swayed in the middle of the yard, blinking. He tilted his head back to look at the sun, then groaned. He peered around the yard. His hand moved aimlessly. "Hello, ol' Jacknife, hello, ol' Tracy. Damned four days, too damned long."

"You better sober up," Jacknife said, worried. "I want to split the money and light out of here."

"Nobody comes to Apache Wells any more," Pawker said. "Tracy, fetch the bottles out o' my saddle bags."

"I don't want a drink," Tracy said. Lola stood in the doorway now, watching, but Pawker did not see her. If he had, he would have seen the disillusionment taking root. Tracy smiled a little. Grabbing the money would be a pleasure.

"Listen, Pawker," Jacknife said, approaching him, "let's divvy the cash and forget the drink—"

Suddenly Pawker snarled and pushed the old man. Jacknife stumbled backward and fell in the dust. Pawker spat incoherent words and his right arm flashed across his body. The pistol came out and exploded loudly in the bright air. A whiff of smoke went swirling away across the old wooden roofs.

Jacknife screamed and clutched his hip. Tracy jumped off the fence and came on Pawker from behind, ripping the gun out of his hand and tossing it away. He spun Pawker around and hit him on the chin. The blond man skidded in the dust and scrabbled onto his knees, some of the drunkenness gone. Glaring, he slid his left hand across his body and down.

Tracy pointed his gun straight at Pawker's belly. "I'd like you to do that," he said. "Go ahead and draw."

Cunning edged across the other man's face. His hand moved half an inch further and he smiled. Then he giggled. "I'm going to throw my gun away, Tracy boy. I don't want trouble. Can I throw my gun away and show you I'm a peaceable man?"

Tracy took three fast steps forward and pulled the gun from its holster before Pawker could seize it. Then he turned his head and said, "Lola, find the satchel and get horses."

Pawker screamed the girl's name unbelievingly, turning on his belly in the dust to stare at her. He began to curse, shaking his fist at her, until Tracy planted a hand on his shoulder, pulled him to his feet and jammed him against the wall of the building with the gun pressing his ribs.

"Now listen," Tracy said. "I'm taking the satchel and I don't want a big muss."

"Stole my money, stole my woman," Pawker mumbled. "I'll get you, Tracy, I'll hunt you up and kill you slow. I'll make you pay, by God." His eyes rolled crazily, drunkenly.

Jacknife was trying to hobble to his feet. "Tracy," he wheezed, "Tracy, help me."

"I'm taking the money," Tracy said.

"That's all right, that's fine, I don't care," Jacknife breathed. "Put me on my horse and slap it good. I just want to get away from him. He's a crazy man."

Tracy shoved Pawker to the ground again and waved his gun at him. "You stay right there. I've got my eye on you." Pawker snarled something else but he didn't move. Tracy helped Jacknife onto his horse. The old man bent forward and lay across the animal's neck.

"So long, Tracy. Hit him good. I want to get away—"

"You need a doctor," Tracy said.

"I can head for some town," Jacknife breathed. "Come on, hit him!"

Tracy slapped the horse's flank and watched him go galloping out of the station yard and across the valley floor. Lola came around the corner of the building leading two horses. The satchel was tied over one of the saddlebags.

Tracy turned his head for an instant and when he turned back again, Pawker was scrabbling in the dust toward his gun which lay on the far side of the yard. Tracy fired a shot. It kicked up a spurt of dust a foot in front of Pawker's face. He jerked back, rolling over on his side and screaming, "I swear to God, Tracy, I'll come after you."

Lola was already in the saddle. The horses moved skittishly. Tracy swung up and said, "Let's get out of here." He dug in his heels and the horses bolted. They headed west across the floor of the valley.

They rode in silence. Tracy looked back once, to see Pawker staggering away from the building with his gun, firing at them over the widening distance. Until they made camp in the early evening at a small grove, with the mountains still looming to the west, Tracy said almost nothing.

Finally, when the meal with its few necessary remarks was over, he said, "Pawker will follow us. We'll have to keep moving."

She answered absently, "I guess you're right." A frown creased her forehead.

"What's the trouble?" He was beginning to sense the growth of a new feeling for this woman beside him. She was as silent and able as the hardened men with whom he had ridden in the last few years. Yet she was different, too, and not merely because she was female.

"I don't know how to tell you this right, Tracy." She spoke slowly. The firelight made faint red gold webs in her hair and the night air stirred it. "But—well—I think you're an honest man. I think you're decent and that's what I need." She stuck her finger out for emphasis. "Mind you, I don't mean that I care anything about you, but I think I could."

Tracy smiled. The statement was businesslike, and it pleased him. He knew that there was the possibility of a relationship that might be good for a man to have.

"I understand," he said. "I sort of feel the same. There's a lot of territory in California. A man could make a good start."

She nodded. "A good start, that's important. I made a mistake, I guess. So did you. But now there's a chance for both of us to make up for that. I'm not asking you if you want to. I'm just telling you the chance is there, and I'd like to see if what I think of you is right."

"I've been thinking the same," he said.

They sat in silence the rest of the evening, but it was a silence filled with a good sense of companionship that Tracy had seldom known. For the first time in several years, he felt things might work out right after all. Right according to the way it had been before the war, not since.

The next morning, they doubled back.

It was a five-day ride to Wagon Bow. The job was carried off at around four in the morning. Tracy rode through the darkened main street at a breakneck gallop and flung the satchel of money on the plank walk in front of the bank. By the time the sun rose he and Lola were miles from Wagon Bow. The only troubling factor was Pawker, somewhere behind them.

He caught up with them when they were high in the mountains, heavily bundled, driving their horses through the lowering twilight while the snow fell from a gray sky. Actually, they were the ones who caught up with Pawker. They saw him lying behind a boulder where he had been waiting. A rime of ice covered his rifle and his yellow boy's beard. His mouth was open. He was frozen to death.

Tracy felt a great relief. Pawker had evidently followed them, knowing the route they would probably take, and circling ahead to wait in ambush. It would have fitted him, rearing up from behind the boulder with his mouth open in a laugh and his avenging rifle spitting at them in the snow.

They stood for a time in the piercing cold, staring down at the body. Then Tracy looked at Lola through the dim veil of snow between them. He smiled, not broadly, because he wasn't a man to smile at death, but with a smile of peace. Neither one spoke.

Tracy made the first overt gesture. He put his thickly clad arm around her and held her for a minute, their cold raw cheeks touching. Then they returned to the horses.

Two days later, they rode down out of the mountains on the trail that led to California.

ELMORE LEONARD

The Boy Who Smiled

One of the three or four best Western novels published in the last quarter-century is Elmore Leonard's Hombre, *the grimly realistic tale of a white man who lived like an Indian and his final act of heroism. (The movie version, starring Paul Newman, is among the best Western films of the past quarter-century as well.) Leonard's other novels include the Westerns* Escape from Five Shadows, The Bounty Hunters, Valdez Is Coming, *and* Forty Lashes Less One *and such first-rate crime novels as* City Primeval, Split Images *and* Cat Chaser. *He has also published numerous Western short stories, the best known of which is probably "3:10 to Yuma," on which the classic film with Glenn Ford and Van Heflin is based. "The Boy Who Smiled," a story of vengeance and a young Apache named Mickey Segundo, ranks as one of Leonard's strongest tales.*

WHEN MICKEY SEGUNDO was fourteen, he tracked a man almost two hundred miles—from the Jicarilla Subagency down into the malpais.

He caught up with him at a waterhole in late afternoon and stayed behind a rock outcropping watching the man drink. Mickey Segundo had not tasted water in three days, but he sat patiently behind the cover while the man quenched his thirst, watching him relax and make himself comfortable as the hot lava country cooled with the approach of evening.

Finally Mickey Segundo stirred. He broke open the .50-caliber Gallagher and inserted the paper cartridge and the cap. Then he eased the carbine between a niche in the rocks, sighting on the back of the man's head. He called in a low voice, "Tony Choddi . . ." and as the face with the wide-open eyes came around, he fired casually.

He lay on his stomach and slowly drank the water he needed, filling his canteen and the one that had belonged to Tony Choddi. Then he took his hunting knife and sawed both of the man's ears off, close to the head. These he put into his saddle pouch, leaving the rest for the buzzards.

A week later Mickey Segundo carried the pouch into the agency office and dropped the ears on my desk. He said very simply, "Tony Choddi is sorry he has caused trouble."

335

I remember asking him, "You're not thinking of going after McKay now, are you?"

"This man, Tony Choddi, stole stuff, a horse and clothes and a gun," he said with his pleasant smile. "So I thought I would do a good thing and fix it so Tony Choddi didn't steal no more."

With the smile there was a look of surprise, as if to say, "Why would I want to get Mr. McKay?"

A few days later I saw McKay and told him about it and mentioned that he might keep his eyes open. But he said that he didn't give a damn about any breed Jicarilla kid. If the kid felt like avenging his old man, he could try, but he'd probably cash in before his time. And as for getting Tony Choddi, he didn't give a damn about that either. He'd got the horse back and that's all he cared about.

After he had said his piece, I was sorry I had warned him. And I felt a little foolish telling one of the biggest men in the Territory to look out for a half-breed Apache kid. I told myself, Maybe you're just rubbing up to him because he's important and could use his influence to help out the agency . . . and maybe he knows it.

Actually I had more respect for Mickey Segundo, as a human being, than I did for T. O. McKay. Maybe I felt I owed the warning to McKay because he was a white man. Like saying, "Mickey Segundo's a good boy, but hell, he's half-Indian." Just one of those things you catch yourself doing. Like habit. You do something wrong the first time and you know it, but if you keep it up, it becomes habit and it's no longer wrong because it's something you've always been doing.

McKay and a lot of people said Apaches were no damn good. The only good one was a dead one. They never stopped to reason it out. They'd been saying it so long, they knew it was true. Certainly any such statement was unreasonable, but damned if I wouldn't sometimes nod my head in agreement, because at those times I'd be with white men and that's the way white men talked.

I might have thought I was foolish, but actually it was McKay who was the fool. He underestimated Mickey Segundo.

That was five years ago. It had begun with a hanging.

Early in the morning, Tudishishn, sergeant of Apache police at the Jicarilla Agency, rode in to tell me that Tony Choddi had jumped the boundaries again and might be in my locale. Tudishishn stayed for half a dozen cups of coffee, though his information didn't last that long. When he had had enough, he left as leisurely as he had arrived. Tracking renegades, reservation jumpers, was Tudishishn's job; still, it wasn't something to get excited about. Tomorrows were for work; todays were for thinking about it.

Up at the agency, they were used to Tony Choddi skipping off. Usually they'd find him later in some shaded barranca, full of tulapai.

It was quiet until late afternoon, but not unusually so. It wasn't often that anything out of the ordinary happened at the subagency. There were twenty-six families, one hundred eight Jicarillas all told, under my charge. We were located almost twenty miles below the reservation proper, and most of the people had been there long before the reservation had been marked off. They had been fairly peaceful then, and remained so now. It was one of the few instances where the bureau allowed the sleeping dog to lie; and because of that we had less trouble than they did up at the reservation.

There was a sign on the door of the adobe office which described it formally. It read: D. J. Merritt—Agent, Jicarilla Apache Subagency—Puerco, New Mexico Territory. It was a startling announcement to post on the door of a squat adobe sitting all alone in the shadow of the Nacimentos. My Apaches preferred higher ground and the closest jacales were two miles up into the foothills. The office had to remain on the mail run, even though the mail consisted chiefly of impossible-to-apply bureau memoranda.

Just before supper, Tudishishn returned. He came in at a run this time and swung off before his pony had come to a full stop. He was excited and spoke in a confusion of Apache, Spanish and a word here and there of English.

Returning to the reservation, he had decided to stop off and see his friends of the Puerco Agency. There had been friends he had not seen for some time, and the morning had lengthened into afternoon with tulapai, good talking and even coffee. People had come from the more remote jacales, deeper in the hills, when they learned Tudishishn was there, to hear news of friends at the reservation. Soon there were many people and what looked like the beginning of a good time. Then Senor McKay had come.

McKay had men with him, many men, and they were looking for Mickey Solner—the squaw man, as the Americans called him.

Most of the details I learned later on, but briefly this is what had happened: McKay and some of his men were out on a hunting trip. When they got up that morning, McKay's horse was gone, along with a shotgun and some personal articles. They got on the tracks, which were fresh and easy to follow, and by that afternoon they were at Mickey Solner's jacale. His woman and boy were there, and the horse was tethered in front of the mud hut. Mickey Segundo, the boy, was honored to lead such important people to his father, who was visiting with Tudishishn.

McKay brought the horse along, and when they found Mickey Solner, they took hold of him without asking questions and looped a rope around his neck. Then they boosted him up onto the horse they claimed he had stolen. McKay said it would be fitting that way. Tudishishn had left fast when he saw what was about to happen. He knew they wouldn't waste time arguing with an Apache, so he had come to me.

When I got there, Mickey Solner was still sitting McKay's chestnut mare with the rope reaching from his neck to the cottonwood bough overhead. His head drooped as if all the fight were out of him, and when I came up in front of the chestnut, he looked at me with tired eyes, watery and red from tulapai.

I had known Solner for years, but had never become close to him. He wasn't a man with whom you became fast friends. Just his living in an Apache rancheria testified to his being of a different breed. He was friendly enough, but few of the whites liked him—they said he drank all the time and never worked. Maybe most were just envious. Solner was a white man gone Indian, whole hog. That was the cause of the resentment.

His son, Mickey the Second, stood near his dad's stirrup looking at him with a bewildered, pathetic look on his slim face. He held on to the stirrup as if he'd never let it go. And it was the first time, the only time, I ever saw Mickey Segundo without a faint smile on his face.

"Mr. McKay," I said to the cattleman, who was standing relaxed with his hands in his pockets. "I'm afraid I'll have to ask you to take that man down. He's under bureau jurisdiction and will have to be tried by a court."

McKay said nothing, but Bowie Allison, who was his herd boss, laughed and then said, "You ought to be afraid."

Dolph Bettzinger was there, along with his brothers Kirk and Sim. They were hired for their guns and usually kept pretty close to McKay. They did not laugh when Allison did.

And all around the clearing by the cottonwood were eight or ten others. Most of them I recognized as McKay riders. They stood solemnly, some with rifles and shotguns. There wasn't any doubt in their minds what stealing a horse meant.

"Tudishishn says that Mickey didn't steal your horse. These people told him that he was at home all night and most of the morning until Tudishishn dropped in, and then he came down here." A line of Apaches stood a few yards off and as I pointed to them, some nodded their heads.

"Mister," McKay said, "I found the horse at this man's hut. Now you argue that down, and I'll kiss the behind of every Apache you got living around here."

"Well, your horse could have been left there by someone else."

"Either way, he had a hand in it," he said curtly.

"What does he say?" I looked up at Mickey Solner and asked him quickly, "How did you get the horse, Mickey?"

"I just traded with a fella." His voice shook, and he held on to the saddle horn as if afraid he'd fall off. "This fella come along and traded with me, that's all."

"Who was it?"

Mickey Solner didn't answer. I asked him again, but still he refused to speak. McKay was about to say something, but Tudishishn came over quickly from the group of Apaches.

"They say it was Tony Choddi. He was seen to come into camp in early morning."

I asked McKay if it was Tony Choddi, and finally he admitted that it was. I felt better then. McKay couldn't hang a man for trading a horse.

"Are you satisfied, Mr. McKay? He didn't know it was yours. Just a matter of trading a horse."

McKay looked at me, narrowing his eyes. He looked as if he were trying to figure out what kind of a man I was. Finally he said, "You think I'm going to believe them?"

It dawned on me suddenly that McKay had been using what patience he had for the past few minutes. Now he was ready to continue what they had come for. He had made up his mind long before.

"Wait a minute, Mr. McKay, you're talking about the life of an innocent man. You can't just toy with it like it was a head of cattle."

He looked at me and his puffy face seemed to harden. He was a heavy man, beginning to sag about the stomach. "You think you're going to tell me what I can do and what I can't? I don't need a government representative to tell me why my horse was stolen!"

"I'm not telling you anything. You know Mickey didn't steal the horse. You can see for yourself you're making a mistake."

McKay shrugged and looked at his herd boss. "Well, if it is, it isn't a very big one. Leastwise we'll be sure he won't be trading in stolen horses again." He nodded to Bowie Allison.

Bowie grinned, and brought his quirt up and then down across the rump of the chestnut.

"Yiiiiiiiii. . . ."

The chestnut broke fast. Allison stood yelling after it, then jumped aside quickly as Mickey Solner swung back toward him on the end of the rope.

It was two weeks later, to the day, that Mickey Segundo came in with Tony Choddi's ears. You can see why I asked him if he had a notion of going after McKay. And it was a strange thing. I was talking to a different boy than the one I had last seen under the cottonwood.

When the horse shot out from under his dad, he ran to him like something wild, screaming, and wrapped his arms around the kicking legs trying to hold the weight off the rope.

Bowie Allison cuffed him away, and they held him back with pistols while he watched his dad die. From then on, he didn't say a word, and when it was over, walked away with his head down. Then, when he came in with Tony Choddi's ears, he was himself again. All smiles.

I might mention that I wrote to the Bureau of Indian Affairs about the incident since Mickey Solner, legally, was one of my charges; but nothing came of it. In fact, I didn't even get a reply.

Over the next few years Mickey Segundo changed a lot. He became Apache. That is, his appearance changed and almost everything else about him—except the smile. The smile was always there, as if he knew a monumental secret which was going to make everyone happy.

He let his hair grow to his shoulders and usually he wore only a frayed cotton shirt and breech-clout; his moccasins were Apache—curled toes and leggings which reached to his thighs. He went under his Apache name which was Peza-a, but I called him Mickey when I saw him, and he was never reluctant to talk to me in English. His English was good, discounting grammar.

Most of the time he lived in the same jacale his dad had built, providing for his mother and fitting closer into the life of the rancheria than he did before. But when he was about eighteen, he went up to the agency and joined Tudishishn's police. His mother went with him to live at the reservation, but within a year the two of them were back. Tracking friends who happened to wander off the reservation didn't set right with him. It didn't go with his smile.

Tudishishn told me he was sorry to lose him because he was an expert tracker and a dead shot. I know the sergeant had a dozen good sign followers, but very few who were above average with a gun.

He must have been nineteen when he came back to Puerco. In all those years he never once mentioned McKay's name. And I can tell you I never brought it up either.

I saw McKay even less after the hanging incident. If he ignored me before, he avoided me now. As I said, I felt like a fool after warning him about Mickey Segundo, and I'm certain McKay felt only contempt for me for doing it, after sticking up for the boy's dad.

McKay would come through every once in a while, usually going on a hunt up into the Nacimentos. He was a great hunter and would go out for a few days every month or so. Usually with his herd boss, Bowie Allison. He hunted everything that walked, squirmed or flew and I'm told his ranch trophy room was really something to see.

You couldn't take it away from the man; everything he did, he did well. He was in his fifties, but he could shoot straighter and stay in the saddle longer than any of his riders. And he knew how to make money. But it was his arrogance that irked me. Even though he was polite, he made you feel far beneath him. He talked to you as if you were one of the hired help.

One afternoon, fairly late, Tudishishn rode in and said that he was supposed to meet McKay at the adobe office early the next morning. McKay wanted to try the shooting down southwest toward the malpais, on the other side of it, actually, and Tudishishn was going to guide for him.

The Indian policeman drank coffee until almost sundown and then rode off into the shadows of the Nacimentos. He was staying at one of the rancherias, visiting with his friends until the morning.

McKay appeared first. It was a cool morning, bright and crisp. I looked out of the window and saw the five riders coming up the road from the south, and when they were close enough I made out McKay and Bowie Allison and the three Bettzinger brothers. When they reached the office, McKay and Bowie dismounted, but the Bettzingers reined around and started back down the road.

McKay nodded and was civil enough, though he didn't direct more than a few words to me. Bowie was ready when I asked them if they wanted coffee, but McKay shook his head and said they were leaving shortly. Just about then the rider appeared coming down out of the hills.

McKay was squinting, studying the figure on the pony.

I didn't really look at him until I noticed McKay's close attention. And when I looked at the rider again, he was almost on us. I didn't have to squint then to see that it was Mickey Segundo.

McKay said, "Who's that?" with a ring of suspicion to his voice.

I felt a sudden heat on my face, like the feeling you get when you're talking about someone, then suddenly find the person standing next to you.

Without thinking about it, I told McKay, "That's Peza-a, one of my people." What made me call him by his Apache name I don't know. Perhaps because he looked so Indian. But I had never called him Peza-a before.

He approached us somewhat shyly, wearing his faded shirt and breechclout but now with a streak of ochre painted across his nose from ear to ear. He didn't look as if he could have a drop of white blood in him.

"What's he doing here?" McKay's voice still held a note of suspicion, and he looked at him as if he were trying to place him.

Bowie Allison studied him the same way, saying nothing.

"Where's Tudishishn? These gentlemen are waiting for him."

"Tudishishn is ill with a demon in his stomach," Peza-a answered. "He has asked me to substitute myself for him." He spoke in Spanish, hesitantly, the way an Apache does.

McKay studied him for some time. Finally, he said, "Well . . . can he track?"

"He was with Tudishishn for a year. Tudishishn speaks highly of him." Again I don't know what made me say it. A hundred things were going through my head. What I said was true, but I saw it getting me into something. Mickey never looked directly at me. He kept watching McKay, with the faint smile on his mouth.

McKay seemed to hesitate, but then he said, "Well, come on. I don't need a reference . . . long as he can track."

They mounted and rode out.

McKay wanted prongbuck. Tudishishn had described where they would find the elusive herds and promised to show him all he could shoot. But they were many days away. McKay had said if he didn't have time, he'd make time. He wanted good shooting.

Off and on during the first day, he questioned Mickey Segundo closely to see what he knew about the herds.

"I have seen them many times. Their hide the color of sand and black horns that reach into the air like bayonets of the soldiers. But they are far."

McKay wasn't concerned with distance. After a while he was satisfied that this Indian guide knew as much about tracking antelope as Tudishishn, and that's what counted. Still, there was something about the young Apache. . . .

"Tomorrow, we begin the crossing of the malpais," Mickey Segundo said. It was evening of the third day, as they made camp at Yucca Springs.

Bowie Allison looked at him quickly. "Tudishishn planned we'd follow the high country down and come out on the plain from the east."

"What's the matter with keeping a straight line," McKay said. "Keeping to the hills is longer, isn't it?"

"Yeah, but that malpais is a blood-dryin' furnace in the middle of August," Bowie grumbled. "You got to be able to pinpoint the wells. And even if you find them, they might be dry."

McKay looked at Peza-a for an answer.

"If Senor McKay wishes to ride for two additional days, that is for him to say. But we can carry our water with ease." He went to his saddle pouch and drew out two collapsed, rubbery bags. "These, from the stomach of the horse, will hold much water. Tomorrow we fill canteens and these, and the water can be made to last five, six days. Even if the wells are dry, we have water."

Bowie Allison grumbled under his breath, looking with distaste at the horse intestine water sacks.

McKay rubbed his chin thoughtfully. He was thinking of prongbuck. Finally he said, "We'll cut across the lava."

Bowie Allison was right in his description of the malpais. It was a furnace, a crusted expanse of desert that stretched into another world. Saguaro and ocotillo stood nakedly sharp against the whiteness, and off in the distance were ghostly looming buttes, gigantic tombstones for the lava waste. Horses shuffled choking white dust, and the sun glare was a white blistering shock that screamed its brightness. Then the sun would drop suddenly, leaving a nothingness that could be felt. A life that had died a hundred million years ago.

McKay felt it, and that night he spoke little.

The second day was a copy of the first, for the lava country remained monotonously the same. McKay grew more irritable as the day wore on, and time and again he would snap at Bowie Allison for his grumbling. The country worked at the nerves of the two white men, while Mickey Segundo watched them.

On the third day they passed two waterholes. They could see the shallow crusted bottoms and the fissures that the tight sand had made cracking in the hot air. That night McKay said nothing.

In the morning there was a blue haze on the edge of the glare; they could feel the land beneath them begin to rise. Chaparral and patches of toboso grass became thicker and dotted the flatness, and by early afternoon the towering rock formations loomed near at hand. They had then one water sack two-thirds full; but the other, with their canteens, was empty.

Bowie Allison studied the gradual rise of the rock wall, passing his tongue over cracked lips. "There could be water up there . . . Sometimes the rain catches in hollows and stays there a long time if it's shady."

McKay squinted into the air. The irregular crests were high and dead still against the sky. "Could be."

Mickey Segundo looked up and then nodded.

"How far to the next hole?" McKay asked.

"Maybe one day."

"If it's got water . . . Then how far?"

"Maybe two day. We come out on the plain then near the Datil Mountains and there is water, streams to be found."

McKay said, "That means we're halfway. We can make last what we got, but there's no use killing ourselves." His eyes lifted to the peaks again, then dropped to the mouth of a barranca which cut into the rock. He nodded to the dark canyon which was partly hidden by a dense growth of mesquite. "We'll leave our stuff there and go on to see what we can find."

They unsaddled the horses and ground-tied them and hung their last water bag in the shade of a mesquite bush.

Then they walked up canyon until they found a place which would be the easiest to climb.

They went up and they came down, but when they were again on the canyon floor, their canteens still rattled lightly with their steps. Mickey

Segundo carried McKay's rifle in one hand and the limp, empty water bag in the other.

He walked a step behind the two men and watched their faces as they turned to look back overhead. There was no water.

The rocks held nothing, not even a dampness. They were naked now and loomed brutally indifferent, and bone dry with no promise of moisture.

The canyon sloped gradually into the opening. And now, ahead, they could see the horses and the small fat bulge of the water bag hanging from the mesquite bough.

Mickey Segundo's eyes were fixed on the water sack. He looked steadily at it.

Then a horse screamed. They saw the horses suddenly pawing the ground and pulling at the hackamores that held them fast. The three horses and the pack mule joined together now, neighing shrilly as they strained dancing at the ropes.

And then a shape the color of sand darted through the mesquite thicket so quickly that it seemed a shadow.

Mickey Segundo threw the rifle to his shoulder. He hesitated. Then he fired.

The shape kept going, past the mesquite background and out into the open.

He fired again and the coyote went up into the air and came down to lie motionless.

It only jerked in death. McKay looked at him angrily. "Why the hell didn't you let me have it! You could have hit one of the horses!"

"There was not time."

"That's two hundred yards! You could have hit a horse, that's what I'm talking about!"

"But I shot it," Mickey Segundo said.

When they reached the mesquite clump, they did not go over to inspect the dead coyote. Something else took their attention. It stopped the white men in their tracks.

They stared unbelieving at the wetness seeping into the sand, and above the spot, the water bag hanging like a punctured bladder. The water had quickly run out.

Mickey Segundo told the story at the inquiry. They had attempted to find water, but it was no use; so they were compelled to try to return.

They had almost reached Yucca Springs when the two men died.

Mickey Segundo told it simply. He was sorry he had shot the water bag, but what could he say? God directs the actions of men mysteriously.

Especially since Mickey had aided God by knowing about a hidden spring.

The county authorities were disconcerted, but they had to be satisfied with the apparent facts.

McKay and Allison were found ten miles from Yucca Springs and brought in. There were no marks of violence on either of them, and they found three hundred dollars in McKay's wallet. It was officially recorded that they died from thirst and exposure.

A terrible way to die just because some damn Apache couldn't shoot straight. Peza-a survived because he was lucky, along with the fact that he was Apache which made him tougher. Just one of those things.

Mickey continued living with his mother at the subagency. His old Gallagher carbine kept them in meat, and they seemed happy enough just existing.

Tudishishn visited them occasionally, and when he did they would have a tulapai party. Everything was normal.

Mickey's smile was still there but maybe a little different.

But I've often wondered what Mickey Segundo would have done if that coyote had not run across the mesquite thicket. . . .

Hired Gun

One of the world's liveliest octogenarians (he was born in 1900), Wil-
liam R. Cox has been delighting fans of the Western story since he began
writing for the pulp magazines in the 1930s and is still going strong with
a novel or two a year. His excellent historical Westerns include Comanche
Moon, Firecreek *and* Jack O'Diamonds; *he has also published several*
mystery novels and some of the best sports fiction to be found in and out
of the pulps, as well as written a number of television scripts. "Hired Gun,"
about an unconventional member of that grim fraternity, is a prime exam-
ple of his sure, professional story-telling.

CHARLIE LANG got off the train in Sirocco and looked curiously around
the station. The last time he had come to the burgeoning town, it had
been aboard a stagecoach. The West was changing, and in Charlie there
was a slight unease.

He was a small man, in striped trousers and a dark jacket and a white
shirt somewhat soiled from flying cinders. He carried a large carpetbag
adorned with sad roses. He saw Daniel Shay at once and went toward him.

Shay was too stout, his head looked smaller than ever. He looked
prosperous, but then Shay could always make money; his trouble was in
consolidating his gains. There was a woman with him, and Charlie
removed his cream-colored Stetson, his vague discontent growing. He did
not like women in on a job.

A man with a badge pinned to his vest sauntered past. This was
Trowbridge, and Charlie was glad he had not worn a gun. Shay had
guaranteed Trowbridge without subduing Charlie's deep distrust of all
lawmen. That was the way it had always been: they didn't like him and
he didn't like them. If it had been different, somewhere in the past, maybe
there wouldn't have been the killing and the hoorahing and all that went
with it.

Shay said to him, "Knew you'd make it, Charlie. By God, you always
make it. This here is Violet Corrivan. She works for me."

The woman was not young: she was medium sized and rather plump.

347

She had fresh skin and she looked directly at Charlie, bowing with the formal elegance peculiar to dance-hall gals in public places. Charlie found himself looking straight into her eyes.

There was something odd about her eyes. They were very blue, with shadings, and they looked at Charlie, not through him. They searched inside him and then she smiled, with good teeth, and he found himself smiling back and this unsettled him, because most women were afraid of him, distrusted him on first sight.

He said to Shay, "We'd better get out of here. I need to wash. You got everything lined up?"

Shay motioned toward a carriage at the platform. "Certainly I got it lined up. Me and Violet been for a drive, so I come over in the rig."

Charlie put his bag in the carriage. Watching the way Shay held the woman when he helped her onto the seat, he knew all he needed to know about them. He felt a twinge of sorrow for the woman.

There were more people in the town, but the street was still dusty. Shay drove to the hotel and bar and gambling joint which bore his name in huge letters, and they clambered down in the alley between the place and a livery stable. Shay couldn't keep his fat hands off the woman. They walked around to the veranda.

Through long habit Charlie used his eyes to cover every detail of the scene. He spotted the H-Bar-H brand on horses at the rack and lagged behind, his hands cold as always. He almost stopped and opened the bag but he knew that was no good and kept on walking.

Three men came down the steps of the hotel porch. One was dark and incisive and reeking with power: the other two were hard-bitten, carefree range riders. The leader was Ring Hatton, and he wore his strength like a cloak. His voice was oddly fuzzy but clear enough and not loud, merely dangerous.

"You strung the fence, didn't you, Shay? You had to cut off the water hole. You asked for it."

"The water hole is on my ranch. I bought that land fair and square and I got a right to the water hole."

"You run off the nesters and you got Loco Barnes to homestead it for you," Hatton said. "He was quite somethin', Loco." He paused, grinned briefly. "You heard me. *Was.* He *ain't*, not now no more. We cut the fence, too. That's why I'm here. To tell you we cut the fence and remind you how it could be with you. Like the Loco. *Was*—but *ain't.*"

The two riders guffawed. They were not experienced, Charlie thought, tough enough, maybe too brave, but not honed by gun war. Hatton was different. Shay had been right when he wrote that his enemy was poison. There was murder in Hatton's furry, slurred tones, in the hands that opened and shut above the gun butts. Charlie had seen his kind all over the frontier and had avoided them whenever possible. They were the kind who liked to kill, and Charlie was rather glad to see this. It made the ending easier.

Shay was clinging to Violet, safe in the tradition that Hatton would not start anything to endanger the woman. "I got the law on my side."

"Town law. And Trowbridge wouldn't scare me if he was honest. I'm givin' you the warning, Shay. Just once."

He stepped aside and for a moment his eyes rested on Charlie, flaring a little, then steadying, studying. Charlie plodded past him, patently unarmed, toting the bag, demure as he could possibly manage, and Hatton seemed satisfied that he was another drummer. Still, Charlie thought, this was not an ordinary man. It would be necessary to be very sure of it with Hatton.

The barroom of the hotel was huge, with two faro tables, four poker tables and a wheel in the rear of the place. The bar ran to the gaming space. There was a dais for a piano against the far wall. The woman went over and sat at a table alone. Shay ordered a double whisky.

Charlie said, "You get drunk and I'm hauling my freight. You picked a dandy this time."

"You can handle him." Shay was sweating. The fear that was always in him did not deter him from his ambition for money and power, but it made him sweat.

"Maybe I can and maybe I can't. Bear that in mind. You can't handle liquor. Lay off."

"They killed Loco."

"You leave a simple halfwit out there alone, he's bound to be killed. If you weren't so cheap, you'd have hired some guns. Hatton—I've seen them like Hatton."

"You can pick your time and place."

"Yeah. Tell you what, Shay. Send word to him that you don't buy his warning. That you're going to restring the fence."

"Now? Right now? You're crazy, Charlie."

"Send word or I'm taking the afternoon train."

Shay poured another drink. "But why? Can't you look around, pick some place and lay for him?"

"You heard me. Send the word." He got a key from the desk and carried his bag upstairs to a large room overlooking the street. Shay was scared, but he would obey because he recognized that it had to be quick: he might not last if it wasn't over soon. There was no sense giving a man like Hatton any time.

He took off his coat and shirt and washed with care. Shay, he thought, a crook with a yellow streak. Always trying to make it big, never quite succeeding. Always running up against real men and yelling for help.

Well, he couldn't shy off from Shay. He had been hired by worse men. Shay paid off, that was for sure. There were times, before he had gone completely cold, when he had not collected his money.

He opened the capacious bag. He took out a .38 revolver and harness and the parts of a stubby, sawed-off shotgun, which he assembled with swift hands. He found a clean shirt and knotted a loose tie at its collar and slid into the harness, which settled the revolver beneath his left armpit. He donned a light alpaca jacket with a single button, a loose garment. He slipped spare shells into his pocket, made sure of both weapons.

There was a tap on the door and he admitted Violet Corrivan, not surprised, anticipating her so that she looked curiously at him.

She said, "Shay sent the word. They'll be coming pretty quick."

"Sure they will."

The woman's gaze was searching. "Can I help?"

"Yes. I was sort of counting on you."

"You were?"

"Why do you think Shay sent you up here? Shay knows about these things."

"Shay knows too much, sometimes. I'm getting sick of Shay, Mr. Lang." Now her eyes opened, bolder. She had been a lovely girl, once.

"He's a good meal ticket."

"You don't know that side of him. You don't know how he is with a woman."

"Maybe I do. Maybe I can guess."

"Shay's no good for a woman."

Her meaning was clear enough. Charlie waited for her to get to the point. She moved toward him, touched his hand. Her fingers were very soft. She exuded a powerful force. Two of them in one day, he thought, Hatton and the woman. Why hadn't they combined to swallow Shay?

She said, "Suppose you were a little slow? Just slow enough? Suppose Hatton got Shay?"

"Who'd pay me?"

She laughed, a carefree sound. "Honey, I know where his poke is hidden. There's an afternoon train. Going west."

"Happens I'm heading that way. California." He hesitated, then said, "Maybe I shouldn't be telling you this. I'm making this my last job."

"California. I've never been there." Now her eyes changed, became hopeful, losing the gleam of avidity. "Life is sudden, sometimes. California."

"Might open a little place, sell booze, deal a game. It's warm in California all year 'round."

"I can sing. I could handle the cash. I'm quick at figures. And I can cook, Charlie, if only somebody would let me cook."

Charlie took her hand, held it. He said, "Can you hide the shotgun under your dress? Can you hand it to me when I give you the signal?"

"I can do it. I'm not one of your red-skinned, shiny nose ranch women, but I can do it." She was excited but she was calm underneath, Charlie saw.

"You're sure you had enough of Shay? No strings?"

"I had plenty of Shay." She snorted. "He's scared of everything and everyone but me. I get it, everything he can't do to other people. I've been sick of him for some time."

He gave her the gun. Her skirts swirled up and it vanished, held in place with one hand. She was as tall as Charlie and once she must have had a wonderful body.

She said, "Make it good, Charlie Lang. Make it real good. You got two reasons, now."

Out in the street a man spoke loudly to a horse. She was staring at him, and he was aware of the silence in the room. He could have kissed her, he could have made some demonstration but he did not stir.

She said, "I've heard plenty about you, Charlie Lang. Not only from Shay. Don't think this is all on the spur of the moment. I know about you."

"Don't let anybody see the gun. Stay close at my end of the bar."

"I'll know what to do. Make it good, Charlie Lang." She went out, moving lightly, quickly, into the hall. She paused one instant, audaciously winked at him, then was gone.

The man in the street yelled again, and the horse whinnied. A carriage squeaked by. There wasn't much time. Charlie thought about the woman.

It was a long time since he had been involved with a female except upon the purchase plan. His wife had run away many years ago, and he had let her go and thought to profit by the experience. This Violet Corrivan had something, all right, something extra. She must have been working Shay for all he was worth.

Well, he thought, fish or cut bait. He had told the truth about California, where he was unknown. He was weary and he had some money in a San Francisco bank. It was time to quit the rat race before he began thinking like a rat.

He went down the steps, past the desk, noting that the lobby was empty save for the clerk and an old man reading an ancient newspaper. He went into the bar and stood at the far end. Violet slid past him, ignoring him, and sat at a table nearby.

At the other end of the bar Shay was drinking despite everything, the perspiration pouring down his cheeks. The bartender was a middle-aged man and Charlie could see that he was not in it. There were no customers, but outside in the street there was a murmur of subdued excitement and then Hatton's odd voice and the sound of hard heels.

Charlie looked once at Violet, about four feet away from him. Hatton and the two men came through the swinging doors. Shay drained his glass, put it down and tried to straighten himself. The bartender dropped the glass he was pretending to polish.

Hatton said to his men, "Like I was saying, a shoat only's got one purpose. To be butchered for the good of people."

This was the moment Shay should have chosen, Charlie knew, before they were set. It never happened that way. If only once someone made the right move at the right time, things would be easier. But Shay just stood there, a big, fat target.

Hatton put both hands on the bar, arching his body away from it, balancing on the narrow toes of his boots. Still Shay did not make his move, fearful of the two riders who remained in back of Hatton, flanking him.

"I don't like the whisky in here. Gimme some of your special stuff."

"We—we only got one kinda whisky," said the barkeep.

"I'll take that bottle." Hatton pointed toward Shay. "The one the shoat's drinkin' out of."

Shay inhaled and stepped away from the bar. He was wearing a gun on his right hip. Hatton took his hands from the bar and the riders moved to give him room. They gave him a lot of space, covering the entire bar from where they made their stand.

They would let Hatton take Shay without interfering, Charlie knew. They were witnesses. On the other hand, Hatton was taking no chances. He looked at Charlie.

"How about a drink for you, stranger? Some of the good stuff?"

" 'Scuse me, I only take sarsap'rilla," said Charlie. He tried to make his voice colorless and vacuous. "Got something wrong with my stomach."

"Then don't wait on us. We got a little business with Mr. Shay."

Charlie grinned weakly. "Oh, that's all right. Don't mind me."

One of the riders laughed. Hatton said, "Couldn't you go somewhere else? Any place, so long as it ain't here."

This could be serious, Charlie thought, unbuttoning his coat with his left hand, trying to appear stupid and without understanding. "I'm all right, thank you."

"Yeah," said Hatton. "You're all right for now." He wheeled around on Shay. "Did you say somethin', Mr. Shoat?"

Charlie stole a quick glance at Violet. She had not moved. She held her hand on the shotgun beneath the skirts. Her face was smooth and quiet. She really did have nice skin.

Shay said, his voice faltering but shrill, "You've got no call to come in here bullyin' people around. Our business is on the range. You got no rights here."

"Why don't you call your town law, Shoat? Why don't you call Mr. Trowbridge, the marshal?"

He was laying a lot of stress on his words, Charlie thought, wasting time. He began to wonder if Hatton was so smart after all, or if he was just murderous. It was hard, sometimes, to tell the difference. He thought Hatton was smart: he thought it better to play the thing that way.

Shay had got up his nerve at last. "I don't need Trowbridge nor anybody else. This is my place. You got no rights here and I'm callin' your bluff."

Charlie made his eyes wide and innocent and tried to look frightened. As a matter of fact he wasn't feeling too brave at the moment. He didn't like the setup. He wished Violet could handle the shotgun: that would do it. He shrank into the corner, managing to get his right hand where it needed to be even as he appeared scared.

Hatton was still talking. Too much palaver, Charlie thought, and the riders weren't acting right.

"You got big and brave all of a sudden, didn't you, Mr. Shoat? You're callin' me out, is that it?"

Maybe that was for the witnesses and maybe it was not, Charlie thought. Talk, talk, talk, he never remembered one where there was so much gab. He stepped away from the bar.

Then Hatton said sharply, "All right. Make your play."

The two cowboys moved again. Charlie's thoughts became clear and sharp and well defined. They knew he was in on it; Hatton was smart after all.

Like all cowards, Shay's fear drove him to action. Hasty, injudicious action, of course, his hand slow in going for the gun. He was counting on Charlie to beat the count.

The two riders were converging, reaching for their weapons. Charlie got out the .38 with a slick, sleek motion. They were a little late or he would have been dead where he stood. He got one in the shoulder, then knocked the woman to the floor and upended the table. A bullet hit Charlie.

Hatton shot Shay twice, but Shay fell behind the end of the bar. Then Hatton turned and his eyes were fox red. Charlie shot the other cowboy.

Hatton was advancing, gun pointed, hand steady. Charlie couldn't walk but he shoved himself away from the table. He had been hit in the hip. Hatton fired once. The bullet nicked Charlie's left shoulder, spinning him, so that Hatton's next bullet missed his head by an inch.

Charlie said, "Ah, there, killer," and held his gun low, pumping three fast shots, emptying all chambers.

Hatton took them in the middle. He folded up like an empty overcoat as they slammed into him. He lay curled on the floor.

Shay was howling, "Charlie, where are you, Charlie? He got me. I'm dying."

People came in, now that the shooting had stopped. Charlie was on his knees, hurting a lot. He had the empty gun in his hand: he stared into the eyes of the woman. He said, "Unload that shotgun."

She was kneeling on the floor, the weapon in her hands. She said, "You —you knocked me out of it."

"You know it."

"You're hurt. You're bleeding."

Shay was pleading and a voice said, "Here's doc. Shay is over yonder.

Looks like Hatton finally jumped him."

Another voice said wonderingly, "Did Shay get the whole kit and caboodle of 'em?"

They could not see Violet and Charlie behind the table. Charlie said, "How much did Hatton pay you?"

"Are you crazy, Charlie? You knocked me out of it." She reached toward him. Her eyes were bright with tears. "You need the doctor."

"Before I got to town. You went to Hatton. You wanted to get away from Shay. You weren't sure about me, but you tipped them just now. They were ready for me."

"No! I didn't. Hatton figured it out. You know Hatton was smart."

"Honey, you played it every way from the middle. You figured to win no matter what happened." The pain was getting bad. He smiled at her. "Hatton would've killed you just as quick as Shay or me. Good thing I shoved you over."

She said, "Charlie, so help me, I didn't. If you hadn't knocked me out of it, I'd have used the greener."

"I saw you knew how to handle it." He took the shotgun from her, then handed it back. "See if you can get it out of here."

"You won't tell that story to Shay? He'd kill me. He could kill a woman."

Charlie felt himself slipping to the floor. He said, "Honey, what the hell. No harm done. I like a smart woman."

So long as he lived, if he lived, he would never forget the look in her eyes at that instant. They lighted up like a Fourth of July fireworks. She slid the gun back beneath her skirts. She leaned forward and kissed him on the mouth.

She stood up. She said, "There's a man here. He's hurt bad. He saved Daniel's life. I think he's a lawman of some kind. You better get over here, doc."

She moved behind the bar, hid the shotgun. Shay was moaning. People were milling about. Two men carried Hatton out onto the veranda. Violet went back to Charlie.

She whispered, "I've got some money of my own. We can't make today's train, but one comes through here every day, Charlie Lang."

He closed his eyes. If he lived, Shay would have a story to convince the tame marshal. The pay would be there, Shay always paid off.

Maybe he wouldn't take the money. Maybe he would take the woman, call it a trade. This was his last job and he sure did take to a clever woman.

She could have killed him with his own shotgun.

Best of all, she hadn't admitted the truth. If you're stuck with a lie, hang onto it, Charlie always believed. The doctor came and shook his head and men lifted Charlie and put him on a faro table and the doc said he was a brave man and that his friend Shay was all right, he would live.

They gave him whisky and murmured as he lay there, letting the doctor probe, grinning a little. They didn't see Violet, hovering, tipping him that sly, promising wink.

STEVE FRAZEE

Due Process

*There have been innumerable stories written about working cowboys,
some good (B.M. Bower's Flying U series, for example) and some not so
good. But there has never been one quite like "Due Process"—a delightfully good-humored account of the shooting of a bully named Obadiah
Smith and the efforts of a bunch of cowhands to disburse his "estate." Its
author, Steve Frazee, produced a large body of similarly first-rate Western
fiction for more than twenty years. Among his most accomplished novels
are* Shining Mountains, The Alamo, Running Target, Hellsgrin *and* High
Cage. *A collection of his best short fiction will be published next year by
Southern Illinois University Press as part of a series of collections by noted
Western writers.*

IT WAS MAYBE two weeks after old Ute Henderson died of the slow
fever at his home place on the Little Peralta.

Spring roundup was on, which meant for four-five days crews from the
five outfits in the southern part of the valley would headquarter at the big
holding corrals not far from Joe Tonso's saloon and store.

Those of us who could get away in the evening after work would go up
to Tonso's, which didn't mean we got roaring drunk every night. We
didn't have that kind of money, and Tonso didn't give that kind of credit.
We did get together for a little fun and talk.

This particular evening the fun was out. Obadiah Smith showed up,
and as usual he was trying to start trouble. He was a whopper-jawed,
scorpion-eyed cuss who fancied himself as a gunfighter. We doubted that
he was, but none of us cared to find out the hard way, and that of course
made it easier for him to be a bully.

Obadiah's specialty was pushing Mexicans around. He worked for Burt
Hamlin, who didn't have any Mexican riders, but there was a fair sprin-
kling of them in other Peralta Valley outfits. They always tried to avoid
Obadiah.

This time it was Ragged Hudnall, one of Obadiah's own crew, that

Obadiah was giving trouble. "Take a man like you, he don't have the guts for gunfighting," Obadiah said.

"You're right," Ragged said.

"Sure I'm right!" Obadiah swung a look around the room. "And the rest of you are the same way."

"Yep," Clum Bronson agreed, and the rest of us just tried to pay no attention. Obadiah was having one of his streaks. The best thing to do was let him run.

Not getting any rise out of us, he tried Joe Tonso. "This is a fine two-bit dump you run here, Joe."

Tonso was slopping glasses in a bucket behind the bar. "I guess you could call it that."

"I am calling it that!"

"Suit yourself," Tonso said.

Nothing makes a bully meaner than lack of resistance. Obadiah was trying to figure who to abuse next when Pistol Pete showed up, getting as far as the doorway before he saw Obadiah. Pete was a grinning, bandy-legged little Mexican who worked for the Circle T, a good rider and about as harmless as they come. We'd nicknamed him because of the big old horse pistol he always carried. Nobody had ever seen him shoot the gun, and some of his nearest friends claimed it was too rusty to go off anyway.

There he was in the doorway, grin wiped out by the sight of Obadiah.

"Come on in!" Obadiah said.

"I think maybe I have some business somewhere."

"Come on, come on! I'll buy you a drink."

Pete's big-toothed grin winked on and off as he came up to the bar. Tonso eyed Obadiah and said, "Don't start no trouble."

"Who's going to start trouble? You worry too much." Obadiah grabbed Pete's arm and hauled him over close, pouring him a drink. Obadiah raised his own glass. "To Pistol Pete, the terror of the Peralta!"

"Si," Pete said, straining to be agreeable. All he wanted was to get out the quickest way he could. He gulped the whisky.

"Another one," Obadiah said. "We'll drink to all the dirty, chili-picking greasers I'm going to wipe out one of these days."

Pete tried to grin. "Gracias," he said, and drank and started to leave.

Obadiah spun him around and threw a glass of whisky in his face. That was one of Obadiah's favorites. He liked to blind a man, gun-whip him down and stomp him into the floor.

I grabbed a singletree off the wall.

Obadiah reached for his gun. No hurry. He grinned as he watched Pete standing with his eyes squinched shut and whisky running off his face.

That was when Pete, blinded and scared, hauled out his rusty old cannon and fired. Talk about roar! Pete was blanked out by the powder smoke.

The slug knocked Obadiah back. He doubled over and hit the floor on his face, deader than a slunk calf.

We stood there with our mouths open.

Pete dropped the gun and ran. He hit the side of the door going out, bounced off and kept going. He was on his horse and away before we grasped the full fact of what had happened.

Tonso came trotting from behind the bar and got down beside Obadiah. "He's done for."

"He had it coming," Ed Glassman said.

Some of the boys carried Obadiah outside into the moonlight and put him alongside the wall.

"He was bought and paid for a long time ago," Tal Hunter said.

We went back inside to talk about it.

Nate Matlock showed up a few minutes later, leading Pete by a rope around his chest and arms. "I was on my way here when I heard the shot. I met Pete, riding like a wild man. He wouldn't stop, so I went after him and roped him. What's going on?"

We told him.

Nate said, "This calls for a little investigation."

"Never mind that lawbook you stuck your nose into once," Glassman said. "There's no problem here."

Nate paid him no attention. "Why'd you run away?" he asked Pete.

Pete cut loose in Mexican so fast and furious that only Tonso could understand. "He says he was afraid the Hamlins would start a war of extermination against the Mexicans in the valley on account of it. He was going to warn them."

Pete nodded vigorously, cut loose again. "He says he thought you were bringing him back here to hang him," Tonso interpreted.

Nate took the rope off. "The facts seem clear. Self-defense—but of course we'll have to take it to a jury."

"Why?" I asked.

"Proper procedure," Nate said. "Due process of law."

Ragged grunted. "Hell! Let's just bury him."

Obadiah's pistol was on the bar. It had fallen out of the holster while we were carrying him outside, and someone had picked it up. "Is that the full extent of the search of the deceased?" Nate asked.

"That's his gun, yep," Tonso answered.

"We'll defer further action along that line." Nate was sure taking charge. "Right now, as a coroner's jury, it's up to us to determine the cause of Smith's death."

"He was shot," I said. "Dead center, by a slug big enough to knock over a buffalo."

Nate shook his head. "Hearsay. Set down, all of you, and let's have the evidence properly presented."

"You mean we haul Obadiah back in here?" Ragged asked.

"That won't be necessary. I want each man to tell carefully and honestly his version of what occurred."

"You don't talk that way all the time," Glassman growled. "What's bit you, Nate?"

"His ma used to stack lawbooks on his chair so's he could set high enough to reach table," Ragged offered. "I think his learning seeped in the wrong end of him."

Nate laughed with the rest of us, but he was some serious when he got started on legal matters. Before long he had things going his way. No wonder Pete got nervous, what with everyone so solemn, and one after another telling how he had killed Obadiah.

Pete decided we were working up a hanging, so he made a break for it. Clum tripped him. We made Pete go sit on a keg of salt pork while we completed the inquest.

Nate announced the finding. "One Obadiah Smith was killed by a bullet fired from a pistol in the hands of Pistol Pete, and the whole mess was self-defense."

"That was a heap of talking to get around to something that even Tonso's hound knew beforehand," Ragged observed. "Now, where do we get our pay?"

"Pay?" Nate shook his head.

"I was on a jury once and I got paid," Glassman argued.

"This wasn't exactly a jury, not the kind that gets paid, leastwise," Nate said. He thought for a while. "Well, I guess each man, including Pete, can have one drink."

"Who pays?" Tonso asked quickly.

"The court will take the matter of payment under advisement," Nate said.

Tonso grunted. "That means I'm stuck for the drinks." He set them out.

I didn't drink, and when I asked for a can of tomatoes, Tonso balked. "You get whisky, or nothing."

Whisky was two bits a shot. Tomatoes cost one buck a can. "All right, give me a cigar," I said. I didn't smoke, either, so I gave the dried-out black stogie to Pete.

Pete still wasn't sure that we weren't going to hang him. The cigar seemed like a last gesture. Once more he started to light out, but someone hauled him back and Tonso at last got it into his head we weren't holding anything against him.

"It's getting late," Ragged said. "We got plenty of hard work again tomorrow, so let's bury Obadiah and get out of here."

"It's not that easy," Nate said. "There's certain legal aspects yet to be taken care of. Tonso, give us your best lantern."

We assembled around the deceased. He didn't look very good in the moonlight.

Nate said, "You know, we haven't actually proved him dead."

"Huh!" I said. "I'm satisfied."

"We really ought to have a doctor say so."

"I hear there's one about seventy miles south," Glassman said. "Go get him, Nate."

"I'll have no levity." Nate studied Obadiah. "Yeah, I'd say there's no doubt about it."

"Where do we bury him?" Ragged asked. "Or does that take another court session?"

"The deceased will have to be thoroughly searched in the presence of witnesses."

"Help yourself," Tonso said.

"Get a pencil and some paper, Joe," Nate ordered. He looked at me. "You're appointed to do the searching."

"Who appointed me?"

"I did."

"I just resigned the appointment!"

"Court order," Nate said. "Get on with it before you're held in contempt."

Everybody else was quick to support him.

I rustled through Obadiah's pockets quick as I could. Found a Mexican dollar, a Piper knife and some crumbly twist tobacco.

"There's a bulge under his shirt," Nate said. "Proceed with the examination of the deceased."

"Why don't you just call him Obadiah? I'm getting sick of that deceased stuff!"

"Proceed," Nate said.

Around Obadiah's waist was a money belt of fine leather. It was heavy. When I gave it to Nate, he ripped some stitches with his knife and out popped a twenty-dollar gold piece.

We went inside where the light was better. Sewn around the belt in little flat pockets were twenty-three more.

"By Ned, he's robbed a bank somewhere!" Ragged said.

Nate looked stunned like the rest of us. He said it would be proper, we still being a jury, to allow certain expenses from the money while deliberating.

We deliberated for three drinks around. For me it was a can of tomatoes.

By that time the jury was some loosened up and ready to deliberate in earnest, but Nate called a halt to further expenses. "How much is his horse and rig worth?"

It was a good outfit. We decided on a hundred and ninety bucks. Glassman said make it two hundred to keep things even.

"His pistol?" Nate asked.

"Twenty bucks," Clum Bronson said, "holster and all."

We agreed that it was a fair price.

"What happens to his stuff?" Ragged asked.

Nate scowled. "That's what I'm trying to figure out. Does anybody know of any relatives?"

Glassman snorted. "He never even had a friend!"

Hunter said, "We got a better idea where he went than where he come from." He hefted Obadiah's pistol. "I *would* give five bucks for this."

"I guess anyone would," Nate said, "but that ain't the way we're handling this business."

"How are we handling it?" I asked.

Nate cleared his throat. He sort of drew himself up, which wasn't hard, since he was about six feet three to start with. "Gentlemen," he said, like he was addressing Congress, "we've got an estate on our hands."

Danged if he didn't make it sound pretty important, but Ragged grunted disgustedly. "Estates are houses and a lot of land and money in a bank and that sort of stuff."

Nate shook his head. "Everything Obadiah left is his estate—money, horse, gun—the whole works. We will have to apply the due process of law to the handling of it. I'm hereby declaring myself administrator and the rest of you deputy administrators."

"Deputies?" Pistol Pete looked uneasy. As a matter of fact, none of us was much taken with the word.

"What's this here administrator thing?" Ragged asked.

"That means we take care of everything Obadiah left until it can be disposed of in a legal way for the benefit of his estate, or heirs."

"How can you benefit the estate by disposing of it?" Clum asked. "And if Obadiah ain't got no heirs—"

"Objection overruled!" said Nate.

"Sounds simple enough," said Glassman. "Let's divvy up the works and be done with it."

Nate looked like he'd been hit in the belly with a corral pole. "We've got to follow proper procedure!"

"Yeah? Well, you name it," Ragged said.

Nate hemmed and hawed. "I'll have to take it under advisement."

"How long does this here advisement last?" Tonso asked.

"Until our next session tomorrow evening."

In the meantime Nate would be doing the same work as the rest of us and getting just as dirty and sweaty, but he made it sound like he was going off to a high-paneled room somewhere to throw a study on all the law that had ever been written.

"I don't want Obadiah laying around out there until tomorrow evening," Tonso said.

We buried Obadiah down in the gulch, where we could do more bank caving than shoveling.

That night when we went to Tonso's, Nate said to me, "I've set four drinks per man as the expenses of each meeting. That means you get one can of tomatoes, or equivalent value in place of four drinks."

"You sure must have been thinking hard today."

"The session is in session," Nate said. "Who's got an idea about Obadiah's estate?"

"I think we ought to consider everything careful before we make any moves," Tonso said.

Glassman snorted. "You're boarding Obadiah's horse and getting paid for it, and making twenty-four cents on every two-bit glass of whisky we drink. We could set on this case all year and you'd be happy."

"I'll have no personalities!" Nate said. "What I want is ideas."

Tonso's blue hound came in and lay down with a sigh near the door. Hunter said, "Let's sell the whole estate to Tonso here, and—"

"Fine!" Glassman nodded. "What do we do with the proceeds?"

"Lemme finish, damn it! Turn the whole works over to Tonso. Then he provides free drinks for any cowboy that shows up, until the estate is gone. Of course, he don't say beforehand that the drinks is free."

Offhand, that sounded like a fine idea. Tonso was nodding agreeably.

"What happens after everybody in the valley finds out about the free drinks?" Nate asked.

"Be quite a rush," Hunter admitted. "But—"

"I know who'd be leading the rush," Glassman said. "What with you staying on the Bragg place all summer, and the rest of us out in the hills in cow camps."

"Calling me a drunkard, huh?" Hunter came around and took a swing at Glassman.

Glassman jumped back and fell over the hound, which let out an awful howl. Nate grabbed Hunter. "Order! Order! We ain't going to have none of that around here!"

"He called me a drunkard!"

"You wanta be cheated?" Glassman yelled.

We didn't get nowhere that night.

As a matter of fact, we didn't get nowhere the following night either. There were some pretty fair ideas about getting rid of Obadiah's estate, but Nate put the kibosh on all of them. We began to call him Old Proper Procedure, and we were getting about as disgusted with him as we were with Obadiah for getting himself killed.

When we were going out to the horses, Ragged proposed, "Let's take the estate and send Nate somewhere to study law."

"Yeah," Hunter said. "Maybe to Europe."

"She is a long way from here," Pistol Pete ventured.

We rode back toward camp.

Ragged said, "You brought on this whole thing, Pete. There ought to be some way we could make you responsible."

"No, no!" Pete said.

"I got it!" Hunter yelled. "All that money Obadiah had proves he was wanted somewhere for robbery. There's a reward out for him, sure as shooting, and it's a cinch it amounts to as much as the estate. Pete killed him, so Pete gets the estate."

That sounded like straight thinking. But Tate said, "There's no proof there was a reward. Even if there was, rewards ain't paid out of a man's estate. Motion overruled."

Hunter got sore. "I quit!"

"You'll be in contempt," Nate warned.

Hunter paused. "What's that?"

"Not showing proper respect for a court and legal procedure."

"Where the hell is the court? You mean us arguing and gabbing every night in Tonso's?"

"We're law, every one of us. We've got to act like it. We're responsible for our actions to the Territorial Courts."

"I quit," Hunter said, but it sounded pretty weak.

"Bury the money in a hole," Pete said. "We shoot the horse. Bury him too. On top we put the lariat so it will turn into a snake if anyone makes to dig."

"Yeah," Ragged said, "and we throw Nate in with the rest of the stuff."

"We ain't burying nothing," Nate said. "We're going to settle this thing all legal and proper."

We had one more night to go. After that, we were going to be scattered all over the Peralta until fall. I didn't see much chance of getting the estate settled.

When we went back to Tonso's that last evening, there was a six-horse team in the corral and a wagon with a hunk of rock on it that must have weighed six tons. My back ached just from looking at that stone.

Tonso introduced us to Jake Foley, a rawboned fellow with a face about like the rock on the wagon. We'd heard about Foley. He'd taken up a claim near Dirty Billy Springs and spent his time blasting.

"Mr. Foley here," said Tonso, "is on his way to sell a gravestone to Ute Henderson's widow."

Ragged began to laugh. Nate rammed him in the ribs.

"What's so funny?" Foley asked.

"I didn't tell him," Tonso said.

Nate took the floor, naturally. "Ute Henderson was married to an Indian, Foley. She and her family got up and left when he died. Far as we know, they took Ute along to bury him somewhere in the rocks up high."

"Why, I'd heard he was one of the leading citizens around here!"

"Reckon he was," Nate said, "but that's what happened to him. You won't be selling no rock down there, Foley."

"Stone." Foley eyed us all with suspicion.

Tonso set out the first round of our expenses. "I persuaded Mr. Foley to wait until you boys had a chance to talk to him about buying his rock for—"

"Stone," Foley said. "For whom?"

"Obadiah Smith," Tonso finished.

"Buy a rock!" Clum said, outraged. "What for? The country's full of rocks."

Nate set his glass down. "A stone for Obadiah! Tonso, I think you've got it!"

"Got what?" Hunter asked.

"We'll use the money to buy a stone for Obadiah," Nate said. "That will settle our problem."

Naturally he didn't want Foley to know it was an estate because the price of everything always goes up where an estate is involved.

Foley said, "Was this Smith a leading citizen?"

Hunter choked on his whisky.

"You could say that," Nate admitted.

You could, sure enough. It was a hell of a lie but you could say it.

"I never heard of him," Foley said.

"You hadn't heard that Ute Henderson was married to a squaw," I said. "There's probably quite a lot you ain't heard."

"Sure!" Tonso said. "If you ever got away from your quarry you'd have heard of him. It'll be a fittin' monument—"

"They don't make the kind of monuments Obe ought to have," Glassman said. "But maybe Foley's rock will do."

"Stone."

Nate asked, "How much were you figuring on getting from Ute's family?"

"Maybe seventy-five dollars."

"Maybe we can come close to that," Nate sighed.

"The price is not everything." Foley showed considerable doubt. "My stones are not just something to be sold. They're cut to last for centuries, and I'm rather particular where they get put."

Trying to run the price up, I thought.

"Fine a piece of granite as I ever quarried."

"We'll pay your price," Nate said.

Foley got a stubborn expression. "It'll have to be a worthy place."

"Right down in the gulch," Hunter said.

Foley looked horrified. "Down in a gulch!"

"We'll work it out," Nate said hastily. "How much?"

"Who was this Obadiah?" Foley asked.

"What's the difference?"

"I'm not placing a stone on the grave of some drifting gambler." Foley was a Vermonter, we found out later. He had narrow views.

Foreseeing the end of court expenses, Ragged was crowding the bottle. "Obadiah was no gambler. He was a loud-mouthed, no—"

"One of us, one of our friends," Nate cut in.

You could see Foley wasn't much impressed with our bunch. That man had a whale of a pride in his granite.

"How did this feller die?" Foley asked.

"I shoot him!" Pete said.

Foley scowled. "I don't like the sound of this. I don't think this corpse was the kind I'd respect."

"What's that got to do with us buying your rock?" Ragged shouted. "We got the money."

"Stone," said Foley.

"I can show you a million tons of the same just by going to the door!"

"Not like mine," Foley said. "Mine is a piece of the finest blue granite. Not a flaw in it."

"Whatever it is, we'll buy it," Ragged grunted. "All you want for it is money."

Foley's blue eyes turned angry. "Money is never the most important consideration in the placing of monumental stones," he said coldly. "My father and his father before him refused large sums to set their stones on the graves of immoral people."

"Who said Obadiah was immoral?" Nate sounded indignant. "You insulting his memory?"

Foley didn't back up. "How did he happen to be killed by him?" He jerked a chin at Pete.

"I will show you how I killed him," Pete said. "He—"

"Never mind that!" Nate smiled at Foley. "Pete's like a kid. Kinda excitable. Might even say he's not quite all there. Why, he wouldn't shoot a magpie."

"Not Pete!" we all cried.

Pete looked a little confused. He started spluttering Mex.

"What's he saying?" Foley asked.

"Telling how he killed twenty-two Injuns single-handed," Nate said.

"See what I mean about him being a little off?"

Foley said, "If he's crazy, why do you let him carry a pistol?"

"A toy," Nate said. "Worthless." He stepped over and grabbed Pete's gun. We'd examined it after Obadiah was killed, and found only two caps on the nipples.

The odds were a hundred to one that Pete hadn't even cleaned it since the shooting.

Nate tipped the cannon up and began pulling the trigger. It clicked three times. "See there?" he said, and should have quit right then, but he went one click too far and the gun like to lifted the roof off.

Tonso's hound let out a howl.

"How could a man kill another man with a gun that hits once out of five times?" Nate snorted. He tossed the pistol back to Pete.

"Four times," Foley said. He coughed in the powder smoke, eyeing the roof. "I guess you've proved your point."

"So you'll sell us the rock—the stone?" Nate asked.

Foley frowned. "How *did* Obadiah die?"

"Caused by something that he was born with, I think," Nate said.

"Sure, he had that trouble all his life," Ragged said.

Foley eyed us narrowly. "He wasn't a sinful man?"

"Good to his horse," I said. "Always took off his hat around women." Those were facts, everything on the good side I could remember.

Some could lie better. They built Obadiah up considerable. He'd been polite, thoughtful, helpful and honest. Before they went too far, Nate shut them off, and just in time, for Foley said dryly, "I never put a stone on the grave of a saint before."

"We'll have to admit that on occasion he did use swear words," Nate said.

"I do a mite of that myself," Foley admitted.

"He was thrifty," Tonso said. "He saved money."

"Ah!" said Foley.

"How much for the rock—the stone?" Ragged asked.

"I won't go less than seventy-five dollars."

"A measly seventy-five bucks for a stone for a man like Obadiah?" Hunter said in an outraged tone.

"I can get a larger one, but that will take time."

"The one outside will do," Nate said, "but we feel that we'll have to spend more for it. One hundred dollars."

"Two hundred," I said.

"Three hundred bucks!" Glassman yelled.

Tonso whacked the bar with his hand. "Four hundred!"

"Four fifty!" Ragged shouted.

"One thousand boocks!" Pete howled.

"Told you he was crazy," Nate said.

Foley figured we all was. He walked out.

"We're not joking!" Nate yelled. "This is serious."

We followed Foley outside, all of us trying to make him believe us. In all my life I never found a man so hard to give money to.

After Nate got us shushed, he talked to Foley over by the wagon. Tonso figured up the bar expenses and a buck and a half for boarding the horse, and came up with a figure that was the entire estate of Obadiah.

"It's our final offer," Nate said. "I can't be responsible for what the boys might do if you don't accept."

We looked tough as we could, although I'm sure that didn't influence Foley in the least.

"Is there something sinful or unlawful about this?"

"Believe me," Nate said, "we're straining ourselves to be as legal as we can."

"It's a damn funny offer." Foley thought a long time. "But I'll take it."

We all breathed with relief.

"I'll show you where the grave is, so you can start setting the stone tomorrow," Nate said.

"In a gulch?" Foley shook his head. "No stone of mine will be placed on loose ground."

Dead or alive, that Obadiah was nothing but trouble.

"You've already made the deal!" Ragged raged.

"Oh, no! The sale of a stone includes the setting, and if I don't have solid ground, I don't sell."

Ragged threw his hat on the ground. "It's fifteen feet down to solid ground in that wash!"

Foley said stonily, "No deal."

"What *do* you want?" Glassman asked.

"Rocky ground." Foley glanced at the point of the hill above Tonso's. "That looks a good place."

"The guy ain't buried there," I protested.

"Move him," Foley said.

Hunter groaned. "By God, up there's all solid rock!"

"Good. My stone will set well in a place like that."

Nate said, "Your stones ain't more important than the people themselves."

"They are to me."

We went back into Tonso's to argue about it. There was no shaking Foley. He wasn't going to set his stone on loose ground, and we couldn't dig a hole in rock.

"You move him, Foley," Ragged suggested. "You're getting enough for the stone to move all the graves from here to the mountains."

"I'm a stonemason, not an undertaker."

Nate had been thinking like sixty. "Foley, ain't it proper to set monuments on land to someone lost at sea."

"Yes."

"All right, put Obadiah's monument on the hill."

You could see that Foley was pretty favorably taken. "You claiming his grave is lost?"

"Yep!" Ragged said. "We buried him at night. I doubt that any of us could say where he's at."

Hunter tried to mess that up. "I know right where he is."

"Not me," I said.

"Me neither," Ragged grumbled. "First big rain—"

Hunter was stubborn. "I kin find him."

Foley shook his head. "The man is right. There's deceit in this. I won't be a party to it."

There we were, stuck fast against Foley's pride and hard morality.

We looked to Nate, but all he said was, "I think I'll remove all restrictions on the expense limit."

The expenses began to flow pretty fast. Foley was right in there, holding his own. His face got red, but I couldn't see that he was loosening up much.

The conversation had got pretty loud and it had extended to about everything under the sun. It was then that Nate brought us back to business. "We'll have a vote to determine whether the grave is lost or not."

Everyone of us except Hunter voted that it was lost beyond reasonable finding, whatever that was.

"No, sir!" Hunter said. "I'll show you where it is."

He lurched away from the bar and started out. He fell over the doorsill and lay there groaning.

"I accept that as evidence that he was incompetent to vote," Nate declared. "Therefore, the grave of Obadiah Smith is lost by unanimous action of this group."

"Second the motion!" yelled Pistol Pete. He was learning something, though not much, about democratic procedure.

We looked at Foley.

"I agree," he declared, solemn as an owl.

"It is, therefore, fitting and proper that Obadiah's stone be erected on a suitable hill in the vicinity where he was last seen," Nate said. "All those in favor—"

"Aye!" we yelled.

"No more expenses," Nate said.

"Hell, I was just beginning to understand law," said Ragged, who could hardly walk by now.

"And what do you want as the inscription?" Foley asked. He took two cuts at the last word before he got it right.

Nate said, "Obadiah Smith, 1881. That's enough."

We all wanted to add something. "In Memory of" or "Rest in Peace" or "He Was a Good Man." I thought "He Died Game" would be pretty good.

Hunter staggered up and came back to the bar. He'd skinned both shins on the high log sill and was feeling ill used. "Just put 'To Hell With Him'!"

Nate had his way. Nothing but the name and date.

We sold Obadiah's gun to Tonso for twenty bucks, and added that to the gold. It was somewhere close to four hundred and fifty bucks, a heap of money for a stone, but getting that estate settled was a big relief.

We'd overlooked something. There was still the horse and the rig, which we'd appraised at two hundred. Tonso called that to our attention.

"You know, of course, Foley, that a horse is involved in the deal," Nate said.

"No, I don't know it." Foley had all the gold before him on the bar. The way he was staring at it, you could tell that his conscience and principles were having a real rough time. "I don't know nothing about a horse. I don't want nothing to do with it."

"You have to take the horse," Nate said.

"I don't even have to take this money." Foley weaved a little, but his eyes were hard and steady. "It's too much."

"The horse is extra for cutting the inscription," Nate said.

"No! That's included."

I had a feeling that it wouldn't take much for Foley to shove that pile of gold back at us.

"I'll buy the horse and rig," Tonso said, "but I won't go any two hundred. I'll go seventy-five."

"It's a deal!" Ragged said.

"No, it ain't," Nate said. "We set the price at two hundred, and that's what we'll get."

Tonso shook his head. "Not from me."

"You ain't shoving the horse off on me either," Foley said.

I tell you that Foley was a hard man to deal with.

But Nate wagged his finger at Foley. "In payment for services to the estate of Obadiah Smith you have just accepted one bay horse, with saddle and bridle, for two hundred dollars."

"Not me," Foley said. "You'll have to do something else with the horse."

"Would you deprive the late lamented of the esteem the world should render by leaving him in an unmarked grave?"

"The grave is lost," Foley said. "I ain't depriving him of nothing."

"You just sold the horse," Nate said.

"Huh?"

"You just sold it to Tonso here for seventy-five dollars. Give him the money, Joe."

Tonso counted out seventy-five dollars and added it to Foley's pile.

"There," Nate said. "Nobody can say it's sinful to lose money on a deal."

"Hah!" said Foley. "That's even more sinful than making too much." Way he stared at that pile of gold on the bar, the more he looked like a dog with a mouthful of bad meat and no place to spit it.

Suddenly he heaved up tall as he could and glared like we was the scum of the earth. "I confess to greed," he said. "I was swayed by the power of gold, but now I renounce the whole deal."

We stood drop-mouthed.

"I will not be a party to deceit and trickery!"

"Nobody asked you to shoot your grandmother," Ragged growled. "Just take the money."

"No!"

Nate cut in smooth and fast. "Of course on transactions of this kind, we do expect a contribution to our cause."

"The wages of sin—What cause?" Foley said. The way he tightened up, you could tell he was not only a hard man to give money to, but a tougher one to take it away from.

"Church fund," Nate said.

"There ain't no church."

"Of course not," Nate said. "That's what our fund is for, to build one." He looked Foley hard in the eye. "I suggest that you contribute all but seventy-five dollars of that money to the fund."

Foley wrassled with that. "I haven't the right."

"Now you're obstructing justice and law."

"That's the first I've heard of any law around here."

"We've got it. You're obstructing it."

Foley counted out seventy-five dollars, put it into his pocket. "For the stone." He shoved the rest away from him. "Do what you wish with it."

"No," Nate said. "We gotta have your statement you're contributing it to the church fund."

"It wasn't mine! I've refused it."

"You took it once. Now you're giving it to the church."

"All right!" Foley yelled. "I'm giving it to the church!"

Nate shoved the money at Tonso. "Deposit this with the rest of the church funds."

"How much have you got?" Foley asked.

"I haven't counted lately," Tonso said, "but it's coming along."

A sudden quiet fell over us. The thing was done.

Smith's monument is still on the hill where Foley set it. You'd be surprised at some of the yarns told today about how come it to be there, about that great pioneer Obadiah Smith.

Hell, maybe he was! His money built the church.

Riverboat Fighter

Before turning to suspense and mainstream novels (Relentless, Death Wish, The Paladin) *and the writing and producing of films* (Hopscotch), *Brian Garfield wrote a large number of excellent historical Westerns, among them* The Lawbringers, The Vanquished, Valley of the Shadow *and* Sliphammer. *His short stories in the Western field number only a few, however, of which "Riverboat Fighter"—a tale of passion and danger aboard a Colorado River steamboat—is perhaps the best. He is also the author of an ambitious and superior Western novel of recent vintage,* Wild Times, *and of a just-published history of Western films.*

CLAY GODDARD came aboard the *Mohave* at Yuma an hour before she was due to depart. He walked around B Deck to his regular tiny stateroom on the portside and remained there only long enough to stow his carpetbag and comb his hair; the cubicle was stifling hot. Coming out on deck, he tugged his brocade vest down and placed his gray hat squarely across his brows. Clay Goddard was a tall man, thin to the point of gauntness, with the hint of a stoop in his broad shoulders. His lion-gray eyes were hooded and his lips were guarded by the full sweep of a tawny mustache.

He was coming around the afterdeck, passing in front of the wide paddlewheel, when his alert eyes shot toward the gangplank. A solid-square man in a dusty blue suit was coming up the plank; sight of that man arrested Clay Goddard: he stood bolt still, watching, while the stocky man ascended to the rail and paused.

A ball-pointed brass star glittered on the newcomer's blue lapel. The ship's captain, coming toward the gangway, nodded and touched the brim of his cap. "How do today, Marshal?"

Marshal Emmett Reese nodded and said something Goddard didn't catch; then the lawman's deliberate voice lifted: "Believe I'll be going up with you this trip, Jack. How's the current running?"

"Slow and easy," Captain Jack Mellon said. He was a legend on the river: he had steamed the Rio Colorado more than fifteen years. It was said he could talk to the river and hear its reply. He said to the marshal,

"Ought to make an easy five miles an hour going up. I figure to make Aubrey's Landing in forty-eight hours."

"That's traveling," Marshal Reese observed. Clay Goddard watched the lawman's profile from his stance under the shadowed overhang of the afterdeck. The captain spoke once more and turned to go up the ladder toward his wheelhouse on the Texas Deck, and Marshal Emmett Reese's glance came around idly. His eyes alighted on Clay Goddard and immediately narrowed; the marshal's whole frame stiffened. Goddard's expression remained bleak, unreadable. Across thirty feet of deck space their glances clashed and held. The revolver butt at Goddard's hip touched the vein of his thin wrist.

Emmett Reese seemed about to advance, about to speak; but then the sound of an approaching buggy clattered toward the wharf, and the marshal ripped his eyes away, swinging heavily around, tramping back down the plank.

Clay Goddard's face revealed no particular relief. He turned with deliberate paces and walked into the ship's saloon. The bartender was its only occupant. Goddard took a cup of coffee, went to a table in the back of the room, and laid out an elaborate game of patience. Brooding over the cards, he sipped the cooling black coffee and ran his glance once around the room.

It was neither so large nor so elegant as the cardrooms on the great Mississippi packets; but then, this was Arizona, and rivers did not run so deep or wide here. It was engineering marvel enough that the *Mohave*, one hundred fifty feet long and thirty-three feet abeam, could carry two hundred passengers and a hundred thousand pounds of cargo and still skim over the Rio Colorado's shallow bottom. The water often ran less than three feet deep; the *Mohave* drew only thirty inches, fully ballasted.

Steamboats had been plying the river for twenty-seven years now, but their interloping presence in the desert country never failed to strike Goddard as an odd phenomenon. The ships of the Colorado Steam Navigation Company regularly made the seemingly impossible run up to Callville, Nevada—six hundred miles above the river's mouth, and desert country all the way, except where the big ships had to winch themselves up over cascades through the knife-cut tall gorges upriver.

The saloon was a plain oblong room, low ceilinged and plainly furnished —not at all like the velvet-lined rooms of the New Orleans sternwheelers. But the *Mohave* was the pride of the line, and in the far Southwest she was queen. The barkeep wiped his plain mahogany counter and behind it, between racks of labeled bottles, hung a lithographed calendar with today's sailing date circled: August 24, 1879. Regarding that, and recalling the grim square-hewn face of Marshal Emmett Reese on deck, Clay Goddard thought what a long time it had been, how the years had flowed silently by; and he felt quietly surprised. He was thirty-seven this month; his birthday had passed, he suddenly realized, without notice.

His lean hands darted over the wooden table, placing card upon card. Green sleeve garters held the shirt back from his wrists. He pulled out his snap-lid pocket watch—eight-thirty in the morning, and already he was soaked with sweat. It would hit a hundred and ten inside the saloon today.

His gambler's training laid a cool endurance over him; over the years he had developed the ability to stand off from himself and look on, as if from some long distance. Without it, his life would not have been bearable.

The boat swayed gently as heavy freight wagons rolled up the plank onto the cargo decking. Faintly through the door came the hoarse shouts of teamsters, the profane calling of stevedores. Passengers, early arriving, began to drift in and out of the saloon. With a hissing chug and a resigned clatter, the boilers fired up and began to build up their head of steam. Smoke rose from the twin tall stacks at the front of the pilothouse.

His shirt drenched, Clay Goddard unbuttoned his elaborate vest—the uniformed sign of his calling—and bent over his solitaire board in concentration. He was like that, frowning over the merciless cards, when a great force rammed the edge of the table into his belly, slamming him in his chair back against the wall.

Tautly grinning, a hawk-faced man stood hunched toward Goddard, a tall, powerful man with a stiff brush of straight red hair standing up brightly on his head. Hatless, the grinning man held the table jammed against Goddard, pinning Goddard to his chair. In a quiet, soft tone, the red-haired man said. "Somebody told me you were working this boat."

Goddard said with deceptive mildness, "Take the table out of my gut, Miles."

Miles Williams took his hands away from the table and laughed unpleasantly. "I ain't got my gun on just now. That's a piece of luck for you, Clay."

"Or for you."

Miles Williams' eyes met Goddard's without guile. "Nobody said you weren't tough, Clay, and nobody said you weren't fast. But I can take you."

"You can try," Goddard answered evenly. He pushed the table away from him and straightened his rumpled vest, but he kept his seat. The cards had flown into disarray when Williams had violently rammed the table. Goddard gathered them unhurriedly into a pack, never releasing Williams from his gaze.

Williams said, "I've got a lot to settle with you for, Clay. Too much to let pass. I'm going up to Aubrey on this boat and I don't figure both of us will get there alive."

"That's up to you, Miles."

"We're still in port. You can get off now. Maybe I won't follow you —I got business upriver."

Goddard tilted his head slightly to one side. "You'd offer me a chance to skin out, would you? I'm surprised."

"I ain't an unfair man," said Miles Williams. "And I don't like killing. Go on, Clay—get off the boat. Save us both a lot of grief that way."

Goddard considered him over a stretching interval of time; at the end of it he shook his head. "I guess not, Miles."

"Suit yourself." Abruptly, with a snap of his big shoulders, Miles Williams swung away and stalked out of the saloon.

At the bar, a few men with cigars and coffee had watched with careful interest. What Goddard and Williams had said had been pitched too low to reach their ears, but the scene had been too charged with action and hard stares to escape their attention. Sweeping them with his guarded eyes, Goddard maintained his cool expression and proceeded to lay out a fresh, slow game on the table.

Shortly thereafter, however, he got up and walked slowly out of the saloon. A deck hand was coiling in the stern rope. The ship was crowded with army men—two companies of infantry on their way to Ehrenberg, shipping point for the inland Apache-fighting garrisons. Goddard threaded his path among the knots of troopers and entered his little stateroom, where he closed the door in spite of the heat building up. Out of his carpetbag he took ramrod, patches, cloth and oil. After locking the door he dismantled his revolver and gave it a careful, methodical cleaning. Then he put it back together, loaded the cylinder with six .44-40 cartridges and let the hammer down gently between the rims of two shells. Standing up, he slid the weapon into its oiled holster and adjusted the hang carefully. His expression never changed; the mustache drooped over his wide lips. He packed the cleaning equipment away, unlocked the door and stepped out on deck just as the captain shouted from two decks above and the boat slowly churned out into the current.

The wharves and shipyard of Yuma slowly drifted past the starboard beam; there was a last glimpse of Fort Yuma, high on the hill with its precious squares of green lawns, and then the massive rolling paddlewheel drove the ship around the outer curve of the first bend, and the only sight to either side was mosquito-buzzing brushy lowlands and, beyond, the flats and dry-rock hills of the vast Southwestern desert.

Goddard stepped past a lashed-down freight wagon, and halted abruptly.

Coming forward, arms linked, were Marshal Emmett Reese and a slim figure of a woman. Holding the woman's left hand was a girl of six, wide-eyed and with hair the same tawny color as Goddard's own. The woman's mouth opened and, quickly, Emmett Reese stepped out in front of her as though to protect her. Reese said nothing but it was plain by his stance and attitude that he expected Goddard to go on about his business without stopping to speak.

The woman put her hand on Reese's arm. "No, Emmett. We'll be on this boat for two days and nights. It's a small boat. We can't pretend to each other that we don't exist."

Goddard stepped forward with the briefest of cool smiles. "It's been a long time, Margaret." His glance dropped to lie on the little girl. "Six years," he murmured.

The woman had both hands on the little girl's shoulders now. Emmett Reese said, "Come on, Margaret, we can—"

"No," she said. "I want to talk to him, Emmett."

Reese's eyes bored into Goddard, but it was the woman his words addressed: "I wish you wouldn't."

"Take Cathy with you, will you? I'll meet you in the lounge." The woman's voice was firm.

Troubled, the marshal reached down to take the little girl's hand. He said to Goddard, "Miles Williams is on board."

"I know."

"This boat's in my jurisdiction. I don't want trouble."

"I won't be starting any trouble," Goddard said.

The little girl watched with her head tilted on one side, looking up at Goddard and then the marshal, puzzled but silent. Soldiers milled past in pairs and groups. An officer moved through the crowd, creating a stir of saluting and mumbled greetings. The woman, tossing her head impatiently, said, "Go on, Emmett." She bent down. "Go with the marshal, sweetheart. Mummy will be along soon."

The little girl stared at Goddard. "Who's he?" she demanded accusingly.

The woman looked up and away; her eyes turned moist. Emmett Reese said gently, "Come on, Cathy," and led the little girl away by the hand, casting one warning glance back toward Goddard.

Goddard moved toward the rail, pushing a path through for the woman. She came up and stood beside him, not looking at him, but watching the muddy flow of the river. Her eyes were still clouded with tears; there was a catch in her throat when she spoke: "I'm sorry. I knew this moment would come. I meant to be strong—I didn't mean it to be this way. But when she asked *who you were*—"

"She looks a little like me," he said musingly.

"She has your hair, your eyes—every time I look at her I—" The woman's head turned sharply down against her shoulder, hiding her face. Goddard's hand came out toward her, but stayed, and he did not touch her. A solemn mask descended over his face. He murmured, "Well, Meg."

He took a folded handkerchief from his vest and offered it to her. She pressed it to the corners of her eyes. She was a blue-eyed woman, slim and pretty but no longer in the smooth-cheeked paleness of youth: the veins of her hands and the creases around her eyes revealed that she was near Goddard's own age.

He said, "You're traveling with Emmett?"

"In separate staterooms," she said dryly, and then shook her head. "He wants to marry me—marry us, that is. He loves Cathy."

"Maybe," Goddard said softly, "that's because he's had the chance to love her."

Her eyes lifted dismally to his. Plainly gathering herself, she used both palms to smooth back her brown hair. "I am going to be strong, Clay," she said, measuring out each word for emphasis. "You and I, we had our chance together."

"And I ruined it," he finished for her.

"You," she agreed, "and that." She was looking at the worn-smooth handle of his revolver. "And now Miles Williams is here. He's been looking for you a long time, Emmett said. You killed two of his friends in a card game."

"I caught them cheating together. They drew against me."

"Is that an explanation, Clay?" she asked. "Or just an excuse?" She reached out; her fingertips touched the walnut gun grip. "You love that thing."

"No. I hate it, Meg."

She swung half way, facing the river again, the marshes drifting past. The huge paddlewheel left a pale yellow wake stretching downstream with the current. "I wish I could believe you," she said. "If it's true then you've changed."

"I have," he agreed simply.

She threw her head back. Her voice was stronger: "We were married once. It didn't work. I've no reason to believe it would work again."

He nodded; but his eyes were sad—he was looking forward, toward the lounge where the little girl had gone. He said, "What will you tell her about me? She wants to know who I am."

"I don't know," she said, almost whispering. "I wish I did." She turned from him and walked away, moving briskly. He watched the way she walked, head turned over his shoulder, both hands gripping the rail so tightly his knuckles shone white.

A tall, red-topped figure swayed forward, pushing soldiers aside roughly with hands and elbows. Miles Williams reached Goddard's side and grinned around the cigar in his teeth. "Who's the lady, Clay?"

When Goddard made no reply, Williams said, "I saw you talking to Emmett Reese. With him on board, we're going to have a little problem, you and me. Either one of us starts trouble, he's likely to step in. So I've got a little proposition for you. I gave you your chance to get off the ship. You stayed, so I guess that means you want to play the game I called. All right, we'll lay down some ground rules. We wait, you and me. These soldier boys get off at Ehrenberg in the morning and the boat'll be less crowded tomorrow. Tomorrow night the decks ought to be pretty clear. We wait until everybody's asleep. No witnesses, that way. We have at each other, and no matter who's standing up afterward, ain't nobody can tell Emmett Reese who started the fight. The winner claims self-defense, and Reese can't dispute it, see? No law trouble, no trouble afterward for the one of us that's still alive."

"You're a coldblooded buck," Goddard observed without much emphasis.

"I just like to keep things neat," Miles Williams said, and turned aft. A holstered pistol slapped his thigh as he walked through the crowd.

Showing no sign of his feelings, Clay Goddard went into the saloon,

picked a table, and set the pack of cards out, advertising his calling. It was
not long before five soldiers were gathered round his table, playing low-
stake poker.

The day passed that way for Goddard, bar sandwiches and coffee and
poker—a steamy hot day that filled the room with the close stink of sweat
weighted with tobacco smoke and the smells of stale beer and whisky. He
did not leave the saloon until suppertime, when he went forward into the
dining salon. He saw Emmett Reese and Margaret and little Cathy at the
captain's table. His eyes lingered on the blond little girl. Margaret's eyes
found him once, but turned away quickly; she swung her head around,
tossing her hair, to respond to some light remark of Captain Jack Mellon's.

Miles Williams was not in the room. Goddard took his customary place
at the first officer's table, between the deck steward and an Army doctor,
and ate a silent meal. Afterward he had a cigar on deck, and returned to
the saloon for the evening's trade. The crowd was thoroughly penny ante;
he made a total of seven dollars for the day's gambling, and went on deck
at midnight. He had to pick a path over the heaps of sleeping soldiers.

The heat had dissipated with darkness. He lay down on his bunk,
knowing he needed sleep in order to be alert for the following night's
encounter; but sleep evaded him and he lay in the dark cabin with his
hands laced under the back of his head, staring sightlessly at the ceiling.
The engines throbbed soporifically, but he was still awake at three when
the boat scraped bottom on a sand bar and the engines reversed to take
her off. She lurched forward once again, going around the bar, and finally
Goddard drifted into a semiwakeful drowsiness that descended into fitful
sleep.

He was awake and dressed at dawn when the *Mohave* berthed at
Ehrenberg. The town was a drab oasis at best. Miles Williams came by
and said, "You could still get off right here and wait till the boat comes
back down. But then maybe you'd rather not wait another three years for
me to come after you again."

"Never mind," Goddard told him.

"All right," Williams drawled. The sun picked up glints in his bush of
red hair. He grinned and ambled away. Goddard noticed Emmett Reese
standing not far away, watching him inscrutably; it was hard to tell
whether Reese had heard what had been said.

The soldiers disembarked with their baggage and wagons, and thus
lightened, the boat made faster headway upstream. Its decks were lashed

with wagonloads of mining machinery for the camps served by Audrey's Landing, but pedestrian traffic was light and there was hardly any trade in the saloon all day.

After supper he was on deck, savoring his cigar, when Margaret came out of the dining room and sought him out. If he was surprised, he did not show it. She said, in a voice that showed how tightly throttled were her emotions, "That may be your last cigar. Have you thought of that?"

"Yes."

"How can you keep such a rein on yourself, Clay? Aren't you frightened?"

He made no answer. He squinted against the cigar smoke and Margaret said, "You're scared to death, aren't you?"

"I guess I am."

"Then that's changed, too."

"Maybe I've learned to care," he said. He turned to look at her. "Sometimes it takes a long time to learn a simple thing like that."

His talk appeared to confuse her. She folded her arms under her breasts. "Cathy still wants to know about you."

"Have you decided what to tell her?"

"I'll tell her the truth. But I'm going to wait until tomorrow."

He said quietly, "You think I'll be dead by then, don't you, Meg?"

"One way or the other," she said. "Dead to us, anyway. Whether you're still walking and breathing won't matter." She dropped her arms to her sides; her shoulders fell. "Emmett told me that Miles Williams gave you the chance to get off at Ehrenberg."

"I might have taken it," he said, "except for you and Cathy. I wanted to have another day—this is as close as I've ever been to her. I couldn't give it up."

She said in a muted voice, "If you'd gotten off the boat," and did not finish; Goddard finished it for her:

"You'd have come with me?"

"I don't know. How can I say? Maybe—maybe."

Twilight ran red over the river. The great paddles slapped the water and a lone Indian stood on the western bank, silhouetted against the darkening red sky, watching the boat churn past into gathering night. A shadow filled the dining room doorway, blocky and sturdy—Emmett Reese, who wore the star. Reese stood there, out of earshot, watching but not advancing. Goddard said, "I guess he loves you."

"Yes."

"And you him?"

She didn't answer right away. There was a sudden break in Goddard's expression and he seemed about to reach out and grasp her to him, but he made no motion of any kind and his face resumed its composure. He said slowly, "I have always been in love with you. But I have to meet Miles Williams tonight and my love for you can't stop that."

"Nor my love for you?" she cried out.

"I'm sorry," he said dismally.

Her voice subsided in resignation. "I can't give my little girl a father who fights to kill."

"What about Emmett Reese?" He was looking at Reese, outlined in the doorway, still as a mountain.

"It's his job. Not his pleasure." Her lip curled when she said it.

"It's no pleasure to me either," he said. "God knows there are a lot of things I regret, Meg."

"But you won't give up your pride."

"Would I be a man without it?"

She had no answer for him. She turned and walked from him, toward the waiting shadow of the marshal.

The cigar had gone dry and sour. Goddard tossed it overboard and went into the saloon. Lamplight sent rays through the smoky air; the crowd was thin and for an hour no one came to Goddard's table. He sat with the pack of cards before him; he sat still, his head dipped slightly like a tired man half asleep.

Miles Williams came at ten-thirty and sat down opposite him. Williams had a cheroot uptilted between his white teeth. His face was handsome and brash, the eyes half-lidded. "A friend is a close and valuable thing," he said. "I lost two friends one night."

"They forced it on me."

"Then they should have won." Williams picked up the deck of cards and shuffled it. "Blackjack suit you?"

And so they played a macabre game of cards while the hours ran out, while the passengers drifted away one by one and lamps winked out around the ship. The engines thrummed, the paddles hit the water with a steady slap-slap, and when the saloon was empty but for the bartender, Miles Williams said in a suddenly taut voice, "All ready, Clay?"

"Here?"

"On deck. Loser goes overboard. Neat—neat that way."

"All right," said Clay Goddard.

Williams thrust his chair back with his knees and stood. "After you?"

"Right beside you," Goddard answered, and they left shoulder to shoulder.

The decks were deserted; lamps were off, except two decks higher up on the Texas, where the keen-eyed captain swept the river vigilantly for shifting sand bars. Miles Williams said, "Jack Mellon's got eyes in the back of his head. We'll go on down to the afterdeck—he can't see that from up there."

They tramped along the port B deck and Goddard felt moisture on his palms; he wiped them on his vest and heard Williams chuckle. "Got you nervous, ain't I? Get a man nervous, you got the edge." Williams was flexing his fingers. Starlight glittered on the river. Not a single lamp glowed in the after section of the ship. The two men reached the platform behind the cabin structure. Here the smash of the paddles against the water was a loud racket in the night; the paddles lifted overhead and swept down, splashing drops of water against the stern and the aft yard or two of deck planking. The iron railing protected passengers from the cruel, deliberate power of the great paddlewheel.

Miles Williams stopped six feet from the rail and wheeled, planting his feet wide apart. "You can step back a way," he said calmly, "or do you want it point-blank?"

"Right here will do," Goddard said. "A man wouldn't want to miss his shot for bad light."

A startled brightness gleamed from Williams' eyes. "You steadied down quick, didn't you?" he observed. Then he laughed with raucous brashness. But the laugh fell away and his face grew long. The brush of his hair stood up against the sky and he suddenly cried, *"Now!"*

Williams' hand spilled for his gun butt. Close in to the man, Goddard did not reach for his own gun; instead he lashed out with his boot. The hard toe caught Williams' wrist just as the gun was rising. The gun fell away, bouncing off Goddard's instep; and Williams, rocked by the kick, windmilled back, off balance. His feet slipped on the wet planking; the small of his back rammed the stern rail and Goddard, rushing forward, was not in time to prevent Williams from spilling over backward into the descending paddlewheel.

The paddles caught Williams and dragged him down relentlessly; there was a brief awful cry, and that was all.

Gripping the rail, Goddard looked down into the churning blackness of the descending paddles. His eyes were hollow. Heavy footsteps hurried toward him along the deck and he turned, nerved up to high pitch.

Emmett Reese said, "I couldn't stop it before it started. But I saw it. He wasn't fast at all—you could have outdrawn him with no trouble."

"I knew that."

"You didn't figure on this?"

"No. I expected a good beating might have changed his mind." Goddard smiled bleakly. "I was always pretty good with my fists."

"Better than guns," Reese said quietly, staring at the heavy falling paddles. He added in a murmur that was barely audible over the slapping wheel, "You're a far better man than I gave you credit for, Clay."

Reese's hand reached out and clenched Goddard's arm. Goddard shook his head slowly back and forth, as if to clear it. He pulled away and walked forward along the empty deck.

He was in his cabin, unhooking his gun belt, when light knuckles rapped the door. When he opened it, Margaret stepped inside. The lamp washed her face in warm light.

She said, "Emmett told me what happened. You could have drawn on him. You could have shot him down, but you didn't—you tried to save his life."

"I told you," he said wearily. "A man learns a few things as time goes by, Meg."

She said, "Cathy's asleep now, and I didn't want to wake her. But in the morning when she asks me who you are, I'll be able to tell her. We'll have breakfast together, the three of us."

"What about Reese?" he said.

She moved into the circle of his arms. "He understands," she said. She turned her face up toward him.

EVAN HUNTER

Snowblind

*Evan Hunter is of course well known for his fine mainstream novels
(*The Blackboard Jungle, Sons, Last Summer, Love, Dad*) and for his
highly acclaimed series of police procedurals, written under the pseudonym
of Ed McBain, featuring the men of the 87th Precinct. He has not often
written of the Old West, but when he has—in the novel* The Chisholms,
*for instance, and in "Snowblind," which was first published early in his
career, he has shown a deft hand with the Western form.*

HE RODE the big roan stiffly, the collar of his heavy mackinaw pulled
high on his neck. His battered stetson was tilted over his forehead,
crammed down against his ears. Still, the snow seeped in, trailing icy
fingers across the back of his neck.

His fingers inside the right-hand mitten were stiff and cold, and he held
the reins lightly, his left hand jammed into his pocket. Carefully, he
guided the horse over the snow-covered trail, talking gently to him. He
held a hand up in front of his eyes, palm outward to ward off the stinging
snow, peered into the whirling whiteness ahead of him.

The roan lifted its head, ears back. Quickly, he dropped his hand to the
horse's neck, patted him soothingly.

He felt the penetrating cold attacking his naked hand, withdrew it
quickly and stuffed it into the pocket again, clenching it into a tight fist,
trying to wrench whatever warmth he could from the inside of the pocket.

"Damnfool kid," he mumbled. "Picks a night like this."

The roan plodded on over the slippery, graded surface, unsure of its
footing. Gary kept staring ahead into the whiteness, looking for the cabin,
waiting for it to appear big and brown against the smoke gray sky.

His brows and lashes were interlaced with white now, and a fine sifting
of snow caked in the ridges alongside his eyes, lodged in the seams
swinging down from his nose flaps. His mouth was pressed into a tight,
weary line. He kept thinking of the cabin, and a fire. And a cup of coffee,
and a smoke.

It was the smoke that had started it all, he supposed. He shook his head

386

sadly, bewildered by the thought that a simple thing like a cigarette could send a kid kiting away from home. Hell, Bobby was too young to be smoking, and he'd deserved the wallop he'd gotten.

He thought about it again now, his head pressed against the sharp wind. He'd been unsaddling Spark, a frisky sorrel if ever there was one, when he saw the wisp of smoke curling up from behind the barn. At first, he thought it was a fire. He swung the saddle up over the rail and took off at a trot, out of breath when he rounded the barn's corner.

Bobby had been sitting there, his legs crossed, gun belt slung low on his faded jeans, calm as could be. And puffing on a cigarette.

"Well, hello," Gary'd said in surprise.

Bobby jumped to his feet and ground the cigarette out under his heel. "Hello, Dad," he said soberly. Gary remembered wondering why the boy's face had expressed no guilt, no remorse.

His eyes stared down at the shredded tobacco near the boy's boot. "Having a party?" he asked.

"Why, no."

"Figured you might be. See you're wearing your guns, and smoking and all. Figured you as having a little party for yourself."

"I was headin' into town, Dad. Feller has to wear guns in town, you know that."

Gary stroked his jaw. "That right?"

"Ain't safe otherwise."

Gary's mouth tightened then, and his eyes grew hard. "Feller has to smoke in town, too, I suppose."

"Well, Dad . . ."

"Take off them guns!"

Bobby's eyes widened, startling blue against his tanned features. He ran lean fingers through his sun-bleached hair and said, "But I'm goin' to town. I just told . . ."

"You ain't goin' nowheres. Take off them guns."

"Dad . . ."

"No damn kid of mine's goin' to tote guns before he's cut his eye teeth! And smoking! Who in holy hell do you think you are? Behaving like a gun slick and smoking fit to . . ."

Bobby's voice was firm. "I'm seventeen. I don't have to take this kind of . . ."

Gary's hand lashed out suddenly, open, catching the boy on the side of his cheek. He pulled his hand back rapidly, sorry he'd struck his son, but unwilling to acknowledge his error. Bobby's own hand moved to his cheek, touched the bruise that was forming under the skin.

"Now get inside and take them guns off," Gary said.

Bobby didn't answer. He turned his back on his father and walked toward the house.

The snow started at about five, and when Gary called his son for supper at six, the boy's room was empty. The peg from which his guns usually hung, the guns Gary'd said he could wear when he was twenty-one, was bare. With a slight twinge of panic, Gary had run down to the barn to find the boy's brown mare gone.

Quickly, he'd saddled the roan and started tracking him. The tracks were fresh in the new snow, and before long Gary realized the boy was heading for the old cabin in the hills back of the spread.

He cursed now as the roan slipped again. Damned if he wasn't going to give that boy the beating of his life. Seventeen years old! Anxious to start smoking and frisking around, anxious to wrap his finger around a trigger. It would have been different if Meg . . .

He caught himself abruptly, the old pain stabbing deep inside him again, the pain that thoughts of her always brought. He bit his lip against the cold and against the memory, clamped his jaws tight as if capping the unwanted emotions that threatened to overflow his consciousness again.

This was a rough land, a land unfriendly to women. For the thousandth time he told himself he should never have brought her here. He'd made a big mistake with Meg, perhaps the biggest mistake of his life. He'd surrendered her to a wild, relentless land, and he was left now with nothing but a memory and a tombstone. And Bobby. He would not make the same mistake with Bobby.

How long ago had it been, he asked himself. *How long?*

Was Bobby really seventeen, had it really been that long?

"All right, mister," the voice said.

He lifted his hand, tried to shield his eyes. The snow whirled before them, danced crazily in the knifing wind. Through the snow, he made out the shadowy bulk of three men sitting their horses. His hand automatically dropped to the rifle hanging in the leather scabbard on his saddle.

"I wouldn't, mister," the same voice said.

He squinted into the snow, still unable to make out the faces of the three riders. "What's this all about, fellers?" he asked, trying to keep his voice calm. Through the snow, he could see that two of the riders were holding drawn guns.

"What's it all about, he wants to know," one of the men said.

There was a flurry of movement and the rider in the middle spurred his horse forward, reining in beside Gary's roan.

"Suppose you tell *us* what it's all about, mister."

Gary's eyes dropped inadvertently to the holster strapped outside his mackinaw, the gun butt pointing up toward his pocket.

"Don't know what you mean, fellers."

"He don't know what we mean, Sam."

The rider close to Gary snickered. "What you doin' on this trail?" His breath left white pock marks on the air. Gary stared hard at his face, at the bristle covering his chin, at the shaggy black brows and hard eyes. He didn't recognize the man.

"I'm lookin' for a stray," Gary said, thinking again of Bobby somewhere on the trail ahead.

"In this weather?" Sam scoffed. "Who you kiddin', mister?"

Another of the riders pulled close to the pair, staring hard at Gary. "He's poster-happy, I think," he said.

"Shut up, Moss," Sam commanded.

The third rider sat his horse in the distance, his hands in his pockets, his head tucked low inside his upturned collar. "Moss is right, Sam. The old geezer's seen our pictures and . . ."

"I said shut up!" Sam repeated.

"Hell, ain't nobody chases strays in a storm," the third rider protested.

Sam lifted the rifle from Gary's scabbard, then took the .44 from the holster at his hip. Gary looked down at the empty holster, raised his eyes again.

"Ain't no need for this," he said. "I'm lookin' for a stray. Wandered off before the storm started, and I'm anxious to get him back 'fore he freezes board-stiff."

"Sure," Sam said, "you're lookin' for a stray. Maybe you're lookin' for *three* strays, huh?"

"I don't know what you're talking about," Gary said. "You feel like throwing your weight around, all right. You're three and I'm one, and I ain't goin' to argue. But I still don't know what you're talking about."

"We gonna freeze out here while this bird gives us lawyer talk?" Moss asked.

The third rider said, "You know of a cabin up here, mister?"

"What?" Gary asked.

"You deaf or some . . ."

"Rufe gets impatient," Sam interrupted. "'Specially when he's cold. We heard there was a cabin up here somewheres. You know where?"

"No," Gary said quickly.

"He's poster-happy," Moss insisted. "What the hell're we wastin' time talking for?" He pulled back the hammer of his pistol, and the click sounded loud and deadly beneath the murmur of the wind.

Gary combed his memory, trying to visualize the "wanted" posters he'd seen. It wasn't often that he went to town, and he didn't pay much attention to such things when he did ride in. He silently cursed his memory, realizing at the same time that it didn't matter one way or the other. He didn't know why these men were wanted, or just what they were running from. But he sure as hell knew they *were* wanted. The important thing was to keep them away from Bobby, away from the cabin up ahead.

"Seems I do remember a cabin," he said.

"Yeah? Where is it?"

Gary pointed down the trail, away from the cabin. "That way, I think."

"We can't afford thinkin'," Rufe said. "And we can't afford headin' back toward town either, mister."

"That ain't the way to town," Gary said softly.

"We just come from there," Sam said. He yanked his reins, pulling his horse around. "I think we'll go up this way, mister. Stay behind him, Moss."

Rufe, up the trail a ways, turned his horse and started pushing against the snow, Sam close behind him. Gary kept the roan headed into the wind, and behind him he could hear the labored breathing of Moss's horse.

"We'll have to hole up for tonight," Rufe said over his shoulder.

"Yeah, if we can find that damn cabin," Sam agreed.

"We'll find it. The old geezer ain't a very good liar."

They rode into the wind, their heads bent low. Gary's eyes stayed on the trail, searching for signs beneath the tracks of the lead horse. Bobby had sure as hell been heading for the cabin. Suppose he was there already? The boy was wearing his guns, and would probably be fool enough to try shooting it out with these killers. Maybe they weren't killers, either. Maybe they were just three strangers who weren't taking any chances. Then why had the one called Moss kept harping on posters, and why had

Rufe mentioned pictures of the trio? *Stop kidding yourself,* Gary thought. *They'd as soon shoot you as look at you.*

"Well, now ain't that funny!" Rufe shouted back. "Looks like the cabin was up this way after all, mister."

Gary raised his eyes, squinted at the squat log formation ahead on the trail. The ground levelled off a bit, and they walked the horses forward, pulling up just outside the front door. Sam dismounted and looped his reins over the rail outside. Gary felt the sharp thrust of a gun in his back.

"Come on," Moss said.

Gary swung off his saddle, patting the roan on its rump. "These animals will freeze out here," he said.

"You can bring out some blankets," Sam said. Together, he and Rufe kicked open the door of the cabin, their guns level. Gary's heart gave a lurch as he waited for sound from within.

" 'Pears to be empty," Rufe said.

"Ummm. Come on, Moss. Bring the old man in."

They stomped into the cabin, closing the door against the biting wind outside. Sam struck a match, fumbled around in the darkness for a lantern. There was the sound of a scraping chair, the sudden thud of bone against wood.

"Goddamnit!" Sam bellowed.

Gary waited in the darkness, the hard bore of Moss's pistol in his back. The wick of the lantern flared brightly, faded as Sam lowered it.

"Right nice," Rufe commented.

"Better get a fire going," Sam said.

Rufe crossed the room to the stone fireplace, heaped twigs and papers into the grate, methodically placed the heavier pieces of wood over these. He struck a match, held it to the paper, watched the flames curl upward as the twigs caught.

"There," he said. He shrugged out of his leather jacket. "This ought to be real comfy."

"There's some blankets on the bunk," Sam said. "Take 'em out and cover the horses, mister."

Gary walked to the bunk, filled his arms with the blankets, and started toward the door. Just inside the door, he stopped, waiting.

Moss shrugged out of his mackinaw. "Go on," he told Gary. "We'll watch you from here. Too damn cold out there."

Gary opened the door, ducked his head against the wind and ran toward the horses. He dropped the blankets, gave one quick look at the door, and then swung up onto the roan's saddle.

"You want a hole in your back?" Sam's voice came from the window.

Gary didn't answer. He kept sitting the horse, staring down at the blankets he'd dropped in the snow.

"Now cover them horses and get back in here," Sam said. "And no more funny business."

Gary dropped from the saddle wearily. Gently, he covered all the horses, feeling the animals shiver against the slashing wind and snow. He was grateful that Bobby hadn't been in the cabin, but he was beginning to wonder now if the boy hadn't been lost in this storm. The thought was a disturbing one. He finished with the horses and headed back for the cabin. Moss pulled open the door for him, slamming it shut behind him as soon as he'd entered.

"Get out of those clothes," Sam said, "and sit over there by the table. One more fool stunt like that last one, and you're a dead man."

Gary walked over to the table, folding his mackinaw over the back of a chair. Rufe was sitting in a chair opposite him, his feet on the table, the chair thrust back at a wild angle.

Gary sat down, his eyes dropping to Rufe's hanging gun.

"Wonder how long this'll last," Sam said from the window.

"Who cares?" Moss said. He was poking around in the cupboard. " 'Nough food here to last a couple of weeks."

"Still, we should be moving on."

"You know," Rufe drawled, "maybe we shoulda split up."

"What the hell brought that on?" Sam asked impatiently.

"Just thinkin'. They'll be lookin' for three men. They won't be expectin' single riders."

"That's what the old man's for," Sam said, smiling.

"I don't follow."

"They won't be expectin' *four* riders, either. The old man's coming with us when we leave."

"The hell I am," Gary said loudly.

"The hell you *are*," Sam repeated.

Gary looked at the gun in Sam's hand. He made a slight movement forward, as if he would rise from his chair, and then he slumped back again. They were treating him like a kid, like a simple, addlebrained . . . He caught his thoughts abruptly. He suddenly knew how Bobby must have felt when he'd slapped him this afternoon.

Sam walked away from the window, stood warming the seat of his pants at the fireplace.

"Four riders," he said. "A respectable old man and his three sons." He looked at Gary and chuckled noisily.

He was still chuckling when the front door was kicked open. Gary turned his head swiftly, his eyes widening at sight of the white-encrusted figure in the doorway. The figure held two guns, and they gleamed menacingly in the firelight.

Sam clawed at his pistol, and a shot erupted in the stillness of the cabin. The gun came free, and Sam brought it up as the second shot slammed into his chest. He clutched at the stone mantel, swung around, his legs suddenly swiveling from under him. He dropped down near the fire, his hand falling into it in a cascade of sparks.

The men in the room seemed to freeze. Moss with his back to the cupboard, Rufe with his feet propped up on the table, the figure standing in the doorframe with smoking guns.

Gary looked at the figure, trying to understand that this was Bobby, that this was his son standing there, his son who had just shot a man.

And suddenly, action returned to the men in the room. Moss pushed himself away from the cupboard in a double-handed draw. At the same instant, Rufe began to swing his legs off the table.

Gary kicked out, sending the chair flying out from under Rufe. From the doorway, Bobby's guns exploded again and Moss staggered back against the glass-paned cupboard, his shoulders shattering the doors. Bobby kept shooting, and Moss collapsed in a shower of glass shards. Rufe sprawled to the floor, tried to untangle himself from the chair as Gary reached down and yanked the gun from his holster, backing away from the table quickly. Rufe crouched on the floor for an instant, then viciously threw the chair aside and reached for his remaining gun. Gary blinked as he saw flame lance out from the gun in his fist. The bullet took Rufe between the eyes, and he clung to life for an instant longer before he fell to the floor, his gun unfired.

Bobby came into the cabin, hatless, his hair a patchwork of snow.

"I figured you were trailin' me," he said. "I swung around the cabin, trying to lose you."

"Lucky you did," Gary said softly. He stood staring at his son. For a moment, their eyes met, and Bobby turned away.

"I ain't goin' back with you, Dad," he said. "A . . . a man's got to do things his own way. A man can't have . . ."

"Suppose we talk about it later, Bob," Gary said.

He saw his son's eyes widen. He'd never called him anything but Bobby until this moment.

Gary smiled. "Suppose we talk about it later," he repeated. "After we've had a cup of coffee." And then, though it was extremely difficult, he added, "And a smoke together."

The Hanging Man

Bill Pronzini, who has been an active member of the Western Writers of America for the past several years, is the author of numerous short stories and two novels in the Western field, the latest of which is The Gallow Land, *which will be published early next year. He amply demonstrates his considerable talent in this genre in "The Hanging Man," an offbeat story about a stranger found hanging in a small Northern California town in the late 1890s, and the efforts of the local sheriff's deputies to learn who he was and why he died in such a bizarre fashion . . .*

It was Sam McCullough who found the hanging man, down on the river bank behind his livery stable.

Straightaway he went looking for Ed Bozeman and me, being as we were the local sheriff's deputies. Tule River didn't have any fulltime law officers; just volunteers like Boze and me to keep the peace, and a fat-bottomed sheriff who came through from the county seat two or three days a month to look things over and to stuff himself on pig's knuckles at the Germany Café.

Time was just past sunup, on one of those frosty mornings Northern California gets in late November, and Sam found Boze already to work inside his mercantile. But they had to come fetch me out of my house, where I was just sitting down to breakfast. I never did open up my place of business—Miller's Feed and Grain—until 8:30 of a weekday morning.

I had some trouble believing it when Sam first told about the hanging man. He said, "Well, how in hell do you think *I* felt." He always has been an excitable sort and he was frothed up for fair just then. "I like to had a hemorrhage when I saw him hanging there on that black oak. Damnedest sight a man ever stumbled on."

"You say he's a stranger?"

"Stranger to me. Never seen him before."

"You make sure he's dead?"

Sam made a snorting noise. "I ain't even going to answer that. You just come along and see for yourself."

I got my coat, told my wife Ginny to ring up Doc Petersen on Mr. Bell's invention, and then hustled out with Sam and Boze. It was mighty cold that morning; the sky was clear and brittle-looking, like blue-painted glass, and the sun had the look of a two-day-old egg yolk above the tule marshes east of the river. When we came in alongside the stable I saw that there was silvery frost all over the grass on the river bank. You could hear it crunch when you walked on it.

The hanging man had frost on him, too. He was strung up on a fat old oak between the stable and the river, opposite a high board fence that separated Sam's property from Joel Pennywell's fixit shop next door. Dressed mostly in black, he was—black denims, black boots, a black cutaway coat that had seen better days. He had black hair, too, long and kind of matted. And a black tongue pushed out at one corner of a black-mottled face. All that black was streaked in silver, and there was silver on the rope that stretched between his neck and the thick limb above. He was the damnedest sight a man ever stumbled on, all right. Frozen up there, silver and black, glistening in the cold sunlight, like something cast up from the Pit.

We stood looking at him for a time, not saying anything. There was a thin wind off the river and I could feel it prickling up the hair on my neck. But it didn't stir that hanging man, nor any part of him or his clothing.

Boze cleared his throat, and he did it loud enough to make me jump. He asked me, "You know him, Carl?"

"No," I said. "You?"

"No. Drifter, you think?"

"Got the look of one."

Which he did. He'd been in his thirties, smallish, with a clean-shaven fox face and pointy ears. His clothes were shabby, shirt cuffs frayed, button missing off his cutaway coat. We got us a fair number of drifters in Tule River, up from San Francisco or over from the mining country after their luck and their money ran out—men looking for farm work or such other jobs as they could find. Or sometimes looking for trouble. Boze and I had caught one just two weeks before and locked him up for chicken stealing.

"What I want to know," Sam said, "is what in the name of hell he's doing *here?*"

Boze shrugged and rubbed at his bald spot, like he always does when he's fuddled. He was the same age as me, thirty-four, but he'd been losing his hair for the past ten years. He said, "Appears he's been hanging a while. When'd you close up last evening, Sam?"

"Six, like always."

"Anybody come around afterwards?"

"No."

"Could've happened any time after six, then. It's kind of a lonely spot back here after dark. I reckon there's not much chance anybody saw what happened."

"Joel Pennywell, maybe," I said. "He stays open late some nights."

"We can ask him."

Sam said, "But why'd anybody string him up like that?"

"Maybe he wasn't strung up. Maybe he hung himself."

"Suicide?"

"It's been known to happen," Boze said.

Doc Petersen showed up just then, and a couple of other townsfolk with him; word was starting to get around. Doc, who was sixty and dyspeptic, squinted up at the hanging man, grunted, and said, "Strangulation."

"Doc?"

"Strangulation. Man strangled to death. You can see that from the way his tongue's out. Neck's not broken; you can see that too."

"Does that mean he could've killed himself?"

"All it means," Doc said, "is that he didn't jump off a high branch or get jerked hard enough off a horse to break his neck."

"Wasn't a horse involved anyway," I said. "There'd be shoe marks in the area; ground was soft enough last night, before the freeze. Boot marks here and there, but that's all."

"I don't know anything about that," Doc said. "All I know is, that gent up there died of strangulation. You want me to tell you anything else, you'll have to cut him down first."

Sam and Boze went to the stable to fetch a ladder. While they were gone I paced around some, to see if there was anything to find in the vicinity. And I did find something, about a dozen feet from the oak where the boot tracks were heaviest in the grass. It was a circlet of bronze, about three inches in diameter, and when I picked it up, I saw that it was one of those presidential medals the government used to issue at the Philadelphia Mint. On one side it had a likeness of Benjamin Harrison, along with his name and the date of his inauguration, 1889, and on the other were a tomahawk, a peace pipe and a pair of clasped hands.

There weren't many such medals in California; mostly they'd been supplied to army officers in other parts of the West, who handed them out to Indians after peace treaties were signed. But this one struck a chord in my memory: I recollected having seen it or one like it some months back. The only thing was, I couldn't quite remember where.

Before I could think any more on it, Boze and Sam came back with the ladder, a plank board and a horse blanket. Neither of them seemed inclined to do the job at hand, so I climbed up myself and sawed through that half-frozen rope with my pocket knife. It wasn't good work; my mouth was dry when it was done. When we had him down we covered him up and laid him on the plank. Then we carried him out to Doc's wagon and took him to the Spencer Funeral Home.

After Doc and Obe Spencer stripped the body, Boze and I went through the dead man's clothing. There was no identification of any kind; if he'd been carrying any before he died, somebody had filched it. No wallet or purse, either. All he had in his pockets was the stub of a lead pencil, a half-used book of matches, a short-six seegar, a nearly empty Bull Durham sack, three wheatstraw papers, a two-bit piece, an old Spanish *real* coin and a dog-eared and stained copy of a Beadle dime novel called *Captain Dick Talbot, King of the Road; Or, The Black-Hoods of Shasta.*

"Drifter, all right," Boze said when we were done. "Wouldn't you say, Carl?"

"Sure seems that way."

"But even drifters have more belongings than this. Shaving gear, extra clothes—at least that much."

"You'd think so," I said. "Might be he had a carpetbag or the like and it's hidden somewhere along the river bank."

"Either that or it was stolen. But we can go take a look when Doc gets through studying on the body."

I fished out the bronze medal I'd found in the grass earlier and showed it to him. "Picked this up while you and Sam were getting the ladder," I said.

"Belonged to the hanging man, maybe."

"Maybe. But it seems familiar, somehow. I can't quite place where I've seen one like it."

Boze turned the medal over in his hand. "Doesn't ring any bells for me," he said.

"Well, you don't see many around here, and the one I recollect was also a Benjamin Harrison. Could be coincidence, I suppose. Must be if that fella died by his own hand."

"If he did."

"Boze, you think it *was* suicide?"

"I'm hoping it was," he said, but he didn't sound any more convinced than I was. "I don't like the thought of a murderer running around loose in Tule River."

"That makes two of us," I said.

Doc didn't have much to tell us when he came out. The hanging man had been shot once a long time ago—he had bullet scars on his right shoulder and back—and one foot was missing a pair of toes. There was also a fresh bruise on the left side of his head, above the ear.

Boze asked, "Is it a big bruise, Doc?"

"Big enough."

"Could somebody have hit him hard enough to knock him out?"

"And then hung him afterward? Well, it could've happened that way. His neck's full of rope burns and lacerations, the way it would be if somebody hauled him up over that tree limb."

"Can you reckon how long he's been dead?"

"Last night some time. Best I can do."

Boze and I headed back to the livery stable. The town had come awake by this time. There were plenty of people on the boardwalks and Main Street was crowded with horses and farm wagons; any day now I expected to see somebody with one of those newfangled motor cars. The hanging man was getting plenty of lip service, on Main Street and among the crowd that had gathered back of the stable to gawk at the black oak and trample the grass.

Nothing much goes on in a small town like Tule River, and such as a hanging was bound to stir up folks' imaginations. There hadn't been a killing in the area in four or five years. And damned little mystery since the town was founded back in the days when General Vallejo owned most of the land hereabouts and it was the Mexican flag, not the Stars and Stripes, that flew over California.

None of the crowd had found anything in the way of evidence on the river bank; they would have told us if they had. None of them knew anything about the hanging man, either. That included Joel Pennywell, who had come over from his fixit shop next door. He'd closed up around 6:30 last night, he said, and gone straight on home.

After a time Boze and I moved down to the river's edge and commenced a search among the tule grass and trees that grew along there. The day had warmed some; the wind was down and the sun had melted off the last of the frost. A few of the others joined in with us, eager and boisterous, like it was an Easter egg hunt. It was too soon for the full impact of what had happened to settle in on most folks; it hadn't occurred to them yet that maybe they ought to be concerned.

A few minutes before ten o'clock, while we were combing the west-side bank up near the Main Street Basin, and still not finding anything, the Whipple youngster came running to tell us that Roberto Ortega and Sam McCullough wanted to see us at the livery stable. Roberto owned a dairy ranch just south of town and claimed to be a descendant of a Spanish conquistador. He was also an honest man, which was why he was in town that morning. He'd found a saddled horse grazing on his pastureland and figured it for a runaway from Sam's livery, so he'd brought it in. But Sam had never seen the animal, an old swaybacked roan, until Roberto showed up with it. Nor had he ever seen the battered carpetbag that was tied behind the cantle of the cheap Mexican saddle.

It figured to be the drifter's horse and carpetbag, sure enough. But whether the drifter had turned the animal loose himself, or somebody else had, we had no way of knowing. As for the carpetbag, it didn't tell us any more about the hanging man than the contents of his pockets. Inside it were some extra clothes, an old Colt Dragoon revolver, shaving tackle, a woman's garter, and nothing at all that might identify the owner.

Sam took the horse, and Boze and I took the carpetbag over to Obe Spencer's to put with the rest of the hanging man's belongings. On the way we held a conference. Fact was, a pair of grain barges were due upriver from San Francisco at eleven, for loading and return. I had three men working for me, but none of them handled the paperwork; I was going to have to spend some time at the feed mill that day, whether I wanted to or not. Which is how it is when you have part-time deputies who are also full-time businessmen. It was a fact of small-town life we'd had to learn to live with.

We worked it out so that Boze would continue making inquiries while I went to work at the mill. Then we'd switch off at one o'clock so he could give his wife Ellie, who was minding the mercantile, some help with customers and with the drummers who always flocked around with Christmas wares right after Thanksgiving.

We also decided that if neither of us turned up any new information by five o'clock—or even if we did—we would ring up the county seat and make a full report to the sheriff. Not that Joe Perkins would be able to find out anything we couldn't. He was a fat-cat political appointee, and about all he knew how to find was pig's knuckles and beer. But we were bound to do it by the oath of office we'd taken.

We split up at the funeral parlor and I went straight to the mill. My foreman, Gene Kleinschmidt, had opened up; I'd given him a set of keys and he knew to go ahead and unlock the place if I wasn't around. The barges came in twenty minutes after I did, and I had to hustle to get the paperwork ready that they would be carrying back down to San Francisco —bills of lading, requisitions for goods from three different companies.

I finished up a little past noon and went out onto the dock to watch the loading. One of the bargemen was talking to Gene. And while he was doing it, he kept flipping something up and down in his hand—a small gold nugget. It was the kind of thing folks made into a watch fob, or kept as a good-luck charm.

And that was how I remembered where I'd seen the Benjamin Harrison presidential medal. Eight months or so back a newcomer to the area, a man named Jubal Parsons, had come in to buy some sacks of chicken feed. When he'd reached into his pocket to pay the bill he had accidentally come out with the medal. "Good-luck charm," he'd said, and let me glance at it before putting it away again.

Back inside my office I sat down and thought about Jubal Parsons. He was a tenant farmer—had taken over a small farm owned by the Siler brothers out near Willow Creek about nine months ago. Big fellow, over six feet tall, and upwards of two hundred twenty pounds. Married to a blonde woman named Greta, a few years younger than him and pretty as they come. Too pretty, some said; a few of the womenfolk, Ellie Bozeman included, thought she had the look and mannerisms of a tramp.

Parsons came into Tule River two or three times a month to trade for supplies, but you seldom saw the wife. Neither of them went to church on Sunday, nor to any of the social events at the Odd Fellows Hall. Parsons kept to himself mostly, didn't seem to have any friends or any particular vices. Always civil, at least to me, but taciturn and kind of broody-looking. Not the sort of fellow you find yourself liking much.

But did the medal I'd found belong to him? And if it did, had he hung the drifter? And if he had, what was his motive?

I was still puzzling on that when Boze showed up. He was a half hour early, and he had Floyd Jones with him. Floyd looked some like Santa Claus—fat and jolly and white-haired—and he liked it when you told him so. He was the night bartender at the Elkhorn Bar and Grill.

Boze said, "Got some news, Carl. Floyd here saw the hanging man last night. Recognized the body over to Obe Spencer's just now."

Floyd bobbed his head up and down. "He came into the Elkhorn about eight o'clock, asking for work."

I said, "How long did he stay?"

"Half hour, maybe. Told him we already had a swamper and he spent five minutes trying to convince me he'd do a better job of cleaning up. Then he gave it up when he come to see I wasn't listening, and bought a beer and nursed it over by the stove. Seemed he didn't much relish going back into the cold."

"He say anything else to you?"

"Not that I can recall."

"Didn't give his name, either," Boze said. "But there's something else. Tell him, Floyd."

"Well, there was another fella came in just after the drifter," Floyd said. "Ordered a beer and sat watching him. Never took his eyes off that drifter once. I wouldn't have noticed except for that and because we were near empty. Cold kept most everybody to home last night."

"You know this second man?" I asked.

"Sure do. Local farmer. Newcomer to the area, only been around for—"

"Jubal Parsons?"

Floyd blinked at me. "Now how in thunder did you know that?"

"Lucky guess. Parsons leave right after the drifter?"

"He did. Not more than ten seconds afterward."

"You see which direction they went?"

"Downstreet, I think. Toward Sam McCullough's livery."

I thanked Floyd for his help and shooed him on his way. When he was gone Boze asked me, "Just how did you know it was Jubal Parsons?"

"I finally remembered where I'd seen that presidential medal I found. Parsons showed it when he was here one day several months ago. Said it was his good-luck charm."

Boze rubbed at his bald spot. "That and Floyd's testimony make a pretty good case against him, don't they?"

"They do. Reckon I'll go out and have a talk with him."

"We'll both go," Boze said. "Ellie can mind the store the rest of the day. This is more important. Besides, if Parsons *is* a killer, it'll be safer if there are two of us."

I didn't argue; a hero is something I never was nor wanted to be. We left the mill and went and picked up Boze's buckboard from behind the mercantile. On the way out of town we stopped by his house and mine long enough to fetch our rifles. Then we headed west on Willow Creek Road.

It was a long cool ride out to Jubal Parsons' tenant farm, through a lot of rich farmland and stands of willows and evergreens. Neither of us said much. There wasn't much to say. But I was tensed up and I could see that Boze was, too.

A rutted trail hooked up to the farm from Willow Creek Road, and Boze jounced the buckboard along there some past three o'clock. It was pretty modest acreage. Just a few fields of corn and alfalfa, with a cluster of ramshackle buildings set near where Willow Creek cut through the northwest corner. There was a one-room farmhouse, a chicken coop, a barn, a couple of lean-tos, and a pole corral. That was all except for a small windmill—a Fairbanks, Morse Eclipse—that the Siler brothers had put up because the creek was dry more than half the year.

When we came in sight of the buildings I could tell that Jubal Parsons had done work on the place. The farmhouse had a fresh coat of white-wash, as did the chicken coop, and the barn had a new roof.

There was nobody in the farmyard, just half a dozen squawking leg-horns, when we pulled in and Boze drew rein. But as soon as we stepped down, the front door of the house opened and Greta Parsons came out on the porch. She was wearing a calico dress and high-button shoes, but her head was bare; that butter-yellow hair of hers hung down to her hips, glistening like the bargeman's gold nugget in the sun. She was some pretty woman, for a fact. It made your throat thicken up just to look at her, and funny ideas start to stir around in your head. If ever there was a woman to tempt a man to sin, I thought, it was this one.

Boze stayed near the buckboard, with his rifle held loose in one hand, while I went over to the porch steps and took off my hat. "I'm Carl Miller, Mrs. Parsons," I said. "That's Ed Bozeman back there. We're from Tule River. Maybe you remember seeing us?"

"Yes, Mr. Miller. I remember you."

"We'd like a few words with your husband. Would he be somewhere nearby?"

"He's in the barn," she said. There was something odd about her voice —a kind of dullness, as if she was fatigued. She moved that way, too, loose and jerky. She didn't seem to notice Boze's rifle, or to care if she did.

I said, "Do you want to call him out for us?"

"No, you go on in. It's all right."

I nodded to her and rejoined Boze, and we walked on over to the barn. Alongside it was a McCormick & Deering binder-harvester, and further down, under a lean-to, was an old buggy with its storm curtains buttoned up. A big gray horse stood in the corral, nuzzling a pile of hay. The smell of dust and earth and manure was ripe on the cool air.

The barn doors were shut. I opened one half, stood aside from the opening, and called out, "Mr. Parsons? You in there?"

No answer.

I looked at Boze. He said, "We'll go in together," and I nodded. Then we shouldered up and I pulled the other door half open. And we went inside.

It was shadowed in there, even with the doors open; those parts of the interior I could make out were empty. I eased away from Boze, toward where the corn crib was. There was sweat on me; I wished I'd taken my own rifle out of the buckboard.

"Mr. Parsons?"

Still no answer. I would have tried a third time, but right then Boze said, "Never mind, Carl," in a way that made me turn around and face him.

He was a dozen paces away, staring down at something under the hayloft. I frowned and moved over to him. Then I saw it too, and my mouth came open and there was a slithery feeling on my back.

Jubal Parsons was lying there dead on the sod floor, with blood all over his shirtfront and the side of his face. He'd been shot. There was a .45-70 Springfield rifle beside the body, and when Boze bent down and struck a match, you could see the black-powder marks mixed up with the blood.

"My God," I said, soft.

"Shot twice," Boze said. "Head and chest."

"Twice rules out suicide."

"Yeah," he said.

We traded looks in the dim light. Then we turned and crossed back to the doors. When we came out Mrs. Parsons was sitting on the front steps of the house, looking past the windmill at the alfalfa fields. We went over and stopped in front of her. The sun was at our backs, and the way we stood put her in our shadow. That was what made her look up; she hadn't seen us coming, or heard us crossing the yard.

She said, "Did you find him?"

"We found him," Boze said. He took out his badge and showed it to her. "We're county sheriff's deputies, Mrs. Parsons. You'd best tell us what happened in there."

"I shot him," she said. Matter-of-fact, like she was telling you the time of day. "This morning, just after breakfast. Ever since I've wanted to hitch up the buggy and drive in and tell about it, but I couldn't seem to find the courage. It took all the courage I had to fire the rifle."

"But why'd you do a thing like that?"

"Because of what he did in Tule River last night."

"You mean the hanging man?"

"Yes. Jubal killed him."

"Did he tell you that?"

"Yes. Not long before I shot him."

"Why did he do it—hang that fellow?"

"He was crazy jealous, that's why."

I asked her, "Who was the dead man?"

"I don't know."

"You mean to say he was a stranger?"

"Yes," she said. "I only saw him once. Yesterday afternoon. He rode in looking for work. I told him we didn't have any, that we were tenant farmers, but he wouldn't leave. He kept following me around, saying things. He thought I was alone here—a woman alone."

"Did he—make trouble for you?"

"Just with words. He kept saying things, ugly things. Men like that— I don't know why, but they think I'm a woman of easy virtue. It has always been that way, no matter where we've lived."

"What did you do?" Boze asked.

"Ignored him at first. Then I begged him to go away. I told him my husband was wild jealous, but he didn't believe me. I thought I was alone too, you see; I thought Jubal had gone off to work in the fields."

"But he hadn't?"

"Oh, he had. But he came back while the drifter was here and he overheard part of what was said."

"Did he show himself to the man?"

"No. He would have if matters had gone beyond words, but that didn't happen. After a while he got tired of tormenting me and went away. The drifter, I mean."

"Then what happened?"

"Jubal saddled his horse and followed him. He followed that man into

Tule River and when he caught up with him he knocked him on the head and he hung him."

Boze and I traded another look. I said what both of us were thinking: "Just for deviling you? He hung a man for that?"

"I told you, Jubal was crazy jealous. You didn't know him. You just— you don't know how he was. He said that if a man thought evil, and spoke evil, it was the same as doing evil. He said if a man was wicked, he deserved to be hung for his wickedness and the world would be a better place for his leaving it."

She paused, and then made a gesture with one hand at her bosom. It was a meaningless kind of gesture, but you could see where a man might take it the wrong way. Might take *her* the wrong way, just like she'd said. And not just a man, either; women, too. Everybody that didn't keep their minds open and went rooting around after sin in other folks.

"Besides," she went on, "he worshipped the ground I stand on. He truly did, you know. He couldn't bear the thought of anyone sullying me."

I cleared my throat. The sweat on me had dried and I felt cold now. "Did you hate him, Mrs. Parsons?"

"Yes, I hated him. Oh, yes. I feared him, too—for a long time I feared him more than anything else. He was so big. And so strong-willed. I used to tremble sometimes, just to look at him."

"Was he cruel to you?" Boze asked. "Did he hurt you?"

"He was and he did. But not the way you mean; he didn't beat me, or once lay a hand to me the whole nine years we were married. It was his vengeance that hurt me. I couldn't stand it, I couldn't take any more of it."

She looked away from us again, out over the alfalfa fields—and a long ways beyond them, at something only she could see. "No roots," she said, "that was part of it, too. No roots. Moving here, moving there, always moving—three states and five homesteads in less than ten years. And the fear. And the waiting. This was the last time, I couldn't take it ever again. Not one more minute of his jealousy, his cruelty . . . *his* wickedness."

"Ma'am, you're not making sense—"

"But I am," she said. "Don't you see? He was Jubal Parsons, the Hanging Man."

I started to say something, but she shifted position on the steps just then—and when she did that her face came out of shadow and into the sunlight, and I saw in her eyes a kind of terrible knowledge. It put a chill on my neck like the night wind does when it blows across a graveyard.

"That drifter in Tule River wasn't the first man Jubal hung on account of me," she said. "Not even the first in California. That drifter was the Hanging Man's eighth."

The Patriarch of Gunsight Flat

Wayne D. Overholser is one of a handful of "grand masters" of Western fiction, having begun his career in the Western pulps in the 1930s and having earlier this year published his one hundredth novel, Danger Patrol. *He has twice won Western Writers of America Spur Awards for Best Novel of the Year, for* Lawman *(under his pseudonym of Lee Leighton) in 1953 and* The Violent Land *in 1954. As is the case with Steve Frazee, a long overdue collection of his finest short stories—this sensitive and superior tale of a homesteading family in Oregon among them—is scheduled for publication by Southern Illinois University Press next year.*

THE SINS OF MAN are many. He will kill. He will take that which belongs to others—money and cattle and all that can be turned into money. Aye, and other things: a good name; a woman's virtue; a man's home; a friend. And who can say with certainty that murder is a greater crime than thievery?

Dave Cray was hitching up when gramp hobbled out of the cabin and came across the trodden earth of the yard. Sometimes Dave wondered if he hated the old man. The years had made his hair white, had scarred his gaunt face with deep lines. They had brought rheumatism to his gnarled and twisted muscles until there were days when he could not walk. But gramp didn't hate nor speak ill of anybody.

No, it wasn't that gramp had ever done anything wrong. It was just that he'd brought Dave out here to Gunsight Flat to dry up with the wind. There'd come a day when Dave's bones would whiten under a hammering sun set in a brassy sky. A million years from now somebody would dig them up like the Gable kids had dug those queer-looking bones out of the sand dunes to the north, bones that must have gone through uncharted eons since some misty day when creatures that were no longer here walked the earth.

"Don't lose your head with Solly," gramp said in the same even tone he used whether it was a good day or a bad day, whether the rheumatism was giving him its special brand of hell or had for the moment forgotten him.

"I ain't making no promises," Dave replied, climbing into the buckboard.

"You got Luke's list?"

"I've got it."

Dave spoke to the team and wheeled out of the yard, keeping his gaze ahead on the twin tracks that cut straight north through the sagebrush. He didn't hate the old man. He knew that. You couldn't hate a man who had waited for death with the uncomplaining fortitude gramp had. It was just that Dave Cray's life would have been different if gramp hadn't settled here. . . .

There were the early treasured years in the Willamette valley with its people and cities. There was Dave's gem box of memories: the valley in spring and the smell of its rich life-swelling earth; the first lamb tongue; Indian summer days when the Cascades were blurred by smoky distance; the cries of other children as they played tag through a July twilight; the thrill of the game itself; and his first kiss when he had caught Ruthie Norton back of the big oak.

Dave had been twelve when the news of Lee's surrender came to Oregon. That was when gramp sold the place. "Ain't much sense in going west—just fall into the Pacific. We'll go the other way, and I aim to keep on believing what I believe."

So they had gone east—over the Cascades, through the Douglas firs and then the pines on the east slope, around the lava flows that an enraged nature had spewed out upon the earth like the fiery vomit of an animated prehistoric gargoyle.

Across the Deschutes—the Crooked River—the John Day: searching, always searching, while the empty miles twisted behind in trackless solitude. Rimrock and sage and pine forest—or pine forest and sage and rimrock. No reception committee, unless it might be a marauding handful of Snake Indians. No band to blare out a brassy welcome—only the lonely miles.

Then gramp found it—Gunsight Flat, an emerald in a gray sage setting; pines in the nearby mountains; a crystal-clear creek; fish, antelope, deer, bear and hay land in the flat that would never want water, for water was always there.

Dave, watching gramp, knew this was the end of the search. The twisting, seeking tracks would go no farther. But the empty miles were there, all around them, running away in any direction as far as Dave could see and on beyond into the unmeasured distance.

"We won't starve," gramp had said. "Fish and game a-plenty. A fine land to become a man in." He pulled at his beard that had been black then, and a glint was in his eyes that comes only to a man when he feels the ultimate in satisfaction. "A land where a man can think what seems fitting to think."

They had gone back the next summer for more horses and stock, for seed and tools. It was the last time they had seen the Willamette valley. Others had come: Luke Petty, Fred Gable and his cabinful of kids, Jared Frisbie, loud-talking Abe Mack, and more and more, until the whole flat was taken.

Then came Smiling Jim Solly with his wagons and cattle and his fine riding buckaroos; and there was pigtailed Ann Solly, riding a bay mare up at the head of the column alongside Smiling Jim. Seeing her that first time, Dave thought her corn yellow hair was as fine as real silk, as beautiful as gold in the sun.

Aye, the sins of man are many . . . Standing with the thief and the murderer is the one who says his daughter shall not see the man she loves. If they run away together, he will follow them and hang the man and black-snake his girl and bring her back. Smiling Jim Solly would have done exactly that—and kept his smile through all of it.

"Don't lose your head with Solly," gramp had said.

Well, maybe Dave wouldn't lose his head, but he'd kill Smiling Jim Solly. Ann wouldn't hate him for it. . . .

The buckboard left the sage flat and climbed the bald face of the rimrock by a twisting route, dropped over, and came down to Solly's store. There was no money in Gunsight Flat except what Solly had brought, but there was a deal of swapping. Solly had cattle and winter shelter, but he had no hay land. The flatters, as they were called, had hay. Every autumn, wagons rumbled into Solly's canyon with the hay and built credit for the flatters at the store.

Only this winter it would be different, for Solly had steadily built a carry-over of hay until now he wouldn't need any for another year. Dave, his eyes sweeping the long row of round weather-browned stacks, choked with the fury of his anger. Smiling Jim Solly would look at you and say you could buy his sugar and salt and coffee and dried peaches if you had money. That was the way it had been with Jared Frisbie and loud-talking

Abe Mack—the week before, when they had come.

As Dave tied his team in front of the store he saw Ann working in her yard. He grinned; he wanted to yell; he wanted to get up on the buckboard seat and holler like a rooster when a hen comes off the nest with fifteen chicks. Smiling Jim Solly could laugh in your face and say he'd starve you to death if you didn't sell to him, but he couldn't keep his girl from loving one of the flatters he despised.

Dave picked up a rock and weighted down the letter he'd written the night before to Ann. Smiling Jim Solly was slick, but he wasn't as slick as his daughter and one Dave Cray. Solly would raise Cain if he ever found out. Dave's jaw set stubbornly. Let him find out. It had to come to a showdown sometime.

Smiling Jim Solly was in the back of the store, one of his long cigars tilted at a cocky angle between his teeth. Half a dozen buckaroos squatted on the floor or sat on a counter, listening and laughing to the big tale Solly was telling. He was a bragger, Smiling Jim was. He liked to talk, and he liked to hear his audience laugh.

There were some flatters over there, too. Jared Frisbie and Abe Mack were helping themselves out of the cracker barrel, only Abe wasn't as loud as usual. The only racket he made was when Solly finished his story. Then Abe laughed louder than any other two men in the store.

Dave stood there in the door, half turned so he could watch Ann run across to his buckboard and get his note. It was the way they always worked it. If Dave stepped out of the doorway, Ann knew her father was watching.

As soon as Ann had the letter and had slipped it inside the bosom of her dress, Dave stalked into the store. Smiling Jim saw him, all right, but he didn't pay any attention. He tilted his cigar a little higher and started on another windy.

There were several things crowding Dave, but mostly it was Abe Mack and Jared Frisbie coming back after the way they'd been turned down cold last week. It was worse standing there filling their bellies with Solly's crackers. But it was a hell of a lot worse for Abe to laugh like that at Solly's sorry jokes.

"Here's some things gramp wants." Dave shoved a ragged corner of paper under Solly's nose. "Likewise there's Luke Petty's list."

Solly looked mad because Dave had butted into his yarn. He chewed on his cigar a minute. His mouth was still smiling, but his eyes weren't. He said, "Got any money?"

"No, but we've got hay."

"You know damned well I ain't taking no hay."

"How do you expect us to eat?"

"Eat your hay, if you've got so much."

They laughed—especially Abe Mack. Funny about that laugh: it sounded like a mule's bray. The flatters eating hay might be funny to Solly's buckaroos; but it wasn't funny to a flatter, and Abe was a flatter.

"Maybe you're horse enough to eat hay, Solly," Dave said evenly, "but we ain't. You don't need to get so smart about not taking any hay, neither. There's gonna be another year."

"By that time you flatters will be starved out, and you'll sell your places to me like I've been asking you to for the last five years."

"Then you're nothing but a thief."

When a man was rich like Smiling Jim Solly and had the power and dignity that money gave him, and when he liked to have other folks bow and scrape around, you didn't call him a thief—not more than once. Solly wasn't smiling. Nobody was laughing. It was the first time Dave had seen Solly when he wasn't smiling.

"You're a brave man or a fool," Solly said slowly. "Either way I'm telling you something you'd better listen to. Get out of this country and don't never come back."

Dave laughed. So Smiling Jim was going to run him out of the country! Suddenly everybody was still. Nobody else had laughed. Dave took a long breath. He said, "Solly, what would you do if your hay burned up?"

He shocked them. Seems it's all right for a man like Jim Solly to make threats and talk tough, but the little fellows like Dave Cray weren't supposed to do that.

They had forgotten to breathe. Everybody but Abe Mack, who took an extra-deep breath—the way a man does when an idea has crawled up his spinal cord into his brain.

"You threatening me?" Solly asked.

"No. I'm just giving you something to chew on along with that cigar. I reckon big talk can blow both ways."

Solly laughed. "Only I wasn't making big talk, kid. I'm just telling you that if you stay in these parts, you're likely to meet up with an accident."

They all laughed then, all but Dave. The laughs were a little shaky, as if it wasn't real funny but they knew Solly expected them to laugh. Abe Mack's was the biggest and loudest.

Dave said, "I'm sure gonna run, Solly. I'm gonna run like hell." He picked Abe Mack up, turned him over and dropped him headfirst into the cracker barrel. Then he walked out.

Ann wasn't in sight when Dave stepped into the buckboard. That was the way it should be. She'd come. He turned the team and wheeled up the grade to the top of the rim. He was a little uneasy about what gramp would say when he heard the way things had gone.

A dozen times since Smiling Jim Solly had come to the canyon, gramp had said, "He's a bad one. You can't trust a man who smiles all the time. There'll come a day when we'll have to have it out; and if we don't handle it right, there'll be some shooting."

Dave hadn't handled it right. Uneasiness deepened in him. He felt he shouldn't have called Solly a thief. It was up to Dave now to fight or run, and he didn't want to do either. Not till gramp said it was time.

He turned off the road when he reached the plateau above the rim and followed it until he came to a cluster of junipers. There he waited—and presently Ann came, as he knew she would.

Looking at Ann was like seeing a million stars flash across a sky that was gloomy black a moment before. When he kissed her, he forgot his uneasiness, he forgot about the empty miles and the lonely years, forgot the childhood memories that had been his treasury. He even forgot that Smiling Jim Solly was her father.

Then she was motionless in his arms, head on his chest, and his heart was pounding with great hammering thuds. He was remembering things now, the things that he had forgotten a moment before.

"It can't be this way," he said. "Turn your horse loose. He'll go back."

"I can't."

What he saw in her brown eyes frightened him. He had seen something like that in a doe's eyes when she was badly hurt. He said more roughly than he intended to, "You don't owe him anything. You owe it to yourself—and to me!"

She drew his arms away from her and walked to the rim. The wheel ruts of the road were like tiny threads laid through the sage. The flat lay below her, the dots that were houses, the brown haystacks squatting in the grass stubble.

"No, I don't owe him anything," she said, "but I have seen him kill men. I know the pride that is in him, and I know what it will do. I couldn't stand it if he killed you."

She mounted and rode away. That was the end of it. The stars were gone. It was a black sky again, gloomy black, and the years lay ahead like the twin tracks through the sage. Only they didn't end here in the flat. Somewhere out there, beyond the horizon, lay Dave Cray's destiny. It wasn't here.

Ann Solly was gone. Dave would never look back again; there was nothing to hold him now. Gramp would be dead soon. There was a world to see, a distant world that waited out there beyond where the twin tracks disappeared in a sea of sage.

But he didn't go that day. Gramp listened to what had happened in the store. He packed his pipe and lighted it, eyes narrowed with feeling, face lines as deep as irregular furrows plowed across a brown and aged field. But there was no reproof.

"It's been a good place to live," gramp said at last, "but I knowed, the day Jim Solly drove his herd across the flat, that we'd have to fight. I've been hoping we'd get it settled afore you had to plant me. Saddle up, Dave. Tell the folks to meet here tomorrow night."

Dave rode that day, uneasiness biting at him again. He couldn't leave today—nor tomorrow. He'd have to wait until he'd buried gramp up there on the rim, a spot he'd picked out years before. It was a gossamer bond, but it held him as no clanking chain or jail bars could have held him.

He told them all, and they said they'd come. Smiling Jim Solly would have to get up in the morning if he wanted their places. It'd take more than a year to starve them out. They'd got along before he'd started his store. They'd sent their own freight wagons to The Dalles, and they'd do it again. Dave didn't have the heart to tell them that they had had money in those days, and didn't now. They had hay, but they couldn't haul hay across those unmarked miles, and nobody would buy it if they did.

Even loud-talking Abe Mack listened, a grin on his lips that was meant to be friendly; but his eyes had a way of touching Dave's face and sliding off like the slimy trail that marks a snail's passing.

"I'll be there," Mack promised. "Solly ain't gonna push us off this flat."

They were there, with the sun still showing a red arc above the western horizon, the promise of tomorrow a shining brightness above the edge of the earth.

They hadn't brought their women, for this was men's business. Nor had they brought their guns. First there would be the talk. Then the fighting if it had to come. But there was no talking yet. They respectfully waited for gramp to start it. All but Abe Mack, who had much to say whether anybody listened or not.

Then gramp got up from where he'd been sitting under a poplar, a poplar he'd planted the second year he'd come to the flat. He knocked the dottle from his pipe into the palm of his hand. They stopped their chatter. Even Abe Mack braked his tongue to silence.

"We all came here for our own reasons," gramp said in his even-toned voice. "That ain't of no importance. What is important is that we put a part of our hearts, aye, our souls, into what we've made home. When folks do that, they don't move off 'cause Smiling Jim Solly gets it into his head to have what is ours.

"Trouble is, Solly's smart. He knows it's too late in the year to get wagons to the Dalles and back. Besides, we ain't got money. Now I've been thinking about this ever since Dave came back from the store yesterday, and I can't see no way out. Come spring, most of us will be riding over to the store with our tails dragging. We'll be begging Solly to give us anything he feels like for our places."

It was true. What would life be without coffee, or tobacco, or salt? They had always stocked those things in the fall when Solly's wagons got in from the Dalles. It was late summer now, and they were out. There was no hope except from the shelves of Jim Solly's store.

"We can steal from him," Fred Gable said. "He's fixing to steal from us."

"You reckon a winter's supply of coffee is enough to pay your kids for the loss of their pappy?" gramp asked. "That ain't the way, Fred."

They were silent then. They knew that gramp was right. They looked at one another, a hopelessness spreading among them like a psychic plague. The sun was almost gone now, just a red slash along the horizon. The glitter of the sunset had spread to be echoed by clouds low in the east. The deep purple and dusk began building below the rimrock. It seemed to move in now, as it always did when the day had spun its allotted thread.

They were still silent when they heard the thunder of hoofs on the road between them and Solly's store. They fell back, edging toward their horses, thinking of their women at home, of the guns they did not have.

"Don't nobody go," gramp said. "Solly's a patient man. He won't be pushing—not yet."

It was Ann. Dave recognized her before the others, bent low on her horse's neck, riding as only a girl raised in the saddle can ride.

She came thundering into the yard and pulled up, dust rolling around her. She coughed and stepped down into Dave's arms. She coughed again, and he led her out of the dust.

There was no telling what they thought. Even gramp stared at her with cold eyes. They didn't know, and Dave didn't tell them—not then. He waited, like the others—not knowing and, like them, a little scared.

"Somebody burned our stacks," she said. "Dad's coming with his men."

They stood like chiseled granite, thinking of this and what it meant, but mostly they thought about what Smiling Jim Solly would do and what this gave him a right to do. But to Dave Cray it meant something else. It meant that Ann had at last cut loose. She was giving to him what a woman owed to the man she loved. Suddenly the golden childhood memories were gone. This was his life. This was his home. Here was his destiny. His arm tightened around her to hold this thing that was his.

"Thank you, Ann," gramp said. "Does he know you're here?"

"No."

Dave had never told gramp about him and Ann, but gramp saw it now. He had a way of knowing things like that.

"Go inside, girl," gramp said. "I think the way has been shown us."

She went without question. They waited while that last trace of the sun was lost to sight and the scarlet began to fade in the west, while purple slid out across the flat from the rimrock. They heard the horses. "A dozen," Luke Petty said. "We ain't got a weapon amongst us, gramp. What have you got inside?"

"The weapons I've got inside will stay there," gramp said, more sternly than he usually spoke. "This ain't the night for fighting."

They shuffled uneasily, and Mack muttered; but they stayed until Smiling Jim Solly came out of the dusk, a dozen buckaroos fanning out on both sides, guns cased on their hips.

"My stacks were burned today," Smiling Jim Solly said coldly. "Nobody was home but Ann. She was in the store, so she didn't see who done it. Rest of us was north on Cold Creek, but I don't have to have anybody tell me. Cray, you asked me yesterday what I'd do if my stacks burned. You denying you fired 'em?"

"*I* didn't do it!" Dave shouted. "It'd be like you to fire 'em yourself —just to blame it onto me."

Solly's cold smile broke now into a raking laugh. "No, I wouldn't do that, Cray. I told you yesterday to get out of the country. I reckon you're fixing to, but first you had to fire my stacks so I'd buy your crop this year."

Dave, staring at the man, knew that was the way it would look to anyone. He said, "I didn't do it, Solly. Gramp knows I was here all day."

Solly lashed them with his raking laugh again. "So you think I'd believe the old coot? Not me, Cray. I knew about this meeting you was having, and I'm guessing you figgered you'd boost the price on me. All right. I'll make a deal, but I'll make it my way: I'll buy your places, and I'll pay you a fair price—but you're turning in this year's crop for nothing, to pay for what Cray burned."

"Hell, Solly, you can't do that!" Abe Mack yelled. "We've got to have stuff out of your store this winter."

It was plain enough to Dave. Jared Frisbie, who had been in the store with Mack the day before, must have had the same thought, for he said in cold fury, "Abe heard Dave ask Solly what he'd do if his hay burned. You knew Solly would jump Dave, didn't you, Abe?"

"How would I know?" Mack cried, and backed away.

"How did you hear about this meeting, Solly?" gramp asked.

"Mack told me," Solly said. "He told me he saw Cray riding over the rim early this morning."

"You got a limb that'll hold Mack's carcass?" Fred Gable bellowed. "We don't want the likes of him around."

"There will be no act of that kind," gramp said sternly. "Mack, be out of the country by morning. You've got no family to hold you. What you did was bad enough, but putting it off on Dave was worse. Git, now!"

Mack left in haste and without dignity. Solly said darkly, "Don't make no difference who done it. Mack was a flatter. You'll make that hay good."

"You can have Mack's hay," gramp said quietly, "but you'll pay the rest of us. I wouldn't be surprised if you put Mack up to burning your hay just to give you an excuse for shoving us off the flat. I know what you are, Solly. You came after the rest of us were here. You came after we'd made it safe for your money and your cattle, all the time thinking you'd work it around to own the land that's ours. We'll never go, Solly. If you murder us, our blood will be on your shoulders. It will be in your dreams and in your soul."

"I ain't worried about my dreams," Solly said contemptuously.

"We've had our dreams, Solly, dreams about our homes. You had money to hire your work done. We had our two hands. Maybe we won't live to see the day, but it will come when a million people live in this country. A million people with hands and faith. Your kind can live with us if they want to. If they don't, they'll have to go like Abe Mack went."

"You're a fool, old man," Solly raged. "I ain't worrying about the million people. I'm worrying about the hay I've got to have to get me through the winter."

"You'll have it for a fair price. You'll be fair with us, Solly, because you've got to live with us the same as we've got to live with you. You think your money gives you the power to ride us down. That makes you a fool. Your money can't even buy you the thing you want more than anything else in the world."

There was silence with only the breathing of thirty men rasping into the stillness. Then Smiling Jim Solly, who had lost his smile a moment before, asked, "What do you mean?"

"Ann!" gramp called.

She came out of the cabin and across the yard until she stood beside Dave. Her hand sought his. She held her head high, proud and defiant.

"Tell him why you're here, girl," gramp said.

"Go home," Solly said through gritted teeth.

"It's not my home now. I'm staying here."

"You see how it is, Solly," gramp said. "All the money and power and pride in hell can't buy your girl's love, and it can't keep her away from the man she loves. We understand that, Solly, but you don't. You'll have to work for her love if you ever have it."

Aye, the sins of man are many, and there must be compensation for them. There must be life, as there is death; there must be love, as there is hate. Smiling Jim Solly shriveled in the eyes of those who looked at him. Dignity garbed gramp like a cloak, but there was no dignity about Solly. He turned his horse and rode away, his men lining out behind him.

"You can go home and sleep well tonight," gramp said. "That was the only way anybody could touch Jim Solly."

Then it was just Dave and Ann and gramp, and the sound of horses' hooves dying across the flat. There would come a day when the empty miles would not be empty, when train whistles and the shrill scream of whirring saws slicing pine into lumber would cut the high thin air. There would be people and cities; there would be the echo of children's laughter. There must be compensation, the companionship of tomorrow to replace the loneliness of yesterday, the goodness of the gramps to balance the sins of the Jim Sollys. It takes time to understand these things: time and human dignity and a willingness to understand.

And Dave Cray did understand. It was a fine land to become a man in—a land where a man could think what it seemed fitting to think.

Rainbow Captive

This exceptional story about a kidnapped Arapahoe Indian boy first appeared in a special popular fiction issue of the literary magazine Antaeus *—and is proof positive that the talent Stephen Overholser inherited from his father, Wayne D. Overholser, is considerable indeed. Since he began publishing in 1970, Steve has produced a number of outstanding works, among them* A Hanging in Sweetwater *(which won the Western Writers of America Spur Award for Best Western Novel of 1974),* Search for the Fox, Field of Death *and a series of novels about Molly Owens, a female operative for a Pinkerton-modeled detective agency in the 1890s.*

THE FIGHT ON Rainbow's main street raised so much dust that the dozen onlookers stood upwind in a tight, quiet semicircle. Behind them three dogs paced back and forth in the rutted street, nervous as the gusting prairie wind.

Young Eagle, an Arapahoe boy of eight summers, sat in the bed of a farm wagon, watching the fight between the bearded man and the cowboy. The farm wagon was stopped across the street from Rainbow's one remaining business with any claim to prosperity, the Shoo-fly Saloon.

Rainbow was an eastern Colorado Territory town whose life had been drained by a route change in the Union Pacific rail line. False-fronted buildings along the narrow main street stood empty; clapboard houses that clustered near to what was to have been the heart of a new Western town were now stripped of all furnishings and most doors and windows.

Young Eagle was naked beneath the tattered blanket that he pulled around himself against the wind. These prairie winds smelled of snow. The blanket also covered Young Eagle's broken right leg, a leg that was now swollen and dark below the knee.

Young Eagle watched the fight without knowing the sense of it. He spoke no words in the white man's language. He understood only a few cuss words he had heard at the Indian agent's store, enough to make him believe that white men despised their women. Young Eagle could often guess the whites' meaning by their exaggerated gestures or by their tone of voice, but this fight made no more sense to him than why he had been brought here.

Fourteen days ago the bearded man had stolen Young Eagle from Soaring Eagle's camp on the reservation. For five days Young Eagle was bound hand and foot in the bed of the bearded man's farm wagon. He traveled only by night, leading Young Eagle to believe he was the spirit of death. By day the bearded man concealed the wagon in trees or in heavy brush while he ate jerked venison, drank from one of the jugs he kept beneath the wagon seat, or slept.

On the sixth day of his captivity, Young Eagle had managed to work the ropes off his feet. He had tried to escape, but was in such a weakened condition that the bearded man easily caught him. The bearded man threw Young Eagle to the earth and stomped on his shin with one hobnailed boot.

When they reached the open prairie, they traveled by day. The first town they came to was Rainbow. Young Eagle felt mystified here, and frightened. Most of the whites' frame dwellings, squat and ugly to his eye, were obviously abandoned. Even on the street where the bearded man stopped the wagon, Young Eagle saw few signs of life. Aside from the Shoo-fly Saloon, the store buildings were dark-windowed and apparently empty.

Young Eagle had watched the bearded man enter the saloon. Half a dozen horses were tied at the rail outside, all branded *Circle B*. As the bearded man opened the door, Young Eagle heard a woman's shrill laughter, but that one human sound was cut off by the closing door.

Presently the bearded man came outside, followed by six cowboys and an equal number of townspeople. The cowboys were slender men who wore boots with pointed toes, chaps over their trousers, dark flannel shirts, and large, sweat-stained hats. The six townspeople, all men, were not so distinctive. One was pudgy and red-faced, another was lanky. One wore patched clothes, another wore a dark suit and a derby hat. In the open doorway of the Shoo-fly Saloon stood a huge white woman. She was nearly as wide as the doorway. Young Eagle noticed that she wore bright red coloring on her cheeks and lips, and while he stared at her, their eyes met and held until Young Eagle looked away.

Young Eagle saw no sign of anger in any of the white men, only silent determination. Was this the secret of their strength? he wondered as he watched the bearded man and one thick-necked cowboy face one another, circling, fists raised.

The cowboy, hatless now, was quick and agile. He feinted, then punched the bearded man in the face. The bearded man was rocked back, but kept his footing.

The bearded man charged, swinging both fists in wide arcs. Even though the cowboy managed to slug the bearded man once, he was driven back by the attack. The bearded man pressed his advantage and punched the cowboy in the nose, with all of his weight behind the blow. A gasp came from the onlookers, as though they themselves had been struck.

The cowboy went down, but was quickly back on his feet. He bled steadily from his nose. The bearded man, sensing victory, charged again. but this time the cowboy smoothly sidestepped him and slugged him on the temple as he stumbled past.

Every time the fighting whites came together, Young Eagle noticed, their feet stirred powdery dust in the street as if the men had plunged their boots into dry puddles. Gusts of wind took the dust away in a brown streak, away from the silent onlookers, and away from the dogs.

The cowboy had lost none of his quickness from being knocked down. He rapidly punched the bearded man with his right fist, followed by a left. The bearded man tried to rush him, but the cowboy eluded him.

For a time the fight became a pursuit of the cowboy by the bearded man. The semicircle of onlookers, maintaining a safe distance, followed the fighters as they came close to the farm wagon, then moved back across the street near the Shoo-fly Saloon.

Even though the bearded man was the pursuer, he got the worst of the fight. The cowboy chose openings and hit his adversary with smooth combinations of rights and lefts before ducking away.

Then the bearded man, his face puffy and bleeding, stepped close to the cowboy and planted his hobnailed boot on the cowboy's foot. The bearded man drew his right arm back and swung, underhanded. He struck the cowboy below his belt buckle, very hard. The cowboy fell to the street. He writhed. The bearded man, aiming for the crotch, kicked him. The cowboy cried out hoarsely.

Several onlookers cursed the bearded man. The oldest among them, a cowman whose hair streamed out from under his battered hat like fine silver, spoke in a low, growling voice:

"Let him up, you bastard. Don't kick him no more."

The bearded man, breathing raggedly, backed away a step, warily watching the cowboy struggle to his feet. Someone shouted encouragement, but the cowboy was clearly hurt. He straightened up and tried to raise his fists, but could bring them no higher than his waist.

The bearded man moved in close. Half-turning, he drew his right arm back and swung. His fist came around in a great, wind-ripping arc, striking the cowboy squarely on the jaw.

The blow sent the cowboy tumbling to the street. He rolled through the dust and came to rest against the hind legs of the horses tied at the rail. One speckled gelding squealed in panic and reared. The horse beside him, a muscular stallion whose eyes rolled wide, lashed out with his hoofs at the prone man. One shod hoof struck the cowboy's head with a report that Young Eagle heard over the sound of the wind.

The fat woman in the doorway of the Shoo-fly Saloon shrieked. All of the onlookers, until then hushed in a moment of shock, rushed to the fallen cowboy. They pulled him away from the horses. Young Eagle caught a glimpse of the cowboy's face and saw that it was open-mouthed and still.

The silver-haired cowman knelt beside the cowboy, then stood. He pulled off his hat and slapped it against his thigh. "Skull's mashed in."

The bearded man, standing spread-legged in the street, wiped a hand through his shaggy beard. The hand came away red. "Is he dead?" he asked in a blurred voice.

Several of the onlookers nodded, but none spoke. They stared down at the cowboy in disbelief.

"I whupped him," the bearded man said. "You seen me whup him. The bet's still good."

All of the townspeople and cowboys ignored the bearded man. In a louder voice he went on: "We had twenty-five dollars riding on this fight—"

The silver-haired cowman whirled and faced the bearded man. "Shut your mouth, mister. The man's dead. Show some respect."

"Wasn't my fault he got kicked," the bearded man said. "All I'm saying is that I got twenty-five dollars coming to me."

The old cowman switched his battered hat from his right hand to his left and drew his revolver from the holster on his hip. He aimed it at the bearded man. "Goddamn it, I told you to shut your mouth. You shut it, or I'll shut it for you—permanent."

A tense moment passed while the bearded man and the cowman stared at one another. Then the bearded man abruptly turned and walked across the street to his wagon. Behind him, the cowman holstered his revolver. The four cowboys gathered around him.

The bearded man, mumbling to himself, reached under the wagon seat. He tried to lift out a brown jug with his right hand, but winced with pain. He brought the jug out with his other hand and pulled the cork with his teeth. Young Eagle saw blood on the cork when he dropped it. Young Eagle watched him tip the jug over his forearm. The bearded man filled his mouth and spat reddened whiskey into the street. Then he tipped the jug to his mouth and drank.

Young Eagle turned and looked at the cowboys. They listened intently to the silver-haired cowman, then all of them walked slowly to the fallen cowboy. They lifted the body and placed it over the saddle of one of the horses. The silver-haired cowman ran a lariat over the body and beneath the horse, tying the ends to the saddle horn. The cowboys swung up into their saddles. Young Eagle saw that the silver-haired cowman rode the stallion that had kicked the cowboy.

The five men of the Circle B Ranch rode out of Rainbow, leading the horse that carried the body of the cowboy. The bearded man watched them go, softly cursing them. He drank from the jug again. Across the street the fat woman stood on the boardwalk, looking in his direction. The men of the town stood in a knot a short distance away. Near them the three dogs sat with their backs against the wind.

The bearded man called across the street to the woman. "Well, I just got robbed out of twenty-five dollars. Ain't there law in Rainbow?"

The fat woman said, "I'd be surprised if you had two dollars to your name, mister."

"That ain't what I asked you, woman," he said. "I said, ain't there law here?"

"There ought to be a law against a man like you being alive," the fat woman said. "I reckon every man here would vote in favor of that."

"I ain't asking you to like me," the bearded man said. "You don't have to stand there looking at me, either."

"I'm not looking at you," she said. "I'm looking at that boy in your wagon. Full-blood Indian, isn't he?"

The bearded man glanced back at Young Eagle, then nodded once in reply.

"What are you doing with him?" she asked.

"You look after your business, woman," he said. "I'll do the same."

The fat woman came off the boardwalk with surprising speed and grace and strode to the bearded man, her lace-up shoes sending up clouds of dust before her.

"Don't use that kind of talk on me, mister," she said. "I asked you a question. I want an answer."

Under her glare and threatening bulk, the bearded man retreated a step. "That injun's off the reservation down south. I brung him up here."

"What for?" she demanded.

"Reasons of my own," the bearded man said.

The woman turned away from him and moved down the length of the wagon bed. She lifted a corner of the tattered blanket.

"Hell, he don't have a stitch on!" she exclaimed.

"Don't matter," the bearded man said. "Injun's skin is thick as rawhide."

Young Eagle was frightened. He tried to pull away from the woman and cover himself. She spoke soothingly to him. Then she lifted the edge of the blanket that covered his right leg.

"Oh, my God, he's hurt," she said.

The bearded man set the jug down on the wagon seat. "Leave him be."

The fat woman caught him by surprise when she pulled up her long skirt, exposing one thick white leg. Above her calf a small holster was strapped to her leg. She stooped and pulled out a double-barreled derringer. She pointed the weapon at the bearded man's face.

"I can see there's only one language you understand, mister," she said. "I've never killed a man before, but I know I could blow a hole in your face and never lose a minute's sleep over it."

The bearded man swallowed hard. He held up both hands in front of him. "Don't . . . don't. . . ."

The fat woman called to the townspeople and asked for help. Then she motioned downward with the derringer. "Mister, sit down right there. Sit up against the wheel of your wagon."

The bearded man dropped to one knee and sat down. He looked up sullenly as the fat woman spoke to one of the men.

Pointing to a length of rope in the wagon bed, she said, "Take that rope and tie this gent to the wheel. Maybe that'll keep him out of trouble for a while."

The fat woman aimed her derringer at the bearded man while he was being tied. The rope that had been used to bind Young Eagle's hands and feet now was looped around the bearded man's chest and through the spokes of the wagon wheel. When the rope was knotted, the fat woman raised her skirt, to the great interest of all the men present, and put the derringer back in its holster.

At first Young Eagle fought when the fat woman tried to lift him out of the wagon. But she spoke softly to him and calmed him. She lifted him slowly and carefully so that none of his weight rested on the injured leg. She carried him across the street into the Shoo-fly Saloon.

Inside, the saloon was long and narrow and high-ceilinged. Lanterns were suspended overhead on wires. Young Eagle saw a pot-bellied stove in the middle of the room. A bar with a dully gleaming brass rail at its base ran the length of the room. In front of the bar, all the way to the wall and the back of the saloon, were round gaming tables, captain's chairs, and a roulette wheel. Young Eagle's eye was caught by the roulette wheel. He wondered if it was a symbol of the whites' spiritual beliefs, as he had been told the cross was.

Young Eagle felt a glow of warmth from the pot-bellied stove when the fat woman set him down on a table that was nearby. She pulled the blanket off him and dropped it to the floor. She inspected Young Eagle's swollen leg by poking it with her fingers and watching his face. Young Eagle fought the pain. But tears streamed from his eyes as the fat woman probed and pressed her hands against his leg.

"Leg's swolled up so bad that I can't tell if it's busted," she said. She thought a moment. "Better put a splint on it. If the bone's busted, it'll heal straight." She rummaged through the kindling box beside the pot-bellied stove until she found two short boards. She set them on the table beside Young Eagle's leg.

The fat woman walked behind the bar. She stooped down and came up with a dark blue flannel shirt and a piece of torn bar towel. She returned to the table and put the shirt on Young Eagle and buttoned it. The flannel shirt was man-sized and reached to his knees. The fat woman rolled the sleeves up above Young Eagle's hands.

Young Eagle watched the fat woman tear the towel into strips. With the help of one of the men, she placed the boards on either side of Young Eagle's leg, pressed them tight against the swollen flesh, and tied them in place with the strips of cloth.

Pain made Young Eagle sweat. Now he chilled. The fat woman made him lie back on the table. She gathered the shirt around him and tucked it beneath him. In a few minutes Young Eagle felt warm and drowsy.

The fat woman picked up the tattered blanket and left the saloon through the front door. Outside, the three dogs intercepted her and followed across the street. The bearded man sullenly watched the fat woman. His beard was caked with drying blood. The dogs bounded ahead of the woman and sniffed cautiously around the bearded man, but slunk away when he spoke.

"You ain't going to get away with this," he said.

"I'll turn you loose," she said, dropping the blanket at his feet, "when you answer some questions."

"Such as what?" he asked.

"When was the last time that boy had anything to eat?" she asked.

"I fed him regular," he said.

"You didn't overfeed him," she said sarcastically. "He's thin as wire." When the bearded man only shrugged in reply, she said, "You never did answer my question. Why did you take that boy off the reservation? Is he yours?"

"Hell, no," the bearded man said. "I had my reasons. That's all you need to know."

The fat woman looked at the team of horses hooked to the farm wagon. "Be a real shame if someone spooked that team while you're tied to the wheel."

The bearded man stared at her. "Goddamn, you're a hard one, ain't you?"

"Answer my questions," she said. "I'll be easier to get along with."

After a moment the bearded man said, "Hand me down that jug."

She lifted the jug from the wagon seat and gave it to him. She watched him drink by tipping the brown jug over his left forearm. His right hand was swollen and appeared immobile.

"Savages killed my brother," the bearded man said. "I was out hunting and came back to camp and found him. They cut him to pieces. Cut his balls off and stuffed them in his mouth."

He muttered, "Savages," and drank again. He set the jug on his thigh. "I knew where their camp was. I watched it for two days, figuring a way to get back at them. Then I seen this boy swimming in a water hole. He was all by hisself. I grabbed him and brung him north."

"What were you doing on the reservation?" the fat woman asked.

"Prospecting," the bearded man said. He added defensively, "It's a free country. We never done those savages harm. . . ."

He was interrupted by the drumming sounds of running horses. The fat woman looked up the street and saw the five cowboys from the Circle B Ranch coming at a dead run. The last horse carried the flopping body of the dead cowboy. A cloud of wind-swirled dust rose up behind them like a dark ghost in pursuit.

The silver-haired cowman pulled his stallion to a sliding halt near the fat woman. "The country's crawling with Indians. Must have broke the reservation. There's a war party of maybe fifty, sixty braves headed this way. Take cover. Between us, maybe we can hold them off."

"Cut me loose," the bearded man said, struggling against the rope. "Cut me loose!"

"That war party must be tracking him," the fat woman said to the cowman.

"What for?" he asked.

"He stole a boy off the reservation," she said.

The bearded man demanded, "Ain't you white, too? Cut me loose!" He looked around frantically. "Give me a running chance!"

"You kidnapped that boy?" the cowman asked him. "What'd you do a fool thing like that for?"

"I aimed to let him go," the bearded man said. "Set him loose now. The savages will take him and go. They won't bother you folks."

One of the cowboys across the street shouted, "I seen one! An Indian ran between those buildings!"

The cowman looked up the street where the cowboy pointed, "A scout, likely. They're coming."

"Cut me loose!" the bearded man cried.

The cowman ignored him and called to his men. "Grab up your rifles and get into the saloon. We'll fort up there." He turned to the fat woman. "Come on."

They walked across the street. The bearded man, sobbing, pleaded with them to release him, then cursed them as they entered the saloon.

Three mounted Indians appeared at the far end of the street. They rode slowly toward the saloon. Behind the three, and on either side, were between forty and fifty Arapahoe warriors on foot. They were armed with rifles, bows and arrows, or war clubs. All were painted and stripped for combat.

The tallest of the three mounted warriors wore a single eagle's feather in his hair. He carried a repeating rifle, a rare prize among this tribe. The man was Soaring Eagle, leader of the war party.

"Here they come!" shouted a cowboy who peered out of a saloon window that faced the street.

The silver-haired cowman had positioned all of the men at the front and rear doors and windows of the Shoo-fly Saloon. They were well armed, but had little ammunition. The cowman had told the men not to shoot until the Indians were very close. An immediate, devastating show of force might rout them.

The fat woman strode to the table where Young Eagle lay. Despite the commotion, he had not awakened. When the fat woman scooped him up into her fleshy arms. Young Eagle blinked and opened his eyes.

"What's happening?" he asked in Arapahoe.

The question was almost echoed in English by the silver-haired cowman. "What the hell are you doing?"

The fat woman did not reply. She pushed her way past a cowboy stationed at the saloon's front door. She shoved the door open with her foot and went outside.

The fat woman crossed the boardwalk and walked into the street. The advancing Arapahoes, less than a hundred feet away now, stopped. Across the street the bearded man sobbed and babbled senselessly.

"Father!" Young Eagle exclaimed.

Soaring Eagle nodded at his son, but made no move to dismount. He looked at the bearded man, then at the saloon windows. Behind the front glass, white men peered out. One aimed a rifle at him through the open door.

Soaring Eagle asked his son. "What has happened to you? Did the white woman injure you?"

"No, Father." Young Eagle said. He pointed over the fat woman's shoulder. "The white man took me. He hurt my leg. Father, he is the spirit of death who travels by night."

The fat woman came a few steps closer and held out the Indian boy. "Here, take him," she said.

Soaring Eagle swung a leg over his pony and slid to the ground. He handed his rifle to the mounted warrior who rode next to him, and walked to the fat woman. He examined the splint, then took his son in his arms. He carried the boy to his horse and placed him on the war pony's back.

Soaring Eagle walked to one of the warriors who carried a war club. The club was a fist-sized stone wrapped in buckskin and attached to a length of tree limb. Soaring Eagle took the club and walked to the bearded man.

The bearded man sobbed uncontrollably as Soaring Eagle stood over him. Soaring Eagle raised the war club high over his head. He paused a moment, then swiftly brought the war club down, striking the bearded man's outstretched leg below the knee. The bearded man cried out.

Soaring Eagle returned the war club to its owner, then mounted his pony behind Young Eagle. The Indian beside him handed the repeating rifle to him. Soaring Eagle turned and led the Arapahoe war party down the street the way they had come.

The fat woman watched the Indians go. The three dogs, tails buried between their legs, came out of hiding and sniffed the ground around the fat woman. The silver-haired cowman, followed by the cowboys of the Circle B and the men of Rainbow, came out on the boardwalk. Across the street the bearded man's cries had turned to low moans.

A short distance away from the white man's village, Soaring Eagle halted and gathered his warriors around him. He asked Young Eagle to tell what had happened to him and to describe what he had seen during his captivity. While Soaring Eagle listened to his son, he looked back at the square buildings on the prairie. When Young Eagle finished, Soaring Eagle spoke.

"Listen while I tell what I have learned. Many summers ago the white tribes came to the land of our fathers. The whites fought us and defeated us with their weapons and their diseases. They dug into the sacred earth. They brought the iron horse and the singing wires. They sent us to barren lands far away where we were told to live forever.

"But now see what has happened to the white tribes. All but a few have gone away. The whites left behind fight among themselves. Soon all the whites will be gone, victims of their own cruelty. The lands of the Arapahoe will be ours once again."

CLAY FISHER

The Trap

*Two highly respected names in contemporary Western literature are
Will Henry and Clay Fisher; both are pseudonyms of Henry Wilson Allen,
a lifelong student of Western history and a writer of remarkable talent. He
has won more Spur Awards from the Western Writers of America—four
—than any other writer; these include two Best Historical Novel Spurs, for*
From Where the Sun Now Stands *(1960) and* Gates of the Mountains
*(1963) and a pair for Best Short Story: "Isley's Stranger" (1962) and "The
Tallest Indian in Toltepec" (1965). "The Trap," which first appeared in
his collection,* The Oldest Maiden Lady in New Mexico and Other
Stories *(as by Clay Fisher), is an outlaw story and a chase story—and better
than just about any of either type you're likely to read.*

CANADY felt the horse beginning to go rough beneath him. He had
been expecting it. On this rocky going no mount could make it for long
when he was already ridden out in coming to it. "Easy, easy," he said to
the laboring animal. "It's only a posse." The horse seemed to understand
the tone of the words, for it slowed and went better and steadier for a
ways. "We'll rest on the rise ahead," Canady said. "I can see back a few
miles and you can catch some wind and we'll go on. We'll make it."

He knew they wouldn't. He knew it before they came to the rise and
he got down and walked out on the overhanging spur of gray-black basalt
that gave view down the canyon behind them for ten miles. It wasn't a
canyon, really, but a narrowing valley. The canyon proper lay before them.
Canady grinned and wiped his streaming face. It was hot, and going to
get hotter. "Hoss," he said, "they're pushing. They mean to take us. They
must know the country ahead. They don't ride like there's any hurry."
The horse, now, did not respond with its ears and a turning of its soft eyes,
as it had before. It stood, head-down, blowing out through its distended
nostrils. Canady came back and squatted down and put his hand below
the nose of the horse, where the moisture of its pained breathing would
strike his palm. "Damn," he said softly. "Blood."

He got his field glasses from the saddle pocket and examined the

430

pursuers through them. "Eight," he said aloud, "and six ropes. I wonder how come it is that they always fetch so many ropes? Never saw a posse yet didn't feel they'd each of them ought to have a rope."

His fingers went to his sunburned neck. They felt it tenderly, and he grinned again. "Son of a gun," he said, "it could happen."

Canady's grins were not the grimaces of a fool, or of an unfeeling man. They were the grins of a gambler. And of an outlaw. And a thief. Canady knew where he was and where he had been and, most apparently, where he was going. It did not frighten him. He would grin when they put the loop over his head. That was his kind. He wouldn't curse or revile, and he wouldn't pray. Not out loud, anyway.

"Hoss," he said, "what do you think?"

The animal, slightly recovered, moved its ears and whickered gruntingly. Canady nodded, turning his back to the approaching posse and glassing the country ahead. "Me too," he agreed. "A grunt and a whicker is all she's worth. We haven't got no place to go." He tensed, as he said it, the glasses freezing on an opening in the rearing base rock of the closing valley. It was to their right. A good horse, fresh and sound, could take a man up to that gap in the cliff. The spill of detritus and ages-old fan of boulders and stunted pine that lay below its lip would permit of perilous mounted passage. There was water up there, too, for Canady could see the small white ribbon of the stream splashing down a rainbow falls to mist up upon the lower rocks in a spume of red and yellow and turquoise green lights, splendid with beauty in the early sun. "I take it back," he said. "Maybe we do have a place to go. Pretty, too, and handy to town. You can't beat that."

Directly ahead was a level sunlit flat, dotted with tall pines and scrub juniper and house-sized boulders. The clear stream from the high hole in the right-side valley wall watered the flat, growing good mountain hay upon its sandy red loam and making a ride across it a thing to pleasure the heart of any Western man.

"Come on," said Canady to his horse. "You canter me across the flat and I'll climb the fan afoot leaving you to pack up nothing but the saddle and the grub sack. You game? Least we can do is make those birds scratch for their breakfast. And who knows? Our luck might change. We might get up there and into that hole-in-the-wall before they come up to the rise, here, and spot us. If we can do that, there's a chance they'll ride on by, up the valley, and we can double back tonight and make it free."

He was talking to Canady, now, not to the horse. It was the way of men much alone and when they needed to do some figuring. They would do it out loud, the way Canady was doing. It sounded better that way, more convincing, and more as though it might really come off. Canady even swung into the saddle believing his own advice, telling himself what he wanted to know, then accepting it as a very good chance indeed. Again, it was his way. A man didn't live by the gun and the good fast horse without acquiring a working philosophy with lots of elastic in it.

"Move out," he repeated to the horse. "It's your part to get us across the flat in time."

The little mustang humped its back and shook itself like a wet dog. Running sweat, and caked, as well, flew from its streaked hide. Its gathering of itself in response to the rider's words was a visible thing. The horse was like the man. It wouldn't quit short of the last second, or step, or shot. They were of a kind with the country around them. It was all the edge they had ever needed.

Canady panted. He wiped the perspiration from his eyes and started upward again. Behind him, the little horse came on, unled, the reins looped over the horn so as not to trail and be stepped on. He followed the man like a dog, panting with him, struggling where he struggled, sliding where he slid, and lunging on as he did, after each setback.

They had made nearly the top of the fan of fallen rock below and leading into the opening of the side canyon. In another four or five minutes they would be clear of the climb. They would be off the slide and safely into the notch in the high wall of the valley. They would be out of sight of the posse, and the posse still had not come into view of them on the rise back across the pine flat.

"Easy, hoss," gasped Canady. "We're going to make it."

But Canady was wrong. Thirty yards from the top, the mustang put its slender foreleg into a rock crevice and drew back quickly. The movement set the slide moving and caught the leg and crushed it like a matchstick below the knee. When the horse had freed itself and was standing hunched and trembling behind Canady, the shattered leg hung sickeningly a'swing and free of the ground, and Canady cursed with tears in his eyes. It was not the luck of it that brought his angry words, but the shame of it. It was his pity and his feeling for a gallant companion that had given its all and almost found it enough.

The hesitation, the wait there near the top of the slide, near the safety of the hole-in-the-wall, was the natural thing for a Western man. His

horse was hurt. It was hopelessly hurt. He would have to leave it, but not
like that. Not standing there on three legs hunched up in the middle with
pain and fright. Not standing there watching him with those liquid brown
eyes. No, he couldn't leave his horse like that.

But how else? He couldn't shoot the mustang, for the noise would key
the posse to his location. Had he had a knife he could cut its throat. Or
had he an ax he could have crushed its skull above the eye-socket and put
the poor devil down painlessly. With a rock he might be able to stun the
brave little brute, but he could not be sure of killing it cleanly. The same
held true for the butt of his Colt or the steel-shod heel of his Winchester.
He could stun the horse, likely put it to its knees, but not, still, be able
to go on knowing it would not recover and try to get up again and go on,
and so suffer as no horse-riding man could think to let his mount suffer.
But, damn it, this was *his* life he was arguing with himself about. It wasn't
the damned horse's life. If he didn't do something and do it quick, the
posse would be over the rise and he and the horse could go to hell together.
Well, he would use the Colt butt. He knew he could hit the exhausted
animal hard enough with it to put it down for the necessary time for
himself to get on into the hole-in-the-wall and for the posse to ride by and
on up the valley. That was all the time he needed, or at least it was all
he could ask for. He pulled the Colt and started back to the horse sliding
and stumbling in his hurry to get to the trembling beast and knock it
down. But when he got up to its side, when he looked into those dark eyes,
he couldn't do it. He had to be sure. "The hell with the posse," he said
to the little horse, and spun the Colt in the air and caught it by the handle
and put it behind the ragged ear and pulled the trigger. The smoke from
the shot was still curling upward, and the little pony just going slowly
down, when the first of the pursuing riders came up over the rise across
the flat and yelled excitedly back to his comrades that the game was in
sight, and on foot.

Canady went up the little stream. Behind him, where it fed the rainbow
falls leaping outward into the main valley, the possemen were just topping
the detritus fan and closing in on "the hole." Back there Canady had
made a decision. It was not to stay and fight from the entrance cleft of
the hole, where the little rivulet went out of the side canyon. He did not
know what lay on up the side canyon, and feared there might be a way
by which the possemen, familiar with this territory, could ride a circle and
come in behind him. He could not risk that, he believed, and must go on

up the creek as far as he could, hoping it would be far enough to find a place where he could put his back to the wall and fight without their being able to get behind him.

Now, going along, the way becoming steeper and narrower and the creek bank little more than wide enough to pass a good horse and rider, he saw ahead of him a basalt dike, or cross dam of rock, which cut across the narrowing floor of the side canyon. Here the stream took another plunge, this of about thirty feet. Above the dike, Canady could see the boles of pine trees and hence knew that the ground above the dike lay fairly level. The cross-laying of rock apparently served as a barrier against which the winter erosions of snow, ice and thaw had worked with the spring floodings of the creek to bring down and build up a tiny flat.

Canady's gray eyes lit up. His brown face relaxed and he said aloud, "By God, maybe this is it," and went on with renewed strength and some hope of keeping his life a little longer. Up there, above that rock cross-bank, a man with a good carbine and plenty of shells could hold down most eight-man posses for several afternoons. Well, two or three, anyway. Or one. For certain, until nightfall. Twelve, fifteen hours, say. It was better than nothing.

His luck held. There was a good angling trail going up that thirty-foot vertical face of rock. It was a game trail, and somewhat of a cow trail, too. He made out the droppings of elk, blacktail deer, range steers and, then, suddenly and strangely, a fairly fresh piling of horse sign. This latter find sent a chill through him. He was on his knees in the instant of the sighting, but then he straightened, grinning. It was all right. The pony was unshod. Moreover, he suspected, from the hard round prints that it left, that it never had been shod and was one of a bunch of broomtails —wild mustangs—that came into this rocky depth for the water that flowed so green and cool in the stream.

Clearing the top of the stone dam, Canady's grin widened. The flat above lay precisely as he had imagined it did. He laughed softly, as a man will who is alone. Now, then, it would be a little different from the way those hungry lawmen had planned it. This was perfect. At the apex of the triangle of the flat he saw the thick stand of sycamore and cottonwood, aspen, laurel and willow, and he knew that the water headed there. A moment later, he made out the source of the stream, a large artesian spring gushing from the native rock under great pressure. The spring was set above the grove some few feet, its stream falling rapidly to plunge into the foliage. Likely it pooled up there under the trees and at the foot of the down-plunge. That's what lured in the wild horses and the other game and the cattle, too, what few of the latter were hardly enough to come this far into the mountains for feed. All a man would need to do, now, was hole up in those boulders that girded the spring, up there above the trees, and he could command with his Winchester the whole of the small, open flat between the spring grove and the stone cross-dam that Canady had just clambered up. Taking a deep breath, the fugitive started across the flat, toward the spring and its hole-up boulders. It was not until he had climbed safely into this haven at the canyon head and laid down pantingly to look back on his trail and get ready for the possemen, that he saw where he had come.

Below him in the trees the spring pooled up exactly as he had expected it would. Also the rim of the pool showed the centuries of wear of the hoofed animals coming to its banks for water. But there was something else—two other things—that he had not expected to see there, and his grin faded and his gray eyes grew taut and tired and empty.

The first thing was the wild horse. It had not gone on up out of the little side canyon as Canady had hoped, showing him the way to follow its tracks and escape over the rim where no mounted man might follow. It was still in the grove of trees that sheltered the springpool waterhole, and it wasn't still there because of its thirst. Beyond the trees, back where Canady had come from, and so skillfully blended and built into the natural cover of the canyon that even his range-wise eyes had missed them, were the two woven brush and pole wings of the second thing Canady had not dreamed to find there. Those were the manmade wings of a mustang corral down there. Canady had stumbled into a wild horse trap. And he was caught there, with this unfortunate lone mustang that now cowered in the trees and could not get out of the trap any more than could he, and for the same reason—the posse and the box canyon.

"Steady on," Canady called down softly to the terrified horse. "We'll think of something."

Two hours after high noon the sun was gone from the canyon. Canady could see its light splashing the far side of the main valley still, but in the side canyon all was soft shade, and hot. Canady drank enough water to keep himself from drying out, yet not enough to log him. He noted that the wild mustang did the same thing. It knew, as Canady knew, that to be ready to fight or fly called for an empty belly. "Smart," said Canady, "smart as hell." The horse heard him and looked up. *"Coo-ee, coo-ee,"*

Canady called to him reassuringly. "Don't fret; I'll figure something for us." But it was a lie and he knew it was a lie.

He had gone down, right after he first lay up in the spring boulders and saw the trap and the wild broomtail in it, and closed off the narrow gate of the funnel-winged corral with his lariat. He had done that in a hurry, before the posse had worked up into the canyon and taken its position along the top of the cross-dam. His one thought had been that the broomtail was a horse, wild or not, and that so long as a man had a horse he wasn't out of it in that country. And he had wanted to keep hidden from the posse the fact that he did have a horse up there in that headwaters timber. The mustang had played with him in that last part of it, lying up shy and quiet as a deer in the trees and brush, not wanting any more than Canady wanted for the men to know that it was there. "It" in this case was a scrubby little stallion, probably too small and old to hold a band of mares. The little horse had not only the fixtures but the temperament of the mongrel stud animal. Watching him lie still in the spring brush and keep his eyes following every move of the men below him, as well as of the single man above him, Canady knew that he and the trapped horse were friends. The only problem was proving it to the horse.

Sometimes these old scrub studs had been ridden long ago and would remember man's smell and voice. He tried a dozen times to talk the mustang up toward his end of the spring pool. But the animal gave no sign that the sight, scent or sound of mankind was familiar to him, or welcome. He bared his teeth silently and pinned his ears and squatted in the haunches ready to kick like a pack mule on a cold morning. He did this every time Canady said more than three or four words to him, or accompanied his talk with any movement that might mean he was coming down to see the horse, if the horse would not come up to see him.

What possible good the horse could do him, even if, by some miracle Canady might gentle him down and put his saddle and bridle on him, Canady didn't know. Then, even in thinking that far, he laughed and shrugged. His saddle and bridle were down there on that rock slide below the hole-in-the-wall. He'd had no time and no reason to take them off his dead mount. So if he went out of there astride that broomtail it would be bareback, and that was about as good a bet as that the crafty old stallion would sprout wings and fly up out of the canyon. A bridle, of sorts, he could rig from splitting and unraveling a short length of his lariat. It would be sort of a breaking hackamore arrangement and might do to give simple directions of right and left and whoa-up. But even if he rigged this Sioux headstall and got it on the shaggy little horse, then what? That was, even if the rascal wanted to be good, or had been ridden in the past, and remembered it of a sudden? Nothing. Not a damned thing. Canady couldn't ride out of that canyon if he had the best saddle mount in Montana waiting and eager to make the try with him. It was all crazy, thinking of that wild stud. But just finding any horse up there was bound to start a man's mind going. Especially when he had just shot his own mount and was fixing to put his back to the best rock he could find and go down with lead flying. But it was crazy all the same. All Canady could do was what the old broomtail stud could do—fight the rope to the last breath he had in him, then kill himself, if he could, before the others did it for him.

The afternoon wore on. The heat in the deep-walled little canyon was enormous. The deerflies swarmed at the spring pool and bit like mad cats. They nearly drove Canady wild, but he fought them with hand and mind and swathed neckband and, when evening came, they lifted up out of the canyon on the first stir of the night wind. In the early part of the waiting there had been some desultory talk between the posse and Canady, talk of Canady coming out peacefully and getting a fair trial, but the fugitive had not bothered to take that offer seriously. He knew the trial he would get. The posse had its own witnesses with it. They would bring up these two or three men who had "seen" the shooting and say to them, "Is that him?" and the men would say, "Yes, that's him," and the trial would be over. Witnesses! thought Canady. God, how he hated them. It wasn't that he minded being identified if he was the man. In his business no feeling was held against the witness who *had* seen something. It was those devils, like the ones with the posse, who had *not* seen the job and yet who were always ready to raise their right hands and be sworn, who were the ones Canady hated. There had not been any witnesses to what passed between him and that teller. All the other bank people had been on the floor behind the cage, and there had been no customers in the bank, or out in front of it. The shooting had happened and Canady had made it to his horse in back of the bank, and made it away down the alley and into the sagebrush south of town before he had passed a living soul. Then, it was two farm wagons, both carrying kids and driven by women, that he had ridden by well out of Gray's Landing. How those good folks—and they were the only real witnesses, save the cashier and the other teller on the bank floor—how they could identify him as anything other than a horseman not of that area, Canady did not know. As for the three shots that had killed the teller, and they must have killed him or the posse would not have pushed so hard, those shots had been fired *after* both barrels of the .36 caliber derringer that the teller brought up out of the cash drawer had been triggered and put their slugs, one in Canady's chest, and one in the ceiling of the Second National Bank of Gray's Landing, Montana. But the only witness to that fact was dead. Canady had reacted as all men with guns in their hands react to other men with guns in their hands. He had fired by instinct, by pure conditioned reflex of long experience, when the first .36 bullet went into the pectoral muscles of his left chest.

Armed robbery? Certainly. Twenty years in the territorial prison? Of course. A man expected that. But to be run down like a mad dog and cornered and starved out and then strung up on a naked cottonwood like a damned Indian drunk or a common horse thief was not right or fair. Murder? Could you call it murder when the other man was a professional in his business and he could see that you were a professional in yours? When you told him he would be killed if he tried anything funny? Then, when on top of the fair warning, you gave him the first shot? Could you call it murder, then, if you shot in answer to his try at killing you? Self-defense was the actual verdict, but of course an armed robber could not plead self-defense. But he was not guilty of murder, or even of assault with a deadly weapon, or even of intent to commit murder, or of a damned thing, really, but to sack that cash drawer and clear out of Gray's Landing just as fast and peaceably as he and the old horse might manage.

Canady grinned, even as he exonerated himself.

It was no good. He knew it was no good. A man had to be honest with himself. If he was in another business he wouldn't need a gun to conduct his trade. Needing and using a gun, he was always in the peril of being forced to use it. The teller was an honest man. Frank Canady was a crook. The teller was a dead honest man and Canady was a live dishonest man. Canady was a killer.

"No!" he yelled down to the posse. "I won't do it; I shot second; I didn't mean to harm that fellow. He pulled on me and shot first. But he's dead, ain't he? Sure he is. And you say to me to come on down peaceable and you'll see I get a fair trial? With a dead teller back there on the floor of the Second National. That's rich. Really rich."

The possemen were startled. It had been two hours since the fugitive had made a sound. Previously he had refused to come down and they had thought he meant it. Now, did they detect a change? Was it that he wanted to reconsider and was only protecting his ego by the defiant outburst.

"That's right, you heard us right," the leader of the posse called up to him. "You come down here and we'll guarantee to take you back to Gray's Landing and get you to either Cheyenne or Miles City, wherever the court is sitting, by train and under armed guard. You'll get the trial we promised, and the protection beforehand." He waited a significant moment, then demanded, "What do you say? There's no use any more people getting hurt."

Canady's gray eyes grew tired again.

"That's so," he called back. "It includes me, too. I don't want to see anybody else get it, either. 'Specially me. No thanks, Mr. Posseman. I'll stay up here. I don't fancy that you brung along all them ropes just to tie me up for the ride back to Gray's Landing."

There was a silence from below the cross-dam of rock in the upper throat of the canyon that lasted perhaps two, perhaps three stretching minutes. Then the posseman called back. "All right," he said, "you'll have it your way. When it's full dark we're going to come for you, and you know what that will mean. There are eight of us, all good shots, and you won't have the chance of a rat in an oatbin. We've got bull's-eye lanterns to light you out. We will set them up behind boulders where you can't snipe them, and yet where they will throw light up there around you like it was bright moonlight. We mean to stomp you out. There will be no trial and no talk of a trial. You're dead right now."

Canady sank back behind his breastwork of basalt and gray-green granite. He hawked the cottony spittle from his throat and spat grimacingly down toward the mustang stud. The animal had been crouching and listening to the exchange of voices intelligently like some big gaunt sandy-maned dog. Seeing him, and noting his apparent interest, Canady managed a trace of his quiet grin.

"What do *you* say, amigo?" he asked.

The horse looked up at him. It was the first time in all the long hours that Canady had tried gentle-talking to him that the animal had made a direct and not spooked response to the man's voice. Now he stomped a splayed and rock-split forehoof and whickered softly and gruntingly in his throat, precisely as Canady's old horse had done.

"All right," said Canady, for some reason feeling mightily warmed by the mustang's action, "so we've each got one friend in the world. That isn't too bad. As long as you have a friend you have a chance. Rest easy; let me think. We'll still make it, you and me. . . ."

It was dusk when the old steer came down the cliff trail. He was a ladino, one of those mossy-horned old rascals that had successfully hidden out from the gathers of a dozen years. He was old and crafty and cautious as any wild animal, but he had to have water and he was coming down to the spring pool to get it. He certainly saw the men of the posse, and winded their mounts, but they did not see him and he knew that they did not. His yellow buckskin hide with the dark "cruz" or cross-stripe on the shoulders, and the dark brown legs and feet, blended perfectly into the weathered face of the cliff, and he made no more sound coming down that hidden trail than a mountain doe might have made. But he had failed to see Canady or to separate his scent, or the scent of the mustang stud, from the other horse and man scents coming from below. He came on, carefully, silently, yet quickly down the wall of the canyon from the rim above and Canady, seeing him, was suddenly lifted in mind and heart. He had been right in the first place! There *was* a trail up out of that blind box of a side canyon. A track up that dizzy sheer cliff, up there, that would pass a desperate man, or a catlike wild mustang, but not a mounted man or a man going afoot leading his tamed and trained saddle mount. "Come on, come on," he heard himself whispering to the old outlaw steer. "Come on down here and let me see how you do it. Let me see how and where you get off that damned wall and down here where we are."

He grinned when he said that, when he said "we," meaning himself and the wild stud, without thinking about it. It was funny how a man took to anything for a friend when he had run out of the real McCoy and was in his last corner. He supposed that if a sidewinder crawled along at the final minute and that was all he had to talk to, a man would find some excuse to think kindly of the snake tribe. Well, anyway, he was thinking with deep kindness about the animal kingdom just then. Especially the horse and cow part of it. And extraspecially about the latter half. "Come on, keep coming on, don't slip, for God's sake," he said to the gaunt dun steer. "Easy, easy. Let me see you do it, just don't fall or spook or get a bad smell and change your mind. That's it, that's it. Easy, easy. . . ."

He talked the steer down that cliff trail as though his life depended on it, and it did. And the steer made it. He made it in a way that caused Canady to suck in his breath and shake his head in wonderment. He made it in a way that even caused Canady to think for a moment about there being something to the idea of a divine providence, for it was the sort of thing no man could have figured out by himself, the weird, crazy, wonderful kind of a last-second reprieve that no force but God Almighty could have sent to a man in Canady's place. It was a miracle.

The dun steer performed it with an easy quickness that defied belief, too. He came to that place on his side of the canyon where it seemed to Canady that the trail must end. The man could see the sheer face of the rock dropping sixty feet to the creek bed. A giant outcropping of granite hid the exact end of the right-side trail, but Canady could see, and with absolute certainty, that the trail did not continue downward past that outcrop that hid its actual terminus. But as he watched the steer disappear behind the outcrop and as he wondered what would happen next, he saw the lean yellow body launch itself in a graceful leap from behind the outer edge of the outcrop, and sail outward through the thin air of the canyon's dark throat. It appeared as though the leap would smash the ribby brute into the rearing face of the opposite, left-hand canyon wall, which lay no more than fifteen or twenty feet from the rightside wall. But again the steer disappeared, this time seemingly into the very face of the opposing cliff.

There was a tricky turn in the rock wall of the canyon's left side at just that point, however, and while Canady could see the creek's raggedly broken bottom, he could not see where the steer hit into the wall. All he was sure of for the moment was that the animal had made his landing somewhere other than in the creek bottom. Difficult as it might be to accept, that old outlaw steer had somehow made it from one side of the wall to the other. But, even so, then what? Where was he now? The questions were soon answered when the missing steer appeared to walk right out of the waterfall that came down from Canady's elevated vantage to strike into and begin following the brief section of creek bed into the pool grove. While Canady gaped, the animal stole swiftly to the pool, drank sparingly, returned and disappeared again behind the curtain of misty water cascading down from the spring above.

So that was it. As simple and as remarkable as that. A trail ran from behind the waterfall up the left-hand wall. At a point opposite the right-side trail's end, it, too, terminated. But it was obvious that there was room enough for a running jump and opposite safe landing, to and from either wall, with both takeoff and landing spots completely masked from the lower canyon.

Gauging the distance of the jump, Canady knew that he could make it. With his boots off and laced about his neck, or better, thrown over with his Colt and the saddlebags with the bank money, the Winchester being slung on his back, alone, he could make that distance through the air. But, then, what of that? He made the jump safely and went on up the right-side cliff trail behind the ladino steer and gained the rim; then what? He would still be afoot in a hostile land in midsummer's blazing heat without food, water or a mount. That was the rub. Even if he made that jump and the cliff climb beyond it and got to the rim, he would have to have a horse. Otherwise, the possemen, within an hour or two of dark, having come for him and found him gone, would go back out and climb out of the main valley and cut for his sign on both rims of the side canyon, and they would still get him. They would get him, easy, with them mounted and he afoot.

No, he had to take that broomy studhorse with him.

Somehow, he had to get that mustang to go with him up the cliff. If he could do that, could get the little horse to make the jump with him on its back—it would have to be that way for he could never trust the brute to follow him or to wait for him if he allowed it to jump first—if he could make that gap in the canyon on the back of that little wild horse, then stay with him, hand-leading him up the cliff trail, then, oh then, by the dear good Lord, he would make it. He and the horse would make it together. Just as he had promised the raunchy little devil. Up on the rim, he would remount the tough wiry mustang and together they would race away and Canady would have his life and the broomtail stud would have his freedom and the Gray's Landing posses would have their ropes unstretched and their vengeance unadministered and left to God where it belonged.

The thought of the Almighty came very strong to Canady in that moment of desperate hope. He turned his face upward to peer out of the narrow slit of late twilight far above him where the walls of the canyon seemed almost to touch at the top and where, far, far up there, he could not see the yellow steer climbing the last few steps of the steep trail and humping himself over the rim and losing himself to a canyon's view. Canady nodded and said to the dusk-hushed stillness about him: "If you'll let me make it, too, Lord, me and that little hoss down yonder, I will try to set things as right as I can. I'll take this money, Lord, the bank don't need it and I won't want it any more after this night, and I will give this money to the widow of that poor teller. I will figure some way to do it, Lord, that she don't know where it came from. And I'll turn loose this little wild hoss, if you will let me gentle him enough to get on him and push him to that jump, up yonder. I'm going to try it, Lord. I'm going down there to the pool and try putting my loop on him right now. You reckon you could help me? I surely hope so, as I think you wouldn't send that ladino steer down here to show a man the way out, and then not help him to make it. Nor likewise do I think you would put that little old mustang studhorse down there in that trap by the pool unless you wanted him used. It looks to me, Lord, as if you truly wanted to pull me out of this here trap, and if that's the way it is, why thank You and I'll do my best. . . ."

In the little light remaining, Canady went down from his rocks by the spring to try for the trapped wild horse. He took his rope from the trap gate and closed the gate, instead, with brush and poles, hoping it would turn the stud should he break past him when he came at him with the lariat.

The actual catching went, as such things perversely will, with a strange easiness. Oh, the little horse fought the loop when he felt it settle on him, but he did not do so viciously. The very fact that he permitted Canady to come close enough to dab the loop on him to begin with was peculiarly simple. It made the matter suspicious to Canady and he thought the little stud was merely stalling on him, was trying to tempt him in close where he could use his teeth and hooves on him. He knew the small mustangs would do this. They would fight like panthers in close, using their teeth like carnivorous animals, and their feet with all the savagery of elk or moose fighting off wolves. But this was not the case with the tattered broomtail in the mustang trap. When Canady got up near enough to him, he saw the reason why, or thought that he did. The telltale white marks of the cinch and saddle, the places where white hair had grown in to replace the original claybank sorrel hairs, showed clearly in the darkening twilight. Canady's first thought that this horse had been handled before was now assured. And it certainly explained the change in the animal the moment the man snugged the loop high up on his neck, under the jaw, in a way that showed the horse he meant to hold him hard and fast, and to handle him again as he had been handled years before. Memory is a strong force. The stud made Canady throw him on the ground, using the loose end of the rope to make a figure-8 shake and roll it around the front legs to bring the little pony down, but once he had been thrown and permitted to stand up again, it was all over. This man had gentled many horses. He had spent his life with them. Their smell had become his smell.

The very sound of his voice had a horse sound in it. The mustang had heard it the first word of the day. He had sensed his kinship with this particular man, then, and he sensed his mastery of the horsekind, now. He submitted to Canady and stood quietly, if still trembling, while the man stroked him and sweet-whispered to him and got him to ease and to stand without shaking, and without dread or apprehension.

Then Canady cut and wove the makeshift breaking halter, the Plains Indian's simple rope rein and bridle arrangement, continuing to talk all the while to the small mustang. When, in half an hour more, it was full dark and the split-ear hackamore-bridle and its short reining rope were finished and put upon the horse, the animal was to all practical purposes reduced to a usable saddle horse. It was a piece of the greatest luck, Canady knew, that he had been able to catch and work the little brute. But it was not so entirely luck that it had no sense or possibility to it, and his success only made the fugitive believe that his hunch of higher help was a true one, and this thought, in turn, strengthened him and made his spirits rise.

"Come on," he murmured to the little horse, "it's time we got shut of here. Come along, *coo-ee, coo-ee*, little hoss. That's good, that's real good. Easy, easy. . . ."

They went in behind the creek falls, as the yellow ladino steer had done. The mustang pulled back a bit at the water but once it had hit him he steadied down and followed Canady's urging pull on the lariat as well and as obediently as any horse would have done in similar straits. Beyond the sheet of the falls, the left-hand trail went sharply but safely upward and around the trunklike bulge of the canyon's wall which had hidden it from Canady's view at the spring. Around the turn was the expected straight run at the leapover. It was better, even, than Canady hoped. There was some actual soil in its track and, here and there, some clumps of tough wire grass to give footing and power for the jump.

"Steady, now," said Canady, and eased up onto the crouching mustang. The little mount flinched and deepened his crouch, but he did not break. Canady sighed gratefully and nodded upward to that power which clearly was helping him now. He took his grip on the rope rein and put the pressure of his bowed knees to the mustang's ribs. Beneath him, he felt the little horse squat and gather himself. Then he touched him, just touched him, with his left bootheel. The wild stud uncoiled his tensed muscles, shot down the runway of the trail, came up to the jumpacross as though he had been trained to it since colthood. Canady felt his heart soar with the mighty upward spring in the small brute's wiry limbs. He laughed with the sheer joy of it. He couldn't help it. He had never in his life felt a triumph such as this one; this sailing over that hell's pit of blackness down there beneath him; this gliding spring, this arching, floating burst of power that was carrying him high above those deadly rock fangs so far below, and was carrying him, too, up and away from those blood-hungry possemen and their winking, glaring, prying bull's-eye lanterns, which he could just see now, from an eye-corner, coming into view down-canyon of his deserted place at the spring above the pool and the peaceful grove of mountain ash and alder and willow there at the head of Rainbow Creek in Blind Canyon, sixty and more miles from the Second National Bank and that fool of a dead teller in Gray's Landing, Montana. Oh, what a wondrous, heady thing was life! And, oh! what a beholden and humble man was Frank Canady for this gift, this chance, this answer to his fumbling prayer. He would never forget it. Never, never, never.

They came down very hard at the far end of the jump. The concussion of the horse hitting the ground rattled Canady's teeth and cracked his jaws together as loud as a pistol shot. He saw lights behind his eyes and heard wild and strange sounds, but only for a second or two. Then all was clear again and he and the little horse were going together up the right-side cliff trail, Canady leading the way, the little horse following faithful as a pet dog behind him. It seemed no more than a minute before they were where it had taken the yellow steer half an hour to climb, and it seemed only a breath later that they had topped out on the rim and were free.

Canady cried then. The tears came to his eyes and he could not help himself. He didn't think that the little mustang would care, though, and he was right. When he put his arms about the shaggy, warm neck and hugged the skinny old stud, the mustang only whickered deep in his throat and leaned into Frank Canady and rested his homely jughead over the man's shoulder. They were of a kind. They belonged to each other, and with each other, and that was true; for that was the way that the possemen found them when they came probing carefully up the bed of the creek in its brief run from the deserted pool grove to the foot of the spring's waterfall. The horse had fallen with the man beneath him, and neither had known a flash or a spark or a hint of thought, in the instant their lives had been crushed out among the granite snags of the creek bed below the jumping place of the yellow ladino steer.

Sweet Cactus Wine

Marcia Muller is the author of three novels and several short stories, a number of which have Western themes. She shows her considerable talent in this field in "Sweet Cactus Wine," one of the few Western stories about pioneer women and how they coped with the myriad problems of the frontier. In this wry-humored, ironic and immensely satisfying story, we meet the widow Katy (or Kathryn, as she prefers to be called), a spritely woman not to be trifled with. When a rejected suitor starts shooting up her cacti, why, she just naturally sets out to do something about it. Something very fitting, indeed . . .

THE RAIN STOPPED as suddenly as it had begun, the way it always does in the Arizona desert. The torrent had burst from a near-cloudless sky, and now it was clear once more, the land nourished. I stood in the doorway of my house, watching the sun touch the stone wall, the old buckboard and the twisted arms of the giant saguaro cacti.

The suddenness of these downpours fascinated me, even though I'd lived in the desert for close to forty years, since the day I'd come here as Joe's bride in 1866. They'd been good years, not exactly bountiful, but we'd lived here in quiet comfort. Joe had the instinct that helped him bring the crops—melons, corn, beans—from the parched soil, an instinct he shared with the Papago Indians who were our neighbors. I didn't possess the knack, so now that he was gone I didn't farm. I did share one gift with the Papagos, however—the ability to make sweet cactus wine from the fruit of the saguaro. That wine was my livelihood now—as well as, I must admit, a source of Saturday-night pleasure—and the giant cacti scattered around the ranch were my fortune.

I went inside to the big rough-hewn table where I'd been shelling peas when the downpour started. The bowl sat there half full, and I eyed the peas with distaste. Funny what age will do to you. For years I'd had an overly hearty appetite. Joe used to say, "Don't worry, Katy. I like big women." Lucky for him he did, because I'd carried around enough lard for two such admirers, and I didn't believe in divorce anyway. Joe'd be surprised if he could see me now, though. I was tall, yes, still tall. But thin. I guess you'd call it gaunt. Food didn't interest me any more.

I sat down and finished shelling the peas anyway. It was market day in Arroyo, and Hank Gardner, my neighbor five miles down the road, had taken to stopping in for supper on his way home from town. Hank was widowed too. Maybe it was his way of courting. I didn't know and didn't care. One man had been enough trouble for me and, anyway, I intended to live out my days on these parched but familiar acres.

Sure enough, right about suppertime Hank rode up on his old bay. He was a lean man, browned and weathered by the sun like folks get in these parts, and he rode stiffly. I watched him dismount, then went and got the whiskey bottle and poured him a tumblerful. If I knew Hank, he'd had a few drinks in town and would be wanting another. And a glassful sure wouldn't be enough for old Hogsbreath Hank, as he was sometimes called.

He came in and sat at the table like he always did. I stirred the iron pot on the stove and sat down too. Hank was a man of few words, like my Joe had been. I'd heard tales that his drinking and temper had pushed his wife into an early grave. Sara Gardner had died of pneumonia, though, and no man's temper ever gave that to you.

Tonight Hank seemed different, jumpy. He drummed his fingers on the table and drank his whiskey.

To put him at his ease, I said, "How're things in town?"

"What?"

"Town. How was it?"

"Same as ever."

"You sure?"

"Yeah, I'm sure. Why do you ask?" But he looked kind of furtive.

"No reason," I said. "Nothing changes out here. I don't know why I asked." Then I went to dish up the stew. I set it and some corn bread on the table, poured more whiskey for Hank and a little cactus wine for me. Hank ate steadily and silently. I sort of picked at my food.

After supper I washed up the dishes and joined Hank on the front porch. He still seemed jumpy, but this time I didn't try to find out why. I just sat there beside him, watching the sun spread its redness over the mountains in the distance. When Hank spoke, I'd almost forgotten he was there.

"Kathryn"—he never called me Katy; only Joe used that name—"Kathryn, I've been thinking. It's time the two of us got married."

So that was why he had the jitters. I turned to stare. "What put an idea like that into your head?"

He frowned. "It's natural."

"Natural?"

"Kathryn, we're both alone. It's foolish you living here and me living over there when our ranches sit next to each other. Since Joe went, you haven't farmed the place. We could live at my house, let this one go, and I'd farm the land for you."

Did he want me or the ranch? I know passion is supposed to die when you're in your sixties, and as far as Hank was concerned mine had, but for form's sake he could at least pretend to some.

"Hank," I said firmly, "I've got no intention of marrying again—or of farming this place."

"I said I'd farm it for you."

"If I wanted it farmed, I could hire someone to do it. I wouldn't need to acquire another husband."

"We'd be company for one another."

"We're company now."

"What're you going to do—sit here the rest of your days scratching out a living with your cactus wine?"

"That's exactly what I plan to do."

"Kathryn . . ."

"No."

"But . . ."

"No. That's all."

Hank's jaw tightened and his eyes narrowed. I was afraid for a minute that I was going to be treated to a display of his legendary temper, but soon he looked placid as ever. He stood, patting my shoulder.

"You think about it," he said. "I'll be back tomorrow and I want a yes answer."

I'd think about it, all right. As a matter of fact, as he rode off on the bay I was thinking it was the strangest marriage proposal I'd ever heard of. And there was no way old Hogsbreath was getting any yesses from me.

He rode up again the next evening. I was out gathering cactus fruit. In the springtime, when the desert nights are still cool, the tips of the saguaro branches are covered with waxy white flowers. They're prettiest in the hours around dawn, and by the time the sun hits its peak, they close.

When they die, the purple fruit begins to grow, and now, by midsummer, it was splitting open to show its bright red pulp. That pulp was what I turned into wine.

I stood by my pride and joy—a fifty-foot giant that was probably two hundred years old—and watched Hank come toward me. From his easy gait, I knew he was sure I'd changed my mind about his proposal. Probably figured he was irresistible, the old goat. He had a surprise coming.

"Well, Kathryn," he said, stopping and folding his arms across his chest, "I'm here for my answer."

"It's the same as it was last night. No. I don't intend to marry again."

"You're a foolish woman, Kathryn."

"That may be. But at least I'm foolish in my own way."

"What does that mean?"

"If I'm making a mistake, it'll be one I decide on, not one you decide for me."

The planes of his face hardened, and the wrinkles around his eyes deepened. "We'll see about that." He turned and strode toward the bay.

I was surprised he had backed down so easy, but relieved. At least he was going.

Hank didn't get on the horse, however. He fumbled at his saddle scabbard and drew his shotgun. I set down the basket of cactus fruit. Surely he didn't intend to shoot me!

He turned, shotgun in one hand.

"Don't be a fool, Hank Gardner."

He marched toward me. I got ready to run, but he kept going, past me. I whirled, watching. Hank went up to a nearby saguaro, a twenty-five footer. He looked at it, turned and walked exactly ten paces. Then he turned again, brought up the shotgun, sighted on the cactus, and began to fire. He fired at its base over and over.

I put my hand to my mouth, shutting off a scream.

Hank fired again, and the cactus toppled.

It didn't fall like a man would if he were shot. It just leaned backwards. Then it gave a sort of sigh and leaned farther and farther. As it leaned it picked up momentum, and when it hit the ground there was an awful thud.

Hank gave the cactus a satisfied nod and marched back toward his horse.

I found my voice. "Hey, you! Just what do you think you're doing?"

Hank got on the bay. "Cactuses are like people, Kathryn. They can't do anything for you once they're dead. Think about it."

"You bet I'll think about it! That cactus was valuable to me. You're going to pay!"

"What happens when there're no cactuses left?"

"What? What?"

"How're you going to scratch out a living on this miserable ranch if someone shoots all your cactuses?"

"You wouldn't dare!"

He smirked at me. "You know, there's one way cactuses *aren't* like people. Nobody ever hung a man for shooting one."

Then he rode off.

I stood there speechless. Did the bastard plan to shoot up my cacti until I agreed to marry him?

I went over to the saguaro. It lay on its back, oozing water. I nudged it gently with my foot. There were a few round holes in it—entrances to the caves where the Gila woodpeckers lived. From the silence, I guessed the birds hadn't been inside when the cactus toppled. They'd be mighty surprised when they came back and found their home on the ground.

The woodpeckers were the least of my problems, however. They'd just take up residence in one of the other giants. Trouble was, what if Hank carried out his veiled threat? Then the woodpeckers would run out of nesting places—and I'd run out of fruit to make my wine from.

I went back to the granddaddy of my cacti and picked up the basket. On the porch I set it down and myself in my rocking chair to think. What was I going to do?

I could go to the sheriff in Arroyo, but the idea didn't please me. For one thing, like Hank had said, there was no law against shooting a cactus. And for another, it was embarrassing to be in this kind of predicament at my age. I could see all the locals lined up at the bar of the saloon, laughing at me. No, I didn't want to go to Sheriff Daly if I could help it.

So what else? I could shoot Hank, I supposed, but that was even less appealing. Not that he didn't deserve shooting, but they could hang you for murdering a man, unlike a cactus. And then, while I had a couple of Joe's old rifles, I'd never been comfortable with them, never really mastered the art of sighting and pulling the trigger. With my luck, I'd miss Hank and kill off yet another cactus.

I sat on the porch for a long time, puzzling and listening to the night sounds of the desert. Finally I gave up and went to bed, hoping the old fool would come to his senses in the morning.

He didn't, though. Shotgun blasts on the far side of the ranch brought me flying out of the house the next night. By the time I got over there, there was nothing around except a couple of dead cacti. The next night it happened again, and still the next night. The bastard was being cagey, too. I had no way of proving it actually was Hank doing the shooting. Finally I gave up and decided I had no choice but to see Sheriff Daly.

I put on my good dress, fixed my hair and hitched up my horse to the old buckboard. The trip into Arroyo was hot and dusty, and my stomach lurched at every bump in the road. It's no fun knowing you're about to become a laughingstock. Even if the sheriff sympathized with me, you can bet he and the boys would have a good chuckle afterwards.

I drove up Main Street and left the rig at the livery stable. The horse needed shoeing anyway. Then I went down the wooden sidewalk to the sheriff's office. Naturally, it was closed. The sign said he'd be back at two, and it was only noon now. I got out my list of errands and set off for the feed store, glancing over at the saloon on my way.

Hank was coming out of the saloon. I ducked into the shadow of the covered walkway in front of the bank and watched him, hate rising inside me. He stopped on the sidewalk and waited, and a moment later a stranger joined him. The stranger wore a frock coat and a broad-brimmed black hat. He didn't dress like anyone from these parts. Hank and the man walked toward the old adobe hotel and shook hands in front of it. Then Hank ambled over to where the bay was tied, and the stranger went inside.

I stood there, frowning. Normally I wouldn't have been curious about Hank Gardner's private business, but when a man's shooting up your cacti you develop an interest in anything he does. I waited until he had ridden off down the street, then crossed and went into the hotel.

Sonny, the clerk, was a friend from way back. His mother and I had run church bazaars together for years, back when I still had the energy for that sort of thing. I went up to him and we exchanged pleasantries.

Then I said, "Sonny, I've got a question for you, and I'd just as soon you didn't mention me asking it to anybody."

He nodded.

"A man came in here a few minutes ago. Frock coat, black hat."

"Sure. Mr. Johnson."

"Who is he?"

"You don't know?"

"I don't get into town much these days."

"I guess not. Everybody's talking about him. Mr. Johnson's a land developer. Here from Phoenix."

Land developer. I began to smell a rat. A rat named Hank Gardner.

"What's he doing, buying up the town?"

"Not the town. The countryside. He's making offers on all the ranches." Sonny eyed me thoughtfully. "Maybe you better talk to him. You've got a fair-sized spread there. You could make good money. In fact, I'm surprised he hasn't been out to see you."

"So am I, Sonny. So am I. You see him, you tell him I'd like to talk to him."

"He's in his room now. I could . . ."

"No." I held up my hand. "I've got a lot of errands to do. I'll talk to him later."

But I didn't do any errands. Instead I went home to sit in my rocker and think.

That night I didn't light my kerosene lamp. I kept the house dark and waited at the front door. When the evening shadows had fallen, I heard a rustling sound. A tall figure slipped around the stone wall into the dooryard.

I watched as he approached one of the giant saguaros in the dooryard. He went right up to it, like he had the first one he'd shot, turned and walked exactly ten paces, then blasted away. The cactus toppled, and Hank ran from the yard.

I waited. Let him think I wasn't to home. After about fifteen minutes, I got undressed and went to bed in the dark, but I didn't rest much. My mind was too busy planning what I had to do.

The next morning I hitched up the buckboard and drove over to Hank's ranch. He was around back, mending a harness. He started when he saw me. Probably figured I'd come to shoot him. I got down from the buckboard and walked up to him, a sad, defeated look on my face.

"You're too clever for me, Hank. I should have known it."

"You ready to stop your foolishness and marry me?"

"Hank," I lied, "there's something more to my refusal than just stubbornness."

He frowned. "Oh?"

"Yes. You see, I promised Joe on his deathbed that I'd never marry again. That promise means something to me."

"I don't believe in . . ."

"Hush. I've been thinking, though, about what you said about farming my ranch. I've got an idea. Why *don't* you farm it for me? I'll move in over here, keep house and feed you. We're old enough everyone would know there weren't any shenanigans going on."

Hank looked thoughtful, pleased even. I'd guessed right; it wasn't my fair body he was after.

"That might work. But what if one of us died? Then what?"

"I don't see what you mean."

"Well, if you died, I'd be left with nothing to show for all that farming. And if I died, my son might come back from Tucson and throw you off the place. Where would you be then?"

"I see." I looked undecided, fingering a pleat in my skirt. "That *is* a problem." I paused. "Say, I think there's a way around it."

"Yeah?"

"Yes. We'll make wills. I'll leave you my ranch in mine. You do the same in yours. That way we'd both have something to show for our efforts."

He nodded, looking foxy. "That's a good idea, Kathryn. Very good." I could tell he was pleased I'd thought of it myself.

"And, Hank, I think we should do it right away. Let's go into town this afternoon and have the wills drawn up."

"Fine with me." He looked even more pleased. "Just let me finish with this harness."

The will signing, of course, was a real solemn occasion. I even sniffed a little into my handkerchief before I put my signature to the document. The lawyer, Will Jones, was a little surprised by our bequests, but not much. He knew I was alone in the world, and Hank's son John was known to be more of a ne'er-do-well than his father. Probably Will Jones was glad to see the ranch wouldn't be going to John.

I had Hank leave me off at my place on his way home. I wanted, I said, to cook him one last supper in my old house before moving to his in the morning. I went about my preparations, humming to myself. Would Hank be able to resist rushing back into town to talk to Johnson, the land developer? Or would he wait a decent interval, say a day?

Hank rode up around sundown. I met him on the porch, twisting my handkerchief in my hands.

"Kathryn, what's wrong?"

"Hank, I can't do it."

"Can't do what?"

"I can't leave the place. I can't leave Joe's memory. This whole thing's been a terrible mistake."

He scowled. "Don't be foolish. What's for supper?"

"There isn't any."

"What?"

"How could I fix supper with a terrible mistake like this on my mind?"

"Well, you just get in there and fix it. And stop talking this way."

I shook my head. "No, Hank, I mean it. I can't move to your place. I can't let you farm mine. It wouldn't be right. I want you to go now, and tomorrow I'm going into town to rip up my will."

"You what?" His eyes narrowed.

"You heard me, Hank."

He whirled and went toward his horse. "You'll never learn, will you?"

"What are you going to do?"

"What do you think? Once your damned cactuses are gone, you'll see the light. Once you can't make any more of that wine, you'll be only too glad to pack your bags and come with me."

"Hank, don't you dare!"

"I do dare. There won't be a one of them standing."

"Please, Hank! At least leave my granddaddy cactus." I waved at the fifty-foot giant in the outer dooryard. "It's my favorite. It's like a child to me."

Hank grinned evilly. He took the shotgun from the saddle and walked right up to the cactus.

"Say good-bye to your child."

"Hank! Stop!"

He shouldered the shotgun.

"Say good-bye to it, you foolish woman."

"Hank, don't you pull that trigger!"

He pulled it.

Hank blasted at the giant saguaro—one, two, three times. And, like the others, it began to lean.

Unlike the others, though, it didn't lean backwards. It gave a great sigh and leaned and leaned and leaned forwards. And then it toppled. As it toppled, it picked up momentum. And when it fell on Hank Gardner, it made an awful thud.

I stood quietly on the porch. Hank didn't move. Finally I went over to him. Dead. Dead as all the cacti he'd murdered.

I contemplated his broken body a bit before I hitched up the buckboard and went to tell Sheriff Daly about the terrible accident. Sure was funny, I'd say, how that cactus toppled forwards instead of backwards. Almost as if the base had been partly cut through and braced so it would do exactly that.

Of course, the shotgun blasts would have destroyed any traces of the cutting.